STEPHEN JONES is the winner of two World Fantasy Awards, three Horror Writers Association Bram Stoker Awards and The International Horror Critics Guild Award as well as being a ten-time recipient of the British Fantasy Award, and a Hugo Award nominee. A full-time columnist, television producer/director and genre movie publicist and consultant (the first three *Hellraiser* movies, *Night Life*, *Nightbreed*, *Split Second*, *Mind Ripper*, *Last Gasp* etc), he is the co-editor of *Horror: 100 Best Books*, *The Best Horror from Fantasy Tales*, *Gaslight & Ghosts*, *Now We Are Sick*, *H.P. Lovecraft's Book of Horror*, *The Anthology of Fantasy & the Supernatural* and the *Best New Horror*, *Dark Terrors*, *Dark Voices* and *Fantasy Tales* series. He has written *Stephen Jones' Essential Monster Movie Guide*, *The Illustrated Vampire Movie Guide*, *The Illustrated Dinosaur Movie Guide*, *The Illustrated Frankenstein Movie Guide* and *The Illustrated Werewolf Movie Guide*, and compiled *The Mammoth Book of Terror*, *The Mammoth Book of Vampires*, *The Mammoth Book of Zombies*, *The Mammoth Book of Werewolves*, *The Mammoth Book of Frankenstein*, *The Mammoth Book of Dracula*, *Shadows Over Innsmouth*, *Dancing With the Dark*, *Dark Detectives*, *Exorcisms and Ecstasies* by Karl Edward Wagner, *The Vampire Stories of R. Chetwynd-Hayes*, *James Herbert: By Horror Haunted*, *Clive Barker's A-Z of Horror*, *Clive Barker's Shadows in Eden*, *Clive Barker's The Nightbreed Chronicles* and *The Hellraiser Chronicles*.

WEST BEND LIBRARY

Also available

The Mammoth Book of Vintage Science Fiction
The Mammoth Book of New Age Science Fiction
The Mammoth Book of Fantastic Science Fiction
The Mammoth Book of Modern Science Fiction
The Mammoth Book of Great Detective Stories
The Mammoth Book of True Murder
The Mammoth Book of Short Horror Novels
The Mammoth Book of True War Stories
The Mammoth Book of Modern War Stories
The Mammoth Book of the Western
The Mammoth Book of Ghost Stories
The Mammoth Book of Ghost Stories 2
The Mammoth Book of the Supernatural
The Mammoth Book of Astounding Puzzles
The Mammoth Book of Terror
The Mammoth Book of Vampires
The Mammoth Book of Killer Women
The Mammoth Book of Historical Whodunnits
The Mammoth Book of Werewolves
The Mammoth Book of Golden Age Detective Stories
The Mammoth Book of Contemporary SF Masters
The Mammoth Book of Erotica
The Mammoth Book of Frankenstein
The Mammoth Book of Battles
The Mammoth Book of Astounding Word Games
The Mammoth Book of Mindbending Puzzles
The Mammoth Book of Historical Detectives
The Mammoth Book of Victorian & Edwardian Ghost Stories
The Mammoth Book of Dreams
The Mammoth Book of Symbols
The Mammoth Book of Brainstorming Puzzles
The Mammoth Book of Great Lives
The Mammoth Book of International Erotica
The Mammoth Book of Pulp Fiction
The Mammoth Book of The West
The Mammoth Book of Love & Sensuality
The Mammoth Book of Chess
The Mammoth Book of Fortune Telling
The Mammoth Puzzle Carnival
The Mammoth Book of Dracula
The Mammoth Book of Gay Short Stories
The Mammoth Book of Fairy Tales
The Mammoth Book of New Sherlock Holmes Adventures
The Mammoth Book of Gay Erotica
The Mammoth Book of the Third Reich at War
The Mammoth Book of Best New Horror
The Mammoth Book of Tasteless Lists
The Mammoth Book of Comic Fantasy
The Mammoth Book of New Erotica
The Mammoth Book of Arthurian Legends
The Mammoth Book of Eye-Witness History
The Mammoth Book of True Crime (New edition)

THE
MAMMOTH BOOK OF
BEST NEW
HORROR

VOLUME NINE

Edited and with an Introduction by
STEPHEN JONES

Carroll & Graf Publishers, Inc.
NEW YORK

Jones, Stephen, ed.
Title

Carroll & Graf Publishers, Inc.
19 West 21st Street
New York
NY 10010–6805

First published in the UK by Robinson Publishing 1998

First Carroll & Graf edition 1998

Collection and editorial content
copyright © Stephen Jones 1998

All rights reserved. No part of this publication
may be reproduced in any form or by any means without
the prior written permission of the publisher.

ISBN 0–7867–0585–X

Printed and bound in the United Kingdom

10 9 8 7 6 5 4 3 2 1

CONTENTS

For
Mam
v. 9

ACKNOWLEDGEMENTS

I would like to thank Kim Newman, Sara Broecker, Mandy Slater, Stefan Dziemianowicz, Bill Congreve, Michael Marshall Smith, Gordon Van Gelder, Andrew I. Porter, David Pringle, Frederick S. Clarke, William K. Schafer, Stuart Hughes, Andy Cox, Peter Coleborn, Jo Fletcher, Nicholas Royle, Basil Copper, Roger Dobson and David J. Howe for their help and support. Special thanks are also due to *Locus*, *Interzone*, *Science Fiction Chronicle*, *Variety* and all the other sources that were used for reference in the Introduction and the Necrology.

INTRODUCTION: HORROR IN 1997 copyright © 1998 by Stephen Jones.

DYING WORDS copyright © 1997 by David J. Schow. Originally published in *Midnight Graffiti* No.8, Winter/Spring 1997. Reprinted by permission of the author.

THE WINDMILL copyright © 1997 by Conrad Williams. Originally published in *Dark Terrors 3: The Gollancz Book of Horror*. Reprinted by permission of the author.

THE RIGHT ENDING copyright © 1997 by John Burke. Originally published in *Time Out Net Books*. Reprinted by permission of the author.

SWALLOWING A DIRTY SEED copyright © 1997 by Simon Clark. Originally published in *Midnight Never Comes*. Reprinted by permission of the author.

THIS IS YOUR LIFE (REPRESSED MEMORY REMIX) copyright © 1997 by Pat Cadigan. Originally published in *Dark*

Terrors 3: The Gollancz Book of Horror. Reprinted by permission of the author.

CHRISTMAS FOREVER copyright © 1997 by Christopher Fowler. Originally published in *Independent on Sunday*, 21 December 1997. Reprinted by permission of the author.

FOUR FAMINES AGO copyright © 1997 by Yvonne Navarro. Originally published in *Terminal Frights*. Reprinted by permission of the author.

THE CRAWL copyright © 1997 by Stephen Laws. Originally published in *Dark of the Night: New Tales of Horror and the Supernatural*. Reprinted by permission of the author.

SERPENT EGGS copyright © 1994, 1997 by David Langford. Originally published in this form in *The Third Alternative*, Issue 14, 1997. Reprinted by permission of the author.

NO ONE YOU KNOW copyright © 1997 by Dennis Etchison. Originally published in *Rage* Vol.2, No.3, October 1997. Reprinted by permission of the author.

THE DRIPPING OF SUNDERED WINESKINS copyright © 1997 by Brian Hodge. Originally published in *Love in Vein II: Eighteen More Original Tales of Vampiric Erotica*. Reprinted by permission of the author.

THE BELLS WILL SOUND FOREVER copyright © 1997 by Thomas Ligotti. Originally published in *In a Foreign Town, In a Foreign Land*. Reprinted by permission of the author.

THE WORD copyright © 1997 by Ramsey Campbell. Originally published in *Revelations*. Reprinted by permission of the author.

THE MAP TO THE HOMES OF THE STARS copyright © 1997 by Andy Duncan. Originally published in *Dying for It*. Reprinted by permission of the author.

EMPTINESS SPOKE ELOQUENT copyright © 1997 by Caitlín R. Kiernan. Originally published in *Secret City: Strange Tales of London*. Reprinted by permission of the author.

SAVE AS . . . copyright © 1997 by Michael Marshall Smith. Originally published in *Interzone* 115, January 1997. Reprinted by permission of the author.

COPPOLA'S DRACULA copyright © 1997 by Kim Newman. Originally published in *The Mammoth Book of Dracula: Vampire Tales of the New Millennium*. Reprinted by permission of the author.

GRAZING THE LONG ACRE copyright © 1997 by Gwyneth Jones. Originally published in *Interzone* 127, January 1998. Reprinted by permission of the author.

THE ZOMBIES OF MADISON COUNTY copyright © 1997 by Douglas E. Winter. Originally published in *Dark of the Night: New Tales of Horror and the Supernatural*. Reprinted by permission of the author.

NECROLOGY: 1997 copyright © 1998 by Stephen Jones and Kim Newman.

USEFUL ADDRESSES copyright © 1998 by Stephen Jones.

This one is for Ellen,
in friendly rivalry and sincere admiration.

INTRODUCTION

Horror in 1997

ONCE AGAIN, THE NUMBER OF HORROR TITLES published in 1997 was down slightly on previous years on both sides of the Atlantic, with young adult books accounting for around a third of everything published in the genre. Despite it being the centenary of the publication of Bram Stoker's *Dracula*, even the ever-popular vampire sub-genre dropped in numbers from the previous year, although there were still plenty of books about the undead lurking around the bookshelves.

As part of a reported $270 million 'restructuring', Harper-Collins US cancelled more than one hundred contracts for (mostly overdue) books. Attempts to convince the authors to repay their advances, or assign a percentage of any resale fee based on receiving the balance of the advance, were eventually relaxed after an outcry from authors, agents and writers organisations.

For the fiscal year ending 30 June, HarperCollins' profits dropped $195 million, but in August the publisher and its parent company News Corp. denied rumours that the company was up for sale. Meanwhile, the money-making HarperPrism imprint, under publishing director John Silbersack, was expanded into a stand-alone division of HarperCollins, with more tie-in books planned. The imprint also entered into the customized card game market with Clive Barker's *Imajica* and *Aliens Predator*.

AnoNova, Avon Books' science fiction line, changed its name to Avon Eros in February with redesigned book covers and increased marketing and support in the trade. In March, Zebra cancelled its horror line, the oldest in American mass-market publishing.

In Britain, Simon & Schuster announced a new science fiction and fantasy imprint under the control of editor John Jarrold, the former editorial director of Legend Books and Orbit. However, the name had to be changed from 'Spectrum' to 'Earthlight' when the American imprint Bantam Spectra complained that the names might become confused.

Meanwhile another UK publisher, Random House, decided to pull out of the SF/fantasy/horror market entirely (except for the occasional blockbuster) and sold its Legend imprint to Little, Brown, publisher of the Orbit SF line.

After seventeen years and more than twenty books with Viking in America, Stephen King signed a three-book deal with Simon & Schuster, agreeing to drop his price from just under $16 million per book to around $2 million – but with a profit sharing deal that could add up to 50–75 per cent royalties.

The author toured Australia on a Harley motorcycle during October and gave a talk and reading, winning over his audience with a tale about his epic battle with a real Australian hamburger.

King's *Wizard and Glass*, illustrated by Dave McKean, was the fourth and longest volume to date chronicling gunslinger Roland's mystical quest for the Dark Tower. Although this was mostly a prequel to the previous books, according to the authors afterword, there are still three more volumes to come. In America, a boxed and signed limited edition of 1,250 copies was issued in two volumes by publishers Donald M. Grant at $175.00, while Britain's Hodder & Stoughton offered a 500-copy slipcased hardcover, bound in red leather with a tipped-in limitation plate signed by the author, at £100.00.

Originally published in six parts, King's 1996 story cycle, *The Green Mile*, finally appeared in a single volume with a new introduction by the author.

Novelist Olivia Goldsmith and publisher HarperCollins were forced to issue a public apology for a passage in the 1996 book *The Bestseller* in which a character referred to an audit requested by Dean Koontz, the results of which indicated that he was owed $4 million in royalties by his publisher. The offending passage was cut from paperback editions of the novel.

Koontz also published an open letter warning collectors about novels by Shane Stevens, "Owen Brookes" and "David Axton" (a military thriller) being incorrectly attributed to him. He also pointed out that a notated original manuscript recently sold for $4,000 was in fact a xerox marked up by the editor, not him. The author also revealed that all his early drafts are shredded and he has all his original material still in his possession. He also noted that collectors have paid hundreds of dollars for letters that are forgeries. "Those who most ardently collect my work are among my most vigorous supporters," said Koontz, "and I dislike seeing them lose money on bogus novel manuscripts and associational material of questionable origin."

Koontz's new blockbuster novel, *Sole Survivor*, featured a depressed crime reporter who learned that family members were receiving a bizarre message from the only survivor of a plane crash that wiped out his family. Meanwhile, Chris Snow, the protagonist of Koontz's second novel of the year, *Fear Nothing*, suffered from *xeroderma pigmentosum* and was unable to endure daylight, which was a bit of a problem when he stumbled upon a government conspiracy involving genetic engineering. The first in a three-book series, CD Publications produced a signed limited edition of 698 copies, illustrated by Phil Parks. In Britain, Headline also published the first hardcover of Koontz's revised edition of his movie novelisation of *Demon Seed*.

Violin by Anne Rice involved a phantom violinist who preyed upon the heartbroken heroine. Rice and violin virtuoso Leila Josefowwicz joined forces to create the CD *Leila Josefowicz – Violin for Anne Rice*, which was released in October. Meanwhile, the author also teamed up with Santa Barbara wine-maker Bryan Babcock to establish Cuvee Lestat wines, with labels illustrated by her husband, Stan Rice.

After thirty years, Ira Levin's *Son of Rosemary* was the disappointing Millennial sequel to his classic *Rosemary's Baby*. *Heart Song* and *Unfinished Symphony* were the second and third volumes respectively in the 'Logan Family' Gothic horror series published under the byline of V.C. Andrews®. These books are still probably written by Andrew Neiderman, who also published *The Dark* under his own name.

The House of Doors: Second Visit was Brian Lumley's belated sequel to his 1990 novel. A TV docudrama about axe murderer

Lizzie Borden was the catalyst for a series of gruesome murders in Dennis Etchison's enjoyable *giallo* novel, *Double Edge*, while *Symphony* and *In the Mood* were the first and second books respectively in Charles L. Grant's Millennium Quartet, inspired by the apocalyptic horrors of the Four Horsemen of the Apocalypse.

The Dealings of Daniel Kesserich, subtitled 'A Study of the Mass Insanity at Smithville', was a short Lovecraftian-inspired novel that the late Fritz Leiber had written in the mid-1930s and intended for *Unknown Worlds*. Mislaid for more than half a century, it was originally published by *Omni* in an online version in 1996 before appearing as a slim hardcover, illustrated by Jason Van Hollander.

The survivors from the first novel investigated a series of cannibalistic murders beneath New York City in *Reliquary*, Lincoln Child and Douglas Preston's sequel to their bestselling *Relic*. When a near-bankrupt couple agreed to the wife becoming the surrogate mother of a stranger's child, their luck began to supernaturally change in *The Truth* by Peter James, which also marked a change of publisher for the author in the UK.

Thomas Tessier's *Fog Heart* was about two couples who began to receive messages from their long-dead relatives, and in James P. Blaylock's *Winter Tides* a man was haunted by the ghost of a twin girl he couldn't save from drowning.

Bestselling authors not normally associated with horror included Terry Brooks, whose *Running With the Demon* was subtitled 'A Novel of Good and Evil' and involved a Knight of the Word and a demon battling over the soul of a fourteen year-old girl during the 4th July weekend. The third volume in the series that began with *Witchlight* and *Ghostlight*, Marion Zimmer Bradley's *Gravelight* continued the exploits of parapsychologist Truth Jourdemayne. Michael Swanwick's *Jack Faust* was a retelling of Goethe's Faust legend in a science fiction novel.

A number of strange gifts dispatched from an apparently condemned asylum sent the townspeople insane in John Saul's *The Blackstone Chronicles*, which was published in six slim monthly paperbacks. Despite early bestseller success and combined in-print copies of more than six million, it didnt have quite the same impact as Stephen King's *The Green Mile*. However, The Science Fiction Book Club reprinted the series in an omnibus hardcover.

The author also had a stand-alone novel published – *The Presence* was about an archaeological dig in Hawaii that uncovered more than it expected.

Graham Masterton continued the exploits of his latest character, a psychic schoolteacher of special children, in *Tooth and Claw: The Second in the New Jim Rook Series*. Also from Masterton, *The Chosen Child* was about a series of decapitations set in Poland, where the author has been the bestselling writer of supernatural thrillers since the collapse of communism. In *Disturbia* by Christopher Fowler a working-class journalist was forced to travel across London and solve a series of riddles so that he could expose a wealthy secret society.

Set in the nineteenth century, *Darker Angels* by S.P. Somtow was a historical horror novel that revolved around an old voodoo priest who could raise the dead from the battlefields of the American Civil War. Brent Monahan's *The Bell Witch* was a fictional memoir supposedly based on a schoolteacher's account of America's first widely reported poltergeist incident, which took place in Tennessee in 1818.

Although the fast-paced *Bad Karma*, about a fixated female serial killer, was the debut novel by "Andrew Harper", the author behind the pseudonym was actually Douglas Clegg. *After Midnight* was another psycho-sexual murder thriller by Richard Laymon.

A sequel to her novel *Dark Cathedral*, Freda Warrington's *Pagan Moon* was about a haunted schoolgirl and the crazed owner of a TV network. *Light Errant*, about a criminal family with psionic powers, was Chaz Brenchley's sequel to *Dead of Light*. *Burning Bright* by Jay Russell was a sequel to *Celestial Dogs* and featured actor-detective Marty Burns in London.

Nicholas Royle's eclectic third novel, *The Matter of the Heart*, was about Victorian horrors and historical influences. It was also the winner of the *Literary Review* Bad Sex in Fiction Prize.

An evil spirit from the Holocaust was reincarnated just in time for the Millennium in Thomas F. Monteleone's *The Night of Broken Souls*. In *The Chalice* by Phil Rickman, subtitled 'A Glastonbury ghost story', a woman's lifelong obsession with the resting place of the Holy Grail led to the discovery of an anti-Grail, The Dark Chalice. There were more ghosts in *The Shadowy Horses* by Susanna Kearsley and Lucy Sussex's *Black Ice*.

Screenwriter Peter Atkins' long-awaited second novel, *Big Thunder*, was about a young woman and a fictional 1930s pulp vigilante confronting an ancient malevolence. Broadcaster Muriel Gray's second novel *Furnace* took its inspiration from M.R. James, as a truck driver stopped in the eponymous small Virginia town where something evil was happening. Ex-rock star Greg Kihn's second novel, *Shade of Pale*, involved a New York psychiatrist trying to find his sister who was being hunted by a Banshee.

In Steve Harris' latest novel, a teenager and his friends spent a bizarre summer holiday investigating the supernatural surrounding an old house in *The Devil on May Street*, while *Longbarrow* by Mark Morris was another haunted house chiller, about the legend of the Seven Sleepers and a forthcoming battle between the forces of good and evil in the Yorkshire village of the title. After a nervous breakdown, a whizz-kid City dealer re-experienced his monstrous childhood nightmares of the *Scissorman* in the novel by Mark Chadbourn, and the Earth itself destructed while civilisation collapsed in *King Blood* by Simon Clark. An exclusive extract from the novel appeared in the February issue of *SFX* magazine.

Black River by Melanie Tem dealt with the sudden death of a beloved child, and Ray Garton's *Shackled* involved modern Satanism, computer networks and child abuse all wrapped up in the author's trademark graphic violence.

Despite being packaged as a crime novel (with cover blurbs by King, Lansdale, Gorman and Bryant), Norman Partridge's *Saguaro Riptide* was a quirky mystery that was set in the Saguaro Riptide Motel and crossed genre boundaries. Much the same could be said about Joe R. Lansdale's *Bad Chili*, the fourth volume in his dark suspense series featuring Hap Collins and Leonard Pine. This time Leonard was implicated in a murder.

Like his previous novel, *The Death Prayer*, David Bowker's *The Butcher of Glastonbury* was a horror novel masquerading as crime when Chief Superintendent Vernon Laverne used his supernatural powers to hunt down a serial killer while being shadowed by an FBI agent. *The Cold Heart of Capricorn* by Martha C. Lawrence was the second volume in the series featuring psychic detective Elizabeth Chase, while *The Haunting* by P.C. Doherty was set in 1865 and introduced a new psychic detective, Fr. Oliver Grafield.

* * *

Compared with Clive Barker and Dean Koontz on the cover, *God's Gift* by John Evans was about a supernatural book that possessed its readers in return for wealth and power. Occult scholar Gerald Suster's *The God Game* featured Arthur Machen as a character, who discovered his fictional creations were coming back to torment him. The author followed it with *The Labyrinth of Satan*.

People stopped noticing Bob Jones, the protagonist of Bentley Little's *The Ignored*, while the same author's *Guests* concerned a town that appeared to be killing off its inhabitants. In *A Dry Spell* by Susie Maloney, a small North Dakota town was struck down by a drought and a sinister evil.

Dark secrets were hiding in the tunnels beneath *The House at the Top of the Hill* by Kathlyn S. Starbuck, and a woman became obsessed with a haunted painting in *Painting in the Dark* by Liane Jones. A pianist was haunted by his mentor's ghost in Noel Hynd's *The Prodigy*, while a man found his ex-mentor impossible to kill in *Angry Moon* by Terrill Lankford.

In a homage to Hollywood B movies, Richard Ryan's *Funnel-web* involved giant spiders and corrupt politicians, while Steve Alten's *Meg* and Charles Wilson's *Extinct* both featured prehistoric sharks. Leigh Clark's *Carnivore* involved the thawing out of a T-Rex egg discovered by scientists in the Antarctic.

The Pastor by Philip Trewinnard was an erotic horror novel about a woman's hunt for her missing twin sister in the world of fetishistic sado-masochism. Two girls shared each other's dreams and nightmares in *Dream Girl* by Brian Rieselman, and *The Witching Hour* was the third medical horror novel about nurse Rachel and her companion Razoxane by John Pritchard, following *Night Sisters* and *Angels of Mourning*.

Dark Dreams by Jane Harrison was a horror/romance involving dark angels, while *The Shores of Midnight* by Janet Tanner was another romantic novel, this time dealing with ghosts and reincarnation.

A young widow was seduced by Satan in *The Snake* by Melanie Desmoulins, and the perfect husband turned out to be a centuries-old member of a secret cult in Tananarive Due's *My Soul to Keep*. There was more of that old black magic to be found in Guy N. Smith's *Water Rites* and Brian Scott Smith's *When Shadows Fall*.

Bright Shadow by Elizabeth Forrest (aka Rhondi Salsitz)

involved a mysterious cult, and an American woman encountered witchcraft in Britain in Barbara Michaels' *The Dancing Floor*. *Witchcraft* by Bill Michaels featured an evil witch who needed the blood of a white witch's child to rule the Earth, and *The Stone Circle* by Gary Goshgarian blended Native American mythology with Celtic superstition.

The Cybernet was behind the horrors of *Fragments* by James F. David. *Cain* by James Byron Huggins featured a possessed serial killer resurrected by science, and an attempt to manufacture a ghost had a bizarre side-effect in *Superstition* by David Ambrose. *1999* by Philip Caveney was set in Manchester as the Millennium approached, and involved a new designer hallucinogenic drug, while *Rage of Spirits* by Noel Hynd was a political thriller set early in the new Millennium in which a curse had put the President of the USA into a coma.

A girl had the power to jump into another reality populated by the dead in *Jumpers* by Patrick R. Gates. A group of people were transported to the *World of the Impossible* and ended up fighting man-eating plants, a shape-changing magician and a two-headed dragon in the latest novel by R. Chetwynd-Hayes. *Thorn: An Immortal Tale* by Frances Gordon was another horrific reworking of a fairy tale.

Being a serial killer was just a *State of Mind* by John Katzenbach, *The Seeker* by Jane Brindle (aka Josephine Cox) involved a supernatural hitchhiker, and *Children of the Dusk* was the third in the 'Madagascar Manifesto' by Janet Berliner and George Guthridge. Other horror novels published during the year included *Man on a Murder Cycle* by Mark Pepper, *Drawn to the Grave* by Mary Ann Mitchell, *Into the Black* by David Aaron Clark and *Silent Scream* by Dan Schmidt.

It was one hundred years since Bram Stoker first published *Dracula*, and Freda Warrington's *Dracula the Undead* was a sequel to Stoker's novel, set eight years after the ending of that book and featuring many of the same characters.

Tom Holland's *Deliver Us from Evil* was about a seventeenth century England invaded by a demonic blood-sucking army of the dead. In *Slave of My Thirst* the author also continued the exploits of his vampiric hero Lord Byron, which he began in *The Vampyre* (aka *Lord of the Undead*).

There were more historical bloodsuckers in *Writ in Blood: A Novel of Saint-Germain* by Chelsea Quinn Yarbro, set in Eastern Europe on the eve of the First World War. An enigmatic European count complicated the comeback of a beautiful actress in the vampire romance *The Ruby Tear* by Rebecca Brand (aka Suzy McKee Charnas), and a woman's biological mother wanted her blood in *Blood Relations* by Clare McNally.

A jungle explorer encountered Nazi vampires in *Night of the Dragon's Blood*, a comedy novel by William Prodgen (aka Ronald L. Ecker). An archaeologist uncovered *The Vampire Virus* by Michael Romkey, and a Romanian hit-man was hired to kill the leader of a San Francisco cult in Jonathan Nasaw's vampire novel *Shadows*. Michele Hauf's *Dark Rapture* was a romance novel featuring a time-travelling vampire, and Australian poet Tracy Ryan created a jealous bloodsucker in her debut novel *Vamp*.

Vixens of the Night was the fifth in an erotic vampire series by Valentina Cilescu. Praised by one critic for her "believable lavender prose", Karen Marie Christa Minns' *Bloodsong* was a lesbian vampire novel and a sequel to the author's *Virago*. *The Darker Passions: Carmilla* was a sexually explicit reworking of the short novel by J. Sheridan Le Fanu by Amarantha Knight (aka Nancy Kilpatrick).

Tanya Huff's vampiric ex-police detective Victory ('Vicki') Nelson returned in her fifth mystery, *Blood Debt*. This time she was out to stop some angry ghosts from haunting the undead Henry Fitzroy. *The Killing Dance* was the sixth volume in Laurell K. Hamilton's series about Anita Blake, Vampire Hunter, who in this volume has to choose between her undead or lycanthropic boyfriends.

A werewolf detective investigated a haunted schoolroom in Henry Garfield's *Room 13*, the sequel to *Moondog*, while *Opalite Moon* was Denise Vitola's follow-up to *Quantum Moon*, and featured lycanthropic detective Ty Merrick investigating the murder of cult members in the near future. A family curse and the conjuring of dark forces threatened a small town in John R. Holt's *Wolf Moon*, and more lycanthropes surfaced in *When Wolves Cry* by Chris N. Africa and Christine Tanasiuk's *Howl*.

British author Ray Bryant's debut novel, *The Satisfaction House*, was an horrific look at childhood and the winner of the *YOU*

Magazine/Little, Brown "Write a Blockbuster Novel Competition".

In Kwadwo Agymah Kamau's first novel, *Flickering Shadows*, the inhabitants of a Caribbean island were helped in their battle against a corrupt government by ghosts. Australian Kim Wilkins' *The Infernal* involved an underground musician whose fans started turning up dead and hideously mutilated, and an entrepreneur encountered a thief of souls in a strange hotel in Alan Richards' first novel, *By Charon to Aidoneus*.

With $12.7 million in secured claims against the company, and apparently owing large amounts of royalties to authors R.A. Salvatore and Margaret Weis and Tracy Hickman, amongst others, TSR, Inc. was bought for an undisclosed sum by rival game-playing company Wizards of the Coast in June, after threatening bankruptcy if suppliers were not willing to substantially reduce their claims. Having started the whole fantasy role-playing field with *Dungeons and Dragons* in 1975, TSR was the largest of the games companies. However, it was forced to lay off staff and cut costs by a downturn in the industry in 1996. Wizards of the Coast subsequently paid off TSR's debts.

Meanwhile, Wizards of the Coast, developer and publisher of *Magic: The Gathering* since 1993, was also granted a patent by the US Patent Office on "the Trading Card Method of Play", making them the only company authorized to manufacture games using the "method of game play and game components that in one embodiment are in the form of trading cards".

In a controversial move that upset authors and agents alike, Bantam and Pocket Books decided to drop the 2 per cent royalty on new contracts for their hugely successful *Star Wars* series of novelizations. Instead, they offered a higher flat-fee payment instead of an advance against royalties. Although Bantam president Irwyn Applebaum dismissed the controversy, in October Lucasfilm moved all future *Star Wars* publishing and audio rights to Ballantine Books/Del Rey for a rumoured fee of $50–60 million guaranteed against a 20 per cent or higher royalty rate. A few days earlier, Bantam Doubleday Dell also lost the rights to the *Babylon 5* novelizations to Del Rey.

It was also discovered that since mid-1993 the Pocket Books imprint had not paid royalties on sticker-priced copies of *Star*

Trek books exported for sale in Britain and Australia. It was finally decided that authors in dispute would receive a one-off second advance of $500.00 (hardcover) or $200.00 (paperback) for those overseas editions, whether the book had earned out or not, and the publisher agreed to pay a 2 per cent royalty on all titles exported in future.

After publishing a number of new books under the Borealis imprint, White Wolf returned to its successful *World of Darkness* franchise with *The Road to Hell* and *The Ascension Warrior* by Robert Weinberg, the first two volumes in the "Horizon War" trilogy, about an apparently mythical warrior who returned to bring peace and unity among warring mages, based on the role-playing game *Mage: The Ascension*.

A madness of relentless hunger gripped the vampire world in *The Devil's Advocate* and *The Winnowing* by Gherbod Fleming, the first two books of "Trilogy of the Blood Curse", based on the game *Vampire: The Masquerade*. *To Sift Through Bitter Ashes* and *To Speak in Lifeless Tongues* by David Niall Wilson were the first volumes in "The Grails Covenant" trilogy. They pitted the vampire Montrovant against the Knights Templar and were set in the world of the role-playing game *Vampire: The Dark Ages*, which was also the basis for *Dark Tyrants*, an original anthology edited by Justin Achilli and Rob Hatch.

Werewolf: Watcher by Charles Grant was also based on a role-playing game, while *The Essential World of Darkness* was a 700-plus page omnibus edited by Stewart Wieck and Anna Branscome that included five novels based on various role-playing games by Robert Weinberg and Mark Rein-Hagen (the only reprint), Owl Goingback, Scott Ciencin, David Niall Wilson and Esther M. Friesner.

Robert McLaughlin's *Cthulhu Live* was a live action horror game from Chaosium that included guidelines for costuming and building your own monsters. For the same publisher, busy series editor Robert M. Price selected and introduced *The Nyarlathotep Cycle* containing sixteen stories by H.P. Lovecraft, August Derleth, Robert E. Howard and Robert Bloch; *The Xothic Legend Cycle: The Complete Mythos Fiction of Lin Carter* included fifteen stories, two in collaboration with Price and HPL and another a solo story by the editor, while *The Scroll of Thoth: Simon Magus and the Great Old Ones* featured twelve Lovecraftian stories by Richard L. Tierney. *Singers of Strange Songs: A Celebration of Brian Lumley* was edited by David Scott Aniolowski and included two reprint stories and a poem by Lumley plus eleven other Lovecraftian tales by Donald R. Burleson, Don D'Ammassa and others.

Ravenloft: Lord of the Necropolis by Gene DeWeese was based on the TSR role-playing game, and Jane Jensen's *Gabriel Kight: Sins of the Father* took its inspiration from a popular series of CD-Rom games.

Movie novelizations continued with *Alien Resurrection* by A.C. Crispin, *Men in Black* by Steve Perry, *The Fifth Element* by Terry Bisson, *Event Horizon* by Steven E. McDonald, *Spawn* by Rob MacGregor, *Steel* by Dean Wesley Smith and *Kull the Conquerer* by Sean A. Moore. *Godzilla 2000* by Marc Cerasini was an original Millennial novel in which the big green monster was forced to battle Rodan, Varan and King Ghidorah in an attempt to avert a fiery Apocalypse.

With *The X Files* books alone apparently generating $11 million in revenues for HarperPrism, it was no surprise that *Antibodies* was the third *X Files* novelisation from Kevin J. Anderson. Meanwhile, *The Calusari* by Garth Nix was the first in a series of *X Files* TV novelizations aimed at young adult readers aged twelve and upwards. It was followed by *Eve* and *Empathy* by Ellen Steiber, *Bad Sign* by Easton Royce, *Our Town* by Eric Elfman, *Control* by Everett Owens, and *Fresh Bones* and *The Host*, both by Les Martin.

Chris Carter's pilot script for *Millennium* was adapted into the slim novel *The Frenchman* by Elizabeth Hand, followed by *Gehenna* by Lewis Gannett.

The surprise success of *Buffy the Vampire Slayer* quickly led to a series of novelizations that included *The Harvest* by Richie Tankersley Cusick, *Halloween Rain* by Christopher Golden and Nancy Holder, and *Coyote Moon* by John Vornholt. Proving that even a cancelled series was still popular amongst vampire fans, *A Stirring of Dust* by Susan Sizemore and *Intimations of Mortality* by Susan M. Garrett were both based on the TV show *Forever Knight*, about an undead detective living in Toronto.

The TV series *Highlander* was also novelized in *Measure of a Man* by Nancy Holder, *The Path* by Rebecca Neason, and *Zealot* by Donna Lettow. *Sabrina, the Teenage Witch* by David Cody

Weiss and Bobbi J.G. Weiss was followed by *Showdown at the Mall* by Diana G. Gallagher, and *Quantum Leap XIV: Loch Ness Leap* by "Sandy Schofield" was actually written by Kristine Kathryn Rusch and Dean Wesley Smith.

Paul Cornell's *The Uninvited* was an adaptation of the awful body-snatching aliens series based on an "original" idea by actor Leslie Grantham.

BBC Worldwide regained the publishing rights to *Doctor Who* following the expiration of the license to Virgin Publishing in May. Among the first titles in the BBC's new series were *Vampire Science* by Jonathan Blum and Kate Orman and *The Body-snatchers* by Mark Morris, the latter featuring the eighth Doctor investigating a case of grave robbing in Victorian London. Virgin continued to publish "The New Adventures" each month, using spin-off characters, but not the Doctor himself. Meanwhile, *A Book of Monsters* by David J. Howe was an illustrated guide to all those rubber-suited creatures in the show.

The Sex Files: File 1: Beyond Limits by Carl K. Mariner was the first in a sexually explicit series inspired by you-know-which TV series. It was quickly followed by *File 2: Forbidden Zone* by Nick Li, *File 3: Unnatural Blonde* by John Desoto, and *File 4: Double Exposure* by S.M. Horowitz (aka Valentina Cilescu).

Christopher Golden's *Hellboy: The Lost Army* was a novelization based on the Dark Horse comic, illustrated by creator Mike Mignola.

According to newspaper reports in October, a long-lost story by Mary Shelley was discovered in a chest in a house in Italy's Tuscan hills. A sentimental tale about a runaway boy and an old fisherman, written two years after *Frankenstein*, "Maurice, or the Fisher's Cot" was mentioned in the author's journal, but had not been seen until it was found by the descendent of one of the circle of friends Mary and Percy Shelley had while living in Italy.

First published in this edition in 1989, Dedalus reissued Honoré de Balzac's 1834 novel *The Quest of the Absolute*, about an obsessed alchemist, translated from the French by Ellen Marriage with an afterword by Christopher Smith. From the same publisher, *Torture Garden* was an 1899 novel by Octave Mirbeau, translated by Michael Richardson with an afterword by Brian Stableford.

The Dover edition of *The Complete John Silence Stories* marked the first time that all six of Algernon Blackwood's psychic detective tales had appeared between the same covers.

The impressive triumvirate of Richard Dalby (who supplied the introduction), Stefan R. Dziemianowicz and S.T. Joshi edited Dover's *Best Ghost and Horror Stories* by Bram Stoker, which included fourteen classic stories by the author of *Dracula*. And *Dracula: Authoritative Text, Contexts, Reviews and Reactions, Dramatic and Film Variations, Criticism* edited by Nina Auerbach and David J. Skal was a comprehensive critical edition of Stoker's novel from Norton.

Joshi also edited *The Annotated H.P. Lovecraft*, which contained four stories, plus various appendices, illustrated with photographs and artwork. *Tales of H.P. Lovecraft: Major Works Selected and Introduced by Joyce Carol Oates* collected ten classic tales by the master of cosmic horror, from Ecco Press.

Barnes & Noble's *The Cthulhu Mythos* was a welcome omnibus collecting seventeen stories by August Derleth (including the entire contents of *The Mask of Cthulhu* and *The Trail of Cthulhu*) along with an introduction by Ramsey Campbell.

With all this renewed interest in Lovecraft's Cthulhu Mythos, it was perhaps not surprising that a micro-brewery in Providence, Rhode Island, created Lovecraft Draft Cider with HPL's many-tentacled creation depicted on the label.

When the Scholastic Corporation announced that sales of its *Goosebumps* series was slowing down, resulting in a 2.4 per cent fall in sales to $210.7 million and a third-quarter net loss of $12.5 million in 1996, the company's shares fell by 40 per cent, the third-biggest percentage loss on the US stock market. According to one analyst, sales of the series of Young Adult horror books had apparently peaked after four years.

However, *Goosebumps* creator R.L. Stine signed a deal, reportedly for around $13 million, for Golden Books Family Entertainment to publish the next 65 books in his *Fear Street* series. Pocket Books, who had published around 75 volumes in the series over the past decade, retained the rights to the backlist through its Archway imprint.

Stine's latest *Fear Street* titles included *Runaway*, *Cat* and

Trapped, while *Fear Street: Fear Hall: The Beginning* and *Fear Street: Fear Hall: The Conclusion* were spread over two volumes.

Fear Street Super Chiller: Cheerleaders: The Evil Lives! was another new series, and Stine's *Fear Street: Goodnight Kiss: Collector's Edition* was an omnibus containing the novels *Goodnight Kiss* (1992) and *Goodnight Kiss II* (1996) along with a new short story, "The Vampire Club". The British omnibus *Goosebumps Flashing Special: Chicken Chicken, Dont Go to Sleep!* and *The Blob That Ate Everyone* came complete with a flashing-eyed skull cover.

Titles in the spin-off series *R.L. Stine's Fear Street Sagas*, apparently written by different authors, included *The Hidden Evil* and *Daughters of Silence* by Wendy Haley, *Children of Fear* by Brandon Alexander, *Dance of Death* by Cameron Dokey, and *Heart of the Hunter* and *The Awakening Evil* both by Eric Weiner.

Christopher Pike's latest books included *Execution of Innocence* and *The Star Group*. *The Bell, the Book, and the Spellbinder* by Brad Stickland continued the late John Bellair's "Johnny Dixon" series, and *Gulliverzone* by Stephen Baxter, *Dreamcastle* by Stephen Bowkett, *Untouchable* by Eric Brown and *Spiderbite* by Graham Joyce were the first four titles in *The Web*, a new six-part series of linked short novels set in the year 2027.

Obviously inspired by *The X Files*, M. (Mark) C. Sumner's *Extreme Zone* series kicked off with *Night Terrors* , *Dark Lies*, *Unseen Powers*, *Deadly Secrets*, *Common Enemy*, *Inhuman Fury* and *Lost Soul*, in which teens investigated strange dreams and alien psychic powers.

At Gehenna's Door by Peter Beere, *Circle of Nightmares* by Malcolm Rose, *Sweet Sixteen* by Franccsca Jeffries (aka Gail Herman), *The Vanished* by Celia Rees, *Unquiet Spirits* by K.M. Peyton, *The Girl in the Blue Tunic* by Jean Ure and *The Carver* by Jenny Jones all appeared as part of the UK's Point Horror series from Scholastic Press.

The Diary of Victor Frankenstein was a retelling of the original story by Roscoe Cooper, illustrated by Timothy Basil Ering, and William Sleator's *The Beasties* was about a race of creatures who survived by stealing human body parts. *The Golem* was a condensed retelling of the Jewish legend for young adults by Barbara Rogasky, illustrated by Trina Schart Hyman.

Three children searched Sydney's rail network for a mysterious zombie king in Bill Condon and Robert Hood's *Loco-Zombies*, the seventh volume in a proposed nine-book series. Having taken in *The Stray Cat*, Nathan and his mother discovered that the creature was more than it seemed in Steven Paulsen's short novel, published as part of Australia's After Dark series.

A ghost helped a girl become a nicer person in *Deal With a Ghost* by Marilyn Singer, *Ghost Story* by Julian Thompson involved child pornography, and two friends fell in love with a ghost in *Ghost of a Chance* by Laura Peyton Roberts. In Chelsea Quinn Yarbro's *Monet's Ghost*, a girl who could project herself into paintings encounters the ghost of the titular artist, *Music from the Dead* by Faas Bebe Rice was about a summer home in Maine haunted by ghosts, and more phantoms turned up in *Patchwork of Ghosts* by Angela Bull and *Ghost Chamber* by Celia Rees. *Dark Beneath the Moon* by Christine Purkis was a ghost novel supposedly based on a true story.

I'll See You in My Dreams by Ilene Cooper involved a girl whose dreams predicted her future. A young girl dreamed about the *Nightmare Stairs* by Robert Swindells, and in *Belin's Hill* by Catherine Fisher more children were haunted by nightmares. Lynne Reid Bank's *Angela and Diabola* were psychic sisters, one good and the other evil. *Gallow's Hill* by Lois Duncan was about a girl who had visions of the Salem Witch trials, and Frances M. Wood's *Becoming Rosemary* was set during the witch hunts. In Wendy Morgan's *Obsession*, two identical teens used voodoo.

A young boy moved to California and found himself involved with a half-human girlfriend who tried to decide if she wanted to be a vampire like her father in *The Vampire's Beautiful Daughter* by S.P. Somtow. Set in a New England where vampires were commonplace, a teenage boy also fell in love with one of the undead, who are under an automatic sentence of death, in M.T. Anderson's *Thirsty*.

The Chosen, *Soulmate*, *The Huntress*, *Black Dawn* and *Witchlight* were the latest volumes in L.J. Smith's vampire/romance series *Nightworld*.

Elvira: Camp Vamp by Elvira and John Paragon was the second in the series, while *Blood and Chocolate* by Annette Curtis Klause involved a 16-year-old werewolf. Other novels aimed at young adults included *The Darkling* by Charles Butler, *The Powerhouse* by Ann Halam (aka Gwyneth Jones), *The Grave-Digger* by Hugh Scott, *Night People* by Maggie Pearson and *Theres No Place Like Home* by A.G. Cascone.

Christopher Pike's *Tales of Terror 1* collected six stories, each introduced by the author. Introduced by Ophelia Dahl, Ralph Steadman and Tom Maschler, *The Roald Dahl Treasury* collected seventy-six pieces by the late author, including novel excerpts, unpublished poems, recipes and letters, illustrated by Quentin Blake and others.

Technofear: A Collection of Tales of Tomorrow included seven original techno-horror stories by Laurence Staig. *MindTwisters* by Neal Shusterman contained eight original stories, and *Nightcomers* featured nine original ghost stories by Susan Price. *Scared in School* by Roberta Simpson Brown collected 17 linked stories set in the 13th Street School.

Chills in the Night: Tales That Will Haunt You by Jackie Vivelo contained eight ghost stories, half of them original. Vivian Vande Velde's *Curses, Inc.* included ten twisted fairy tales, while Emma Donoghue's *Kissing the Witch: Old Tales in New Skins* featured thirteen retellings of old fairy stories.

Bruce Coville's Book of Nightmares II contained twelve mostly original stories by the editor, Al Sarrantonio, Michael Stearns and others. Dennis Pepper edited *The Young Oxford Book of Nasty Endings*, while *Bad Dreams* and *Weird and Wonderful*, both edited by Wendy Cooling, each featured six original stories.

Slow Chocolate Autopsy was another of Iain Sinclair's dark fantasies set in the underbelly of London's history, with illustrated sections by Dave McKean. Set in London and Budapest, *Signs of Life* by M. John Harrison involved a courier to the genetics industry and a woman's attempts to turn her fantastic dreams of flying into reality.

A Face at the Window was a literary ghost novel by Dennis McFarland, about a man who became obsessed with a phantom in a London hotel. Robert Girardi's *Vaporetto 13* was a romantic ghost story set in Venice, and there were more literary spooks in *If He Lived: A Modern Ghost* by Jan Stephen Fink.

James Hyne's *Publish and Perish*, subtitled "Three Tales of

Tenure and Terror" included a humorous pastiche of M.R. James' "Casting the Runes". Nick Bantock's *The Forgetting Room* involved a surreal puzzle of alchemy and revenge, while *Out of the Body* by Thomas Baum was a psychic mystery novel.

A New York woman lawyer constructed a golem in Cynthia Ozick's *The Puttermesser Papers*. The self-explanatory *Confessions of a Flesh-Eater* by the pseudonymous "David Madsen" was published by Dedalus.

Published under the Phoenix Originals list, James Lovegrove's *Days* was about a day in the life of a giant department store and was the author's second solo novel after *The Hope* (1990). After originally appearing as the world's first fully interactive Internet novel, Geoff Ryman's *253* told the stories of 253 people on board a London tube train during a seven minute journey. Each story was a single page comprising 253 words.

Mrs. Rochester by Hilary Bailey was a sequel to Charlotte Bronte's *Jane Eyre*, while the same author's *Miles and Flora* was a follow-up to Henry James' *The Turn of the Screw*. Jeremy Reed's *Dorian*, a sequel to Oscar Wilde's *The Picture of Dorian Gray*, was also published in a special limited holograph edition.

Robert Poe's *The Black Cat*, written by a distant relative of the original author, was a retelling of Edgar Allan Poe's story set in a small town and involving modern paganism.

Ray Bradbury contributed a brief afterword to *Driving Blind*, his second new collection within a year. It featured 21 stories, only four of them previously published, mostly written between 1949-56.

Although not amongst her best work, *Just an Ordinary Day* by Shirley Jackson collected 54 stories by the late writer, the majority of which were unpublished during Jackson's lifetime. *Missing the Midnight: Hauntings & Grotesques* collected 12 literary ghost stories by Jane Gardam.

Richard Laymon's *Fiends* included the original short horror novel of the title plus reprints of a dozen short stories from over the past three decades. Dean Koontz contributed an introduction.

The two volumes of *Brian Lumley's Mythos Omnibus* each contained three previously-published novels (*The Burrows Beneath*, *The Transition of Titus Crow*, *The Clock of Dreams* and *Spawn of the Winds*, *In the Moons of Borea*, *Elysia*, respectively) featuring his Titus Crow character and based on Lovecraft and Derleth's famed Cthulhu Mythos. In America, they were published in three volumes, each containing two novels apiece.

Edgeworks 3 and *4* were two hefty hardcovers from White Wolf Publishing, reprinting *The Harlan Ellison Hornbook* and *Harlan Ellison's Movie* in the first volume, and Ellison's excellent collections *Love Ain't Nothing But Sex Misspelled* and *The Beast That Shouted Love at the Heart of the World* in the second; both with new introductions by the author.

Probably the most important original horror anthology of last year was Douglas E. Winter's *Revelations* (which appeared under its original title *Millennium* from the British publisher, who was not concerned that it would be confused with the TV series of the same name). Top and tailed with a short novel by Clive Barker, it charted a decade-by-decade journey through the twentieth century by Joe R. Lansdale, David Morrell, F. Paul Wilson, Poppy Z. Brite and Christa Faust, Charles Grant, Whitley Strieber, Elizabeth Massie, Richard Christian Matheson, David J. Schow and Craig Spector, and Ramsey Campbell. A slipcased, limited edition signed by all the contributors was available from CD Publications for $100.00.

The non-themed *Dark Terrors 3: The Gollancz Book of Horror*, edited by Stephen Jones and David Sutton, featured twenty mostly new stories by Ray Bradbury, Poppy Z. Brite, Ramsey Campbell, Dennis Etchison, Christopher Fowler, Neil Gaiman, Michael Marshall Smith and others.

The fourth volume of *Northern Frights*, edited by Don Hutchison and published by Canada's Mosaic Press, included twenty non-themed stories either set in Canada or written by Canadians. The seventh volume of *Palace Corbie* was another nice-looking trade paperback edited by John Marshall and Wayne Edwards that contained thirty-nine stories by Brian Hodge, Steve Rasnic Tem, William F. Nolan, Yvonne Navarro, J.N. Williamson, Douglas Clegg, Edward Lee, John Pelan and D.F. Lewis, amongst others.

Destination Unknown was an non-themed anthology from White Wolf Publishing, edited by Peter Crowther and introduced by Anne McCaffrey. It contained sixteen original stories by Ian Watson, R.A. Lafferty, Christopher Fowler, Lisa Tuttle, Terry

Dowling, Ramsey Campbell, Storm Constantine and others. From the same editor and publisher, *Tales in Time* featured 13 reprint stories about time-travel from Jack Finney, H.G. Wells, Ray Bradbury, Harlan Ellison and others, introduced by John Clute.

White Wolf also attempted to resurrect *New Worlds*, once again edited by David Garnett and featuring new stories by Pat Cadigan, Kim Newman, Brian W. Aldiss, Howard Waldrop, Ian Watson, Garry Kilworth, Michael Moorcock and William Gibson.

Gothic Ghosts edited by Wendy Webb and Charles L. Grant featured 19 traditional-style ghost stories by such authors as Rick Hautala, Nancy Holder, Kathryn Ptacek, Brian Stableford, Esther M. Friesner and Lucy Taylor.

Editor Gardner R. Dozois' *Dying For It* was billed as "More Erotic Tales of Unearthly Love" and contained 17 stories (four reprints) by Tanith Lee, Ian R. MacLeod, Pat Cadigan, Steve Utley, Michael Bishop, Ursula K. Le Guin, Nancy Kress and others.

The Hot Blood Series: Kiss and Kill was the eighth in the series edited by Jeff Gelb and Michael Garrett and contained 16 stories of erotic horror by Graham Masterton, Brian Hodge, Gary Brander, Thomas Tessier and Nancy Holder, amongst others. The next volume, *Crimes of Passion*, introduced a new look to the series with 14 stories (three reprints) by Ramsey Campbell, Brian Lumley, Brian Hodge, Joyce Carol Oates, Lawrence Block, Melanie Tem, Greg Kihn and others.

Urban Legends edited by Josepha Sherman and Keith R.A. DeCandido contained 25 stories inspired by contemporary urban myths by such writers as S.P. Smotow and Kristine Kathryn Rusch.

The Time Out Book of New York Short Stories edited by Nicholas Royle featured 23 stories about the Big Apple by such authors as Kim Newman, Joyce Carol Oates, Michael Moorcock, Jonathan Carroll and Christopher Fowler.

Veteran editor Mike Ashley had a busy year, and along with such anthologies as *The Chronicles of the Round Table* and other similar books, he also published *Shakespearean Whodunits*, which featured murders and mysteries based on Shakespeare's plays by such authors as Stephen Baxter, Louise Cooper, Tom

Holt, Patricia McKillip, Kim Newman, Darrell Schweitzer and Peter Tremayne. The indefatigable Ashley also edited *The Mammoth Book of New Sherlock Holmes Adventures*, which featured 21 new stories and four reprints by Michael Moorcock, Stephen Baxter, Simon Clark, Basil Copper, Peter Tremayne, Guy N. Smith, David Langford and others, plus an excellent chronology of cases and a bibliographical listing of stories compiled by the editor.

The Mammoth Book of Dracula: Vampire Tales for the New Millennium edited by Stephen Jones was a "fictionalized history" of the Count during his centenary year. It contained 31 new and reprint stories by such diverse writers as Ramsey Campbell, Christopher Fowler, Thomas Ligotti, Brian Lumley, Paul J. McAuley, Kim Newman, Michael Marshall Smith, F. Paul Wilson and others, plus the first publication of the *Prologue* to Bram Stoker's 1897 stage-play of *Dracula, or the Un-Dead*, a poem, and a foreword by Stoker's great-nephew, Daniel Farson.

Blood Thirst: 100 Years of Vampire Fiction edited by Leonard Wolf and illustrated by Max Douglas, included twenty-seven reprint stories by Stephen King, Anne Rice, Tanith Lee, Roger Zelazny, Woody Allen, Charles Beaumont, Joyce Carol Oates and others. *Vampires, Wine & Roses* edited by John Richard Stephens covered much of the same material with thirty-four stories, poems and excerpts from such authors as Anne Rice, Woody Allen, William Shakespeare, Rod Serling, Lenny Bruce, H.P. Lovecraft and Sting.

Cherished Blood edited by Cecilia Tan contained ten erotic vampire stories and *Brothers of the Night: Tales of Men, Blood, and Immortality* edited by Michael Rowe and Thomas S. Roche collected eleven tales of gay erotica by Edo van Belkom and others. Poppy Z. Brite contributed one of the eighteen stories in *Grave Passions: Tales of the Gay Supernatural* edited by J. William Mann.

At one time set to be called *Razor Kiss, Love in Vein II: Eighteen More Original Tales of Vampire Erotica* was edited by Poppy Z. Brite and Martin H. Greenberg and included seventeen original stories by Caitlín R. Kiernan, Christopher Fowler, Lucy Taylor, Roberta Lannes, Brian Hodge, Nicholas Royle, Richard Laymon and David J. Schow, plus a reprint by Neil Gaiman.

With Lawrence Schimel (who supplied the introduction), Greenberg also edited *Blood Lines: Vampire Stories from New England* featuring ten stories (one original) from H.P. Lovecraft, Manly Wade Wellman, Chelsea Quinn Yarbro, Esther Friesner and others. Schimel and Greenberg also teamed up on *Southern Blood: Vampire Stories from the American South*, which included twelve stories by Dan Simmons, Fred Chappel and others, and *The Fortune Teller*, which contained sixteen original stories and a poem by Neil Gaiman about prognostication. The latter also included a new Vicki Nelson vampire story by Tanya Huff.

With Richard Chizmar, Greenberg edited *Screamplays*, which collected seven scripts by Harlan Ellison, Stephen King, Joe R. Lansdale, Richard Matheson and others, along with an introduction by Dean Koontz.

On his own, Greenberg edited *Vampires: The Greatest Stories*, which featured fifteen stories by Robert Bloch, Philip K. Dick, Roger Zelazny, Jane Yolen, S.P. Somtow and others in an instant remainder edition from MJF Books. *Haunted Houses: The Greatest Stories* was another instant remainder anthology from Greenberg, containing sixteen stories by Lovecraft, Bloch and others.

Martin Greenberg was also the series editor on David Drake's *A Century of Horror 1970–79*, the first in a projected decade-by-decade series which contained 21 classic stories by such authors as Richard Matheson, Tanith Lee and David Morrell, with an introduction by Stefan R. Dziemianowicz.

As usual, he also teamed up with Dziemianowicz and Robert Weinberg for more instant remainder volumes from Barnes & Noble. *Girls' Night Out: Twenty-Nine Female Vampire Stories* was arranged alphabetically with stories by Robert Aickman, Robert Bloch, Pat Cadigan, Hugh B. Cave, August Derleth, Barbara Hambly, K.W. Jeter, Tanith Lee, Fritz Leiber, Richard Matheson, Joanna Russ, Brian Stableford, Manly Wade Wellman and Everil Worrell, amongst others. The same team was also responsible for the superb anthology of short shorts, *100 Fiendish Little Frightmares*, and both books contained knowledgeable introductions by Dziemianowicz.

The Best of Interzone edited by David Pringle was the first *Interzone* anthology for six years and featured 29 previously uncollected stories from Britain's premier science fiction magazine by such authors as J.G. Ballard, Richard Calder, Thomas M.

Disch, Graham Joyce and Peter F. Hamilton, Garry Kilworth, Ian R. MacLeod, Kim Newman, Brian Stableford, Ian Watson and Cherry Wilder.

Bodies of the Dead and Other Great American Ghost Stories edited by David G. Hartwell reprinted 13 classic tales by Bierce, Hawthorne, Poe, and others. *Twelve Tales of the Supernatural* and *Twelve Victorian Ghost Stories*, both edited by Michael Cox for Oxford Paperbacks, featured stories by M.R. James, Marjorie Bowen, Shamus Frazer, J. Sheridan Le Fanu, Henry James and Amelia B. Edwards.

As part of the Oxford World Classics series, *The Vampyre and Other Tales of the Macabre* edited by Robert Morrison and Chris Baldick collected together fourteen stories from 1819-38, from such authors as John Polidori, J. Sheridan Le Fanu and James Hogg, plus a long introduction by the editors.

In *Restless Spirits: Ghost Stories by American Women 1872-1926*, editor Catherine A. Lundie arranged the twenty-two stories thematically, by authors such as Edith Wharton, Mary Wilkins Freeman and Charlotte Perkins Gilman.

Weird Tales: Seven Decades of Terror edited by John Betancourt and Robert Weinberg was a Barnes & Noble instant remainder collection of twenty-eight stories that originally appeared in *Weird Tales* from the 1920s to the 1990s, published in chronological order. Also from Barnes & Noble, *American Gothic* edited by Elizabeth Terry and Terri Hardin collected twenty-five Gothic stories by Poe, Robert Chambers, Charlotte Perkins Gillman, Washington Irving and others. The first hardcover edition of *The Book of Vampires* edited by Stephen Jones also appeared as an instant remainder from Barnes & Noble.

As part of a promotion with *Focus* magazine, Victor Gollancz published *Future Visions: Tale from Beyond 200*, a free sampler featuring novel extracts by Paul J. McAuley, Simon R. Green and Arthur C. Clarke, plus short stories from Nicholas Royle, Ian Watson, Peter F. Hamilton, Ian McDonald and Michael Marshall Smith.

The Year's Best Fantasy and Horror: Tenth Annual Collection edited by Ellen Datlow and Terri Windling contained 39 stories and four poems. It weighed in at over 600 pages, more than a hundred of which contained annual summaries by the editors and others. Running just over 500 pages, *The Mammoth Book of Best*

New Horror Volume Eight featured 24 stories and novellas, including two by Terry Lamsley, plus an overview of the genre in 1996, a detailed Necrology and a listing of useful addresses.

During 1997, more horror was published by the semi-professional and specialty presses than ever before.

In January, small press publisher Ash-Tree Press relocated to Canada from Britain, but still managed to maintain its prolific output of limited edition hardcovers of ghost stories and the supernatural. *Imagine a Man in a Box* was a reprint of H.R. Wakefield's 1931 collection of 13 stories, around half of which were supernatural. The volume also included an introduction by Barbara Roden and a bibliographic afterword by Jack Adrian. *Someone in the Room: Strange Tales Old and New* was the third volume in a projected four-book series collecting the bulk of A.M. Burrage's supernatural fiction. Edited by Jack Adrian, it contained twenty-eight stories, including seven published in book form for the first time and two articles about ghosts by Burrage.

Reprinted from 1947, *Unholy Relics* by M.P. Dare contained thirteen stories about investigators into the supernatural Gregory Wayne and Alan Granville, plus an extra story and a novel excerpt. *In Ghostly Company* by Amyas Northcote was reprinted from 1921 and featured an extensive biography by Richard Dalby and another bibliographic tailpiece by Jack Adrian.

The Rose of Death and Other Mysterious Delusions contained eight stories by Julian Hawthorne (the only son of the more famous Nathaniel) and was edited and introduced by Jessica Amanda Salmonson. Richard Dalby edited and supplied the introduction to *The Haunted Chair and Other Stories* by Richard Marsh (aka Richard Bernard Heldmann). This volume featured eighteen stories by the author of the 1897 novel *The Beetle* and Robert Aickman's grandfather.

The Ash-Tree Press Annual Macabre 1997 was the first in a proposed series of obscure reprints edited by Jack Adrian and scheduled to appear between Halloween and Christmas every year. The theme of the first volume was four weird stories by women writers, published between 1911–36. *Midnight Never Comes* edited by Barbara Roden and Christopher Roden was the first Ash-Tree Press anthology and contained seventeen ghost stories by Stephen Volk, Terry Lamsley, John Whitbourn, Jonathan Aycliffe, Marni Griffin, Ron Weighell, Rhys Hughes and Simon Clark, amongst others.

Ash-Tree also published the first hardcover edition of Terry Lamsley's World Fantasy Award-winning debut collection *Under the Crust: Supernatural Tales of Buxton*, which the author originally self-published in 1993.

Fedogan & Bremer continued to produce some of the best books in the Arkham House tradition with *Don't Dream*, edited by Philip J. Rahman and Dennis E. Weiler, which collected twenty-six horror and fantasy stories (two previously unpublished) by the late pulp writer Donald Wandrei, along with prose poems, essays and other fragments. It was introduced by the author's next door neighbour, Helen Mary Hughesdon, and included a substantial historical afterword by D.H. Olson.

A tribute to the late Karl Edward Wagner edited by Stephen Jones, *Exorcisms and Ecstasies* contained thirty-two uncollected stories and two poems, personal reminiscences by Peter Straub, Frances Wellman, David J. Schow, Ramsey and Jenny Campbell, David Drake, James R. Wagner, Brian Lumley and C. Bruce Hunter, a working bibliography, artwork by J.K. Potter and sixteen pages of photographs.

To celebrate their authors' appearance as special guests at the 1997 World Fantasy Convention in London, Fedogan & Bremer launched *The Door Below* containing twenty-five stories by Hugh B. Cave, published chronologically from over five decades, with a new foreword by the writer, and *The Vampire Stories of R. Chetwynd-Hayes* edited by Stephen Jones, featuring fifteen often humorous tales of the undead (including a new Fred and Frances story), along with an introduction by Brian Lumley, an exclusive interview with the author and illustrations by Jim Pitts.

All the Fedogan & Bremer books were published in attractive trade editions plus 100-copy signed and slipcased limited editions.

Pumpkin Books was a new British small press publisher that launched itself at the World Fantasy Convention with two new hardcovers: *Dark of the Night: New Tales of Horror and the Supernatural* was edited by Stephen Jones and contained fourteen original stories and a poem by Stephen Baxter, Ramsey Campbell, David Case, Christopher Fowler, Paul J. McAuley, Kim Newman, Michael Marshall Smith, Douglas E. Winter and others.

Edited and annotated by Sylvia Starshine, Bram Stoker's *Dracula: or the Un-Dead: A Play in Prologue and Five Acts* marked the first publication of the only surviving copy of the author's play-script, performed just once at London's Lyceum Theatre on 18 May 1897, with eight pages of photographs and illustrations. Starshine and friends organized a five-and-a-half hour read-through of the play at the historic Spaniard's Inn pub, Hampstead, on 18 May 1997. Both books were also available in very reasonably priced signed and slipcased editions limited to 250 numbered and twenty-six lettered copies.

As its official souvenir book, the World Fantasy Convention published an original anthology entitled *Secret City: Strange Tales of London* edited by Stephen Jones and Jo Fletcher. Available as a large-size paperback and in a limited hardcover edition of just 300 copies, it included fiction and articles by Iain Sinclair, Joan Aiken, Hugh B. Cave, R. Chetwynd-Hayes, Clive Barker, Karl Edward Wagner, Michael Marshall Smith, Kim Newman, Christopher Lee, Les Daniels, Basil Copper, Caitlín R. Kiernan, Christopher Fowler and many others, plus a special section celebrating the centenary of *Dracula*.

New trade paperback releases from Tanjen included the novels *Eyelidiad* by Rhys H. Hughes, *The Parasite* by Neal L. Asher, *Recluse* by Derek M. Fox, *Prisoners of Limbo* by David Ratcliffe, *Mesmer* by Tim Lebbon and *Scattered Remains* by Paul Pinn. *Scaremongers* was an anthology edited by Andrew Haigh that included twenty-five new and reprint stories by Ramsey Campbell, Dennis Etchison, Poppy Z. Brite, Joan Aiken, Michael Marshall Smith, Peter Crowther and others, plus a poem by Ray Bradbury, with royalties being donated to three animal charities.

From Tartarus Press came three more volumes by Arthur Machen: *Tales of Horror and Supernatural* was effectively thirteen of the best of Machen's stories and novellas with a new introduction by Roger Dobson, published in an edition of 500 limited and twenty marbled presentation copies. From the same publisher came a revised edition of Machen's more obscure tales, *Ritual and Other Stories*, in a limited edition of 200 copies, including twenty marbled for presentation. *Ornaments in Jade* was the first complete British collection of ten atmospheric prose poems written in the 1890s, with an introduction by Machen admirer Barry Humphries. Available in a limited edition of 400 copies plus twenty-five marbled presentation copies, this volume was published in association with Caermaen Books. Another Tartarus publication was *A Night with Mephistopheles* by Irish writer Henry Ferris, a collection of stories and essays by a contemporary of Poe and Le Fanu, edited and with an introduction by S.T. Joshi and limited to 200 numbered copies.

Durtro Press published 400 copies of *The Book of Jade*, a reprint of David Park Barnitz's scarce decadent collection of poetry from 1901. Praised by H.P. Lovecraft, this edition included two extra poems, an introduction by Mark Valentine and an afterword by Thomas Ligotti. Limited to 2,000 copies, Ligotti's own *In a Foreign Town, In a Foreign Land*, was a small fifty-six page hardcover from Durtro comprising four interconnected new stories together with a CD of music by UK cult band Current 93 which accompanied the text. Two-thirds of the run were sold through the group's record distributor. *Studies of Death: Stories by Stanislaus Eric, Count Stenbock*, was another attractive hardcover, limited to 300 copies, reprinting the 1894 decadent collection plus an extra story, two translations and a fascinating introduction by David Tibet.

The White Road by Ron Weighell was published by the Ghost Story Press and limited to 400 copies. The first book in a planned series of rare reprints from Caliban Press was C.D. Pamely's *Tales of Mystery & Terror*, issued in a hardcover edition of just 250 copies, with an introduction by Brian Stableford, an afterword by Richard Dalby, and illustrations by publisher David Fletcher.

Besides various limited editions of mainstream books, CD Publications also issued *A Fist Full of Stories (and Articles)* by Joe R. Lansdale which, as the title indicated, was a bit of a mixed bag and included a dozen stories, a novel excerpt, five essays and a play. *Things Left Behind* was a large collection of thirty-nine related stories, vignettes to novellas (twenty-three original) by Gary A. Braunbeck. It also included a preface by J.N. Williamson, an introduction by William F. Nolan and an afterword by Ed Gorman. Illustrated by Allen Koszowski, it was limited to 500 signed copies. The first edition of the long-delayed Horror Writer's Association anthology *Robert Bloch's Psychos* attributed the editing to the late author and included twenty-two stories by Stephen King, Charles Grant, Richard Christian Matheson, Jane Yolen, Ed Gorman and others.

A decade after it was first published, CD was also responsible for a welcome reissue of Ray Garton's contemporary vampire novel *Live Girls* in a 500-copy signed and slipcased hardcover, with a new introduction by the author and a CD "soundtrack" to the book, created by Scott Vladimir Licina. Richard Laymon's 1980 novel *The Cellar* was another reprint given the signed and slipcased treatment by CD in an edition of 500 copies with an introduction by Bentley Little and an endnote by the cover artists.

The Good, the Bad, and the Indifferent was a nice-looking hardcover collection of early or obscure stories and other miscellaneous material by Joe R. Lansdale, including sixteen never-before-published tales. It was available from Subterranean Press in a 600-copy signed and numbered edition and twenty-six signed and lettered copies, leatherbound in a hand-made slipcase with one of the author's rejection slips dating from the late 1970s or early '80s included. Subterranean also published a hardcover reprint of Lansdale's rare first novel, the western *Texas Night Riders*. Written in eleven days and originally published in 1983 as by "Ray Slater", it was available in a signed limited edition of 500 copies and a $125 lettered edition with a new introduction by the author.

Robert Bloch, John Carradine, Davis Grubb, Stephen King, John Landis, Ira Levin, David Morrell, Roman Polanski, Diana Rigg and Orson Welles were among the many characters sampled and re-mixed by Eugene Byrne and Kim Newman in *Back in the USSA*, an alternate history set in the United Socialist States of America, originally serialised in *Interzone* and published in hardcover by Mark V. Ziesing Books.

Whitley Strieber's first collection, *Evenings with Demons*, which also included a miscellany of previously unpublished fragments, appeared in a 350-copy signed edition from Borderlands Press, which quickly sold out.

From the Overlook Connection came a handsome "corrected definitive" hardcover of Jack Ketchum's (aka Dallas Mayr) 1989 novel *The Girl Next Door* with a new introduction by Stephen King, afterwords by Christopher Golden, Lucy Taylor, Edward Lee and Philip Nutman, plus an interview with the author by Stanley Wiater. Limited to 500 copies, there was also a fifty-two mahogany-boxed lettered edition signed by all the contributors for $300.00.

Gauntlet Press owner Barry Hoffman published his own serial killer novel *Hungry Eyes* with an introduction by William F. Nolan and an afterword by Rick Hautala in both a trade hardcover and a signed, limited edition of 500 copies. Terminal Fright's first publication was *The Throne of Bones* by Brian McNaughton, a collection of fourteen stories (half of them original) set in a fantasy world of ghouls, with an introduction by Alan Rodgers and an afterword by S.T. Joshi. It was subsequently reprinted by the Science Fiction Book Club. Also from Terminal Fright, the anthology *Terminal Frights* edited by Ken Abner featured twenty-two stories by Peter Crowther, Yvonne Navarro, J.N. Williamson and others.

The Mirror of Night was a long-awaited collection of ten stories by Roberta Lannes with a non-introduction by Harlan Ellison. It was published by John Pelan's Silver Salamander Press in a trade paperback edition of 500 copies, a limited hardcover of 300 copies and a deluxe leatherbound edition of fifty copies. Also from Silver Salamander, *Painted in Blood* was the third collection by Lucy Taylor, and like the Lannes volume it was available in a deluxe edition of fifty copies, a limited edition of 300 and a trade paperback of 500. *Notes from the Darkside* was an irregular newsletter about recent and forthcoming releases from Silver Salamander and the Darkside Press.

Edward Lee's southern Gothic *The Bighead* appeared in both hardcover and paperback from Necro Press, and Lee was also one of the contributors to Necro's anthology *Inside the Works*, along with Gerard Daniel Houarner and Tom Piccirrilli.

From Dark Regions Press came the Bentley Little collection *Murmerous Haunts* and *Horizon Lines* by Jeffrey Osier. The latter included seven stories (one original) with an introduction by Elizabeth Massie and was also available in a twenty-six copy deluxe limited hardcover edition. *Leavings* was a collection of thirteen (seven original) *Twilight Zone*-type stories by P.D. Cacek with a foreword by Edward Bryant, published by StarsEnd Creations.

The Best of Weird Tales: 1923 was the first volume in a proposed series edited by Marvin Kaye and John Gregory Betancourt published by Wildside Press/Bleak House. It included thirteen stories from the first year of the pulp magazine by authors H.P. Lovecraft, Frank Owen, editor Farnsworth Wright and others.

From California's Zapizdat Publications came *Monsters from Memphis*, a trade paperback anthology edited by Beecher Smith, featuring thirty-one stories set in or around the Tennessee city by Brent Monahan, Don Webb, Tom Piccirilli, Trey R. Baker and others, including two by the editor. New York's Gryphon Books published *Professor Challenger in Secrets of the Dreamlands* by Ralph E. Vaughan, a lost world/Lovecraftian novel featuring Conan Doyle's adventurer.

After leaving Arkham House because he was accused of publishing too much science fiction, editor and packager James Turner created his own imprint, Golden Gryphon Press. His first release was James Patrick Kelly's *Think Like a Dinosaur and Other Stories*, a collection of fourteen stories reprinted from *Asimov's*, including the Hugo Award winning novelette of the title, with a forward by John Kessel. One of Turner's last books for Arkham House was *Voyages by Starlight*, the impressive first collection from British author Ian R. MacLeod, with most of the ten stories again reprinted from *Asimov's* and a foreword by Michael Swanwick.

From Ripping Publishing came two debut novels by British authors: Brian Hughes' humorous *Hobson & Co (Paranormal Investigators)* was illustrated by the author, while Simon M. Shinerock's *The Dark Lagoon* was about a demon living off the coast of Florida.

Noctet: Tales of Madonna-Moloch by Albert J. Manachino was a collection of this small press author's stories, with an introduction by Charles R. Saunders, from Argo Press. *A Cold at Heart* was Brian Hopkin's novel about werewolves in the Arctic, published by Sovereign Seal Books.

Published by Australia's Ticonderoga Publications, Steven Utley's long-awaited first short collection, *Ghost Seas*, collected fourteen stories written over a twenty-seven year period with a preface by Michael Bishop and an introduction by Howard Waldrop. A signed, limited edition of fifty copies was also available. From Australia's Galley Press, *Penumbra* was Stephen Studach's first collection of seven stories, six of which were previously unpublished.

Quetzalcon was a clever short story disguised as a programme booklet for "The Kingston Dunstan Convention" by Kim Newman, designed by Michael Marshall Smith and published by Airgedlámh Publications in an edition of 800 signed and numbered copies for the 1997 World Fantasy Convention in London.

New chapbooks from Subterranean Press included *Blood Brothers*, a non-supernatural thriller by Richard T. Chizmar, and *Between Floors* by Thomas F. Monteleone, about a man trapped in an elevator with a mad bomber. *Doughnuts* by James Blaylock with cover art by Tim Powers was a reprint of a hard-to-find story about a man obsessed by the eponymous snack food, while *Website* by Ray Garton was a new story about a madman obsessed with the Internet. All four publications were each limited to 250 signed and numbered copies and twenty-six lettered copies.

From The Ministry of Whimsy Press, *The Final Trick of Funnyman and Other Stories* by Bruce Taylor collected thirty stories (six original) mostly reprinted from the small press, and *Feeding the Glamour Hogs* by Mark McLaughlin collected eight stories, most of them reprints. *The Troika* was a surreal debut novel by Stepan Chapman, about three travellers crossing an endless desert who were manipulated by unseen forces.

Darrell Schweitzer's *Poetica Dementia: Being a Further Accumulation of Metrical Offenses* was a humorous booklet of thirteen Lovecraftian poems (three original), illustrated by Thomas Brown and published by "Zadok Allen". *Tales of Sesqua Valley* by W.H. Pugmire was a chapbook of ten Lovecraftian stories (two original) published by Necropolitan Press.

Black Walls, Red Glass from Georgia's Marietta Publishing collected three original horror stories by Jeffrey Thomas, illustrated by the author. *The Dog Syndrome & Other Sick Puppies* by Tom Piccirilli contained six stories illustrated by seven artists, and was limited to 500 signed copies.

Canadian author Cliff Burns' collection of fifteen stories, *The Reality Machine (Tales of the Immediate Future)*, was published in a print run of 1,000 signed copies by Black Dog Press and included an introduction by Kim Newman. From Tsathoggua Press came two volumes of "The Early Cannon", *The Thing in the Bathtub and Other Lovecraftian Tales* and *Tales of Lovecraftian Horror and Humor*, which between them collected fifteen HPL pastiches by Peter H. Cannon.

Hobgoblin Press issued chapbook editions of such classic

Victorian tales as Robert W. Chambers' *The King in Yellow*, Arthur Machen's *The Hill of Dreams* and R.H. Benson's collection *The Light Invisible*. Edited by Jessica Amanda Salmonson for publisher Richard H. Fawcett, *The Shell of Sense* contained a quartet of ghost stories written nearly a century ago by Olivia Howard Dunbar.

Roger Johnson's *I am Dracula. Welcome to My House*, published by The Pyewacket Press, was a minimal stage adaptation of Stoker's story and a background to vampire literature. From Macabre, Inc., Nancy Kilpatrick's *Endorphins* collected two original vampire stories with illustrations by Chad Savage and an introduction by Karen E. Taylor.

The Exorcist by Mark Kermode, *The Thing* by Anne Billson, *Blue Velvet* by Michael Atkinson and *The Cabinet of Dr. Caligari* by David Roinson were among a number of titles published as part of The BFI Modern Classics series.

After taking over from Kristine Kathryn Rusch with the May issue of *The Magazine of Fantasy & Science Fiction*, new editor Gordon Van Gelder continued the digest's forty-eighth year of publication with stories by Brian Stableford, Ron Gulart, Nancy Etchemendy, Mary Soon Lee, Kathe Koja and Barry N. Malzberg, Nancy Springer, Jack Williamson, Michael Blumlein, Esther M. Friesner, Nina Kiriki Hoffmann, David Bischoff and many others, plus book review columns by Charles de Lint, Elizabeth Hand, Robert K.J. Killheffer and Douglas E. Winter.

Although David Pringle's *Interzone* did not have as much as usual to offer in the areas of horror or dark fantasy, there was still a lot to admire, including Brian Stableford's two-part historical vampire novella "The Black Blood of the Dead", stories by Michael Marshall Smith, Ian Watson, Terry Dowling, Paul J. McAuley, Lisa Tuttle, Stephen Baxter, Kim Newman and Eugene Byrne, Stephen Baxter, Gwyneth Jones and Graham Joyce; interviews with Smith, Neil Gaiman, Dyana Wynne Jones, Peter Crowther and James Lovegrove, Gene Wolfe, M. John Harrison, Judith Merril, and Pat Cadigan; Stableford's articles on James Blish, Fritz Leiber and Hugo Gernsback; a tribute to Sam Moskowitz by Mike Ashley, and all the usual columns and book reviews.

After an issue numbered '0' appeared in September/October,

mostly reprinting material from its role-playing sister magazine *Valkyrie*, new British science fiction and fantasy magazine *Odyssey* made its debut in November/December, edited by Liz Holliday. Published by Partizan Press, the first bi-monthly issue included a story by Stephen Baxter, an interview with Terry Bisson and columns by Colin Greenland, David Langford and others.

Before being cancelled for the second time, Larry Flint's thinking man's porno magazine *Rage* included new and reprint fiction by David J. Schow, Poppy Z. Brite (who also posed naked as well), Kim Newman, Paul J. McAuley and Dennis Etchison, an article about the *Dracula* centenary by David J. Skal, and interviews with John Carpenter, Clive Barker, David Cronenberg, J.G. Ballard, Troma's Lloyd Kaufman, and Rob Zombie.

The 26 April-2 May issue of *TV Guide* included a rare reprint of Stephen King's prologue to *The Shining* plus an alternative cover painting by Bernie Wrightson, and Nicholas Royle contributed a new Halloween story to the London listings magazine *Time Out*.

As usual, the Hallowe'en edition of *AB Bookman's Weekly* was a special issue on science fiction, fantasy and horror to tie in with the World Fantasy Convention. It included a profile of the career and writings of Avram Davidson, plus reviews and numerous ads for dealers.

Edited by Dave Golder, *SFX* continued to offer the most eclectic overview of the SF/fantasy/horror genres with each monthly edition packed with news, reviews, features and gossip. Among those interviewed in its glossy pages were Forrest J Ackerman, Grant Morrison, David Cronenberg, Freda Warrington, Peter Jackson, George Romero, Douglas Winter, Phil Rickman, Tom Holland, R. Chetwynd-Hayes, Jack Hill and John Landis. In August, *SFX*'s Future Publishing also launched *CultTV*, a messy-looking monthly which featured articles on old and new TV shows, including *ScoobyDoo* and *The Avengers*.

Under the guiding hand of editor David Miller, Visual Imagination's *Shivers* remained a solid read for horror media fans. Monthly issues featured interviews with Russell Mulcahy, Wes Craven, Andrew Kier, Rick Baker and Guillermo del Toro, along with a series of articles celebrating the 100th anniversary of Dracula and Ingrid Pitt's appallingly self-indulgent column,

"The Pitt of Horror". Sister publication *Starburst*, edited by Stephen Payne, celebrated its twentieth anniversary with the December issue. Along with its monthly coverage of *Star Trek*, *Red Dwarf*, *Star Wars*, *The X Files* and *Babylon 5*, it also published three specials and a Yearbook.

As well as the expected double-issues devoted to *Star Trek* and *The X Files*, Frederick S. Clark's always excellent *Cinefantastique* profiled *Mars Attacks!*, the twentieth anniversary of *Star Wars* and the special effects of *The Empire Strikes Back*, *Space Truckers*, MTV's animated *Aeon Flux*, Disney's Hercules, *Batman & Robin*, *Contact*, *Spawn* and *Starship Troopers*, amongst numerous other movies.

Sci-Fi Entertainment, edited by Scott Edelman, was billed as "The Official Magazine of the Sci-Fi Channel". Along with endless pages of advertising, it also included news and features about the latest film and TV releases, plus retrospective articles on Hammer films and vampire movies. Several regular writers for the British horror magazine *The Dark Side* withdrew their services owing to non-payment of invoices, a problem which also resulted in the collapse of its sister SF magazine, *Infinity*.

Tim and Donna Lucas' Bram Stoker Award-nominated *Video Watchdog*, subtitled "The Perfectionists Guide to Fantastic Video", produced six more excellent issues. Alongside the usual reviews of video, laserdiscs, DVDs, soundtracks and books, the magazine also included profiles of the *Highlander* series, George Romero's *Dead* trilogy, the missing scenes from *E.T.*, a career interview with Italian screenwriter Ernesto Gastaldi, Dan Curtis' two *Dark Shadows* movies, the career of Edgar G. Ulmer, the two versions of *Doctor X*, and Cronenberg's controversial *Crash*.

Michael J. Weldon's *Psychotronic Video* included fascinating interviews with John "Bud" Cardos, Larry Buchanan, Julie Edge, James Karen, Monte Hellman and make-up man Harry Thomas, plus a tribute to horror host Ghoulardi and numerous reviews of obscure movies.

In its twenty-ninth year, *Locus*, edited by Charles N. Brown and Marianne S. Jablon, continued to be the most reliable news and reviews magazine in the science fiction, fantasy and horror field. With most monthly issues averaging around seventy pages, authors interviewed included Dan Simmons, Jane Yolen, Jonathan Lethem, and Gardner Dozois. Andrew I. Porter's *Science Fiction Chronicle* only managed four irregular issues in 1997 (which was one more than the previous year's total). They included interviews with Jonathan Carroll, Brian Stableford and Stephen Jones.

Ably edited by Debbie Bennett and David J. Howe, The British Fantasy Society's bi-monthly *Newsletter* pointlessly changed its name to *Prism UK*, but otherwise remained the same, with plenty of news and reviews of books, films and small press publications, plus regular columns by Nicholas Royle and Tom Holt. *The Best of Prism UK* was a sampler published for the 1997 World Fantasy Convention.

Also produced by the BFS, Peter Cannon's chapbook *Long Memories: Recollections of Frank Belknap Long* included an afterword by Ramsey Campbell. It was a fascinating, often hilarious, but ultimately depressing memoir of the pulp author and his eccentric wife Lyda during their final years in New York. Another excellent BFS booklet was *Shocks*, a reprint collection of four stories by R. Chetwynd-Hayes, with an introduction by David J. Howe.

For anyone interested in the books published by Ash-Tree Press, then The Ghost Story Society (also run by Barbara and Christopher Roden) offered three more issues of its journal, *All Hallows*, including a Dracula special. Along with news and reviews, these nicely-produced volumes included articles on Russell Kirk, illustrators of M.R. James, Le Fanu's "Carmilla", the history of Hallowe'en, and fiction by Tina Rath, John Whitbourn and others.

The Fall 1997 issue John B. Rosenman and Joe Morey's *Horror Magazine* included interviews with Dan Simmons, S.P. Somtow, Joseph Mugnaini and David B. Silva.

Besides offering regional events for its members around Britain, The Vampire Society also published *The Velvet Vampyre*, which included book reviews by Tina Rath and a bizarre article about customised hearses. Issue 22 of Thee Vampire Guild's *Crimson* was a special fiction issue, featuring D.F. Lewis and others, while No. 24 included an interview with Caroline Munro.

Edited by Aaron Sterns, the latest three issues *Severed Head: The Journal of The Australian Horror Writers* included articles on Australian Gothic, a history of censorship in Australia, the search for Australia's first fictional vampire, a look at Australian horror comics plus all the usual news and letters.

Richard T. Chizmar's *Cemetery Dance* managed three issues featuring fiction by Ed Gorman, Jack Ketchum, William F. Nolan, Terry Lamsley, Peter Crowther and James Lovegove, Joe R. Lansdale, Richard Laymon, Hugh B. Cave and Melanie Tem, plus interviews with Laymon, Dean Koontz, Douglas Clegg, Richard Matheson and Norman Partridge, non-fiction from Lansdale and Stanley Wiater, and the usual columns by Thomas F. Monteleone, Charles L. Grant, Ed Bryant, Paul Sammon, Ed Gorman and Tyson Blue.

The eighth *Midnight Graffiti* was a special "Killers" issue, edited by Jesse Horsting, with an article by Stephen King, fiction from David J. Schow and an interview with Neil Gaiman. Al Shevy's *World of Fandom* included interviews with David Lynch, David Cronenberg, Joss Whedon, Guillermo del Toro, Jesus Franco, Tony Scott and artist S. Clay Wilson.

Concerned over worries about his health, W. Paul Ganley decided to bring his long-running *Weirdbook* to a close in style with No.30 – a large-size hardcover which was combined with a long-awaited new issue of Stuart David Schiff's *Whispers*. The Ganley section featured a cover by Stephen E. Fabian and fiction and poetry by Darrell Schweitzer, Jessica Amanda Salmonson, Ardath Mayhar, Brian McNaughton, John Maclay and John Gregory Betancourt, amongst others. When the book was flipped over, the Schiff section boasted a cover and several 'Weirdisms' by veteran *Weird Tales* artist Lee Brown Coye plus six unpublished stories from the *Whispers* files by Joseph Payne Brennan, Hugh B. Cave, Ken Wisman, Avram Davidson, Chet Williamson and David Drake.

Andy Cox's *The Third Alternative* published three more glossy issues containing "slipstream" fiction by Joel Lane, Jason Gould, Rhys Hughes, Mark Morris, Jeff VanderMeer, Nicholas Royle, Peter Crowther and James Lovegrove, amongst others, an interview with Royle, a portfolio of J.K. Potter's art, and Rick Cadger's usual rambling column.

The second edition of Shade Rupe's *Funeral Party* was a handsome, perfect-bound volume subtitled "A Celebratory Excursion into Beautiful Extremes of Life, Lust & Death". It lived up to that description with its "adults only" tag and interviews with Jack Ketchum and Ulli Lommel, a full colour art portfolio, and fiction by Ketchum, Lucy Taylor, John Shirley and others.

The first edition of Paula Guran's *Wetbones* was a promising debut that included fiction by Marc Laidlaw, Nancy Kilpatrick, Don Webb and Sean Doolittle, along with opinion columns by John Shirley, Philip Nutman and others. It was followed by the second and final number, featuring stories by Shirley, Nancy A. Collins, Edward Lee and Caitlín R. Kiernan, plus a tribute to Karl Edward Wagner by David J. Schow.

Gordon Linzner's *Space & Time* celebrated its thirtieth anniversary with issue 87, featuring a cover by Jill Bauman and fiction and poetry by Don D'Ammassa, Sue Storm, Don Webb, Mary Soon Lee and others.

The eighth issue of Mark McLaughlin's *The Urbanite* was devoted to "Fabulous Creatures" with stories from Caitlín R. Kiernan, Hugh B. Cave, Joel Lane, M.R. Scofidio and others. Subtitled "Surreal & Lively & Bizarre", the following edition spotlighted Basil Copper as the featured author with two stories, and also included fiction by Nancy Kilpatrick, Hugh B. Cave, Thomas Wiloch, Marni Scofidio Griffin and William H. Pugmire.

The fourteenth issue of Ann Kennedy's *The Silver Web* included featured artist Rodger Gerberding being interviewed by Poppy Z. Brite, interviews with Jonathan Carroll and Jack Ketchum, plus fiction from Joel Lane, Alan M. Clark and others.

The fourth issue of *Squane's Journal*, published and edited by Simon Wady, was a special Ramsey Campbell issue featuring a foreword by Stephen Jones, an introduction by Stephen Laws, and contributions by Jenny Campbell, Dennis Etchison, Douglas E. Winter, Poppy Z. Brite, Peter Atkins, Graham Joyce, Peter Crowther, Mark Morris, Conrad Williams, J.K. Potter, Nicholas Royle, Stephen Gallagher, Ed Gorman, Mark Chadbourn, Kim Newman, Joel Lane and others. Profusely illustrated with photographs, this attractive booklet came with a supplement, *Ramsey's Appendix*, containing more tributes. Also published by Squane's Press, the chapbook *Challenging the Wolf* by Steve Harris contained the titular novella and an extract from the author's unpublished "nasty" novel, *The Switch*.

Following the nineteenth and final issue of *The Scream Factory*, which looked at horror in the comics, co-editors Peter Enfantino and John Scoleri created a new magazine, *bare.bones*. The pocket-sized publication debuted in December with articles about bondage art on vintage paperbacks, the history of *Super Science Fiction*, an interview with Bill Warren and much more.

The first three issues of editor Tom Piccirilli's *Epitaph: Tales of Dark Fantasy & Horror* contained interviews with Jack Ketchum and Edward Lee, Richard Laymon, and Graham Masterton, along with fiction and poetry. The second issue of Tracy L. Craigen's Canadian fanzine *Shiver* featured an interview with Clive Barker.

The sixth and seventh issues of *Kimota*, edited by Graeme Hurry for The Preston Speculative Fiction Group, included fiction by Stephen Gallagher, Conrad Williams, Paul Finch, Peter Tennant, Paul Pinn and Nicholas Royle, along with an interview with Michael Marshall Smith. Rod Heather's *Lore* No.8 included fiction by Brian Lumley (an original SF story) and Richard Lee Byers.

As usual, Stuart Hughes' *Peeping Tom* published four issues, with new and reprint fiction from Ramsey Campbell, Stephen Gallagher, Chaz Brenchley, Guy N. Smith, Jack Wainer, Mark Chadbourn, D.F. Lewis (including a collaboration with Paul Pinn), Tim Lebbon and others. No.25 included a guest editorial by Chadbourn. Stuart Hughes' first collection *Ocean Eyes* marked the debut publication of Peeping Tom Books. It contained eleven stories illustrated by Madeleine Finnegan.

The first issue of editor John B. Ford's *Terror Tales* was subtitled "An Anthology of Traditional Horror Fiction" and included stories by William Hope Hodgson, D.F. Lewis and Derek M. Fox. Ford's own fiction was collected in the chapbooks *Macabre Delights & Twisted Tales*, introduced by Simon Clark, and *Within the Sea of the Dead*, which comprised two stories written as a tribute to and in the style of Hodgson. All three items were published by B.J.M. Press.

John Benson's *Not One of Us* No.17 included fiction and poetry by Mark McLaughlin and Barbara Rosen, and D.F. Lewis was the featured writer in the seventh issue of Anthony Barker's *Night Dreams*, which included an interview and the author's 1,000th story along with fiction by Allen Ashley and the editor. Issue 8 featured an interview with Mark Chadbourn, who also contributed a story. D.F. Lewis was also one of the writers featured in Dennis Kirk's *Outer Darkness* No.12.

The third issue of Daniel Paul Medici's *Vampire Dan's Story Emporium* included fiction by Yvonne Navarro and John B. Rosenman and an interview with Tom Piccirilli. No.4 featured an interview with Ken Wiseman. Edited and published by M. Malefica Grendelwolf Pendragon Le Fay (aka Michael Pendragon), *Penny Dreadful: Tales and Poems of Fantastic Terror* published four quarterly issues.

The Fall 1997 issue of the Science Fiction Research Association's *Extrapolation*, edited by Donald M. Hassler, included an article on H.P. Lovecraft, along with scholarly features about Philip K. Dick, Olaf Stapledon, Arthurian romance and Victorian fantasy. Issue 31 of Carl B. Yoke and Roger C. Schlobin's academic journal of the International Association for the Fantastic in the Arts, *Journal of the Fantastic in the Arts*, also included a piece on Lovecraft, as well as Bram Stoker and James Joyce.

Issues 105 and 106 of *The New York Review of Science Fiction* included features about the work of Fritz Leiber and K.W. Jeter. No.111 contained "The Communicants", an early, unfinished piece of fiction by Leiber, and the following issue featured articles on the works of Karl Edward Wagner and Joyce Carol Oates on H.P. Lovecraft.

From TTA Press, *Zene* was a useful guide to the independent press, with numerous guidelines, short articles and reviews by Rhys Hughes, Gary Couzens, Peter Tennant, Andy Cox and others.

Necronomicon Press published its usual four issues of *Necrofile: The Review of Horror Fiction*, edited by Stefan Dziemianowicz, S.T. Joshi and Michael A. Morrison. It included perceptive insights from such reviewers as Donald R. Burleson, Peter Cannon, T.E.D. Klein, Brian Stableford, Chet Williamson and others, Ramsey Campbell's regular column, and an address given at the 1997 World Horror Convention by Darrell Schweitzer.

Also from Necronomicon came two issues of S.T. Joshi's *Studies in Weird Fiction*, with articles on H.P. Lovecraft, new-wave vampires, Edgar Allan Poe and M.R. James, along with two issues of Joshi's *Lovecraft Studies*. Edited by the prolific Robert M. Price, *Crypt of Cthulhu* managed three new issues that included two articles by Lin Carter and the text of a 1963 Lovecraft symposium featuring Robert Bloch, Fritz Leiber and others, with notes by August Derleth. Containing more Lovecraftian fiction and poetry, Price's *Cthulhu Codex* and *Midnight Shambler* also totalled three issues apiece and *Tales of Lovecraftian Horror* managed just one. Also in single digits were *The Lovecraft Collector* and *The Dark Man: The Journal of Robert E. Howard Studies*, a long-delayed academic journal edited by Rusty Burke.

In His Own Write: Brian Lumley: Necroscribe collected three previously-published Lovecraftian stories and a new foreword by the author to commemorate Lumley's appearance at NecronomiCon 3. Peter Cannon's *The Chronology Out of Time: Dates in the Fiction of H.P. Lovecraft* was a revised second edition aimed at the HPL fanatic, and *Mosig, at Last: A Psychologist Looks at H.P. Lovecraft* was a collection of essays by Dirk W. Yozan Mosig, with appreciations by the author's daughter, S.T. Joshi and others.

Ghor, Kin-Slayer, edited by Jonathan Baker, was a round-robin story based on a fragment by Robert E. Howard. Contributing authors included Karl Edward Wagner, Michael Moorcock, Manly Wade Wellman, Brian Lumley, Frank Belknap Long, Ramsey Campbell, H. Warner Munn and Marion Zimmer Bradley. The first twelve chapters were originally published in *Fantasy Crossroads* magazine, with the remaining five appearing for the first time in the trade paperback from Necronomicon Press.

After two issues from new American publisher Implosion, Steven Proposch announced in December that he was withdrawing from his position as fiction editor of *Bloodsongs*, the magazine he created in Australia. He cited "artistic differences" and added that the position did not live up to his expectations. And after being published for eight years, the eighth and final issue of Rod Williams's Australian reviewzine *Skintomb* was given away free to readers.

The much-anticipated *The Encyclopedia of Fantasy*, edited by John Clute and John Grant, with help from a lot of other people, weighed in at more than a million words and over 1,000 pages. It contained plenty of material to interest horror fans amongst its 4,000 entries.

Edited by Stanley Wiater, *Dark Thoughts: On Writing* was subtitled "Advice and Commentary from Fifty Masters of Fear and Suspense" and collected quotes and comments about writing horror from Stephen King, Clive Barker, Dean Koontz, Anne Rice and others. Meanwhile, David Morrell, Joyce Carol Oates, Joe R. Lansdale, Alan Rodgers and Robert Weinberg were among the authors who contributed forty articles to the "Handbook by the Horror Writers of America", *Writing Horror*, edited by Mort Castle and published by Writers Digest.

Shaking a Leg: Journalism and Writings collected essays, articles, reviews and other pieces by the late Angela Carter, edited by Jenny Uglow.

In the Shadow of the Vampire: Reflections on the World of Anne Rice by Jana Marcus was a photo-record of the author's fans, along with interviews and an introduction by Katherine Ramsland. *The Anne Rice Reader* was edited by Ramsland and contained seventeen articles about the author's works plus two previously uncollected early stories by Rice. Ramsland was also responsible for *Dean Koontz: A Writer's Biography*, which included chronologies of books, stories and articles.

From Borgo Press, *The Work of Stephen King* by Michael R. Collings was an updated and expanded edition of the author's 1986 book *The Annotated Guide to Stephen King*, covering its subject's output through 1994. Also from Borgo, *A Subtler Magick: The Writings and Philosophy of H.P. Lovecraft* was the second edition of S.T. Joshi's detailed critical guide to the work of HPL, expanded from the 1983 edition, and Lee Prosser's *Running from the Hunter: The Life and Works of Charles Beaumont* was a survey of the late author's work with a primary biography by William F. Nolan.

In *The Fantastic Worlds of Robert E. Howard*, editor James Van Hise collected twenty-one articles, mostly from The Robert E. Howard United Press Association, plus numerous illustrations. *Clark Ashton Smith: The Sorcerer Departs* by Donald Sidney Fryer was a booklet from Tsathoggua Press about the Californian writer, poet and artist.

A Companion to Poe Studies edited by Eric W. Carlson included twenty-five critical essays, from Greenwood Press. The subject of Mark Edmundson's *Nightmare on Main Street: Angels, Sadomasochism, and the Culture of the Gothic* was pretty much summed up by the title.

Edited by Stephen Jones, *Dancing With the Dark: True Encounters with the Paranormal by Masters of the Macabre* contained seventy-three accounts of confrontations with the unexplained or the supernatural by Clive Barker, Robert Bloch, Ramsey Campbell, Neil Gaiman, M.R. James, Stephen King, John Landis, H.P. Lovecraft, Brian Lumley, Arthur Machen, Richard Matheson, Anne McCaffrey, Edgar Allan Poe, Vincent Price, F. Paul Wilson and many others, arranged alphabetically. *Clive Barker's A-Z of Horror*, also compiled by Jones, was a thematically arranged tie-in to the disappointing BBC-TV series, profusely illustrated with artwork by Barker, book covers, movie stills and posters.

In *Fangoria: Masters of the Dark*, editor Anthony Timpone collected twenty-seven articles on and interviews with Clive Barker and Stephen King from the horror media magazine by such writers as Stanley Wiater, Bill Warren, Phil Nutman, Skipp and Spector, Jessie Horsting, Linda Marotta and Douglas Winter.

Peter Haining and Peter Tremayne teamed up to chronicle the influences and research that contributed to Stoker's novel in *The Un-Dead: The Legend of Bram Stoker and Dracula*. *Dracula: The Connoisseur's Guide* by Leonard Wolf was a series of ten essays exploring Stoker's character in books and movies, while *Dracula: Celebrating 100 Years* edited by Leslie Shepard and Albert Power, and *Dracula: The First Hundred Years* edited by Bob Madison, covered the Count's creation from an Irish and movie viewpoint, respectively.

Edited by Joan Gordon and Veronica Hollinger and published by the University of Pennsylvania Press, *Blood Read: The Vampire as Metaphor in Contemporary Culture* was a collection of fourteen academic essays by Suzy McKee Charnas, Rob Latham, Brian Stableford, Nina Auerbach and others, with a foreword by Brian Aldiss.

Published by Underwood Books, with an introduction by James Blaylock, the first volume of *The Selected Letters of Philip K. Dick 1938-1971* presented a fascinating insight into the often bizarre mind of the late science fiction author.

Pete Tombs' *Mondo Macabro* covered many obscure movie titles, as its subtitle "Weird & Wonderful Cinema Around the World" indicated. With knowledgeable chapters about film-making in Hong Kong, the Philippines, Indonesia, India, Turkey, Brazil, Argentina, Mexico and Japan, it was packed with little-known details about a host of unusual movies, illustrated with rare stills and posters.

Forrest J Ackerman's World of Science Fiction was the first in a proposed series of lavishly illustrated hardcovers in which the world's biggest sci-fi fan shared his knowledge and collection with readers. It also included a preface by A.E. van Vogt and a foreword by John Landis.

To celebrate forty years of Hammer horror, *The Hammer Story* by Marcus Hearn and Alan Barnes was a beautifully illustrated history of the famous horror studio, complete with a foreword by Christopher Lee. Lee also updated his entertaining 1977 autobiography *Tall, Dark and Gruesome*, but despite sixteen pages of photographs it concentrated more on his Italian ancestry and war-time experiences than his horror movie career. *Do You Want it Good or Tuesday? From Hammer Films to Hollywood! A Life in the Movies* was the convoluted title of Hammer scriptwriter Jimmy Sangster's enjoyable autobiography.

The Avengers and Me was a personal reminiscence of the cult TV series by star Patrick Macnee with Dave Rogers, illustrated with many rare behind-the-scenes photographs, while *The Avengers Companion* was a reprint of a 1990 French guide by Alain Carrazé and Jean-Luc Putheaud.

Bright Darkness: The Lost Art of the Supernatural Horror Film by Jeremy Dyson, with a foreword by Peter Crowther and eight pages of stills, was a critical study of the supernatural horror film from Val Lewton's 'B' films of the 1940s to Robert Wise's *The Haunting* in 1963.

McFarland published Bill Warren's *Set Visits: Interviews With 32 Horror and Science Fiction Filmmakers*, which included interviews with Rick Baker, Joe Dante, John Landis, Christopher Lee and Sam Raimi, many of which were originally published in *Starlog* and *Fangoria* magazines. *Science Fiction, Fantasy and Horror Film Sequels: An Illustrated Filmography, With Plot Synopses and Critical Commentary* by Kim R. Holston and Tom Winchester included a foreword by Ingrid Pitt.

The fourth volume of Donald C. Willis' indispensable guide *Horror and Science Fiction Films* was published in large-format hardcover by Scarecrow Press.

The third edition of Roger Fulton's *The Encyclopedia of TV Science Fiction* from Boxtree/TV Times added plenty of new material to another indispensable reference work. However, Alan Morton's apparently self-published *The Complete Directory to Science Fiction, Fantasy and Horror Television Series* was even more impressive, weighing in just short of 1,000 packed pages.

The MiXtake Files by Michael French was an unofficial nit-picker's guide to *The X Files*, aimed at very sad people. Marc Shapiro's *The Anderson Files: The Unauthorized Biography of Gillian Anderson* was another inconsequential attempt to jump on the *X Files* bandwagon, as was *The Lexicon: An Unofficial X-Files Guide to People, Places and Proprietary Phrases*, an illustrated trivia book by Canadian author N.E. Genge, who also published two volumes of *The Unofficial Millennium Companion: The Covert Casebook of the Millennium Group*.

From Underwood Books, *Spectrum 4: The Best in Contemporary Fantasy Art* was once again edited by Cathy Fenner and Arnie Fenner with Jim Loehr and featured a review of the year and over 200 full colour pieces of art chosen by a jury, plus the Chesley Award winners.

"Repent Harlequin!" Said the Ticktock Man, also from Underwood and designed by Arnie Fenner, reprinted Harlan Ellison's 1965 Hugo and Nebula Award-winning short story, illustrated in full colour by Rick Berry. With a new foreword by the author, it was available in a trade hardcover and a 1,000-copy deluxe signed edition.

Subtitled "Original Cover Paintings for the Great American Pulp Magazines", *Pulp Art* edited by Robert Lesser reproduced some beautiful work by Hannes Bok, Virgil Finlay, Frank R. Paul, Edd Cartier, J. Allen St. John, Norman Saunders, Rafael de Soto and George Rozen, along with eighteen short essays by Forrest J Ackerman, Sam Moskowitz and Jim Steranko, amongst others.

Learn to Draw Fantasy Art by novelist Mike Jefferies was a large-format "how-to" book, illustrated with the author's art throughout.

1997 was definitely the year for Monster stamps. On 13 May, the Royal Mail in Britain celebrated home-grown horror with a set of four stamps depicting Dracula, Frankenstein, Dr. Jekyll and Mr. Hyde and The Hound of the Baskervilles. Unfortunately, the artwork by Ian Pollock was terrible. Slightly better were Canada's haunted house stamps, issued on 1 October, portraying a werewolf, a goblin, a ghost and a vampire. The same day, Ireland celebrated the centenary of *Dracula* and the 150th anniversary of the birth in Dublin of his creator, Bram Stoker, with a set of four photo-artwork scenes featuring the undead Count rising from his coffin, preparing to bite the neck of Lucy Westenra, surrounded by bats in his Transylvanian castle, and lurking in the woods with a glowing-eyed wolf. However, best of all were the set of Classic Movie Monsters stamps issued by the United States Postal Service on 30 September, with a ceremony at California's Universal Studios. The five beautifully-painted images featured Boris Karloff as the Frankenstein Monster and The Mummy, Lon Chaney, Jr. as The Wolf Man, Lon Chaney, Sr. as The Phantom of the Opera, and Bela Lugosi as Dracula. A stamp decoder revealed hidden images on the sheets, and the launch was supported by a wide range of merchandise, including T-shirts, buttons and mouse mats.

Staying with the Universal Studios Monsters theme, over Hallowe'en the Burger King chain on both sides of the Atlantic offered action toys of Dracula, the Frankenstein Monster, The Wolf Man and The Creature from the Black Lagoon with its Kids Club meals. Along with glow-in-the-dark stickers, the promotion was supported by monster masks and illustrated meal boxes.

Neil Gaiman and Charles Vess' *Stardust* was a four-issue miniseries in illustrated text format from DC Comics. Set in Victorian England, it was about a young man of magically mixed parentage who fell in love with a fairy girl.

Gaiman's *Death: The Time of Your Life* featured the three issue mini-series collected in trade paperback with a cover by Dave McKean, an introduction by Claire Danes, a gallery of classic Death portraits and a new four-page story by Gaiman and artists Mark Buckingham and Mark Pennington. *The Wake* was the tenth and final collection in *The Sandman* series by Gaiman, which came complete with enthusiastic quotes from Stephen King and Norman Mailer.

Dust Covers collected Dave McKean's distinctive photo-illustrated covers for *The Sandman* between 1989-97, with a new story and commentary by Neil Gaiman and the artist. McKean also supplied the illustrations for Gaiman's humorous children's

book *The Day I Swapped My Dad for Two Goldfish*, published
in hardcover by White Wolf's Borealis imprint.

Meanwhile, Caitlín R. Kiernan continued Gaiman's *The
Dreaming* for the DC Vertigo line with the three-part story
"Souvenirs", illustrated by Peter Doherty.

Hellblazer No.120, was a double issue written by Paul Jenkins
and John Ney Rieber that marked the tenth anniversary of the
title, as downbeat detective John Constantine took the reader on a
London pub-crawl of his dark universe. From the same writing
team, *Hellblazer/The Books of Magic* was a two-issue mini-series
that reunited Constantine with his student, Tim Hunter.

In October it was announced that a bank settlement of Marvel
Entertainment Group's Chapter 11 bankruptcy case had fallen
through.

Marvel's *Man-Thing* and DC's *The Creeper* returned after long
absences, and Dark Horse and DC Comics teamed up for *Batman
Aliens*, in which the Dark Knight of Gotham City battled H.R.
Giger's acid-dripping monsters, illustrated by Bernie Wrightson.
It was followed by *Batman vs. Predator III*, a four-part series
illustrated by Rodolfo Damaggio. The Predator also met Judge
Dredd in a three-part series written by John Wagner with covers
by Brian Bolland.

From Hellboy creator Mike Mignola and Pat McEown came
Dark Horse's *Zombie World*. Action Planet Comics' *Monster-
man* was a four-issue series featuring a character who was
transformed by a curse and forced to confront his evil twin,
while the fifteenth issue of Image Comics' *Big Bang* was a Special
Hallowe'en "Spooktacular" featuring Dr. Weird battling swamp
creature Bog, with a cover by Steve Bissette.

Chaos! Comics' four-issue *Classic Monsters: Nightmare Theater* was hosted by Mr. Mischief and Psychotica and set in a
haunted movie theatre with a monstrous audience. The series
featured beautiful painted covers by Bernie Wrightson and the
line-up of talent involved included Alan Moore, Rick Veitch,
Richard Christian Matheson, Mick Garris and Christopher Gold-
en. From the same company came *The Lost*, a vampiric reworking of the Peter Pan myth in a four-issue black and white mini-
series.

Billed on its cover as "The best comic book on Earth", David
Britton's *Meng & Ecker: Lord Horror's Creep Boys* was a large

format graphic novel from Savoy containing the much-praised or much-reviled (depending on your opinion) comic strip, illustrated by Kris Guidio.

From Jayde Design came a reprint of Druillet's illustrated adaptation of Michael Moorcock's *Elric The Return of Melnibone*. *Occurrences: The Illustrated Ambrose Bierce* was a trade paperback collection from Mojo Press featuring six Bierce stories with a biographical introduction by Debra Rodia.

Frank Plowright's *The Slings & Arrows Comics Guide* was an A-Z critical assessment of over 2,500 comic books from the 1930s to the present. *Comic Book Rebels: Conversations with the Creators of the New Comics* by Stanley Wiater and Steve R. Bissette included interviews with Richard Corben, Dave Sim, Kevin Eastman, Alan Moore, Eddie Campbell, Neil Gaiman, Dave McKean, Frank Miller, Todd McFarlane and Will Eisner, amongst others, and was published in a deluxe signed and slipcased edition of 750 numbered copies by Underwood Books.

The Complete Guide to the Outer Limits was an eighty-one card collectors set from DuoCards, illustrating both the classic 1963 series and its latest incarnation, with production information, unpublished interviews and rare photos.

Following the surprise success of *Scream*, screenwriter Kevin Williamson continued to pump out his own brand of revisionist teen horror with *I Know What You Did Last Summer* (a return to the stalk 'n' slash genre, based on a young adult book by Lois Duncan) and *Scream 2*, once again directed by Wes Craven. Disney's stock reportedly rose three per cent on the New York market following the record-breaking $39.2 million weekend opening for the inevitable sequel.

With Craven as executive producer and script by Peter Atkins, *WishMaster* was the beginning of a new franchise and featured cameos by horror icons Robert Englund, Tony Todd and Kane Hodder. Al Pacino and Keanu Reeves starred in Taylor Hackford's *Devil's Advocate*, based on a 1990 novel about Satanic lawyers by Andrew Neiderman. Sculptor Frederick Hart successfully sued the producers for using his work as "inspiration" for the film's designs.

An American Werewolf in Paris, Anthony Waller's belated sequel to the 1981 original, was neither as funny nor as horrific as it could have been, as Tom Everett Scott saved a suicidal Julie Delpy from a cult of CGI-created lycanthropes. *Darklands*, starring Craig Fairbrass and Jon Finch, was best described a Welsh *Wicker Man*.

After five months delay, David Cronenberg's controversial version of J.G. Ballard's *Crash* was finally released, and Lynne Stopkewich made her directing debut with *Kissed*, about a woman obsessed with necrophilia. David Lynch's bizarre *Lost Highway* followed two parallel stories and featured Robert Blake as the spooky Mystery Man, while Dario Argento's *The Wax Mask* was yet another version of *Mystery of the Wax Museum*.

Tom Sizemore and Penelope Ann Miller were trapped in a museum with Stan Winston's scaly jungle monster in Peter Hyams's *The Relic*, and a documentary film crew encountered John Voight's psychopathic German and a monstrous man-eating snake in the silly *Anaconda*. Guillermo del Toro's giant bug thriller, *Mimic*, was based on a pulp story by Donald A. Wollheim, while Steven Spielberg took us back to *The Lost World Jurassic Park*, based on Michael Crichton's 1995 novel, for another encounter with the CGI dinosaurs.

After her character committed suicide in the previous film, Sigourney Weaver returned as Ripley, cloned by mad scientists and once again battling the aliens on a military spaceship in Jean-Pierre Jeunet's *Alien Resurrection*, scripted by the talented Joss Whedon. Artist H.R. Giger complained that Twentieth Century Fox "cheated" him out of a screen credit on the movie.

In *Event Horizon*, a mission sent to salvage the eponymous spaceship discovered it had returned from a hellish dimension and the rescue crew were soon experiencing their own worst nightmares. Adding to the confusion, director Paul Anderson's film was apparently cut by forty minutes prior to release.

Based on the series from Malibu Comics, Barry Sonnenfeld's *Men in Black* featured Tommy Lee Jones and Will Smith as the titular heroes who had to confront Rick Baker's inventive alien atrocities. Paul Verhoeven's *Starship Troopers* battled CGI-created alien insects, and Bruce Willis was a cab driver reluctantly recruited to save the world in Luc Besson's *The Fifth Element*. In Andrew Niccol's *Gattaca*, Ethan Hawke tried to work his way up through a world controlled by genetic engineering.

Less successful was Stuart Gordon's *Space Truckers* with

Dennis Hopper, while Kevin Costner had to take the blame as both director and star of *The Postman*, based on the novel by David Brin. Christopher Lambert starred in Albert Pyun's *Adrenalin Fear the Rush*, about the hunt for a cannibalistic maniac in the catacombs beneath an abandoned prison.

George Clooney was the latest actor to don the bat costume in Joel Schumacher's disappointing *Batman & Robin*. This time the Caped Crusader battled Arnold Schwarzenegger's Mr. Freeze and Uma Thurman's Poison Ivy with the help of Chris O'Donnell's Boy Wonder and Alicia Silverstone's plump Batgirl. At least horror veteran Michael Gough was back as Alfred the butler.

As *Spawn*, based on the comic character created by Todd McFarlane, Michael Jae White returned from Hell to battle John Leguizamo's demonic Clown. Former basketball star Shaquille O'Neal pulled on the tights and mask in Kenneth Johnson's *Steel*, based on the DC Comics character.

Kevin Sorbo starred as Robert E. Howard's barbarian king *Kull the Conquerer*, battling an evil Egyptian queen, while Anthony Hickox's *Prince Valiant* was another cut-price fantasy, based on Hal Foster's classic comic strip.

In *Austin Powers International Man of Mystery*, Mike Myers played both the eponymous British superspy, frozen since 1967, and his arch-nemesis Dr. Evil.

While Disney's animated musical *Hercules* took some liberties with Greek mythology, the Twentieth Century Fox cartoon *Anastasia* meddled with Russian history. At least the latter featured a zombiefied Rasputin (voiced by Christopher Lloyd) revived by sorcery.

Photographing Fairies and *Fairy Tale A True Story* were both period pieces covering the same event.

The Texas Chainsaw Massacre: The Next Generation was the new title of Kim Henkel's 1994 production *The Return of the Texas Chainsaw Massacre*, finally given a limited theatrical release in America because leads Renee Zellweger and Matthew McConnaughey had subsequently become big Hollywood stars. Director F.W. Murnau's 1922 film *Nosferatu, A Symphony of Horrors* was re-issued in a restored and newly tinted version which featured a specially-composed music score by Hammer's James Bernard.

* * *

Christopher Walken returned as the avenging angel Gabriel in
Greg Spence's direct-to-video release *The Prophecy II: Ashtown.*
Casper: A Spirited Beginning was a direct-to-video sequel to the
1995 movie, starring Steve Guttenberg and Rodney Dangerfield.

For Full Moon, director Ted Nicolaou returned to his Romanian undead in *Vampire Journals, Hideous!* concerned a group of
rival freak collectors, and Charles Band's *The Creeps* was shot in
3-D and featured diminutive versions of such classic monsters as
Dracula, Frankenstein, the werewolf and a mummy.

The crew and passengers of a crashed orbital plane were
exposed to bio-hazard material that mutated them into homicidal
maniacs in *Ravager.* Corbin Bernsen starred as *The Dentist* for
director Brian Yuzna, and Joseph Parda's super-8 *5 Dead on a
Crimson Canvas* was a low budget homage to the Italian *giallo*
thrillers of the 1960s and '70s.

Unavailable for legal reasons since early 1950s, the 1945
thriller, *Strange Confession* (aka *The Missing Head*), finally made
its video debut on a series of value-for-money *Inner Sanctum*
double-bills from Universal. Lon Chaney, Jr. starred as a nice-guy
chemist who has his life destroyed by his scheming boss (a
villainous J. Carroll Naish).

The original uncut version of Amando de Ossorio's 1971 *La
Noche del Terror Ciego* (aka *Tombs of the Blind Dead*) was
digitally remastered on video from a new 35mm print, struck
from the original negative. This story about a group of people
trapped in an abandoned monastery by the skeletal corpses of an
evil cult of thirteenth century Knights Templars was presented in
its original theatrical aspect ratio, with Spanish dialogue and
English subtitles.

At more than four hours, Mick Garris' TV mini-series remake of
The Shining was tediously overlong, despite some occasionally
impressive horror set-pieces. It also included mostly pointless
cameos by writer/executive producer Stephen King, Sam Raimi,
Frank Darabont, Christa Faust, Peter James, Richard Christian
Matheson and David J. Schow, amongst others.

Based on an inconsequential story by King, Mark Pavia's *The
Night Flier* starred Miguel Ferrer as a ludicrously cynical tabloid
photo-journalist on the trail of a vampire, who arrived at remote
airfields in his private airplane and slaughtered the inhabitants.

Trucks was a remake of King's own *Maximum Overdrive*, as if we needed one, and Christopher Lloyd linked Mick Garris's silly *Quicksilver Highway*, based on Clive Barker's story "The Body Politic" and King's "Chattery Teeth". The Barker segment included cameos by the author as a mugging anaesthetist and John Landis playing a surgical assistant.

Co-executive producer Dean Koontz's *Intensity*, a four-hour mini-series, starred John C. McGinley as a brilliant psychopath. Sigourney Weaver played the wicked stepmother in Michael Cohn's *Snow White A Tale of Terror*, a dark, often disturbing reworking of the Grimms's fairy tale. Peter Medak's *The Hunchback* starred Mandy Patinkin under the make-up as Quasimodo, while Kim Delany discovered she was *The Devil's Child* in another *Rosemary's Baby* rip-off.

Despite Peter Cannom's impressive special make-up effects for the vampire, werewolf and Frankenstein's sympathetic creature, *House of Frankenstein* was a three hour mini-series that never overcame its cliched script, poor production values and terrible performances. Christopher Lee was one of many stars who turned up in *The Odyssey*, a sub-Harryhausen slice of epic mythology.

Robin Cook's Invasion, directed by Armand Mastroianni, was a four hour mini-series written by Rockne S. O'Bannon and based on an original story by Cook. It was about an alien virus that invaded Phoenix, Arizona, and soon spread around the globe, transforming its victims into alien hybrids. Bradford May's *Asteroid* was another ridiculous three hour mini-series, about a giant rock on a collision course with the Earth. When lasers were used to break up the asteroid, Dallas, Texas, was destroyed by the fragments.

Moira Armstrong's dull *Breakout* concerned a stolen biological test sample that was accidently released into the British countryside with potentially disastrous results. The irritating Neil Morrissey starred as Nick Cameron who, as a result of experiments by a secret corporation, turned invisible when wet in Maurice Phillip's pilot movie *The Vanishing Man*. A two-part adaptation of Wilkie Collins' *The Woman in White*, scripted by David Pirie, came in for a lot of criticism for its condensation and altered ending.

Steve Guttenberg and Kirsten Dunst investigated the Hallowe'en disappearance of a famous Hollywood child star nearly sixty years earlier in the *Tower of Terror*. Ian Richardson gave a surprisingly low-key performance in yet another version of Oscar Wilde's *The Canterville Ghost* which, despite a cast that included Pauline Quirke and Rik Mayall, totally lacked any charm. The *Doom Runners* were a group of children who attempted to evade capture by Tim Curry's cyborg troopers after the eco-collapse.

A spin-off from the 1992 movie of the same name, Joss Whedon's *Buffy the Vampire Slayer* was a mid-season replacement that was fast, fun and frightening and quickly became one of the best genre shows on television. In Sunnydale, a town built over the mouth of Hell, Sarah Michelle Gellar's eponymous high school heroine and her friends encountered the vampiric mummy of a beautiful Inca princess, a reanimated football star who wanted a girlfriend created from stolen body parts, plus all manner of undead minions of The Master.

Chris Carter's *The X Files* continued to baffle with its plots about UFO encounters and government conspiracies, but FBI agents Mulder and Scully still took time out to investigate a sighting of The Great Mutato, the grotesque result of illegal genetic experiments by the mad Dr Polodori.

Along the same lines, the Canadian *Psi Factor Chronicles of the Paranormal* was hosted by a laughably unconvincing Dan Aykroyd and supposedly inspired by the actual case files of The Office of Scientific Investigation and Research. Matt Frewer took over from Paul Miller as the O.S.I.R. team leader whose investigations included a family that had survived for more than a century without ageing, by drinking blood. *Poltergeist the Legacy* was another continuing Canadian show, about a San Francisco-based secret society led by Derek Rayne (Derek de Lint), which protects others from the supernatural creatures that inhabit the shadows and the night.

Cancelled in America after only two episodes, *Sleepwalkers* was about a team of researchers at The Morpheus Institute, headed by Dr Nathan Bradford (Bruce Greenwood), who had discovered a deeper stage of sleep that allowed them to travel into dreams.

Chris Carter's downbeat *Millennium* included a spooky Hallowe'en episode, written by executive producers Glen Morgan and James Wong, in which psychic investigator Frank Black (a bravura performance by Lance Henriksen) discovered through a series of bizarre messages that he had become a legendary Bogeyman himself. The French/Canadian *Highlander* series included a sequence of supernatural episodes in which a shapechanging Zoroastrian demon returned to the Earth after a thousand years to begin a new cycle of evil. It tricked Duncan MacLeod (Adrian Paul) into killing his friend Ritchie and attempted to convince the immortal's associates to betray him.

Granada Television and Channel 4's *Springhill* was a bizarre, short-lived soap opera set in Liverpool with more than a touch of the supernatural about it.

The Hunger was a new made-for-cable erotic horror series, obscurely hosted by Terence Stamp, which adapted stories by such established authors as Robert Aickman, F. Paul Wilson, Brian Lumley, David J. Schow and Karl Edward Wagner, amongst others.

In *Sliders*, inventor Quinn Mallory (Jerry O'Connell) and his companions pursued Neil Dickson's brain-eating villain Rickman between parallel Earths and found themselves on a devastated planet where most of the population had been transformed into cannibalistic zombies; a world where Wade (Sabrina Lloyd) became involved with Goth rock band Stoker, which was made up of centuries-old vampires; and, in what was supposed to be the final episode of the briefly-cancelled series, a tropical island where the mad Dr. Vargas (Michael York) was experimenting with genetic mutations and creating human-animal hybrids in an uncredited rip-off of H.G. Wells' *The Island of Doctor Moreau*. *Sliders* was subsequently picked-up by the Sci-Fi Channel.

It was *Invasion of the Body Snatchers* time again in Zenith Productions' *The Uninvited*, a four-part series about a photographer who discovered that an entire British seaside village, along with important people in industry and civil defence, had been replaced by glowing-eyed aliens. *Space Island One* was a dull series set in the year 2005 on first generation space station Unity in orbit 240 miles above the Earth. Chloë Annett's Kochanski became a regular crew member for the seventh season of the BBC cult comedy *Red Dwarf*.

The war with Earth reached its finale in J. Michael Straczynski's *Babylon 5*, and *Babylon 5 In The Beginning* was the first in a series of TV movies designed to fill the gaps in the regular series. Producers Dean Devlin and Roland Emmerich passed on the *Stargate SG-1* series, based on their 1994 movie hit, and instead they got behind *The Visitor*, yet another variation on *The Fugitive*. John Corbett played the US pilot, who disappeared over the Bermuda Triangle fifty years before. When his UFO was shot down and crashed in the Utah mountains, he travelled around the country helping people until the series was cancelled.

Earth Final Conflict was based on an old Gene Roddenberry script and starred Kevin Kilner as William Boone, a human assigned as an aide to the alien Taelons. *Dark Skies*, a mixture of historical fact and alien conspiracy, was cancelled after its first season, despite an appeal in the trade magazines by fans of the show. The new series of *The Outer Limits* continued to turn out stories of alien invasions and misguided scientists, while *Timecop* was another short-lived series based on a hit movie.

The BBC's *Crime Traveller* was a mindless series about two detectives (Michael French and Chloë Annett) who used an experimental time machine to solve cases. However, the corporations time travel sitcom *Goodnight Sweetheart*, starring the nation's favourite Nicholas Lyndhurst as an adulterous husband cheating on his wife with a 1940s barmaid, proved much more popular with viewers.

Xena Warrior Princess began to develop a dark edge amongst the swordfights and brawls, while her stablemate in *Hercules The Legendary Journeys* found himself battling a monstrous spider woman who either burned off the faces of her victims with acid or impregnated them with her murderous offspring. Compared with these two, Ed Naha's cheap-looking *The Adventures of Sinbad* and Brian Yuzna's *Tarzan The Epic Adventures* appeared decidedly juvenile, despite their magic and monsters. Even more disappointing was Yuzna's *Conan* series, with weight-lifter Ralph Möeller bringing little dignity to Robert E. Howard's mighty barbarian. Bizzarely, the pilot movie included a computer-created image of the late Richard Burton as Crom, the God of War.

Despite the return of H.G. Wells (Hamilton Camp) and his time machine, *Lois & Clark The New Adventures of Superman* was finally cancelled. Glen A. Larson's *Night Man*, who used his prototype weapons suit to defeat evil, was based on the Malibu Comics character created by Steve Englehart, and Todd

McFarlan's *Spawn*, voiced by Keith David, also turned up as an adults-only animated series on HBO.

Deepwater Black (aka *Mission Genesis*), the name of a spaceship carrying six adolescent clones on a mission to restore life to a Earth they have never known, was based on the novels by Ken Catran. In one episode they brought a psychic vampire on board. Much more fun was *Honey, I Shrunk the Kids*, based on the movie series, with Peter Scolari as the scatter-brained scientist.

Three young children with superpowers teamed up with a ghost, the Frankenbeans Monster, Count Fangula the vampire, Mums the mummy and Wolfgang the werewolf to battle the evil Magnavors in *Big Bad BeetleBorgs*.

Like R.L. Stine's popular *Goosebumps* series, *Frighteners* was a half-hour series aimed at young adults that involved various hauntings. One episode of the new *Teen Angel* series featured Melissa Joan Hart as *Sabrina The Teenage Witch*.

The animated *Casper* was based on characters created by Joseph Oriolo for Harvey Comics, filled with numerous in-jokes and inspired by the 1995 movie. The four teenage offspring of the original Ghostbusters continued the family business by battling some scary supernatural creatures in a new cartoon, *Extreme Ghostbusters*. K and J, two members of a secret organisation dedicated to hunting down illegal aliens within Earth's atmosphere, were back in the animated *Men in Black The Series*, based on the Malibu comic created by Lowell Cunningham.

Christopher Lee was the sepulchral voice of Death in Cosgrove Hall's *Wyrd Sisters* and *Soul Music*, both based on Terry Pratchett's popular Discworld novels, and *The Simpsons Halloween Special VIII* included spoofs of *The Omega Man* and *The Fly*, plus a segment where Marge was revealed to be a seventeenth century witch who helped create the tradition of Trick or Treating.

Introduced by the author, *Clive Barker's A-Z of Horror* was a series of six shows from the BBC that, despite the title, were grouped thematically instead of alphabetically. These included 'American Psycho' (Ed Gein and *Psycho*), "Beyond Good and Evil" (*Rosemarys Baby*, Barbara Steele and H.P. Lovecraft), "Broken Homes" (John Carpenters *Halloween*), "The Devil You Know" (*The Exorcist*), "A Fate Worse Than Death" (*The Crow*) and "The Kingdom of the Dead" (*Night of the Living Dead*).

Jack Palance hosted AMC's *Monster Mania* from a mad

scientist's laboratory. An hour-long celebration of the classic movie monsters, it included many familiar trailers and a few TV clips. "Children of Frankenstein" was the first episode of Channel 4's *The Sci-Fi Files*, a four-part documentary series about how biological experimentation has influenced or been influenced by science fiction ever since Mary Shelley's novel. To celebrate forty years of Hammer horror, the Sci-Fi Channel's *Hammer A-Z* used some nice-looking clips to look at everything from "Anniversary" to "Zenith", with commentary by Valerie Leon, Ingrid Pitt, Roy Skeggs, Francis Matthews, James Bernard and Tudor Gates, amongst others.

From December 1997 until the following May, London's The Museum of the Moving Image hosted "Hammer Horror", a tribute to forty years of horror from the British studio. The exhibition included original sketches by Peter Cushing, press memorabilia, props and costumes, as well as recreations of Count Dracula's Castle, Frankenstein's laboratory and the Mummy's tomb. An ongoing series of Hammer Films poster postcards were also produced by the London Post Card Company.

On the British stage, Liz Lochhead's play *Blood and Ice*, about the writing of Mary Shelley's novel *Frankenstein*, opened at the Royal Lyceum Edinburgh in February with Molly Gaisford as a depressed Mary. Chris Bond's stage spoof *The Blood of Dracula* toured the UK and featured Dickon Tyrrell's Count dealing with hapless Transylvanian honeymooners, while a stage version of the 1950s cult movie *The Fly* opened in Oxford in April.

For two days in September and again in November, the London Actors Theatre Company staged an ambitious multi-media presentation of Edgar Allan Poe's *The Masque of the Red Death*. The audience found themselves surrounded by poetry, music and song, as the cast, drawn from various art and drama-based groups, presented adaptations of several classic Poe stories and related fiction. In October, the same company also presented *The Murder of Edgar Allan Poe* by Sophia Kingshill, a murder mystery in which Poe became the detective. In America, John Astin toured as *Edgar Allan Poe – Once Upon a Midnight*, a one-man show written by Paul Day Clemens and Ron Magid.

*   *   *

BBC Radio 2 produced a pilot sitcom entitled *Things That Go Bump in the Night*, starring Jean Boht as Madam Lavinia Bullock, an expert on the supernatural and a woman who has devoted her life to battling against the forces of evil in Victorian England.

In February, BBC Radio 4 began broadcasting a six-part serialisation of Stephen King's *Pet Sematary*, featuring John Sharian, Briony Glassco and Lee Montague. Two months later, Jenny Agutter, Brian Glover and John Woodvine recreated their film roles in an updated radio version of *An American Werewolf in London*, broadcast over ten weeks on BBC Radio 1 with original director John Landis as creative consultant. BBC audio cassettes and CDs of both serials followed.

Dracula – A Birthday Tribute was an hour-long programme on Radio 2 in which Ann Mann travelled to Whitby to interview members of the local Dracula Society. The show also included contributions from Stoker's great-nephew Daniel Farson and Christopher Lee reading extracts from the novel. For the same station, Hywel Bennett read an eight-part adaptation of Stoker's *Dracula* in the evenings.

Susan Cooper's classic fantasy *The Dark is Rising* was dramatised in four parts for BBC Children's Radio 4 in November. During the run-up to Christmas, the author himself introduced six half-hour dramatized versions of his stories for Radio 4's *Ray Bradbury's Tales of the Bizarre. The Female Ghost* was a series of three half-hour ghostly dramas by women that featured "The Cold Embrace" by Mary Baddon, "Man Sized in Marble" by Enid Nesbit and "Afterward" by Edith Wharton.

Also over the holiday season, Radio 2 presented four classic re-mastered and restored radio dramas under the umbrella title *Hollywood Christmas*. The first starred Vincent Price as Lesley Charteris' The Saint in *Christmas Eve Problems* directed by Helen Mack, and the series concluded with Richard Widmark in a version of Walter Van Tilburg Clark's *Track of the Cat*.

One-off productions on Radio 4 included John Van Druten's *Bell, Book and Candle* and Willa Cather's ghost story *The Affair at Grover Station*, while December ended with *The Late Book* broadcasting five fifteen-minute adaptations of M.R. James' classic *Ghost Stories*. Produced and abridged by Paul Kent, the series featured "Canon Alberic's Scrapbook", "Lost Hearts", "A School Story", "The Haunted Doll's House" and "Rats".

Jon Pertwee, Hayley Mills, Dennis Waterman, Colin Baker, Roger Daltrey, Peter Davidson, Bernard Cribbins, Prunella Scales, June Whitfield and Honor Blackman were among the many unlikely celebrities who read stories by Robert Eastland and others on *Creatures of the Night*, *Haunted Houses* and *Fright Time*, a trio of two-tape sets featuring ten horror stories, ghost stories and nail-biting thrillers respectively, from Telstar Talking Books.

The Wendigo by Algernon Blackwood/*Dream Woman* by Wilkie Collins and *The Screaming Skull* by F. Marion Crawford/*The Old Nurses Story* by Elizabeth Gaskell were two sound tapes from Tangled Web Audio featuring heavily abridged radio plays first broadcast by the Canadian Broadcasting Corporation under the title *Mystery Theatre*.

World Horror Convention 1997 was held from 8-11 May in the Hotel Niagara, Niagara Falls. Despite the dilapidated surroundings and inclement weather, the small number of attendees welcomed guests of honour Ramsey Campbell, Poppy Z. Brite, Joe R. Lansdale, editor Darrell Schweitzer, artist Rick Berry, media guest Gunnar Hansen and toastmaster Edo van Belkom. The Life Achievement Award went to Peter Straub, who was unable to attend.

The 1996 Bram Stoker Awards for superior achievement in the horror field were presented by Gahan Wilson on behalf of the Horror Writers Association in New York City over the weekend of 20-21 June. Stephen King's *The Green Mile* won in the Novel category, *Crota* by Owl Goingback won for First Novel, "The Red Tower" by Thomas Ligotti picked up the award for Novelette and P.D. Cacek's "Metalica" topped the vote for Short Story. Ligotti also won for Collection with *The Nightmare Factory*, S.T. Joshi's *H.P. Lovecraft: A Life* was the winner in the Non-Fiction category, and Life Achievement awards went to Ira Levin and Forrest J Ackerman.

The winners of the Third Annual International Horror Guild Awards were announced at Dragon*Con, held in Atlanta over 26-29 June. Mark Laidlaw's *The 37th Mandala* won Best Novel, Del Stone Jr.'s *Dead Heat* won in the First Novel category, S.P. Somtow's "Brimstone & Salt" won for Short Form, and Graham Masterton's "Underbed" was considered Best Short Story. Best

Collection was Terry Lamsley's *Conference With the Dead*, Best Anthology was *Darkside: Horror for the New Millennium* edited by John Pelan, and Richard Chizmar's *Cemetery Dance* was voted Best Publication. Best Artist was Timothy Bradstreet, Mike Mignola's *Hellboy: Wake the Devil* was Best Graphic Story, and *Scream* won for Best Film. Edward Bryant won the Living Legend award, and a Special Award went to the late Lou Stathis.

The third NecronomiCon, dedicated to celebrating H.P. Lovecraft and the Cthulhu Mythos in all it forms, was held as usual in Providence, Rhode Island, over 15-17 August. Guest of honour was Brian Lumley, with HPL scholar Dirk W. Mosig as special guest.

The winners of the World Fantasy Awards were announced at The 1997 World Fantasy Convention, held over 30 October - 2 November in London. This was only the third occasion the convention had moved outside the United States and the second time it had been held in Britain. Rachel Pollack's *Godmother Night* won Best Novel, Mark Helprin's *A City in Winter* was voted by the judges as Best Novella and James P. Blaylock's "Thirteen Phantasms" (from Omni Online) picked up Best Short Fiction. *Starlight 1* edited by Patrick Nielsen Hayden was the winner of Best Anthology, Jonathan Lethem's *The Wall of the Sky, the Wall of the Eye* won Best Collection and the Best Artist award went to Moebius (aka Jean Giraud). Michael J. Weldon's *The Psychotronic Video Guide* won the Special Award – Professional, and the Special Award – Non-Professional went to Barbara and Christopher Roden for Ash-Tree Press. Co-Special Guest of Honour Hugh B. Cave accepted the Special Convention Award, and the Life Achievement Award went to Madeleine L'Engle.

The British Fantasy Society's FantasyCon XXI was held in conjunction with the World Fantasy Convention. Voted for by the membership of the society, Graham Joyce's *The Tooth Fairy* was considered Best Novel, Martin Simpson's "Dancing About Architecture" (from *The Silver Web/The Third Alternative*) was chosen as Best Short Story, and the Best Anthology/Collection award went to Thomas Ligotti's collection *The Nightmare Factory*. Jim Burns picked up Best Artist, S.T. Joshi's *H.P. Lovecraft: A Life* was presented with the award for Best Small Press Publication and Jo Fletcher was the recipient of the inaugural Karl Edward Wagner Special Award.

California book dealer Barry R. Levin announced his Tenth Annual Collectors Awards with Stephen Baxter voted the Most Collectable Author of 1997, Mark V. Zeising Books won the Most Collectable Book of the Year for the limited edition of *Slippage* by Harlan Ellison, and S.T. Joshi received the special Lifetime Collectors Award for his outstanding contributions to the bibliographical and biographical knowledge of H.P. Lovecraft.

It was around a decade ago that a small group of young-ish (mostly male) American writers banded together and called themselves "Splatterpunks". They dressed and behaved like the rock stars they wanted to be and set out to revolutionize the horror field, rallying against what they saw as the establishment – those proponents of "quiet" or "gentle" horror who, in many cases, had only come to prominence in the genre themselves less than ten years before. Like the British "New Wave" in science fiction during the 1960s and exponents of so-called "slipstream" fiction in the 1990s, they attempted to shake up and eventually overthrow the established order and, for the most part, they briefly succeeded in their aims. They blurbed each other's work and published each other in their anthologies, and for a while publishers and readers saw them as the Hottest Thing in Horror.

Because of the way they looked and acted, and with the support of a few journalists who were desperate to jump on the bandwagon, the Splatterpunks had their brief moment of fame before being consigned to the footnotes of horror history. Like any literary movement, they quickly discovered that attitude was simply not enough. Sometimes you need to back it up with talent, and as they began to fall out with each other and their book sales started to plunge, so the best of them were absorbed into the horror mainstream, where they continue to toil today, while the less talented practitioners quietly faded away into other careers.

A decade later, and so-called "Extreme Horror" is now the flavour of the month. A group of not-quite-so-young (mostly male) middle-class American writers have loosely banded together to create another literary movement within the field. But this time the fiction is mostly misogynistic, gratuitous and often puerile. Its almost as if Beavis and Butt-head decided to become horror writers, sniggering to themselves over the detailed depictions of extravagant sadism and lingering over almost clinical depictions of female sexual organs. Although often published under the nomenclature, their work is usually anything but "erotic" horror.

This time they have a thriving small press to support them as they blurb, review and publish each other's work in various signed and limited hardcover editions and chapbooks. And once again journalists (in some cases, the very same ones that exalted the Splatterpunks ten years before) cannot wait to hail them as the Next Hot Thing in Horror.

Of course, we've seen it all before. You can go back as far as Matthew Gregory Lewis' *The Monk* (1796) or the so-called "Shudder Pulps" (*Horror Stories, Terror Tales* etc.) of the 1930s and '40s. Then there were the EC comics of the 1950s, the British horror novels of the 1970s that were branded "Nasties", or even the Splatterpunks themselves.

As with all literary movements, Extreme Horror will not last. Those writers who have more than a modicum of talent will go on to establish themselves with professional publishers and become part of the established horror field, while the majority will eventually disappear back into the obscurity they deserve.

It is perhaps only coincidence that the horror boom of the 1980s began to collapse around the same time that the Splatterpunks formed themselves into a splinter group. With horror publishing still struggling to re-emerge from a slump that has already lasted for too many years, it is unlikely that Extreme Horror will cause too much damage to field. Meanwhile, many of those authors who the Splatterpunks railed against are still successfully working in the genre and those Splatterpunks who survived are themselves now fast approaching middle-age.

The way any literature survives and grows is through the introduction of new talent and original ideas. Obviously, the ability to be able to write is also an asset. Yet despite their back-slapping praise of each other and their moderate success amongst a relatively small readership and collectors of limited editions, most exponents of Extreme Horror have yet to prove that they have anything worthwhile and meaningful to say in their fiction. Detailed descriptions of gruesome violence and twisted sexuality are simply not enough. Unless they learn this lesson soon, like their illustrious black-clad predecessors of a decade ago, their flame will shine brightly and briefly before they are destined to end up as yet another marginal notation in the history of a much bigger field.

The Editor
July, 1998

DAVID J. SCHOW

Dying Words

DAVID J. SCHOW'S LATEST COLLECTION of stories is entitled *Crypt Orchids*, recently published by Subterranean Press, which includes an introduction for the volume written by Robert Bloch in 1992. A recipient of the World Fantasy Award, his other books include the novels *The Kill Riff* and *The Shaft*, plus the collections *Seeing Red*, *Lost Angels* and *Black Leather Required*. The author himself has also created a lavish new edition of his definitive non-fiction guide, *The Outer Limits Companion*.

Schow has lived in Hollywood for seventeen years, and during that time he has written a number of scripts and tele-plays, including *The Texas Chainsaw Massacre III*, *Critters 3*, *The Crow* and, most recently, *The Furthest Place* for James Cameron's Lightstorm Entertainment and Twentieth Century Fox.

About the following story, he explains: "Astute readers will note that Chan McConnell, referenced in this story as a writer who occasionally works under pseudonyms, also penned two stories for the *Book of the Dead* anthology series, volumes 1 and 2, respectively. Even more astute readers will note that Chan's buddy Oliver Lowenbruck published several stories in *The Twilight Zone Magazine* in the 1980s.

"This story represents their only known collaboration and takes place, more or less, within the universe of George Romero's *Dead* trilogy of films. Rather than recap the mythos, I found that Karl Edward Wagner's preamble (written for one of the zombie entries in *The Year's Best Horror Stories*) works best: 'It seems that the world has been over-run by flesh-eating zombies, see – and then . . .'

"As for Oliver's demise, all I can say is that his tombstone can be seen in the motion picture *The Crow*. The cemetery from that film was blown away by a hurricane, but I do still have the headstone in my office."

T HE COLD ICHOR OF *projectile vitreous humor spurted in snotty globules from the zuvembie's punctured eyeball. Steve tried to recoil but fell on his ass, thinking GAAAH, this crap didn't even have body temperature! The monster eagerly trying to gnaw out his larynx was dead, stone cold dead, lacking either a lurching, corrupt heartbeat or a whiff of dogshit breath. The skull-face champed. Steve heard the moist crunch of his own sundering tendons, and knew that pretty soon he would have to choose his own dying words; something quippy and tart, or perhaps just a scream of –*

"Ahh, fuck it!"

Oliver dealt his monitor a frustrated whack. Processed words goosed themselves, then resettled. The ambient hum of his machine, nicknamed The Damned Thing, goaded him, forever begging the question of input. To punch SAVE would only make Oliver feel worse, as though he was *about* to suffer a headache he had not yet earned.

Save? Save this anal mung? For what?

For promises. For deadlines – now *there* was an intriguing word, in context. For the bitter truth that in one fleeting second of beery confidence, he had sold his soul and agreed to hock up a chunk of fiction for some goddamned storybook about walking corpses who eat people.

Swell. *New Yorker*, here I come, and is it Art yet?

The market rate for Oliver's soul – this week – was six big American pennies per word. Those lacking critical sanction need not apply unsolicited. For a book about zombies, for fuck's sake.

A book about zombies in a world where prose had all but croaked outright, and bookstores went down like the Titanic beneath the gross tonnage of macerated pulp that *looked* like books, had pages and type like books, but were superficial mimics of books . . . the way zombies were mimics of human beings. Between shelves handily labeled according to one inapt genre or other, Oliver felt assaulted on all sides by such "books" – artless pastiches, Mad Lib fill-in-the-adjective timewasters with paint-by-the-numbers plots, crutching through bloated chapters gorged on overfed phraseology, from vile cliche to exhausted simile, with all the grace of a piano shoved off a tall building. Here were the lame "beach reads" which aspired to best-sellerdom; over here, another movie script novelized when the so-called writer's lame screenplay failed to strike a spark. There was a reason the technique was called "formula"; like pabulum or biowar poison, lukewarm or toxic, it was whipped up like Nestle's Quik or ground out like hamburger without enough beef, the net product equaling a foregone conclusion that took too many thousands of words to reach.

Where Oliver sought meat, there was only starch, and he was a starving man. Mediocre wordage engulfed and threatened to drown him. Too long had he tread water in a stormy ocean of doorstop books full of typing, not writing. Their only positive function was to serve as negative reinforcement, the eternal dare to do better. To make some kind of Art out of a flesh-eating zombie story, just as Val Lewton had when he interpreted *Jane Eyre* into *I Walked With A Zombie*.

Oliver abandoned his miracle of home tech and retreated to his legal pad. For starters, how about a better title? 'I Eat Your Face' was not destined to catapult him into *Who's Who* anytime soon. Pen in mouth, he pondered. Ruminated. Then wrote:

'Insatiable Hungers'. He muttered the title to himself. Less a sop to category. At least it had not been amputated from some Shakespearian quotation.

Good kickoff. Make sure we have it by the first of the month.

He sighed and lit a smoke, remembering the seminar on urgency addiction: Work to the task, not the clock.

So, what's it about? Gimme the log line.

It's about time you pounded through this mammy-jammer, he thought. So you can get back to your latest unsold novel. You'll be lauded for your diction and punctuality. Then you can wax proud about *Beast at the Gate*, *The Bullet*, and *Serpent's Smile*.

Consider the possibilities of a novel in which four Confederate soldiers, boyhood friends, slowly betray and turn upon one another in the hell of Andersonville . . . that had been *Beast*, Oliver's notorious but inevitable "first novel".

Unsold and unpublished.

Or trace the origins of *The Bullet*, a .357 Magnum cartridge, from its manufacture to its ultimate use in a murder, and the assorted lives it touches and corrupts enroute to the gunbarrel, from the ammo maker, sick with self-doubt, to the killer, religiously pure in his purpose . . .

Sold, but never published. Book politics.

Or his latest disappointment, *Serpent's Smile*, nominally a horror chug-a-lug about . . .

Published, but only just, its poor track record certain to doom the sale or promotion of Novel #4, yet untitled.

Jezus Christos, he was getting depressed, as one will over deceased or crippled children, one baby step away from bagging the whole writing operation and pouring on the Bass ale. Suitably besotted, he could then drag forth the boxed manuscripts, one-two-three, and drip upon them. Try to magick them to life. To make these dead walk.

Then he could get in another thousand words on Book #4 before bed.

At least the anthologies were still asking for stories. At least 'I Eat Your Face' could lumber forth and make Oliver feel current, the integrity of his wiring intact for one more day, a still-operative force for prose in a wordscape devoid of a good, chewy sentence. Minuscule comfort, and chilly, yet enough to drag him a few pages closer to the end.

THE END. Boyoboy.

He was in fine morbid fettle now. He was writing himself sick, skipping meals, shambling from bed to word processor on yesterday's stiffened pizza. He needed fuel, a diversion, a break. Pool.

Chan's big showoff specialty was the long, baize-spanning V-bank. He parked his cigarette, lined up, stuck out his tongue like a sniper, and plugged the eight ball dead into the side pocket.

"Told you I'd win the next three games." He had, too, the son of a bitch.

"Yeah, but can you shoot the whole rack of balls out your ass in numerical order?" Oliver gathered strays into the wooden rack while Van Halen and Metallica hammered from the PA system – linear, thudding, uncomplicated tunes; good junk to shoot to.

Chan fired up a fresh smoke with an Air Force Zippo, one-handed, and summoned a beer refill from a dishwater blonde waitress in a sports getup. The good heft in her tray arm ran to her breasts; she had no problem with people looking at her legs. So far this evening, she had deigned to speak to Chan and Oliver twice as much as the losers playing on either side of their table, and Chan *always* interpreted this as a positive omen. Her name – she told them, but no one else – was Kath, and there was much experience in her eyes, little knowledge, and no ring on the deadly finger. Chan fell in love.

Chan himself was a piece of work. His costume plan ran to charcoal gray shirts and black leather ties (authority intimidates, he'd say) beneath a ghost-white brush cut and a dangling axe earring of solid 24K. He could easily afford stylistic affectations by the grace of television residuals. He, like Oliver, had started out as a writer of short stories. *I dabble*, he'd say.

"Got a real weenie in the mail today," he said. Chan chalked before each and every shot, wore a three-fingered nylon glove to avoid using powder, and liked to fidget with the tip of his cue as though constantly modifying it, bending it into some enchanted shape which would guarantee his next victory. "This'll change the world: *Sploot!* BODY-BAG HORROR FOR THE NINETIES." He squared his hands, like a director framing a turd. "Edited by none other than Jazz Remora."

"Cutting edge splootmeister of the Nineties", said Oliver. "Bald spot, bay window, flip-flops and all. The master of Hawaiian shirt horror. He once tried to con me into a book he called *Grind Up Chuck*."

"I remember that – UNDIFFERENTIATED MEAT HORROR FOR THE EIGHTIES. I love his approach; he should be a mobster." Chan held off lighting his next smoke until Oliver had missed an easy shot. Cigarette mojo really can work. "Is he still bugging you for a story?"

"Does gum think to pull itself off your shoe?"

Chan sighted and let fly, Robin Hood in the green felt forest. He bagged three lowballs in a row, then finally lit his cigarette. "What're you working on right now?"

"Zombie story."

"Ah. ROTTING CADAVER HORROR FOR THE MILLENNIUM."

"It's recreational writing, to get me back up to speed." Oliver stranded himself with a pocket-hanger. "Shit, I hate it when it does that."

"I did one for the first volume." Chan enjoyed reaping credit in premiere anthologies and the very first issues of new magazines. "You should give Adrian a holler. Pound out a script for *Boneyard*. You can write a half-hour teleplay in two days; it's not like *real* writing. It's cable – no Standards and Practices, no censors to worry about." He shrugged and rechalked. "Think of it as subsidizing your next prose epic."

Oliver had been meaning to follow-up on *Boneyard*. It was pretty much a slam-dunk; Chan was practically walking him in . . . and Oliver had not made the call. He thought of it as a cookie, to hold out for that future you read about . . . the one that never comes.

"Vampire novel. Vampires are big."

"Vampires are the *Star Trek* of horror. Sooner would I nail my hand to a flaming building."

"You couldn't nail your hand to a flaming building; how would you hold the nail?"

"Sooner would I nail my *penis* to a flaming building."

"That's better. Earthier. You must be one of them writer dudes."

Oliver felt the ball skew as soon as his stick kissed it. "Shit. Go ahead and knock that one in for me, would you."

"No chance, Minnesota."

Oliver's newest superstition was that he shot better when he did not banter so much, so he tried shutting up and Chan began to look at him all funny. Chan won anyway.

They toasted the death of prose. Then Oliver winked and said Chan's magnetization back to the printed page was unavoidable. "You'll see the light. In your own novels, you get to direct."

"Maybe we can collaborate."

Chan could not realize how prophetic his words were. When they finished, he promised to call later, not knowing that tonight's disport was the last time he would see his pal Oliver alive.

Oliver caught his latest sneeze. The stuff glistening back from his palm was gross, unnatural, worse each time. Whatever he was coming down with, it was more immediate and serious than his fanciful – and comparatively livable – literary constipation.

When in doubt, phone real friends in the dead of night. That's what friends were for: psychic storage batteries, support systems, and emotional sponges that could leach away mental toxins as if by biological modem and recharge one's will to work . . . or, at least, to continue being a consumer.

Then again, there are those of us with cursed telephones.

Oliver felt the bad vibes working when he lifted his receiver and heard not a dial tone, but a voice already on the line. At least it meant his phone was still hooked up.

"Ahhr . . . hallo? Ollie? You there? Hallo?"

Oliver's guts trilled. Fresh stomach acid flushed. He had been ensnared and bushwhacked by his own phone.

"Coney Freewick calling."

The voice coming at him was shrill and anti-masculine, bent into migraine frequencies by the uncomplimentary filter effect of the phone. Oliver felt like rubbing his face, the way Brian Keith used to do on *Family Affair* whenever Buffy or Jody had really pissed him off, as if when your hand came away you'd be staring at a new day, a clean slate, a fresh start. He began searching his desk clutter for his pocket microcassette recorder and managed a noncommittal grunt to indicate he was still listening.

"I can't believe how lucky you are, dude", Freewick whined. "You're aces, tippy-top on my hit list. I got a new book, and thought I'd call you first a'cause –"

– a'cause I need a story that goes all the way, break those taboos, dude, cutting edge, state of the art, there are no limits, get splattery, get punky, fuck it till it bleeds, I wanna read something that'll MAKE ME VOMIT!

How about *make you die*, thought Oliver.

"– and fuckin do me, baby, write me something WET. Oh, yeah, and it's gotta be an original."

"A wet original. Like a diaper?"

"Huh? Oh, I get it, that's a good one –"

Oliver pressed PLAY and aimed the tape unit at the mouthpiece. A prerecorded *click-click* issued into the phone, raced along miles of filament, and registered inside one of Coney Freewick's grease-clotted ears. "Oops," said Oliver. "Sorry. Got a call on the other line."

"S'cool, dude, I'll hold, right, I mean, you're the father of –"

Oliver hung up on him. In point of sheer fact, he had never sprung for call waiting. He pressed FLASH to clear the line and hit Chan's number on the speed dialer. The only time Chan ever answered his phone in person was when *he* was engaged in a call on *his* other line. Chan had owned call waiting from day one.

For Oliver, the game of Which Caller Is Cooler began. Whoever was on Chan's other line, lost.

"How's the weather in zombie-land?"

"Bite me," said Oliver. This is a cry for help from a tortured soul."

"I bet Coney Freewick called you. He called me an hour ago. Wanted a story for a book called *Suck On This*."

"BRAIN CURD DEVOURING HORROR FOR THE TURN OF THE CENTURY, no doubt. And I bet you were tippy-top on his hit list."

"It's like, when you realize the head bobbing at your groin is Coney's, you wonder if you have enough time to shove a gun in your mouth."

"I'd rather nail *your* dick to a flaming building."

Chan blew a raspberry. "Burgess called that 'lip music.'"

"We fairly seethe with oral metaphor tonight."

"Don't toss big scientific words at me. I'll quote famous people and then go spend too much money on upwardly mobile trifles to assuage my creative inferiority."

"You have my pity. Listen, Chan –"

"It smells like favor time. Have you been good?"

"No."

"Correct. You win a favor. Or would you try to care for what Jay is bringing in this box down the aisle . . . it's . . . it's a *severed human head*!"

"Just what I always wanted. Now please shut up a minute."

"What's the favor?"

"It's Number Nine of the Ten Stupidest Questions in Writing."

"*Will you read my manuscript?!*" Chan mock-screamed into the phone loud enough to make Oliver wince. "That's Number Eight, anyway. What manuscript?"

"No conditions. Think of it as exercise."

"Okay," said Chan. "You take that *Boneyard* meeting on Monday and I'll help you rescue your zombie story."

"Deal. Come alone. No girlfriends."

"Michelle is a wonderful woman."

"I thought it was Holly. Never mind. Where'd you meet Michelle?"

"The hospital."

"There's nothing wrong with you."

"I went there for a bit of emergency room research. On a slow night you wouldn't believe what these people will talk about. She looked like a prime-time network TV fashion model nurse, and I caught her undressing me with her eyes, so I undressed her with my hands, then she tied me up, then I cuffed –"

"I think I get the picture," said Oliver. "That's why no lady friends. No parade. If you want me to sign an affidavit saying how manly you are, I will. Would you please just get over here tonight?"

"Soon as I catch a shower." *Click-click*, for real. "Oops, got a call on the other line."

"That's what I told Coney."

"Good for you."

"See you in, what?"

"Two hours. Just vacuum, okay?"

The other caller was cooler, so Oliver lost. He set his machine, an old one, with dual cassettes, to screen calls for the rest of the night.

Chan favored knickknacks. Emplaced on his work desk, atop a riser of matched plastic file trays, was one of those lucite oblongs that seesawed, simulating an endless ocean wave.

"You left your bag, you know," Chan told his new caller.

"Probably as a sneaky excuse to come back and retrieve it", Michelle said from her end of the line. "But not, alas, tonight. It looks like they're keeping us overtime at gunpoint. The ER is a nightmare; they're double-teaming the berths and one doctor has dropped already from exhaustion. You should see the switchboard."

"Just as well, I guess," Chan said, not believing her story. He watched the glycerine or whatever it was roll to and fro. "I've got a writer emergency."

"That sounds suspiciously like *I've got to spend the night with a sick friend*."

"Oliver is no competition for you, love. He's stuck in word

gridlock. It's my duty to help pry him loose. It's in the union contract."

"You need material, just come here. Tonight's the weirdest it's been in ages. We got our own units, plus freelancers, plus fire department ambulances, plus wagons from our friendly coroner – all bi-parked and honking. It's not even a weekend, for shit's sake."

"Chained to the job?"

"Yeah – chains are heavy, cold, oppressive and leave marks. *Not* a pleasure."

Unlike pantyhose, thought Chan, who had thoroughly inventoried Michelle's wayward bag before speaking to its owner. Silk scarves, self-sticking athletic bandages, scissors, two pairs of handcuffs with keys, body paint, Astro-Glide, condoms in various flavors and/or colors, several pre-cut lengths of leather cord, a vinyl mask with a mouth zipper. Plus the pantyhose, for bondage – much less stressful than metal links, it was true. Plus surgical gloves, catheters wrapped in plastic, an enema bag, and syringes for piercing. After all, Michelle *was* a medical professional.

"I could just drop it off later."

"That's really sweet, but it's a loony bin. Trust me. I'd prefer a raincheck . . ."

He overrode her. "But I stay up incredibly late."

"Say goodbye now, Chan. I've got too many blinking lights to deal with. Call me in the morning. *Your* morning – lunchtime."

"Will do."

"I'll think about you, meanwhile."

They traded good-nights. Chan despised predestination, the feeling of having his own decisions made for him. Tonight it was fated to be Guy Night with the too-tragic Oliver. It was in the stars or something. He tossed Michelle's fun-bag into the back seat of his Taurus, just he case he saw her later tonight after all.

Michelle's duty clock put her off at one o'clock in the morning – barely enough time to shed her whites and rendezvous with Jessie at the Shaggy Dog Pub before last call. Jessie was an amazingly virile cowboy who had been Michelle's backup liaison through several "official" boyfriends in a row. By 2:05, with no letup and no relief on the horizon, Michelle capitulated to the compensations of golden time. The world at large seemed to have different plans for her this evening.

Casualties in, casualties out. It didn't take much to make the ER into a circus. Paperwork would kill them all if the stress did not. The coroner's meatwagons had been rolling in and out, two by two. What a gag – the DOAs and overdosed junkies were turning out not to be so dead after all. One guy with no heart and a big shotgun blast hole in his chest had still been spunky enough to unzip his own bag and bite a quarter-pounder out of Mitch, the junior pathology resident. Now Mitch was busy throwing up – projectile emesis, from some sort of unidentified toxin – and getting *rabies* shots, for god's sake.

Cops, firefighters, virtually every employee of the country coroner's office, and hospital staff (in roughly that order) had become increasingly more vocal and disenchanted with the night's rash of dead body calls since Michelle had started her shift. By three A.M. the flood was relegated to triage priority status.

By three-thirty, Michelle had shifted to a backup plan that might save her a tiny piece of the night. Tired and cranky, but relieved at last, she sought to stealth her way into Jessie's shower. Jessie would not mind. He'd think it was sexy.

If Jessie was not alone tonight, then Chan was probably still up, good as his word.

Michelle had no way of knowing that the amazingly virile Jessie had died of several gunshot wounds at 1:30, and had been left butt-up in a dumpster at 1:32. The parking lot of the Shaggy Dog was no place to dispute with Jamaicans over drug prices. An especially useless death, considering that Jessie had been grooming Michelle, a medical professional, so he could cadge drugs from her.

Having tried to cope with the chaos and madness at the hospital, Michelle now fantasized about the hour or so left to her before dawn. The big punchline of her life would be that she had no way of guessing that she, too, would be dead long before the sun came up.

Because Jessie had returned from his parking lot mishap, and homed back to his apartment. Despite being dead, he had a whole new menu of hungers Michelle would never even guess.

*   *   *

It was the first time Chan had ever seen his pal, Oliver, naked.

Over the course of several fine drunks and the odd bout of midnight oil-burning, Oliver had more than once mentioned his propensity for writing in the buff. Spoke of grumping awake, grabbing coffee, and attacking the machine before vital post-dream images could be flattened by the time wasted in dressing. Talked about how he was usually good for a fast thousand words on this sort of autopilot. Reasoned, what good was it to have one's own garret, if not to facilitate striding forth in the nude to do battle with the keyboard? A sky-clad literary warrior, was Oliver.

The computer was in SLEEP mode, and as far as Chan could tell, so was Oliver. His left hand was spidered across the keyboard as if frozen in mid-stroke. The right side of his face also rested on the keys, turned toward his hand. His lips were parted. Drool had dried. Chan wondered if his saliva had short-circuited something and electrocuted Oliver.

"You've *got* to get out more," Chan started in. "This place smells like a jock sock."

No response from Oliver. No startled awakening, no jerks, no twitches of doggy dream-sleep.

"I've come to slap you into obeisance," Chan said, more loudly. Nada. He tilted Oliver backward. The swivel chair squeaked. Oliver's head lolled, unhinged, and Chan inadvertently recoiled, despite every stupid horror movie he had ever seen.

This was starting to stink real, and Chan preferred fiction.

He hung up on 911 after twenty rings. The hospital from which Michelle had phoned was not picking up, either. Average Los Angeles response time for an emergency was forty-seven minutes on a *good* day, and so far this was a day that classified as the shits.

Oliver's body was, in fact, lifeless and unbreathing. Chan dragged it to the sofa (strictly thrift-shop, and sprinkled with food crumbs) and covered it with a bedsheet (mildewy, dingy, and begging to be laundered). Oliver's entire apartment smelled like gangrene. Chan forced open two of the paint-welded casement windows, which had shade material stapled over the glass. You don't write in the altogether for the world to see, and Oliver had a quirk about letting daylight invade his eyrie. By working strictly under artificial light, he avoided the distractions of the moving sun outside.

In a bad horror story, he would have just been a vampire and that would be that.

Oliver's window obsessions struck Chan as sort of romantic, really – the kind of feeling Chan honestly wished he could say he felt more often. Oliver *felt* things; Chan always provided a correct or witty response, a reaction that mimicked a human feeling. Writing too many scripts could rebuild you that way, until you were always cued for the next line.

Both of them had read most of the scary stories involving writer characters who happened to die in mid-phrase, from Lovecraft all the way to Bloch; stories in which death utterances always transposed to actual type as *it's coming . . . it's in the room! . . . it has its fingers around my throat . . . it . . . auuuuugggghhhh . . .*

Or the Bloch one, about the guy whose fingers crumble as he attempts to continue typing.

Figuring a minimum safety net of three quarters of an hour before anything exciting happened, Chan decided to read what Oliver had written – the tale now destined to be just another unfinished story by just another writer dead before his prime.

". . . what we really need is a poison control 1–800 number for all the victims of shitty writing," argued Shade, who began to fling steatopygous paperbacks from the review stack. "*Look* at this crap! Gerund titles, drippy letters, black spines that should be yellow. These aren't horror novels, they're the *corpses* of books that have been murdered by hacks!"

"Zombie literature?" Blake cracked a smile.

Shade lifted another lurid example: Foil, holograms, die-cuts, and a water-weight bloat to the prose that would make Jenny Craig's entire philosophy beg for mercy. *The Hosing*. She pinched it between two fingers like roadkill, and quoted the blurbs. "*Dabney Abbott delivers a big eleven on the fright scale*, says the reviewer from Tentacles of Yentacle. Woo, scary! *Dabney Abbott is the new Steven King*, claim the Horror Scriveners of Provi-

dence, which spells King's name wrong. Who the hell
is Dabney Abbott?"

"I thought he was the new Steven." At least Blake
was finding this entertaining.

"Wrong! He's a yoyo who sold this stiff to Maelstrom
Books for $1800, and he needs to be decapitated!"

"Do YOU have a burning urge to write?"

"*A small New England town . . . after centuries of
waiting, the evil was poised to commence afresh . . .*"

"Please stop, I beg you."

"This is a living dead book, Blake!"

Blake appreciated the notion. "Yes – it schlumps out
into the world, it preys on you for six bucks . . . then it
EATS."

"It eats. Precisely."

Chan noticed that Blake and Shade were sounding suspiciously
like two guys named Chan and Oliver.

You cunning monster, he thought of the shape beneath the
mouldering sheet. You used our conversation to build the subtext
of a story you could not write because it had no heart.

Like the Cowardly Lion, Oliver's story had found its heart, its
theme – *the murder and subsequent zombiatic revivification of
prose itself!*

Got to watch those mental italics, thought Chan. Too frantic,
like Dr. Frankenstein, declaiming.

He read 'Insatiable Hungers' through. Blake and Shade, it
turned out, were two women, and lovers. Oliver had strategically
placed a lovemaking scene right up front, to snag the reader like a
pit bull, and not relinquish. It was a seduction, a trick of writing
that worked as surely as the synaptic fire of orgasm.

. . . she rolled her eyes, now glazed in that satiated cat
way, as Shade surfaced from between her legs. She
saw appraisal, there in the cafe au lait irises; questions, in the arch of jet-black brows.

"God, that must have been five. Six."

"If you can still count them, they don't count," said
Shade evilly. "Warm up, before worn out." She
grabbed Blake's forearms and trapped her, arching

her rudely upward in order that she might observe
any and everything Shade planned, while she was
gloriously open and wet and helpless.
"I don't think I can make it any more, baby . . ."
"Wrong," said Shade, and proved it.

Chan scrolled the story to the point where it broke off in mid-
line.

"It would be very easy to believe we're the only people
really alive among all the walking dead out there,"
Shade said, bleakly, taking care to angle her gaze
through the slanted blinds, so that from the outside
it would look as though

Interesting term, "scrolling." Hadn't writers been scrolling, so to
speak, ever since papyrus? And what was a scroll but rolled up
paper? Didn't you smack uncooperative dogs with a rolled-up
paper? And weren't writers essentially *bad* dogs? Didn't publishers and producers constantly admonish them to *do it on the
paper,* like right *now?*

The zany, loose-limbed Mr. Calm puppet in Chan's brain
dropped by long enough to note: *Easy. You're losing your
fucking mind, Boss.*

He paced his breathing and Zenned his cardio back to normal.
Control. No commotion of ambulance arrival had distracted him
from his read of the story so far.

Oliver had insisted on giving Chan a set of apartment keys two
years ago. Perhaps this was why; Oliver had suspected he might
wind up unexpectedly dead, tragically youthful. Wasn't that a
promotable angle, a guaranteed sale, given talent? Wasn't the lust
of publishers for dead writers one of the few ironclads left? It
made royalties so much simpler; the dead did not complain or
write stiff letters when you skimmed more. This happenstance
might garner Oliver an audience when nothing else could. Chan
had seen all three of his friend's novels; all were good, each was
kinky and original, with memorable and stimulating characters
and a twisty-turny plot structure. Each book evidenced expo-
nential growth, and that, too, was a pattern that might be
exploited.

Good trick, Chan thought. I've just been appointed de facto executor of Oliver's literary estate, because he knows – knew – I won't let him go down unsung. *Congratulations, you fucker!*

Chan found himself at the window. He milled about the apartment, trying not to look back at the outline beneath the dirty sheet. Staring through a tear in the shade, he tried to put himself in the place of Oliver's character, also named Shade. There was nothing out in the courtyard. An interloper would have to work hard to peep, only to be rewarded with the silhouette of some naked writer, writing.

Chan peeled the grimy shade off the windowpane. It was dusty; it resisted. There was nothing to look at outside except a sort of anti-view. After a moment, he booted up Oliver's story again and completed the unfinished line.

. . . so that from the outside it would look as though some stranger was pausing to browse. It was the fishbowl effect in reverse; no one would ever know a naked woman looked out from these anonymous rooms. All the outside world would ever perceive was a pair of shielded eyes, examining them.

Chan left the cursor blinking. He tried 911 again and got a recording. He would not hold, nor was there any message he cared to leave after the beep.

In the bathroom, he splashed water on his face and groped for one of the three towels Oliver had owned since he was seventeen. All were transparently threadbare, and the muggy odor never left them no matter how clean they were. Chan reviewed his own face for a bit in the cataracted mirror, wondering who the hell he was supposed to be.

Until the typing sounds from the front room snatched his attention away.

sounds snatched awy herr notice like cellllophane criklingto simulat fire on some fake radio dramma blake was stufing pages form the deadlyy books into hr mout andeating them shade ws at firrrst shokd then curious blake seemd to be derivin g g

nourishmnt from th dead bodysx of fiction so
shade e eee abrptly an d shokin ly
wondred what blake might t taste lik now

Chan understood that the first rule of the zombie playbook was
that walking dead-ites tried to replicate whatever constituted
their fundamental behavior in life. Couch potato zombies
locomoted to the nearest mall. Soldier zombies herky-jerked
through a retarded version of military drill. And writer zombies,
well . . .

As soon as Chan peered over Oliver's shoulder to read what
was on the screen, Oliver orally voided a glurt of pinkish catarrh,
twisted his head on squeaking tendons, and tried to bite Chan's
nose off. Chan backpedaled and fell broad-assed over the foo-
tlocker which served as Oliver's coffee table.

Oliver had been the *late* Oliver – dead – for over two hours, by
Chan's watch.

But Oliver had asked Chan to help. Chan's definition of help
did not extend to providing parts of himself as food so Oliver
could complete his short story. There were some things friends
just did not let friends do.

A half-hour of wisely invested time turned their situation
around quite nicely. If Chan had an inborn talent, it was for
finding the upside.

It was no longer carnal desire that Blake fostered
for her best friend; not now, no. It was hunger,
pure, primal, and elemental. A need of instinct.

And Shade, who had never denied herself any sensation, found that she was not repulsed by the truth.
No. She was *fascinated*.

Michelle's leather and nylon bondage paraphernalia proved
adequate to the need to strap Oliver's forearms to his chair at
precisely the textbook angle of wrist-slant required for typing.
Her handcuffs, attached to the tubular steel of the computer
trolley, permitted Oliver's hands the play of the keyboard. The
zippered vinyl mask kept Oliver's bite reflex in check. Just in time,
too . . . since Oliver had apparently forgotten how to space
between words altogether.

Chan stood off Oliver's left shoulder, leaning in to correct or complete spelling, insert punctuation, indent new paragraphs, and supply whatever other skills Oliver would lose in the next five minutes due to catching a nasty case of death. He had literally chained Oliver to his word processor, and quite naturally felt like the worst caricature in the world of an overbearing, unfeeling editor. He was forcing Oliver to do it on the paper for the last time.

And when it is a done thing, Chan thought, it'll be time to jam one of Michelle's syringes straight into the dysfunctional cottage cheese of Oliver's dead-ass brain, right through the ear hole, and click him off. Chan imagined the moist noise the penetration would bring. Chan found it tough to rein in his imagination right now.

In this way, together, they grimly marched toward the conclusion of this invented fiction. After THE END . . . then what?

Revisions, was what. Polishing.

Chan busied himself in the prettification of 'Insatiable Hungers', annotating the hard copy with red ink marks until the pages seemed adorned with shallow razor cuts. During this, the late Oliver chowed down on bloody, fat-rich ground round, a family-pack.

The 24-hour market had been an adventure in itself. Chan saw much more crowd action than the usual three A.M. gaggle of the city's walking wounded, metalheads seeking munchies, and derelicts pretending not to shoplift. Tonight there were too many normal citizens in the mix – house frumps in slippers and bathrobes, weekend warriors in fatigues, skittish young couples with puppies in tow – all gazing blankly at the shelves as if awaiting mystic revelations, or stocking up as if a nuclear strike had been announced. Something was askew out here in the real world, too, not just back at Oliver's garret, but it only made Chan more anxious to return to his personal piece of the chaos, the part he could control.

Chan's writing habit was to not annotate work draft copy so much as draw cabalistic circles and arrows on it, visual benchmarks which could remind him of each intended amendment. A private code. While secure in his method, he now doubted the integrity of the end product. This doubt was his rationale for never becoming an editor himself; any changes he might suggest would inevitably slant the story, making it less representative of the author than of Chan himself. The impulse was second nature to anyone who had ever sat staff on a TV show – the imposition of a uniform identity on the writing. Chan hated the automatic nature of this, and his own inability to transcend it. Was *this* all he owed his good friend, his pool-playing partner?

He needed to ask questions. To be directed. Oliver was incapable of supplying navigational tips. Oliver could not do anything except numbly pound the keys, and Chan's reserve tank of inner drive was close to fumes.

Chan owed it a try, anyway: "So, uh . . . what do you think?" He laid the stack of copy in Oliver's lap.

Oliver writhed and slobbered and tried to eat the last seven pages. He would have, too, if the mask had not been zipped. Chan accepted this as criticism, and rewrote the seven pages from a new angle. The sun came up. Chan closed all the windows. Oliver's lighting trick worked pretty well, as it turned out.

Chan chained Oliver to the kitchen sink pipe and assumed the pilot seat for himself, repeating the whole process until he, too, slumped face-first into the keyboard, exactly as Oliver had when he died.

"You've painted yourself into a corner," said the Editor, flipping up Page 29 of the story and finding nothing underneath.

"Bite me," said the Writer, who had pounded down about a gallon of the Editor's iced tea and blazed through half a pack of smokes, suffering the desultory read in the silence of the damned.

"I mean, it's kind of obvious this Chan guy has got to wind up dead, too," said the Editor. "End of story. So how does the fictional story they're writing get to where it's going, I mean, to the poor son of a bitch who's editing the zombie book? Who prints it out, who mails it, who delivers it? Is this trip really necessary?"

"What difference does it make," said the Writer. "Do you really need it tied up into a granny knot? If you can't see the subtext, I can't wave my magic wand

and grant you divine sight. The point is *there*, and why write it past the point? The guts are *there*. You don't need to spotlight either of them.''

"You think readers are smarter than publishers do."

"I'm not writing for *publishers*, goddammit."

"Humor me. Open it up. Let it breathe just a hair. Don't wire it so tight metaphorical."

"Okay," said the Writer, expelling a long plume on concentrated smoke. "Think TV: Cops burst in and find two dead writers. Like Quasimodo and Esmerelda, except that both Chan and Oliver have chewed each other up pretty good. There are only enough body parts left to make a single person . . . but nobody can distinguish which part belongs to who."

"*Whom*. Why would anyone care?"

"The important part is the writing itself. No one can tell where Ollie leaves off and Chan begins."

"You mean like that Poe story finished by Robert Bloch?"

" 'The Lighthouse,' " said the Writer. "All the high-and-mighty literary sleuths assumed Bloch had picked up Poe's unfinished story at the point where the plot makes a radical left-hand turn. In fact, Bloch wrote the section *preceding* the shift in gears, and I think he did it on purpose, to mimic Poe perfectly, then drop in a false lead for all the nitpickers to trip over."

The Editor waved the stack of pages. Editors frequently waved paper around as though it lent weight to their criticisms. "So, am I to assume here that the double-death of the collaborators makes the story notorious enough to become famous, as in make money?"

"Except that the disenfranchised body parts are all still moving around. And they're trying to keep writing. The collaboration, you see, is enough of a success that publishers ask immediately for the novel version."

"Which means somebody has to shepherd the zombie parts together and make them behave long enough to produce more output.''

"Correct – you have the first bestseller written by a dead guy who actually *is* dead. With a third hand governing the process, neatening the manuscript, making it all presentable to the norms in publishing.''

"Who? Another dead writer?''

"No,'' said the Writer. "Too many cooks. What they obviously need is an Editor of the Living Dead. That character would be you, for example.''

"What you need is for one of those friendly West Hollywood sheriffs to shine a baton flashlight up your ruby red asshole to see what drugs you've been pooping.''

"Come on. It'll play and you know it.''

"I think it needs more development.'' Editors frequently said this a lot, too.

The Writer rummaged in his briefcase. "I'm way ahead of you. Here's how it works: 'Chan' and 'Oliver' are pseudonyms; they were *always* secret identities. So no one can say that the narrative did not occur actually as presented.''

"You mean the only real need is to get the editor, having gotten the writers.''

"This is the beauty part,'' said the Writer.

Before the Editor could ask what that meant, the Writer's fist came up from the briefcase wrapped around a Sig Sauer 226 and grouped a close trio of nine-millimeter slugs to frame the Editor's heart. At this time of night, nobody would give a shit about gunshots in *this* neck of Hollywood. The Editor, bearing the ultimate expression of bugfuck betrayal, slumped back onto the sofa without time for a grunt of surprise.

"Welcome to the winning team,'' said the Writer as he zipped up the Editor's corpse into a sleeping bag brought for just this purpose. "We're all going to be rich and famous.''

Murder? Not here, not now.

Not when there were real zombies roaming the sidewalks, eating people, making more zombies. In times of societal stress, people always turned to escapist entertainment, and who was to say their behavior would change just because some of them died? *En masse* they could form a new and burgeoning audience which would *always* crave the next book, and the next, any book, so long as they could continue reading, and keep deluding themselves that nothing horrific was happening in *their* world, that the news on TV must have gotten it wrong somehow. A public that wanted *even more* stories about the walking dead . . . because they had so much in common with them.

There are those who eat, and those who get eaten, thought Chan. Yet *all* of them were consumers. Herbivores need not apply. He dumped the corpse of his newest collaborator, the Editor, into the trunk of his Taurus, where a set of handcuffs and a recycled bondo mask already had the Editor's name on them.

It was time to go forth into the new world, and feed.

THe en . . .

CONRAD WILLIAMS

The Windmill

CONRAD WILLIAMS IS A past winner of the British Fantasy Award and the Littlewood Arc prize. Although this is his first appearance in *The Best New Horror*, his story "The Bone Garden" was published by the late Karl Edward Wagner in his final volume of *The Year's Best Horror Stories*.

As the author explains: "The idea for 'The Windmill' came to me on the night I stayed in a windmill on the Norfolk coast. Much of what appears in the story actually happened. It contains two themes which I am particularly fascinated by: the decay of relationships and isolation."

The latter is explored more fully in Williams' debut novel, *Head Injuries*, published in 1998 by The Do-Not Press. A second novel, *London Revenant*, is currently doing the rounds and an excerpt from it has appeared in *This Is* magazine. His work has also appeared in *Dark Terrors 2, 3* and *4*, *The Mammoth Book of Dracula*, *The Ex Files*, *A Book of Two Halves*, *Sirens and Other Daemon Lovers*, *Scaremongers*, *Last Rites & Resurrections*, *Darklands 2*, *Blue Motel* and many others. The author is currently working on his next novel, *Softsuck*.

A S THEY DROVE PAST the gutted skeleton of the Escort, Claire tensed.

"What's wrong?" asked Jonathan, easing off the accelerator.

"There was someone in that," she said, twisting against his seat belt to look out of the back window. "Stop. Go back."

He shook his head. "Will you stop messing about Claire? I can never tell when you're being truthful. You should have been an actress."

The car diminished. It was standing on its hubs, the tyres having melted, in a pool of oil. Claire squinted at the driver's side: a black shape was bolt upright in what remained of the seat.

She turned around.

Jonathan was fiddling with the tuner, trying to find some music. The only station that cropped up on the automatic search was a thin grainy hiss, punctuated by a slow *whump . . . whump* sound.

"Welcome to Radio Norfolk," said Claire, trying to forget. *He'd had no lips. Just a gritted sheet of white. His fat had oozed through the black shell of his skin and hung in yellowish loops, like cheap pizza cheese.*

The Fens reached out beyond the hedgerows muscling against the car, green fields splashed with red poppies and sprigs of purple lavender. Claire wound down the window and breathed deeply, trying to unwind. This was meant to be a relaxing weekend but already she felt that she'd made errors. And that riled her.

"Norfolk? Why are you going to *Norfolk?"* they'd asked her back at the office. She'd felt the need to defend the place, even though the nearest she'd ever been to the county was a day trip to Mablethorpe as a child.

"There's lots of unspoilt coastline," she said. "I want long, windswept beaches to walk along. And there's a stack of wildlife. Apparently."

"You should try Suffolk instead," a colleague, Gill, had said, almost desperately, while her deputy looked at her with an expression approaching pity.

Jonathan had suggested they go to Paris but she quashed that idea because she didn't want to spend too much money. And anyway, what was the point of going away for a weekend to another busy, polluted city? But that wasn't strictly true. Her negativity had more to do with the fact that the break was Claire's baby: she wanted to come up with the plan. Now, as they swept through mile after mile of flat, sunbleached land, she was beginning to wish that she'd thought of Paris first. And she was also thinking of Jonathan's disappointment and the "told you so" triumphs of her workmates once she got back. Jonathan was aware of her frustration. He rubbed her leg. "We'll stop for a drink, hey?" he said. "Next pub we come to. We'll try some good old local brew."

"There was someone in that fucking car," she snapped.

"Fine," he said, braking hard. "Get out and go and save him."

They sat in silence, the heat building. Claire strained for some sound to massage the barrier loose between them but none was forthcoming. They hadn't seen a car, a moving car, for an hour or so. The buildings they'd passed were gutted and crippled, the life seemingly sucked from their stone into the sallow pastures that supported them.

"I'm sorry," she said. "I just – it's work, you know? It's been getting me down. I just want this weekend to be perfect. I need this break and maybe . . . maybe I haven't realised that you need it just as much. You've driven all the way from London and . . ." she trailed off, lamely. Work excuses were crap, she knew that and so did he.

Jonathan didn't say anything. He started the car and moved off.

"Put a tape on then," he said. "Anything. I'm getting antsy with all this bloody quiet."

She dug for a cassette from the pile on the back seat. Most were hers although there were one or two tapes from his past, recorded on blanks by ex-girlfriends and scribbled over with red kisses. Alexander O'Neal. Luther Vandross. He had some new stuff, Fugees and Skunk Anansie but she couldn't get the irritation out of her where those older albums were concerned. It wasn't so much the music – it was shite, that went without saying – it was thoughts of what he'd been up to while she listened to it. Why would you play Luther Vandross if you weren't doing what he was singing about?

Her fingers settled on a Pavement album they both liked. The tension between them relaxed a little but Claire was glad to be able to point out a pub – it would be good to get out of the car and make the distance between them an optional thing.

"Where are we, navigator?" Jonathan asked, parking the car in the gravel forecourt. Behind them, a stone building with no discernible purpose was the only other sign of life around.

"Um, Cockley Cley. Just south of Swaffham."

"Right. Let's get re-fuelled. Hungry?"

A man wearing sunglasses and a padded Parka uncoiled from the corner of a bench outside the pub, where he had been sunning himself. He snaked out a hand to the adjoining picnic table and withdrew a pallid sandwich from a paper bag. His flask was attached to a sling around his shoulder. Jonathan nodded as they walked by but if the man reacted, Claire didn't see it.

Inside, three men were hunched over their meals, whispering conspiratorially. A cold meat buffet under hot lights reminded Claire of a Pantone chart of greys. To their left, the lounge was empty: two men were sitting at the bar, exchanging lowing, long-vowelled words. Claire wanted to leave.

"Jonathan – "

The man facing her wore a shirt opened to his navel. His gut lolled there, a strip of sweat banding his sternum. His nose was a sickening chunk of discoloured flesh, bulbous and misshapen, hanging down almost to his top lip. She watched, fascinated and repulsed, as he dragged a handkerchief across it, threatening to smear it even further. It looked as though it was melting. His companion was dressed in a cheap suit with a purple shirt. His hair was greased back, one blade of it swung menacingly in front of his eyes. His grin was loose and slick with spit. She could see his dentures, behind the pitted white flaps of his lips, clacking loosely around his mouth.

She edged towards her boyfriend as the landlord appeared from behind a gingham curtain. She was conscious of movement behind his arm: a swift descent of something silver, a hacking noise. She backed into a chair and sat down.

"Pint of Flowers. And, er –" Jonathan looked at her and she saw a little boy lost. The men eating their dinner had looked up at his softly blunted northern tones. They looked confused, as if they ought to act upon this invasion but didn't know what course to take.

"Glass of fresh orange," she said, her voice too loud.

The landlord poured their drinks and took Jonathan's money. He had the look of a pathologically strict Sergeant-Major. His moustache and his accent were violently clipped. His eyes were unpleasantly blue.

They took their drinks outside and sat on the bench adjacent to the man with the flask. He was still eating his sandwiches. He gave them a cursory once over and zipped his Parka closer to his throat.

"Jesus," whispered Jonathan, downing half of his drink. "Jesusing Christing piss."

"Did you see that man's *nose*?" hissed Claire, fidgety with nervous excitement. She was close to guffawing. "What do you think it was? Syphilis? Cancer?"

Jonathan polished off his pint. "Demonic possession," he said, standing. "Drink that, bring it or leave it. We've been here seven minutes too long."

They spewed gravel getting out of the car park. Claire looked back and saw the Sergeant-Major step out of the door, his hand raised, a stricken look on his face.

Neither of them said anything until they hit the relative bustle of Swaffham. Even then, their relief could only manifest itself in gusts of laughter.

"I love you," she said, surprising herself. It seemed easy to say after the minor trauma of the pub. It was a comfort.

"I love you, too," he replied, although she hadn't meant it as a cue. "I thought we were goners. I thought we were going to end up as part of a very disappointing Scotch egg."

She laughed again and then suddenly felt like crying. Her upset was nebulous, there was no real reason for it, no rational reason. They'd just been people, strange only because they were slightly more different to her than she was used to. Must be exhaustion. She closed her eyes and through the reddish dark of that unshareable interior, she immediately saw the measured sweep of a deeper blackness across her vision. She opened her eyes but there weren't any boringly equidistant trees to cast their shadows, no houses since Swaffham now lay behind them. She shut out the light again and yes, here it was, a slow black glide from the top of her eyes to the bottom. And again. And again. Again.

Her heartbeat then, she reasoned, not without some discomfort. But before she could offer any satisfying alternative, she was asleep.

She swam out of the dark, panicking that she wouldn't grasp Jonathan's question and be able to answer it before he lost patience with her. But it wasn't a question, he was merely talking to himself, loud enough for her to infer that he was pissed off with her sleeping while he did all the work.

"Sea view, they said. A sea view at the hotel. Oh yes, certainly, if you've brought the Hubble telescope along with you."

He looked at her and she could tell why; both to check she was awake and that she appreciated his joke. God, he really could be a minor irritant sometimes. "Wells-Next-The-Sea, they call this place," he continued. "Mmm, and my name's Jonathan-Two-Dicks-Chettle."

"We're here then?" Claire stretched in her seat, and blinked against the late morning sunshine. A clutch of beached boats seemed to cling to each other in the distance. Well beyond them, a silvery grey line – like a mirror seen edge on – marked the leading strip of the tide.

"Yes, arrival can usually be said to be on the cards when the driver is in parking mode. And hey! We're in a car park. Well done. Super."

"Oh shut up, Jon," Claire sneered. Twin glints of light drew her gaze towards a range of thin trees forming a paltry windbreak against the sea's muscle. Someone was looking in their direction with a pair of binoculars.

"Birdwatchers," Jonathan said, with a mock shudder. "This place'll be crawling with them. Come on, let's go and christen our room."

They checked into the B&B and were led up a grand staircase past mounted blunderbusses and badly stuffed seabirds. Their room looked out on the car park but was only slightly higher up, giving a better view of the acres between the hotel and the sea. Jonathan pressed up against her while she took in the tangy air. She let him peel down her jeans and panties, take her from behind even though she was dry. His pleasure, transmitted into grunts and selfish stabs, did nothing for her, but it was better than arguing about sex. She wondered why she had suggested this holiday as he withdrew and came on her buttocks. She wondered if, as he wiped himself against her, it was to prove to herself that she didn't want him any more.

"Quick walk before dinner?" he said, tucking himself away and kissing the back of her head. "I'll wait downstairs. See if they can recommend some good restaurants."

She masturbated to a swift, shallow orgasm, then cleaned

herself up and pulled on a pair of shorts. Jonathan was leaning against the door outside, absently sniffing his fingers. He looked at her, obviously irritated that he'd had to wait so long, then motioned with his head and set off for the road before she'd reached him. They followed its uneven surface towards the boats then struck out across the fields, past dun-coloured cows. Thick reeds nestled in a gulley off the track, hissing.

The quick, unexpected smell of camomile pleased her, a scent she'd always associated with long summer walks as a child with Dad through the woods behind their house. She'd ask him where they were going and he'd reply: "The land of far beyond." They never arrived, though she'd soon lose her excitement of that unseen place in favour of his soft words as he told her about the plants and the buildings and the animals they saw. More often than not, she'd end up in his arms, too tired to walk, as twilight drew around them.

"What are you smiling at?" Jonathan asked.

"Sorry," she said, reluctant to share her memory. He'd probably only scoff. "I thought this was a holiday. I thought I'd be able to smile without being invited."

"Do you have to be such a snidey bitch all the time?"

"Only when I'm with you, lover."

Violently quiet, they approached an expanse of mud. Riven with trenches and pits, its scarred surface stretched out towards the sea. At this landlocked end, dry, stunted plants sprouted from its surface sheen. The acrid smell of salt was accompanied by something cloacal: oil bound up in its organic processes, farting silently through moist fissures.

"Jesus," said Claire. 'Fucked if I'm wading through *that*."

"This holiday was your idea, kid," Jonathan sang. "We could have been sipping *serré* outside Café de la Mairie by now."

It took the best part of an hour to cross the mud, by which time they were hot and cross with the way the mud sucked their feet in easily enough but was reluctant to give them back without a fight. Eventually the land solidified and gave itself over to a tract of well-packed sand. They squelched towards a band of shallow water and rinsed their feet. At the other side, they headed towards the boats, parallel to the path they'd taken. Two hundred yards away, a man collecting shellfish in a carrier bag cast featureless glances at them while a dog scampered at his feet.

The journey back seemed free of obstacles and they were able to relax and enjoy the walk. The sea breeze flirted gently with them, taming the sun's heat. Claire was able to laugh at one point, at some lame crack or other that Jonathan came out with. She didn't care. The water that they'd crossed had broadened and it soon became apparent they'd have to re-cross it to get back to their hotel. It seemed much deeper, with a fast running spine.

"Shit," Jonathan spat. "We could swim it."

"I'm not swimming anything. I've got my sunglasses on and money in my pockets. And my watch isn't waterproof."

"And God fucking forbid you should smudge your fucking make-up!"

Claire flinched from his rage and inwardly threatened herself not to cry. She wouldn't do that in front of him again. She wasn't happy with her silence – a mute response might only goad Jonathan further – but if she opened her mouth she'd start bawling. She couldn't remember how their relationship had started. It was as passionless and inexorable as a driver grudgingly picking up a hitchhiker on the road.

While he judged the depth and keenness of the water, she watched the tide in the distance, creaming against the slate-coloured sand at a tempo to match the beat of her resentment towards him.

"I'm going to try this, try walking across. To show you. Then you'll be safe."

Do I hate him? she thought, bitter with her redundancy in this situation and angry that he should be illustrating her uselessness by making such a sacrifice. My hero. Suddenly, she didn't care if he disappeared into the sand and drowned. She wouldn't dive in to help him, she wouldn't scream for assistance. She might just sit down on the sand here for a while and count the bubbles.

"Nah," he said, waist-high in water. "Sand's giving way. Too dangerous for you."

She gritted her teeth and looked back along the flow. She saw a place where it chuckled and frothed and padded over to it. Shallow land. She'd skipped across to the other side while Jonathan was still struggling to free himself of the beach's suck. She had to turn away from him to conceal her laughter. He caught up to her, red and soaking.

"You might have told me, you twisted little cunt," he hissed into her ear, and strode off.

Yes, she thought, *yes I do*.

Shocked and hurt by his attack on her, more than she wanted to admit, Claire rinsed her feet in the sink while Jonathan languished in the bath. It seemed his good mood had revived somewhat. His hand was gripping the head of his straining cock.

"Hey, baby," he said, in a mock cowboy voice. "Why don'cha mosey on over here 'n' milk my love udder."

"Fuck off," she muttered, leaving him to it.

She dressed and went downstairs. Ordered a drink from the bar. An hour later, Jonathan was with her. Her distress was a palpable thing, spinning out from her like barbed hooks: a blind, flailing defence against his insinuative cruelty. She felt subsumed by his personality, as if he were trying to ingest her. Maybe it was the drink, but she was convinced his feelings for her were as shy of respect and concern as she'd suddenly come to realise for him.

"Sorry about that whole 'cunt' thing. Bit strong. You know I love you. What shall we have for dinner?"

She picked at a chicken and apricot pie while he polished off a bowl of mussels. "Christ," he said. "This sea air! I'm knackered!" He looked at her hopefully.

"I'll stay down here for a while," she said. "I'm not ready for bed yet."

He saluted and trotted upstairs. She swallowed hard. It seemed an age ago that she'd been able to think of him as attractive and warm. As – God, had she *really*? – a potential life-partner.

She took a drink with some of the other tourists, middle-aged women in oatmeal coir jumpers and Rowan bags. They tolerated her presence although she could tell she unnerved them for some reason. The hotel owner came in and lit the fire, asking everyone if they wanted brandy and she was going to start a game of whist if anyone was interested.

Claire bid everybody goodnight and went up to her room, the skin of her nape tightening when she heard the word "blood" mentioned behind her, by one of the women.

Did you smell the strength of her blood? She thought maybe that was what she'd said. Jonathan was snoring heavily. The TV was on, a late night film starring Stacey Keach. She switched it off and went to the bathroom where she undressed quietly. And stopped.

Her period had begun.

Did you smell the strength of her blood?

"Oh," she said, feeling dizzy. "Okay." She cleaned herself up and slipped into a pair of pyjamas. Stealthily, praying she wouldn't wake Jonathan, who'd read her clumsiness as a prompt for sex – or an argument – she climbed into bed and willed sleep into her bones before her mind could start mulling over the steady, sour creep of their relationship. She failed. She was awake as the full moon swung its mocking face into view, arcing a sorry path across the sky that might well have been an illustration of her own trajectory through darkness. Jonathan's ragged breathing ebbed and flowed in time with the tide of disaffection insistently eroding her from within.

As dawn broke, she managed to find sleep, although it was fragmented, filled with moments of savagery and violence that were instantly forgettable even as they unfolded shockingly before her.

Gulls shrieking as they wheeled above the hotel woke her. Jonathan had left a note on the pillow: *Didn't want to wake you for breakfast – you were well out of it. Nipped out for a newspaper. Enjoy your toast. Love, J*

He'd wrapped two pieces of wholemeal toast and marmalade in a napkin and left them by her bed. The gesture almost brought her back from the brink but she guessed he considered it a chore. *If he mentions it to me later*, she thought, *I'll know he's after a reward, a pat on the back. I'll know it's over*. She giggled a little when she thought the death of their relationship should come down to a few slices of Hovis but that wasn't really the case; it was just a tidy way to cap it all, a banal necessity to make the enormity of her realisation more manageable.

An hour later, they were piling along the A149 coastal road, Jonathan singing loudly to a Placebo song. The sea swung in and away from them, lost to bluffs and mudflats before surprising Claire with its proximity once more. She didn't like the sea here. It appeared lifeless and sly. Where it touched land, grey borders of scum had formed. It simply sat there, like a dull extension of the Norfolk coastline.

They pulled off the road for a cup of tea at a small café. While

Jonathan argued with the proprietor, who was loath to accept a cheque under five pounds, Claire watched an old woman attempting to eat her Sunday lunch. Her hands shook so badly that she couldn't cut her meat; her cutlery spanked against the side of her plate like an alarm. The winding blades of an old-fashioned fan swooped above them all. Something about its movement unsettled Claire.

"Come on," said Jonathan, imperiously. "We'll have a drink when we get to Cley." He turned to the café owner, who was now flanked by her waitresses, alerted by the fuss.

"Suck my dick, Fatso," Jonathan said, and hurried away. Claire raised a placatory hand but the proprietor only looked saddened. The woman eating her meal raised her jerking head and showed Claire what she was chewing.

"Jon! How could you say that? How could you embarrass me like that?"

"Us Chettles don't suffer fools lightly, Claire. I'm not about to start now."

She wanted to leave him, to just go home, but it was his car and she didn't know where the nearest railway station was. Sheringham, probably, a good twenty miles away. She hadn't seen a bus or taxi since they were in Ely the day before yesterday.

"I don't feel as though I'm on holiday, Jon. I haven't been able to relax. All we've done is drive and argue. And I really needed this break."

"Hey, it was your choice."

"Oh, like it would have been different if we were in Paris?"

He was nodding. "Paris is the city of romance. It's impossible to have an argument there."

She snorted. "There's a word for people like you. Dumbfuck, I think it is."

He let that one go, but she could see his jaw clenching, his knuckles whitening on the wheel.

She was the first to see the windmill. It rose up from a coppice beyond a low range of roofs, its naked, motionless blades seeming to pin the sky into position. She pointed it out and Jonathan nodded, turning the car on to a gravel track. They crested a small humpback bridge over a stream choked by rushes. The windmill was white, tall and solid. Some of its windows were open; lace curtain wagged in the breeze.

Jonathan parked the car and got out without looking at Claire. He walked through the heavy wooden door at the windmill's base. Claire collected the bags and stood for a while, looking out towards the dunes. On the path, a cluster of bird-spotters in brightly coloured windcheaters alternated their focus between her and a clump of gorse. Occasionally, one of them would raise their sunglasses and favour her with a brilliant stare. A woman in a fluorescent green beanie trotted further down the path and the others followed. Claire laughed. They looked intense and foolish.

At the door, she paused. She couldn't see anybody inside.

"Jon?"

There was a visitors' book open on a bureau next to a coffee cup. A small jar of lollipops on the windowsill had been dis-coloured by the sunlight. "Hello?"

She left the bags by the door and headed towards the room to her left. The door was ajar; an old woman was turning back the covers on the bed.

"Oh, hello?" said Claire, raising her hand. The woman looked up and smiled.

"Hang on dear," she said, fiddling with her ear. Claire saw she was wearing a hearing aid. "I keep it turned off when I work. Nice to have silence every now and again."

"My name's Claire? Claire Osman? I booked a double room for tonight."

She moved past Claire and checked her name in the ledger. "Yes. Room for two. Where's your partner?"

"He went in ahead of me."

The old woman gave her an askance look before shuffling towards the other end of the room. She twisted the handle on the door at the end but it was securely locked.

"Nobody came in here, my love. Are you sure?"

"I'm certain!" Claire blurted. "I saw him come in before me. He must have gone through that door."

"Aye, if he was a spirit. That's the door to the windmill. It's always locked unless we have a party of schoolkids come round, or enthusiasts, you know."

"The other guest room then. He must be joking with us."

"There's someone already in that, my love."

"He *must* be in there." Claire felt sick. She'd have been happy to see the back of Jonathan in any other circumstances but this was just too weird. Suddenly too final.

She pressed up close against the old woman's back when she disturbed the other guests, who were sorry they couldn't help, but no, they hadn't seen a soul in the past half hour. Claire felt her head filling with grey. She smelled Trebor mints and Earl Grey on the woman's cardigan. The next thing she was aware of, she was sitting on a high-backed wooden chair in the dining room, her eyes fixed on a cut glass bowl filled with boxes of Kellogg's Variety. The old woman had her hand between hers. The other guests – a woman in a pair of khaki shorts and a fleece; a willowy woman in a track suit sucking vampirically at a cigarette – watched, concerned from the corner of the room.

She introduced herself as Karen and looked as though she'd smoked herself thin. The type of woman who hurried a meal, picked at it really, just so that she could have the cigarette afterwards. Claire wondered if that was the way she had sex too. She drew the smoke so deeply into her lungs that it was almost without colour when it returned.

Her partner, Brenda, offered to call the police and look around the dunes outside. "The tide here is pretty innocuous but, you know, water is water."

Claire sat in the room, looking at Jonathan's travel bag. It hadn't been zipped up properly; a corner of his Bolton Wanderers flannel was sticking out of it. Two WPCs arrived. She told them what she knew, which was nothing. They made notes anyway. Checked the car. Told her to relax and there'd be someone to talk to her in the morning. Best not to go anywhere tonight. In case Jonathan should return.

"He's got the car keys anyway," she said. The policewomen laughed, although she hadn't meant it as a joke.

She watched them go back to their car. They talked to the old woman for a while, one of the policewomen turning to look at her through the window for a few seconds.

She ate with the other couple at the ridiculously large dining table, Brenda quick to let her know what a sacrifice this was as they'd aimed to go to The Red Lion in Upper Sheringham for food. Karen puffed before and after courses and during mouthfuls. Her cheeks seemed permanently hollowed.

"Has he ever done this before?" she asked.

Claire started to cry through her food, something she hadn't done since her childhood. She'd forgotten how hard it was to eat and cry at the same time. It was quite interesting to try, really.

"I can't talk. I'm sorry." She left them and went to her room. She drew a hot bath and soaked for twenty minutes, tensed for his knock at the door and his impatient, stabbing voice. She never realised she'd miss him so much.

Later, she watched the dark creep into the sky. Mars clung, a diamond barnacle, to the underside of a raft of cloud. The birdspotters were still out there, a mass of coloured Kangol clothing and Zeiss lenses. There was even a tripod. Cows stood in a far-off field like plastic toys.

Pale light went on outside. A soft looking young girl carrying a hose slowly drifted around the perimeter of the windmill's grounds wetting the plants and the lawn. An overweight dog ambled alongside her. Claire listened to the fizz of electricity until it calmed to a dull murmur and then went to bed.

Sleep claimed her quickly, despite her loneliness and the alien posture of the low-slung room. Her dreams were edgy, filled with savage angles and lurid colours, as though she were a film director trying too hard. She was in a car too big for the road, ploughing through a village where there were no men. She was heading towards a windmill in the distance that didn't seem to get any closer. Occasionally she'd drive over some indistinct shape in her path. Before long, the roadkill became larger. Some of it wore clothes. It didn't impede her progress; she drove straight over it.

whump . . . whump . . . whump . . .

Shanks of flesh squirted up on to the windscreen. The engine whined as it bounded through the bodies.

whump . . . whump . . . whump . . .

Awake. Grainy blackness separated into the lumpen shapes of furniture and pictures on the wall. Imperfect light kissed at the curtains, turning them into powdery tablets of neon.

"Jonathan," she whispered, softly, hopefully.

whump . . . whump . . .

A deep creaking noise punctuated that heavy sound. The window filled with black, then cleared again after an age. Blackness once more. Then soft light.

She opened the curtain. A blade of the windmill swung past her, trailing ragged edges of its sail. Down towards the end of the lawn, a huddle of people sat, a pinkish mass in the gloaming. Were they having a midnight party? Why hadn't she been invited? Maybe they wanted to leave her to her grief.

She shrugged herself into her towelling robe and picked her way through the shadows to the main door. The air was sharp with salt and still warm. She followed the path round to the garden, stepping through an arch crowded with roses. The windmill creaked and thudded, underlit by strange, granular arcs from lamps buried in the soil.

She was halfway across the lawn when she saw they were naked. They were surrounding something, dipping towards it and moving away. She recognised the young girl who'd watered the lawn, the old woman and Karen, who was lying back, cigarette in one hand, Brenda's thigh in the other. Brenda was talking to some other women. Claire realised she hadn't seen a man since the pub in Cockley Cley. The Sergeant-Major bustling out of the door. Holding up his hand. Mouthing something.

whump . . . whump . . .

The windmill hadn't born sails when they arrived that morning. She took another, hesitant step forward when she was spotted. One of the policewomen pointed at her. They all turned to look, peeling away from the dark, wet core of their interest. She saw their bodies were painted with blood. The old woman wore feral slashes of deep red across her forehead and neck.

Claire felt a thick, hot release against her thigh as she turned to look at the blades of the windmill, wrapped in the still wet hide of her boyfriend. Turning back to the women, who were advancing towards her now, she reached beneath the folds of her robe, sank her fingers into her own blood and began to paint.

JOHN BURKE

The Right Ending

JOHN BURKE WAS BORN in Rye, Sussex, and grew up in Liverpool, where his father became Chief Inspector of Police. During the 1930s he and Charles Eric Maine started *The Satellite*, one of the first science fiction fan magazines in Britain. He had several short stories published before winning the Atlantic Award in Literature for his first novel, *Swift Summer*. He worked in publishing, the oil business, and as European Story Editor for Twentieth Century-Fox Productions before becoming a full-time writer.

Burke has published more than 140 books, including such film and TV novelizations as *Look Back in Anger*, *Those Magnificent Men in Their Flying Machines*, *A Hard Day's Night*, *The Bill*, *London's Burning*, *Moon Zero Two*, *Dr. Terror's House of Horrors* and two volumes of *The Hammer Horror Omnibus*. He edited and contributed to three volumes of *Tales of Unease*, while *The Devil's Footsteps*, *The Black Charade* and *Ladygrove* comprise his "Dr. Caspian" trilogy about a Victorian psychic detective.

He has also written a number of science fiction novels and, in collaboration with his wife, he is the author of three Victorian Gothic romantic novels, *Darsham's Folly*, *The Eye Stones* and *The Florian Signet*, under the pen-name "Harriet Esmond". The author's latest thriller, *Bareback*, was recently published by Robert Hale.

T HE TABLE WAS LONG and had a heavy glass top. Books were piled neatly beside his left elbow – dozens of copies of the same book.

He took one from the top of the heap and briskly autographed it. The woman with the floral hat and the beads went pink with pleasure. "Thank you, oh, thank you so much." She clutched the copy and hurried away. The queue moved up like travellers at a railway station putting down their fares. Only here it was the same fare each time and the same destination: escape via the same route, into the world of Martin Paget.

Most of them were women. They shuffled forward with their carrier bags or neatly tied packages, all stamped with the convoluted logo of the vast store. Some crept around the author as if wondering whether to succumb to what was known in the trade as impulse buying and have Paget wrapped, delivered, and charged to their account, or to save their money for the lingerie department. Others looked coy when they met his gaze, challenging him to put them in a book just as he had put Valerie in a book.

Only of course it wasn't Valerie. A few traits here and there, it had to be admitted; a possible real-life situation imaginatively developed; wasn't there a taste of that in all creative a fiction? And anyway the character was called Melanie and not Valerie.

"I wonder if you'd autograph it for my husband." A large woman was thrusting a copy of his book peremptorily at him. "*To Harry with best wishes*, or something on those lines. He likes that kind of thing."

He didn't know whether the kind of thing Harry liked was a Martin Paget novel or Martin Paget's signature plus best wishes; but obligingly he signed.

Some gushed. Some were tongued-tied. Some seized the chance to play at being literary critics or psychologists.

A blue-rinsed customer wafted Carven and mid-afternoon gin towards him and said huskily: "How do you know so much about women, Mr Paget?"

He could have wished, just for once, that Valerie was standing behind him, listening, fuming. *There*, he said silently to her, wherever she might be now. *There . . . you see*?

"That character is so striking, Mr Paget. So true. So dreadful, but so true."

There was a breathing space as the next one in line turned to argue some unintelligible point with the department manager, standing to one side. Martin looked between them, towards the entrance.

A woman in a lime-green wool dress, with a short cape drooping casually from her right shoulder, smiled at him. He smiled back. She provoked that flicker of uneasy recognition you get when you meet someone who later turns out to be second or third cousin to someone you have known a lifetime. Only her smile was so direct and . . . well, knowledgeable.

She was probably one of the aviary of chattering birds he had met when discussing tonight's late-night television interview, and had been sent along to check on how the signing session was going. Only it was odd that he could have forgotten, or half-forgotten, anyone so beautiful.

"Based on fact," another of them was saying to him across the table. "It must be. It rings so true."

"It's kind of you to say so."

"So haunting. You must have known a great deal of suffering."

He nodded, and she went away happy, eager to tell her friends that she had wormed the author's secret out of him.

The next customer could surely not have pushed herself to the head of the queue, not just like that, without arousing some protest. Yet here she was. Green dress matched by drowsy green eyes, and a drowsily appreciative voice. Definitely not one of the telly twitterers. She was older than he had thought at a distance: older, calm, quietly assured.

"Such a very convincing book." The tone was so musical yet with an uncomfortable, sardonic edge to it. Somehow he sensed, without understanding why, that nobody but himself could hear a word she said. "But the ending isn't right, is it?"

"You think not?"

"From the point of view of the fictional *hero*" – again that harsh edge – "I suppose it fits. But really it's not right. And *you* know it isn't."

Before he could decide whether the argument was worth pursuing she had moved away and he was signing a copy not for her but for a young woman who managed in thirty seconds to tell him how many dozens and dozens of articles she had written for her local paper and how she intended to become a great writer one day just like he was, and . . . and . . .

He blinked. The place was too warm. Clashes in colours of book jackets, carpets and display panels began to shout at him. He would be glad to leave.

On the way out he went through the stationery department and bought a pad of that particularly smooth cream-laid paper on which he loved to write. That was a big point they made in all the publicity about Martin Paget and his books. Of course in this day and age the end product had to be bashed out on a word processor, and the publishers were more interested in knowing whether he could supply disks from the machine than in what the quality of his work might be. But Martin Paget was known to produce all his first drafts lovingly (and of course exquisitely) with an old-fashioned pen on old-fashioned paper.

Tonight he would listen uninterrupted to Bach, or maybe Bartók, and jot down some notes for a new book.

Difficult, though, to find a theme quite as compelling as that of Valerie . . . Melanie, rather.

The woman in green passed and smiled, not at him but into a distance which might hold the perfume counters, the notions room; or nothingness.

He drove home to relax before setting off for the television studio.

Home was a flat at the top of a Chelsea Embankment block. It was also the home of pictures which Valerie had detested, CDs and cassettes whose sound she couldn't stand, and the drinks cabinet which she had once smashed open when he had hidden the key.

It was quiet without her. Quiet and free from her malicious fidgetings, the obsessive rearranging of her collection of tiny porcelain frogs on their display shelves, knowing how it would spoil his concentration on his favourite music, and the noisy opening and closing of the drinks cabinet's glass doors; free from her innumerable, inexplicable silent resentments.

That character is so striking, Mr Paget. So true. So dreadful, but so true.

He poured himself a glass of chilled white port and put on a CD of the second Janáček Quartet.

For once it failed to coax him down its complex, entrancing

byways. He heard it without interruption yet could not concentrate. Valerie's voice was no longer there, her fidgetings and creakings were no longer there; yet he was still waiting for her to slouch into the room, to sneer across the music, to sneer at everything he most cared for. Valerie was dead. But the echo of her still resonated through the flat, still refusing to forsake him.

He no longer hated her. He kept telling himself that. He was haunted only by a lingering sadness.

Haunted.

Suddenly she was there. Not Valerie but the woman in green. Her head on one side, she seemed to be listening and smiling. He had always wanted someone who would listen in this way, drinking in the music as it was meant to be drunk. The tangle of sound took on shape and significance for him again.

Then he knew this was all absurd. "How did you get in?"

"I've always been here. Waiting."

The sound of the telephone struck a jangling discord through Janáček and through the woman with the loving smile. She vanished.

The voice at the other end of the line said that the producer of tonight's programme had been struck with one or two last-minute angles on the subject. Paget suspected the producer had only just got round even to thinking about it, and was panicking into a dazzle of ideas off the top of his head. But anyway, they were wondering whether Mr Paget could consider having a few answers ready for questions they would want to throw at him with calculated spontaneity. Were women being pampered too much in our society? Were men naively offering them too many legal safeguards while leaving themselves defenceless? And was the pain of a break-up any less for a man than for a supposedly more sensitive woman?

And could he get along twenty minutes earlier than arranged, so they could spark off a few new concepts together?

When the telephone was back in its cradle, he pressed the button to continue the music. There was a long delay before at last he detected the faint tremor of her movement across the room, began to see the turn of her shoulder, hear her faint intake of breath.

Yet she refused to materialise. And the music refused to take on meaning.

He glanced at the clock. If he left now he would be there far too early, and sitting around those studios would be even more frustrating than simply sitting here.

He got up and took that latest novel from the shelf, skimming through the last chapter to reassure himself that it really was as good as all the critics had said – and as he himself knew it to be. Uncompromising in its honesty. Savage, true, excoriating. Ruthless yet filled with compassion. Such a tragic yet inevitable climax. The only right ending.

In reality it had been much cruder. It had taken all his creative talent to weave literary beauty from the memories of screaming rage, rasping obscenities, drunken abuse. And at last the crazy car drive on her own out into Surrey: the crash, and the crushed mess of her corpse, and then her eternal silence. He had let her drive off on her own, knowing the state she was in, and still could not feel guilty; she had asked for it, he could predict what the ending would be, and it was one of her own choosing. All that he had known then and still knew was that he simply hadn't wanted to make the effort to do a damn thing about it.

Too brutish, too sudden. Reality had had none of the skill, the poetic beauty-in-horror, which suffused his novel.

The woman in green was standing at his shoulder and looking down at the open page.

"That's not how it ought to have been."

"The book?" he asked. "Or the reality?"

"In the book there are excuses. Very plausible ones. Very clever. In reality . . ."

"She was asking for it."

"Oh, no," cried the beautiful woman with the proud head and the yearning smile. "No. That wasn't what I asked for. Never, Martin, never."

Earlier today, in the store, he had felt uncomfortably warm. Now she was making him feel cold. Very cold. "You?" he protested. "You're not Valerie. Nothing like her."

"I'm what she *could* have been."

The lines in the corners of her eyes and mouth were aged by a sweet, tolerant humour, where Valerie's had been sour and derisive. Yet he could almost recognise them.

He said: "It's a mockery."

"I'm what you could have had. I'm the Valerie you could have created instead of the one you did create."

Now, his stomach lurching with a terrible sense of loss, he knew that truly he was haunted, devoured by a nostalgia for something which had never even existed.

"What are you doing here?"

"Waiting."

"For what?"

"For the right ending."

He dropped the book and reached for her. She did not appear to evade him yet remained always a few inches away, smiling, seeming to dance with him.

"If we could start again," he said desperately. "You and I . . ."

"You can't have me now. Not here. You wrote me out of existence a long, long time ago."

"Then what do you want now?"

"The right ending," she said again.

He looked again at the clock. It was time to be moving. He would walk past her, drive off to the studio, and her wraith could go wherever it pleased.

He reached for the original notes they had provided for the programme and went downstairs, quickening his pace out into the early evening as he headed for his car.

She was sitting in the passenger seat.

As he got in beside her he wondered what easy dismissal he could summon up: some ready-made incantation, or simply the blinking of his own eyes to free him from this waking dream. Yet somehow he was not surprised at her remaining there as he drove off, smiling ahead at the road as if this was the nicest drive they had ever taken together, the nicest beginning to a long, long holiday.

As the corner came up he knew that he was about to take it at a speed which was quite impossible. And he didn't try to slow; and didn't really care any more. He turned for a last quick glance at Valerie.

And once more it had become Valerie's face as he had always known it – the lines clawed deeper into it, the mouth turned down in bitter glee.

"I might have known," he sobbed, trying to hold the wheel as they hit the bend, but knowing he had no more strength. "Always wanting to get your own back, but never knowing what for."

"For all I never had," she screeched. "For all the things you would never allow me to be."

As the car and the world dissolved in a splintering and shrieking of metal, he heard her voice fall away into gentleness again, just as he had always wanted it to be – not vengeful but tranquil as it died with him in the suddenly fiery wreckage, as though she were thankful for him as much as for herself.

"The right ending," she said.

SIMON CLARK

Swallowing a Dirty Seed

SIMON CLARK LIVES IN DONCASTER, South Yorkshire. His own roots lie in the small press which published his first short stories, two of which were reprinted by the late Karl Edward Wagner in *The Year's Best Horror Stories*, and half-a-dozen appeared in the increasingly rare 1990 collection *Blood & Grit* from BBR Books.

Hodder & Stoughton has published five of his novels, beginning with *Nailed by the Heart* in 1995 (which was nominated for the British Fantasy Award). Others include *Darker* (nominated for the Dracula Society's award for Best Novel) and a hard-hitting post-apocalypse story, *King Blood*. His most recent novel, *Vampyrrhic*, will be followed by *The Fall* and a short story collection, *Salt Snake & Other Bloody Cuts* from Silver Salamander Press.

As Clark reveals, "The inspiration for 'Swallowing a Dirty Seed' stems from a fascination with the other-worldly landscape of North Wales, where seldom are things what they really seem. This piece continues the story, of one Stephen Carter began in 'Acorns – A Bitter Substitute for Olives'. He is someone else whose fascination with the dark magic of the Welsh mountains and deep valleys won't let him go."

"COULD YOU SPARE US some food?"
  "Food?"
"We haven't eaten all day. We were camping up the valley."
"We lost the rucksack with our supplies," the man added.

It was five in the afternoon. Despite the new electric oven causing the main's fuses to blow every forty minutes, I'd cooked my first proper meal in the cottage. A leg of Welsh lamb in rosemary; to accompany that, fresh vegetables and an apple and walnut stuffing of which I was particularly proud. The oven had behaved itself, nothing had been burnt, or emerged raw. And I'd just poured myself a glass of crisp white wine, so chilled the glass immediately frosted. That's when I heard the knock on the door.

The cottage, tucked deep in a Welsh valley, was miles from the nearest village and at first I thought it was the man from the garage returning my car a day early.

Instead, there on the doorstep, looking as if they'd just hiked back from the Antarctic, stood a man and woman in their early twenties. Both looked exhausted. Dark rings underscored their strangely glittery eyes; the man leaned forward, one elbow against the door frame to support his weight. He was slightly built with dark curly hair. He wore a corduroy jacket and jeans; the girl wore a brown suede jacket with black trousers. If anything she looked physically stronger than the man. Statuesque would be a description to suit her; she'd tied her long blonde hair back into a pony tail; her brown eyes fixed on me without a hint of shyness.

Both wore trainers. For campers they were pretty poorly equipped. I saw no sign of tents or sleeping bags.

"We can pay," the girl prompted. She unzipped a pocket on the inside of her jacket and pulled out about two pounds in change. The man leaned forward, trying not to look too obvious, but I could see he was drawing the aromas of the roasting lamb through his nostrils, as if he'd be nourished on the scents alone.

I smiled. Heck, I could afford to play the good Samaritan now I'd finally managed to sell my flat in Manchester and put down six months rental on this place.

"Come on in," I said, "I'm just about to eat anyway. Roast lamb okay? No, put the money in your pocket. The pair of you look as if you could do with a drink. White wine?"

"God, yes." The man sounded shocked by my generosity. "Brilliant. Thanks."

"Thank you very much, Mr?" The girl held out her hand.

"Stephen Carter." I shook her hand.

"My name's Dianne Johnson."

Her grip was firm, even vigorous. By contrast, the man lightly held my fingers when I shook hands with him. He said his name was Ashley May. I could easily have imagined he was a young Church of England vicar who'd gone on a camping holiday only to find that the girl or the weather, or both, were more than could cope with.

"Pretty lousy weather for camping," I said, pouring the wine. "This is the driest day we've had in a week."

"That's Wales in April." The girl made polite conversation. "We thought it might be warmer."

"I came here for the light," Ashley said in a small voice. "Here in April you get good light."

"Good light?"

The girl explained quickly. "Ashley's a landscape painter. He's been commissioned by a gallery in Bangor to paint three land-scapes. They'll print a limited edition."

"To sell to tourists." Ashley shook his head and drained the glass of wine in one. "It would have paid the rent, too."

Would have paid the rent? He sounded as if some catastrophe had struck.

"Here, Ashley," I said, "let me fill your glass. Top up, Dianne?"

"Please . . . lovely wine."

They drank as if they needed it. Both were trembling as they lifted the glasses to their lips.

They've just had one hell of a shock, I realised, surprised at my sudden insight. Yes. They've come through something terrible.

Now they were trying to pretend they were tired campers; and forcing themselves to make polite conversation with me; but it looked as if at any moment the self-control would break and they would run screaming down the hillside all the way to Criccieth.

I served them huge platefuls of lamb and vegetables. They ate every scrap. I offered seconds; they hungrily accepted.

When they had finished, Dianne looked at Ashley in a way that asked a question. He nodded. Then Dianne looked back at me.

"I don't like to ask this. You've been so generous. But would you mind driving us to the nearest town?"

"Normally, I'd be delighted to oblige. But my car's at the garage."

"Then may we telephone for a taxi?"

"I'm terribly sorry. I'm still waiting to be connected. I've only just moved in."

"Is it far to town? Could we walk there before it gets dark?"

"I'm sorry to have to keep being so negative. But there's not a chance I'm afraid. It would be a good two hour walk."

Ashley glanced out of the window. He looked frightened.

"God . . . it's nearly dark now. *Dianne?*"

"Don't worry, Ashley. You won't be like him. There's no sign of anything?"

"No. But I can feel it."

"Ah, sorry to intrude," I asked awkwardly. "But are you in any kind of trouble?"

Dianne looked at me sharply. "Trouble? We're not on the run from the police or anything like that."

"Sorry. I didn't mean to imply that. It's just both of you seem . . . un-nerved."

"We're fine," said the girl firmly.

Ashley shot her a startled look as if she'd just told the lie of the century.

"We lost our tents." Dianne attempted to sound matter-of-fact, as if they faced a minor glitch in their plans. "You wouldn't allow us to sleep here tonight?"

"We're so tired," Ashley said. "The tents went yesterday evening."

"Went?"

"Stolen." Dianne shrugged. "We'd gone for a walk. They had been taken by the time we got back."

Come on, Stephen, I told myself, you can't turn them out a day like this. Well . . . evening would be a better description now. It was falling dark early as rain clouds avalanched over the Welsh hill-tops. Already lights from cottages on distant hillsides twinkled like stars.

I smiled. "No problem. I've got a single bed in the spare bedroom. Someone will have to make do with the sofa I'm afraid."

"That's fine." Ashley yawned. "I could sleep like a baby on that stone floor."

"I'll just switch on the immersion heater," I told them. "Then you can have hot baths."

"A hot bath." Dianne looked at Ashley with a delight that was near child-like. "Would you be able to manage a bath?"

"I think so." Again he spoke in a voice that was as watery as it was hesitant.

I walked through into the kitchen and switched on the immersion heater. They were a peculiar couple. I shook my head. It takes all sorts, I suppose.

I plugged in the cappuccino coffee maker that the office bought me for a leaving present (they'd also surprised me with a box of chocolates, an REM CD and a video entitled *Speak Welsh The Easy Way* – ha, ha, thanks lads and lasses of Messrs. Dyson & Clarke, solicitors of Manchester). My finger hovered over the mains switch.

Best not risk it if the electric immersion heater's on, I told myself. The main's fuses had repeatedly blown when the electric oven had been used. The cottage's dicky old wiring just couldn't cope with too much juice running through it.

I filled the kettle and put it on the gas hob to boil.

On my memo sheet, magnetted to the refrigerator door, I jotted down: *Call out electrician.* Then I scratched out: *Thursday – W Motors to collect car for MOT.*

It was a few seconds before I realised that Ashley and Dianne were whispering to each other. I think it must have been the tone and way they were whispering that caught my attention. They whispered the words urgently to each other as if they'd given a sixty-second deadline to solve a problem. Ashley's voice had a tremoring quality to it. The man was scared out of his wits.

I spooned coffee into the cups, poured milk into the jug. Their problem was no business of mine. I tried not to hear individual words – believe me, I'm no eavesdropper – but some part of my mind picked up that these people were discussing a subject of vital importance.

"Leaves, Dianne . . . there were so many leaves."

"Don't think about it, Ashley."

"Don't think about it? *How can I stop?*"

"What about Michael?"

"What can we do to help him now?"

"Maybe find him again?"

"How? There's thousands up there."

"He was . . . bringing in . . . too dark. Far too dark. I think . . ."

The sound of the kettle coming to boil was enough to drown

out most of their whispering. What I had heard made little sense to me anyway. As the kettle began to whistle I turned off the gas.

I could hear the whispering again: "It started down there. He could feel it start down there I tell you."

"Ashley. We'll get you to a doctor."

"A doctor will believe me?"

"They'll believe all right when they see it with their own eyes."

"I'm frightened Dianne. What if it hurts?"

"Don't worry. I'll see you get help."

I poured the hot water into the cups, put them onto a tray with the milk and a plateful of biscuits and carried them through. I noticed they'd switched on the lights – *all* the lights! – even though it was only just dusk.

Immediately they were silent. Dianne forced herself to smile. "We were just saying . . . lovely cottage."

"Thanks. I've only just moved in so even I'm not sure which room is which."

Dianne gave a polite laugh. Ashley looked preoccupied with his own worries.

Whatever those were.

"Would you like some apple tart?"

"*No!*"

Ashley flushed and looked confused as if he'd not realised he'd shouted the *No!* in such a panic stricken way.

He swallowed. "Eh . . . no . . . thank you. No apple tart."

Then the man visibly shivered one of those someone-just-walked-over-my-grave-shivers. I realised Ashley was hiding a terrible secret. Curiouser and curiouser.

"Eh, not for me either, Stephen. I'll take a biscuit, thank you." Dianne nibbled a digestive. All the time she shot Ashley little anxious glances like a mother worrying over a feverish baby.

Ashley sat quietly. He sipped his coffee; stared at the table lamp, his eyes slipping into a far away gaze as he turned some problem over in his mind.

Dianne forced herself to make small talk. She liked the cottage, she told me. How old was it? Did I like Wales? Did I work locally? You've just retired from working a solicitor's office? You're too young to retire. You can't be more than thirty-five. Oh, a joke. So you're taking a sabbatical? Self-employed? As a proof-reader for publishers of law books . . . and so on for the next hour.

She seemed livelier for eating the meal – the wine and coffee probably helped, too. I found myself enjoying her company. After losing Anne I promised myself a moratorium on women for a while. But I had begun to wonder lately if I would end up being lonely up here in the cottage – after all, it was slap bang deep in the heart of nowhere.

I finished eating the biscuit then said, "The water should be hot enough now. I've left out clean towels."

"You first, Ashley," she said.

Meekly, he obeyed.

After he'd gone upstairs, I asked Dianne if she'd like a gin and tonic. She accepted gratefully. Her face had flushed now, and the smile seemed more genuine. I'd just unscrewed the top from the Gordon's and began to pour when, *bang!* the fuse blew again.

Instantly the cottage lights went out.

The scream that followed turned my blood to ice. The shock caused me to hold my breath, dimly I realised I was pouring all over the table top. But that scream. It had been driven out of the man's mouth by sheer terror.

I slotted the ceramic fuse holder back into the fuse box.

Click!

The lights came on killing the darkness. The fridge shuddered into life.

I found my hands were still clammy with sweat. The scream had disturbed me more than I could adequately describe. If a man realised he was about to have his throat cut, he'd probably scream in the same way – an outpouring of shock, despair and absolute horror. Ashley must have a clinical phobia of the dark.

I returned to the living room. All the lights had been switched on again as if to compensate for the three minutes or so of darkness earlier.

"Is he all right?"

Dianne looked up at me, her face pale. "Fine. You'll have the bath now, Ashley?"

He looked up at her his eyes wide. "When the light went out . . . they moved. *They moved.*"

She shot me a look as if to say, "Please don't listen to what he's saying. It means nothing."

"In the dark," Ashley murmured as if he'd finally understood some terrible truth. "*In the dark*, Michael had said. In the dark."

I stood there, cold shivers running from head to foot. There was such a charge in that room. A charge of cold, blue fear.

I was in bed by eleven on that April night. The wind blew down along the valley. It moaned round the chimney pots drawing strange musical notes that sounded like a surreal composition for pan pipes – a song for souls lost in darkness and achingly alone. The wind carried a flurry of hail to rattle against the windows. In the next room slept Dianne Johnson. Ashley May had the sofa downstairs. As I came back from the bathroom I'd peeped over the bannister down into the living room. All I could see of him beneath the blanket was an expanse of glistening forehead. He was sleeping with the table lamp on.

It must be terrible to be afraid of the dark.

Shaking my head I returned to bed, then switched out the light. Burning out of the darkness were the red numerals on the clock radio. They read 11:04.

Disaster struck. I sat up blinking in the darkness; my heart pounded. I didn't know what had woken me. I didn't know what had happened.

But something had. I sensed it: an oppressive sense of dread seemed to push down at me from the darkness. I looked to the clock radio for the time. I could see nothing.

There was only the dark.

Then I sensed movement at the foot of the bed.

Hell, someone was in here with me. A figure moved through that all encompassing darkness.

Crash.

That was the chest of drawers at the foot of my bed being struck.

A weight thumped across my legs.

I thought: *You're being attacked! Fight back!*

I swung my fist.

Nothing. I'd swiped at fresh air. But still that weight stopped me from moving my legs.

Next I grabbed. A head. My fingers closed round long hair.

"Please!"

"Dianne?"

"Please help me."

"What's wrong?"

"It's Ashley . . . The lights went out."

I looked back at the clock radio. Damn, damn, Stephen. You forgot to switch the immersion heater off; now it's only gone and blown the fuse again.

"It's okay," I said. "I've got a torch . . . there . . ."

Dianne's face suddenly appeared in the blaze of torchlight. Her hair was wild; deep dread lanced through her brown eyes. "The lights went out. Now I can't find Ashley."

"You can't find him?"

"He's gone. Like Michael."

"Michael? Who's Michael?"

"He was on the camping trip with us. He went first, but . . . look, please. Can we just try and find Ashley? I'll tell you everything when we find him."

My head was spinning. I remembered Ashley's terrified scream when the light went out earlier in the evening. He had a phobia about the darkness. At least that's what I surmised. Had that phobia driven him to run wildly from the cottage?

If he had, I might not be able to find him. I still didn't know the area. Beyond the cottage garden and the orchard there were woods and fields running for miles in the direction of the hills of the Lleyn Peninsula. You could hide entire armies out there.

"Dianne. You looked in all the rooms?"

"I tried. I found a box of matches. As far as I could see he's not in the cottage."

"Damn."

"God, I'm sorry . . . I'm sorry."

"Don't worry. We'll find him. Take this torch; I've a spare in the kitchen."

First I replaced the blown fuse with the standby ceramic fuse holder. The lights came on. The fridge gave that wobbly shudder as the compressor fired up again.

I pulled on my boots, and slipped a wax jacket over my pyjamas. Dianne had already dressed. She followed me outside and we walked across the lawn calling his name.

"Ashley? *Ashley?*"

The torch lights splashed across grass being blasted into flurries of ripples by the wind. The discordant pan pipe boomed as the wind caught the chimneys – that serenade for lost souls was as dismal as ever.

"*Ashley?*"

We followed the garden wall until we reached a gate.

"Where does this lead?" called Dianne above the wind.

"The orchard," I said, following her as she hurried through the gate.

The wind whistled through the branches of the apple trees. I watched as Dianne walked slowly along the lines of fruit carefully shining the torch into the whipping mass of branches if she expected to find her friend clinging to them monkey-like – his face twisted into a mask of sheer terror.

After an hour searching the wood and surrounding fields we returned to the garden. Again Dianne shone the light into the fruit trees. I followed suit. Half expecting to see Ashley's frightened face peering out from the mass of branches.

Suddenly she asked, "How many trees are there?"

It seemed a bizarrely inappropriate question. "I don't know," I said. "Actually, it's the first time I've been in – "

She suddenly turned and walked back to the cottage.

Once inside she quickly stripped off her jacket. "Stephen. I want to tell you something." She spoke briskly. "It's too late for Ashley. We won't find him."

"This fear of the dark. Has it happened before?"

"It's nothing to do with being afraid of the dark. Sit down please." She sat down and patted the sofa cushion beside her.

I sat down, puzzled. Earlier she seemed so concerned for her friend: now she seemed to almost dismiss him from her thoughts.

I said, "I think it's best if I walk down to the farm and phone for help."

"No."

"We should telephone the police. Ashley might be hurt."

"No. Please just listen to what I have to say first. It's too late for Ashley. It might also be too late for me."

"For you? Look, just give me half an hour. I can run down to the farm at – "

"Please, Stephen." She squeezed my hand. "I want to – no – I *need* to tell you what happened to us."

The pan pipe notes boomed discordantly down the chimney –

the mournful song for lost souls becoming that bit more desperate.

"I was camping with Ashley and our friend Michael. We'd all been to college together. It was still a tradition we'd go on holiday as a threesome. This year Ashley had been given the commission to paint the landscapes. So we decided to go camping in North Wales." She gave a little smile. "I imagine you noticed we weren't very well equipped – or experienced.

"Anyway," she continued. "There we were, camping miles from anywhere. Ashley painted. Michael and I explored the valley. The weather was awful. Every morning you'd see the clouds come racing across the sky. We had hail, rain, even snow. The wind blew out the stove all the time." She sighed. "On the Monday afternoon the three of us went for a walk. And there, deep in a wood, Michael found an apple tree growing amongst the oaks. He was really delighted with the find. He picked one of the apples and – "

"Just a minute," I said puzzled. "This is April. You wouldn't find fruit on an apple tree at this time of year."

"This had. Even though it hadn't any leaves yet. The apples were red – as red as strawberries. Michael cut slices with his penknife and we all ate a piece." She frowned as she remembered. "They were very sweet, but they had a sort of perfume flavour to them; you know, like the taste of Earl Grey tea. It was only as I was eating that I noticed the apple didn't have a core with pips. It was simply apple flesh all the way through. Then, do you know what I found?"

I shook my head. I wasn't going like the outcome of what she was telling me.

She tilted her head to one side, her eyes far away. "I found the seeds. They were just under the skin of the apple. And they were white and soft like tomato seeds."

"Just under the skin? Then it can't have been an apple."

She shrugged, her eyes faraway. "It looked like an apple."

"These apples. They had something to do with what happened to Michael and Ashley?"

"Yes." She pushed her long hair back from her face. "We have swallowed the seeds." Suddenly she lifted her sweatshirt to show me her exposed midriff. "You can feel them under my skin."

"*Your skin? Feel what under your skin?*" It was if a series of electric shocks had just tingled across my own skin. "Dianne, what can you feel?"

"Touch." She grasped my hand and pressed my fingers against her stomach. "Hot isn't it? Michael and Ashley started like that and . . ." She shrugged. "And now you can feel them growing under my skin."

I looked at her, my eyes wide.

"You can feel the roots," she said.

I could feel nothing but skin and firm stomach muscle beneath.

"Dianne," I began as calmly as I could. "Don't you think – "

"And there." She pointed to a dark growth on her side, just above the hip. "That's where one of the buds is already forcing its way through. It doesn't hurt. But I'm conscious of them pressing out through my flesh. It makes it very sensitive. All the time I'm aware of my clothes against my skin. To slow down the growth I should take off my clothes and sit beneath bright lights. That seems the only way to retard it. In darkness they grow at an explosive rate. That's why Ashley was so afraid of the dark. And that's why Ashley disappeared when the lights failed. He would have felt the branches bursting through his skin; the pricking of the roots as they wormed out through the soles of his feet. He would have felt an overwhelming compulsion to run from the house –"

"Dianne –"

"If you count the trees in the orchard in the morning, you'll find there will be one more than yesterday.

"Dianne. I think I really do need to make a phone call. Will you be all right here by yourself?"

She's mentally ill.

The revelation had perhaps been too long coming. But I realised the truth now. She and Ashley had absconded from a hospital somewhere. No, probably it wasn't even that dramatic. This so-called Care in the Community policy for people suffering mental illness put the onus of care on the patient themselves. Perhaps for some reason, she and Ashley had stopped taking their medication.

"Stephen, why don't you believe me? Look at my stomach. You can see the bud there, breaking through the skin."

"It's not a bud. It's a mole; just a mole, Dianne. Now –"

"Touch it."

"No."

"You're afraid aren't you, Stephen?"

"No."

"Press your finger against it."

"Dianne –"

"Press hard, Stephen."

"Dianne, please –"

"Press. You can hear the bud casing crack."

"It's a mole."

"Just a mole?"

"Yes."

"Here, watch closely, Stephen."

"It's a mole."

"Watch as I scratch the top off it."

"Dianne, don't –"

"When I scratch the top off you'll see the green leaf all curled up tight as a parcel inside."

"Dianne, stop it!" I gripped her fists in my hands, held them hard. "Don't hurt yourself – *please*."

"Okay, Stephen." She looked up at me, meek as a scolded child. "I'm sorry, but I just wanted so much that you believe me."

I looked into her brown eyes. They seemed so calm now. As if she'd accepted a terrible calamity would soon overtake her.

"Look," I said gently. "Will you be all right here by yourself?"

"You're going to phone the police, aren't you?"

"Yes . . . not because I think you're mad. But we need to find Ashley. He'll die of exposure out there on a night like this."

She sighed sadly. "I don't think he'll feel the cold now."

"Stay in here with the door locked and the lights on. I looked at the wall clock. It's three o' clock now. I can be back by four."

"Okay." She spoke in a small voice. "Don't worry about me, I'll be all right."

"Good girl."

"Stephen?"

"Yes?"

She looked up into my eyes. Lightly she rubbed her bare stomach with one hand. "Will you do something for me?"

"Whatever I can, yes."

"I'm frightened, so please . . . well . . . will you kiss me?"

*   *   *

I ran along the track. The torchlight flashed against the tractors ruts, then against the steep banking at either side, illuminating bushes and grass. The wind blew hard, sending out brambles to whip horizontally across the track. Sometimes they lashed against my wax jacket with a crack. By this time I was panting hard; the thump of my boots hitting the ground transmitted juddering shocks up into my neck.

Briefly I stopped to zip up the jacket. The gales repeatedly caught it, causing it to balloon around my body.

Then I ran on. Above me the trees creaked and groaned in the wind. The skin on my back, rubbed by the heavy winter jacket, began to chafe. I wore nothing but pyjamas beneath it.

What a night, I thought in astonishment. Just think of the letter you can write to big Jim back at the office. Maybe in a few days I'd look back on all this in amusement. But I couldn't now. Although those two strangers had only walked into my life just hours ago, I was worried about them.

I hadn't wanted to leave the girl alone in the cottage. But what options had I got? If I had waited until morning Ashley would surely have died of hypothermia out here in this gale. But would Dianne be all right? Perhaps I should have hidden the knives? I would have had to hide the screwdrivers and aspirin, too. But I didn't have time to do everything. Maybe the girl was only delusional, not suicidal.

Her manner had changed, too. She seemed somehow elated after I left her.

Perhaps that was the kiss.

She'd asked me to kiss her. Poor kid, at the moment that was all I could give her. Anyway I'd left her listening to the CD player; she seemed calm enough.

Ahead I saw the outline of the farmhouse through the darkness. The early-to-rise farmer was already up. I could see him moving about in the kitchen. At least I wouldn't have to stand hammering at the door. I crossed the yard and knocked.

I arranged to meet the police back at my cottage. I ran back up the lane home. The sweat streamed down my chest. All I wanted was to get out of the sweat soaked pyjamas and ease my body into a steaming hot bath.

I took the short cut over the wall, ran through the orchard; the

branches of the trees rattled in the wind; then I pushed the gate
into the cottage garden.

I stopped dead.

Damn.

I don't believe it, I thought, heart sinking; I don't damn well
believe it. *It's only gone and done it again!*

The cottage lights were out. The fuse had blown.

I ran across the lawn. The torch light illuminated the grass
being ripped this way and that by the gale blasting down the
valley. The cottage door slammed open-shut-open-shut.

I ran inside. Then stood there, hauling in great lungfuls of cold
air. Just a second of shining the torch around the room told me it
was deserted. And within a few moments I'd checked every other
room in the cottage. All deserted.

I went back downstairs. I played the torch over the furniture,
the table with the bottle of gin and two empty glasses. The wind
blew the branches of a tree to tap against the room window pane.
In here, the only thing to be disturbed was a single chair, tipped
onto its back as if someone had pushed by it in a frantic rush to
escape the house.

She'd gone.

The emotion took me by surprise, but I felt a sudden aching
loss. I'd really liked her. I remembered the way she'd asked me to
kiss her. Her brown eyes, gentle and trusting. Her hair, the way
the wind had mussed it into a light froth that poured down
around her shoulders.

She'd kissed me so passionately. Her hands had gripped my
head as she held my mouth to hers.

That kiss. Suddenly I shivered. Quickly I rubbed the back of my
hand across my mouth as if to clean dirt from my lips. But it was
too late.

Far, far too late.

I shivered again; points of ice crawled across my stomach.
When she kissed me it felt as if she'd transferred something from
her mouth to mine. I must have imagined it, surely.

But no. It had felt as small as a seed. When she stopped kissing
me and moved her head back I'd felt for it with my tongue. There
was nothing there. I couldn't have swallowed it, could I? That
small seed-like particle that I'd felt slide between my cheek and
gum.

The perspiration irritated my skin. I unzipped my wax jacket and rubbed my stomach. God, I needed a bath. A red hot bath.

The kiss began to trouble me. I shouldn't have let her kiss me. Suddenly I wished I could turn the clock back, then when she asked, I'd firmly say, "No, I won't kiss you." As simple as that.

But it's too late. Much too late.

My skin felt acutely sensitive. I rubbed my stomach and my chest. The wind blew the branches to tap against the glass again. Those damn branches . . . tapping, tapping, tapping.

I felt uneasy.

No, I didn't.

I felt frightened.

Because I knew no tree grew so close to the cottage that its branches could touch the glass.

Holding the torch in front of me, I walked outside. I swung the light to my left.

Tap, tap, tap . . .

There was the tree.

Its slender trunk, rooted deeply into the edge of the lawn; its branches swayed to and fro like the limbs of a graceful dancer.

And the branches kept tap, tap tapping at the glass.

As if it strived to attract my attention.

There had been no tree there yesterday. I was certain of that. Fear prickled through me. I looked back at the house. No, I wasn't going back there. I couldn't bear to hear those branches at the glass. Tap, tap tapping . . .

The wind blew; it caught the chimney pots and the pan pipe notes boomed loud and madly discordant.

With a shiver I zipped up my wax jacket. There was no alternative. I would –

No –

This couldn't be happening . . .

At that moment the torch died on me. The bulb went from glowing an incandescent white, to yellow, to orange . . .

– to red.

– to dull red

– then to nothing. I slapped the torch into the palm of my hand.

My skin itched. All I could hear was the damned wind, the mad pan pipe music, and the rattle of branches against the window pane.

The torch is dead, I told myself as calmly as I could, even though the shiver running through my body had become a deep tremble that would not stop; a tremble that intensified until my teeth clacked together like dry bones being shaken hard in a sack. I threw the torch savagely into the grass – the bloody thing had betrayed me.

"*It doesn't matter, Stephen,*" I panted. "*It doesn't matter. It's going to be light in an hour.*"

Better still, the police would be here soon. I'd wait for them in the lane.

I found my way to the wall in the darkness. Then by sense of touch I reached the gate to the orchard.

Cross the orchard, Stephen; then wait in the lane.

Soon you'll see the lights of the police car as it brings a couple of down-to-earth Welsh coppers up to the cottage.

The orchard seemed full of trees. I groped my way through. The branches snagged my jacket, pricked my face, caught my hair.

The wind whipped through the trees with a howl, like it was a wild animal, ferociously savaging the branches of a pear tree there, clawing at the grass here, before pawing hungrily at coat.

God, I wish I could see. The darkness was total.

I was growing tired now. I could hardly move. My skin itched. I thought of that kiss. Now I was convinced Dianne had transferred something into my mouth. I couldn't stop myself imagining this picture: *Dianne opening her mouth. It is packed with seeds. Like when you slice open a melon. Hundreds of seeds all neatly packed, all so tightly packed, there inside the fruit.*

Shut out the picture, Stephen. My head spun dizzily. Shut the damn thing out!

I thought: *The seed . . . I've swallowed it. I'm sure I've swallowed the damned seed.*

Must be nearly at the lane. The fruit trees tugged at me. They were everywhere, blocking my path, scratching my face, pulling my hair.

Then I was free of them. Along the lane I could see the lights of the police car coming up the track. I tried to run toward the wall that separated the orchard from the lane. I made it to within five paces.

Then I stopped.

I was too exhausted to move another step. The police car approached. I held up my hands to flag it down.

They drove past, not seeing me.

I tried to lower my arms. I couldn't. For some reason I'd frozen in that position. My face, too, had seized into some kind of frozen mask as I'd shouted. I couldn't move my feet. I couldn't move them at all.

I was rooted to the spot.

"Mum!"

"What's is it, what's wrong!"

"Mum, come and look at this?"

"Joel, I thought we were making a snowman up on the lawn."

"I wanted to look in the orchard."

"Keep your coat fastened up, it's cold. And be a good boy or we won't go to the café for lunch."

"But I wanted to show you this."

"Oh, go on then, Joel. What is it?"

"That apple tree near the wall. There's a coat stuck in the tree."

"Ugh, probably belonged to a tramp."

"It's a wax jacket like Dad's, and someone's pushed the branches through the sleeves like arms."

"Leave it, it's dirty. Now come back and finish the snowman with me."

"But Mum?"

"But Mum what?"

"There's still apples on the tree. Can I eat one?"

"Certainly not. They'll give you stomach ache. Now, come with me."

The two walked back hand in hand through the snow to where the snowman stood. Next to it, grew the slender tree at the edge of the lawn. The breeze blew. Gently, it tapped a branch against the window pane.

As if it were cold and lonely.

And it wanted to come inside.

PAT CADIGAN

This is Your Life (Repressed Memory Remix)

PAT CADIGAN'S MOST RECENT books are *The Making of Lost in Space*, her first non-fiction volume, and *Tea from an Empty Cup*, an urban murder mystery set in a multimedia future. Two of her previous novels, *Synners* and *Fools*, have won the Arthur C. Clarke Award. Her short fiction has been featured in many anthologies, including *Dark Terrors 3*, *The Ex Files*, *Disco 2000*, *New Worlds*, *Alien Sex* and *Dying For It*. Formerly a resident of Kansas, she now lives in North London with her husband, the Other Chris Fowler.

About the following story, she recalls: "I wrote this after reading *Victims of Memory* by Mark Pendergast, a compelling and thoroughly researched study of False Memory Syndrome. One unfortunate victim, accused by his adult children, dutifully turned himself in, confessed to atrocities he hadn't committed, and served time for them, figuring that if his children remembered it, it must have happened, even if he couldn't recall anything himself. Now that's scarier than just about anything else I've heard lately . . ."

B Y THE TIME SHE was on the flight back to Massachusetts, Renata had grown weary of condolences. You're forty years old, your father dies. If you haven't been close to him for most of your life, you're not going to suddenly discover a deep well of emotion connected to him.

Of course, she had to remind herself, it wasn't that way with a lot of people. A good many of her co-workers, for example, would not have had to fly to get home for a family funeral, and they'd have been pretty torn up about it. But that was how you felt when you lost someone who had been one of the mainstays of your life.

Her friend Vinnie had been nonplused to know that she didn't consider her father one of the mainstays of her own life. Brought up in a large extended Italian family, Vincenza Marie Fanucci was a curious mix of highly independent, uncompromising professional and Old World filial piety. Vinnie regarded her father as a big kid ensconced in the body of a flawed minor deity who permeated, even now, the lives of his five children with his paternal . . . oh, hell, Renata didn't even know what to call it. Paternal existence. Paternal paternity. Daddy-ish-ness. Staring down unseeing at the inflight magazine in her lap, Renata thought that she probably knew more of the substance of Vinnie's father than she ever had of her own.

It wasn't that her father hadn't loved her, or that he had rejected her. She could remember times when she was little that her father had taken her to the movies or to the circus, or even just out to the playground on Saturday. Just her alone – in those days, her brother Jules had been only a baby. Her father had dutifully pushed her on the swings, spun the go-round for her till she had gotten dizzy almost to the point of nausea, caught her at the bottom of the slide.

No, not just *dutifully*. That was unfair. He had been pleasant. She had even believed that he'd been having fun, but no child could believe that anyone wouldn't have fun in a playground. Any more than, she supposed, any child – any very young child – could believe that she wasn't the only thing of any real importance in her parents' world.

Eventually, you'd know better. By then, however, you had usually achieved adolescence and if you gave that sort of thing any thought at all, it was probably more with satisfaction than anything else, maybe a fleeting sense of relief as you left the house to go meet friends. As Renata had always understood it, this was called *flying the nest*. Except some people worked out some kind of compromise, where they left but acceded to a kind of place-holder that marked a bit of territory that they would always belong to, rather than vice versa.

My, but our thoughts are heavy today, for someone claiming not to be terribly affected by her father's death.

She turned a page and frowned down at a photo of an impossibly plush hotel in some ridiculously inaccessible vacation region. Perhaps that was because, instead of mourning her father, she was mourning the profound and lasting connection they had failed to achieve. As she had gotten older, he'd just had less and less time for her, or her brother Jules. She thought now that probably he'd barely had time for their mother. But that had just been the way things were back then. His draftsman's job consumed more of his time and attention. The company he'd worked for had been switching over to Computer Aided Design, trying to keep up with the rest of the corporate Joneses, and her father had had to re-train himself almost from scratch in a job that he had been proficient in – had *thought* he'd been proficient in – for almost twenty years. New developments had eaten up his time and hadn't left much in the way even of bare bones behind.

And hadn't it been that way for a lot of other families as well? Sure. *We can't all be jolly Italian dynasties, now, can we? No, we sure can't.*

What sadness there was for her in the occasion had much more to do with the absence of the man's effect on her rather than the absence of the man himself. Maybe that was sadder than his death, she thought, and actually felt her throat begin to tighten.

Now, now. Let's not go to pieces just because it's an occasion that usually calls for it, she thought, sneaking a look at her seat-mate on the right as she pretended that she wasn't dabbing tears from her eyes. No worries there; the woman had dozed off with her mouth open and her reading glasses a centimeter from the end of her prominent nose. She was a plump, middle-aged blonde made even plumper by masses of blonde hair extensions artfully braided into her natural hair. Naturally-*grown* hair, Renata amended to herself; the color was as acquired as the extra tresses. It wasn't a bad job. Renata wouldn't have known except that one tiny connection knot was peeking out at her near the woman's left temple. She smiled at it, absently patting the greying brown hair fluffing over the back of her own collar.

Tell you what, Blondella, Renata thought at her; *you don't notice my tears and I won't notice your hair-falsies. Is it a deal?*

The woman went on sleeping silently, her breath inaudible in spite of her open mouth. Too bad. A snore as an inadvertent reply would have made her laugh at least inwardly and dried up her tears. She should have known, Renata chided herself, looking down at the ridiculous vacation hotel ad again. Comic timing, like so many other things, was just never *there* in real life. At least, not in *her* real life.

Her surprise at finding her brother waiting to meet her at the airport was almost enough to be honest shock. He was standing at the top of the escalators that slid down to the baggage carousel area, his face sad, worried, and portentous, which was even more disconcerting. She had always described Jules to everyone as the sort of person the term *even-tempered* had been invented for. Unflappable Jules Adrian Prescott, who had raised his voice maybe three times a year, usually to say "Ow!" after stubbing his toe or something. There had been times she had felt like telling him they could trade birth order and he could be the older Prescott kid, as he had always been more mature than she. Sometimes, though, she wondered if he didn't frustrate the hell out of his wife, Lena.

The thought of Lena made her automatically look at Jules' left hand; his wedding ring was gone. Now she *was* shocked, almost enough to draw back as he leaned forward to kiss her cheek and say something, but he looked so fraught that she shut up instead and submitted. For all she knew, he had accidentally left his ring in the bathroom after showering. Why add a stupid, intrusive, and erroneous question to a time like this?

A time like *what*, though? Jules hadn't been terribly close to their father, either.

"How are you feeling?" he asked her as he took her carry-on bag and steered her onto the escalator.

"Okay, I guess, Julio," she said, using the old childhood nickname, in which the j was pronounced improperly as j and not h. "But you don't look too good –"

"Yeah, well, a time like this," he said almost offhandedly, and she felt a *frisson* as he unknowingly echoed her thoughts. "It's all so –" he shook his head and a sudden stray breeze rifled his thick brown hair like invisible fingers searching for something concealed there.

She looked up at him, puzzled. *It's all so what, Julio?* she wanted to say, but the pain in his expression stopped her. Maybe if the non-relationship with their father saddened her, she thought suddenly, it was even more so for Jules. Maybe he'd been reflecting on everything he hadn't had as his father's son, on memories that should have been there to comfort and reassure but were not, never could have been, never would be. Did Lena understand, she wondered, anxious for him now.

They collected her one small bag from the carousel and then followed a silly, over-complicated route made even more convoluted by detours around awkwardly-placed areas of renovation hidden behind impassive wooden walls. Signs warned of dangers hidden behind their featureless façades. Apparently there were things back there that could maim you, cripple you, kill you without warning. But nothing reached out to harm them, or so much as scare them as they made their way to Jules' car in the parking garage. The walk took a good twenty minutes and during that time, Jules never did manage to complete the sentence that had ended with *everything being so* and she thought again that he was probably suffering from the realization that it was all just *So what?*

Her first thought was that her mother needed heart pills. Everything about her was *grey,* in a way that went beyond old age. Her skin looked as if it had been dusted with ashes only a few shades lighter than her hair, her lips might have moved a doctor to pronounce her cyanotic, and even the pupils of her eyes seemed to have lost all pigmentation. She sat, or rather sagged on a chair at the dining room table, while Renata's Aunt Daisy stood over her like a sentinel or a household servant waiting for instruction, occasionally squeezing one of her mother's plump, rounded shoulders.

Daisy's name was one of those ridiculous mistakes people sometimes made in christening their children. For Renata, the name *Daisy* had always suggested capriciousness and whimsy to the point of complete foolishness. But Daisy was serious, often humorless, and almost never emotional in any way. The only remotely daisy-ish thing about her was her yellow hair which was actually natural and looked dyed. It gave Renata another pause. Did anyone in her family ever get *anything* right? she wondered.

Jules had allowed her to carry in her own suitcase. Now he had vanished into another part of the house or into thin air, Renata wasn't sure which. Daisy's twin daughters were both there, one with her husband, the other with her female partner. The four of them were huddled near the antique sideboard where the good china and crystal sat safely in the dark of the cabinets most of the year, emerging only for Christmas season dinners. On the mirror-shiny surface, kept that way by her mother's monthly polishings, a collection of photos of various family members gazed out over the room as if the frames were actually funny little windows in so many sizes and shapes that each subject had just happened to wander up to, and were now staring through with vague unease at all that went on.

Renata's own vague unease snapped into precise clarity. There were no pictures on the sideboard now. Someone had removed them, every single one, and she had never known that to happen, outside of her mother's regularly-scheduled cleaning sessions. She put her bag down where she stood and looked around, unease beginning to mutate into suspicion.

On the other side of the room, Mrs. Anderson from next door was standing by a tall bookcase with the O'Briens from across the street. The three of them looked exhausted, as if something–her father's death, or something unrelated except for timing?–had been draining them of every bit of energy and endurance. It was how another of her co-workers, a pretty young woman in accounting services, had looked after seeing her sister through a long and terrible death from AIDS.

But if Mrs. Anderson and the O'Briens had been through something similar, it couldn't have been with *her* father, Renata thought. Her father's final heart trouble had dragged on a bit, but it had not been that kind of ordeal. Even if it had been, she couldn't imagine that these people would have been involved to such an extent.

The O'Briens' son Dan was sitting on a stool by the television, his elbows on his knees and his big hands folded under his chin. Dan was her age and looked about the same as he had the last time she had seen him several years before, except there was a little less of his greying, light brown hair and a little more round softness in his face. He was watching her with an intensity that almost frightened her, that *would* frighten her if he kept it up.

If he does *keep it up,* she decided, *I'll go over there and give him one upside the head, as the kids say. Knock that stupid look right off his face.*

Her Aunt Daisy was watching her with almost the same expression, she realized suddenly. They *all* were. They were *watching* her, as if they expected her to do something strange and dangerous. A chill spread out over her scalp and down her neck, and she knew that if her hair could actually have stood on end, it would have.

She thought absurdly of the woman on the plane. *Too bad I don't have* that *hair to stand on end – that would* really *give them something to stare at.* And now she was staring right back at all of them, each and every one in turn, and the fact that they weren't the least bit put off by this, that not a one of them felt compelled to look away or even blink was the worst of all.

"What?" she said finally, trying to force down the panic that was lifting so rapidly inside of her that she had to gasp for breath. "What? *What is it?* What the hell are you all looking at me like this for?"

There was a moment of utter silence, not long, but if it had stretched out any longer, she would have screamed into it. Abruptly, Dan O'Brien got up from the stool over by the television and gestured at it. "Renata, there's something you have to see before the funeral."

She gave her head a quick, minute shake. "What – an old re-run of *Masterpiece Theatre?*"

"Please," he said, and his voice was as frightening as everything else, because it was so damned *calm.* "This hasn't been easy on your mother or Jules, it isn't easy for any of us, and it won't be easy for you. But you have to see this. You do. And after you see it, you'll understand. Everything will be clear."

Renata looked to her mother for some sign but her mother had buried her face in Daisy's waist, while Daisy held her, stroking her hair and glaring at Renata as if she were to blame. "Where's Jules?" she asked Dan, glancing at her twin cousins and their respective partners.

"Jules has seen it," Dan said, suddenly sounding prim.

She wanted to make a smart remark about how they all had cable where she lived, so she had probably seen it herself, but something in her gave out and she sat down on the stool instead. *Just get it over with,* she told herself firmly. *If it's something utterly horrid, just leave. Don't even stay for the funeral.*

Dan put on the TV and then reached down to the VCR on the shelf underneath. Renata had a glimpse of a greasy man standing in front of a chat-show panel of even greasier people and then her father was looking earnestly out at her from the television screen. She jumped, putting one hand to her chest. God, but it looked and sounded so *much* like him, it was positively scary.

Then she suppressed a groan. It was one of these ghoulish videotaped will things that people knew would be played back after their deaths. So *ghoulish*. She felt her stomach turn over. Didn't anyone ever consider what it would be like for the survivors to watch something like this? No wonder Jules was hiding out.

"My darling Renata," her father said, folding his hands and leaning forward, as if he really were seeing her in the lens of the camera focused on him. He had been videotaped sitting at the head of the dining room table. How much she and her father had resembled each other, she thought, much more than her father and Jules, or even herself and Jules. There was no missing the similarity of the shape of their faces and eyes, and even their voices shared a certain timbre. "My darling daughter Renata, this is the hardest thing I have ever had to do. Harder, in some ways, than dying, really. I know I *am* dying. I can feel my heart becoming weaker every day. If my hearing were good enough, I would probably hear the blood in my veins and arteries slowing down, swashing and gurgling, getting ready to stop."

Renata took a deep, careful breath to control her nausea. Maybe her father *did* know what sort of effect this would have and he was doing it on purpose, some kind of weird revenge of an angry, dying man on his still-living relatives.

"So I must – *must* – make a clean breast of things. I cannot die carrying the guilt and the shame of what's happened between us any longer."

Her nausea melted into bewilderment. "The guilt and shame of what had happened between them?" Being a distant, mostly absent father figure was a source of *guilt* and *shame?* The poor man, she thought in a sudden rush of pity. Then her bewilderment returned, along with a dash of irritation. If it had bothered him *that* much, he could have apologized, in person, while he'd still been alive.

"No parent should ever put a child through the terrible things I put you through," he continued. "When I think of the hell you endured, I want to –"

"Stop it," Renata snapped suddenly and jumped up from the stool. "Stop it *right now.*"

Dan O'Brien looked startled but obediently pointed a slender remote control at the VCR. Her father's face froze in mid-word. Everyone in the room was looking at her as if she were displaying the worst manners possible, except for her mother who was slumped against Daisy and sobbing softly into a wad of tissues.

"I refuse to listen to another moment of this travesty," Renata said, angrily. "Obviously Dad went a little wonky before he died. I'm awfully sorry about that, it's a terrible thing to happen. But now he's gone. His troubles are over, and there's no good reason to torture ourselves with this kind of thing."

There was no answer except the sound of her mother's sobbing.

"Where's Jules?" Renata said, disgusted. "I want my suitcase. I'm going. If Jules won't drive me back to the airport, I'll take a cab or I'll even walk if I have to, but I'm not going to stay here –"

"Please," Dan said and she turned to him in surprise. "You don't know how important this is."

"You're probably right about that. You're not family to me, however – "

"Well, no, I'm not. Though in some ways, I may be even closer." Dan's face was frighteningly sincere as well as serious. "I'm your father's therapist. I treated him for two years before he died."

Renata turned to her mother for confirmation, but her mother wouldn't look at her. Her gaze went to the O'Briens to see what their reaction was. They had none, or none that she could see, except for the same strange quiet that everyone except her mother was hell-bent on maintaining. She turned back to Dan. "I didn't know you were a doctor. I thought you went to business school."

"I did, but I switched direction a little while ago. Now I'm a therapist. Not a doctor in the sense that I could prescribe medications, but most of that stuff is poison anyway." Renata was sure that Dan's smile was meant to look benevolent but to her it seemed more vacant than anything. "I do a lot of work with hypnosis."

"Fine," Renata said. "But don't expect me to make an appointment just because my father did. I'm a lousy subject for hypnosis, I just don't have the attention span." She raised her voice. "Jules! Jules, *dammit*, where are you, I want to –"

Dan caught her arm as she was about to walk out of the room. "Renata, you're making a hard situation all but impossible. Sit down and watch the tape, and then you'll understand everything."

Her gaze went from his face to his hand, still gripping her upper arm just a little too tightly and back again several times. Astoundingly, he failed to get the message. "Let *go* of my fucking *arm*," she said finally. He glanced over at his parents, who turned as one to Mrs. Anderson. Mrs. Anderson's gaze went to the twins, who passed the look to their respective partners before raising their eyebrows at their mother.

They were all crazy, Renata realized suddenly. She didn't know what brand of psychosis they were sharing, what it involved or whether it was dangerous, but they were nuts and she wasn't and by god, she was getting out of there. She bolted for the door, deciding she could live with the loss of her overnight bag and collided with someone else, someone too strong for her to twist away from, who struggled her back from the doorway, bruising her forearms with a hard grip and forced her down onto the couch in front of the television set.

"Jules! What –"

He grabbed the stool she had been sitting on and planted it just to her left, sat down on it and seized her arms again. *"Shut up!"* he bellowed into her face, so close that she could feel how hot his breath was. It was that sensation more than anything that shocked her. She could not remember ever being that physically close to her brother.

"Now, *listen*," he growled at her and she was horrified to see tears welling in his eyes. "*Listen* and *watch*. The suffering is – " He stopped, breathing hard and deep through his nose, glaring at her.

And again he left the sentence unfinished. *At a time like this. Everything is so. The suffering.*

Then her father was speaking to her from the television again, the live man performing the task that the dead man had delegated.

". . . to punish myself in more hideous ways than the state would, I think. I *had* thought of turning myself in, as a matter of fact, but your mother talked me out of it. She said that a man in my health, so many years later – well, the only thing that would really make a difference would be if we could – if *I* could, actually – try to make it up to you in some way. To get you the help that you're going to need, for the rest of your life."

Renata made a disgusted noise. "Oh, Christ, what is it? Was there a trust fund and he embezzled – "

"Shut up," her brother warned her quietly.

"– can never give you back those years of your childhood that I stole." Her father's voice was beginning to sound whiny. "All I can do is tell you I was wrong, beg for your forgiveness from here, beyond the grave, and assure you that you will get only the very best counselors, doctors, hospitalization when you need it – "

"*Hospitalization?*" Warning bells went off in her head to the point where she could not have told the difference if she had been hearing them outside. Abruptly she remembered a basic self-defense move Vinnie had taught her, a way to twist your wrist to get out of a man's grip so that no matter how big and strong he was, he would have to let you go. *My brothers taught me this one*, Vinnie had said, *they told me that if any guy was gonna beat me up, it would be them, not some stranger. Of course, they never did beat me up, not that I recall, anyway –*

She pushed Jules away and stood up. To her surprise, Jules launched himself at her and pinned her down on the couch with his body. Renata cried out, more in anger than anything else. The worst part about it was that no one else in the room had moved, *no one*, not to help her, not to help Jules, not to do *anything*, and all the while her father's voice went on and on and on, talking and talking and talking. *Dead Man Talking*, she thought, and bit her lip to keep from laughing hysterically.

"... to treat my beloved daughter in such a hideous fashion. I don't know what drove me to it, to act out my vile needs on your innocence, to soil and betray your trust in me as your father, your protector ..."

"What?" Renata said, trying to push Jules off her. "What? Stop that! Turn that fucking TV *off!*"

But no one moved, and her father's voice whined on. "... and you, so pure, so loving, so unwilling to believe that life would have such ugliness in it that you completely repressed all memory of what I had done to you. It was as if your sweet little mind said, 'All right, then, if he won't be a father to me out here, then I will create the loving father that he isn't in my mind.' "

"*What?*" She arched her back, trying to buck her brother off but he seemed to get heavier and heavier.

" ' – and if I can't get anyone to protect me or help me out here, then I will create the support group that I need in my mind – ' "

Support group? Had her father just said *support group?* Renata was beyond disbelief. This was some kind of horrible joke, it had to be. Some kind of absurd practical joke put on by Jules and her mother. They had been driven mad with grief, the –

"– hypnotic regression to recover my memories, we've determined that I've observed you displaying at least thirteen different personalities, just to help you cope with the terrible things I've done to you – "

"*What?*" Renata looked from her father's earnest image on the TV, babbling away about *abuse* and *multiples* and *recover memories* to Jules' tormented, painful face above her. "Julio, what in God's name is he talking about?"

He turned to look at Dan. "This must be the one Dad referred to as 'Cleo.' She always denied all knowledge of anything that was going on."

"*Who's* Cleo?" Renata demanded. "What are *you* talking about now?"

"Cleo," Jules said to her. "Short for Cleopatra. Queen of Denial?" Pause. "You get it?"

"No, wait a minute. And get *off* me, goddammit–" Renata arched her back again, trying to throw him off.

"Careful!" Dan called. "Maybe that isn't Cleo, it could be Lilith just *pretending* to be Cleo so she can molest you – "

Jules made a disgusted noise, started to get off her and then didn't, instead, planting his knee in the center of her stomach without letting go of her wrists. "What do we do?" he asked, frightened.

Dan was at his side in a moment. "Well, the first thing we do is, we keep our heads. Remember, I told you that doing an intervention can be an incredibly emotional experience. You can't start panicking as soon as things get hairy. It's going to get worse before it gets better, it's going to get a *lot* worse, and Renata needs all of us to be strong and calm for her – ".

"Hey, asshole," Renata said angrily, "I'm right here, not in the next room. Now get my crazy brother off me and stop talking about me in the third – "

"Should I call an ambulance?" asked one of the twins in a tight, anxious voice.

"Not yet," Dan said. "Some of these personalities can be incredibly strong, we don't want any innocent paramedics to get hurt. As soon as she's calmer, we'll call a private service and have them take her out to Wood Grove." He knelt down beside the couch and brushed Renata's hair out of her face. "I want to speak with Renata, please. Or The Boss. That's what your father always called her," he added to Jules. "The Boss was the one who always took charge when things got a little loose around the edges and threatened to fall apart." He turned back to her and spoke clearly into her face, over-enunciating as if she were stupid.

"I said, send out Renata *right now*. We want to talk to *Renata*."

"Dan," she said, trying to sound calm but hearing the shakiness in her voice. "Dan, stop a minute. What are you doing? At least, tell me what you think you're doing? We've known each other all our lives. We played together, went to the same school. Hell, you even took me to the Christmas dance one year when my boyfriend came down with the shingles." She swallowed hard. "Remember that?"

Dan's face took on an expression so sad that she wanted to cry for him. "You see, Jules? You see how insidious this thing is? She remembers going to a dance she never went to, because it's far better than remembering what *really* happened that night, that her father forced me to bring her to that motel where he was meeting with that group he called The Sex Club –"

"Dan, there are *pictures, photos* of us together at the dance –"

"Faked," Dan said, with authority. "All faked. So you'd go on believing that you'd had a happy childhood and a good life, and not the horror that you really had to live with." He bowed his head for a moment. "And so I could repress the memory of my part in what you suffered."

The rest of them had gathered around the couch now, even her mother, sniffling and dabbing at her eyes and clutching Mrs. Anderson for support. They all looked down at her as if she were some kind of strange, unidentifiable creature that had somehow landed, injuring and frightened, in the middle of an ordinary, suburban living room.

"This is *wrong*," Renata told them desperately. "This is *wrong*, this is *not* what happened. Can't you hear me, don't you understand me? *None of this is true.* It didn't happen. *It didn't happen!*"

One of her cousins reached down and touched her shoulder gently. "I know it's hard to believe. The human mind is so amazing, there are all sorts of things that it can do, including repressing memories that are too horrible for us to live with. But don't worry. Wood Grove is a good place. They've got a great staff there, including Dan – " she paused to smile over at him. "And it's completely covered by insurance. They helped me. They and Dan helped me."

"And me," said the other twin, and put her hand on Jules' shoulder. "And they've performed miracles with your brother. His personalities will never be integrated the way ours were, but he's learned how to manage them better than a traffic cop in New York rush hour."

Everyone gave a polite titter at her joke and Jules' expression was an impossible combination of pride and nausea.

Dan leaned forward and put his hands on both sides of her face, turning her head gently so he could stare into her eyes. "The important thing to do right now," he said, "is relax. You're among friends, you're safe, you can stop denying and pretending. You're a bad subject for hypnosis? Don't worry, I can fix that. I can make you a good subject. I can. I'm a very good at what I do."

She tried to draw back but there was nowhere to go.

"Next month at this time," Dan said gently, "next month, you'll remember it all. You'll have all those memories and you'll be able to take them on and cope with them. I promise." He looked up at one of the twins. "You can phone for the ambulance now."

CHRISTOPHER FOWLER

Christmas Forever

CHRISTOPHER FOWLER'S MOST RECENT books include a new collection of short stories, *Personal Demons*, and a novel, *Soho Black*. Among his earlier volumes are *Roofworld* (currently being developed as a big-budget action horror movie by Granada Television), *Rune*, *Red Bride*, *Disturbia*, *Spanky* and *Psychoville* (also in development as a vehicle for the new "Britpack" stars), while *Menz Insanza* is a large graphic novel from DC Comics, illustrated by John Bolton.

He is not the same Chris Fowler who is married to Pat Cadigan.

" 'Christmas Forever' was originally a commission for the *Independent on Sunday* magazine," reveals the author, "something to bring heartwarming cheer into the lives of its readers at Christmas. So I like to think that, in my own way, I put the blocks on that.

"By a weird coincidence, the story was inspired by an article I had read in the Indie the year before about something called the Finland Tongue breaking off. This section of frozen fjord helped to create the Gulf stream, and I liked the idea that one of the first effects of global warming might be a new ice age in Britain. Call me perverse . . .

"Typically, this story, which was admirably followed through in the Indie for months, failed to make other newspapers who had the more urgent matter of the Spice Girls and Gazza to report."

H E HAD BEEN GINGERLY attempting to unfold a copy of the *Independent*, but the newspaper snapped apart in his hands and shattered into dozens of pieces. Kallie swore angrily as he shovelled the shards into a pile with his boot; the broken edges were razor-sharp. There was nothing else to read in the apartment except his father's books, but there was no way of getting them off the shelves without a blowlamp, which he figured would somewhat defeat the object. Someone had given him some old magazines, but these were now stuck fast to the kitchen table, their covers rippled together in an iridescent mosaic.

Kallie wondered how much longer Bennett would be. He had gone to the shops three days ago – or was it four? Perhaps he'd run into friends and gone to stay with them for Christmas. Well, good riddance. Bennett had been camping out on the sofa for over two months now. Not bad for a guy who was "just passing through the neighbourhood". He had supposedly called in to see how his old schoolfriend was faring, but in the last eight weeks all he had done was empty the larder and try to repair the refrigerator. The refrigerator! Why in the name of everything perverse would he want to do that? Kallie had tried to throw it out but it would not fit through the kitchen door that his father had replaced after drunkenly burning the old one two years ago.

He walked over to the window and rubbed away a patch of ice with the back of his glove. Across the street was the bus depot where no buses ever ran. Not too many people passed by, either. Most had learned their lesson the hard way, leaving the comparative warmth of their homes only to become disoriented in the blizzards and stumble into snowdrifts. It didn't take long for a body to cool down in these temperatures. His father had been fond of describing a time when you could see the curving green meadow of Primrose Hill from the bedroom windows. All Kallie had ever seen was a perpetual ice-haze hanging in the air, obscuring a sun as watery as an uncooked egg.

There was little point in trying to lead a normal life now. Everything conspired against it. The solution, his eternally optimistic father had always told him, was to stay busy. Edward had stayed busy right until the end, refusing to acknowledge the fact that he was slowing down, moving with increasing decrepitude, like a clockwork toy at the end of its winding. Finally he had overestimated his stamina on a trip to town and had failed to make it back to safety before a storm of truly biblical proportions had set in. The blizzard lasted for over three months. When it subsided, the landscape had changed its proportions entirely, and his father had become part of the great permafrost ridge that separated North London from the city centre.

The problem with Bennett not coming back was that Bennett had taken his wallet, ostensibly to buy food. The reason for deciding to trust a man who had never shown an ounce of reliability was obscure to him now. He looked over at the telephone, willing it to ring. It wouldn't, of course, even if Bennett had bothered to note the number. The mechanism was encrusted in ice, as indeed was the entire exchange, although he had heard a rumour that MPs could still operate some kind of closed circuit telecommunication system – presumably for use in emergencies.

Well, what was it now if not an emergency? The entire apartment, the entire building, the entire city, the entire country was frozen solid, and had been for eighteen years. With each passing year it grew a little colder, a little more still and silent as the national heartbeat slowed to a weak and distanced blip.

Kallie was twenty, but held no memory of those fabulous sunsoaked times before the great freeze. Like a man blind from birth, he had not been granted the pleasure of memories. Bennett was a year older, and swore he could recall laying in long grass with the sun in his eyes, so light and bright it hurt to look into the sky. But almost everything that came out of his mouth was a lie. He said he had once seen Selfridges open. He said he knew people who could take them South, far beyond the reach of the ice. He said if they waited inside long enough the government would find a way to make it warmer. All lies. But he was right about one thing; they could not survive without food. That was why Kallie let him go. They had been living on beans and tinned luncheon meat, which was edible if you made a couple of holes in the lid of the can and gently heated it over the stove. But ten days ago the last gas ring had ceased to work, even though the council had promised to keep the pipes clear.

And perhaps Bennett had found a pub open somewhere and was spending his money with a bunch of his drunken mates. Kallie knew there was nothing for it but to find out for himself. He would certainly die if he stayed here. His last source of heat – the gas ring – had packed in. The electricity still worked intermittently, but there were no electric radiators to be had, not unless you were rich enough to buy one on the black market.

What would happen to him? He no longer cared to know. It would be easy to escape this bitter place; he just had to open all the windows, remove his greatcoat and lay down on the bed for a few minutes. Perhaps that was his only choice. But not before he visited the outside world one last time.

He struggled into his greatcoat, dug out leather gloves with split seams, tucked his jeans into the tops of his battered Caterpillar boots. When he unlatched the front door and looked out, he was surprised to find snow drifting in the hall. It had been nearly two months since his last foray into the streets of what had once recognisably been Camden Town. The tall windows at the end of the floor were broken, and the snow had formed a drift below the sill. If any of his neighbours still lived in the building, they would not answer his knock. The times were too strange to recklessly open doors. Good neighbour rules were no longer in force; now it was every man for himself. One would have thought this new ice age would draw people together, but it had encouraged the British to increase their insularity. The Blitz spirit was lost to a post-war nation raised on the solitary pleasures of television. People jealously hoarded their heat sources. Who could blame them? Heat was hard to share; if you opened the circle it dissipated.

Down the icy stairwell – the lift had not worked for nine years – to the front door, so frozen shut that Kallie assumed no-one had been in or out since Bennett had left with his wallet. Deadening whiteness glared in through the window panels. He would need to find sunglasses. He had tried to pick up ski equipment from Lilley & Skinner the last time he was in town, but – surprise, surprise – they had sold out. Only a handful of staff still manned the store, loyally maintaining the old conventions. He had worked there himself once, bored out of his mind, waiting to seize upon the odd straggling customer who had made it in through the snow. That was back when the free market was still trying to cope with the crisis, when the rich warm nations were still exporting to their poor frozen neighbours. Now that those neighbours had ceased to earn wages, there was no point in supplying them with affordable products. The milk of human kindness had been the first thing to freeze.

Throwing his weight against the door, he shifted it wide enough to push his way through. Bayonets of ice divorced themselves from the lintel and fell about him, cutting stencils into the swathes of snow that crusted the steps. Kallie raised his face into the biting wind and looked along the street, in the direction of the city. The air stole his breath. It was far colder than anything he had experienced before.

The Christmas scene that greeted him was absurdly picturesque, a postcard snowscape. Snow dunes, sparkling like hills of granulated jewels, swept in great unspoilt arcs across a bleached Sahara of roads and pavements. This was a bad sign; the route had been passable the last time he ventured out. But now even those high-profile charity missions the government was fond of announcing had ceased while everyone sorted out the problems in their own back yards.

On his last trip, Kallie had seen a few heavy-traction vehicles lumbering toward town. No people, though. There were hardly ever any people. It was simply too dangerous to set out on your own. He vaguely recalled a shopping expedition with his parents, and some friends of theirs who owned a car fitted with snowtyres. His mother had bought crazy things, pointless things, high-heeled shoes and summer blouses she would never be warm enough to wear. Anxious to be rid of their stock, the storekeepers had been bargained down to nothing. He would always remember his mother posing in front of the mirror as she held diaphanous chiffon against her. Ironically, her refusal to lose hope had brought her life to a protracted, painful end.

What had instilled his parents with such unreasoning optimism? Was it because they remembered a time when their world was a cacophony of movement and sound, when trees still flowered, when their vision was saturated with rainbow colours? Had they never lost sight of life's possibilities? Is that why they had allowed him to be born?

It took forty minutes to reach the deserted high street, silent but for the wind that moaned eerily between the buildings like a widow at a wake. At Camden Lock the ice in the canals had expanded and crushed itself upwards into fantastic twisted geometries. Kallie pulled the fur hood of his coat tighter around his face and concentrated on placing one foot before the other. The secret was to keep moving through the crystalline streets.

There were no shops open at all in the high street. This was a worrying new development. Surely some signs of life still existed? There had been a steady exodus to the southern hemisphere. Some had chosen to stay, determined to continue living in the radically altered climate. And there were the others, the ones who had no money and no way of leaving alive.

As he trudged on, staying wide of the treacherously deep drifts, he peered in at the frosted store windows. The warm bright pigments of their advertising posters were gone now. The sheer white force of snow and ice blotted every other colour from the landscape.

He resolved to walk as far as the giant supermarket at the end of the road. Beyond lay the crusted ridge of permafrost that had built up in the warring crosswinds of the Euston Road. Passing near it always unnerved him; there were people in the ice, frost-blackened hands and faces staring out like half uncovered statues. It wasn't right that they had been left there, but what could anyone do? After a few years the ice turned to stone, shifting and rupturing like the tectonic plates of the earth.

The Priceway car park was almost empty. The attendant's barrier was up, and from the lack of tyre tracks it looked like nothing had driven in or out for days. The long glass wall of the supermarket glittered with frost, and was covered in starburst cracks where the great weight of snow was slowly pushing it in, but at least the lights were still on inside, and that meant the store was open for business. Kallie had no money on him, but with luck there would be no staff to operate the tills. Many people continued to conduct a semblance of normal life, as if determined to prove that the British could remain polite in the direst of circumstances, but were easily turned from their daily tasks. Nothing could be relied upon anymore, beyond the fact that the situation would worsen.

The only advantage of the new cold climate was that food stayed fresher. Just as well; supplies were sporadic and perverse. Trucks would deliver great quantities of razorblades or suntan lotion, but there would be no bread or meat. Sometimes fresh-looking food would prove to have been frozen for years, and was impossible to thaw. Unscrupulous dealers would refreeze thawed meat, spreading illness.

The temperature inside the store was, oddly enough, too high.

Because of the value of its vast cold storage capacity, Priceway operated on its own generator, but the thermostats must have become damaged in the recent storms. To be hit by the smell of rotting meat was one final cruel consumerist joke to play on the few half-starved members of the public who still ventured through its doors. "Joy To The World" blared wonkily from the public address system. Kallie unbuttoned his coat and fought the desire to vomit as he tried to ignore the sweet, ripe smell of putrifying vegetables. He would have to stick to tins again.

"Happy Christmas, Kallie." He looked along the aisle to see an old friend of his mother's, Mrs Quintero, waving her bad hand at him. She had lost three fingers to frostbite last winter, and had not had the wounds properly dressed. The black stumps of her distended knuckles suppurated through filthy bandages. He was not surprised to see her; she lived here in the store. Besides, there were only a few people who visited the outside world with any regularity these days, and one tended to see the same faces.

"The heating came back on, Kallie, can you believe it? Seventy six degrees! Everything's gone off. The one place it needed to be cold."

"Hasn't the professor been able to fix it?"

"He hasn't a practical bone in his body. I wish you would take a look."

"Have there been any shipments lately?" he called back, ignoring her request. If he moved any closer she would come over and hug him, and he wanted to avoid that at all costs. He hated anyone touching him.

"Barbie dolls. Tinned mandarins. Jars of sun-dried tomatoes. No medical supplies." She shoved a wedge of peroxided hair from her dark-rimmed eyes. He wondered why on earth she still bothered to wear makeup. "You heard anything?"

It was the most common question of all. Everyone expected some kind of government-authorised announcement to be made. Crisis over, it's safe to come out, that kind of thing. But it had not happened in his lifetime, and he doubted it could ever happen, or that there was still a government that could make any sort of announcement. Things had moved too far away from the norm. How could their former lives ever be restored?

"We've had a few people call in, but nobody with any news. Been ages since we had news. A crowd of rough kids came by this week, stole the coffee vending machine, really noisy types. Of course, you don't remember when the whole world was noisy." She looked around, too sharp, too anxious. "It's so quiet now. The snow deadens everything, but oh! it never used to be like this."

"Things change," Kallie shrugged, keen to move on.

"I used to work in an office," she continued, desperate to be understood, "I was good at my job, and always busy, no time to stop. And the noise! Telephones, typewriters, and buses out in the street, people calling to each other. Televisions just left on. Singing at Christmas as we left the pub. Sometimes you had to shout to be heard. Now you can almost hear yourself think. Noise was life." She blinked and shook her head, too frightened to speak.

"I have to go, Mrs Quintero."

"Wait a moment!" She tore open a carton and produced a Christmas cracker. "These just arrived. Make a wish." She held it out with an air of desperation. "Want something, Kallie."

They pulled, but the snap didn't go off. A whistle, a joke, a motto and a party hat fell out. The joke was; "Where Does A Policeman Live? 999, Letsby Avenue". The motto was "Make Hay While The Sun Shines".

"The professor's in the stock room giving a class." She had turned away, unwilling to share her distress. "My two are in there with him."

"I'll look in and say hi," he assured her, even though he did not want to.

"There's lychees in syrup on Aisle 6, and pesto sauce in jars," she added listlessly. "Make sure you take some. You need to keep your strength up."

Why? he thought. What the hell for? "Thanks, Mrs Quintero. Take care." He set his metal basket aside and decided to look in on the professor first. He wasn't really a professor; he just looked and sounded like everybody's idea of one.

The stockroom had long been cleared of produce, and folding metal chairs had been set in rows. The metal was cold to sit on, but everything wooden had been burned. Anyone could attend the professor's lectures. Kallie was sure he would continue to make them even if no-one showed up at all. Today he was teaching Mrs Quintero's children, and another boy he had not seen before. He stood at the back and raised his hand in silent gesture. The professor did not take kindly to being interrupted.

"Cores drilled from the centre of the Greenland ice-sheet should have warned us." His dull monotone blunted the most interesting facts. The kids looked bored, and exhibited the distracted mannerisms of the unwell. "They proved that the climate of the Earth fluctuates far more than was ever previously realised. The last ice age took very little time to occur, perhaps just a decade or two, and lasted for over a hundred thousand years. Chance plays a large part in the survival temperature of our planet. In the seas of the world there are five natural pumps that drive the great currents of the oceans. The European Sub-Polar Ocean Programme found that one of these, the Odden Feature, powers a deep cold current that helps to control the circulation of the North Atlantic Ocean. It is caused by a vast tongue of ice in the Greenland Sea."

Kallie quietly helped himself to a tray of sausage rolls Mrs Quintero had defrosted. They tasted like putty.

"Back in February 1993, Greenland's winter ice receded due to global warming, and the tongue of ice failed to form, dissolving into pancake ice." He paused here to write the word PANCAKE on the wall with a blue crayon. One of Mrs Quintero's boys started repeating the word aloud.

"Without a pump to drive it, the Gulf Stream, one of the sea's warmest currents, stopped almost overnight. The Gulf Stream kept Britain and northern Europe warm, and now it's gone. Then, in less than a decade, the other great pumps died, transforming the weather patterns of the world in the wink of an eye. We are in uncharted territory now. The Royal Commission of Environmental Pollution's report into the flooding of Egypt and southern China – "

But the children were all saying "Pancake, pancake," and the professor's lesson, always the same lesson, was wasted. They were too young to understand, anyway. They would learn soon enough.

"You were listening, weren't you, Kallie?" he asked wearily, throwing his crayon away.

"Heard it all before, prof. Nothing we can do, right?"

"Right. A friend of yours was in the other day. Tuesday."

Kallie could not imagine why he still bothered to work out the names of individual days. Nobody else did. "What was his name?" he asked.

"Mr Bennett. Sat in the beverage department all day. He was very drunk when he left. I warned him not to go outside, but he wouldn't be stopped. Wouldn't even take his jacket. Became very belligerent when challenged." He clicked his tongue disapprovingly.

That was it, then. No chance of getting his wallet back now. It was hard enough staying alive when you were sober, let alone drunk.

"Someone else was looking for you," said the professor, an almost playful tone in his voice. Without asking, Kallie knew who.

"How is she?" he said finally. The professor grinned. 'Missing you, naturally. She always asks after you. She still talks about the time – "

"I know." He cut the conversation short, uninterested in hearing an embroidered account of how, a year ago, he had saved Shari's life. "I have to go."

"I understand," the professor answered with mock solemnity. "You're a busy man. You know, I think it's time you considered moving in here with us while the generator still holds out. You get used to the smell, and it's worth it to be warm."

"Thanks for the offer," he mumbled, rebuttoning his coat. "I'll keep it in mind." Moving in meant being a part of the professor's ever-changing extended family, which meant looking after sick kids and hysterical, gangrenous parents.

"Shari will be sorry she missed you."

I'll bet, he thought. He was suspicious of Shari since the accident; she was too nice to him now. "Say hi to her for me." He waved to Mrs Quintero as he pushed against the exit door.

Outside, the rising wind drove the temperature still lower. He reached the bottom of the slope below the supermarket and saw what he initially took to be a pile of brown rags, but closer inspection revealed a rigid hand, its fingers clutching the gelid air as if trying to take hold on life itself. Crystals of ice had formed over the corpse's eyes like luxuriant cataracts. Kallie cracked open its jacket and felt around for his wallet, but found nothing. Bennett had either dropped it in his drunken stupor, or had been robbed.

He knelt and bowed his head for a moment. No prayer, just a few seconds of stillness. They had spent their childhood years together; he owed Bennett something. Then he rose and turned into the wind.

On a suicidal impulse he decided to push further on into the city centre, something he had not done for over four years. He wanted to see the Thames, to prove for himself that this life-channel still existed. It meant he would be trapped there overnight, because it would take him until sunset just to reach Piccadilly Circus, and it was virtually impossible to travel alone after dark without being well prepared. Still, he wanted to see Eros once more. See it, perhaps, one last time.

As he passed the cylindrical ruin of the Telecom Tower, he thought of Shari; how she had been passing him somewhere near here on her way back to the supermarket, and how the Red Cross van had swung wildly around the corner. He remembered the lethal guillotine of ice sliding from its roof in a broad oblong sheet, and how he had thrown himself at her with a shout, slamming her body to the pavement as the ice shattered above their heads. It was the first time he had touched a girl. Up until then, the thought of physical contact with anyone had made him shudder uncontrollably. Shari had hugged him tight, clinging to the life she had nearly lost. Kallie had gently disentangled himself, embarrassed. He had shunned her ever since.

The freezing wind sucked at his greatcoat as he waded knee-deep through the intersection at Charlotte Street. His right foot had gone numb; a dangerous sign, one which suggested he should at least find a warm place to rest up for a while. As he passed shuttered, padlocked stores in Leicester Square, he reached a decision. The river would no longer be a point in his journey, but the point of the journey.

In Rathbone Place he passed a dying dog, a red setter, half buried in an avalanche of dislodged ice. The shards that sparkled in its diamante fur lent it an air of ostentatious glamour.

Oxford Street. Once a cheap-and-cheerful marketplace thronged with shoppers, according to his father. Now a wind-ravaged tunnel of ice, black-spotted in places where the corpses of foolhardy pedestrians poked up through the snowdrifts. Soho was impassable. The narrow streets were blocked with abandoned trucks and crags created by the sheet-ice that slid continuously from the rooftops. The upper floors were skeined with billowing crosshairs of ice that caught the dying light like the wings of giant dragonflies.

Kallie skirted around into Regent Street, the great curve of Nash's terrace pockmarked by the blown-in windows of department stores. Here the wind was at its fiercest. A double-decker bus lay on its side, almost buried by drifts. A diamond shop had lost its panes, the ground floor now extravagantly filled with opalescent icicles, so that it appeared little changed from its window-dressed heyday.

The snow in the circus was sullied by the discharges of overturned trucks and the tracks of pilgrims who had come here in the vain hope that reaching this gaudy apex of civilisation might somehow end their own spiritual loss. As man descended once more into beast, the manufactured tokens of a forgotten world took on the power of talismen. Kallie watched as an elderly woman floundered past with a green plastic Harrods bag on her head. Earlier that day he had seen two young men dragging an electronic exercise machine toward a tube station, perhaps planning to install it as an object of veneration.

And here was poor Eros, intended as an inspiration to Londoners, now twisted from its perch so that only a leg and an elegant silvery wing of Gilbert's famous statue could be seen thrusting hopelessly up from the dunes in the centre of the roundabout. Kallie stood before the fallen god and grimaced in despair, heaving in gulps of stinging knife-sharp air as he stared at the upturned calf and ankle, the feathered wingtip almost lost in snow and discarded chunks of scaffolding. He clawed at the statue in a desperate attempt to free it from the swamped remains of the desecrated fountain. Uncovering even another inch proved impossible. Others had tried to remove the permafrost trellis that encased it like a crystal shroud, in vain.

Kallie stumbled on until he came up against the steel-shuttered doorway of a record store. There was nothing for him here, and nowhere to go. Unable to think or move, he remained completely still. As night fell, the warmth within him slowly faded. At his back, giant cutouts of forgotten rock stars struck poses of defiance, icons of redundant anarchy.

Dying was as easy as he had hoped it would be. You just had to do nothing, and let the insidious numbness colonise your limbs.

The cloudbase reflected the whiteness of the city, and finally ceased to move, as if the world could no longer be bothered to turn upon its axis. He closed his eyes and rested his head against the ice-jewelled shutters, allowing life to quietly slip away.

The explosion of noise that followed blasted him to his feet. Somebody was playing loud music inside the building. He could feel the bass tones vibrating the window panes. He stepped back, trying to see beyond the reflections into the rear of the ground floor. Someone – some *thing* – was gyrating insanely to the music, raging the entire length of the store.

It took him a while to discover the forced door of the delivery bay at the side of the building. He climbed over buckled steel struts – they must have been rammed with a vehicle – to the interior, and was deafened by the surrounding, saturating noise. Someone had used a bright yellow forklift truck to break in. Piles of cracked and broken CD cases littered the floor. A primitive set of disco lights pulsed red and blue diamonds at the back of the floor near the stairwell. The dancer was a short, slim woman in her late forties. Her body retained the litheness and aggression of a professional performer. She swung and slammed and span, kicking out, punching the chill air with a series of gutteral grunts. Her greying red hair was tied back with a green bandana. She wore a red satin leotard with the leggings hacked off above the knee, and a yellow scarf carelessly knotted around her waist. She looked ablaze with anger and energy.

Kallie dropped behind a record rack and watched as her music twisted through a dozen different styles. Now that there was no more culture, the abrupt changes did not shock. When the last song ceased in mid-track she crossed to the DJ booth and flipped the tape – obviously an item she had personally assembled – and continued dancing. The second side began with "We're Havin' A Heatwave", sung by Marilyn Monroe, and Kallie caught himself grinning. Wondering where the power was coming from, he searched the floor and saw that a pair of car batteries had been rigged to the system with jump leads.

Now he was able to observe her properly for the first time, bent over the light in the booth, feeling for the controls. She was unable to see, permanently blinded by time spent lost in the snowy wastes. There were no fingers at all on her swollen right hand, and just two on her left. She had deftly flipped the tape with her thumbs. He tried to catch sight of her feet, dreading to imagine their damaged state, knowing that every step she took must be agonising, but she was already off and away, pounding across the floor to the brassy orchestrations.

Finally, even the deafening music failed to keep him awake. Comforted by the weight of sound, with his greatcoat pulled about his head, he slept on through the long, loud night.

He awoke soon after dawn to find the store silent, the lights and the sound system turned off to conserve power. The dancer was asleep on a patchwork duvet beside the DJ booth, snoring lightly. Studying her, he was tempted to think that the tiny crosshatched lines around her mouth and eyes were caused by laughter, not fear, even though he saw that her feet were little more than swollen stumps. For a moment he wanted to ask her how she could dance in the face of all reason, when the world and her own body were steadily failing her, how it was possible to experience pleasure without hope. But waking her up, he realised, would be a mistake. Better to let her sleep on and rebuild her energy. Gingerly stepping between CD cases, he made his way back to the delivery bay door and left.

The sky had cleared to a sapphire-hard blue and the wind was keen, but at least the snow had stopped. He passed four people on his way to the river, but none were prepared to acknowledge him, or even look up. For the first time he began to sense just how completely the cold had closed them all off. The shimmering ebony band ahead drove him forward along the half-buried embankment, until he was standing in the silent centre of Waterloo Bridge, above the strangled stream that had once been the mighty Thames.

When he looked down into the spangled black water and saw that it still ran, determinedly chugging around the encrusted floes and over mounds of industrial debris, on through the heart of the city, he began to cry, but his tears turned to ice.

Something inside him opened, fanning into faint life, growing warmer until his gut was burning. He turned and bellowed from the bridge, out across the sub-zero city, up into the frozen sky where hardy white gulls still wheeled and screamed, yelling until he was hoarse and dizzy from the exertion.

As that first great release subsided, he knew; that hope was false, a misleading hollow nonsense obscuring all that was real and true. The truth was that the world would die and take him with it, today, tomorrow, years from now, in agony, in terror, in unreadiness, and it didn't matter. What mattered was the time left to live.

Kallie looked out across the glittering, foolish river, to the weakling sun climbing in a pointless sky, where a dancing mad-woman whirled in scraps of fire on crippled feet, beyond the laws of gravity, the threshold of pain, the bounds of rationality. He removed a glove and wiped his eyes until they were clear and dry. Heavy grey snowclouds were amassing on the estuary horizon. It was time to head North before the temperature fell further.

He wondered what Shari was doing, and whether, in the face of all reason, she too was smiling. It would be Christmas forever, and it was too cold to be alone.

YVONNE NAVARRO

Four Famines Ago

YVONNE NAVARRO LIVES IN A small town west of Chicago and has
been publishing fiction since 1984, when her first story appeared
in *Horror Show* magazine.

Her books include *AfterAge*, *Species* and *Species II*, *Deadrush*
and *Aliens: Music of the Spears*, while her most recent novels are
Babylon 5: The River of Souls and *Red Shadows*, which is a
sequel to her award-winning *Final Impact*.

As the author explains, " 'Four Famines Ago' grew solely from
its title. Several years ago I was having a conversation with writer
Jeff Osier (who is one of the smartest men I know) about Africa
and the famine that had struck in Somalia. He used this phrase to
place it in time, then went on to talk about some of the more
current food shortages there. I started wondering how it would be
if the term 'four famines ago' was used by someone who was
basically heartless, what could happen, and how, ultimately, it
could be used to teach that person a lesson."

S HOCKED SILENCE FELL ACROSS the people seated around the
polished conference room table. A few mouths gaped at him,
others just looked embarrassed. Only Aisha spoke, her lovely
ebony face held in rigid control.

"I beg your pardon?"

"I said this film is obsolete," Paul repeated. "It – "

"No," she interrupted. "You said 'This film was shot *four*

famines ago.' That is the most tasteless thing I believe I've ever heard."

Paul folded his arms. "Does it matter? I'm not here to be tactful, Aisha. Leave that to public relations. My job is to review the films and make sure they're ready to hit the market." He jabbed a finger toward the case of the video he and the other attendees had just finished watching. "This one is out of date."

"But what you said – " she sputtered.

He raised a hand for silence – and wasn't it amazing the power the hand of a senior VP had? – and shrugged. "The only effect who's starving in Africa has on the people in this room is that it means we have to bring this project current." The others were carefully examining their fingernails or shuffling through notes, afraid to make eye contact. Only Aisha refused to lower her glittering black eyes, and her boldness got her the prize. He gave the tape a sharp push and it slid across the shining wood of the table like a beer mug on a wet bar. "You got it. I want re-shot footage in two weeks."

She gasped. "But I'll have to schedule camera people, guides, airfare – the costs on a short term like that will be tremendous!"

"Not as much as the losses we'll pull on the advertising we've dropped into this series, all of which announced it would be ready by the end of this month. Need I remind you of the price of television spots in today's markets?" Paul glared at her. "I didn't think so." He looked at his watch, then stood and pulled on his jacket. "I'm due at another meeting. Send the disbursements to my secretary." He paused at the door for one more comment to the Marketing Manager, who was tugging nervously at his collar and trying to look inconspicuous. "Dave, I would seriously recommend that you never let another project go as far out of date as the Africa series."

Paul stopped at the restroom to rinse his face and hands and run a comb through his carefully trimmed hair before heading up to the budget meeting. This one would be tougher; too many others there wielded considerably more power than him and he would have to explain the overspends in his department, not to mention warn them in advance of the costs looming on the Africa shoot. If they decided to pull the project despite the advertising – though he was sure they wouldn't – he would still have time to stop Aisha before she bought tickets and paid advances to photographers and other workers. He couldn't help grinning at his reflection in the mirror. Too bad they hadn't liked his line about the famines; he'd thought it was pretty clever and damned effective at halting the worthless excuses those fools had been bandying around the table. Then again, Aisha was actually from Somalia and maybe this whole project just hit a little too close to the heart for her. Well, welcome to the business world.

Two weeks later Aisha walked into his office and handed him a tape. She looked thinner, as though the trip and the shoot had sucked away something, a piece of her essence. "Are you all right?" he asked, peering at her curiously. "I didn't mean for you to run yourself down."

She stared at him, her eyes like melted tar. "That's not the impression I got at the marketing meeting, Paul. A two week deadline will run anyone down." She nodded at the tape. "I was there, you know, right in the middle of it. Somalia is a terrible place, full of useless death and utterly lacking in hope. The tape will never show it in its awful truth."

"And it shouldn't," he said briskly. "We want people to *buy* the series, not turn away because they can't handle it." He swung his chair around and inserted the tape into the video player, then thumbed the remote and watched the rough footage that began to roll across the thirty-inch monitor on the wall. Aisha said nothing as the scenes passed and he studied them critically. Skeletal children with distended bellies stared at the camera, hardly making the effort to brush away the flies crawling over their cracked lips; a sea of people sprawled in a camp filled with tattered, filthy blankets, scraping a few tablespoons of gruel from gritty bowls with their fingers; a pair of twiglike hands gently pulled a grey blanket over an infant's tiny corpse. Paul frowned and leaned forward. What was that? Had he just seen a well-fed child working among the starving, carrying buckets of water on a branch strung across her shoulders? A volunteer? No, of course not; there were no well-fed children in the area of Somalia that had been taped on this film. His eyes were tired, that's all.

After five minutes he shut off the player without bothering to rewind or remove the tape. "It's too raw," he said.

Aisha leaned towards him, the hollows beneath her eyes and her cheeks deep purple smudges within the mahogany gleam of her skin. "But that's the way it *is*," she said. "We do educational films, not Hollywood. How can we disguise the truth?"

"I'm not telling you to disguise it," he replied. "Just tone it down. We're going after the high school as well as college audience here, remember? I can tell you right now that eighty-five percent of this country's high school teachers wouldn't show this film in human studies, even to the classes that are talking about enlisting in the Peace Corps. Those high schools are a high percentage of our target market."

"All right." Aisha stood and Paul's eyes narrowed. Was she actually trembling? "You can keep that copy," she said. "I've got another in my office."

"How much weight have you lost and why?" he asked. "Are you actually well enough to handle this?"

Her return stare was stony. "I'm fine. I just couldn't justify eating American-size meals while I was over there, you know?" Her eyes tried to trap him and he found himself ducking her gaze. "But I have to eat better now." Her voice trailed away without explanation.

Paul started to ask why, then let it pass. Of course she would eat better now that she was back home and away from all those starving people. He reached over and gave her a quick, bland pat on the hand. "Well, you take care of yourself. How long before you can get this edited?"

"Give me three days and it'll be ready."

"You've got two. Get busy." He picked up the telephone and she nodded and left.

Later, at the end of a very difficult day, he rewound the tape and played it again, watching it more carefully now that he didn't have Aisha's accusing stare boring into his back. He had to admit that it *was* a terrible thing to witness, and he would stand by his judgment that it was too harsh for the high school audience. Oddly, here and there throughout the film he caught glimpses of children who were a little heavier than the others, not by a huge amount but obviously not walking the tightrope of starvation as were their peers. He tried to freeze the tape at these points but could never quite catch the shots, though he was sure he saw these children wandering in and out of the scenes, carrying water and supplies to other, smaller children. He thought he even glimpsed one digging a small grave, but couldn't be positive when once again the frame eluded the freeze feature on the tape player.

Amid the starving people, one emaciated child in particular caught his eye, a girl of about five with the same wood-colored skin as Aisha, the same liquid tarpit eyes staring at him from twelve thousand miles away via the miracle of electronics. His finger fumbled with the remote and he caught this one easily, a full front of the tiny girlchild. Her hungry eyes pierced into his own, mesmerizing him through the monitor until his mind suddenly filled with an unspeakable, unanswerable question:

Just how hungry is she?

Inexplicably he tried to imagine it then, to let the sensation spill into his mind: the empty stomach, day after day, swollen until a child who'd lived less than half a decade looked nine months' pregnant. Hunger induced headaches at first, then fading to a dull pang that the small girl didn't understand. He had asked his question, but what was hers?

Why doesn't someone make the hunger go away?

Why, indeed? Paul's fingers involuntarily reached towards the screen and he traced the shape of the little girl's nearly hairless head, his fingertips crackling with static electricity against the glass. What would she feel like if he held her in his arms? A helpless, innocent bundle of living sticks – frail, a bowl of soup away from early, undeserved death. He felt a sudden profound regret that he had made that reckless and so callous remark in the meeting two weeks ago.

The tape player clanked, then jammed; he blinked as the picture zigged and went out. When he ejected the tape and peered at the machine, he could find no damage and no reason for the tape to have stopped, and when he reinserted the tape it played just fine, although he had lost his place in the footage. No matter; it was almost seven o'clock and past dinner, and he was absolutely ravenous.

The small girl swats at the biting flies that circle her head and try persistently for her cracked lips and the moister corners of her eyes. The hunger is bad enough without the flywelts itching along the line of her mouth and eyes when she wakes, little mounds of festering flesh which refuse to heal. Her belly is a dark, swollen circle in the sickly light of the African moon, the skin a tight, dark shadow stretched across the line of her vision as she raises her head wearily; she cannot see her own feet. Huddled beneath a worn blanket as meager protection against the insects, she sleeps and dreams of a faraway, unknown place and a white man she's never seen. He looks and dresses differently than the Red Cross volunteers at her camp, as though he is soft enough for the harsh African wind to sweep away and grind into sand. She dreams, too, that he eats a meal the likes of which she has never imagined, plate after plate of unidentifiable food with rich aromas that make her mouth water even in her sleep. When she wakes in the morning she thinks of him and feels better; her belly is not so swollen, her head not so painful, and when a volunteer presses a bowl of gruel into her hands she eats only three spoonfuls then surreptitiously divides the remainder between two of the more sickly children who slept beside her the previous night.

Paul's fingers were doing a frustrated drumbeat on the remote control when Aisha walked into his office two days later and dropped the edited version on his desk. He said nothing, just kept going back and forth with the remote, trying without luck to freeze the shot of the little girl who had caught his attention the last time he'd played the tape. He felt like throwing the damned remote to the floor and stomping on it. Why couldn't he catch that shot, damn it?

"Having problems?" Aisha sounded amused.

"I can't get this stupid thing to stop where I want," he said through gritted teeth. "I want it to pause . . . right . . . there – *damn* it! See how it skips? What the hell's the matter with this thing?"

"Nothing."

He blinked at her tone and looked up, the remote momentarily forgotten. "Well sure there is. You saw it."

"Sure I saw it. But what did *you* see, Paul?" Her eyelids lowered, the lashes drooping over her eyes. "You look like you've lost some weight," she said softly.

"A little," he said curtly. Paul found himself staring at his own hands and gave a shake of his head. He offered her the remote. "Here, see if you can get it to work."

"All right. What are you trying to find?" She hit the PLAY button.

"There!" He pointed excitedly. "That little girl, I'm trying to pause it on her."

Aisha hit the REWIND button. "What's so special about her?"

"She –" Paul cleared his throat. "Well, I don't know. I think the tape's . . . distorted, or something. She . . ." He hesitated, then plunged on. "She looks *different*." He frowned and finally met Aisha's unwavering gaze. "Is it my imagination or do some of the children on this tape – not a lot, but *some* – look like they've been eating fairly decently?" He shook his head. "Sounds crazy, I know."

"Not at all."

He jerked and stared at her. "It doesn't?"

It was her turn to shake her head. "Some of them *are*," she said. "For instance," she aimed the remote and the tape sped ahead, then slowed to normal speed as she lifted her finger from the FAST FORWARD button. "Watch. You'll see a little boy wearing a green T-shirt with the left sleeve missing, right . . . here. See him?"

Paul nodded. "Why didn't you pause it?"

"Because the tape won't stop on those children."

"Bullshit. Put it on the editing machine and find it."

"It won't be there," she said blandly.

He slammed his fist on the desktop. "Why the hell *not?*"

"Because the film only stops on the starving ones. And like your little girl, my little boy isn't starving anymore."

Paul opened his mouth, then shut it again; whatever he'd been about to yell had vanished like water spilled on blistering desert sand. "I guess I don't know what you're talking about," he said slowly. "And maybe I don't want to."

Without being told, Aisha stepped back to the door of his office and closed it, then returned to the chair in front of his desk and settled herself on it. The thinness that had stayed with her since her trip to Somalia became her; wearing a dress printed in shades of pale green, she looked like the branch of a tall willow tree as it swayed gracefully in the breeze. "You don't have that choice anymore," she said. "You chose a child –"

"I did what?"

"– and she accepted. Now she's your responsibility."

"What do you mean 'I chose' a child?" Confused, Paul glanced back at the despairing footage still flickering across the screen. "What child?"

"The little girl you keep trying to capture on the tape. You must have done something –"

"I stopped the tape on her," Paul interrupted. "I was curious, that's all. I certainly didn't have any contact with her or anything." His eyes narrowed. "Not like you had with the children on your trip."

Aisha shrugged delicately. "I suppose it doesn't matter." She looked away, her gaze tracking his richly-appointed office. "A personal touch, I mean. The Peace Corps and Red Cross workers over there whisper about cases like this – they say it's some kind of weird empathetic link that transfers to the physical world. It never happens to them while they're *there*, where everyone's starving. Only when they go back home . . . where they can eat well and carry the burden."

"What happens?" Paul demanded. "What *burden*? Aisha, what the hell is going on here?"

"You chose a child to sustain," she explained patiently. "That little girl on the videotape. Now you have to feed her."

Paul snorted and swiveled his chair around. "You spent too much time around the locals out there, Aisha. Do you really think I'm going to swallow this?"

"How's your appetite been, Paul?"

He turned back to stare at her. Her eyes met his steadily, refusing to look away. They were disturbingly similar to the those of the child, that same small girl whose gaze haunted his dreams at night. The same one he'd thought of every day as he sat down to eat each meal, three squares a day, same as always . . .

Well, *almost* the same. A little more, perhaps.

Not a little. Nearly twice as much as he used to eat.

Still Aisha didn't say anything. She just sat, waiting for him to make the connection, to take the jump into what the writing workshops always called *suspension of disbelief*. Two weeks ago he wouldn't have been able to do it; he was a practical, educated man who had no time for that kind of nonsense.

Amazing how easily practicality could be usurped by fear and hope.

"I thought I had cancer," he managed to croak. "I dropped ten pounds in three days for no reason, and I was hungry all the time. I started eating and eating and eating, and finally got the weight back . . . but the hunger's always there."

Aisha nodded sympathetically. "It is for them, too," she said softly.

"But I can't eat like this forever!"

"Why not?" It was her turn to become demanding. "Don't you understand yet? You're not eating just for you anymore, you're eating for *her*, and then for her sisters, or cousins, or for whomever." She leaned forward and placed her hands palms down on the desk top. He could smell her breath and something she'd eaten – potato chips? – and the scent made his mouth suddenly water. He felt like an idiot, and maybe more than just a little crazy. "If you stop, Paul, or you diet or do something really stupid like fast – which you obviously don't need – she'll die. And it'll be your fault."

"For how long?" Desperation clawed at him and he suddenly saw it all too clearly: decades of chowing down and never gaining weight, ridiculous food bills – the least of his worries, really – but how did you explain this to a companion, a wife, or your co-workers? Call it a high metabolism? He'd have to eat normally in front of normal people, then continue the job when he was alone. And let's face it; most people would gag at the quantity of food he'd been consuming. Horrified, he raised his eyes to Aisha and recognized everything reflected in her eyes: he would be alone with his child for the rest of his life.

She stared back at him, and for the first time Paul saw something like sympathy flicker in the dark pools of her eyes.

"I'm starved," she said softly. "Join me for dinner?"

STEPHEN LAWS

The Crawl

STEPHEN LAWS WAS BORN IN Newcastle-upon-Tyne, where he continues to live and work. He became a full-time writer in 1992 after working in local government, and his nine horror-thrillers have been widely translated around the world: *Ghost Train*, *Spectre*, *The Wyrm*, *The Frighteners*, *Darkfall*, *Gideon* (winner of the Children of the Night Award), *Macabre*, *Daemonic* and *Somewhere South of Midnight*. His tenth novel, *Chasm*, was published in 1998.

Chariot Films is currently developing *Darkfall* as a feature film, for which he has written the screenplay, while several other scripts for the movies and television are in development. His award-winning short stories have appeared in various anthologies, magazines and newspapers, and he is the regular host of the Manchester Festival of Fantastic Films where, in his own words, he is able to put to useful purpose "a youth spent sitting in the back rows of local fleapits, escaping into other worlds and other times."

The author clearly remembers where he got the idea for following story: "In the words of the story's narrator, '. . . the whole thing began on the A1 just a half-mile from Boroughbridge.' It's the first time that an image has leapt into my mind, apparently from nowhere.

"Just like the couple in the story, my wife Melanie and I were driving home after an Easter stay with her parents. Unlike the fictional couple, we weren't having an argument at the time. But just as we passed a roadway sign that read BOROUGHBRIDGE: HALF-MILE, I had the most alarming and intense image that a scarecrow figure was going to step out from the hard-shoulder and lay a hand-scythe across the windscreen, shattering the glass. Now, don't get me wrong. I don't live in a state of perpetual anxiety, waiting for things like this to happen. And I hadn't been thinking of anything beforehand that might lend itself to such a violent fantasy.

"It was such a powerful and disturbing image that I grabbed up my briefcase, found my scribbling pad and jotted it down, together with the exact location.

" 'You alright?' asked Melanie (who was driving), not understanding my sudden energetic activity, and my apparent discomfort.

" 'Yeah,' I said in a puzzled sort of way. 'I think so.'

"I didn't get around to the story straightaway. But when I did, some months later, the power of that image hadn't gone away. And when I began to write, it was as if the story already existed and was just waiting to be discovered. I finished it in a high fever, suffering one of the worst bouts of influenza I've ever experienced. When it was done, I remember thinking: Now where the hell did *that* come from?

"Which makes me wonder a little.

"Do you suppose that maybe . . . I mean, just maybe . . . the thing that pursues our fictional husband and wife in this story really *is* out there on the highways and by-ways somewhere? No, it couldn't be that the thing is still stalking through the underbrush, striding down dusty roads and looking for passers-by.

"Could it . . . ?"

T HE DAYS ARE BAD, but the nights are always worse. Since it all happened and I lost my job, it seems as if the front door is always the focus of my attention, no matter what I'm doing. I try to keep myself occupied, try to read, try to listen to music. But all of these things make it much worse. You see, if I really *do* become preoccupied in what I'm doing, then I might not hear it if . . .

If he . . . if it . . . comes.

I've recently had all my mail redirected to a post office box where I can go and collect it, since the clatter of the letterbox in the morning and afternoon became just too much to bear. I had to nail it up against junk mail and free newspapers. The house has become a terrible, terrible place since I lost Gill. God, how I miss her.

And in the nights, I lie awake and listen.

The sound of a car passing on the sidestreet is probably the worst.

I hear it coming in my sleep. It wakes me instantly, and I'm never sure whether I've screamed or not, but I lie there praying first that the car will pass quickly and that the engine won't cough and falter. Then, in the first seconds after it's moved on I pray again that I won't hear those familiar, staggering footsteps on the gravel path outside; that I won't hear that hellish hammering on the front door. I listen for the sounds of that hideous, hoarse breathing. Most nights I'm soaked in sweat waiting for the sound of the door panels splintering apart. Sometimes I dream that I'm down there in the hall, with my hands braced against the wood of that front door, screaming for help as the pounding comes from the other side.

Sometimes I dream that I'm in bed, that he's got in and he's coming up the stairs.

That same slow, methodical tread.

I run to the door, trying to slam it shut as he reaches the landing. In slow motion, I turn and scream at Gill to get out quickly through the bedroom window as I heave the bedside cabinet across the floor to the door. But as I turn, Gill isn't there. She's in the bathroom at the top of the landing, so now I'm frantically tearing the cabinet away from the door as he ascends, but Gill doesn't hear him because the shower's running and I slowly pull open the door screaming her name just as the shadow reaches the landing and Gill turns from the wash basin and . . .

If I started by telling you that the whole thing began on the A1 just a half mile from Boroughbridge, you might suppose that it has some kind of relevance for the horror that came afterwards. If it does, then that relevance has eluded me. Believe me, I've been over the whole thing many times in my mind, trying to make sense of it all. No, like all bad nightmares, it defied any logic. It seemed that we were just in the wrong place at the wrong time; like a traffic accident. Thirty seconds earlier or thirty seconds later, and maybe I'd be able to sleep at night a little better than I do these days. But since all stories start somewhere, the A1 turn-off half-a-mile from Boroughbridge was our somewhere.

The day had started badly.

We had spent Easter weekend with my wife's parents, and on the trip home Gill and I weren't speaking. There had been a party at her folks' house on the Sunday evening (we'd been there since Thursday), and that bloody personnel manager friend of theirs had been invited. I'd been made redundant from an engineering firm three years previously, and it was two years before I found another job. Not easy, but things were going fine again at last. Nevertheless, the use of my previous firm's psychometric testing to "reduce staffing levels" was a bug-bear of mine. ("What is the capital of Upper Twatland? You don't know? Then sorry, you're sacked.")

We were driving home on Easter Monday, and I had promised not to drink during the evening so that we could take turns behind the wheel. But this bastard personnel man (who I'd never met before, but whose profession didn't endear himself to me) was standing there all night, spouting off his in-house philosophy about big fish eating little fish, and only-the-strongest-will-prevail. My anger had begun as a slow-burn, and I'd had a drink to dampen the fuse. But then a second had begun to light it again. And by the third, I was just about ready for an intervention. By my fourth, I'd burned it out of my system, was having a chat with Stuart and Ann and their light-hearted banter was making everything okay again. Then, the personnel-man was left on his own and, having bored his companion to tears, decided to move over to us. If he'd kept off the subject, everything would have been okay. (But then again, if we hadn't been on the A1 half-a mile out of Boroughbridge, none of this would have happened either.)

Disregarding anything we were talking about, he started again where he'd left off.

And I'm afraid that was it. All bets off. Fuse not only rekindled, but powder-keg ignited. I could probably go on for three pages about our conversation, but since this tale is about the worst thing that ever happened to me, and not one of the best, it seems a little pointless if I do. Just let's say that without giving in to the urge for actual bodily harm, I kept a cold fury inside. I dispensed with any social airs and graces or the rules of polite party-conversation, and kept at his throat while he tried to impress us with his superior "if-they-can't-hack-it, out-they-go" credo. Like a terrier, I kept hanging at his wattles, shaking him down and finishing with a "who-lives-by-the-sword-dies-by-the-sword". Sounds obvious, but believe me; as a put-down it wasn't half bad. Maybe you had to be there to appreciate it. He left our company, and kept to other less-impolite partygoers. Stuart and Ann were pleased too, and that made me feel good.

However, I could tell by Gill's face that I wasn't going to get any good conduct medals. At first, I thought that maybe I'd overstepped the mark; been too loud, let the booze kid me that I was being subtle when in fact I was acting like Attila the Hun. But no, her tight-lips and cold demeanour were related to more practical matters than that. I'd seen off at least a half-bottle of scotch, and we had that long drive tomorrow. Remember? Well, no I hadn't. My anger had seen to that.

So by next morning we were in a non-speaking to each other situation.

I tried to hide the hang-over, but when you've been living with someone for ten years it's a little difficult to hide the signs. The two fizzing Solpadeine in the glass were the final insult. I stressed that I would take care of the second-half of the journey, but this didn't seem to hold water. Did I mention that she'd lost a baby, was still getting over it physically and psychologically, that she was feeling very tired all the time? No? Well, just sign out the Bastard Club form and I would willingly have signed.

Tight-lipped farewells to the In-laws.

And a wife's face that says she's just waiting for the open road before she lets rip.

Well, she let rip. But I probably don't have to draw you a map.

I let it go, knowing that I'd been a little selfish. But Gill always did have a habit of taking things a little too far. My temper snapped, and seconds later it had developed into the knock-down, drag-out verbal fight that I'd been trying to avoid.

BOROUGHBRIDGE, said the motorway sign. HALF MILE.

"That's the last time we spend any time together down here at Easter," said Gill.

"Fine by me. I've got more important things I could be doing."

"Let's not stop at Easter. How about spending our Christmases and Bank Holidays apart, too?"

"Great. I might be able to enjoy myself for a change."

"Maybe we should make it more permanent? Why stop at holidays? Let's just . . ."

". . . spend all of our time apart? That suits me fine."

There was a man up ahead, standing beside the barrier on the central reservation. Just a shadow, looking as if he was waiting for a break in the traffic so that he could make a dangerous run across the two lanes to the other side.

"God, you can be such a bastard!"

"You're forgetting an important point, Gill. It was people like that Personnel bastard who got me the sack. You should be sticking up for me, not . . ."

"So what makes you think we need *your* money? Are you trying to say that what I earn isn't enough to . . ."

"For Christ's sake, Gill!"

The shadow stepped out from the roadway barrier, directly in front of us.

Gill had turned to look at me, her face a mask of anger.

"For Christ's *sake!*" I yelled, and it must have seemed to her then that I'd lost my mind when I suddenly lunged for the steering wheel. She yelled in anger and shock, swatted at me but held fast.

And in the next minute, something exploded through the windscreen.

Gill's instincts were superb. Despite the fact that the car was suddenly filled with an exploding, hissing shrapnel of fine glass, she didn't lose control. She braked firmly, hanging onto the wheel while I threw my hands instinctively up to protect my face. The car slewed and hit the barrier, and I could feel the front of the car on Gill's side crumple. The impact was horrifying and shocking. In that split-second I expected the body of that idiot to come hurtling through into our laps, smashing us back against our seats. But nothing came through the windscreen as the car slewed to a halt on the hard-shoulder, right next to the metal barrier, and with its nose pointed out into the nearside lane.

There were fine tracings of red-spiderweb blood all over my hands as I reached instinctively for Gill. Her hands were clenched tight to the wheel, her head was down and her long dark hair full of fine glass shards. I could see that her hands were also flayed by the glass and with a sickening roll in the stomach I thought she might be blinded.

"God, Gill! Are you alright?"

I pulled up her face with both hands so that she was staring directly ahead through the shattered windscreen. Her eyes were wide and glassy, she was breathing heavily. Obviously in shock, and hanging onto that wheel as if she was hanging onto her self-control.

"Are you alright?"

She nodded, a slight gesture which seemed to take great effort.

Twisting in my seat, making the imploded glass all around me crackle and grind, I looked back.

We hadn't hit the stupid bastard.

He was still standing, about thirty or forty feet behind us on the hard-shoulder. Standing there, unconcerned, watching us.

I kicked open the passenger door and climbed out. Slamming it, I leaned on the roof to get my breath and then looked back at him. He was a big man, but in the dusk it was impossible to see any real details other than he seemed to be shabbily dressed and unsteady on his feet. The sleeves of his jacket seemed torn, his hair awry. A tramp, perhaps. He was just standing there, with his hands hanging limply at his sides, staring in our direction.

"You *stupid* bastard!" I yelled back at him when my breath returned. "You could have killed my wife."

The man said nothing. He just stood and looked. His head was slightly down, as if he was looking at us from under his brows. There was something strange about his face, but I couldn't make it out.

"You stupid *fuck!*"

Then I saw that he was holding something in one hand, something long and curved in a half-moon shape. I squinted, rubbing my shredded hands over my face and seeing that there was also blood on the palms, too. The sight of more blood enraged me. Fists bunched at my side, I began striding back along the hard shoulder towards the silently waiting figure.

After ten or fifteen feet, I stopped.

There *was* something wrong with this character's face. The eyes were too dark, too large. The mouth was fixed in a permanent grin. I couldn't see a nose.

And then I realised what it was.

The man was wearing a mask.

A stupid, scarecrow mask.

It was made from sacking of some sort, tied around the neck with string. From where I was standing, I couldn't tell whether he'd drawn big, round black eyes with peep holes in the centre, or whether they were simply ragged holes in the sacking. I could see no eyes in there, only darkness. Ragged stitchwork from ear to ear gave the mask its permanent grin. Bunches of straw hair poked from under the brim of the ragged fishing hat which had been jammed down hard on the head. That same straw was also poking out between the buttons of the ragged jacket. More string served as a belt holding up equally ragged trousers. The sole had come away from the upper on each boot.

As I stood frozen, taking in this ridiculous sight and perhaps looking just as stupid, the figure raised the long curved thing in its hand.

It was a hand scythe.

This one was black and rusted, but when the scarecrow raised it before its mask-face it seemed as if the edge of that blade had been honed and sharpened. Then I realised that it was this that had smashed our car windscreen. The bastard had waited for us to pass, had stepped out and slammed the damned thing across the glass like an axe.

And then the man began to stride towards me.

There was nothing hurried in his approach. It was a steady methodical pace, holding that scythe casually down at his side. His idiot, grinning scarecrow's face was fixed on me as he moved. There was no doubt in my mind as he came on.

He meant to kill me.

He meant to knock me down and pin me to the ground with one foot, while he raised that hook, and brought it straight down through the top of my skull. Then he would kick me to one side, walk up to the car and drag Gill out of the driving seat . . .

I turned and ran back to the car. As I wrenched open the passenger door, I glanced back to see that the figure hadn't hurried his pace to catch up. He was coming at the same remorseless pace; a brisk, but unhurried walk. Inside the car, Gill was still hunched in the driving seat, clutching the wheel.

"Drive, Gill!" I yelled. "For God's sake, *drive!*"

"What . . . ?"

I tried to shove her out of the driving seat then, away from the wheel and into the passenger seat. Still in shock, she couldn't understand what the hell was wrong with me. She clung tight to that wheel with one hand and started clawing at my face with the other. I looked back as we struggled. In seconds, that maniac would reach the car. He was already hefting that hook in his hand, ready to use it.

"Look!" I practically screamed in Gill's face, and dragged her head around to see.

At the same moment, the rear windscreen imploded with shocking impact.

Everything happened so fast after that, I can't really put it together in my head. I suppose that the scarecrow-man had shattered the glass with the hand scythe. There was a blurred jumble of movement in the ragged gap through the rear windscreen. And I suppose that Gill must have realised what was happening then, because the next thing I heard was the engine roaring into life.

"*Go!*" someone yelled, and I suppose it must have been me. Because the next thing I remember after that was me sitting in the back of the car, swatting powdered glass off the seat. Then I heard another impact, and looked up to see that the scarecrow was scrabbling on the boot of the car. The scythe was embedded in the metalwork, and the scarecrow was clinging on tight to it. I thrust out through the broken window and tore at the man's ragged gloves, pounding with my fists. The car bounced and jolted, something seemed to screech under the chassis, and I prayed to God that it was the madman's legs being crushed. We were moving again, but Gill was yelling and cursing, slamming her hands on the wheel. The engine sounded tortured; the car was juddering and shaking, as if Gill was missing the clutch bite-point and "donkeying" all the time.

The scythe came free from its ragged hole and the madman fell back from the boot. There was a scraping, rending sound as the hook screeched over the bodywork. To my horror, I saw that he had managed to snag the damned thing in the fender and now we were pulling him along the hard-shoulder as he clung to its handle. With his free hand, he clawed at the fender; trying to get a proper grip and pull himself upright again. His legs thrashed and raised dust clouds as we moved. Somehow, I couldn't move as I watched him being dragged along behind us. The car juddered again and I almost fell between the seats. Lunging up, I seemed to get a grip on myself.

The madman had lost his hold on the fender. We were pulling away from where he lay. I saw one arm flop through the air as he tried to turn over. Perhaps he was badly hurt? Good.

We were still on the hard shoulder, near to the barrier, as traffic flashed past us. But something had happened to the car when it hit that roadside barrier. Something had torn beneath the chassis, and Gill was yanking hard at the gear lever.

"It's stuck!" she shouted, nearly hysterically. "I can't get it out of first gear."

"Let me try . . ." I tried to climb over into the passenger seat, but in that moment I caught sight of what was happening in the rear view mirror. The scarecrow was rising to his knees, perhaps fifty feet behind us now. I lost sight of him in the bouncing mirror, twisted around to look out of the window again, just in time to see him stand. There was something slow and measured in that movement, as if he hadn't been hurt at all. He had retrieved the scythe.

And he was coming after us again.

Not running, just the same methodical stride. As if he had all the time in the world to catch up with us.

I faced front again. Gill was still struggling with the gears, and the speedometer was wavering at five miles an hour. As we juddered along on the hard shoulder, it seemed as if we were travelling at exactly the same pace as the man behind us.

"Hit the clutch!" I yelled, lunging forward again as Gill depressed the pedal. I yanked at the gearstick, trying to drag it back into second gear. The best I could do was get it into the neutral position, and that meant we were coasting to a halt. Behind us, the man started to gain. Gill could see him now, slapped my hand away and shoved the gearstick into first again.

"Who *is* he?" she sobbed. "What does he want?"

I thought about jumping out of the car and taking over from Gill in the driving seat. But by the time we did that, the madman would be on us again, and anyway, Gill was a damn sight better driver than me. There seemed only one thing we could do.

"Steer out onto the motorway," I hissed.

"We're travelling too slowly. There's too much traffic. We'll be hit."

"Maybe he'll get hit first."

"Oh *Christ* . . ."

Gill yanked hard on the wheel and the car slewed out across the motorway.

A traffic horn screamed at us and a car passed so close that we heard the screech of its tyres and felt the blast of air through the shattered windscreen as it swerved to avoid us. I looked at the speedo again. We were still crawling.

I moved back to the rear window.

The radiator grille of a lorry filled my line of vision. The damned thing was less than six feet from us, just about to ram into our rear; crushing the boot right through the car. I yelled something, I don't know what; convinced that the lorry was going to smash into us, ram us both up into the engine block in a mangled, bloody mess. Perhaps it was the shock of my yell, but Gill suddenly yanked hard at the steering wheel again and we slewed to the left. I could feel the car rocking on its suspension as the lorry passed within inches, the blaring of its horn ringing in our ears. But we weren't out of danger yet. I reared towards the dash as another car swerved from behind us, around to the right, tyres screeching.

"You were travelling too *fast*, you bastard!" I yelled after it. "Too bloody *fast!*"

More horns were blaring and when I flashed a glance back at Gill I could see that she was hunched forward over the wheel. Her face was too white, like a dead person. There were beaded droplets of sweat on her forehead. In the next moment, she had swung the wheel hard over to the left again. Off balance, I fell across my seat, my head bouncing from her shoulder. I clawed at the seat rest, trying to sit up straight again. Suddenly, Gill began clawing at me with one hand. I realise now that my attempts to sit were hampering her ability to pull the wheel hard over. To my shame, I began clawing back at her; not under- standing and in a total funk. She yelled that I was a stupid bastard. I yelled that she was a mad bitch. And then I was up in my seat again as Gill began spinning the wheel furiously back, hand over hand. Glancing out of the window, I could see that she had taken us right across the motorway and was taking a slip-road. The sign said: BOROUGHBRIDGE.

She had done it. She had taken us right across those multiple lanes without hitting another vehicle. We were still crawling along, but at least we had got away from the madman behind us. I knew then that everything was okay. When we found the first emergency telephone, we would stop and ring for the police.

"Okay," I breathed. "It's okay . . . you've done it, Gill . . . we're okay now."

Until I turned in my seat and looked back to see that everything was far from okay.

The man in the fancy-dress costume was walking across the highway towards us, perhaps fifty yards back. His steps were measured, still as if he had all the time in the world, the scythe hanging from one hand. Grinning face fixed on us. Even as I looked, and felt the sickening nausea of fear again, a car swerved around him, tyres screeching. Its passage made his ragged clothes whip and ruffle. Straw flew from his shoulders and his ragged trousers. By rights, it should have rammed right into him, throwing him up and over its roof. But just as luck had been with us, crossing that busy motorway, it was also with him.

Our car began its ascent of the sliproad, engine coughing and straining. Gill fumbled with the gears, trying without success to wrench them into second. The engine began to race and complain.

"He's there . . ." I began.

"I *know* he's fucking *there!*" yelled Gill, eyes still fixed ahead. "But we *can't go any faster!*"

The speedo was wobbling around fifteen miles an hour; even now as we ascended the sliproad, the gradual slope was having an affect on our progress. The needle began to drop . . . to fourteen . . . to thirteen.

When I looked back, I could see that nevertheless, we were putting a little distance between us and the madman. When a car flashed past, between the scarecrow and the entrance to the sliproad, I could see that fate wasn't completely on his side, after all. He wasn't invulnerable. He had waited while the car had crossed his path, and that slight wait had given us a little time. Not to mention a certain relief. The man might be mad, but he was human and not some supernatural creature out of a bad horror movie. As the car passed, he came on, the scythe swinging in his hand as he moved.

It came to me then.

There was a tool kit in the boot. If Gill pulled over, I could jump out and yank the boot open, grab a screwdriver or something. Threaten him, scare him away. Show him that I meant business.

"Pull over," I said.

"Are you joking, or what?" asked Gill.

When I looked at her again, something happened to me. It had to do with everything that had occurred over the last forty-eight hours. It had to do with the stupid fights, with my stupid behaviour. But more than anything, it had to do with the expression on Gill's face. This was the woman I loved. She was, quite literally, in shock. And I'd just lashed out at her when she'd been acting on my instruction and taken us across the motorway, away from the maniac and – against all the odds – avoided colliding with another vehicle. I'd let her down badly. It was time to sort this thing out.

"Pull over!" I snapped again.

"He's still coming," she said. Her voice was too calm. Too matter of fact.

Then I realised. At this speed, I could open the door and just hop out.

Angrily, that's what I did.

I slammed the door hard as I turned to face our pursuer; just the way that people do when there's been a minor traffic "shunt" and both parties try to faze out the other by a show of aggression, using body language to establish guilt before any heated conversation begins. Inside the car, I heard Gill give a startled cry as the car shuddered to a halt.

The scarecrow was still approaching up the ramp.

I stood for a moment, praying that he might at least pause in his stride.

He didn't.

I lunged at the boot, slamming my hand on it and pointing hard at him; as if some zig-zag lightning bolt of pure anger would *zap* out of my finger and fry him on the spot.

"You're fucking *mad* and I'm fucking telling *you!* You want some aggro, *eh?* You want some fucking *aggro?* I'll show *you* what fucking *aggro* is all *about!*" If the "fuck" word could kill, he should be dead already.

But he was still coming.

I swept the remaining frosting of broken glass from the boot and snapped it open. There was a tyre-wrench in there. I leaned in for it, without taking my eyes off the clown, and my hand bumped against the suitcase. In that moment, I knew that the wrench must be at the bottom of the boot and that all our weekend luggage was on top of it. I whirled around, clawing at the suitcase, trying to yank it aside. But I'd packed that boot as tight as it's possible to get. The only way I was going to get that wrench was by yanking everything out of there onto the tarmac.

And the scarecrow was only fifty feet from us.

I looked back to see that he was smacking the scythe in the palm of one hand, eager to use it.

"*Shit!*" I slammed the boot again and hurried back around the car.

The scarecrow remained implacable. From this distance, I could see how tall he was. Perhaps six-feet-seven. Broad-shouldered. Completely uncaring of my show of bravado. And, Good Christ, I could hear him now.

He was *giggling*.

It was a forced, manic sound. Without a trace of humour. It was an insane sound of anticipation. He was looking forward to what he was going to do when he reached us. As I dragged open the passenger door, I had no illusions then. If I engaged in a hand-to-hand physical confrontation with this lunatic, he would kill me. There was no doubt about it. Not only that, but he would tear me limb from limb, before he turned his attentions to Gill. I stooped to yell at her, but she was already yanking at the gear-stick and the car was moving again; the engine making grinding, gasping sounds.

The scarecrow's pace remained unaltered.

There was a car coming up the sliproad behind him.

Some mad and overwhelming darkness inside myself made me *will* that car to swerve as it came up behind the scarecrow. I wanted to see it ram him up on the hood and toss him over the fence into the high grass. But then I knew what I had to do. I skipped around the front of our own car and into the road as the car swerved around the scarecrow and came up the sliproad towards us. I ran in front of it, waving my arms, flagging it down. I can still hardly believe what happened next.

The driver – male, female, it was impossible to tell – jammed their hand on the horn as the car roared straight at me. I just managed to get out of the way, felt the front fender snag and tear my trouser leg as it passed. I whirled in the middle of the road, unbelieving. The car vanished over the rise and was gone from sight. I turned back.

The scarecrow was still coming.

"For Christ's sake!" snapped Gill. "Get in."

I stumbled back into the car and we began our juddering crawl again. I wasn't in a sane world anymore. This couldn't possibly be happening to us. Where was everyone? Why wouldn't anyone help as we crawled on and on with that madman behind us? I turned to say something to Gill, studied her marble-white face, eyes staring dead ahead; but I couldn't find a thing to say. The scarecrow behind us was still coming at his even stride. If he wanted to, he could move faster, and then he'd overtake us. But he seemed content to match his speed with our own. At the moment, he was keeping an even distance between us. If our car failed or slowed, he would catch up. It was as simple as that.

We reached the rise. Down below, we could see that the road led deep into countryside. I'd lost all track of where the hell Boroughbridge might be, if it had ever existed at all. On either side of the road were fields of bright yellow wheat.

At last, God seemed to have remembered we were here and wasn't so pissed off with us, after all. As our car crested the ridge and began to move down towards the fields, it began to pick up speed.

"Oh thank God . . ." Gill began to weep then. The car's gearbox was still straining and grinding, but we *were* gathering speed. Leaning back over the seat I watched as the lip of the hill receded behind us. When the scarecrow suddenly reappeared on the top of the rise, silhouetted against the skyline, he must surely see that we were picking up speed. But he didn't suddenly alter his pace, didn't begin to run down after us. He kept at his even march, right in the middle of the road, straight down in our direction. Following the Fucking Yellow Brick Road. Soon, we'd leave him far behind.

I swung around to the front again, to see that we were doing thirty, the engine straining and gasping. I gritted my teeth, praying that it wouldn't cut out altogether. But it was still keeping us moving. When I looked back again, the silhouette of our attacker was a small blur. Another vehicle was cresting the rise behind him. I heard its own horn blare at the strange figure in the middle of the road, watched the small truck swerve around him. It seemed to me that someone was leaning out of the truck window, and the driver was giving the idiot a piece of his mind. The vehicle came on towards us, picking up speed. Should I chance our luck again? Slow the car, jump out and try to flag down help?

"No you're not," said Gill, without taking her eyes from the road. She had been reading my mind. "I'm not slowing this car down again. I'm keeping my foot down and we're getting out of here . . ."

When I looked at the speedo, I felt as if I was going to throw up; there-and-then.

". . . and we're never, *ever* coming back to this fucking hellhole of a place," continued Gill, her voice cracking and tears streaming down her face, "As long as I ever live. Do you hear me, Paul? Not never, *ever!*"

"I've got to stop that truck before it passes us."

"You're not listening! I'm not stopping. Not for anything!"

"We *are* stopping, Gill! Look at the speedo! We got extra speed on the incline, that's all. Now we're slowing down on the straight. Look."

Gill shook her head, refusing to look.

The needle had fallen from thirty to twenty and was still descending.

"Will you just *look!*"

"*No!*"

I lunged around. The truck was less than two hundred yards behind us, and soon to overtake.

"Gill, look! It's a *tow-truck!* From a breakdown service. It's stencilled on the side. Look!"

"*No!*"

With the needle wavering at ten miles an hour, I did what I had to do. I kicked open the passenger door. Gill refused to take her eyes from the road, but clawed at my hair with one hand, screaming and trying to drag me back into the car. I batted her off and hopped out into the middle of the sun-baked dirt road.

A cloud of dust enveloped me. I just made it in time. Five seconds later, and the tow truck would have overtaken us and been gone. But now the driver could see my intent. He slowed, and then as I walked back towards him, the truck trundled on up behind us, matching an even time at ten miles an hour as I hopped up onto the standing-board.

The man inside had a big grin. He was about sixty, maybe even ready for retirement. Something about my action seemed to amuse him.

"Don't tell me," he said, without me having to make any opening conversation. "You're in trouble?"

Something about his manner, his friendliness, made that fear begin to melt inside me. Now it seemed that the world wasn't such a hostile and alien place as I thought it had suddenly become. I was grinning now too, like a great big kid.

"How could you tell?"

"My line of business. Been doing this for thirty-five years. People always come to me. I never go looking for them. How can I help you?"

Suddenly, looking back at the scarecrow, now perhaps two or three hundred yards away and still coming down that dirt road towards us, I didn't know what to say.

"Well . . . the car. We had a bash and . . . and it's stuck in first gear. Can't get it any faster than five, six miles an hour. Got some speed on the incline there, but it won't last."

"Okay," said the old man with the lined face and the rolled up sleeves. "Just pull her over and I'll take a look."

If my smile faltered, the old man either didn't notice or failed to make anything of it. I hopped down from the board and, realising that I was trying to move too nonchalantly, moved quickly back to the car. Running around the front, I leaned on the window-edge, jogging alongside where Gill was still hunched over the driving wheel, still staring ahead with glassy eyes.

"We're in luck. It *is* a tow-truck. He says he'll help us."

Gill said nothing. The car trundled along at seven miles an hour.

"Gill, I said he'll help us."

Somewhere, a crow squawked, as it to remind us that the scarecrow was still there and was still coming.

"Come on, stop the car."

Gill wiped tears from her eyes, and returned her white-knuckled, two handed grip on the steering wheel.

"Stop the car!"

This time, I reached in and tried to take the keys.

Gill clawed at me, her fingernails raking my forehead. I recoiled in shock.

"I . . . am . . . not . . . stopping the car. Not for you. Not for anybody. He's still coming. If we stop, he'll come. And he'll kill us."

I thought about making another grab, then saw that the old man was leaning out of his window behind us, watching. He wasn't smiling that big smile anymore. I made a helpless, "everything's fine" gesture and stood back to let our car pass and the tow truck catch up. Then I jumped up on the standing-board again as we trundled along. Behind us, I could see that the scarecrow had gained on us. The silhouette was bigger than before. Had he suddenly decided to change the rules of the game and put on a burst of speed to overtake us? The possibility made me break out into another sweat. The old man seemed to see the change in me.

"Got a problem?" His voice was much warier this time.

"Well, my wife. She . . . she won't . . . that is, she won't stop the car."

"Why not?"

"She's frightened."

"Of you?"

"Me? God, no!" I wiped a hand across my forehead, thinking I was wiping away sweat, only to see that it was covered in blood. Gill's nails had gouged me. The old man was only too aware of that blood.

"Well if she won't stop the car I can't inspect it, can I ? What's she want me to do? Run alongside with the hood opened?"

"No, of course not. It's just that . . ."

"So what's she frightened of?"

"Look, there's a man. Can you see him? Back there, behind us?"

The old man leaned forward reluctantly, now suddenly wary of taking his eyes off me, and adjusted his rear view mirror so that he could see the ragged figure approaching fast from behind.

"Yeah, what about him?"

"He . . ." My throat was full of dust then. My heart was beating too fast. "He's trying to kill us."

"To *kill* you?"

"That's right. That's why the car's damaged. And he just keeps coming and won't stop and . . ." I was going to lose it, I knew. I was babbling. The old man's eyes had clouded; the sparkle and the welcoming smile were gone.

In a flat and measured voice, he said: "I don't want any trouble, mister."

"Trouble? No, no. Look, we need your help. If you just . . . well, just stop the truck here. And stand in the road with me. Maybe when he sees that there're two of us, he'll back off. Maybe we can scare him away. Then you can give us a tow. We'll pay. Double your usual rate. How's that sound?"

"Look, I just wanted to help out. I could see your car was in trouble from way off. Steam coming out from under the hood. Oil all the way back down the road. But I don't want to get involved in no domestic dispute."

"*Domestic* dispute?"

"Anything that's happening between you and the lady in the car and the fella behind has nothing to do with me. So why don't you hop down and sort your differences out like civilised people?"

"Please, you've got it all wrong. It's not like that, at all. Look, have you got a portable telephone?"

"Get off my truck."

"Please, the man's *mad!* He's going to kill us. At least telephone for the police, tell them what's happening here . . ."

"I said, get *off!*"

The flat of the old man's calloused hand came down heavy where I was gripping the window-edge, breaking my grip. In the next moment, he lunged sideways and jabbed a skinny elbow into my chest. The pain was sharp, knocking the breath out of my lungs; the impact hurling me from the standing board and into the road. I lay there, engulfed in a cloud of choking dust, coughing my guts out and unable to see anything. All I could hear was the sound of the truck overtaking our car as it roared on ahead down the country road, leaving us far behind. When I tried to rise, pain stabbed in my hip where I had fallen. I staggered and flailed, yelling obscenities after the old man.

The dust cloud swirled and cleared.

The tow-truck was gone from sight.

Behind me, the scarecrow was alarmingly close; now perhaps only a hundred yards away and still coming with that measured tread. Despite my fears, he didn't seem to have put on that burst of speed. Relentless, he came on.

Gill hadn't stopped for me. The car had moved on ahead, itself about fifty yards further down the road. Perhaps she hadn't seen what had happened between the old man and myself, didn't realise my plight. So it was hardly fair of me to react the way that I did. But I reacted anyway. I screamed at her, just as I'd screamed at the departing old man. I screeched my rage and blundered after the car, the pain in my hip stabbing like fire. Even with my staggering gait, it didn't take long to catch up with the car, making the evil mockery of the scarecrow's relentless approach all the more horrifying. If he just put on that extra spurt of speed, he could catch up with us whenever he liked. I threw open the back door of the car and all but fell inside. I tried to yell my rage, but the dust and the exhaustion and the pain all took their toll on my throat and lungs. When I stopped hacking and spitting, I tried to keep my voice calm but it came out icy cold.

"You didn't stop, Gill. You didn't stop the car for me. You were going to leave me there."

Gill was a white-faced automaton behind the wheel. She neither looked at me or acknowledged my presence. In her shock I had no way now of knowing whether she could even hear what I was saying. I wiped more blood from my forehead, and struggled to contain the crazy feeling that I knew was an over-reaction to outright fear.

There was someone up ahead on our side of the road, walking away from us. He was a young man, his body stooped as if he had been walking a long while; with some kind of holdall over his shoulder. He didn't seem to hear us at first; his gaze concentrated downwards, putting one foot in front of the other. I moved towards Gill but before I could say anything, she said:

"Don't!"

"But we should . . ."

"No, Paul. We're not stopping."

I had no energy. Fear and that fall from the tow-truck had robbed me of strength. But as I leaned back, I saw the young man ahead suddenly turn and look at us. Quickly, he dropped his holdall to the ground and fumbled for something inside his jacket. We were close enough to see the hope in his eyes when he pulled out a battered cardboard sign and held it up for us to read: HEADING WEST.

I looked at the back of Gill's head. She never moved as the car drew level and began to pass the young man. The hope in his eyes began to fade as we trundled past. Did he think we were travelling at that speed just to taunt him? I looked back over my shoulder to see that the scarecrow was still closing the gap, still coming. The fact that I was looking back seemed to give the young man some encouragement. Grabbing his holdall, he sprinted after us. I wound down the side window as he drew level.

"Come on, man." His voice was thin and reedy. He jogged steadily at the side of the car as we moved. "Give me a lift. I've been walking for hours."

"That man . . . back there . . ."

The young man looked, but didn't see anything worth following up in conversation.

"I'm heading for Slaly, but if you're going anywhere West that's good enough for me. How about it?"

"That man . . . he's mad. Do you hear me? He tried to kill us."

Now, it seemed that he was seeing all the evidence that there was something wrong about this situation. The quiet woman with the white face and the staring eyes. The broken windows and the sugar-frosted glass all over the seats. The dents and scratches on the car as it lurched and trembled along the road, engine rumbling. And me, lying in the back as if I'd been beaten up and thrown in there, blood all over my forehead.

"You and me. If we square up to him, we can frighten him off. I'll pay you. Anything you want. And then we'll drive you where you want to go."

"I don't think so," said the young man. He stopped and let us pass him by. I struggled to the window and leaned out to look back at him. He waved his hand in a "Not for me" gesture.

"Yeah?" I shouted. "Well, thanks for fucking nothing. But I'm not joking. That guy back there is a *psycho*. So before he catches up, I'd head off over those fields or something. Keep out of his way. When he gets to you, you're in big trouble."

The young man was looking away, hands on hips as if deciding on a new direction.

"I'm telling you, you stupid bastard! Get out of here before he catches up!"

I fell back into the car, needing a drink more than I've ever done in my life. Up in front, Gill might have been a shop mannequin, propped in the driving seat. She was utterly alien to me now, hardly human at all.

"You've killed him," I said at last. Perhaps my voice was too low to be heard. "You know that, don't you? The guy back there is as good as dead."

When I turned to look back again, I could see that the young man was still walking in our direction. The scarecrow was close behind him. But still in the middle of the road. Perhaps something in the tone of my voice had registered with him, because he kept looking over his shoulder as he moved and the scarecrow got closer and closer. I couldn't take my eyes away from the rear window. There was a horrifying sense of inevitability. When it seemed that the scarecrow was almost level with him, I saw the young man pause. He seemed to speak to the scarecrow. Then he stopped, just staring. Perhaps he had seen the scarecrow's face properly for the first time.

I gritted my teeth.

The young man shrank back on the grass verge.

I could see it all in my mind's eye. The sudden lunge of the scarecrow, wielding that scythe high above his head. The young man would shriek, hold up his hands to ward off the blow. But then the scarecrow would knock him on his back, grab him by the throat and bring the scythe down into his chest. The young man would writhe and thrash and twist as the scarecrow ripped that scythe down, gutting him. Then it would begin ripping his insides out while he was still alive, the man's arms and legs twitching feebly, and then he would lie still forever as the scarecrow scattered what it found into the surrounding fields.

Except that it wasn't happening like that at all.

The man was shrinking back on the verge, but the scarecrow was still walking.

And now the scarecrow had walked straight past the young man without so much as a sideways glance. He was coming on, after *us*, at the same relentless pace. Now, the young man was hurrying back in the opposite direction; stumbling and fumbling at first, as if he didn't want to take his eyes off this figure in case it suddenly changed its mind and came lunging back at him. The man began to run, then was heading full pelt back in the opposite direction.

The scarecrow was coming on.

It only wanted *us*.

"You bastard!" I yelled through the shattered windscreen. "You fucking, fucking *bastard!* What was the matter with *him*, then? What do you want from us? What the hell do you *want* us for?" I think I began to weep then. Maybe I just went over the edge and became insane. But I seemed to lose some time. And I only came out of it when I realised that I could still hear weeping, and realised that it wasn't mine. When my vision focused, it was on the back of Gill's head again. She was sobbing. I could see the rise and fall of her shoulders. Looking back through the rear window, I could see that the man had continued to gain on us. He was less than fifty yards behind, and the engine was making a different sound. I pulled myself forward, and it was as if the tow-truck driver was whispering in my ear at the same time that my gaze fell on the petrol gauge.

I could see your car was in trouble. Oil all the way back down the road.

The gauge was at "empty". We'd been leaking petrol all the way back to the motorway. Soon we'd be empty and the car would roll to a stop.

Fear and rage again. Both erupting inside to overcome the inertia and engulfing me in an insane, animal outburst. I kicked open the door, snarling. My hip hurt like hell as I staggered into the middle of the road. I tried to find something else to yell back at the approaching figure. Something that could encompass all that rage and fear. But even though I raised my fists to the sky and shook like I was having a fit, I couldn't find any way of letting it out. I collapsed to my knees, shuddering and growling like an animal.

And then, crystal clear, something came to me.

I don't know how or where. It was as if the damned idea was planted by someone else, it felt so utterly *outside*. Maybe even in that moment of pure animal hate, a cold reasoning part of me was still able to reach inside and come up with a plan. Had I had time to think about it, I would have found dozens of reasons not to do what I did. But instead, I acted. I clambered to my feet again. The

scarecrow was thirty yards away; close enough for me to see that
idiot, grinning face and the black-hollowed eyes. I hobbled after
the car, braced my hands on the metalwork as I felt my way along
it to the driver's door. I knew what would happen if I spoke to
Gill, knew what she would do if I tried to stop her.

So instead, I pulled open the door, lunged in and yanked both
her hands off the steering wheel. She screamed. High-pitched and
completely out of control. The violent act had broken her out of
that rigid stance. She began to scream and twist and thrash like a
wild animal as I dragged her bodily out of the car, hanging onto
her wrists. When she hit the rough road, she tried to get purchase,
tried to kick at me. She was yelling mindless obscenities when I
threw her at the verge. She fell badly and cried out. Twisting
around, she saw the scarecrow – and could no longer move. In
that split-second as I dived into the car, already slewing towards
the verge and a dead-stop, I didn't recognise her face. The eyes
belonged to someone else. They were made of glass.

I jammed on the brakes, felt so weak that I was afraid I
couldn't do what I was going to do. My hand trembled on the
gearstick.

Yelling, I rammed the gear into reverse. It went in smooth. I
revved up the engine and knew that if it coughed and died from
lack of petrol I'd go quite mad.

Then I let up the clutch, and this time the car shot backwards.
Maybe it was twenty, thirty miles an hour. Not so fast maybe, but
three or four times faster than we'd been travelling on this Crawl.
And it felt like the vehicle was moving like a fucking bullet. I was
still yelling as I leaned back over the seat, twisting with the wheel
to get my bearings right – and the scarecrow began to loom large
in my sight-line, right smack centre in the rear window. Dust and
gravel spurted and hissed around me.

The scarecrow just came on.

Filling the ragged frame of that rear window.

I just kept yelling and yelling as the scarecrow vanished in the
dust cloud the car was making. It gushed into the car, making me
choke and gag.

And then there was a heavy *crunching* thud, jarring the frame
of the car. It snapped me back and then sharp-forward in the seat.
The engine coughed and died. The car slewed to a stop.

I had hit the bastard – and I had hit him hard.

The car was filled with dust. I couldn't see a thing. I threw the door open and leapt out, feeling that stab of pain in my hip but not giving one flying fart about it. I dodged and weaved in the cloud, crouching and peering to see where he had been thrown. I wanted to see blood in that dry dust. I wanted to see brains and shit. I wanted to see that he'd coughed up part of his intestine on impact and that he was lying there in utter agony. I wanted to see his legs crushed; his head split apart, his scythe shattered into hundreds of little bits.

The dust cloud settled.

I warily walked around the side of the car, looking for the first sign of a boot or an outstretched hand. I strained hard to listen in the silence for any kind of sound. I wanted to hear him moaning or weeping with pain.

But there was no sound.

Because there was no one lying behind the car.

I hobbled to the grass verge. The car was still in the centre of the road, so there was a chance that it had thrown him clear into one of the fields at either side. But there was no one in the grass at the left side, and when I skipped across the road to the other field, there was no sign of a body there either. I knew I had hit that bastard with killing force. But at that speed, surely he couldn't have been thrown the two hundred feet or so into the stalks of wheat out there. It couldn't be possible, unless . . . unless . . .

Unless he wasn't very heavy.

Unless he hardly weighed anything at all.

Like, maybe, he weighed no more than your average scarecrow.

The thought was more than unnerving. I cursed myself aloud. He'd had real hands, hadn't he? I'd seen them up close. But then a little voice inside was asking me: *Are you sure you saw them properly? Wasn't he wearing gloves?*

On a sudden impulse, I ducked down and looked under the car. There was nothing there.

When I straightened up, I could see that Gill was staggering down the road towards me. She looked drunk as she weaved her way towards the car. I leaned against the dented framework, holding my arms wide, imploring.

"I know I hit him," I said. "I *know* I did. I felt the car hit him. He must be dead, Gill. I didn't want to do it, but it was the only way. Wasn't it? I'm sorry for what I did to you, just then. I shouldn't have. But I had to at least try and . . ."

She was almost at the car now; face blank, rubbing her eyes as if she might just have woken up. I felt the temptation to retreat into that safe fantasy. To pretend that none of this had happened. Lost for words, I shook my head.

I was just about to take Gill into my arms when she screamed, right into my face.

I don't know whether the shock made me react instinctively. But suddenly, I was facing in the opposite direction, looking back to the rear of the car.

And the scarecrow was right there.

Standing on the same side of the car, right in front of me, about six feet away. Grinning his stitched and ragged grin. Straw flying around his head. That head was cocked to one side again, in that half-bemused expression that was at the same time so horribly malevolent. Something moved in one of the ragged eye sockets of his "mask", but I don't think it was the winking of an eye. I think it was something alive in there; something that was using the warm straw for a nest.

The scythe jerked up alongside my face.

I felt no pain. But I heard the *crack!* when the handle connected with my jaw.

In the next moment, I was pinned back against the car. Instinctively, I'd seized the scarecrow's wrist as it bent me backwards. My shoulders and head were on the roof, my feet kicking in space as I tried to keep that scythe out of my face. He was incredibly strong, and I tried to scream when I saw that scythe turn in and down towards my right eye. But no sound would come, and I couldn't move. Somewhere behind, I could hear Gill screaming. Then I saw her behind the scarecrow, tearing at its jacket and yanking handfuls of straw away.

I slid, the impetus yanking me from the thing's grip as I fell to the road. Stunned, dazed, I saw one of the car wheels looming large; then turned awkwardly on one elbow as the scarecrow stepped into vision again. The sun was behind him, making him into a gigantic silhouette as he lifted the scythe just the way I'd envisaged he'd do it for the hitch-hiker. This wasn't real anymore. I couldn't react. I couldn't move. It wasn't happening. Somewhere, a long way away, Gill was screaming over and over again; as if someone was bearing her away across the fields.

Then the car horn rang, loud and shocking.

It snapped me out of that inertia, and everything was real again.

Somehow, the scarecrow's arm was stayed.

It just stood there, a black shape against the sun, the weapon raised high.

And then the horn rang again. This time, a gruff man's voice demanded: "You put that down, *now!*"

Someone had grabbed my arm and was tugging hard. I grabbed back, and allowed myself to be pulled out of the way and around to the rear of the car. Everything focused again, out of the sun's brilliance.

Gill had pulled me to my feet, and clung tight to me as we both leaned against the battered bodywork. Neither of us seemed able to breathe now.

A car had pulled up on the other side of the road. Only fifteen or twenty feet separating the vehicles. A man was climbing out, maybe in his forties. Thick, curly grey hair. Good looking. Checked shirt and short sleeves. Perhaps he was a farmer. He looked as if he could handle himself. His attention remained fixed on what stood by the side of our own car as he slammed the door with careful force.

"I don't know what's happening here. But I know you're going to drop that."

The scarecrow had its back to us now. Its head was lowered, the scythe still raised; as if I was still lying down there on the ground, about to be impaled.

"You alright, back there?" asked the farmer.

All we could do was nod.

"Drop the scythe, or whatever it is," continued the farmer slowly. "And everything will be okay. Okay?" He moved towards our car, one hand held out gentle and soothing, the other balled into a fist just out of sight behind his back. "And you take off the fright mask, alright? Then we'll calm down and sort everything out."

The scarecrow looked up at him as he approached.

The man halted.

"Take it . . ." he began.

The scarecrow turned around to face him.

". . . easy," finished the farmer. Suddenly, his expression didn't seem as confident as it had before. He strained forward, as if studying the "mask".

The scarecrow stepped towards him.

"Oh Christ Jesus," he said, and now he didn't sound at all like the commanding presence he'd been a moment before. He backed off to his own car, groping for the door handle without wanting to turn his back on what stood before him. He looked wildly at us. "Look, mister," the farmer said to me. "If we both rush him. Maybe we can take him. Come on, that's all it needs . . ."

I moved forward, but Gill held me tight and pinned me back against the car.

The scarecrow took another step towards the farmer.

"Come *on!*" implored the farmer, fumbling with the handle.

I tried to say something. But what would happen if I opened my mouth, and the scarecrow should turn away from him and look back at *me* again?

"Please," said the man. "Help . . . help . . . me . . ."

The scarecrow held out the scythe to the farmer, a hideous invitation.

I wasn't going to speak, but Gill put a hand over my mouth anyway.

The man yelped and dodged aside as the scarecrow lunged forward, sweeping the scythe in a wide circle. The tip shrieked across the bodywork of the car, where the farmer had been standing a moment before. Flakes of paint glittered in the air. The man edged to the rear of his car as the scarecrow jammed the scythe down hard onto the roof of the vehicle. With a slow and horrible malice, the scarecrow walked towards him. As it moved, it dragged the screeching scythe over the roof with it.

"Please help me!" shouted the man. "*Please!*"

The scarecrow walked steadily towards him.

We saw the man run around the back of his car.

We saw him look up and down the road, trying to decide which direction. He held both arms wide to us in a further appeal.

"For God's sake, please *help!*"

We clutched each other, trembling.

And then the man ran off into the nearest field of wheat. He was soon swallowed by the high stalks. We watched them wave and thrash as he ran.

The scarecrow followed at its steady pace.

It descended into the high stalks, but didn't pause. It did not, thank God, turn to look back at us. It just kept on walking, straight into where the farmer had vanished, cutting a swathe ahead with its scythe. Soon, it too was swallowed up in the wheat. We watched the grass weave and sway where it followed.

Soon, the wheat was still.

There were no more sounds.

After a while, we took his car. The keys were in the dash. I drove us back to the nearest town and we rang for the police. We told the voice on the other end that we'd been attacked, and that our attacker had subsequently gone after the man who had ultimately been our rescuer. We were both given hospital treatment, endured the rigorous police investigations and gave an identical description of the man who had pursued us in his Hallowe'en costume. The police did not like the story. It didn't have, as one of the plain-clothes men had it, the "ring of truth". The fella in the tow-truck was never traced, neither was the hitch-hiker. They could have given the same description, if nothing else.

But the man who stopped to help us – Walter Scharf, a local farmer, well liked – was never seen again. And he's still missing, to this day. Despite every avenue of enquiry, the police still couldn't link us to anything.

That's what they began to think at the end, you see? That Scharf was somehow the attacker (maybe some sort of love-triangle gone wrong), that he was responsible for the damage to the car and/or us. And that we had killed him, and hidden him. I got a lot of hate mail from his wife. But they couldn't link us to anything.

So we got out of it alive, Gill and I.

But there was something neither of us told the police.

Something that neither of us discussed afterwards.

We never talked about the fact that when the first person to stop and volunteer to help, asked us . . . *begged* us . . . to help him: we kept quiet. We said nothing, and did nothing. And because of it, the thing went after him instead of us.

And we were *glad*.

But the darkness of that gladness brought something else into our lives.

Shame. Deep and utter shame. So deep, so profound and so soul-rotting that we couldn't live with ourselves anymore. Gill and I split up. We couldn't talk about it. We live in different cities, and neither of us drives a car anymore.

I know that she'll be having the same nights as me.

The days are bad, but the nights are always worse.

The front door is always the focus of attention, no matter what I'm doing. I'll try to keep myself occupied, try to read, try to listen to music. But all of these things make it much worse. You see, if I really *do* become preoccupied in what I'm doing, then I might not hear it if . . .

If he . . . it . . . comes.

And in the nights, I'll lie awake and listen.

The sound of a car passing on the sidestreet is probably the worst.

I'll hear it coming in my sleep. It wakes me instantly, and I'm never sure whether I've screamed or not, but I lie there praying first that the car will pass quickly and that the engine won't cough and falter. Then, in the first seconds after it's moved on I'll pray again that I won't hear those familiar, staggering footsteps on the gravel coming up the path; that I won't hear that hellish hammering on the front door. I listen for the sounds of that hideous, hoarse breathing.

Sometimes, I'll wonder if I can hear Walter Scharf distantly screaming as he runs through the dark fields of our dreams, the scarecrow close behind. Perhaps those screams aren't his, they're the screams of the next person who crossed its path. They'll fade and die . . . and the quiet of those dreams is sometimes more horrible than the noise.

And to this day, there are two things that terrify me even more than the sounds of a car, or someone walking up the drive, or the noise of that letterbox before I nailed it down.

The first is the sight and the sound of children playing "tag".

The second is a noise that keeps me out of the countryside, away from fields and wooded areas. A simple, everyday sound.

It's the sound of crows, cawing and squawking.

Perhaps frightened from their roosts by something down below and unseen, thrashing through the long grass.

Now, this crow stays home.

And waits.

And listens.

And crawls from one room to the next, making as little noise as possible.

The days are bad, but the nights are always worse . . .

DAVID LANGFORD

Serpent Eggs

DAVID LANGFORD WAS BORN in 1953. He spent some significantly formative years as an Atomic Weapons Research Establishment physicist from 1975 to 1980, and has been freelancing ever since. In 1998 he won his fifteenth Hugo Award for SF/fantasy reporting and humorous commentary, making his Hugo collection the second largest in the world.

Recent writing includes the official Discworld quizbook *The Unseen University Challenge*, and substantial chunks of such reference works as *The Encyclopedia of Fantasy* edited by John Clute and John Grant, and *The St. James Guide to Horror, Ghost and Gothic Writers* edited by David Pringle. He also contributes regular columns to the UK magazines *Interzone*, *Odyssey* and *SFX*.

As the author explains, "Revisions of 'Serpent Eggs' have haunted me since 1977, when I took a monstrously lopsided attempt at the story to my first-ever Milford (UK) SF Writers' Conference. Its defects were laid bare with deadly kindness and the manuscript reduced to charred fragments. After various unsatisfactory rewrites, I put the thing to rest by wrenching out one central notion and transplanting this into a 1984 humorous novel where it may have looked a trifle lost. The idea wouldn't lie down, though, and in the 1990s it occurred to me that I'd originally used the wrong narrator, the wrong tone and the wrong ending. I started again, and one night woke to find this monstrous prose creation at my bedside, gazing at me with watery yet speculative eyes . . ."

May 9

W HEN THE ISLAND FIRST SHOWED itself as a formless dark blot on the shifting greys of sea and sky it should have been a moment full of significance, of boding . . . but my attention was elsewhere. One of its people is actually on this boat. And yes, and yes, she has something of what I have been calling the Droch Skerry "look". Besides that odd patchiness of the hair and the dark bruises under each eye, there are points only hinted by the newspaper photograph that first caught my curiosity months ago and on the far side of the Atlantic. A peaked unhealthiness, a greyish, shrunken aspect – well, it's hard to put in words.

Otherwise she would be an ordinarily attractive young woman. Her name is Lee something. "Just call me Lee. It'll be great to have a new face on the island." She's loaded with small oddments for people in the Droch Skerry community. Out here on the edge of the Shetlands, going shopping is a major expedition planned weeks ahead. We clung to an icy rail and made small talk on the heaving deck, surrounded by all her sprawling bags and parcels. Luckily I had already picked up a smattering of this alternative-energy lore from books bought *en route*.

For the record – and this casebook might as well carry a complete record – I would not have made the long journey for something as nebulous as a "look". Other sources (the UFO journals, the *Fortean Times*, even the *National Enquirer*) carry tales, recent tales, of this being a region where "something fell out of the sky". Maybe I am even the first to spot what might well be a significant nexus.

Later

What a place. A lone bare lump in the ocean. Grey rock, damp concrete, mist and endless chill . . . they say that Spring comes early to the Scottish Islands but they must have meant some other islands.

And the alternative-technology angle! There are straggling windmill towers on the heights, both the ordinary and the vertical-axis kind, flapping in a dispirited way; there are salt-crusted solar panels aimed up into the fog; the toilets are ideologically correct, and stink. Even the quay is low-tech, a sort of natural spit of rock humped like a brontosaur and squared off with wobbly stonework, glistening and slippery from the spray; I nearly killed myself getting my suitcases to firm ground.

The commune was out in force to greet Lee and the shipment from the mainland. Their clash of dingy anoraks and fluorescent cagoules looks cheerful enough until you come closer and see their faces. In various degrees, like Polaroid snaps frozen at twenty different stages of their development, they have that wasted look. Most are quite young.

Stewart Wheatley is the man I corresponded with before coming. He owns Droch Skerry, I think, and runs the commune by his own whims. They led me to him in one of their squat energy-saving houses, and he greeted me under a yellow light that waxed and waned with (I suppose) the wind overhead.

Is there a grey look about Wheatley too? Hard to tell in that pulsating light. He's big and completely bald, looks like a retired wrestler, has one of those arc-lamp personalities whose glare backs you up against the wall like a strong wind. He was throbbingly glad I'd come to join the group, insisted I must call him Stewart, everyone would call me Robert, no formalities on Droch, knew I'd get the most tremendous satisfaction from working alongside this truly dedicated team . . .

Somehow I never even got around to my carefully prepared story of research work for a magazine article.

There was a meal: all twenty-odd of the islanders at one long table. We ate some sort of meat loaf from tins, wizened vegetables out of the grey salty garden plots I'd seen, and horribly naked shellfish that some of the team (a third of them seemed to be called Dave) had chipped laboriously from the rocks at low tide. Whelks, limpets, some vile winkle things called buckies, and worse. It seemed impolitic to shut my eyes, but they looked as bad as anything described in the grimoires.

The stuff in the chipped tumblers tasted of lime-juice, and a bottle of multivitamin capsules went round the table like the port decanter at some old Oxford college . . . so a tentative theory of mine was abandoned. *Not* merely a case of deficiency disease. Good.

Conversation: subdued. They keep one eye on Wheatley, huge at the head of the table. I said, not strictly truthfully, that the shabby wind-farm was impressive.

"You should hear what they cost," said Lee at once with an edge in her voice. "Low technology is our watchword, Robert. We've set ourselves free from industrial civilization, except the bits that sell wind generators."

"Have to start somewhere," muttered a scanty-haired, haggard man who I gathered was called Rich.

Wheatley told me, "Lee would like us to live in caves and eat roots – Rich is disappointed that in five years we haven't yet covered the skerry with dams and refineries."

I asked him which he favoured, and he said rather grandly that he was an eco-opportunist who made the best use of whatever was available: money, weather, materials . . .

"Mussels," said a voice to my right, not with enthusiasm. "Eggs."

I do not know how to convey the chill that crept into that long, stuffy eating hall. Some seemed as puzzled as myself by the sudden silence; some looked sidelong at Wheatley as though expecting a cue.

"Dave," he said gently. "Not, not you, *you*. I've just remembered . . . it's your turn to go on watch tonight."

The indicated Dave gave a small nod. Clearly it had not been his turn. It was a punishment. Disciplinary.

On watch? Where and for what?

Later

Or might it conceivably be sickness after all? Wheatley alone has a private room. In the men's dormitory before lights-out, much pallid flesh was visible. Those with more pronounced cases of the "look" seem to suffer unusually from bruises on their arms and legs – great piebald splotches.

Of the toilets I do not choose to write more. ("We return *everything* to the soil." The sooner the better. These people's digestive systems do not seem in good order.) The bathrooms are tolerable and give a few minutes' privacy to bring these notes up to date. How the heating systems are shared between the windmills, diesel generator and those joke solar cells remains a dark mystery, but after a tepid start the shower surprised me by running hot.

Tufts of thin hair lie on the floor, sticking to my wet feet. I have seen it coming out in wads on their combs.

In my locked suitcase there are certain signs and wards that may offer a little protection against . . . against? I have followed up some odd cults (not with any great success) in a dozen decayed holes of old Britain and New England, but have rarely known such a compelling sense of being *too close*.

May 10

Already I have to pay the price of offering myself as a willing worker. Today's choice is limpet-work on the western shore, or some nameless task involving a cranky and obstinate biomass converter which will one day heat the buildings with methane or blow them sky-high . . . or plain digging. That sounded the safest. Four hours scratching with an undersized fork at a vast tract of ground which was to blossom with yams, kiwifruit or something equally unlikely. Occasional jets thundered overhead according to the whim of the Royal Air Force, thick as flies in these "remote" parts. Seagulls and scrawny hens pecked after me for worms. It offered time to think.

The impression I have is that the commune members who are further gone in the "look" are those who have been here longer. Rich is one of the original few and has it very badly. He said hello just now, on his way to "look over the number-two windmill cable – it's leaking to earth." Not keen to have me come and see. "I get uptight if people watch me working."

I watched him scramble up the slope, though, up beyond the weak fingers of greenery that reach towards the central granite gnarl. The rocky climb is rotten with industrial archaeology: cable runs, abandoned scaffolding, the wreck of a windmill that hadn't been anchored right, pipes snaking this way and that to tap what I suppose must be fresh-water springs. In one or two places there are ragged wisps of steam. A long scar of raw stone marks where Wheatley had (according to Lee) tried to blast the foundations for something or other. Rusty stains bleed down the rock. The place is a mess.

There were tolerant smiles for me when I staggered into the kitchen, aching and blistered, clammy with sweat despite the chill air. Lee and someone called Anna cracked age-old jokes about feeble city muscles; another of the Daves offered me soup hot from the midget electric stove that is another of Droch Skerry's compromises with self-sufficiency. There is a certain sardonic amusement in counting just how many compromises there are. Boxes and boxes of Kleenex tissues, not even recycled!

(But a tiny puzzle is lurking there too. Longer-standing members of the group will sometimes snatch a few tissues and turn aside from whatever is going on, not sneezing but quietly pressing the things to nose or mouth. Once or twice as the wadded-up tissue goes into the fire, I have thought to detect a splash of red.)

So I've worked for Droch Skerry and am halfway to being accepted. Coming a little way in makes one oddly sensitive to divisions further in, before you reach Wheatley and the centre. As though there were things which A and B might speak of together but not discuss with an outer circle of myself and Lee and half a dozen others.

May 11

Something fell out of the sky. The vague UFO rumours are sober truth.

In between work shifts it's quite allowable to go for a walk. "But when you know the place by heart," said Lee with half a smile, "the fun goes out of it rather."

Even in this eternal weeping mist, there ought not to be enough of Droch Skerry to become lost in. Its many granite shoulders are hunched and knotted, though; the grassy folds between them twist in a topologist's nightmare; the closer you look, the longer any journey becomes. Especially, of course, when you're not in the least sure what you hope to find.

Granite, gorse, granite, rabbit droppings, matted heather, gorse, granite, endlessly repeated . . .

It was in the tenth or twentieth coarse wrinkle of the ground that the irregular pattern seemed to break. Less of the prickly gorse here, perhaps, and more of it withered and brown? This fold of the island dipped further down than most, a long sheltered combe or glen that ended at a cliff over deep water. I pulled gingerly at the nearest dead gorse and it came up in my hand, roots long broken and dry. Then, coming to the edge of a roundish depression in the ground, I tripped over something like a doormat.

Not a doormat. A slab of turf that hadn't taken root. And next to it another, and another.

Part of the combe had been painstakingly re-turfed in chequerboard squares. Some of these turves had dried and died before they could knit into a smooth carpet of salt grass. When I stood back, the oval hollow in the ground rearranged itself in my mind's eye. It was a crater where something had impacted, hard, from very high up. One bulging granite rock nearby was marked with a bright smear of metal. I could imagine Wheatley's little workforce laboriously covering up what had happened, and . . .

What had it been and where was it taken?

The only further information I thought I could extract from this fold of the island was that – it seemed – a large and heavy bulk might have been dragged to or from the cliff edge. I had a hazy vision of something vast and formless rising from the sea, or returning to it.

Not long after, a dim shape along roughly those lines came looming out of the thin mist. It resolved itself into Wheatley, carrying a shotgun and the bloody rags of several rabbits strung into a bunch. The gun barrel wavered erratically, sometimes pointing at his own foot, or mine. "Our Rich catches the little buggers in humane snares," he said in a conversational tone, "but where's the challenge in that? You shouldn't come this way on your own. It's treacherous."

I had not found it so, and said something non-committal.

"Believe me. See you've had a fall already."

It was ridiculous to feel guilty, trapped, as my eyes followed Wheatley's down to the muddy and grass-stained knees of my jeans. Was it so obvious that I'd spent time minutely studying the ground?

"Oh," he said, "and I should avoid the heights altogether. If I were you."

May 13

I constantly feel the circles within circles at these strange meals in that close, smelly room. (Deodorants do not seem to figure largely in the alternative life; no matter how often we all resort to the showers, we aren't a salubrious lot *en masse*.) There is what you might call a Lee faction which does not like relying on the dark gods of Western industrial civilization even for microchips, paracetamol or the band-aids that decorate every other hand. The inner ring have a more Robinson Crusoe approach, feeling justified in snatching anything from the world's wreck as the pelagic deeps close over it. Sometimes they seem to be talking in code about some great and significant coup along these lines. "Power for the people," they say, and it means something more than an empty slogan. Wheatley watches over this with a curious air of controlled force, fraught with doom and significance, as though by lifting one finger he could abolish any of us. I think he may be an adept.

We are a democracy here and decide everything by show of hands, but suggestions not to the master's liking are never put to the vote. People change their minds in mid-proposal, turned by his pale gaze.

A special treat tonight: after some days' accumulation, the island's bedraggled hens have provided eggs all around. I never met boiled eggs so small and odd-tasting, but appetites here are small. Rich, who looked very bad tonight, collected a dozen half-shells and idly (it seemed, until I saw others' faces) arranged them on the table, unbroken end up, in a ring. A circle of power. It had some kind of power, because I saw Wheatley frowning like thunder. He rose early and the meal was over.

In the dormitory late on, eyes tight shut, I overheard a brief exchange. One of the Daves, the black one from Jamaica, was not looking forward to some coming night duty. "Man. Every hour on the hour. That light up there really genuinely gives me the creeps." He was answered, not quite intelligibly from where I lay in "my" clammy bunk. But I believe a Name was pronounced. It is a central axiom of the old knowledge, of which I have learned so desperately little, that the forces that crawl under the thin bright reality we know all have their separate names, and may be called.

On watch. "Up there."

Avoid the heights.

May 16

Where does the time go? You can lose yourself in a community like this: hoeing, hunting for driftwood, carrying water in the twenty-litre plastic drums that are comfortably liftable and an agony after thirty seconds' walk. There are a hundred running jokes about life here – away from the mainland, the job centre, the dole. Apart from the occasional strange no-go areas in conversation, I like these people.

But.

You can't get newspapers here, nor a decent steak or cup of coffee. We sit in a shivering circle around the radio and hear the pulse of the world, but see nothing. Lee says there is always going to be satellite TV on the skerry *next* month. It was a shock to leaf through mouldy old magazines stacked in the store-hut against some dim future notion of recycling, and be reminded of normal faces; of the fact that something on Droch is *wrong*, no matter how easily one becomes used to the ruined look people wear here. I ran, almost, to scan my own face in a shaving-mirror. Anxious and none too clean, but not (yet?) wearing that mark . . .

It is not lack of vitamins. Precautions are taken. It does not appear to be any of the legendary miscegenations of the literature – the notorious "Innsmouth look" or the seal-man hybrids of Island folklore – but something subtler. These people have no lifelong roots here. From personal knowledge of a friend who died, I think it is not AIDS.

Tonight I plan to watch the watcher on the heights.

Later

Bright light-bulbs indoors mean gales outside, the windmills screaming up above. Rather him than me.

In brief: when I heard the wind take the front door and slam it, I counted an interminable five minutes of seconds ("one and-a-pause, two and-a-pause, three and-a-pause"). Then I got up as naturally as possible and padded off towards the toilet. Out in the upper-floor passage, thick and smeary windows show part of the hillside behind the commune buildings; I hoped I might see a light.

To my surprise I saw it quite soon, a flicking torch beam that danced to and fro impatiently while its invisible source mounted the rocks with infinite slowness and care. Lacking survey equipment, I did what I could and knelt to watch one-eyed, chin on the deep window-ledge, tracing each position of the light by touching my pen to the window-glass. In the grey of morning the marks might show up and indicate a path, or not . . .

The light vanished. Surely it could not have reached and passed the crest? I waited another age, shivering in my pyjamas, and suddenly found the flicker again – now unmistakably descending.

A memory: "every hour on the hour," I'd overheard. The watch was not a continuous one. Somehow this made it even odder and more disturbing.

May 17

After the usual unsatisfactory breakfast, the upstairs passage seemed full of comings and goings I'd never noticed before. I dodged guiltily to and fro, unable to be alone with my window; in the end I invented a story about a touch of diarrhoea (common enough here), and then felt I had to brood in the lavatory for the sake of verisimilitude each time.

Eventually I was able to squint from what I hoped was the right position, and see how the blurred smears of ink on the glass overlaid the hillside. The end of the dancing light's journey must have been in *that* area, above the raw scar in the rocks, some way to the left of that tangle of old iron.

After a while I thought I saw a patch of black . . . an opening? The old places under the Earth. With a wholly disproportionate effect of dread, a wisp of fog seemed to trail from the blackness like dog's breath on a chill morning.

I must record that I have played around with these investigations in libraries and ancient college archives, and have never before reached a position where the next logical step is to climb a hill in slippery darkness and crawl into a black cavity. I record that I am sick with fright.

Since I am officially frequenting the toilets, I'm thus today's logical choice to carry all the buckets out for return to the soil and cleansing in the sea. As I trudged back from the fourth trip Wheatley chose to waylay me and say, "You're settling in nicely, Robert." And as a seeming afterthought: "You should get more sleep at night."

When next upstairs I remembered to wipe my felt-pen tracing from the window. If anyone had noticed, it could have meant nothing to them. Surely.

Light relief of the evening: Anna, who is interested in something called biodynamic gardening, said we should preserve our excrement, stuff it into sterilized cow horns and bury them at the winter solstice to be transmuted by cosmic and telluric forces. Dug up in Spring, minute quantities of the result would make Droch Skerry bloom like the garden of Findhorn. Wheatley laughed out loud and scoffed at her mercilessly. I noticed that Anna, like most of the women here, wears a headscarf all day long; it covers the thinning hair.

I judge that Lee will need a scarf soon. I *like* Lee. Something ought to be done about the shadow on this damned place.

Tonight, then.

Later

Inventory. Plenty of wellington boots, anoraks and electric torches for night emergencies, waiting in the big kitchen. A little shamefacedly I am wearing a scrap of parchment inscribed with certain elder signs, carrying a vial of powder compounded from a protective formula. One does not wholly believe in these things and yet they can offer comfort.

What do I expect to see? I don't know. If there's anything in sortilege, though, my eye fell today on a balloon in the Krazy Kat collection from our ramshackle library: "I sense the feel of evil – Every nerve of me vibrates to the symphony of sin – Somewhere, at this moment, crime holds revel." That's it.

May 18, around 1:20 a.m.

The cave mouth. It is a cave; could be natural. Water streams from it and is lost in the rocks. Warm water.

The climb was very bad; my shins must be bleeding in a dozen places. Bitter wind. I think it was Rich making the every-hour-on-the-hour visits at midnight and one. Plenty of time before two. Keep telling myself, Rich and several others have stared again and again into whatever abyss waits there, and come out unscathed.

Except for the worrying way they *look* . . .

Shortly after

Have to stoop slightly and splash my way. Firm underfoot except when I trip over the ubiquitous pipes. A warm breath blowing from further in, a seaside reek. There seems to be a bend ahead, and a hint of blue light when I click off the torch. "That light gives me the creeps." The hiss and moan of the wind in the cave mouth drowns out another sound ahead, I think; in the lulls it seems to be a faint . . . bubbling?

Later

I cannot get over that terrible glare he gave me at the last.

The chamber might be natural, and the spring that pours into it, but the deep, brimming pool is surely not. (I remembered those scars of abortive blasting activities.) The pool holds something bleak and alien. All in a ghostly blue light.

There are things down there, eight things like great eggs, each the size of a man's skull, suspended in a complex cradle of ropes anchored to the stony floor around the rim . . . a precisely spaced ring of devil's eggs, a diagram of power, a gateway? All around them the water glows in deadly blue silence. Bubbles rise from them, every bubble a blue spark, the whole pool fizzing and simmering. Thick, choking warmth in the air.

One half-remembered phrase kept writhing through my mind like a cold worm: "*. . . a congeries of iridescent globes . . .*" It was a long while before I could even look away from the incomprehensible blue horror that held me with a snake's gaze.

A rack of rust-caked tools: hammer, chisel, knife. More coils of rope. A prosaic notebook hanging from a nail on the wall, damp pages full of scribble in different handwritings. "17/5 0100 OK no adjust – R." I shuddered most of all at the innocent-looking pipe that led away, and down the slope outside, towards the houses.

Then I heard the scraping down the passageway and knew that I was caught. Beyond the troubled pool the floor and roof became a wedge-shaped niche for dwarfs, and after that nothing at all.

Wheatley, gigantic in this low-ceilinged space, was not carrying the shotgun as carelessly as he had in the open. I backed away uselessly over granite slippery and treacherous with condensation.

"You probably know already: no one can climb up here after dark without showing a light to half the island," he said reasonably, pacing my slow retreat around the pool. "Now what are we going to do with you?"

"What *is* that monstrosity? What force makes the light?" I said, or something of the sort.

"A very well-known one. Never heard of Cherenkov radiation? Nor me, but Rich understands all this stuff. My God, can't you imagine how we felt when that Eurostealth bomber came down smash on top of Droch Skerry? Over the cliff with it, except for the cores, and there they are. Talk about swords into plough-shares, talk about power for the people. We might have had some leakage trouble early on, but we're the first community with its own alternative-technology reactor. Piping-hot water for all our showers, all our . . ."

I understood only that in his raving he had allowed the gun barrel to wander again. The plastic phial of Ibn Ghazi powder was in my hand by then; logically I should have cast it into the accursed waters, but I threw it at Wheatley instead. Common salt, sulphur, mercury compounds; all more or less harmless, but perhaps it had some virtue, and he caught it in the eyes. With a not very loud grunt he lurched off-balance, the shotgun fired and rock chips exploded from the floor, the recoil (I think) took him over backwards, and his head struck hard on a spur of granite as he splashed into the warm seething water.

I could not bring myself to dive after him. The sinking body spun lazily down towards the terrible eggs and their aura of hellish radiance. For an instant Wheatley's whole face glowed translucent blue, and the light somehow filled his eyeballs, a final unseeing glare at me from eyes that were discs of blue fire. Then he floated slowly to the surface and became a lumpish silhouette against the evil light below. He no longer moved.

It must be stopped. This rot, this ulcer, this tumour in the clean rock. The circle of "cores" lets in something bad from outside the world we know. Break the circle. Break the symmetry.

The old knife from the rack haemorrhages wet rust at every touch, but it has the remnants of an edge beneath. Hack through the ropes and the strange eggs will no longer be arranged in that terrible sigil; they'll sink and nestle together in a ragged bunch at the bottom of the water. Whatever esoteric contract is fulfilled by that careful spacing will be broken apart.

The logic cannot be faulted. I don't know why I find myself hesitating.

May 2???

It is very hard to write now. Around dawn they found me half-conscious on the rocky hillside. I suppose I slipped and fell. My nerve had failed me as the loosed eggs glowed hotter, cracked as though about to hatch, while raw steam erupted from the foaming pool. By the time I'd stumbled to the cave mouth there was a superheated blast in pursuit, a roar of dragon's breath. The rest of that bad night has sunk out of memory, apart from the jags of pain. RAF helicopters came clattering down in the morning light to investigate the tall plume of steam and something else that still wound snakelike into the sky.

"Jesus Christ, we've got our own Chernobyl," I heard one of the uniformed crowd mutter.

The mark of Droch Skerry is fully on me now. My hair flees by handfuls, I bleed too easily, food is hateful and fever sings in my blood. Lee has visited me, and wept. Wheatley's tomb is said to be sealed with a monstrous plug of concrete. That is not dead which can eternal lie. They say the others can nearly all be saved. To one or two I am a kind of hero. They say.

I still do not wholly understand . . .

DENNIS ETCHISON

No One You Know

DENNIS ETCHISON LIVES IN CALIFORNIA and is a winner of both the World Fantasy Award and the British Fantasy Award. Some of his best short stories are collected in *The Dark Country*, *Red Dreams* and *The Blood Kiss*, while his novels include *The Fog*, *Halloween II* and *III*, *Videodrome*, *Darkside*, *Shadowman*, *California Gothic* and *Double Edge* (recently published in a handsome hardcover edition by Pumpkin Books). His latest novels are *Blue Screen* and *Tuesday Night*, both psychological thrillers set in Los Angeles.

"I grew up at a time when radio drama was still a significant part of American culture," reveals the author. "*Suspense*, *Escape*, *The Whistler*, *Inner Sanctum*, *X Minus One* and *Dimension X* held me spellbound week after week. These were science fiction and horror shows calculated to give you a chill, especially if you listened with the lights off. So, a few years ago, I was delighted to write the script for UNICEF's annual ninety-minute network radio special, to be broadcast live on Halloween night, and featuring adaptations of stories by Richard Matheson, Stephen King and William F. Nolan, along with an original of my own.

"I had an idea for a closing piece that would use only two characters and minimal sound effects: a telephone and a gun. A man dials a woman's number and plays Russian roulette; after a plot twist, the drama ends when the gun goes off.

"There was just one problem. It was too depressing to end the show, which was supposed to be a charity fund-raiser, especially following such grim tales as 'The Children of Noah' and 'The Monkey'. So I had to come up with another, less downbeat finish. But ideas are never discarded, they're only put on hold, and eventually 'No One You Know' was written not as a radio play but as a minimalist short story, with an even colder ending.

"I know you aren't able to read it with the lights off, but I hope it gives you a chill just the same."

T HIS TIME THE PHONE rang for ten minutes before she picked it up.

"Michael, stop. Or I'll call the police."

"We need to talk," he said.

She put the book down on the bed, took off her glasses and rubbed her eyes so hard that they made little squeaking sounds in their sockets.

"There's nothing to talk about."

"It wasn't what you think . . ."

"What was it, a mercy fuck?"

"I'm not going to lie to you. I made a mistake – *once*, that's all. It didn't mean anything . . ."

"I'm sure it didn't to her. What's thirty seconds, one way or the other?"

"You don't have to be nasty about it."

The young woman sighed, blowing air into the mouthpiece. She took the last of her Virginia Slims from a crumpled pack and searched the night table for a match.

"Oh, I get it," she said, "it's *my* fault now. You didn't do anything. You weren't even there, right?"

"One mistake and you're cutting me off. Just like that. I thought we had something . . ."

"Maybe we did, but it's over."

The cigarette hung from her lips at an odd angle. When she lit it nothing happened. There was a break in the middle and a thin stream of blue smoke wafted up and into her eyes before reaching her mouth. She dropped the match into a full ashtray but kept the cigarette clamped so tightly between her teeth that the filter deformed into a flattened oval.

"Listen . . ." he said.

"You just don't get it, do you? What is there about this that you can't understand? *Finis*. Do you hear what I'm saying?"

"Do you hear this?"

On the other end of the line, there was a click.

She sighed again.

"It's one o'clock in the morning. Good night, Michael."

"Or *this?*" he said.

Then there was a second click, closer and sharper. It sounded like he had struck the mouthpiece with a pencil.

"What about it?" she said.

"That makes two out of six."

She opened her eyes and stared across the bedroom, trying to focus. The cigarette fell from her lips and onto the front of her nightgown. When she picked it up the teeth marks in the filter were so deep that it was bitten almost completely through, but she did not notice.

"Look, whatever your game is, I don't want to play, all right? I have to go to work in six hours . . ."

"This isn't a game," he said. "It's a matter of odds."

"What is?"

"I'm betting that you won't throw it all away."

"Don't be stupid."

"Then come over."

"What for?"

"We'll talk it out."

"I told you, no!"

"One more and it's fifty-fifty."

There was something different about his voice now. The tone was no longer smooth and conciliatory. It was not even desperate. It was mocking.

She sat up straight.

"What are you doing?"

"I'm a gambler, Jeannie. Are you?"

"What's that supposed to mean?"

"I always liked roulette. Here goes . . ."

"Wait."

"I could come over there."

"Do that and I call the police."

"Then listen up."

"Why?"

"I want you to hear it. So you'll never forget."

There was a third click in her ear, as loud as a piece of metal snapping. It must have been right next to his mouth.

"Michael, stop this! Whatever you're – "

"You lucked out," he said. "This time."

"I'm hanging up."

"You know I love you, don't you?"

"Good-*bye*!"

She broke the connection.

She dialed another number almost immediately.

"Mara, it's me."

"What time is it?"

"Sorry to bother you. I know it's late . . ."

"What's wrong?"

"Michael."

"Is he there?"

"No. But he won't give up."

"Just a minute." There was a faint clicking as Mara turned on her lamp. "Now. What about Michael?"

"He wants to come over."

"The creep."

"I know. But he sounds like . . ."

"What?"

"I can't describe it. His voice isn't – normal."

"*He's* not normal. Get that through your head."

"He's doing something."

"Oh, dirty phone calls! Listen, girl, there's a law . . ."

"I just want him to leave me alone."

"I hear that."

"He's been calling all night."

"So take the phone off the hook."

"I can't."

"Why not?"

"I'm afraid of what he might to do."

"To you?"

"To himself."

"So let him! At least you'll get a good night's sleep."

"I can't, now."

"He isn't worth it, Jeannie."

"But what if he – does something?"

"That's your ego talking. This isn't about you. It could be anyone. He just likes the melodrama."

"I think he means it this time."

"Listen. He's a manipulator. He's trying to dominate you. It's the old passive-aggressive bit – control is the name of the game. Take my advice and don't play. Cut it off right now. Clean."

"I tried that. Only . . ."

"Only *what?* He's gambling on your weakness. Be strong. Once he finds out he can't make you jump anymore, he'll lose interest. Trust me."

"Maybe I should see him one more time," she said after a pause. "Just to be sure."

"Of what?"

"I don't know. That he's okay."

"You're crazy!"

"He only cheated once . . ."

"How do you know that?"

"We always told each other everything."

"Oh, really?"

"Well . . ."

"If he did it before, he'll do it again."

"He says it didn't mean anything."

"Sure. It was just his prick. Like it doesn't even belong to him. He found it in his pocket and thought he better try it out. What the hell."

"It's different for men."

"You got that right. They're not human."

"What's her name?"

"No one you know. Some bimbo with roots. Just his type."

"I think he has a gun."

"Did he threaten you?"

"No."

"Then he's just blowing smoke. Where would he get a gun?"

"His father's a cop. Was. He blew his brains out when Michael was nine."

"Don't worry about it. He doesn't have the guts. Besides, it's none of your business now. Do you hear what I'm saying?"

"I guess."

"You want to come over here?"

"I have to get up in the morning."

"Then take some NyQuil and zone out. Tomorrow you won't remember any of this."

"Are you sure?"

"I'm sure."

"Thanks, Mara."

"Anytime."

As soon as Mara put the phone down it rang again.

She tried to ignore it. She turned the TV on in her bedroom while the electronic chirping continued for another five minutes. When it finally stopped, she reached for the phone and punched in a series of numbers with such force that her long fingernail clicked against the keypad and left gouges in the plastic.

He answered right away.

"What is this bullshit about a gun?" she said.

"I knew it was you."

"You don't know jack shit. What are you trying to pull?"

"You talked to Jeannie."

"She's my best friend, remember?"

"I only called to see how she's doing."

"You lying sack of shit."

"I'm worried about her. I swear."

"Well, you can forget it. The girl is fine."

"Is that what she told you?"

"None of your business."

"She's unstable. When I told her I was through with her, she broke down."

"Give me a break!"

"We need to talk."

"You need to go fuck yourself."

"Just talk, that's all. I can be there in twenty minutes."

"You're certifiable, you know that?"

"What more do you want from me?"

"Don't even go there."

"Listen."

There was the sound of metal on metal.

"What are you doing?"

"Cocking the hammer."

"Don't you dare jerk me around! Your father was the one with the balls. Not you."

"This is number four."

"Michael –"

"One out of three, now. You like those odds?"

"Cut the crap or I'll call the cops! They'll put you in the psycho ward!"

"I only want to talk. You know I love you . . ."

"Go to hell."

She slammed down the phone.

He set the cordless telephone in front of him.

There was a notepad and pencil on the living room table, alongside a drinking glass, a fifth of Dewar's scotch, a nickle-plated Smith & Wesson .38 Police Special and a box of Remington hollow-point cartridges. The top of the box was open. None of the rounds were missing.

He picked up the phone and entered a number. When no one answered, he dialed a second number.

After a few minutes he put the handset down again, poured out an inch of the scotch, held it up in the light from the lamp and emptied the glass.

Then he took the Smith & Wesson in one hand. He swung the cylinder out, spun it with his other hand sighted through the chambers to be sure they were all empty, then snapped it closed.

He laid it on the table and studied the notepad before taking up the phone again.

This time he got an answering machine.

"Hi," he said. "I just wanted to see if you're all right. Oh, by the way, I didn't get the check. I thought you said you mailed it. If it doesn't get here by Wednesday, I'll have to come over. You don't want me to do that. Anyway, say hello to Dad for me. You know I love you, don't you, Mama?"

As he broke the connection, a white light swept over the front window.

He blinked and looked up.

Now red lights flashed on the other side of the curtains. They might have been taillights but it was hard to be sure.

He lifted the gun, opened it, inserted one of the cartridges and pointed the muzzle across the room.

A car door closed and footsteps started up the walk to the porch.

There was a knock on the door.

He drew the hammer back and waited, not moving a muscle.

The footsteps went away and passed along the side, down the driveway toward the back.

A moment later there was a click in another part of the house.

He turned around in his chair.

A shadow entered the living room from the kitchen.

He squinted into the darkness.

"Jesus," he said. "It's you."

"I used my key," she said.

"I thought you were going to call the cops."

"What do you think you're doing?"

"What do you care?"

She walked over to the table and stood looking down at him.

"I don't," she said. "I just wanted to be sure you're okay."

"I'm fine," he said, "now. I told you, it's over with her."

She saw the box of cartridges with one shell missing. "What the hell is this?"

"My dad's," he said.

"And this?" She reached for his arm under the table, where he had the pistol. "Give it to me."

"Want to play?"

"My God." Her eyes grew wide, then glassy as tears spilled down her cheeks. "It's true. Oh, my God."

He raised the gun.

She took a step back.

He eased the hammer back down, turned the gun around and held it out to her.

"Go ahead. If I can't have you, I don't care."

She snatched it from him and held it in front of her with both hands. Her knuckles were white.

"You're a player, aren't you?" he said. "It's still one out of two. Or two to one. I forget."

"I should do it," she said. She nodded at the pad and pencil. "What's that, your suicide note? Perfect! I must have been out of my head. I only went to bed with you because you were so pathetic, always crying about her . . ."

"I told you, it's over. We don't have to sneak around anymore."

"I should fucking do it." Her face twisted up and she started to sob. "But I can't. I just can't . . ."

He closed the box of ammunition and placed it in the drawer, tore the top sheet off the notepad before she could see what was written there, crumpled it and dropped it into the wastebasket. Then he got out of the chair and faced her.

She stared at him, her lips trembling.

He took the gun from her.

"Stay," he said.

She kept staring, her eyes so bright that they seemed to give off sparks.

"God damn you," she said.

"We can talk about it in the morning."

She flung her keys down so hard that they gouged the floor-boards and skittered away into the darkness.

Then she turned and crossed to the bedroom.

"Thanks for coming over," he said. "I can't stand to be alone. You know I love you, don't you, Mara?"

She slammed the door.

He smiled and threw his head back, laughing silently.

He started for the bedroom with a bounce in his step.

When he was halfway there he stopped and returned to the table. He reached down into the wastebasket and retrieved the sheet of paper from the pad. On it was written a list of women's names, at least a dozen of them, with telephone numbers after each one.

He smoothed the paper and slipped it into the drawer.

Then, just to be sure, he stuck the gun into the waistband at the back of his trousers before he followed her to the bedroom, closing the door behind him with a gentle click.

BRIAN HODGE

The Dripping
of Sundered Wineskins

BRIAN HODGE'S BOOKS INCLUDE *Dark Advent*, *Oasis*, *Nightlife*, *Deathgrip*, *The Darker Saints*, *Prototype* and the collection *The Convulsion Factory*, which was a finalist nominee for the Bram Stoker Award. A second collection, *Falling Idols*, featuring stories with spiritual and outre religious themes, is published by Silver Salamander Press, while his most recent novel, *Wild Horses*, was sold by auction to William Morrow and is slated as a lead title in 1999.

About "The Dripping of Sundered Wineskins", he explains: "This is the second in a cycle of linked novellas that began with 'The Alchemy of the Throat' (reprinted in *Best New Horror Volume Six*). I didn't initially plan it that way, it's just that each story contains ample seeds for something else, and sooner or later they start to sprout.

"There are a couple more storylines that I've noted, and it's just a matter of getting to them when they feel ready to be born. I've made tentative plans to have the next one published in a doubles-book shared with Caitlín Kiernan.

"But this one, 'Wineskins', does seem to fry a few synapses. I keep hearing from people for whom it's been their introduction to my work, and they really want to know what else is out there. So I'm very pleased with the impact it has, and in particular that some readers, at least, appear to be tapping into the intended currents of thought and inquiry and aesthetics that went into this.

Now, obviously I'm not advocating the slaughter of priests. Just their doctrine."

I. Media vita in morte sumus

I T'S SAID THAT WILLIAM BLAKE spent nearly all of his life experiencing visitations by angels, or what he took to be angels, but my first time came when I was only seven, and I'd never heard of William Blake and was unaware that anything miraculous was happening. It may have been that my young age kept me from seeing her as anything other than entirely natural, much as I took for granted the checkpoints and the ever-present British soldiers who tried in vain to enforce peace in the Belfast of my childhood.

Or, more likely, I was in shock from the bomb blast.

It was years before I understood what was known as, with wry understatement, the Troubles: the politics and the hatreds between Protestants and Catholics, amongst Catholics ourselves, loyalists and republicans. As I later came to understand that day, the pub that had been targeted was regarded by the Provo I.R.A. as a nest of opposition, lovers of queen and crown. To those who planted the bomb that should have killed me, a few more dead fellow Irish were but part of the cumulative price of independence. Funny, that.

Belfast is working-class to its core, and made mostly of bricks. They rained from the blast erupting within the pub across the street from where two friends and I were walking home from school, late and chastised for some forgotten mischief we'd gotten up to. I knew the grey calm of an early autumn day, then fire and a roar, and suddenly I stood alone. One moment my friends had been walking one on either side of me, and in the next had disappeared.

"Don't look at them," she said, in a gentle voice not of the Emerald Isle, the first of two things I fully recall her telling me, even if I don't know where she'd come from. It was only later, from the odd translucence of her otherwise light brown skin, that I realized she was unlike any woman I'd ever seen. "Don't look."

But look I did, and I remember the feel of her hand atop my head, although not to turn me from the sight; lighter, it was, as if even she were rendered powerless by my schoolboy's curiosity. *Well, now you've done it,* her touch seemed to be telling me. *Now you've sprung the lid on the last of that innocence.*

They both lay where they'd been flung, behind me, cut down by bricks propelled with the velocity of cannonballs. Nothing have I seen since that's looked any deader, with more tragic suddenness; and there I stood between them, untouched but for a scratch across my bare knee that trickled blood down my hairless shin.

I felt so cold my teeth chattered, and thought she then told me I must've been spared for a reason. It's always made sense that she would. It's what angels say. And whatever reason she had, in the midst of an afternoon's chaos, for stooping to kiss away that blood from my knee, I felt sure it must've been a good one.

"Oh yes," I think she said, her lips soft at my knee, as if something there had confirmed her suspicions that in my survival there lay design.

Even today I can't say that the mysterious touch of her mouth didn't inspire my first true erection, if stubby and immature.

She looked up, smiling at me with my young blood bright upon her mouth. She nodded once toward the smoking rubble of the pub, once at the pitiful bodies of my lads, then said the other thing I clearly recall: "Never forget – this is the kind of work you can expect from people who have God on their side."

When I told my mother about her that night, how the smiling woman had come to me, I left out the part about her kissing away my blood. It had been one of those moments that children know instinctively to separate from the rest, and keep secret, for to share it would change the whole world. I saw no harm in sharing what she'd said to me, though; but when I did, my mother shook me by the shoulders as if I'd done something wrong.

"You mustn't ever speak of it again, Patrick Kieran Malone," she told me. Hearing my full name used meant no room for argument. "Talk like that sounds like something from your Uncle Brendan, and a wonder it is *he's* not been struck by lightning."

The comparison shocked me. The way she normally spoke of her brother, Brendan was, if not the devil himself, at least one of his most trusted servants. I protested; I was only repeating what the angel-lady said.

"Hush! Word of such a thing gets round, they'll be showing up one day to sink us to the bottom of a bog, don't you know."

Of course I wondered who she meant, and why they would feel so strongly about the matter, but as I think about it now I don't believe she even fully knew herself. She knew only that she had one more reason to be afraid of something at which she couldn't hit back.

There are all kinds of tyranny employed around us. Bombs are but the loudest.

To those things that shape us and decide the paths we take, there is no true beginning, not even with our birth, for many are in motion long before we draw our first breath. Ireland's monastic tradition predates even the Dark Ages, when the saint I was named for returned to the island where he'd once been a slave, to win it for Christianity. While that tradition is now but a sliver of what it used to be, when thriving monasteries housed hundreds of monks and friars, on the day I joined the Franciscan order my whole life felt directed toward the vows of poverty, chastity, and obedience.

For as long as I could recall, the mysteries of our Catholic faith had sparked my imagination, from the solemn liturgy of the priests, to the surviving architecture of our misty past, to the relics that had drawn veneration from centuries of believers. Ever thankful for my survival, my parents exposed me to as much of our faith as they could. They took me to visit the Purgatory of St. Patrick, and to his retreat on Cruachan Aigli in County Mayo. Down in County Kerry we undertook pilgrimages to Mount Brandon, and to the shrine of the Blessed Virgin in Kilmalkedar. I touched Celtic crosses that had been standing for a millennium, the weathered stone hard and sacred beneath my fingers.

Most mysterious of all to me was the 300-year-old head of the newly-canonized Saint Oliver Plunkett, staring from the splendour of his reliquary in Saint Peter's Church in Drogheda. Blackened skin stretched over his bald skull like leather; his upper lip had shrivelled back from his teeth to give him the start of a smile, and I could stare at him in full expectation that those dry lips would continue to move, to whisper some message for me alone.

It held no terrors for me, that severed head of his. I'd seen the dead before, and a damn sight fresher than old Oliver was.

Of the ethereal woman who came and went unnoticed on that

day death had come so close, for years I hoped she might show herself again so I could put to her the questions I was old enough now to ask, and felt a deep ache that she did not. The mind reevaluates what's never validated, giving it the fuzzy edges of a dream, and as I grew taller, older, there were days I almost convinced myself that that was all she'd been; that I'd hallucinated a beautiful, compassionate adult because she was what I needed at the moment, since so many others around me were busy killing each other.

But on those nights I dreamt of her, I knew better. I could never have invented anything so radiant out of thin air. Every few months, a dream so crystalline would unfold inside me it felt as if she were in the same room, watching. Angel, phantom, whatever she was, she was as responsible as anything for my joining the Franciscans of Greyfriars Abbey in Kilkenny, for she had done so much to open my eyes to the things of the spirit, and inspire my hunger to let them fill me.

"Does it hurt to become a saint?" I asked the first time I set eyes on those sunken leathery sockets of Oliver's.

"Some of them were hurt staying well true to the will of the Lord," my mother answered. "But on that day they were made saints they felt only joy, because they'd already been in Heaven a long, long time, in the company of their angels."

"Then that's what I want to be," I declared.

She smiled at such impudence, waiting until later to tell me that no saint had ever aspired to such, as the first thing they'd given up was ambition for themselves. Sainthood was something that happened later, usually decided by people who'd never known them in the flesh.

While I didn't claim to understand why it had to be that way, I tried to put vanity behind me like the childish thing it was . . . and remember I was still alive for a reason that would be revealed in God's own time.

II. Corpus antichristi

The greatest irony about what drove me from the Order of St. Francis is that it was nothing that hadn't been experienced by the very founder himself, nearly eight hundred years before.

The first time it happened to me was a Sunday morning in the abbey chapel, near the close of Mass. The Host had been venerated and the brothers and I knelt along the railing before the altar as Abbot O'Riordan worked his way down the row of us.

"The body of Christ," he would say, then rest a wafer upon a waiting tongue, while in our mouths the miracle would happen again and again – the bread become the actual flesh of our Lord, and the wine His Saviour's blood. "The body of Christ."

Awaiting my turn, I often contemplated the crucifix hanging on the wall before us: life-size, a plaster Christ painted in the vivid colours of His suffering and passion. His dark eyes gazed heavenward, while from His brow and nail-wounds blood streamed in the other direction. Every rib stood out clearly as He seemed to labour in agony for each breath.

"The body of Christ," said the abbot, before me now.

Only when I drew my hands from the railing to cup them beneath my chin, to catch the Host should it fall by accident, did I notice my own blood flowing from each wrist, where a nail might have been driven by a Roman executioner. Beneath my grey robe, my feet felt suddenly warm and wet.

And when the Host slipped from Abbot O'Riordan's fingers, it fell all the way to the hard floor, with no hands there to catch it and spare it from defilement. There it chipped into crumbling fragments of proxy flesh, to mingle with drops of blood that were entirely real.

There was no pattern to the stigmata's recurrence after the first time, just a gradual worsening of physical signs. Initially, blood only seeped like sweat through unbroken skin, but later the wounds themselves manifested in my flesh, deeper on each occasion, layer by layer – for scarcely a minute to begin with, until at last they lingered for as long as two hours before sealing up again.

I was examined over several months by a hierarchy of church representatives, all of them seeking a simple explanation, and I soon realized this was what they were hoping to find. The length and sharpness of my fingernails were checked repeatedly, and my routines became of intense fascination as they sought to discover some habit that might inflict deep blisters which would on occasion burst and bleed.

But Greyfriars was no reclusive monastery far from the modern world, where medieval-minded monks were turned out each sunrise to till the fields. In the quiet neighbourhoods of Kilkenny I taught Latin in the parochial school adjacent to the friary. The closest I came to fieldwork was teaching the declensions of *agricola.*

At least until the day I bled in class, and was removed from active staff.

For a faith founded on the resurrection of the dead, and sustained by centuries of miracles accepted as historically real as wars and plagues, the Church of my era I found to be reluctant to admit to the possibility of modern miracles. Worse, I began to feel I'd become more of an embarrassment than anything, a smudge of unfortunate dust that may have been *only* dust, but that they weren't yet willing to say was not divine, and therefore dust that they above all wished they might sweep aside so they wouldn't have to debate what more to do with it.

I believe what unsettled them most was that the wounds opened on my *wrists*, an anatomical verisimilitude shared by no stigmatic I'd ever heard of. Centuries of art and sculpture have depicted a crucifixion that never would've taken place, not with any self-respecting Roman soldier on the scene with a hammer and a fistful of nails. Say what you will of the Romans, they were no incompetents when it came to killing. They knew better than to nail some poor bugger up by his palms; the bones are too small. Nailing through the wrists was the only way to support the weight of the body and keep it on the cross without its tearing loose. But old images, fixed in the head and worn round the neck, are hard to die, although I should think they'd give anyone a handy means for weeding the miraculous from the merely hysterical: If Jesus were to go to all the trouble of manifesting through the flesh of another, you'd think He'd at least want to get the facts straight.

This, more than anything, was what seemed to keep my priestly examiners from comfortably dismissing the whole matter. It'd been going on for nearly half a year before I was told, finally, that I was to be examined the next day by a tribunal arriving from Rome.

"I would ask you to spend the hours between now and then in prayer and fasting," Abbot O'Riordan told me. We were alone in his office and the door that he almost never closed was shut tight.

"All due respect, Father," I said, "I've been praying for a bit more insight ever since this started."

"Not for insight, that's not what I'm asking of you, but for how you'll answer their questions tomorrow. What you send back to Rome with them . . . *that's* what you need concern yourself with now."

"I thought all I'd send them back with was the simple truth about what's been happening."

"Do you even *know* what's happening to you, Patrick? Can you tell me the cause of it? There's been no getting to the bottom of it for six months, and you don't know how I prayed for an end to it before it got *this* far."

He lowered his head to his hands for a moment, as if he'd said too much; then, with those hands folded loosely together on his desk, he avoided my eyes and looked about the austere room.

"The Church," he said in a slow hush, "is built on a solid foundation of miracles from the past. But it's my belief – and I'm not alone in this – that the past is where they should stay. What's in the past remains fixed and constant. There's no reason to doubt it, no need to demand from it any greater explanation. There's no need to question it . . . only to believe in it. There it is and there it remains for all time, and it need never, ever, change . . . because it's safely protected by time."

I stepped closer to him, aghast. "What threat could I pose to any of that?"

"Have you not yet understood why we've tried to keep this as quiet as we can? Spontaneous healings at shrines and apparitions of Mary are one thing. But give the laity another human being they see miracles in, and it opens up an entirely new channel for their faith. You don't want it any more than I do . . . because *they'll* want more from you. They *will*. No pun intended, Brother Patrick, they'll bleed you dry, and in the end you can only disappoint them because you can't possibly give them as much as they'll want from you. And then they'll doubt, because disappointment can lead to cracks in the foundation of their faith. Cracks that might never appear if we but leave well enough alone."

He looked as sad as any man I had ever seen. "I'd never tell you how to conduct yourself tomorrow, or how to answer their questions. But God gave us a mind, Patrick . . . and the ability to anticipate the consequences of our actions. All I ask is that you go do that for me, and for the sake of the Church."

After the abbot sent me from his office, I paused in the cool empty hall, and stood before a painting that hung on the wall. I'd admired, even envied, it ever since first coming to the abbey.

It showed the martyrdom of Saint Ignatius, having been brought from Antioch to Rome, to be tossed to the beasts in the Coliseum. Left hand on his heart, the right outstretched in glory, as if he were making a grand speech of his suffering, his transcendent old eyes looked wide to the heavens. Supposedly he'd been eaten by two lions, but the beasts set upon him in the painting more resembled savage dogs, although no dogs I'd ever seen, with pig-like snouts and eyes human in their cunning. The paws of the one tearing into his shoulder were spread wide like clawed hands. Often I wondered if they weren't subtly intended to portray demons, instead. But whatever they were, Ignatius had looked forward to meeting them. They were his transport to a Heaven he couldn't wait to get to.

"You were lucky," I whispered. "When you knew what tomorrow was bringing, they hadn't given you any choice in the matter."

I ate nothing for the rest of the day, nor that night, hoping that a fast would clear my mind. Long after Compline, the rest of the brothers asleep in their cells, I remained on my knees before the altar rail in the chapel. The only eyes on me were those of the cruciform Christ hanging on the wall. The only light was cast from the rack of votive candles to my left, filling the sanctuary with a soft glow and warm, peaceful shadows.

For hours I prayed for a resolution between my conflicting loyalties – to the mission of the Church, as well as the purpose of whatever had chosen to work through me. I couldn't see why these two aims had to exclude one another.

In the chapel's hush, I heard the soft plink of drops as they began falling to the floor nearby. Distracted, I checked both wrists but found them dry. Probably some leak sprung in the roof, I told myself. I pushed it from my ears, and from my heart tried to push the pique I felt over that reflex to check for my own blood in the first place, that this ordeal had done such a thing to me.

I prayed for the ugliness rising in me to recede like muddied waters. There should be no place within me for anger, I believed, but felt it more and more as the hours passed. Part of me raged toward Abbot O'Riordan and the others like him, so concerned with the status quo that they preferred to turn a blind eye on anything in their midst that threatened to disrupt their lives of routine.

The dripping sound seemed to become more insistent, as if the flow had increased – or perhaps my growing annoyance with it, I reasoned, was only making it appear louder.

There was more at work here than blood and transitory wounds, yet they all behaved as if what was happening through me happened mindlessly, devoid of purpose. Yet there had to be a logic behind it, and therefore a reason . . . else why should it occur at all?

The dripping grew heavier still, like the thick spatter of rainwater on the ground beneath the clogged gutters of a house. It killed the last of my prayer on my lips. When the chapel's broken hush was ripped by a scream that resounded from the chilly stone, at first I wasn't sure it hadn't come from me.

But no – I hadn't the lungs for any cry as terrible as this.

I stood at the railing, faced the back of the chapel to see who might've walked in on me, but no one was there; the door hung motionless. From the shadows I heard the wet sound of something tearing, and a rustle, then a moist heavy thud, like that of an animal carcass collapsing to the killing floor, except with it came a grunt that sounded unmistakably human.

When I turned round front again, to see if someone might have come through unnoticed from the sacristy, it took several moments for what I noticed to penetrate the layers of disbelief.

The cross on the wall hung empty, no Christ nailed to it now. Blood ran darkly gleaming down the stones from the foot of the cross and from both sides, and from each of these points jutted a crooked spike shellacked with coagulating gore.

From the deep shadows behind the altar there issued a rasp of breath, and a groan of agony. In none of it did I hear any hint of meekness – these were not the sounds of a man who'd gone willingly to his cross. And when from his concealment he began to rise, I started to back my trembling way down the aisle.

By the time I reached the rear of the chapel, he was standing in shadow, little of him to see in the flickering votives but for wet reflections of flame. He doubled halfway over, quaking in pain beyond imagining, as he began to move out from behind the altar.

My first impulse was to retreat all the way to my room – yet what if this truly was meant for me to see? I chose to seclude myself in the flimsy shelter of the confessional – remaining, but giving this apparition every chance to vanish. I drew the curtain behind me as I sat pressed against the far wall and hoped to be spared this sight, hoped that it was no more than a waking dream brought on by one night's hunger and six months of stress.

But closer it came, and even when I could not see it, I heard it. Down the aisle it moved, harsh breath growing more ragged as it neared me, each shuffling footstep louder than the one before, a meaty wet slap of torn flesh on stone.

The Christ seemed to linger outside the confessional, then I heard the rattling of the door to the priest's booth. On the other side of that thin wall the Christ settled heavily upon the seat, bringing with him a stifling reek of blood and sweat.

I pushed the curtain back again and in the dim light thrown by the votives looked down at my wrists, unbloodied, then at the partition separating me from this Christ who'd ripped free of his cross. The panel between us scraped open; through the screen I saw the outline of his head, misshapen with its wrapping of the crown of thorns. Fingers next – they clawed at the screen, then battered away until it buckled and fell out. The hand looked mangled beyond repair, and he held it up so I could see the damage it would never have sustained had that life-size crucifix been accurately rendered.

"Do you understand now?" he asked, in Latin.

"I'm . . . not sure," I whispered, but suspected that I did. If sculptors couldn't get anatomical details right, how much easier might it have been for scribes to propagate other fallacies?

The Christ's head tilted forward to fill the tiny window. I was spared the worst of his burning and pain-mad gaze, his eyes veiled by the hair straggling blood-caked from beneath the thorns.

"Save me," he begged, again in Latin. "Save me from that impotent, slaughtered lamb they have made of me."

"You mean . . . you never died?"

"Everyone dies. Everyone and everything," he said. "But there is no salvation in anyone's death but your own . . . and sometimes not even then."

"What . . . what of your being the Son of God, then?"

"There are many gods. There are many sons conceived by rape." For a moment he was still, almost contemplative; then he reached through the opening with a filthy arm, torn hand clamping upon my wrist. "The things I've seen, the secrets he keeps . . . if babies were born remembering these things, they would tear apart their mothers trying to return to the womb."

His hand felt hot and wet, the splintered bones as sharp as nails, gouging deep scratches where before my flesh had opened of its own accord. He held fast as our blood mingled.

"*Demon est Deus inversus*," he said, a phrase born of ancient heresy, yet coming now from the one I'd thought to be my Saviour.

He released me then, his arm withdrawing like a serpent back to its lair. A moment later I heard him abandon the confessional, and hurriedly I drew my curtain again, so I wouldn't have to see him passing before me, lacerated and limping.

The footsteps receded into the chapel silence. For a moment I thought it might be safe to leave, but what I heard next persuaded me to remain until morning light had driven away every shadow:

The pounding of hammers.

When I came awake a few hours later and left the booth, the dawn showed no blood upon the walls, nor sticky footprints along the aisle. But I don't think I was expecting any, really.

Later on in the day, I told the tribunal from Rome that I'd been causing the stigmata myself, and showed them the fresh wounds on my wrist as evidence. The matter was officially closed. Abbot O'Riordan seemed greatly relieved, and only mildly distressed when I informed him that I planned to leave Greyfriars.

The prior night could have been a dream, and I might've found it easy to convince myself, as I'd nearly done with that spectral comforter who'd at least been substantial enough to kiss the blood from my knee. What evidence to the contrary did I have, except for some deep scratches on my wrist that I could've made myself?

None, but for unshakable conviction . . . and the other thing. It went unnoticed until my last day with the order, as alone I stood in the chapel gazing silently up at the lurid crucifix and its Christ frozen in suffering like an ancient fly trapped in the amber of another epoch. The change in it was so subtle I doubted anyone else would even notice, and if they did, they'd merely dismiss their memories of how it had looked as being mistaken.

Surely, they'd tell themselves, their Saviour had been nailed up there through the wrists all along.

III. Excommunio sanctorum

After the pinched faces and ectomorphic frames of most of my Franciscan brothers, the robust lumpiness of my Uncle Brendan came as a welcome change. He drove me away from Greyfriars with a ruddy scowl for the abbey, and only when we were rolling west through that green and treeless countryside did he break into a relieved grin and slap his big hard hand upon my leg.

"So. Which vow should we have you breaking first?" he asked.

Penniless, I'd turned to Uncle Brendan for help in making my new life. By renouncing the order in disillusion, I had become a shame to my devout family in Belfast. As they'd regarded Brendan the same for as long as I could recall, it was inevitable that two such black sheep as ourselves throw in together. I'd long realized he was hardly the devil my mother – his older sister – had painted him to be, for refusing to set foot in a church since before I was born, and scoffing at nothing less than the Holy See itself.

"Some choose to face the world with a rosary in their hands, and some get more out of holding a well-pulled pint of stout," he said. "Not that one excludes the other, but at some point you *do* need to decide which is more fundamentally truthful."

I lived with him in Killaloe, northeast of Limerick, where at the southern tip of Lough Derg he rented out boats to tourists and wandering lovers. I helped him most days at the docks, on others motoring down to Limerick to earn a little extra money tutoring Latin. In this way I slowly opened up to a wider world.

Early evenings, we'd often find ourselves in one of Brendan's favourite pubs. Great pub country, Ireland, and Brendan had a great many favourites. Poor man's universities, he called them, and we'd further our educations at tables near fires that crackled as warm and welcoming as any hearth in any home.

Guinness for Brendan, always, and in the beginning, shandies for me; I was little accustomed to drinking and inclined to start slow. But they relaxed me, and this I needed, often feeling that I still didn't belong outside cloistered walls. I would look at all these people who knew how to live their days without each hour predetermined as to how they'd pass it, and I'd wonder how they managed, if they knew how courageous they were. I'd listen to them laugh and would feel they had no more than to look at me to see that I was only pretending to be one of them.

More to the heart, I began to regret all the years I'd never truly known my uncle, letting others form my opinion of him for me. When I told him this one night, I was glad to learn he didn't hold it against me, as he waved my guilt aside like a pesky fly.

"You've a great many relatives, but I daresay not a one of them could understand how you'd be feeling now any better than I can," he said. "After all . . . *I'm* the one who once left seminary."

Astounding news, this. I'd never been told; had assumed Uncle Brendan to have been an incorrigible heathen from the very start. "*Father* Brendan, it almost was?" I exclaimed, laughing.

"Oh, aye," he said, mischief in his eyes. "I was going to win souls back from the devil himself, until I began to really listen to those claiming to be out of his clutches already, and started wondering what he could ever want with them in the first place. Not a very bright or ambitious devil, you ask me."

"You left seminary because of . . . who, the priests?"

"Oh, the whole buggery lot of them. Them, and that I woke up one day to realize that all I'd been studying for years? I didn't believe a word of it. Now, love and compassion, aye, they've their virtues . . . but a message that basic doesn't need any act of divine intervention." He winked. "Not as dramatic as your experiences with those collared old pisspots, but you're not the only one to give in to a crisis of faith."

He knew of the stigmata, I'd freely told him of that. Of the rest, that awful Christ come down off the wall, I'd been silent.

"But we're in good company, we are." He toasted his stout to companions unseen. "Hardly the Church's finest hour, not a thing they're any too proud of, you understand, but last century, I think it was, the pope decides he's a bit fagged of hearing the Bible attacked on educated terms. Science, history. If the Church fathers didn't have the wee-est clue what they lived on was round, and orbited the sun, then why in hell assume they knew what they were talking about when it comes to eternity? Or, fifteen hundred years after he's dead, you still had minds like Saint Augustine's setting down doctrine. Augustine had said it was impossible that anyone could be living on the other side of the world, because the Bible didn't list any such descendants of Adam. So the pope, under that big post-hole digging hat, the pope decides he's heard quite enough of this shite, from these smart-arse intellectuals, so he decides to establish his own elite corps of priests who can argue their faith on the same terms . . . scientific, historical, like that.

"Except the more they studied, tried to arm themselves, the more these buggers quit the priesthood altogether." Brendan gulped a hearty swallow of stout and wiped the foam from his mouth with the back of his hand. "Game called on account of brains."

"You're a hostile man, Uncle Brendan," I joked, setting no accusation by it. In truth, I admired the courage it took to make no secret of such opinions in a mostly Catholic country.

"Aye. Ignorance brings out the worst in me, it's true, and the Church has never been much bothered by facts getting in the way of the dazzle. Like a magic show, it is . . . the grandest magic show anyone's ever put on, and the fools who pay their money or their souls are plenty keen on letting themselves *be* fooled." He shook his head. "Like with the relics. Never mind all the saints' bones that actually came from animals – the Vatican won't even keep its own records sensible. What are they up to now, more than a hundred and fifty nails from the crucifixion? Used that many, why, they'd still be taking him down off the cross to this day. What else . . . ? Ah – nine breasts of Saint Eulalia. Twenty-eight fingers and thumbs of Saint Dominic. Ten heads of John the Baptist. Ten! You show me where in the gospels it says anything about John the Baptist being a fucking Hydra, and I'll still not believe it, but at least I'll admire their bloody audacity in trying to pull that one off too."

Quite in my cups by now, I lamented how sad it was that faith and reason were so often at odds with one another. What a joke it would be on the whole planetary lot of us if it turned out that whatever made us in its own image had then filled the books with the most improbable bollocks imaginable, and put incompetents in charge of keeping them, just to make it that much harder on us and weed out everyone but the truest of true believers.

"Who's to say it hasn't happened that very way?" my uncle said. The seriousness with which he was taking this surprised me, even unsettled me. "But what you've got then? It's no god of love and mercy. What you've got then . . . it's a master who wants slaves."

"Uncle Brendan," I said, "I was only joking."

"I know you were. But even jesters can speak the truth. They just do it by accident."

"Forget all the dogma, then," I said. "You don't even believe in something so basic as a god of love?"

"I believe in love itself, oh, aye. But, now, love could just as easily be our own invention, couldn't it? Took a few billion years of bloody harsh survival of the fittest before we'd dragged ourselves out of the mud far enough where we could even *think* of love. So why should we take for granted that something out there loves us any more than we love ourselves? I'll tell you why: Any other alternative is too horrible for most people to contemplate."

I remembered the way my mother reacted when I told her what the blood-kissing angel had said on that day of the bomb. *This is the kind of work you can expect from people who have God on their side.* I'd not made it up, only repeated it, but my mother hadn't wanted to hear another word. Hadn't wanted to know any more about that woman who'd comforted me as my friends lay dead. It hurt me now much more than it had then. How rigid our fears can make us; how tightly they can close our minds. I wondered aloud why the uncomplicated faith that ran like a virus through the generations of our family hadn't been enough for Brendan and me.

"Wondered that myself, I have," he admitted. "Who knows? But I like to think it might be our Celtic blood. That it's purer in us, somehow, than it is in the rest of the family . . . and the blood remembers. Greatest mystics that ever were, the Celts. So you and I . . . could be we're like those stones they left behind."

"How's that – the standing stones?"

"Aye, those're the ones," Brendan said, and I thought of them settled into green meadows like giant grey eggs, inscripted with the primitive ogham alphabet. "Already been around for centuries, they had, by the time the bloody Christians overrun the island and go carving their crosses into the stones to convert them . . . like they're trying to suck all the power out of the stones and turn them into something they were never intended to be. But the stones remember, still, and so do we, I think, you and I . . . because our blood remembers too."

The blood remembers. I liked the sound of that.

And if blood could only talk, what stories might it tell?

The stigmata still came, the flow of blood awe-inspiring to me, still, but there was something shameful about it now, as if leaving the Franciscans had made me unworthy. Worse, it terrified me now more than ever, for I exhibited the wounds of a Christ who had denied himself. They came like violent summons from something beyond me, indifferent to what I did or didn't believe in.

They knew no propriety, no decorum. One night, soon after I'd confessed to my uncle that I'd never been with a woman, he paid for me to enjoy the company of one who certainly didn't live in the area, and then stepped discreetly from the house to share a drink with a neighbour. They'd scarcely tipped their glasses before she ran from the house and demanded he take her back to Limerick. Brendan first came in to see what had upset her so, and found me sitting on the bed with my wounds freshly opened.

"Oh suffering Christ," he said, weary and beaten. "Ordinarily it's the woman who bleeds the first time."

For days I felt stung by the humiliation, and the loneliness of what I was, and tried to pull the world as tight around me as it had been at the friary. Once a cloister, now a boat. I'd leave the docks early in the morning, rowing out onto Lough Derg until I could see nothing of what I'd left behind, and there I'd drift for hours. Chilled by misty rains or cold Atlantic winds, I didn't care how cruelly the elements conspired against my comfort. The dark, peaty waters lapped inches away like a liquid grave.

I often dwelt upon Saint Francis, whose life I'd once vowed to emulate. He too had suffered stigmata, had beheld visions of Jesus. *Francesco, repair my falling house,* his Jesus had commanded him, or so he'd believed, and so he'd stolen many of his father's belongings to sell for the money it would take to get him started. *Repair my falling house.* Whose Jesus was more true? Mine appeared to want from me nothing less than that I tear it down.

But always, my reflections would turn to that which to me was most real: she who had come on the day of the bomb. Who had smiled reassuringly at me with my blood on her lips, then never seen fit to visit again. A poor guardian she'd made, abandoning me. Since I'd been a child kneeling beside my bed at night, I had prayed to every evolving concept of God I'd held. I'd prayed to Saviour and Virgin and more saints than I could recall, and now, adrift on the dark rippling lake, I added *her* to those canonical ranks, praying that she come to my aid once more, to show me what was wanted of me.

"You loved me once," I called to her, into the wind. "Did I lose that too, along with all the blood?"

But the wind said nothing, nor the waters, nor the hills, nor the skies whence I imagined that she'd come. They were as silent as dead gods who'd never risen again.

In the nights that followed these restless days, I learned to drink at the elbow of a master. No more shandies for me – the foamy black stout now became the water of life. Women, too, lost much of their mystery, thanks to a couple of encounters, the greater part of which I managed to remember.

And when I couldn't stand it any longer, I broke down and told my uncle the secrets that had been eating away at me – the one for only a few weeks, the other since I was seven. It surprised me to see it was the latter that seemed to affect him most. Brendan grew deathly quiet as he listened to the story of that day, his fleshy, ruddy cheeks going pale. He was very keen on my recounting exactly how she'd looked – black hair shimmering nearly to her waist, her skin a translucent brown, not like that of any native I'd ever seen, not even those called the Black Irish.

"It's true, they really do exist," Brendan murmured after I'd finished, then turned away, face strained between envy and dread, with no clear victor. "Goddamn you boy," he finally said. "You've no idea what's been dogging your life, have you?"

Apparently I did not.

He sought out the clock, then in sullen silence appeared to think things over for a while. When at last he moved again, it was to snatch up his automobile keys and nod toward the door. Of the envy and dread upon his face, the latter had clearly won out.

IV. De contemptu mundi

"Somebody once said – I've forgot who – said you can take away a man's gods . . . but only to give him others in return."

He told me this on our late-night drive, southwest through the countryside, past hedgerows and farms, along desolate lanes that may well have been better travelled after midnight. A corner rounded by day could have put us square in the middle of a flock of sheep nagged along by nipping dogs.

Or maybe we travelled by the meagre lustre of a slivered moon because, of those things that Uncle Brendan wished to tell me, he didn't wish to do so by the light of day, or bulb, or fire.

"Wasn't until after I'd left seminary that I understood what that really meant. You don't walk away from a thing you'd thought you believed your whole life through without the loss of it leaving a hole in you, hungering to be filled. You've still a need to believe in something . . . it's just a question of what."

Sometimes he talked, sometimes he fell silent, collecting his remembrances of days long gone.

"I *tried* some things, Patrick. Things I'd rather not discuss in detail. Tried some things, and saw others . . . heard still other things beyond those. You can't always trust your own senses, much less the things that get whispered about by people you can't be sure haven't themselves gone daft before you've ever met them. But some things . . .

"That woman you saw? One of three, she is, if she's who I think she was. There's some say they've always been here, long as there's been an Ireland, and long before that. All the legends that got born on this island, they're not *all* about little people. There's some say that from the earliest times, the Celts knew of them, and worshipped them because the Celts knew that the most powerful goddesses were three-in-one."

We'd driven as far down as the Dingle Peninsula, one of the desolate and beautiful spits of coastal land that reached out like fingers to test the cold Atlantic waters. The land rolled with low peaks, and waves pounded sea cliffs to churn up mists that trapped the dawn's light in spectral iridescence, and the country-side was littered with ancient rock – standing stones and the beehive-shaped huts that had housed early Christian monks. Here hermits found the desolation they'd craved, thinking they'd come to know God better.

"There's some say," Uncle Brendan went on, "they were still around after Saint Patrick came. That sometimes, in the night, when the winds were blowing and the waves were wearing down the cliffs, a pious hermit might hear them outside his hut. Come to tempt him, they had. Calling in to him. All night, it might go on, and that horny bugger inside, all alone in the world, sunk to his knees in prayer, trying not to imagine how they'd look, how they'd feel. No reason they couldn't've come on in as they pleased – it was just their sport to break him down."

"Why?" I asked. "To prove they were . . . more powerful than his god was?"

"Aye, now that could be. More powerful . . . or at least *there*. Then again, some say that, by the time the Sisters of the Trinity finally got to their business on those who gave in, all the hours of fear . . . flavoured the monks better."

"Flavoured . . . ? Their blood, you mean?"

"*All* of them. It's said each consumes a different part of a man. One, the blood. One, the flesh. And one, the sperm. It's said that when they've not fed for a good long time? There's nothing of a man left but his bones, cracked open and sucked dry."

I couldn't reconcile such savagery with the tenderness I'd been shown – the sweetness of her face, the gentle sadness in her eyes as she looked upon us, two dead boys and the other changed for life. Only when she'd tasted my blood had anything like terrible wisdom surfaced in her eyes.

The sun had breached the horizon behind us when Uncle Brendan stopped the car. There was nothing human or animal to be seen in any direction, and we ourselves were insignificant in this rugged and lovely desolation. We crossed meadows on foot, until the road was lost to sight. Ahead, in the distance, a solitary standing stone listed at a slight tilt; it drew my uncle on with quickened steps. When we reached it, he touched it with a reverence I'd never thought resided in him, for anything, fingers skimming the shallow cuts of the ogham writing that rimmed it, arch-like.

"It's theirs. The Sisters'. Engraved to honour them." Then he grinned. "See anything missing?"

I looked for chunks eroded or hammered away, but the stone appeared complete. I shook my head, mystified.

"No crosses cut in later by the Christians. It wouldn't take the chisel. Tried to smash the rock, they did, but it wore down their sledges instead. Tried to drag it to the sea, and the ropes snapped. So the legend goes, anyway. Like trying to pull God's own tooth. Or the devil's. If there's a difference." He shut his eyes, and the wind from the west swirled his greying hair. When he spoke again his voice was shaking. "Killed a boy here once. When I was young. Trying to call them up. I'd heard sometimes they'd answer the call of blood. Maybe I should've used my own instead. Maybe they'd've paid some mind to that."

On the wind I could hear the pounding of the ocean, and as I tried to imagine my generous and profane uncle a murderer, it felt as if those distant waves had all along been eroding everything I thought I knew. I asked Brendan what he'd wanted with the Sisters.

"They didn't take the name of the Trinity just because there happens to be three of them. Couldn't tell you what it is, but it's said there's some tie to that *other* trinity you and I thought we were born to serve. Patrick, I . . . I wanted to know what they know. And there's some say when they put their teeth to a man, the pleasure's worth it. So what's a few years sacrificed, to learning what's been covered up by centuries of lies?"

"But what if," I asked, "all they'd have to tell you is just another set of lies?"

"Then might be the pleasure makes up for that, too." He took a step toward me and I flinched, as if he had a knife or garrote as he would've had for that boy whose blood hadn't been enough. Brendan raised his empty hands, then looked at mine.

At my wrists.

"Maybe you've the chance I never had. Maybe they've a use for you they never had for me."

And in the new morning, he left me there alone. I sat against the old pagan stone after I heard the faraway sound of his car.

The blood remembers, he'd once told me, *and so do we.*

Demon est Deus inversus, I'd been told by another. *Save me from that impotent, slaughtered lamb they have made of me.*

On this rock will I build my church, some scribe had written, putting words in the latter's mouth.

The blood remembers.

Three days later my flesh remembered how to bleed.
And the stone how to drink.

Regardless of their orbits, planets are born, then mature and die, upon a single axis, and so the stone and those it honoured had always been to me, even before I knew it. Now that I was here, I circled the stone but wouldn't leave it, couldn't, because, as in space, there was nothing beyond but cold dark emptiness.

They came while I slept – the fourth morning, maybe the fifth. They were there with the dawn, and who knows how many hours before that, slender and solid against the morning mists, watching as I rolled upright in my dew-soaked blanket. When I rubbed my eyes and blinked, they didn't vanish. Part of me feared they would. Part of me feared they wouldn't.

As I leaned back against the stone, she came forward and went to her knees beside me, looking not a day older than she had more than twenty years before. Her light brown skin was still smoothly translucent. Her gaze was tender at first, and though it didn't change of itself, it grew more unnerving when she did not blink– like being regarded by the consummate patience of a serpent.

She leaned in, the tip of her nose cool at my throat as she sniffed deeply. Her lips were warm against mine; their soft press set mine to trembling. Her breath was sweet, and the edge of one sharp tooth bit down to open a tiny cut on my lip. She sucked at it as if it were a split berry, and I thought without fear that next I would die. But she only raised my hands to nuzzle the pale inner wrists, their blue tracery of veins, then pushed them gently back to my lap, and I understood that she must've known all along what I was, what I was to become.

"It's nice to look into your eyes again," she said, as if but a week had passed since she'd done so, "and not closed in sleep."

Since coming to the stone I'd imagined and rehearsed this moment countless times, and she'd never said this. Never dressed in black and greys, pants and a thick sweater, clothes I might've seen on any city street and not thought twice about. She'd never glanced back at the other two, who stood eyeing each other with impatience, while the taller of them idly scraped something from the bottom of her shoe. She'd never simply stood up and taken me by the hand, pulled me to my feet, to leave me surprised at how much smaller she looked now that I'd grown to adulthood.

"He stinks," said the taller Sister. From the feral arrogance in her face, I took her to be the flesh-eater. "I can smell him from here."

"You've smelt worse," said the third. "Eaten it, too."

As I'd rehearsed this they'd never bickered, and my erstwhile angel – Maia, the others called her – had never led me away from the stone like a bewildered child.

"Where are we going?" I asked.

"Back down to the road. Then back home to Dublin," Maia said.

"You . . . you drove?"

The flesh-eater, her leather jacket disconcertingly modern, burst into mocking laughter. "Oh Jesus, another goddess hunter," she sighed. "What was he expecting? We'd take him by the hand and fly into the woods?"

The third one, the sperm-eater by default, slid closer to me in a colourful gypsy swirl of skirts. "Try not to be so baroque," she said. "It really sets Lilah off, anymore."

V. Sanguis sanctus

They were not goddesses, but if they'd been around as long as they were supposed to have been, inspiring legends that had driven men like my uncle to murder, then as goddesses they at least must've posed. They were beautiful and they were three, and undoubtedly could be both generous and terrible. They could've been anything to anyone-goddesses, succubi, temptresses, avengers – and at one time or another probably had been. They might've gone through lands and ages, exploiting extant myths of triune women, leaving others in their wake: Egyptian Hathors, Greek Gorgons, Roman Fates, Norse Norns.

And now they lived in Dublin in a gabled stone house that had been standing for centuries, secluded today behind security fences and a vast lawn patrolled by mastiffs – not what I'd expected. But I accepted the fact of them the same way I accepted visions of a blaspheming Christ, and ancient stones that drank stigmatic blood, then sang a summons that only immortal women could hear. All these I accepted as proof that Shakespeare had been right: there was more in Heaven and Earth than I'd ever dreamt of. What I found hardest to believe was that I could have any part to play in it.

They took me in without explaining themselves. I was fed and allowed to bathe, given fresh clothes. Otherwise, the Sisters of the Trinity lived as privileged aristocrats, doing whatever they pleased, whenever it pleased them.

Lilah, the flesh-eater, aloof and most often found in dark leathers, had the least to do with me, and seemed to tolerate me as she might a stray dog taken in that she didn't care to pet.

The sperm-eater was Salíce, and while she was much less apt to pretend I didn't exist, most of her attentions took the form of taunts, teasing me with innuendo and glimpses of her body, as if it were something I might see but never experience. After I'd been there a few days, though, she thrust a crystal goblet in my hand. "Fill it," she demanded, then pursed her lips as my eyes widened. "Well-do what you can."

I managed in private, to fantasies of Maia.

I'd loved her all my life, I realized – a love for every age and need. I'd first loved her with childish adoration, and then for her divine wisdom. I later loved her extraordinary beauty as I matured into its spell. Loved her as an ideal that no mortal woman could live up to. I'd begun loving her as proof that the merciful God I'd been raised to worship existed, and now, finally, as further evidence that he didn't.

My devotion was reciprocated, and the time we spent together lovers' time. But while I shared her bed and body, I tried not to delude myself that it meant the same thing to Maia as it did me. Millions of people may love their dogs, but none regard them as equals. I kept alive the cut on the side of my lip, where she'd bitten me that first morning, the pain tiny and exquisite. But her teeth never returned to the spot, or sought any other.

"Why not?" I asked one bright afternoon. Now I understood why Aztecs had allowed their hearts to be cut out, and islanders went willingly into live volcanoes. "Is there something wrong with my blood?"

"Is that all you think you are to me?" Maia looked at me with such intuitive depth it felt as if she could take in my whole life between eyeblinks. "I can get blood anywhere."

"I didn't say you had to take it all."

"Yours is special. It shouldn't be wasted."

When I suggested they must be reserving me for something, she only smiled, with mystery and allure. We were out walking, had gotten far from home by this time of day, Maia showing me some of the mundane, everyday sights of Dublin. Her arm looped in mine, she steered me down a side street, more purpose in her stride now than before. When we were across the street from a brick building that looked like a school, we sat atop a low wall. Before long the doors opened to release a flood of young boys in their uniforms – dark blue short pants and pullover sweaters, with pale blue shirts and red ties. We watched them swarm away, and one in particular she seemed to track, until he was lost from sight.

"I had children once . . . but they were killed by soldiers," she said, as if the grief still came unexpectedly sometimes. "Life is cheap enough now but it was even cheaper then. Before I could have any more, things *happened* to me, and then . . . I couldn't. So I just watch strangers, children whose names I never know. I'll pick one out, pretend he or she is mine, and it goes on like that for a year, maybe two. And then I go to another school and pick out a new one, because I've noticed the other's looking older, and I don't want to know what becomes of him. Or her. It's easier to imagine a good future than to deal with the truth, watch all that bright potential start to dim."

"Then obviously I'm an exception."

"Exception. Oh, you're that, all right." When she touched my leg I could feel the thrilling heat of her. "I was following you that day. Like I always did. I'd first noticed you six, seven months before. Such a pious little thing – it was the most adorable trait. Like little American boys growing up wanting to be cowboys, before they find out the world doesn't have cattle drives anymore. I wanted to save you from yourself, if I could. And then the bomb almost took care of it for me."

I'd never once imagined our history predating that day.

"You were standing there between your friends' bodies. Too shocked to cry. I wish I could tell you I steered the bricks away from you in midair, but something like that's a bit beyond me. I think I was as surprised as you that you were okay. But I couldn't walk away without touching you. And then . . . then I saw your knee."

Across the street, the flood of schoolboys had been reduced to a trickle: the laggards, the stragglers, the delinquents.

"Sometimes – and it *is* rare," Maia went on, "I can taste more than life in someone's blood. I can taste all the truth of that person. Lilah's the same way. The blood and the flesh of a special or gifted person are full of images. Take them in and we can learn things they might not even know about themselves." Her eyes locked on mine, clear and hard. "If you think the rite of Holy Communion is only two thousand years old, you're a few thousand short.

"When I licked the blood from your knee that day, I knew you were either going to be a saint, or a butcher."

I thought at first she meant working in a meat shop. Then I realized what sort of butcher she meant.

"From one to the other, that's quite a jump," I said.

Maia shook her head. "They're closer than you think. There's always been a certain type of man, if he can't save a soul, he's willing to settle for exterminating it. Your Church has attracted more than its share. And I tasted that potential in you."

She'd kept track of me ever since, she admitted, always knew where to find me when she felt like watching me sleep. And while it disturbed her to see me hand my life over to the Church, she was patient enough to let it run its course without interfering, knowing all along that it wouldn't last.

"What made you so sure?"

"You were too raw and open for it to last forever. There's no faith in anything so strong it can't be shattered by one moment's glimpse of something it doesn't allow for. And I knew someday you were bound to see one of them . . . and it'd leave its mark on you."

I looked at my wrists. Maia was right. *There, in the flesh, over the veins* . . . Weeks had passed, yet there was still a mark where that tormented Christ had grabbed me with his handful of shattered bones. Since he'd pierced the skin and his blood had mingled with my own, a transfused message that I was to carry inside until, perhaps, I found someone able to read it.

His commission: *Save me from that impotent, slaughtered lamb they have made of me.*

With one fingertip, Maia touched the healing split on my lip. "I've tasted you before," she said, "and I've tasted you after. So I know the difference, Patrick. He's in there. You still carry him. We can use that."

VI. Haereticae pravitatis

I didn't know what she was waiting for, one day being as good as another to bleed. I was used to it. I wondered how much Maia would require; if it made a difference to her where it came from, wrists or throat. Wondered if she alone would be involved, or Lilah too, or maybe all three of them, opening me like a heretical gospel written in flesh and blood and semen. It was Lilah I feared most, because if she were involved, I could only be read once.

Still, I never considered running.

They indulged their appetites, neither flaunting them nor hiding them from me. Only Lilah's necessitated fatality, and as I came to understand their habits, they didn't always feed together, but when they did it was usually at her instigation. Most often, Lilah or Salíce would disappear for a few hours, some nights both of them, coming home after they'd coaxed some man into joining them. As huntresses, they had an easy time of it.

"After more than two and a half millennia," Lilah told me one morning, when she was in especially good humour, "I can personally vouch that one thing about men has stayed exactly the same, and always will." She grinned, relishing the predictability of my gender. "Every one of you thinks you're virile enough to handle more than one woman at a time . . . and you're *soooo* embarrassingly eager for your chance to prove it."

I'd never seen the room where the Sisters took them. It was always locked, like the room where Bluebeard kept dead wives. Nor did I see the men themselves; didn't want to. But on those nights when I knew one would be coming, I'd sit nearby in the dark and listen to their laughter, their ignorance-fuelled anticipation. I'd hear the latching of the door. Then it would go on for some time. Often the men grew vocal in their passion, bellowing like love-struck bulls. The Sisters would laugh and squeal. Eventually I'd hear a sudden snap, or worse, a thick ripping. The overwhelmed voice would screech louder still, but I never could discern any clear division between ecstasy and agony, even after their cries degenerated into whimpers and moans that never lasted very long.

The final cracking open of the bones was the worst.

One morning after they'd fed, Salíce found me huddled before the hearth and a blazing fire. I was dishevelled from having been up all night, and clutched a blanket around my shoulders because I couldn't seem to get warm.

"Awww, look, he's . . . he's *shivering*," Salíce announced to an otherwise empty room. "He misses home, I'll bet."

I wouldn't answer, wouldn't turn around to look at her. Maia and Lilah would still be upstairs sleeping it off. Maia wouldn't let me see her for the next several hours after she'd gorged, but I found that easy to live with.

"Well, he *was* a noisy one, even by the usual standards, I'll admit that much." Behind me, she was coming closer. "Tendons and ligaments like steel bands, Lilah said. What a snap those made."

I could feel her directly behind me, warmer than the fire, and I jumped when she bent down to snake her arms around me in an unexpected hug. Patronizing, I first thought, but when she kissed me atop the head I wondered if instead she wasn't trying, in her way, to tell me that she wouldn't bite.

"Nobody forces you to listen, you know," she said. "There're plenty of places in this house where you wouldn't hear a thing."

I nodded. Salíce didn't need to tell me this, though, just as I shouldn't have had to tell her that listening to them feed was the best way of putting my future in perspective.

"You're worried about the divination? That's all?" She almost sounded amused. "Forget about Lilah, why don't you. So she looks at you like a kidney pie. The thing to remember about Lilah is, if it wasn't for scaring people, she wouldn't have any fun at all."

Salíce told me to wait right there, that she really shouldn't show this to me, but so what. She disappeared into an adjacent room that overlooked the back lawn; it was full of tall windows and sunlight, locked file cabinets and computers. When she came back she handed me a small news clipping.

"It was a bigger story in Italy," she said, "but I'm assuming you don't read Italian."

It was dated the previous week, about a theft from the church of a small village seventy-some kilometres north of Rome. During the night, someone had smashed a spherical crystal reliquary and stolen the relic inside, which wasn't identified, only described as dating from the earliest years of Church history.

"Our friend Julius had this done. He lives in Capua, with a

beautiful castrato boy named Giovanni. He used to throw the best parties, until Vanni deafened him with a pair of nails, so they're pretty sure he's dying now . . . but I think he wanted it that way, because he still loves Vanni after what that little eunuch did." She rolled her eyes. "They want to grow *old* together." Since I didn't know who or what she was talking about, I read the article again. It still struck me as an incomplete puzzle. "I don't understand what this has to do with me, or Maia, or –"

"Don't you get it? The relic – it's for the divination. Lilah can't bother you with those lovely white teeth of hers if she's got them busy on something else, now, can she?"

Ghouls already; now body thieves? Asked what the relic was, Salíce just laughed and told me to be patient, adding only that if it was genuine it could prove to be quite illuminating. Pour my tainted stigmatic's blood into the mix, and it might be their best opportunity yet for stealing the secrets of Heaven and Hell.

"I'd've thought you already knew them," I said.

"You think because we've lived a long time we hold privileged information?" She shook her head. "There's some older than we are, and they're no better off. We've all got our ideas, but there's too much we can never agree on.

"At Julius's last party, two years ago, we managed to summon down and imprison an Ophanim. We thought we might get some answers out of it. But it was already insane. And wasn't flesh and blood like Maia and Lilah are used to. So we raped it and sent it back, out of spite, and that was the end of it. We didn't learn anything that most of us hadn't already suspected.

"But you," she said, with a faint smile. "We're thinking we might learn more from you than even one of Heaven's inmates. We don't even have to summon you down – *you're* already here. And all you have to do . . . is bleed."

When she learned how much Salíce had told me, Maia wouldn't speak to her for two days; after it got to be too much to contain, they shouted at each other for half an hour.

"You didn't have any right!" Maia cried. "*I* should've been the one to tell him those things."

"Then what you were waiting for?" Salíce asked. "Until he got too old and decrepit to run away from you?"

I listened to them argue as I listened to them feed: out of sight, and out of reach.

"The problem with you, Maia, is that there's still a part of you that refuses to admit you're not like the rest of them, and never can be again. Aren't you ever going to accept that? *Ever?*"

"Because I'm not strictly human anymore, that means I can't still be humane?" Maia's voice then turned bitter, accusing. "Of course, you do have to possess that quality before you can slough it off."

"Inhumane – me? They always *thank* me when I feed on them. What *I* take they're already swimming in to begin with; they can't wait to give it away. You can't make any such claim, so don't you even try." Salíce groaned with exasperation. "My god, you still think you can fall in love, don't you? You pick them out when they're children and you dream about what might've been, and on the rare occasion you meet up with one again when he's grown, you think if you put on enough of a front you'll both forget what you are."

"Keep your voice down," Maia warned.

"You're afraid he'll hear something he doesn't already know? Oh, wake up, he's got excellent hearing. The only thing he doesn't know is how you look after a meal. That's the one thing you can't pretend away, isn't it? Not even you're *that* naïve. And damn right you are that most of them would have a problem loving you back if they saw how bloated your belly gets with all the blood."

Whatever Maia said next I didn't hear; I was too busy facing Lilah when I realized she'd been behind me, watching me eavesdrop.

"It'll blow over. It always does," she told me, and nodded in the direction of the argument. "Salíce always has had an attitude of superiority because she never has to get any messier than some little cocksucker bobbing her head beneath a table at Mr Pussy's Café."

"Do you ever resent that?" I asked.

"Do *I*? God, no. But then, I know what really makes Salíce so cocky over it in the first place." She laughed, long hair uncombed and tangled in her face, as she leaned into mine. "Nobody's afraid of her. She hates that. Maia and me – they fear us. But nobody fears Salíce."

"I'm not afraid of Maia, either."

Lilah loudly clicked her teeth. "But you are of me." She stared triumphantly through the crumbling of my self-assurance. "Then maybe you're only half-stupid."

As she'd predicted, the argument soon blustered away, ending when Maia stormed from the house and cooled down out on the back lawn. Through the windows I watched her, a slight distant figure in sombre greys, walking slowly amidst grass and gardens, finally sitting beneath an oak, where she distractedly petted one of the slobbering mastiffs that had the run of the grounds. When I braved the dog and joined her, we sat awhile in that silence that follows the clumsy dropping of another guard from around the heart.

"After that first day, and the bomb," I said, "why didn't you come to me again? I've always wondered that. I'd've followed you anywhere. I'd've been anything you wanted."

"There's your answer, right there. It's too easy for someone like us to take whatever we want. Where's the joy in that? After so long, it's only gratifying one more appetite." She watched her hand scruffing the black fur across the dog's huge head. "It's important to me that if someone like you comes back . . . it's because you do it on your own."

"Because it's more real to you then?"

Maia shrugged, stared off into the grey sky. "What *is* real, anyway?" she asked, and while once I thought I had those answers, now I wasn't even sure of the questions.

In the black-and-white faith I was raised in, there'd been no room outside of Hell for the likes of the Sisters of the Trinity. And while I realized that they weren't goddesses, neither were they demons. I no longer believed in demons, at least not the sort the Church had spent centuries exorcising. Where was the need of them, other than keeping the Church in business? One pontiff with a private army could wreak more havoc than any infernal legion.

Because of Salíce, now I understood that the Sisters weren't the only ones of their kind. When I asked how many of them there were, Maia didn't know, or wouldn't say, and I realized with an unexpected poignancy that whatever monstrous acts it was in their nature to commit, they were no worse than what went on between wolves and deer, and that those who committed them were still as lost in their world as the most ignorant of us mortal fools in ours, working and loving and praying and dying over our threescore and ten.

Black-haired and black-eyed, hair tousled in the breeze, Maia turned her unblinking serpent's gaze on me, so unexpected it was almost alien.

"How much would it take to repulse you?" she said.

At first I didn't know how to respond, then asked why she'd even want to.

"Because it obviously takes more than eating men alive to do it. You don't find that interesting about yourself?" She wouldn't look at me, instead smiled down at the dog. "I've made lovers of grown-up children before, and sometimes they've run and sometimes they've stayed, but do you know who I've noticed is most likely to stay? It's you refugees from Christianity. Now why do you suppose that is?"

I had no idea.

"My guess is it's because, most of you, you were *weaned* on the idea of serving up your god on a plate and in a little cup and eating him in a communal meal. Then when you can't believe in him anymore, and you find us, and see how willing we are to eat others just like you, how we *need* that . . . then isn't a little part of you, deep inside, relieved? Because that means *you're* the god. Your ego is still too fragile to see yourself as just food. So you *must* be God, right . . . ?"

"So let me ask you again: How much would it take to repulse you? To sicken those romantic ideals out of you?"

"I don't want to talk about this anymore, Maia. If you want me to leave, I'll leave, but have the good grace to ask me rather than talking your way around it."

"Hear that, Brutus? Doesn't want to talk about it," she said to the mastiff. "You know, Patrick, where we get these dogs, they claim the lineage runs directly back to war dogs used by the Roman army. Like barrels, they were . . . with legs and teeth and fury and spiked leather armour. And you know something, Patrick? That's no empty claim on the breeders' part, it's absolutely true. Do you know how I know this?"

I shook my head.

"They're extraordinary dogs. With extraordinary bloodlines." She hugged the dog, then slammed it over onto its back, and I could only watch appalled as Maia buried her beautiful face in the coarse fur at the mastiff's bull neck. It yelped once, and those powerful legs kicked and clawed at the air, its body all squirming steel muscle, and yet she held it down with a minimum of struggle. When after several moments Maia tore her face away and let the dog go, it rolled unsteadily to its feet and lurched to a safer spot. Dazed, it looked back at her and whined, then ran off as if in a drunken lope.

She was on me by then, had flipped me back and down before I knew it was happening. She straddled me, her hands gripping my shoulders, then pressed her smeared face to mine and opened her mouth in a violent kiss, let gravity take the blood straight into me. We spit and we spewed, but I couldn't fight her.

It would've been like wrestling an angel.

So I pretended the blood was her own.

When she sat back against the oak, Maia was breathing hard. I was still lying flat and trying not to retch. She wiped her mouth with the back of one hand, and trembled.

"Julius has always hated the dogs," she murmured. "He hated the Romans, so he hates the dogs. He still blames the Romans for what he became. And he hates the dogs."

"Became," I echoed. "None of you were born this way, then?"

"Nobody's ever born this way," she said. When I asked what made them all, she told me it was different on the surface in each case, and sometimes that surface was all they knew. When I asked what made *her*, Maia did not speak for a long time, nor look at me. At last, after we heard the mournful howling of an unseen dog, she said, "If you're still around late tonight, I'll tell you."

VII. Ignominy patris

"We were Assyrian," she began, in our room filled with silks and dried orchids, "and we were just women. Devalued, and with no formal power. But we still had our ways. You know the Bible, so you know the sorts of men who made Assyria, don't you?"

I told her I did. A nation of warrior kings ruling warrior subjects, Assyria had been so feared for its savagery that an Old Testament scribe had called it "a land bathed in blood."

"In Assyria, as in Babylonia," Maia went on, "each woman was expected, once in her life before she married, to go to the temple of Ishtar and sit on the steps until a man came and dropped a coin in her lap as the price of her favours. So off they'd go and their bodies became divine vessels for a while, and that was how a woman performed her duty to the goddess of love.

"My sisters and I decided to go the temple all on the same day, and the men who came then, they showered us with coins and started to fight each other over who'd end up having us. Lilah loved it, thought it was hilarious. At night, in secret, she led us and other women in worshipping the demoness Lilitu . . . the one the Israelites took and turned into Adam's first wife, Lilith, and thought was so horrible just because she fucked Adam from the top instead of lying on her back like a proper woman was supposed to. I'm sure you can see the appeal she had to those of us who didn't feel particularly subservient to men.

"After that first day at the temple, when we saw what kind of power we had over them, we kept going back. Our fame grew, and so did our fortunes, and the rumours of the pleasure we could bring . . . until we were finally summoned by King Sennacherib. He wanted to restore a rite that was ancient even then, from Sumerian times: the Sacred Marriage. The king embodied a god and a priestess stood in for the goddess – by then, we were held in much higher esteem than mere temple prostitutes – and out of that physical union the gods and goddesses received their pleasures of the flesh."

Maia uttered a small laugh. "Lilah never believed Sennacherib really meant any of it, said he only wanted some grandiose excuse for an orgy with us. Probably she was right. After that, we became his most favoured concubines, and whatever in Nineveh we wanted, we had. And I . . . gave birth to twins, a daughter and a son. Of course the king didn't publicly acknowledge them as his own. That was only for children born of his queen. But *I* knew whose they were.

"In 701 B.C. Sennacherib invaded the Israelites. He captured forty-six cities before getting to Jerusalem, but by then, the Jewish King Hezekiah had had an underground aqueduct dug to insure the water supply. Sennacherib besieged the city, as he'd already done at Lachish, but by now they were in a position to outwait us almost indefinitely. I know, because we were *there*. He might leave his queen at home, but Sennacherib wouldn't dare leave us behind. Not with the addiction he had to our bodies. So we were there for it all. Waiting for weeks under that merciless desert sun, a few arrows flying back and forth, an attempt at building a siege ramp . . . but mostly each side just waiting for the other to give up."

Maia seemed to lose herself in the flickering flame of a pillar candle. "Do you remember what supposedly happened to part of our army there?"

I nodded. It was said that an angel from the one true God of Israel came down and in one night slaughtered 185,000 Assyrians.

"Not true, I'm guessing?"

"Do you even have to ask?" she said. "It was closer to four thousand, and it was Sennacherib's own fault. He was starting to fear he might lose the siege, so he went to the priests, the ones he knew practised sorcery . . . and he had them conjure a demon from out of the desert wastes. He'd meant to send it over the city walls and turn it loose on Jerusalem. But the priests lost control of it and it began slaughtering our own soldiers. When they wrote about it later, the Israelites grossly exaggerated the casualties and credited them to the Archangel Michael." Maia shook her head. "They did a lot of that sort of thing. Nothing but propaganda for their god Yahweh.

"What our priests had created, they finally got some control over, but they couldn't get rid of it. I call it a demon, but it's not like *you* think of demon. There've always been spirits, like unshaped clay, waiting to take whatever form someone with enough knowledge or devotion gives it, and that's what the priests had done. But with the appetite they'd given it, and fed on the blood of four thousand warriors, it'd reached a degree of independence. Finally it consented to banishment, but only on condition of a sacrifice. It . . . it wanted flesh and blood from Sennacherib's own lineage. Even then he got the priests to bargain with it. The thing didn't care if what it received was a legitimate heir to the Assyrian throne. It was the flesh and blood alone that mattered.

"*They took my children, Patrick.* He sent soldiers into our tent and they took my beautiful babies and they *fed* them to that thing. It opened up their bellies and spread their insides out on the desert floor, and ate them piece . . . by . . . piece."

Maia was silent for a long time, and I didn't go to her as I might've. I wasn't made to ease grief some 2,700 years strong.

"Hezekiah was horrified by what he'd heard happened, and he eventually paid tribute – he ransomed the city, really – so our army went back home again. Except Sennacherib left us behind, Lilah and Salíce and me. Now that he'd killed my children he couldn't trust us, so he made a gift of us to Hezekiah, to be his own concubines. Seems even *he* had heard of us, from spies he'd sent to Assyria.

"Even though we were betrayed by Sennacherib, we still didn't have any love for the Israelites, or their god. So it was mostly a very antagonistic relationship we had with Hezekiah. But then one night, before he took us, he became very drunk, and we were amazed at what a state of *terror* he was in over their god. He talked to us, I think, because we were the only ones he *could* talk to, the only ones who didn't share his religion.

"He was still haunted by the butchery of my babies. It wasn't their deaths so much as the . . . the consumption of them that was so abhorrent to him. And this one night, drunk, with his guard down, he confessed that he couldn't see any difference between that, and certain things their own god Yahweh had demanded.

"Then he mentioned some text he'd acquired from a Chaldean trader. He wouldn't tell us what it said, specifically – he was too horrified to do that – but he hinted that it was written in angelic script, and that it couldn't be burned, and that it had something to do with Yahweh and the blood sacrifice of a child."

As Maia told me these things, they plucked at old misgivings I'd once chosen to ignore . . . like all those scriptures that plainly had God demanding that his chosen people lay waste to enemies down to the last innocent baby and ignorant animal.

Might these, too, have fed him, along with faith?

"When Hezekiah finally had us that night, something became very different about him. In spite of how drunk he was, he was inexhaustible. His erection had swollen to twice its usual size, and he kept after us long after it was raw. Hours, it must've been, and he still hadn't released once. I don't know if it was something in his eyes, or the way his throat ballooned out, as if his flesh couldn't contain whatever was inside him, but we knew it wasn't Hezekiah any longer. It was the Sacred Marriage, all over again . . . except this time, it was *their* god inside *him*.

"And when we realized this, Lilah and Salíce and I, that was when he orgasmed. His screaming was like a slaughtered pig's.

You can't have any idea what that sounded like echoing down the palace corridors and back again. And his semen . . . was like venom. He held us down and filled us with it, and there wasn't any end to it, and it burned us from the inside out . . ."

When Maia went to the window, pressing her hands to the panes of leaded glass, we both gazed on the risen moon that watched over a land once filled with people who'd had no need of anything from the scorching deserts of Palestine. And I thought how right it was that she and her sisters had come to live amongst the Celts, and wait for that day when some magic in our blood might be turned to their advantage, if only to know the enemy a little better.

"And that was the seed of what we became," she finished. "The punishment from their god for who we were; what we'd heard. He turned us into their idea of what we'd worshipped at home. Turned us into Liliths. And then he turned us away. Forever."

VIII. O magnum mysterium

Even before they came to Dublin for the divination, I'd begun collectively thinking of them as the Misbegotten.

They came from as near as across the Irish Sea; as far away as the other side of the world. They came, and they were not all the same. Some drank blood while others ate flesh; then there was Salíce. The one called Julius? Before his castrato deafened him, Maia told me, it was the resonances of extraordinary sounds that kept him young. I'd been told of an aborigine who'd been eating eyes since the British used Australia as a penal colony, claiming it kept his view into the Dreamtime clear. I'd been told of a Paris artist who could be nourished only with spinal fluid. They walked and talked like men and women, but only if you looked none too close. For one who knew better, it was as though the gates of some fabulous and terrible menagerie had been thrown wide, and its inhabitants allowed to overrun creation.

Nobody's ever born this way, Maia had said, but I saw them as misbegotten all the same, of monstrous second births that had, by chance or perverse design, left them equipped to demand accounting for what they'd all become. And even if in the end they might only shake futile fists at Heaven, I felt sure their voices would carry much farther than the rest of ours.

In a way I envied them.

In a way I regretted they hadn't the power to turn me into one of them.

But to aid their cause, all I had to do was spread wide my arms, fixate my soul upon the Christ, then do what came naturally.

"We're of two minds on God, Patrick," she'd explained to me. "But if he really had a son, and there's even a little bit of him in that son, and if there's even a little bit of that son now in your blood, and in that single tiny scrap of flesh he left behind, then maybe that's enough for us to do what men and women have always wanted to do: understand the true nature of God."

"What tiny scrap of flesh he left behind?" I'd asked.

Having heard stories of their revels and debauches, I'd half-expected them to behave like barbarians as they filled the cellars beneath the house. But they took their places amongst the stones and great oaken beams with grim and solemn faces, and waited with the kind of hungry patience that could only accrue over lifetimes.

When the Sisters came for me I was preparing myself in silent contemplation. The Order of Saint Francis had taught me well in this much, at least. I turned around to find they'd quietly filled the doorway, and when Maia laid her cheek to my bare back, the other two turned theirs, to give us our moment alone.

"We're of two minds on God," she'd explained. "Some fear he might really be the creator of everything. In which case, we have no hope at all. Even if there is some lost paradise that was once promised, we'll never regain it."

They led me into the chamber, in the centre of eyes and teeth and throats, and naked, I lay down upon the waiting cross.

"But there's another way it might be," she'd said, reminding me then of how the Assyrians had made their demon by taking that malleable form and imprinting it with all the traits they desired in it, until they'd fed it to the point of independence, so that it broke away on its own.

They lashed my arms to those of the cross; secured my feet as well. The crown of thorns came last. And when they raised the cross upright, and dropped its foot into the waiting hole, all the old devotions came back to me again, and once more I became as one with Father, with Son, and with Holy Ghost.

Whatever those were.

"*Some of us wonder if religion hasn't gotten it backwards,*" she'd said. "*If what the world now calls God wasn't born in the desert out of the needs of people who had to have something bigger than themselves to worship. So it heard them, and asked for more, and they fed it burnt offerings, and the blood of their enemies, and their devotion, and later on they exported it to the rest of the world. But even before then, it was getting stronger, until after enough centuries had passed, they'd all forgotten where that god of theirs came from and thought it'd always been there, and created them instead . . . and by then, it was ready to feed on them.*"

The Sisters of the Trinity took their places while my weight tugged at the lashes that held me aloft. My every rib stood etched against flesh as I laboured for breath, and now, at long last, the empathy I'd always sought with Christ had come. I was no longer in a Dublin cellar; rather, atop a skull-shaped hill called Golgotha, dying in the hot winds and stinging desert dust.

"*Who better to feed on than those who considered themselves his children?*" she'd explained. "*They've always called themselves his chosen people . . . but chosen for what? You have to wonder. From the time of the Babylonian exile, to the destruction of Jerusalem by the Romans, right up to the Holocaust . . . he's been eating and drinking them all along, like no other people on earth.*"

Salíce stood before me, below, and slowly, reverently, took me into her mouth. Minutes passed, as I writhed upon the cross between the agony of breaths, until it happened anew – the flesh of my wrists splitting layer by layer, the blood freed at last in a gush of transcendence and ecstasy. It trickled first along my arms toward my ribcage, then began to flow heavier, drizzling down into Maia's wide and waiting mouth. So that none would be wasted, bowls were set beneath my other wrist and my feet.

I turned my eyes toward the heavens, wide and seeing so very clearly now, like those of the martyr I'd once dreamt of being: Saint Ignatius, in that painting hanging in Greyfriars Abbey. I'd so admired it, always wondering if I could show his sort of courage when the teeth of the carnivores began to close. Perhaps, now, I'd equalled him, even bettered him; or maybe I'd fallen short by the depth and breadth of the darkest abyss.

There was no truth but this: I was not the father's son I'd once been.

"What tiny scrap of flesh he left behind?" I'd asked.

"Don't forget, he was circumcised. In the temple, when he was eight weeks old. The Holy Foreskin – that's what you papists call it," she'd said, with a teasing shake of her head. *"You people and your morbid relics."*

When I looked down the bloody length of my body, I could see that tiny dark scrap in Lilah's fingers, stolen from its crystal reliquary north of Rome. Still soft and pliable, it was, neither rotted nor gone leathery; incorruptible.

But flesh is flesh, and beliefs something else altogether.

"Save me from that impotent, slaughtered lamb they have made of me," he'd asked, and while I'd never known for sure what impact I might have, perhaps the truth alone would be enough.

The truth, they'd insisted he said, will set you free.

Then again, doubt works miracles too.

Lilah lifted her hand, and touched the foreskin to my flesh, to wet it with my blood; then it disappeared between her teeth.

And in the convulsive rapture of fluids and tissue, in that moment that makes us one with gods, I gave them all they'd asked for, all they needed, all I had to give.

It was explosive.

The greatest revelations usually are.

IX. Descendo ad patrem meum

"You can take away a man's gods, but only to give him others in return."

It was Carl Jung said that. My uncle had only borrowed it.

I nearly bled to death on that night of the divination, the stigmata persistent and reaching for the very core of me. In the weeks that followed, as the Sisters nursed me back to health like a faithful dog they couldn't bear to have put to sleep, I often fondled an old pewter crucifix while my thoughts turned to the subject of fear.

Fear the Lord thy God, we were taught since childhood in my family, and how we quaked. How we trembled. How we fell daily to our knees and supplicated for continued mercy.

I'd long ceased to fear; fear is for children, no matter what their age. But when fear is no more, that's still not the end of it, because beyond fear lies despair, and so far, I don't know if there's any end to despair at all.

Once I was well enough to get about again, to stand without dizziness, to walk and run without weakness pitching me toward the nearest chair, I decided I could no longer spend my life with the Sisters of the Trinity. They, and the rest of the Misbegotten, were so much more than I could ever be. Their eyes saw more, their ears heard more, and with their tongues they tasted it, and their feet had walked it, and their minds comprehended it, and they had lived the histories that others only analyzed, and wrongly . . .

And still they were not gods. They'd have been the first to admit it.

To see them day by day was too hideous a reminder that I was nowhere near their equal . . . and worse, that I'd never really gotten past that deeply instilled need to *believe*, but had now been left with only the Void.

"So what did you learn from it?" I'd asked the Sisters, soon as I could, from my bed; asked more than once. They'd look at one another and smile, with something like sadness and pity and even embarrassment for my sake; but for their own, with maybe just the tiniest ray of hope. Or maybe I saw that only because I wanted to. And then they'd tell me to rest, just rest, their 2,700 years to my thirty-one like quantum mechanics to a dog.

On my own for the first time in my life, I hiked my homeland like a student tourist, my old possessions sharing backpack space with something I thought of as belonging to a newer Patrick Kieran Malone. The knife was large, with a contoured Kraton haft, and a huge killing blade of carbon steel and a sawtoothed upper edge.

I walked an Ireland different from that of the times of the Troubles, when a bomb had left me standing on a new road. Up north there were no more bombs going off, nor bullets flying, the I.R.A. having decided to lay down its arms – for the time being, at least – and I saw that most everyone was caught up in a cautious optimism that people with differing ideas of the same god really could live together after all.

I wondered if, somewhere, in his jealousness, he missed the smoke and blood of those earlier days. But time was on his side. The old blood lusts never die, they just lie dormant.

Saw a bumper sticker while on my way back up to Belfast. *Nuke Gay Whales for Christ*, it said.

Had to come from America.

"So what did you learn?" I'd asked the Sisters, refusing to give up, and finally Maia sat down on the bed where the marrow in my bones frantically churned out new red blood cells.

"How can I tell you this so you understand it?" she said, and thought awhile. *"What's God really like . . . ? Imagine an arrogant and greedy and demented child on a beach, building castles in the sand . . . only to kick them over out of boredom, leaving what's left for the waves. Which of course begs one more question:*

"Where did the sand come from?"

In Belfast I returned to the church I'd grown up in, and as I entered the sanctuary that quiet afternoon, it smelt the same as it always had, old and sweet with wax and incense. It took me back twenty years, more, the shock of it overwhelming and unexpected; smells can do that to you. It was here where my family gave thanks for my life being spared on that day of the bomb, where they lit candles for the souls of my friends who'd been killed.

I genuflected before the altar, out of old reflex.

Or maybe it was disguise.

The priest didn't recognize me at first, but then it *had* been awhile, a decade of monasticism and nearly another year of heresy in between. Such things leave their mark on a man, and even his blood knows the difference. The priest had already heard that I'd left the order; clasped my hands warmly just the same; would be at least sixty now. He told me how deeply my leaving the Franciscans had hurt my mother, dashing so many of her expectations for me.

"Can't help that, Father," I said. "Wasn't my idea, but . . . I've learnt a brand new doctrine. I just count myself lucky that I learnt it while I'm still a relatively young man."

I could see that he was puzzled. And I remembered a childhood friend who'd told me, when we were altar boys, how the Father had put his hands on him, and where. I'd not believed him. Nobody had. Everybody knew that God loves little children.

"Gospel of Matthew," I said. "Remember what Jesus had to say about new doctrines? Comparing them to wine?" The priest nodded, back on familiar ground. "Said you can't go pouring new wine into old wineskins. It'll just burst them, and what've you got then? Spilt wine and a wineskin that won't hold anything else."

From my backpack I took the sleek, dark knife, and when I unsheathed it, the blade seemed to keep on coming.

"Some days," I confessed, "I do wish that fucking bomb had done me in too."

I don't know why I killed the priest. Don't know why I did such a thorough bloody job of it. Or why I killed twelve more in the coming weeks, or how I managed to get away with it for as long as I did. Blessed, I suppose, in my own way.

With that sacrificial blade I opened them, throats and chests and bellies, opened them lengthwise or crossways, and out of each poured their stale old wine. And then I'd have to sit awhile and gaze upon their burst skins, and reflect upon the way they weren't good for anything else now; this was my main comfort. But I could never get them all.

That, too, was my despair.

So I imagined those beyond my blade, Catholic and Protestant alike, shepherding those even more desperate than I to believe, telling them about an impotent, slaughtered lamb whose history and words had been agreed on by committees. And in his captive name, the eager converts would rise from their watery baptismal graves to go forth and seek to propagate the species.

Over those weeks, I was not a particularly beloved figure in Ireland. Knew it couldn't be much longer before I was caught. And when at last I grew too tired, too sick at heart to continue, only then did I return to the one place, the one people, that would have me, and they took me in as one of their own.

I knew better, though.

No matter how much blood I'd drunk, it hadn't made me one of them.

"Hide me," I asked those voracious and beautiful Sisters of the Trinity. "Hide me where they'll never find me. Hide me where they never can."

Of course, they said. Of course we will.

But Maia wept.

X. Consummatum est

And thus finishes this testament of a boy who wanted only to grow up and be a saint.

There are many who'd say he couldn't have fallen any farther short of such a lofty goal. After all, there are saints, and there are butchers, and they believe they know the difference.

But a few – a growing few, perhaps – would say that he achieved his dream all the same. But this depends on your idea of paradise.

"Think of it this way," Lilah tells me. "You struck some of the first blows in a coming war. Oh, you'll be venerated, I don't have any doubt about that. I've seen it before."

And now, at the end of all ambition, where too ends the flesh and the blood and the seed of life, I can't help but thinking of my old hero, obsolete though he may be: Saint Ignatius, on his way to the lions in Rome. Would that he'd had such beautiful mouths to welcome him as I'll soon have.

Take me into you, Maia. Take me in, my angel, my deliverer, and I will be with you always . . . until the end of your world.

Caress then, these beasts, that they may be my tomb, Ignatius wrote in a final letter, *and let nothing be left of my body; thus my funeral will be a burden to none.*

As for me, I'll not mind leaving bones, and I hope they keep them around, gnawed and clean, true relics for the inspiration of disciples yet to come.

THOMAS LIGOTTI

The Bells
Will Sound Forever

THOMAS LIGOTTI'S FIRST COLLECTION of short stories, *Songs of a Dead Dreamer*, was described by Ramsey Campbell as "one of the most important horror books of the decade." He has since followed it with such other collections as *Grimscribe*, *Noctuary*, *The Agonizing Resurrection of Victor Frankenstein and Other Gothic Tales* and the Bram Stoker Award-winning *The Nightmare Factory*, a bumper compilation of previously collected and new stories.

"This story was written as part of a collaborative project done under the influence of David Tibet of Current 93," reveals the author, "who produced a CD of atmospheric music and vocals with which 'The Bells Will Sound Forever', and three other tales with a common setting and cast of characters were issued as *In a Foreign Town, In a Foreign Land*. The title of this volume derives from a line in David Tibet's song 'Falling Back in Fields of Rape'."

I WAS SITTING IN A small park on a drab morning in early spring when a gentleman who looked as if he should be in a hospital sat down on the bench beside me. For a time we both silently stared out at the colorless and soggy grounds of the park, where things were still thawing out and signs of a revived natural life remained only tentative, the bare branches of trees finely outlined against a grey sky. I had seen the other man on previous visits to the park, and when he introduced himself to me by name I seemed to remember him as a businessman of some sort. The words "commercial agent" came to my mind as I sat gazing up at the thin dark branches and, beyond them, the grey sky. Somehow our quiet and somewhat halting conversation touched upon the subject of a particular town near the northern border, a place where I once lived. "It's been many years," the other man said, "since I was last in that town." Then he proceeded to tell me about an experience he had had there in the days when he often travelled to remote locales for the business firm he represented and which, until that time, he had served as a longtime and highly dedicated employee.

It was late at night, he told me, and he needed a place to stay before moving on to his ultimate destination across the northern border. I knew, as a one-time resident of the town, that there were two principal venues where he might have spent the night. One of them was a lodging house on the west side of town that, in actuality, functioned primarily as a brothel patronized by travelling commercial agents. The other was located somewhere on the east side of town in a district of once-opulent but now for the most part unoccupied houses, one of which, according to rumor, had been converted into a hostel of some kind by an old woman named Mrs Pyk, who was reputed to have worked in various carnival sideshows – first as an exotic dancer, and then later as a fortune teller – before settling in the northern border town. The commercial agent told me that he could not be sure if it was misdirection or deliberate mischief that sent him to the east side of town, where there were only a few lighted windows here and there. Thus he easily spotted the VACANCY sign that stood beside the porch steps leading up to an enormous house which had a number of small turrets that seemed to sprout like so many warts across its façade and even emerged from the high peaked roof that crowned the structure. Despite the grim appearance of the house (a "miniature ruined castle," as my companion in the park expressed it), not to mention the generally desolate character of the surrounding neighborhood, the commercial agent said that he was not for a moment deterred from ascending the porch steps. He pressed the doorbell, which he said was a "buzzer-type bell", as opposed to the type that chimed or tolled its signal. However, in addition to the buzzing noise that was made when he pressed the button for the doorbell, he claimed that there was also a "jingle-jangle sound" similar to that of sleigh bells. When the door finally opened, and the commercial agent confronted the heavily made-up face of Mrs Pyk, he simply asked, "Do you have a room?"

Upon entering the vestibule to the house, he was made to pause by Mrs Pyk, who gestured with a thin and palsied hand toward a registration ledger which was spread open on a lectern in the corner. There were no other guests listed on the pages before him, yet the commercial agent unhesitatingly picked up the fountain pen that lay in the crux of the ledger book and signed his name: Q. H. Crumm. Having done this, he turned back toward Mrs Pyk and stooped down to retrieve the small suitcase he had brought in with him. At that moment he first saw Mrs Pyk's left hand, the non-palsied hand, which was just as thin as the other but which appeared to be a prosthetic device resembling the pale hand of an old mannikin, its enameled epidermis having flaked away in several places. It was then that Mr Crumm fully realized, in his own words, the "deliriously preposterous" position in which he had placed himself. Yet he said that he also felt a great sense of excitation relating to things which he could not precisely name, things which he had never imagined before and which, it seemed, were not even possible for him to imagine with any clarity at the time.

The old woman was aware that Crumm had taken note of her artificial hand. "As you can see," she said in slow and raspy voice, "I'm perfectly capable of taking care of myself, no matter what some fool tries to pull on me . . . But I don't receive as many gentleman travellers as I once did. I'm sure I wouldn't have any at all, if it were up to certain people," she finished. *Deliriously preposterous,* Mr Crumm thought to himself. Nevertheless, he followed Mrs Pyk like a little dog when she guided him into her house, which was so poorly lighted that one was at a loss to distinguish any features of the decor, leaving Crumm with the heady sensation of being enveloped by the most sumptuous surroundings of shadows. This feeling was only intensified when the old woman reached out for a small lamp that was barely glowing in the darkness, and, with the fingers of her real hand, turned up its wick, the light pushing back some of the shadows while grotesquely enlarging many others. She then began escorting Crumm up the stairs to his room, holding the lamp in her real hand while simply allowing her artificial hand to hang at her side. And with each step that Mrs Pyk ascended, the commercial agent seemed to detect the same jingle-jangle of bells that he first heard when he was standing outside the house, waiting for someone to answer his ring. But the sound was so faint, as if heavily muffled, that Mr Crumm willingly believed it to be only the echo of a memory or his wandering imagination.

The room in which Mrs Pyk finally deposited her guest was on the highest floor of the house, just down a short, narrow hallway from the door leading to the attic. "By that time there seemed nothing at all preposterous in this arrangement," Mr Crumm told me as we sat together on the park bench looking out at that drab morning in early spring. I replied that such lapses in judgement were not uncommon where Mrs Pyk's lodging house was concerned, at least such were the rumors I had heard during the period when I was living in the town near the northern border.

When they had reached the hallway of the highest floor of the house, Crumm informed me, Mrs Pyk set aside the lamp she was carrying on a table positioned near the top of the last flight of stairs. She then extended her hand and pushed a small button that protruded from one of the walls, thereby activating some lighting fixtures along either wall. The illumination remained dismal – *actively* dismal, as Crumm described it – but served to reveal the densely patterned wallpaper and the even more densely patterned carpeting of the hallway which led, in one direction, to the door opening onto the attic and, in the other direction, to the room in which the commercial agent was supposed to sleep that night. After Mrs Pyk unlocked the door to this room and pushed another small button upon the wall inside, Crumm observed how cramped and austere was the chamber in which he was being placed, unnecessarily so, he thought, considering the apparent spaciousness, or "dark sumptuousness", as he called it, of the rest of the house. Yet Crumm made no objection (nor felt any, he insisted), and with mute obedience set down his suitcase beside a tiny bed which was not even equipped with a headboard. "There's a bathroom just a little ways down the hall," Mrs Pyk said before she left the room, closing the door behind her.

And in the silence of that little room, Crumm thought that he once again could hear the jingle-jangle sound of bells fading into the distance and the darkness of that great house.

Although he had put in quite a long day, the commercial agent did not feel in the least bit tired, or possibly he had entered into a mental state beyond the boundaries of absolute fatigue, as he himself speculated when we were sitting on that bench in the park. For some time he lay on the undersized bed, still fully clothed, and stared at a ceiling that had several large stains spread across it. After all, he thought, he had been placed in a room that was directly below the roof of the house, and apparently this roof was damaged in some way which allowed the rain to enter freely through the attic on stormy days and nights. Suddenly his mind became fixed in the strangest way upon the attic, the door to which was just down the hall from his own room. *The mystery of an old attic*, Crumm whispered to himself as he lay on that miniature bed in a room at the top of an enormous house of enveloping shadows. Feelings and impulses that he had never experienced before arose in him as he became more and more excited about the attic and its mysteries. He was a travelling commercial agent who needed his rest to prepare himself for the next day, and yet all he could think about was getting up from his bed and walking down the dimly lighted hallway toward the door leading to the attic of Mrs Pyk's shadowy house. He could tell anyone who cared to know that he was only going down the hall to use the bathroom, he told himself. But Crumm proceeded past the door to the bathroom and soon found himself helplessly creeping into the attic, the door to which had been left unlocked.

The air inside smelled sweet and stale. Moonlight entered by way of a small octagonal window and guided him among the black clutter toward a lightbulb that hung down from a thick black cord. He reached up and turned a little dial that protruded from the side of the lightbulb fixture. Now he could see the treasures surrounding him, and he was shaking with the excitation of his discovery. Crumm told me that Mrs Pyk's old attic was like a costume shop or the dressing room of a theater. All around him was a world of strange outfits spilling forth from the depths of large open trunks or dangling in the shadows of tall open wardrobes. Later he became aware that these curious clothes, for the most part, were remnants from Mrs Pyk's days as an exotic dancer, and subsequently a fortune teller, for various carnival sideshows. Crumm himself remembered observing that, mounted along the walls of the attic, were several faded posters advertising the two distinct phases of the old woman's former life. One of these posters portrayed a dancing girl posed in mid-turn amidst a whirl of silks, her face averted from the silhouetted heads representing the audience at the bottom of the picture, a mob of bald pates and bowler hats huddled together. Another poster displayed a pair of dark staring eyes with long spidery lashes. Above the eyes, printed in a serpentine style of lettering, were the words: MISTRESS OF FORTUNE. Below the eyes, spelled out in the same grotesque type of letters, was a simple question: WHAT IS YOUR WILL?

Aside from the leftover garments of an exotic dancer or a mysterious fortune teller, there were also other clothes, other costumes. They were scattered all over the attic – that "paradise of the past," as Crumm began to refer to it. His hands trembled as he found all sorts of odd disguises lying about the floor or draped across a wardrobe mirror, elaborate and clownish outfits in rich velvets and shiny, colorful satins. Rummaging among this delirious attic-world, Crumm finally found what he barely knew he was seeking. There it was, buried at the bottom of one of the largest trunks – a fool's motley complete with soft slippers turned up at the toes and a two-pronged cap that jangled its bells as he pulled it over his head. The entire suit was a mad patchwork of colored fabrics and fit him perfectly, once he had removed all of the clothing he wore as a commercial agent. The double peaks of the fool's cap resembled the twin horns of a snail, Crumm noticed when he looked at his image in the mirror, except that they drooped this way and that whenever he shook his head to make the bells jangle. There were also bells sewn into the turned-up tips of the slippers and hanging here and there upon the body of the jester's suit. Crumm made them all go jingle-jangle, he explained to me, as he pranced before the wardrobe mirror gazing upon the figure that he could not recognize as himself, so lost was he in a world of feelings and impulses he had never before imagined. He no longer retained the slightest sense, he said, of his existence as a travelling commercial agent. For him, there was now only the jester's suit hugging his body, the jingle-jangle of the bells, and the slack face of a fool in the mirror.

After a time he sunk face-down upon the cold wooden floor of the attic, Crumm informed me, and lay absolutely still, exhausted by the contentment he had found in that musty paradise. Then the sound of the bells started up again, although Crumm could not tell from where it was coming. His body remained unmoving upon the floor in a state of sleepy paralysis, and yet he heard the sound of the jangling bells. Crumm thought that if he could just open his eyes and roll over on the floor he could see what was making the sound of the bells. But soon he lost all confidence in this plan of action, because he could no longer feel his own body. The sound of the bells became even louder, jangling about his ears, even though he was incapable of making his head move in any way and thus shake the bells on his two-pronged fool's cap. Then he heard a voice say to him, "Open your eyes . . . and see your surprise." And when he opened his eyes he finally saw his face in the wardrobe mirror: it was a tiny face on a tiny fool's head . . . and the head was at the end of a stick, a kind of baton with stripes on it like a candy cane, held in the wooden hand of Mrs Pyk. She was shaking the striped stick like a baby's rattle, making the bells on Crumm's tiny head go jingle-jangle so wildly. There in the mirror he could also see his body still lying helpless and immobile upon the attic floor. And in his mind was a single consuming thought: *to be a head on a stick held in the wooden hand of Mrs Pyk. Forever . . . forever.*

When Crumm awoke the next morning, he heard the sound of raindrops on the roof just above the room in which he lay fully clothed on the bed. Mrs Pyk was shaking him gently with her real hand, saying, "Wake up, Mr Crumm. It's late and you have to be on your way. You have business across the border." Crumm wanted to say something to the old woman then and there, to confront her with what he described to me as his "adventure in the attic". But Mrs Pyk's brusque, businesslike manner and her entirely ordinary tone of voice told him that any inquiries would useless. In any case, he was afraid that openly bringing up this peculiar matter with Mrs Pyk was not something he should do if he wished to remain on good terms with her. Soon thereafter he was standing with his suitcase in hand at the door of the enormous house, lingering for a moment to gaze upon the heavily made-up face of Mrs Pyk and secure another glimpse of the artificial hand which hung down at her side.

"May I come to stay again?" Crumm asked.

"If you wish," answered Mrs Pyk, as she held open the door for her departing guest.

Once he was outside on the porch Crumm quickly turned about-face and called out, "May I have the same room?"

But Mrs Pyk had already closed the door behind him, and her answer to his question, if it actually was one, was a faint jingle-jangle sound of tiny bells.

After consummating his commercial dealings on the other side of the northern border, Mr Crumm returned to the location of Mrs Pyk's house, only to find that the place had burned to the ground during the brief interval he had been away. I told him, as we sat on that park bench looking out upon a drab morning in early spring, that there had always been rumors, a sort of irresponsible twilight talk, about Mrs Pyk and her old house. Some persons, hysterics of one sort or another, suggested that Mrs Glimm, who operated the lodging house on the west side of town, was the one behind the fire which brought to an end Mrs Pyk's business activities on the east side. The two of them had apparently been associates at one time, in a sense partners whose respective houses on the west and east sides of the northern border town were operated for the mutual benefit of both women. But a rift of some kind appeared to turn them into bitter enemies. Mrs Glimm, who was sometimes characterized as a "person of uncanny greed", became intolerant of the competition posed by her former ally in the business. It came to be understood throughout the town near the northern border that Mrs Glimm had arranged for someone to assault Mrs Pyk in her own house, an attack which culminated in the severing of Mrs Pyk's left hand. However, Mrs Glimm's plan to discourage the ambitions of her competitor ultimately backfired, it seemed, for after this attack on her person Mrs Pyk appeared to undergo a dramatic change, as did her method of running things at her east side house. She had always been known as a woman of exceptional will and extraordinary gifts, this one-time exotic dancer and later Mistress of Fortune, but following the dismemberment of her left hand, and its replacement by an artificial wooden hand, she seemed to have attained unheard-of powers, all of which she directed toward one aim – that of putting her ex-partner, Mrs Glimm, out of business. It was then that she began to operate her lodging house in an entirely new manner and in accordance with unique methods, so that whenever travelling commercial agents who patronized Mrs Glimm's west side lodging house came to stay at Mrs Pyk's, they always returned to Mrs Pyk's house on the east side and never again to Mrs Glimm's west side place.

I mentioned to Mr Crumm that I had lived in that northern border town long enough to have be told on various occasions that a guest could only visit Mrs Pyk just so many times before he discovered one day that he could never leave her again. Such talk, I continued, was to some extent substantiated by what was found in the ruins of Mrs Pyk's house after the fire. It seemed there were rooms all over the house, and even in the farthest corners of its vast cellar regions, where the charred remains of human bodies were found. To all appearances, given the intensely destructive nature of that conflagration, each of the incinerated corpses was dressed some outlandish clothing, as if the whole structure of the house was inhabited by a nest of masqueraders. In light of all the stories we had heard in the town, no one bothered to remark on how unlikely it was, how preposterous even, that none of the lodgers at Mrs Pyk's house managed to escape. Nevertheless, as I disclosed to Crumm, the body of Mrs Pyk herself was never found, despite the most diligent search that was conducted by Mrs Glimm.

Yet even as I brought all of these facts to his attention as we sat on that park bench, Crumm's mind seemed to have drifted off to other realms and more than ever he looked as if he belonged in a hospital. Finally he spoke, asking me to confirm what I had said about the absence of Mrs Pyk's body among those found in the ashes left by the fire. I confirmed the statement I had made, begging him to consider the place and the circumstances which were the source of this and all my utterances, as well as his own, that were exchanged that morning in early spring.

"Remember your own words," I said to Crumm.

"Which words were those?" he asked

"Deliriously preposterous," I replied, trying to draw out the sound of each syllable, as if to imbue them with some actual sense or at least a dramatic force of some kind.

"You were only a pawn," I said. "You and all those others were nothing but pawns in a struggle between forces you could not conceive. Your impulses were not you own. They were as artificial as Mrs Pyk's wooden hand."

For a moment Crumm seemed to become roused to his senses. Then he said, as if to himself, "They never found her body."

"No, they did not," I answered.

"Not even her hand," he said in a strictly rhetorical tone of voice. Again I affirmed his statement.

Crumm fell silent after that juncture in our conversation, and when I left him that morning he was staring out at the drab and soggy grounds of that park with the look of someone in a hysterical trance, remaining quietly attentive for some sound or sign to reach his awareness. That was the last time I saw him.

Occasionally, on nights when I find it difficult to sleep, I think about Mr Crumm the commercial agent and the conversation we had that day in the park. I also think about Mrs Pyk and her house on the east side of a northern border town where I once lived. In these moments it almost seems as if I myself can hear the faint jingle-jangle of bells in the blackness, and my mind begins to wander in pursuit of a desperate dream that is not my own. Perhaps this dream ultimately belongs to no one, however many persons, including commercial agents, may have belonged to it.

RAMSEY CAMPBELL

The Word

RAMSEY CAMPBELL'S MOST RECENT suspense novel, *The Last Voice They Hear*, has only been published in America to date, and he is currently at work on his next, *Silent Children*. Other recent books by the author include the novels *The House on Nazareth Hill*, *The One Safe Place* and *The Long Lost*, and such collections as *Waking Nightmares*, *Strange Things Stranger Places*, *Alone With the Horrors* and his latest, *Ghosts and Grisly Things*.

About the following novella, a finalist for the Bram Stoker Award, he recalls: "I still remember the day in 1992 when a phone call from Doug Winter brought about this tale. At first I thought he was ringing to check whether the rare uncut Venezuelan copy of *Chainsaw Sorority Spanking* had arrived (alas, it never did) but quickly learned that he'd been inspired with the idea of a new anthology. Each tale would have as its underlying – not necessarily central – theme the concept of revelations made to someone at the beginning of this century, and each decade would have a tale to itself.

"Creativity can be a contrary business, however, and so while all the contributors to the anthology met Doug's second requirement, I seem to have been alone in working the underlying theme into my story. That didn't prevent me from having my kind of dark fun, and I hope the reader will have some."

NOBODY TRIES TO SPEAK to me while I'm waiting for the lift, thank Sod. Whenever you want to go upstairs at a science fiction convention the lift is always on the top floor, and by the time it arrives it'll have attracted people like a dog-turd attracts flies. There'll be a woman whose middle is twice as wide as the rest of her, and someone wearing no sleeves or deodorant, and at least one writer gasping to be noticed, and now there's a vacuum-head using a walkie-talkie to send messages to another weekend deputy who's within shouting distance. Here comes a clump wearing convention badges with names made up out of their own little heads, N. Trails and Elfan and Si Fye, and I amuse myself trying to decide which of them I'd least like to hear from. Here's the lift at last, and I shut the doors before some bald woman with dragons tattooed on her scalp can get in as well, but a thin boy in a suit and tie manages to sidle through the gap. He sees my *Retard* T-shirt, then he reads my badge. "Hi there," he says. "I'm — "

"Jess Kray," I tell him, since he seems to think I can't read, "and you sent me the worst story I ever read in my life."

He sucks in his lips as if I've punched him in the mouth. "Which one was that?"

"How many have you written that are that bad?"

"None that I know of."

Everyone's pretending not to watch his face doing its best not to wince. "You sent me the one about Frankenstein and the dead goat and the two nuns," I say for everyone to hear.

"I've written lots since."

"Just don't send any to *Retard*."

My fanzine isn't called that now, but I'm not telling him. I leave him to ride to the top with our audience while I lock myself in my room. I was going to write about the Sex, Sects and Subtexts in Women's Horror Fiction panel, which showed me why I've never been able to read a book by the half of the participants I'd heard of, but now I've too much of a headache. I lie on the bed for as long as I can stand being by myself, then I look for someone I can bear to dine with.

We're at Contraception in Edinburgh, but it could be anywhere a mob of fans calling themselves fen take over a hotel for the weekend. As I step into the lobby I nearly bump into Hugh, a writer who used to have tons of books in the shops, maybe because nobody was buying them. Soon books will all he games you play on screens, but I'll bet nobody will play with his. "How are you this year, Jeremy?" he booms.

"Dying like everyone else."

He emits a sound as if he's trying not to react to being poked in the ribs, and the rest of his party comes out of the bar. One of them is Jess Kray, who says "Join us, Jeremy, if you're free for dinner."

He's behaving like the most important person there, grinning with teeth that say we're real and a mouth that says you can check if you like and eyes with a message just for me. I'd turn him down to see how that makes him look, except Hugh Zit says, "Do by all means" so his party knows he means the opposite, and it's too much fun to refuse.

Hugh Know's idea of where to eat is a place called Godfathers. I sit next to his Pakistani wife and her friend who isn't even a convention member, and ignore them so they stop talking English. I've already heard Hugh Ever say on panels all the garbage he's recycling, about how it's a writer's duty to offer a new view of the world, as if he ever did, and how the most important part of writing is research. He still talks like the fan he used to be, like all the fen I know talk, either lecturing straight in your face or staring over your shoulder as though there's a mirror behind you. Only Kray couldn't look more impressed. Hugh Cares finishes his pizza at last and says "I feel better for that."

I say "You must have felt bloody awful before."

Kray actually laughs at that while grimacing sympathetically at Hugh, and I can't wait to go back to my room and write a piece about the games he's playing. I write until I can't see for my headache, and after I've managed to sleep I write about the rest of the clowns at Contraception, until I've almost filled up the first issue of *Parade of the Maladjusted and Malformed*, which is what conventions are. On the last day I see Kray buying a publisher's editor a drink, which no doubt means he'll sell at least a trilogy. At least that's what I write once I'm home.

Then it's back to wearing a suit at the bank in Fulham and having people line up for me on the far side of a window, which at least keeps them at a distance while I turn them and their lives into numbers on a screen. But there's the smell of the people on my side of the glass, and sometimes the feel of them if I don't move fast enough. Playing the game of never saying what I think just about sees me through the day, and the one after that, and the one after that. I print my fanzine in my room and mail it and wait for the clowns I've written about to threaten to sue me or beat me up. The year isn't over when among the review copies and the rest of the unnecessaries publishers send to fanzines I get a sheet about Jess Kray, the most exciting new young writer of the decade, whose first three novels are going to give a new meaning to fantasy.

Sod knows I thought I was joking. I ask for copies to see how bad they are, and they're worse. They're about an alternate world where everyone becomes their sexual opposite, so a gay boy turns into a barbarian hero and a dyke becomes his lover, and some of the characters remember when they return to the real world and most of them try to remind the rest, except one thinks it's meant to be forgotten, and piles of similar crap. I just skim a few chapters of the first book to get a laugh at the idea of people buying a book called *A Touch of Other* under the impression that it's a different kind of junk. Apparently the books go on to be about some wimp who teaches himself magic in the other world and gets to be leader of this one. It's months since I saw Kray talking to the editor, so either he writes even more glibly than he comes on to people or he'd already written them. One cover shows a woman's face turning into a man's, and the second has a white turning black, and the third's got a tinfoil mirror where a face should be. That's the one I throw hardest across the room. Later I put them in the pile to sell to Everybody's Fantasy, the skiffy and comics shop near the docks, and then I hear Kray will be there signing books.

How does a writer nobody's heard of put that over on even a shop run by fen? I'm beginning to think it's time someone exposed him. That Saturday I take the books with me, leaving the compliments slips in so he'll see I haven't bought them. Maybe I'll let him see me selling them as soon as he's signed them. But the moment I spot him at the table with his three piles on it he jumps up. "Jeremy, how are you! This is Jeremy Bates, everyone. He was my first critic."

Sod knows who he's trying to impress. The only customers are comics readers, that contradiction in terms, who look as if they're out without their mothers to buy them their funnies. And the proprietor, who I call Kath on account of his kaftan and long hair, doesn't seem to think much of Kray trying to hitch a ride on my reputation, not that he ever seems to think of much except where the next joint's coming from. I give Kray the books with the slips sticking up, but he carries on grinning. "My publishers haven't sent me your review yet, Jeremy."

I should tell him that's because I won't be writing one, but I'm mumbling like a fan, for Sod's sake. "Write something in them for me."

In the first book he writes *For Jeremy who knew me before I was good*, and *To our future* in the second, and *For life* in what I hope's the last. When he hands them back like treasure I stuff them in my armpit and leaf through some tatty fanzines so I can see how many people he attracts.

Zero. Mr Nobody and all his family. A big round hole without a rim. Some boys on mountain bikes point at him through the window until Kath chases them, and once a woman goes to Kray, but only to ask him where the *Star Trek* section is. Kath's wife brings him a glass of herbal tea which isn't even steaming and with the bag drowning in it, and it's fun to watch him having to drink that. We all hang around for the second half of the hour, then Kath says in the drone that always sounds as if he's talking in his sleep "Maybe you can sign some stock for us."

I can hear he doesn't mean all the books on the table, but that doesn't stop our author. When Kray's defaced every one he says "How about that lunch?"

Kath and Mrs Kath glance at each other, and Jess Kidding gives them an instant grin each. "I understand. Don't even think of it. You can buy lunch next time, after I've made you a bundle. Let me buy this one."

They shake their heads, and I see them thinking there'll never be a next time, but Jess Perfect flashes them an even more-embracing grin before he turns to me. "If you want to interview me, Jeremy, I'll stand lunch. You can be the one who tells the world."

"About what?"

"That'd be telling."

I want the next *PotMaM* to spill a lot more blood, and besides, nobody's ever bought me lunch. I take him round the corner to *Le Marin Qui Rit*, which some French chef with too much money built in an old warehouse by the Thames. "This is charming," Kray says when he sees the nets full of crabs hanging from the beams and the waiters in their sailor suits, though I bet he doesn't think so when he sees the prices on the menu. As soon as we've ordered he hurries through the door that says Matelot until he comes back with his grin and says "Ask me anything." But I've barely opened my mouth when he says "Aren't you recording?"

"Didn't know I'd need to. Don't worry, I remember everything. My ex could tell you."

He digs a pocket tape-recorder out of his trench-coat. "Just in case you need to check. I always carry one for my thoughts."

He heard an ex-success say that at Contraception. A sailor brings us a bottle of sheep juice, Mutton Cadet, and I switch on. "What's a name like Kray supposed to mean to the world?"

"It's my father's name," he says, then proves I was right to be suspicious, because it turns out his father was a Jewish Pole who was put in a camp and left the rest of his surname behind when he emigrated with the remains of his family after the war.

"Speaking of prejudice, what's with the black guy calling himself Nigger when he gets to be the hero?"

"A nigger is someone who minds being called one. Either you take hold of words or they take hold of you."

"Which do you think your books do?"

"A bit of both. I'm learning. I want to be an adventurer on behalf of the imagination."

I can hardly wait to write about him, except here's my poached salmon. He waits until I've taken a mouthful and "What did you like about the books?"

I'm shocked to realise how much of them has stuck in my mind – lines like "AIDS is such a hell you'll go straight to heaven." I want to say "Nothing," but his grin has got to me. "Where you say that being born male is the new original sin."

"Well, that's what one of my characters says."

What does he mean by that? His words keep slipping away from me, and I've no idea where they're going. By the time we finish I'm near to nodding in my pudding, his refusing to be offended by anything I say has taken so much out of me. The best I can come up with as a final question is "Where do you think you're going?"

"To Florida for the summer with my family. That's where the ideas are."

"Here's hoping you get some."

He doesn't switch off the recorder until we've had our coffee, then he gives me the tape. "Thanks for helping," he says, and insists on shaking hands with me. It feels like some kind of Masonic trick, trying to find out if I know a secret – either that or he's working out the best way to shake hands.

He pays the bill without letting his face down and says he's heading for the station, which is on my way home, but I don't tell him. I turn my back on him and take the long way through the streets I always like, with no gardens and no gaps between the houses and less sunlight than anywhere else in town. While I'm there I don't need to think, and I feel as if nothing can happen in me or outside me. Only I have to go home to deal with the tape, which is itching in my hip pocket like a tapeworm.

I'm hoping he'll have left some thoughts on it by mistake, but there's just our drivelling. So either he brought the machine to make sure I could record him or more likely wanted to keep a copy of what we said. Even if he didn't trust me, it's a struggle to write about him in the way I want to. It takes me days and some of my worst headaches. I feel as if he's stolen my energy and turned it into a force that only works on his behalf.

When I seem to have written enough for an issue of *PotMaM* I print out the pages. I have to pick my way around them or tread on them whenever I get up in the night to be sick. I send out the issue to my five subscribers and anyone who sent me their fanzine, though not many do after what I write about their dreck. I take copies to Constipation and Convulsion and sell a few to people who haven't been to a convention before and don't like to say no. When I start screaming at the fanzine in the night and kicking the piles over I pay for a table in the dealers' room at Contamination. But on the Saturday night the dealers' room is broken into, and in the morning every single copy's gone.

It isn't one of my better years. My father dies and my mother tells me my ex-wife went to the funeral. The branch of the bank closes down because of the recession, and it looks as if I'll be out of a job, only luckily one of the other clerks gets his back broken in a hit and run. They move me to Chelsea, where half the lunchtime crowd looks like plain-clothes something and all the litter-bins are sealed up so nobody can leave bombs in them. At least the police won't let marchers into the district, though you can hear them shouting for employment or life sentences for pornography or Islamic blasphemy laws or a curfew for all males as soon as they reach puberty or all tobacco and alcohol profits to go to drug rehabilitation or churchgoing to be made compulsory by law . . . Some writers stop their publisher from sending me review copies, so at least I've bothered them. I give up going to conventions for almost a year, until I forget how boring they are, so that staying in my room seems even worse. And at Easter I set out to find myself a ride to Consternation in Manchester.

I wait most of an hour at the start of the motorway and see a car pick up two girls who haven't waited half as long, so I'm in no mood for any crap from the driver who finally pulls over. He asks what I'm doing for Easter and I think he's some kind of religious creep, but when I tell him about Consternation he starts assuring me how he used to enjoy H. G. Wells and Jules Verne, as if I gave a fart. Then he says "What would you call this new johnny who wrote *The Word*? Is he sci-fi or fantasy or what?"

"I don't know about any word."

"I thought he might be one of you chaps. Went to a publisher and told him his ideas for the book and came away with a contract for more than I expect to make in a lifetime."

"How come you know so much about it?"

"Well, I am a bookseller. Those on high want us to know in advance this isn't your average first novel. Let me cudgel the old brains and I'll give you his name."

I'm about to tell him not to bother when he grins. "Don't know how I could forget a name like that, except it puts you in mind of the Kray brothers, if you're not too young to remember their reign of terror. The last thing he sounds like is a criminal. Jess Kray, that's the phenomenon."

I'd say I knew him if I could be sure of convincing this caricature that he isn't worth knowing. I bite my tongue until it feels as if my teeth are meeting, then I realise the driver has noticed the tears that have got away from me, and I could scream. He says no more until he stops to let me out of the car. "You ought to tell your people about this Kray. Sounds as if he has some ideas that bear thinking about."

The last thing I'll do is tell anyone about Kray, particularly when I remember him saying I should. I wait in my hotel room for my headache to let me see, then I go down to the dealers' room. Instead of books a lot of the tables are selling virtual reality viewers or pocket CD-ROM players. I can't find anything by Kray, and some of the dealers watch me as if I'm planning to steal from them, which makes me feel like throwing their tables over. Then the fat one who always wears a sombrero says "Can I do something for you?"

"Not by the look of it." That doesn't make him go away, and all I can think of is to confuse him. "You haven't got *The Word*."

"No, but Jess sent us each a copy of the cover," he says, and props up a piece of cardboard with letters in the middle of its right-hand side:

JESS KRAY
THE WORD

I can't tell if they're white on a black background or black on white, because as soon as I move an inch they turn into the opposite. I shut my eyes once I've seen it's going to be published by the dump that stopped sending me review copies. "What do you mean, he sent you it? He's just a writer."

"And he designed the cover, and he wants everyone to know what's coming, so he got the publisher to print enough cover proofs for us all in the business."

I'm not asking what Kray said about his book. When Fat in the Hat says "You can't keep your eyes shut forever" I want to shut his, especially when as soon as I open mine he says "Shall we put you down for a copy when it's published?"

"They'll send me one."

"I doubt it," he says, and he'll never know how close he came to losing the bone in his nose, except I have to take my head back to my room.

Maybe he wasn't just getting at me. Once I'm home I ring Kray's new publisher for a review copy. I call myself Jay Battis, the first name that comes into my head, and say I'm the editor of *Psychofant* and no friend of that total cynic Jeremy Bates. But the publicity girl says Kray's book isn't genre fiction, it's literature and they aren't sending it to fanzines.

So why should I care? Except I won't have her treating me as though I'm not good enough for Kray after I gave him more publicity than he deserved when he needed it most. And I remember him thanking me for helping – did he mean with this book? I ask the publicity bitch for his address, but she expects me to believe they don't know it. I could ask her who his agent is, but I've realised how I'd most like to get my free copy of his world-shaking masterpiece.

I don't go to Kath's shop, because I'd be noticed. On the day the book is supposed to come out I go to the biggest bookshop in Chelsea. There's a police car in front, and the police are making them move out of the window a placard that's a big version of the cover of *The Word* – I hear the police say it has been distracting drivers. I walk to a table with a pile of *The Word* on it and straight out with one in my hand, because the staff busy with the police. Only I feel as if Kray's forgiving me for liberating his book, and it takes all my strength not to throw it away.

Even when I've locked my apartment door I feel watched. I hide the book under the bed while I fry some spaghetti and open a tin of salmon for dinner. Then I sit at the window and watch the police cars hunting and listen to the shouts and screams until it's dark. When I begin to feel as if the headlights are searching for me I close the curtains, but then I can't think of anything to do except read the book.

Only the first few pages. Just the prospect of more than a thousand of them puts me off. I can't stand books where the dialogue isn't in quotes and paragraphs keep beginning with "And". And I'm getting the impression that the words are slipping into my head before I can grasp them. Reading the book makes me feel I'm hiding in my room, shutting myself off from the world. I stuff *The Word* down the side of the bed where I can't see the cover playing its tricks, and switch on the radio.

Kray's still in my head. I'm hoping that since it's publication day I'll hear someone tearing him to bits. There isn't a programme about books any longer on the radio, just one about what they call the arts. They're reviewing an Eskimo rock band and an exhibition of sculptures made out of used condoms and a production of *Jesus Christ Superstar* where all the performers are women in wheelchairs, and I'm sneering at myself for imagining they would think Kray was worth their time and at the world for being generally idiotic when the presenter says "And now a young writer whose first novel has been described as a new kind of book. Jess Kray, what's the purpose behind *The Word*?"

"Well, I think it's in it rather than behind it if you look. And I'd say it may be the oldest kind of book, the one that's been forgotten."

At first I don't believe it's him, because he has no accent at all. I make my head throb trying to remember what accent he used to have, and when I give up the presenter is saying "Is the narrator meant to be God?"

"I think the narrator has to be different for everyone, like God."

"You seem to want to be mysterious."

"Don't you think mystery has always been the point? That isn't the same as trying to hide. We've all read books where the writer tries to hide behind the writing, though of course it can't be done, because hiding reveals what you thought you were hiding . . ."

"Can you quote an example?"

"I'd rather say that every book you've ever read has been a refuge, and I don't want mine to be."

"*Every* book? Even the Bible? The Koran?"

"They're attempts to say everything regardless of how much they contradict themselves, and I think they make a fundamental error. Maybe Shakespeare saw the problem, but he couldn't quite solve it. Now it's my turn."

I'm willing the presenter to lose her temper, and she says "So to sum up, you're trying to top Shakespeare and the Bible and the rest of the great books."

"My book is using up a lot of paper. I think that if you can't put more into the world than you take out of it you shouldn't be here at all."

"As you say somewhere in *The Word*. Jess Kray, thank you."

Then she starts talking to a cretic – which is a cretin who thinks they're a critic, such as everyone who attacks my fanzines – about Kray and his book. When the cretic says she thinks the narrator might be Christ because of a scene where he sees the light beyond the mountain through the holes in his hands I start shouting at the radio for quite a time before I turn it off. I crawl into bed and can't stop feeling there's a light beside me to be seen if I open my eyes. I keep them closed all night and wake up with the impression that some of Kray's book is buried deep in my head.

For the first time since I can remember I'm looking forward to a day at the bank. I may even be able to stand the people on my side of the glass without grinding my teeth. But that afternoon Mag, one of the middle-aged girls, waddles in with an evening paper and nearly slaps me in the face with it as though it's my fault. "Will you look at this. Where will it stop. I don't know what the world is coming to."

CALL FOR BAN ON "BLASPHEMOUS" BOOK. I don't want to read any more, yet I grab the paper. It says that on the radio programme I heard Kray said his book was better than the Bible and people should read it instead. A bishop is calling for the police to prosecute, and some mob named Christ Will Rise is telling Christians to destroy *The Word* wherever they find it. So I can't help walking past the shop my copy came from, even though it isn't on my way home. And on the third day half a dozen Earnests with placards saying CHRIST NOT KRAY are picketing the shop.

The police apparently don't think they're worth more than cruising past, and I hope they'll get discouraged, because they're giving Kray publicity. But the next day there are eight of them, and twelve the day after, and at the weekend several Kray fans start reading *The Word* to the pickets to show them how they're wrong. And I feel as though I've had no time to breathe before there's hardly a shop in the country without clowns outside it reading *The Word* and the Bible or the Koran at one another. And then Kray starts touring all the shops and talking to the pickets.

I keep switching on the news to check if he's been scoffed into oblivion, but no such luck. All the time in my room I'm aware of his book in there with me. I'd throw it away except someone might end up reading it – I'd tear it up and burn it except then I'd be like the Christ Will Risers. The day everyone at the bank is talking about Kray being in town during my lunch hour I scrape my brains for something else to do, anything rather than be one of the mob. Only suppose this is the one that stops him? That's a spectacle I'd enjoy watching, so off I limp.

There must be at least a hundred people outside the bookshop. Someone's given Kray a chair to stand on, but Sod knows who's arranged for a beam of sunlight to shine on him. He's answering a question, saying "If you heard the repeats of my interview you'll know I didn't say my book was better than the Bible. I'm not sure what better means in that context. I hope my book contains all the great books."

And he grins, and I wait for someone to attack him, but nobody does, not even verbally. I feel my voice forcing its way out of my mouth, and all I can think of is the question vacuumheads ask writers at conventions. "Where did you get ideas?"

So many people stare at me I think I've asked the question he didn't want asked. I feel as if he's using more eyes than a spider to watch me, more than a whole nest of spiders – more than there are people holding copies of his drivel. Kray himself is only looking in my general direction, trying to make me think he hasn't recognised me or I'm not worth recognising. "They're in my book."

I want to ask why he's pretending not to know me, except I can't be sure it'll sound like an accusation, and the alternative makes me cringe with loathing. But I'm not having any of his glib answers, and I shout "Who are?"

The nearest Kray fan stops filming him with a steadycam video and turns on me. "His ideas, he means. You're supposed to be talking about his ideas."

I won't be told what I'm supposed to be saying, especially not by a never-was who can't comb her hair or keep her lips still, and I wonder if she's trying to stop me asking the question I hadn't realised I was stumbling on. "Who did you meet in Florida?" I shout.

Kray looks straight at me, and it's as if his grin is carving up my head. "Some old people with some old ideas that were about to be lost. They're in my book. Everyone is in any book that matters."

Maybe he sees me sucking in my breath to ask about the three books he wants us to forget he wrote, because he goes on. "As I was about to say, all I'm asking is that we should respect one another. Do me the honour of not criticising *The Word* until you've read it. If anyone feels harmed by it, I want to know."

I might have vanished or never been there at all. When he pauses for a response I feel as if his grin has got stuck in my mouth. The mob murmurs, but nobody seems to want to speak up. Any protest is being swallowed by vagueness. Then two minders appear from the crowd and escort Kray to a limo that's crept up behind me. I want to reach out to him and – I don't know what I want, and one of the minders pushes me out of the way. I see Kray's back, then the limo is speeding away and all the mob are talking to one another, and I have to take the afternoon off because I can't see the money at the bank.

Whenever the ache falters my head fills up with thoughts of Kray and his book. When I sense his book by me in the dark I can't help wishing on it – wishing him and it to a hell as everlasting as my headache feels. It's the first time I've wanted to believe in hell. Not that I'm so far gone I believe wishes work, but I feel better when the radio says his plan's gone wrong. Some Muslim leaders are accusing him of seducing their herd away from Islam.

I keep looking in the papers and listening in the night in case an ayatollah has put a price on his head. Some bookshops in cities that are overrun with Muslims are either hiding their copies of The Word or sending them back, and I wish on it that the panic will spread. But the next headline says he'll meet the Muslim leaders in public and discuss The Word with them.

A late-night so-called arts programme is to broadcast the discussion live. I don't watch it, because I don't know anyone who would let me watch their television, but when it's on I switch out my light and sit at my window. More and more of windows out there start to flicker as if the city is riddled with people watching to see what will happen to Kray. I open my window and listen for shouting Muslims and maybe Kray screaming, but I've never heard so much quiet. When it starts letting my head fill up with thoughts I don't want to have, I go to bed and dream of Kray on a cross. But in the morning everyone at the bank is talking about how the Muslims ended up on Kray's side and how one of them from a university is going to translate The Word into whatever language Muslims use.

And everyone, even Mag who didn't know what the world was coming to with Kray, is saying how they admire him or how they've fallen in love with him and the way he handled himself, and wish they'd gone to see him when he was in town. When I say I've got The Word and can't read it they all look as though they pity me. Three of them ask to borrow it, and I tell them to buy their own because I never paid for mine, which at least means nobody speaks to me much after that. I can still hear them talking about Kray and feel them thinking about him, and in the lunch hour two of them buy *The Word* and the rest, even the manager, want a read. I'm surrounded by Kray, choked by a mass of him. I'm beginning to wonder if anyone in the world besides me knows what he's really like. The bank shuts at last, and when I leave the building two Christ Will Risers are waiting for me.

Both of them wear suits like civil servants and look as though they spend half their lives scrubbing their faces and polishing the crosses at their throats. They both step forward as the sunlight grabs me, and the girl says "You knew him."

"Me, no, who? Knew who?"

Her boyfriend or whatever touches my arm like a secret sign. "We saw you making him confess who he'd met."

"Let's sit down and talk," says the girl.

Every time they move, their crosses flash, until my eyes feel like a whole graveyard of burnt crosses. At least the couple haven't swallowed *The Word*, and talking to them may be better than staying in my room. We find a bench that isn't full of unemployed and clear the McDonald's cartons off it, and the Risers sit on either side of me even though I've sat almost at the end of the bench. "Was he a friend of yours?" the girl says.

"Seems like he wants to be everyone's friend," I say.

"Not God's."

It doesn't matter which of them said that, it could have come from either. "So how much do you know about what happened in Florida?"

"As much as he said when I asked him."

"You must be honest with us. We can't do anything about him if we don't put our faith in the truth."

"Why not?"

That throws them, because they're obviously not used to thinking. Then they say "We need to know everything we can find out about him."

"Who's we?"

"We think you could be one of us. You're of like mind, we can tell."

That's one thing I'll never be with anyone. I nearly jump up and lean on their shining shampooed heads so they won't follow me, but I want to know what they know about Kray that I don't. "Then that must be why I asked him about Florida. All I know is that last time I met him he was going there and he wrote *The Word* when he came back. So what happened?"

They look at each other across me and then swivel their eyes to me. "There are people who came down a mountain almost a hundred years ago. We know he met them or someone connected with them. That has to be the source of his power. Nothing else could have let him win over Islam."

I wouldn't have believed anyone could talk less sense than Kray. "He was like that when he was just a fantasy fan. He's got a genius for charming everyone he meets and promoting himself."

"That must be how he learned the secret that came down the mountain. What else can you tell us?"

I don't mind making them more suspicious of Kray, but I won't have them thinking I tried to help them. "Nothing," I say, and get up.

They both reach inside their jackets for pamphlets. "Please take these. Our address is on the back whenever you want to get in touch."

I could tell them that's never and stuff their pamphlets in their faces, but at least while I've the pamphlets in my fist nobody can take me for a Jess Kray fan. At home I glance at them to see they're as stupid as I knew they would be, full of drone out of the Bible about the Apocalypse and the Antichrist and the Antifreeze and Sod knows what else. I shove them down the side of the bed and try to believe that I've helped the Risers get Kray. And I keep hoping until I see *Time* magazine with him on the cover.

By then half the bank has read *The Word*. I've seen them laughing or crying or going very still when they read it in their breaks, and when they finish it they look as if they have a secret they wish they could tell everyone else. I won't ask, I nearly chew my tongue off. Anyone who asks them about the book gets told "Read it" or "You have to find out for yourself", and I wonder if the book tells you to make as many people read it as you can, like they used to tell you on posters not to give away the end of films. I won't touch my copy of *The Word*, but one day I sneak into a bookshop to read the last page. Obviously it makes no sense, only I feel that if I read the page before it I'll begin to understand, because maybe it can be read backwards as well as forwards. I throw the book on the table and run out of the shop.

At least they've taken *The Word* out of ⌐
room for another pound of fat in a jacket, but I ⌐
reading it in the streets. Whenever I see anything h⌐
I'm afraid it's another copy drawing attention to itsel⌐
feel it beginning to surround me in the night out there, a⌐
myself I've one copy nobody is reading. But I have to take ⌐ ⌐
rides into the country for walks to get away from it – they're the
only way I can be certain I'm nowhere near anyone who's read it.
And coming back from one of those rides, I see him watching me
from the station bookstall.

He looks like a recruiting poster for himself that doesn't need to
point a finger. While I'm pretending to flip through the magazine
I knock all the copies of *Time* onto the floor of the booking hall,
except for the one I shove down the front of my trousers. All the
way home I feel my peter wiping itself on his mouth, and in my
room I have a good laugh at my stain on his face before I turn to
the pages about him.

The headline says WHAT IS THE WORD? in the same typeface as
the cover of his book. Maybe the article will tell me what I need to
put him out of my mind for good. But it says how he bought his
parents a place in Florida with part of his advances, and how *The
Word* is already being translated into thirteen languages, and I'm
starting to puke. Then the hack tries to explain what makes *The
Word* such a publishing phenomenon, as she calls it. And by the
time I've finished nearly going blind with reading what she wrote
I think it's another of Kray's tricks.

It says too much and nothing at all. She doesn't know if the
word is the book or the narrator or the words that keep looking
as if they've been put in by mistake. Kray told her that if a book
wasn't language it was nothing. "So perhaps we should take him
at his, you should forgive it, word." He said he just put the words
on paper and it's for each reader to decide what they add up to. So
she collected a gaggle of cretics and fakes who profess and that
old joke "leading writers" and got them to discuss *The Word*.

If I'd been there I'd have mashed all their faces together. It was
the funniest book someone had ever read, and the most moving
someone else had, and everyone agreed with both of them. One
woman thought it was like *The Canterbury Tales*, and then
there's a discussion about whether it's told by one character or
several or whether all the characters might be the same one in

some sort of mental state or it's showing a new kind of relationship between them all. A professor points out that the Bible was written by a crowd of people but when you read it in translation you can't tell, whereas she thinks you can identify to the word where Kray's voices change, "as many voices as there are people who understand the book". That starts them talking about the idea in *The Word* that people in Biblical times lived longer because they were closer in time to the source, as if that explains why some people are living longer now and the rest of what's happening to us, the universe drifting closer to the state it was in before it formed. And there's crap about people sinning more so their sins will reach back to the Crucifixion because otherwise Christ won't come back, or maybe the book says people have to know when to stop before they have the opposite effect and throw everything off balance, only by now I'm having to run my finger under the words and read them out loud, though my voice makes my head worse. There are still columns to go, the experts saying how if you read *The Word* aloud it's poetry and how you'll find passages almost turning into music, and how there are developments of ideas from Sufism and the Upanishads and Buddhism and Baha'i and the Cabbala and Gnosticism, and Greek and Roman and older myths, and I scrape my fingernail over all this until I reach the end, someone saying "I think the core of this book may be the necessary myth for our time." And everyone agrees, and I tear up the magazine and try to sleep.

I can still hear them all jabbering as if Kray is using their voices to make people read his book to discover what were raving about. I hear them in the morning on my way to the bank, and I wonder how many of them his publisher will quote on the paperback, and that's when I realise I'm dreading the paperback because so many more people will be able to afford it. I'm dreading being surrounded by people with Kray in their heads, because then the world will feel even more like somewhere I've wandered into by mistake. It almost makes me laugh to find I didn't want to be shown that people are as stupid as I've always thought they were.

When posters for the paperback start appearing on bus shelters and hoardings I have to walk about with my eyes half shut. The posters don't use the trick the cover did, but that must mean the publishers think that just the title and his name will sell the book.

At the bank I keep being asked if I don't feel well, until I say I'm not getting my Sunday dinner any more since my mother had a heart attack and died in hospital, not that it's anyone's business, but as well as that I can hardly eat for waiting for the paperback.

The day I catch sight of one there's a march of lunatics demanding that the hospitals they've been thrown out of get reopened, and in the middle of all this a woman's sitting on a bench reading *The Word* as though she can't see or hear what's going on around her for the book. And then the man she's waiting for sits down by her and squashes his wet mouth on her cheek, and leans over to see what she's reading, and I see him start to read as if it doesn't matter where you open the book, you'll be drawn in. And when I run to the bank one of the girls asks me if I know when the paperback is coming out, and saying I don't know makes me feel I'm trying to stop something that can't be stopped.

Or am I the only one who can? I spend the day trying to remember where I put the interview with him. Despite whoever stole all the copies of *PotMam* at Contamination, I should have the tape. I look under my clothes and the plates and the tins and in the tins as well, and under the pages of the magazine I tore up, and under the towels on the floor in the corner, and among the bits of glasses I've smashed in the sink.

It isn't anywhere. My mother must have thrown it out one of the days she came to clean my room. I start screaming at her until I lose my voice, by which time I've thrown just about everything movable out of the window. They're demolishing the houses opposite, so some more rubbish in the street won't make any difference, and my fellow rats in the building must be too scared to ask what I'm doing, unless they're too busy reading *The Word*.

By the end of the week, two of the slaves at the bank have the paperback and will lend it to anyone who asks. And I don't know when they start surrounding me with Kray's words. Most of the time – Sod, all the time – I know they're saying things they've heard someone else say, but after a while I notice they've begun speaking in a way that's meant to show they're quoting. Like the girl at the window by mine would start talking about a murder mystery on television and the one next to her would say "The mystery is around you and in you" and they'd laugh as if they were sharing a secret. Or one would ask the time and her partner in the comedy team would say "Time is as soon as you make it." And all sorts of other crap:

"Look behind the world" or "You're the shadow of the infinite," which the manager says once as if he's topping everyone else's quotes. And before I know it at least half the slaves don't say "Good morning" any more, they say "What's the word?"

That makes the world feel like a headache. People say it in the street too, and when they come up to my window, until I wonder if I was wrong to blame my mother for losing the tape, if someone else might have got into my room. By the time the next catch-phrase takes root in the dirt in people's heads I can't control myself – when I hear one of the girls respond to another "As Kray would say."

"Is there anything he doesn't have something to say about?"

I think I'm speaking normally enough, but they cover their ears before they shake their heads and look sad for me and chorus "No."

"Sod, listening to you is like listening to him."

"Maybe you should."

"Maybe he will."

"Maybe everyone will."

"Maybe is the future."

"As Kray would say."

"Do you know you're the only one who hasn't read him, Jeremy?"

"Thank Sod if it keeps me different."

"Unless we find ourselves in everybody else . . ."

"As fucking Kray would say."

A woman writing a cheque gasps, and another customer clicks his tongue like a parrot, and I'm sure they're objecting to me daring to utter a bad word about their idol. None of the slaves speaks to me all day, which would be more of a relief if I couldn't feel them thinking Kray's words even when they don't speak them. I assume the manager didn't hear me, since he was in his office telling someone the bank is going to repossess their house. But on Monday morning he calls me in and says "You'll have been aware that there's been talk of further rationalisation."

He was talking before that, only I was trying to see where he's hidden *The Word*. At least he doesn't sound like Kray. "Excuse me, Mr Bates, but are there any difficulties you feel I should know about?"

"With what?"

"I'd like to give you a chance to explain your behaviour. You're aware that the bank expects its staff to be smart and generally presentable."

I hug myself in case that hides whatever he's complaining about and hear my armpits squelch, and me saying "I thought you were supposed to see yourself in me."

"That was never meant to be used as an excuse. Have you really nothing more to say?"

I can't believe I tried to defend myself by quoting Kray. I chew my tongue until it hurts so much I have to stick it out. "I should advise you to seek some advice, Mr Bates," says the manager. "I had hoped to break this to you more gently, but I must say I can see no reason to. Due to the economic climate I've been asked to propose further cuts in staff, and you will appreciate that your attitude has aided my decision."

"Doesn't Kray have anything to say about fixing the economy?"

"I believe he does in world terms, but I fail to see how that helps our immediate situation."

The manager's beginning to look reluctantly sympathetic – he must think I've turned out to be one of them after all, and I won't have him thinking that. "If he tried I'd shove his book back where it came from."

The manager looks as if I've insulted him personally. "I can see no profit in prolonging this conversation. If you wish to work your notice I must ask you to take more care with your appearance and, forgive my bluntness, to treat yourself to a bath."

"How often does he say I've got to have one?" I mean that as a sneer, but suppose it sounds like a serious question? "Not that I give a shit," I say, which isn't nearly enough. "And when I do I can use his book to wipe my arse on. And that goes for your notice as well, because I don't want to see any of you again or anyone else who's got room in their head for that, that . . ." I can't think of a word bad enough for Kray, but it doesn't matter, because by now I'm backing out of the office. "Just so everyone knows I know I'm being fired because of what I say about him," I add, raising my voice so they'll hear me through their hands over their ears. Then I manage to find my way home, and the locks to stick the keys in, and my bed.

*   *   *

There's almost nothing else in my room except me and *The Word*. So I still have a job, to stay here to make sure it's the copy nobody reads. I do that until the bank sends me a cheque for the money they must wish they didn't owe me, and I remember all my money I forgot to take with me when I escaped from the bank.

I'm waiting when they open. At first I think the slaves are pretending not to know me, then I wonder if they're too busy thinking Kray's thoughts. A slave takes my cheque and my withdrawal slip and goes away for longer than I can believe it would take even her to think about it, then I see the manager poke his head out of his office to spy on me while I'm tearing up a glossy brochure about how customers can help the bank to help the Third World. I see him tell the clerk to give me what I want, then he pulls in his head like a tortoise that's been kicked, and it almost blinds me to realise he's afraid of what I am. Only what am I?

The slave stuffs all my money in an envelope and drops it in the trough under the window, the trough that always made me wonder which side the pigs were on. I shove the envelope into my armpit and leave behind years of my life. I'm walking home as fast as I can, through the streets where every shop either has a sale on or is closing down or both, when I see Kray's face.

It's a drawing on the cover of just about the only magazine which is still about books. I have to find out what he's up to, but with the money like a cancer under my arm I can't be sure of liberating the magazine without people noticing. I go into the bookshop and grab it off the rack, and people backing away make me feel stronger.

I've only read how *The Word* is shaping up to outsell the Bible worldwide, and how some campus cult is saying there's a different personal message in it for everybody and anyone who can't read it should have it read to them, when a bouncer trying to look like a policeman tells me to buy the rag or leave. I've read all I need to, and I have all I need. The money is to give me time to do what I have to.

Only I'm not sure what that is. The longer I stay in my room, the more I'm tempted to look in *The Word* for a clue. It's trying to trick me into believing there's no help outside its pages, but I've something else to read. I find the Christ Will Rise pamphlets that The Word has done its best to tear up and shove out of my reach, and when I've dragged them and my face out of the dust under the bed I manage to smooth out the address.

It's down where most of the fires in the streets are and the police drive round in armoured cars when they go there at all, and no cameras are keeping watch, and hardly any helicopters. By now it's dark. People are doing things to each other standing up in doorways if they aren't prowling the streets in dozens searching for less than themselves. I'm afraid they may set fire to me, because I see dogs pulling apart something charred that looks as if it used to be someone, but nobody seems to think I'm worth bothering with, which is their loss.

The Risers' sanctuary is in the middle of a block of hundred-year-old houses, some of which have roofs. Children are running into one house holding a cat by all its legs, but I can't see anyone else. I feel the front steps tilt and crunch together as I climb to the Risers' door, and I hold onto the knocker to steady myself, though it makes my fingers feel as if they're crumbling. I'm about to slam the knocker against the rusty plate when a fire in a ruin across the street lights up the room inside the window next to me.

It's full of chairs around a table with pamphlets on it. Then the fire jerks higher, and I see they aren't piles of pamphlets, they're two copies of *The Word*. The books start to wobble like two blocks of gelatin across the table towards me, and I nearly wrench the knocker off the door with trying to let go of it. I fall down the steps and don't stop running until I'm locked in my room.

I watch all night in case I've been followed. Even after the last television goes out I can't sleep. And when the dawn brings the wagons to clean up the blood and vomit and empty cartridges I don't want to sleep, because I've remembered that the Risers aren't the only other people who know what Kray was.

I go out when the streets won't be crawling – when the taken care of have gone to work and the beggars are counting their pennies. When I reach Everybody's Fantasy it looks as if the books in the window and the Everything Half Price sign have been there for months. The rainy dirt on the window stops me reading the spines on the shelf where Kray would be. I'm across the road in a burned-out house, waiting for a woman with three Dobermans to pass so I can smash my way into the shop with a brick, when Kath arrives in a car with bits of it scraping the road.

He doesn't look interested in why I'm there or in anything else, especially selling books, so I say "You're my last hope."

"Yeah, okay." It takes him a good few seconds to get around to saying "What?"

"You've got some books I want to buy."

"Yeah?" He comes to as much life as he's got and wanders into the shop to pick up books strewn over the floor. "There they are."

I think he's figured out which books I want and why until I realise he means everything in the shop. I'm heading for the shelf when I see *The Word, The Word, The Word, The Word* . . . "Where's *A Touch of Other*?" I nearly scream.

"Don't know it."

"Of course you do. Jess Kray's first novel and the two that go with it. He signed them all when you didn't want him to. You can't have sold them, crap like them."

"Can't I?" Kath scratches his head as if he's digging up thoughts. "No, I remember. He bought the lot. Must have been just about when *The Word* was due."

"You realise what he was up to, don't you?"

"Being kind. Felt guilty about leaving us with all those books after nobody came, so he bought them back when he could afford to. Wish we still had them. I've never even seen them offered for sale."

"That's because he doesn't want anyone to know he wrote them, don't you see? Otherwise even the world might wonder how someone like that could have written the thing he wants everyone to buy."

"You can't have read *The Word* if you say that. It doesn't matter what came before it, only what will happen when everyone's learned from it."

He must have stoned whatever brains he had out of his head. "I felt like you do about him," he's saying now, "but then I got to know him."

"You know him? You know where I can find him?"

"Got to know him in his book."

"But you've got the address where you sent him his books."

"Care of his publishers."

"He didn't even give you his address and you think he's your friend?"

"He was moving. He's got nothing to hide, you have to believe that." Having to give me so many answers so fast seems to have used Kath up, then his face rouses itself. "If you want to get to know him as he is, he's supposed to be at Consummation."

"I've given up on fans. The people I meet every day are bad enough."

Kath's turning over magazines on the counter like a cat trying to cover its turds. "There'll be readings from *The Word* for charity and a panel about it, and he's meant to be there. We'd go, only we've not long had a kid."

"Don't tell me there'll be someone growing up without *The Word*."

"No, we'd like her to see him one day. I was just telling you we can't afford to go." He shakes two handfuls of fanzines until a flyer drops out of one. "See, there he is."

The flyer is for Consummation, which is two weeks away in Birmingham, and says the Sunday will be Jess Kray Day. I manage not to crumple much of it up. "Can I have this?"

"I thought you didn't want to know him."

"You've sold me." I shove the flyer into my pocket. "Thanks for giving me what I was looking for," I say, and leave him fading with his books.

I don't believe a whole sigh fie convention can be taken in by Kray. Fen are stupid, Sod knows, but in a different way – thinking they're less stupid than everyone else. I'll know what to do when I see them and him. The two weeks seem not so much to pass as not to be there at all. On the Friday morning I have a bath so I won't draw attention to myself until I want to. For the first time ever I don't hitch to a convention, I go by train to be in time to spy out the situation. Once I'm in my seat I stay there, because I've seen one woman reading *The Word* and I don't want to see how many other passengers are. I stare at streets of houses with steel shutters over the windows and rivers covered with chemicals and forests that children keep setting fire to, but I can feel Kray's words hatching in all the nodding heads around me.

The convention hotel is five minutes' walk from the station. After about ten beggars I pretend I'm alone in the street. The hotel is booked solid as a fan's cranium, and the hotel next to it, and I have to put up with one where the stairs lurch as if I'm drunk and my room smells of someone's raincoat and old cigarettes. It won't matter, because I'll be spending as much time with the fen as I can bear. I go to the convention hotel while it's daylight and there are police out of their vehicles. And the first thing the girl at the registration desk with a ring in her nose and six more in her ears says is "Have you got *The Word*?"

My face goes hard, but I manage to say "It's at home."

"If you'd like one to have with you, they're free with membership."

It'll be another nobody else can read. I tell her my name's Jay Batt and pin my badge on when she's written it, and squeeze the book in my right hand so hard I can almost feel the words mashing together. "Is he here yet?"

"He won't be."

"But he's why I'm here. I was promised he was coming."

She must think I sound the same kind of disappointed as her. "He said he would be when we wrote to him, only now he has to be in the film about him they'll be televising next month. Shall I tell you what he said? That now we've got *The Word* we don't need him."

I know that's garbage, but I'm not sure why. I bite my tongue so I won't yell, and when I see her sympathising with the tears in my eyes I limp off to the bar. It's already full of more people than seats, and I know most of them – I've written about them in my fanzines. I'm wondering how I can get close enough to find out what they really think about *The Word* when they start greeting me like an old friend. Two people have offered to buy me a drink before I realise why they're behaving like this – because I've got *The Word*.

I down the drinks, and more when they're offered, and make sure everyone knows I won't buy a round. I'm trying to infuriate someone as much as their forgiveness infuriates me, because then maybe they'll argue about Kray. But whatever I say about him and his lies they just look more understanding and wait patiently for me to understand. The room gets darker as my eyes fill up with the dirt and smoke in the air, and faces start to melt as if *The Word* has turned them into putty. Then I'm screaming at the committee members and digging my nails into the cover of the book. "Why would anyone be making a film about him? More likely he was afraid he'd meet someone here who knows what he wants us to forget he wrote."

"You mustn't say that. He sent us this, look, all about the film." The chairman takes a glossy brochure out of his briefcase. The sight of Kray grinning on the cover almost blinds me with rage, but I manage to read the name of the production company. "And they're going to do a live discussion with him after the broadcast," the chairman says.

I run after my balance back to my hotel. I can hear machine-guns somewhere, and I have to ring the bell three times before the armed night porter lets me in, but they can't stop me now. I haul myself up to my room, snapping a banister in the process, and fall on the bed to let my headache come. Whenever it lessens I think of another bit of the letter I'm going to write. The night and the sounds of gunfire falter at last, and the room fades into some kind of reality. It's like being part of the cover of a book nobody wants to take out of a window, but they won't be able to ignore me much longer.

I write the letter and check out of the hotel, telling the receptionist I've been called away urgently, and fight my way through the pickpockets to the nearest post office, where I get the address of the television channel. Posting the letter reminds me of going to church when I had to live with my parents, where they used to put things in your mouth in front of the altar. As soon as the letter is out of my hands I don't know if I feel empty or unburdened, and I can't remember exactly what I wrote.

I spend Sunday at home trying to remember. Did I really claim I was the first to spread the word about Kray? Did I really call myself Jude Carrot because I was afraid he'd remember the interview and tell the producer not to let me anywhere near? Won't he just say he's never heard of me? I can't think how that idea makes me feel. I left the other copy of *The Word* in my hotel room as if it was the Bible, and I have to stop myself from throwing the one under the bed out of the window to give them something to fight over besides the trash in the street.

On Monday I know the letter has arrived. Maybe it'll take a few hours to reach the producer of the discussion programme, since I didn't know his name. By Tuesday it must have got to him, and by Wednesday he should have written to me. But Thursday comes, and I watch the postman dodging in and out of his van while his partner rides shotgun, and there's no letter for me. Twice I hear the phone in the hall start to ring, but it could just be army trucks shaking the house. I start trying to think of a letter I could write under another name, saying I know things about Kray nobody else does, only I can't think of a letter that's different enough. I go to bed to think, then I get up to, and keeping doing those is Thursday and Friday morning. Then I hear the van screech to a halt just long enough for the postman to stick a letter through the door without getting out of his cabin, because presumably they can't afford to pay his partner any more, then it screeches away along the sidewalk. And when I look down the stairs I see the logo of the television company on the envelope.

I'd open it in the hall except I find I'm afraid to read what it says. I remember I'm naked and cover my peter with it while I run upstairs, though everyone in the house is scared to open their door if they hear anyone else. I lock all my locks and hook up the chains and wipe my hands on my behind so the envelope won't slip out of them, then I tear it almost in half and shake the letter flat.

Dear Mr "Carrot"
Jess Kray says

Suddenly my hands feel like gloves someone's just pulled their hands out of, and when I can see again I have to fetch the letter from under the bed. I'm already struggling to think of a different name to sign on the next letter I send, though since now I'll know who the producer is, should I phone them? I poke at my eyes until they focus enough that I can see her name is Tildy Bacon, then I make them see what she wrote.

Dear Mr "Carrot"
Jess Kray says he will look forward to seeing you and including you in our discussion on the 25th.

There's more about how they'll pay my expenses and where I'm to go, but I fall on the bed, because I've just discovered I don't know what to do after all. It doesn't matter, I'll know what to say when the cameras are on and the country's watching me. Only something's missing from that idea, and the absence keeps pecking at my head. It feels like an intruder in my room, one I can't see that won't leave me alone. Maybe I know what I'm trying not to

think, but a week goes by before I realise: I can't be certain of
exposing Kray unless I read *The Word*.

I spend a day telling myself I have to, and the next day I drag
the book out of its hiding place and claw off the dusty cobwebs. I
stare at the cover until it feels as if it's stuck behind my eyes, then I
scream at myself to make me open it. As soon as I can see the print
I start reading, but it feels as if Kray's words and the noises of
marching drums and sirens and gunfire are merging into a
substance that's filling up my head before I can stop it, and I
have to shut the book. There's less than a week before I'm on
television, and all I can think of that may work is being as far
away from people as I can get when I read the book.

The next day is Sunday, which makes no difference, since
there are as many people wandering around the countryside
with nothing else to do any day of the week. I tear the covers off
a Christ Will Rise pamphlet and wrap them round *The Word*
before I head for Kings Cross, and I'm sure some of the people I
avoid look at it to see if it's *The Word*. I thump on the steel
shutter until the booking clerk sells me a ticket. While I'm
waiting for the train I see through the reinforced glass of the
bookstall that most of the newspapers are announcing a war
that's just begun in Africa. I catch myself wondering if *The
Word* has been translated in those countries yet, and then I
imagine a world where there are no wars because everyone's too
busy reading *The Word* and thinking about it and talking about
it, and my fingernails start aching from gripping the book so I
won't throw it under a train.

When my train leaves I'm almost alone on it, but I see more
people than I expect in the streets. Quite a few seem to be
gathering in a demolished church, and I see a whole crowd
scattered over a park, being read to from a book – I can't decide
whether it's black or white. All their faces are turned to the sun as
if they don't know they're being blinded. As the city falls away I'm
sure I can feel all those minds clogged with Kray trying to drag
mine back and having to let go like old tasteless chewing gum
being pulled out of my head. Then there are only fields made up of
lines waiting to be written on, and hedges blossoming with litter,
and hours later mountains hack their way up through fields and
forests as if the world is still crystallising. In the midst of the
mountains I get off at a station that's no more than two empty

platforms, and climb until I'm deep in a forest and nearly can't breathe for climbing. I sit on a fallen tree, and there's nothing to do except read. And I make myself open *The Word* and read as fast as I can.

I won't look up until I've finished. I can feel his words crowding into my head and breeding there, but I have to understand what he's put into the world before I confront him. The only sound is of me turning pages and ripping each one out as I finish it, but I sense the trees coming to read over my shoulder, and moss oozing down them to be closer to the book, and creatures running along branches until they're above my head. I won't look, I only read faster, so fast that the book is in my head before I know. However much there is of it, I'm stronger – out here it's just me and the book. I wonder suddenly if the pages may be impregnated with some kind of drug, but if they are I've beaten it by throwing away the pages, because you must have to be holding the whole book for the drug to work. I've no idea how long I've been reading the book aloud, but it doesn't matter if it helps me see what Kray is up to. Though my throat is aching by the time I've finished, I manage a laugh that makes the trees back away. I fall back with my face to the clouds and try to think what the book has told me that he wouldn't want anyone to know.

My body's shaking inside and out, and I feel as if my brain is too. There was something about panic in *The Word*, but if I think of it, will that show me how the book is causing it, or won't I be able to resist swallowing *The Word* as the cure? I'm already remembering, and digging my fingernails into my temples can't crush the thought. Kray says we'll all experience a taste of the panic Christ experienced as we approach the time when the world is changed. I feel the idea cracking open in my brain, and as I fight it I see in a flash what he was trying not to admit phrasing it that way. He wanted nobody to know that he is panicking – that he has something to be afraid of.

I sit up and crouch around myself until I stop shaking, then I go down through the forest. The glade papered with *The Word* seems to have a meaning I no longer need to understand. Some of the pages look as if they're reverting to wood. The night comes down the forest with me, and in a while a train crawls out of it. I go home and lock myself in.

*   *   *

Now it takes me all my time to hold *The Word* still in my head. The only other thing I need to be aware of is when the television company sends me my train ticket, but everything around me seems on the point of making a move. Whenever I hear a car it sounds about to reveal it's a mail-van. At least that helps me ignore my impression that all I can see of the world is poised to betray itself. If this is how having read *The Word* feels . . .

The next day the mail-van screeches past my building, and the day after that. Suppose the letter to me has been stolen, or someone at the television company has stopped it from being sent? I'll pay my own fare and get into the discussion somehow. But the ticket finally arrives, which may mean they'll try and steal it from my room.

I sit with the ticket between my teeth and watch the street and listen for them setting up whatever they may use to smash my door in. Suppose the room itself is the trap? Or am I being made to think that so I'll be driven out of it? I wrap the ticket in some of a Christ Will Rise pamphlet so that the ink won't run when I take it with me to the bathroom, and on the last morning I have a long bath that feels like some kind of ritual. That would be a good time for them to come for me, but they don't, nor on my way to the station, though I'm sure I notice people looking at me as if they know something about me. For the first time since I can remember there are no sounds of violence in the streets, and that makes me feel there are about to be.

On the train I sit where I can watch the whole compartment, and see the other passengers pretending not to watch me. All the way to Hyde Park Corner I expect to be headed off. I'm trudging up the slope to the hotel when a limo pulls up in front of the glass doors and two minders climb out before Kray does. As he unbends he looks like a snake standing on its tail. I pretend to be interested in the window of a religious bookshop in case he tries to work on me before the world is watching. I see copies of *The Word* next to the Bible and the Koran, and Kray's reflection merging with his book as he goes into the hotel. He must have noticed me, so why is he leaving me alone? Because passiveness is the trick he's been playing on me ever since I read *The Word* – doing nothing so I'll be drawn towards him and his words. It's the trick he's been playing on the world.

Knowing that makes me impatient to finish. I wait until I see him arrive in the penthouse suite, then I check in. My room is more than twice the size of the one I left at home. The world is taking notice of me at last. I drink the liquor in the refrigerator while I have another bath, and ignore the ringing of the phone until I think there's only just time to get to the studio before the discussion starts.

A girl's face on the phone screen tells me my taxi's waiting. As soon as we're in it she wants to know everything about me, but I won't let her make me feel I don't know what I am. I shrug at her until she shuts up. There are no other cars on the road, and I wonder if there's a curfew or everyone's at home waiting for Kray and me.

Five minutes later the taxi races into the forecourt of the television studios. The girl with not much breath rushes me past a guard at the door and another one at a desk and down a corridor that looks as if it never ends. I think that's the trick they were keeping in store for me, but then she steers me left into a room, and I'm surrounded by voices and face to face with Kray.

There are about a dozen other people in the room. The remains of a buffet are on a table and scattered around on paper plates. A woman with eyes too big for her face says she's Tildy Bacon and hands me a glass of wine while a girl combs my hair and powders my face, and I feel as if they're acting out some ritual from *The Word*. Kray watches me as he talks and grins at some of his cronies, and once the girl has finished with me he puts a piece of cake on a plate and brings it over. "You must have something, Jeremy. You look as if you've been fasting for the occasion."

So does he. He looks thinner and older, as if he's put almost all of himself into his book, or is he trying to trick me into thinking he'll be easy to deal with? I take the plate and wash a bite of the cake down with some wine, and he gives me the grin. "It's nearly time."

Is he talking about the programme I can see behind him on a monitor next to a fax machine? Someone who might be a professor or a student is saying that nobody he's met has been unchanged by *The Word* and that he thinks it promises every reader the essential experience of their life. Kray's watching my face, but I won't let him see I know how much crap the screen is talking until we're on the air. Then Tildy Bacon says to everyone "Shall we go up? Bring your drinks."

As the girl who ought to learn how to breathe ushers people towards the corridor, Tildy Bacon steps in front of me and looks me in the face. So they've saved stopping me until the last possible moment. I'll wait until everyone else is out of the room, then I'll do whatever needs to be done to make certain she can't follow me and throw me off the air. But she says "We had to ask Jess how to bill you on screen since you weren't here."

If she thinks I'm going to ask what he said I was, she can go on thinking. "I'm sure he knows best," I tell her with a grin that may look like his for all I care, and dodge around her before she can delay me any further, and follow the procession along the corridor.

At first the set-up in the studio looks perfect. The seven of us, including Kray, will sit on couches around a low table with glasses and a jug of water on it while Kray's minders have to stay on the far side of a window. Only I haven't managed to overtake the procession, so how can I get close to him? Then he says "Sit next to me, Jeremy," and pats a leather cushion, and before I have time to wonder what he's up to I've joined him.

Everyone else sitting down sounds like something leathery stirring in its sleep. The programme about Kray is on a monitor in a corner of the studio. A priest says he believes the secret of *The Word* needs to be understood, then the credits are rolling and a woman who I hadn't even realised was going to run the discussion leans across the table and waits for a red light to signal her. Then she says "So, Jess Kray, what's your secret?"

He grins at her and the world. "If I have one it must be in my book."

A man with holes in his purple face where spots were says, "In other words, if you revealed the secret it wouldn't sell."

Is there actually someone here besides me who doesn't believe in *The Word*? Kray grins at him. "No, I'm saying the secret must be different for everyone. It isn't a question of commerce. In some parts of the world I'm giving the book away."

The holey man seems satisfied, but a woman with almost more hair on her upper lip than on her scalp says "To achieve what?"

"Peace?"

Good Sod, Kray really does believe his book can put a stop to wars. Or does he mean he won't be peaceful until the whole world has *The Word* inside them? The woman who was given the signal leans across the table again, reaching for Kray with her perfume and her glittering hands and her hair swaying like oil on water. She means to turn the show into a discussion, which will give him the chance not to be watched all the time by the camera. I'll say anything to bother him, even before I know what. "It's supposed to be . . ."

That heads her off, and everyone looks at me. Then I hear what I'm going to say – that the secret of *The Word* is supposed to be some kind of eternal life. But there is no secret in *The Word*, that's why I'm here. "Jeremy?" Kray says.

I'm wondering if *The Word* has got inside me without my knowing – if it was making me say what I nearly said and that's why he is encouraging me. He wants me to say that for him, and he's talking about peace, which I already knew was his weapon, and suddenly I see what everything has been about. It's as if a light is shining straight into my eyes, and I don't care if it blinds me. "He's supposed to be Christ," I shout.

There's some leathery movement, then someone I don't need to see says "All the characters are clearly aspects of him."

"We're talking about the narrator of *The Word*," the television woman explains to the camera, and joins in. "I took him to be some kind of prophet."

"Christ was a prophet," says a man who I can just about see is wearing a turban.

"Are we saying –" the television woman begins, but she can't protect Kray from me like that. "He knows I didn't mean anyone in his book," I shout. "I mean him."

The words are coming out faster than I can think, but they feel right. "If people don't believe in him they won't believe in his book. And they won't believe in him unless he can save himself."

Ideas are fighting in my head as if *The Word* is trying to come clear. If Christ came back now he'd have to die to make way for a religion that works better than his did, or would it be the opposite of Christ who'd try to stop all the violence and changes in the world? Either way . . . I'm going blind with panic, because I can feel Kray close to me, willing me to . . . He wants me to go on speaking while my words are out of control – because they're his, or because I won't be able to direct them at him? Then I realise how long he's been silent, and I think he wants me to speak to him so he can speak to me. Is the panic I'm suffering his? He's afraid –

afraid of me, because I'm . . . "I think it's time we moved on," the television woman says, but she can't make anything happen now. I turn and look at him.

He's waiting for me. His grin is telling me to speak – to say whatever I have to say, because then he'll answer and all that the world will remember hearing is him. It's been that way ever since the world heard of him. I see that now, but he's let me come too close. As I open my mouth I duck my head towards him.

For a moment it seems I'm going to kiss him. I see his lips parting, and his tongue feeling his teeth, and the blood in his eyes, and the fear there at last. I duck lower and go for his throat. I know how to do it from biting my tongue, and now I don't need to restrain myself or let go. Someone is screaming, it sounds as if the world is, but it can't be Kray, because I've torn out his voice. I lift my head and spit it back into his face.

It doesn't blot out his eyes. They meet mine, and there's forgiveness in them, or something even worse – fulfilment? Then his head falls back, opening his throat so I'm afraid he'll try and talk through it, and he throws his arms wide for the cameras. That's all I see, because there's nothing in my eyes now except light. But it isn't over, because I can still taste his voice like iron in my mouth.

Words are struggling to burst out of my head, and I don't know what they are. Any moment Kray's minders or someone will get hold of me, but if I can just . . . I bang my knees against the table to find it, and hear the glasses clash against the jug. I throw myself forwards and find one, and a hand grabs my arm, but I wrench myself free and shove the glass against my teeth until it breaks. Now the light feels as if it's turning into pain which is turning into the world, but whose pain is it – Kray's or mine? Hands are pulling at me, and I've no more time to think. As I make myself chew and swallow, at least I'm sure I'll never say another word.

ANDY DUNCAN

The Map to
the Homes of the Stars

ANDY DUNCAN WAS A FINALIST for the 1998 Campbell Award for Best New Writer, and the first story he sold, "Beluthahatchie", was nominated for the Hugo Award for Best Short Story the same year.

A native of Batesburg, South Carolina, and a long time resident of North Carolina, he now lives in Tuscaloosa, Alabama, where he teaches composition, American literature and creative writing at the University of Alabama, and is working on his M.F.A. in fiction.

Duncan is a 1994 graduate of the Clarion West Writers' Workshop in Seattle, and his stories have appeared in *Asimov's Science Fiction*, *Dying for It* and the World Fantasy Award-winning anthology *Starlight 1*.

About the following story, the author explains: "Gardner Dozois wrote me that he was putting together an anthology, and did I have any stories that involved sex and ghosts? I was both pleased and embarrassed to answer that I had three and was working on a fourth. He wound up buying two of them. I thank Gardner for that and for his astute rewrite suggestions.

" 'The Map' is set in my hometown, and old friends have recognized the few scraps that aren't made up. Given the opportunity, I dedicate it to the best friend of my adolescence, Richard O'Malley, who is, I'm glad to say, still very much on the map."

L AST NIGHT, I HEARD it again. About eleven, I stood at the kitchen counter, slathered peanut butter onto a stale, cool slice of refrigerated raisin bread, and scanned months-old letters to the editor in an A section pulled at random from the overflow around the recycling bin. READER DECRIES TOBACCO EVILS. ECONOMY SOUND, SAYS N.C. BANKER. The little headlines give the otherwise routine letters such urgency, like telegraphed messages from some war-torn front where issues are being decided, where news is happening. ARTS FUNDING CALLED NECESSARY. As I chewed my sandwich, I turned one-handed to the movie listings, just to reassure myself that everything I had skipped in the spring wasn't worth the trouble anyway, and then I heard a slowly approaching car.

We don't get much traffic on my street, a residential loop in a quiet neighborhood, and so even we single guys who don't have kids in the yard unconsciously register the sounds of each passing vehicle. But this was the fifth night in a row, and so I set down my sandwich and listened.

Tom used to identify each passing car, just for practice.

"Fairlane."

"Crown Victoria."

"Super Beetle."

This was back home, when we were as bored as two seventeen year-olds could be.

"Even *I* can tell a Super Beetle," I said. I slugged my Mountain Dew and lowered the bottle to look with admiration at the neon-green foam.

Tom frowned, picked up his feet, and rotated on the bench of the picnic table so that his back was to Highway 1.

Without thinking, I said, "Mind, you'll get splinters." I heard my mother speaking, and winced.

Now Tom looked straight ahead at the middle-school basketball court, where Cathy and her friends, but mostly Cathy (who barely knew us, but whose house was fourth on our daily route), were playing a pick-up game, laughing and sweating and raking their long hair back from their foreheads. As each car passed behind him, he continued the litany.

"Jeep."

"Ford pickup."

"Charger."

I didn't know enough to catch him in an error, of course, but I have no doubt that he was right on the money, every time. I never learned cars; I learned other things, that year and the next fifteen years, to my surprise and exhilaration and shame, but I never learned cars, and so I am ill-equipped to stand in my kitchen and identify a car driving slowly past at eleven o'clock at night.

Not even when, about five minutes later, it gives me another chance, drives past again in the other direction, as if it had gotten as far as the next cul-de-sac, and turned around.

It passes so slowly that I am sure it is about to turn into someone's driveway, someone's, mine, but it hasn't, for five nights now it hasn't. I couldn't tell you if I had to precisely what make of car it is.

I could guess, though.

Maybe tonight, if, when, it passes by, I'll go to the front door and pull back the narrow dusty curtain that never gets pulled back except for Jehovah's Witnesses, and see for myself what make of car it is. See if I recognize it. But all I did last night, and the four nights before, was stand at my kitchen counter, fingertips black with old news, jaws Peter-Panned shut (for I am a creature of habit), stare unseeing at the piled-up sink, and trace in my head every long-gone stop on the map to the homes of the stars.

Even when all we had were bicycles, Tom and I spent most of our time together riding around town. We rode from convenience store to convenience store, Slim Jims in our pockets and folded comic books stuffed into the waistbands of our jeans. We never rode side by side or single file but in loopy serpentine patterns, roughly parallel, that weaved among trees and parked cars and water sprinklers. We had earnest and serious conversations that lasted for hours and were entirely shouted from bike to bike, never less than ten feet. Our paths intersected with hair-raising frequency, but we never ran into each other. At suppertime, we never actually said goodbye, but veered off in different directions, continuing to holler at each other, one more joke that had to be told, one more snappy comeback to make, until the other voice had faded in the distance, and we realized we were riding alone, and talking to ourselves. I remember nothing of what we said to each other all those long afternoons, but I remember the rush of the wind past my ears, and the shirttail of my red jersey snapping behind me like a hound, and the slab of sidewalk that a big tree root thrust up beneath me in the last block before home, so that I could steer around it at the last second and feel terribly skillful, or use it as a launching ramp and stand up on the pedals and hang there, suspended, invincible, until the pavement caught up with my tires again.

Then we were sixteen and got our licenses. Tom's bicycle went into the corner of his room, festooned with clothes that weren't quite ready to wash yet; mine was hung on nails inside the garage, in a place of honor beside my older sister's red wagon and my late Uncle Clyde's homemade bamboo fishing poles. Tom had been studying *Consumer Reports* and *Car & Driver* and prowling dealerships for months, and with his father's help, he bought a used '78 Firebird, bright red exterior, black leather upholstery, cassette stereo, and a host of tire and engine features that Tom could rattle off like an auctioneer but that I never quite could remember afterward. Being a fan of old gangster movies, Tom called it his "getaway car". Tom and his dad got a great deal, because the getaway car had a dent in the side and its headlights were slightly cockeyed. "Makes it unique," Tom said. "We'll get those fixed right up," his dad said, and, of course, they never did. I inherited the car my father had driven on his mail route for years, a beige '72 Volkswagen Beetle that was missing its front passenger seat. My father had removed it so that he'd have an open place to put his mail. Now, like so many of my family's other theoretical belongings, the seat was "out there in the garage," a phrase to which my father invariably would add, "somewhere".

We always took Tom's car; Tom always drove.

We went to a lot of movies in Columbia and sometimes went on real trips, following the church van to Lake Junaluska or to Six Flags and enjoying a freedom of movement unique in the Methodist Youth Fellowship. But mostly we rode around town, looking – and *only* looking – at girls. We found out where they lived, and drove past their houses every day, hoping they might be outside, hoping to get a glimpse of them, but paying tribute in any case to all they had added to what we fancied as our dried-up and wasted and miserable lives.

"We need music," Tom said. "Take the wheel, will you, Jack?"

I reached across and steered while he turned and rummaged among the tapes in the back seat. I knew it was the closest I ever would come to driving Tom's car.

"In Hollywood," I said, "people on street corners sell maps to the stars' homes. Tourists buy the maps and drive around, hoping to see Clint Eastwood mowing his lawn, or something." I had never been to Hollywood, but I had learned about these maps the night before on *PM Magazine*.

"What do you want? You want Stones? You want Beatles? You want Aerosmith? What?"

"Mostly they just see high walls," I said, "and locked gates." I was proud to have detected this irony alone.

"We should go there," Tom said. "Just take off driving one day and *go*."

"Intersection coming up."

"Red light?"

"Green."

Tom continued to rummage. "Our map," he said, "exists only in our heads."

"That's where the girls exist, too," I said.

"Oh, no," Tom said, turning back around and taking the wheel just in time to drive through the intersection. "They're out there. Maybe not in this dink-ass town, but somewhere. They're real. We'll just never know them. That's all."

I had nothing to add to that, but I fully agreed with him. I had concluded, way back at thirteen, that I was doomed to a monastic life, and I rather wished I were Catholic so that I could take full advantage of it. Monastic Methodists had nowhere to go; they just got grey and pudgy, and lived with their mothers. Tom pushed a tape into the deck; it snapped shut like a trap, and the speakers began to throb.

Lisa lived in a huge Tudor house of grey stone across the street from the fifteenth fairway. To our knowledge she did not play golf, but she was a runner, and on a fortunate evening we could meet her three or four times on the slow easy curves of Country Club Drive. She had a long stride and a steady rhythm and never looked winded, though she did maintain a look of thoughtful concentration and always seemed focused on the patch of asphalt just a few feet ahead, as if it were pacing her. At intersections, she jogged in place, looking around at the world in surprise, and was likely to smile and throw up a hand if we made so bold as to wave.

Tom especially admired Lisa because she took such good care of her car, a plum-colored late-model Corvette that she washed and waxed in her driveway every Saturday afternoon, beginning about one o'clock. For hours, she catered to her car's needs, stroking and rubbing it with hand towels and soft brushes, soaping and then rinsing, so that successive gentle tides foamed down the hood. Eventually, Lisa seemed to be lying face to face with herself across the gleaming purple hood, her palm pressed to the other Lisa's palm, hands moving together in lazy circles like the halfhearted sparring of lovers in August.

Crystal's house was low and brick, with a patio that stretched its whole length. From March through October, for hours each day, Crystal lay on this patio, working on her tan – "laying out," she would have called it. She must have tanned successive interior layers of her skin, because even in winter she was a dusky Amazonian bronze, a hue that matched her auburn hair, but made her white teeth a constant surprise. Frequent debates as we passed Crystal's house: Which bikini was best, the white or the yellow? Which position was best, face up or face down? What about the bottles and jars that crowded the dainty wrought-iron table at her elbow? Did those hold mere store-bought lotions, or were they brimful of Crystal's private skin-care recipes, gathered from donors willing and unwilling by the dark of the moon? Tom swore that once, when we drove past, he clearly saw amid the Coppertone jumble a half-stick of butter and a bottle of Wesson oil.

Gabrielle lived out on the edge of town, technically within the city limits but really in the country, in a big old crossroads farmhouse with a deep porch mostly hidden by lattices of honeysuckle and wisteria. She lived with her grandparents, who couldn't get around so good anymore, and so usually it was Gabrielle who climbed the tall ladder and raked out the gutters, cleared the pecan limbs off the roof of the porch, scraped the shutters, and then painted them. She had long black hair that stretched nearly to the ragged hem of her denim shorts. She didn't tie her hair back when she worked, no matter how hot the day, and she was tall even without the ladder.

Natalie lived in a three-story wooden house with cardboard in two windows and with thickets of metal roosters and lightning rods up top. At school, she wore ancient black ankle-length dresses in all weathers, walked with her head down, and spoke to no one, not even when called upon in class, so that the teachers finally gave up. Her hair was an impenetrable mop that covered her face almost entirely. But she always smiled a tiny secret smile, and her chin beneath was sharp and delicate, and when she scampered down the hall, hugging the lockers, her skirts whispered generations of old chants and endearments. Natalie never came outside at all.

Cynthia's was the first house on the tour. Only two blocks from Tom's, it sat on the brink of a small and suspect pond, one that was about fifty feet across at its widest. No visible stream fed this pond or emptied it, and birds, swimmers, and fishes all shunned it. The pond was a failure as a pond, but a marginal success as an investment, an "extra" that made a half-dozen nondescript brick ranch houses cost a bit more than their landlocked neighbors. Cynthia's house was distinguished by a big swingset that sat in the middle of the treeless yard. It was a swaybacked metal A-frame scavenged from the primary school. In all weathers, day and night, since her family moved to town when she was six, Cynthia could be found out there, swinging. The older she got, the higher she swung, the more reckless and joyful her sparkle and grin. When she was sixteen, tanned legs pumping in the afternoon sun, she regularly swung so high the chains went slack for a half-second at the top of the arc before she dropped.

"Zero gee," Tom said as we drove slowly past. Tom and I didn't swing anymore, ourselves; it made us nauseated.

Once a year Cynthia actually came out to the car to say hi. Each Christmas the people who lived on the pond, flush with their wise investment, expressed their communal pride with a brilliant lighting display. For weeks everyone in town drove slowly, dutifully, and repeatedly around the pond and over its single bridge to see the thousands of white firefly lights that the people of the pond draped along porches and bushes and balustrades, and stretched across wire frames to approximate Grinches and Magi. The reflection on the water was striking, undisturbed as it was by current or life. For hours each night, a single line of cars crept bumper-to-bumper across the bridge, past Santa-clad residents who handed out candy canes and filled a wicker basket with donations for the needy and for the electric company. Painted on a weather-beaten sandwich board at the foot of the bridge was a bright red cursive dismissal: THANK YOU / MERRY CHRISTMAS / SPEED LIMIT 25.

At least once a night, Tom and I drove through this display, hoping to catch Cynthia on Santa duty. At least once a year, we got lucky.

"Hey there, little boys, want some candy?" She dropped a shimmering fistful into Tom's lap. "No, listen, take them, Dad said when I gave them all out I could come inside. I'm freezing my ass off out here. Oh, hi, Jack. So, where you guys headed?"

"Noplace," we said together.

She walked alongside Tom's Firebird, tugging down her beard to scratch her cheek. "Damn thing must be made of fiberglass. Hey, check out the Thompsons' house. Doesn't that second reindeer look just like he's humping Rudolf? I don't know *what* they were *thinking*. No? Well, it's clear as day from my room. Maybe I've just looked at it too long. When is Christmas, anyway? You guys don't know what it's like, all these goddamn lights, you can see them with your eyes closed. I've been sleeping over at Cheryl's where it's dark. Well, I reckon if I go past the end of the bridge, the trolls will get me. Yeah, right, big laugh there. See you later." Then, ducking her head in again: "You, too, Jack."

With the smoothness of practice, Tom and I snicked our mirrors into place (his the driver's side, mine the overhead) so that we could watch Cynthia's freezing ass walk away. Her Santa pants were baggy and sexless, but we watched until the four-wheel drive behind us honked and flashed its deer lights. By the time we drove down to the traffic circle and made the loop and got back in line again, Cynthia's place had been taken by her neighbor, Mr. Thompson.

"Merry Christmas, Tom, Jack," he said. "Y'all's names came up at choir practice the other day. We'd love to have you young fellas join us in the handbells. It's fun and you don't have to sing and it's a real ministry, too." He apologized for having run out of candy canes, and instead gave us a couple of three-by-five comic books about Hell.

*   *   *

Tina's house always made us feel especially sophisticated, especially daring.

"Can you imagine?" Tom asked. "Can you imagine, just for a moment, what our parents would do?"

"No," I said, shaking my head. "No, I can't imagine."

"I think you should try. I think we both should try to envision this. That way we'll be prepared for anything in life, anything at all."

I cranked down the windowpane until it balked. "I don't even want to think about it," I said. I pressed the pane outward until it was back on track, then I lowered it the rest of the way.

"Oh, but you've *been* thinking about it, haven't you? You're the one that found out where she lived. You're the one that kept wanting me to drive past her house."

"It's the quickest route between Laura's and Kathleen's, that's all," I said. "But if it's such a terrible hardship, then you can go around the world instead, for all I care. You're the driver, I'm just sitting here."

He fidgeted, legs wide, left hand drumming the windowsill, fingertips of his right hand barely nudging the steering wheel. "Don't get me wrong, I think she's a babe. But this neighborhood, I don't know, it makes me nervous. I feel like everybody we pass is looking at us."

"Do what you like. I'm just sitting here," I said. I craned to see Tina's house as we drove around the corner.

Tina lived in what our parents and our friends and every other white person we knew, when they were feeling especially liberal, broad-minded and genteel, called the "colored" part of town. Tina's yard was colored all right: bright yellows, reds, oranges, and purples, bursting from a dozen flowerbeds. As so often when she wasn't at cheerleading practice, Tina knelt in the garden, a huge old beribboned hat – her grandmother's, maybe? – shading her striking, angular face. Her shoulders tightened, loosened, tightened again as she pressed something into place. Without moving her hands, she looked up at us as we passed. She smiled widely, and her lips mouthed the word "Hey."

Once we were around the corner, Tom gunned the engine.

"Uh-uh, no sir, hang it *up*," Tom said. "Not in my family, not in this town. Thousands of miles away, maybe. That might work. Oh, but then they'd want *photos*, wouldn't they? Damn. The other week, all my aunts were sitting around the kitchen table, complaining about their daughters-in-law. My son's wife is snotty, my son's wife is lazy, they aren't good mothers, they aren't treating our boys right, and so on and so on. Just giving 'em down the country, you know?"

"Uh-huh. I hear you."

"And I finally spoke up and said, "Well, I know I'm never going to introduce y'all to any wife of *mine*, 'cause y'all sure won't like *her*, either."

"What'd they say to that?"

"They all laughed, and Aunt Leda said, 'Tom, don't you worry, 'cause you're the only boy in the family that's got any sense. We know we'll like *any* girl you pick out.' And then Aunt Emily added, 'Long as she isn't a black 'un!' And they all nodded – I mean, they were serious!"

After a long pause, he added, half to himself, "It's not as if I'm bringing *anybody* home, anyway – black or white or lavender."

"You bring me home with you sometimes," I said.

"Yeah, and they don't like *you* either," he said, and immediately cut me a wide-eyed look of mock horror that made me laugh out loud. "I'm kidding. You know they like you."

"Families always like me," I said. "Mamas especially. It's the daughters themselves that aren't real interested. And a mama's approval is the kiss of death. At this moment, I bet you, mamas all over town are saying, 'What about that nice boy *Jack*? He's so respectful, he goes to church, he makes such good grades,' and don't you know that makes those gals so hot they can't stand it."

Tom laughed and laughed.

"Oh, Jack!" I gasped. "Oh, Jack, your SAT score is so – so *big*!"

"Maybe you should forget the girls and date the *mamas*," Tom said. "You know, eliminate the middleman. Go right to the source."

"Eewww, that's crude." I clawed at the door as if trying to get out. "Help! Help! I'm in the clutches of a crude man!"

"Suppose Kathleen's home from Florida yet?"

"I dunno. Let's go see."

"Now you aren't starting to boss me around, are you?"

"I'm just sitting here."

He poked me repeatedly with his finger, making me giggle and twist around on the seat. "Cause I'll just put you out by the side of the road, you start bossing me."

"I'm not!" I gasped. "Quit! Uncle! Uncle! I'm not!"

"Well, all right, then."

On September 17, 1981, we turned the corner at the library and headed toward the high school, past the tennis courts. The setting sun made everything golden. Over the engine, we heard doubled and redoubled the muted grunts and soft swats and scuffs of impact: ball on racket, shoe on clay. The various players on the adjoining courts moved with such choreography that I felt a pang to join them.

"Is tennis anything like badminton?" I asked. "I used to be okay at badminton. My father and I would play it over the back fence, and the dogs would go wild."

"It's more expensive," Tom said. "Look, there she is. Right on time."

Anna, her back to us, was up ahead, walking slowly toward the parking lot on the sidewalk nearest me. Her racket was on one shoulder, a towel around her neck. Her skirt swayed as if she were walking much faster.

As we passed, I heard a strange sound: a single Road Runner beep. In the side mirror, tiny retreating Anna raised her free hand and waved. I turned to stare at Tom, who looked straight ahead.

"The *horn*?" I asked. "You honked the horn?"

"Well, you waved," he said. "I saw you."

I yanked my arm inside. The windblown hairs on my forearm tingled. "I wasn't waving. I was holding up my hand to feel the breeze."

"She waved at *you*."

"Well, I didn't wave at *her*," I said. "She waved because *you* honked."

"Okay," he said, turning into the parking lot. "She waved at both of us, then."

"She waved at *you*. I don't care, it doesn't matter. But she definitely waved at you."

"Are we fighting?" he asked. He re-entered the street, turned back the way we had come. Anna was near, walking toward us.

"Course we're not fighting. Are you going to honk at her again?"

"Are you going to wave at her again?"

Anna looked behind her for traffic, stepped off the sidewalk, and darted across the street, into our lane, racket lifted like an Olympic torch.

"Look out!"

"What the hell?"

Tom hit the brakes. The passenger seat slid forward on its track, and my knees slammed the dash. Dozens of cassettes on the back seat cascaded onto the floor. Only a foot or two in front of the stopped car stood Anna, arms folded, one hip thrust out. She regarded us without expression, blew a large pink bubble that reached her nose and then collapsed back into her mouth.

"Hi, guys," she said.

Tom opened his door and stood, one foot on the pavement. "For crying out loud, Anna, are you okay? We could've killed you!"

"I was trying to flag you down," she said.

"What? Why?" Tom asked. "What for? Something wrong with the car?" I saw him swivel, and I knew that, out of sight, he was glancing toward the tires, the hood, the tailpipe.

"Nothing's wrong with the car, Tom," she said, chewing with half her mouth, arms still folded. "It's a really neat car. Whenever I see it I think, 'Damn, Tom must take mighty good care of that car.' I get a *lot* of chances to think that, Tom, 'cause every day you guys drive by my house at least twice, and whenever I leave tennis practice, you drive past me, and turn around in the lot, and drive past me *again*, and every time you do that I think, 'He takes mighty damn good care of that goddamn car just to drive past me all the fucking time.' "

Someone behind us honked and pulled around. A pickup truck driver, who threw us a bird.

"Do you ever *stop*? No. Say hi at school? Either of you? No. *Call* me? Shit." She shifted her weight to the other hip, unfolded her arms, whipped the towel from around her neck and swatted the hood with it. "So all I want to know is, just what's the *deal*? Tom? Jack? I see you in there, Jack, you can't hide. What's up, Jack? You tell me. Your chauffeur's catching flies out here."

Looking up at Anna, even though I half expected at any moment to be arrested for perversion or struck from behind by a truck or beaten to death with a tennis racket, purple waffle patterns scarring my corpse, I realized I had never felt such crazed exhilaration, not even that night on Bates Hill, when Tom passed a hundred and twenty. My knees didn't even hurt any more. The moment I realized this, naturally the feeling of exhilaration began to ebb, and so before I lost my resolve I slowly stuck my head out the window, smiled what I hoped was a smile, and called out: "Can we give you a lift, Anna?"

A station wagon swung past us with a honk. Anna looked at me, at Tom, at me again. She plucked her gum from her mouth, tossed it, looked down at the pavement and then up and then down again, much younger and almost shy. In a small voice, she said: "Yeah." She cleared her throat. "Yeah. Yes. That's . . . that's nice of you. Thank you."

I let her have my seat, of course. I got in the back, atop a shifting pile of cassettes and books and plastic boxes of lug nuts, but right behind her, close enough to smell her: not sweat, exactly, but salt and earth, like the smell of the beach before the tide comes in.

"Where to?" Tom asked.

"California," she said, and laughed, hands across her face. "Damn, Anna," she asked, "where did *that* come from? Oh, I don't know. Where are y'all going? I mean, wherever. Whenever. Let's just *go*, okay? Let's just . . . go."

We talked: School. Movies. Bands. Homework. Everything. Nothing. What else? Drove around. For hours.

Her ponytail was short but full, a single blonde twist that she gathered up in one hand and lifted as she tilted her head forward. I thought she was looking at something on the floor, and I wondered for a second whether I had tracked something in.

"Jack?" she asked, head still forward. No one outside my family had made my name a question before. "Would you be a sweetie and rub my neck?"

The hum of tires, the zing of crickets, the shrill stream of air flowing through the crack that the passenger window never quite closed.

"Ma'am?"

"My neck. It's all stove up and tight from tennis. Would you rub the kinks out for me?"

"Sure," I said, too loudly and too quickly. My hands moved as

slowly as in a nightmare. Twice I thought I had them nearly to her
neck when I realized I was merely rehearsing the action in my
head, so that I had it all to do over again. Tom shifted gears,
slowed into a turn, sped up, shifted gears again, and I still hadn't
touched her. My forearms were lifted; my hands were outstretched, palms down; my fingers were trembling. I must have
looked like a mesmerist. You are sleepy, very sleepy. Which
movie was it where the person in the front seat knew nothing
about the clutching hands in the back? I could picture the driver's
face as the hands crept closer: Christopher Lee, maybe? No:
Donald Pleasence?

"Jack," she said. "Are you still awake back there?"

The car went into another turn, and I heard a soft murmur of
complaint from the tires. Tom was speeding up.

My fingertips brushed the back of her neck. I yanked them
back, then moved them forward again. This time I held them
there, barely touching. Her neck so smooth, so hot, slightly –
damp? And what's *this*? Little hairs! Hairs as soft as a baby's
head! No one ever had told me there would be hairs . . .

"You'll have to rub harder than *that*, Jack." Still holding her hair
aloft with her right hand, she reached up with her left and pressed
my fingers into her neck. "Like that. Right – *there*. And there. Feel
how tight that is?" She rotated her hand over mine, and trapped
between her damp palm and her searing neck I did feel something
both supple and taut. "Oooh, yeah, like that." She pulled her hand
away, and I kept up the motions. "Oh, that feels good . . ."

The sun was truly down by now, and lighted houses scudded
past. Those distinctive dormer windows – wasn't that Lisa's
house? And, in the next block, wasn't that Kim's driveway?

We were following the route. We were passing all the homes of
the stars.

Tom said nothing, but drove faster and faster. I kept rubbing,
pressing, kneading, not having the faintest idea what I was doing
but following the lead of Anna's sighs and murmurs. "Yeah, my
shoulder there . . . Oh, this is wonderful. You'll have to stop this
in about three hours, you know."

After about five minutes or ten or twenty, without looking up,
she raised her left index finger and stabbed the dashboard. A tape
came on. I don't remember which tape it was. I do remember that
it played through both sides, and started over.

Tom was speeding. Each screeching turn threw us off balance. Where were the cops? Where was all the other traffic? We passed Jane's house, Tina's house. Streetlights strobed the car like an electrical storm. We passed Cynthia's house – hadn't we already? Beneath my hands, Anna's shoulders braced and rolled and braced again. I held on. My arms ached. Past the corner of my eye flashed a stop sign. My fingers kept working. Tom wrenched up the volume on the stereo. The bass line throbbed into my neck and shoulder blades, as if the car were reciprocating.

Gravel churned beneath us. "Damn," Tom muttered, and yanked the wheel, fighting to stay on the road. Anna snapped her head up, looked at him. I saw her profile against the radio dial.

"I want to drive," she said.

Tom put on the brakes, too swiftly. Atop a surging flood of gravel, the car jolted and shuddered to a standstill off the side of the road. The doors flew open, and both Tom and Anna leaped out. My exhilaration long gone, my arms aching, I felt trapped, suffocating. I snatched up the seat latch, levered forward the passenger seat, and stepped humpbacked and out of balance into the surprisingly cool night air. Over there was the Episcopal church, over there the Amoco station. We were only a few blocks from my house. My right hand stung; I had torn a nail on the seat latch. I slung it back and forth as Tom stepped around the car. Anna was already in the driver's seat.

"You want to sit in front?" Tom sounded hoarse.

"No," I said. "No, thanks. Listen, I think I'll, uh, I think I'll just call it a night. I'm nearly home anyway. I can, uh, I can walk from here. Y'know? It's not far. I can walk from here." I called out to Anna, leaning down and looking in: "I can walk from here." Her face was unreadable, but her eyes gleamed.

"Huh?" Tom said. It was like a grunt. He cleared his throat. "What do you mean, *walk*? It's early yet."

The car was still running. The exhaust blew over me in a cloud, made me dizzy. "No, really, you guys go on. I'm serious. I'll be fine. Go on, really. I'll see you later on."

"We could drop you off," Tom said. He spoke politely but awkwardly, as if we had never met. "Let's do that. We'll drop you off in your yard."

Anna revved the motor. It was too dark to see Tom's expression as he looked at her. Her fingers moved across the lighted instrument panel, pulled out the switch that started the emergency flashers, *ka-chink ka-chink ka-chink*, pushed it back again. "Cool," she said.

"I'll see you later," I said. "Okay? See you, Anna. Call me tomorrow," I said to Tom.

"Okay," he said. "I'll call you tomorrow."

"Okay," I said, not looking back. I waved a ridiculous cavalier wave, and stuck my hands in my pockets, trying to look nonchalant as I stumbled along the crumbling asphalt shoulder in the dark.

Behind me two doors slammed. I heard the car lurching back onto the highway, gravel spewing, and I heard it make a U-turn, away from town and toward the west, toward the lake, toward the woods. As the engine gunned, my shoulders twitched and I ducked my head, because I expected the screech of gears, but all I heard was steady and swift acceleration, first into second into third, as the Firebird sped away, into fourth, and then it was just me, walking.

They never came back.

Tom's parents got a couple of letters, a few postcards. California. They shared them with Anna's parents but no one else. "Tom wants everyone to know they're doing fine," that's all his mom and dad would say. But they didn't look reassured. Miss Sara down at the paper, who always professed to know a lot more than she wrote up in her column, told my father that she hadn't seen the mail herself, mind you, but she had *heard* from people who should *know* that the letters were strange, rambling things, not one *bit* like Tom, and the cards had postmarks that were simply, somehow, *wrong*. But who could predict, Miss Sara added, *when* postcards might arrive, or in *what* order. Why, sometimes they sit in the post office for *years*, and sometimes they never show up at *all*. Criminal, Miss Sara mourned, criminal.

Anna's parents got no mail at all.

I never did, either, except maybe one thing. I don't know that you could call it *mail*. No stamps, no postmark, no handwriting. It wasn't even in the mailbox. But it felt like mail to me.

It was lying on my front porch one morning – this was years later, not long after I got my own place, thought I was settled. At first I thought it was the paper, but no, as usual the paper was spiked down deep in the hedge. This was lying faceup and foursquare on the welcome mat. It was one of those Hollywood maps, showing where the stars can be found.

I spread it across the kitchen table and anchored it with the sugar bowl and a couple of iron owl-shaped trivets, because it was stiff and new and didn't want to lie flat. You know how maps are. It was bright white paper and mighty thick, too. I didn't know they made maps so thick anymore. I ran my index finger over sharp paper ridges and down straight paper canyons and looked for anyone I knew. No, Clint Eastwood wasn't there. Nor was anyone else whose movies I ever had seen at the mall. A lot of the names I just didn't recognize, but some I knew from cable, from the nostalgia channels.

I was pretty sure most of them were dead.

I searched the index for Tom's name, for Anna's. I didn't see them. I felt relieved. Sort of.

"California," I said aloud. Once it had been four jaunty syllables, up and down and up and down, a kid on a bicycle, going noplace. California. Now it was a series of low and urgent blasts, someone leaning on the horn, saying, come on, saying, hurry up, saying, you're not too late, not yet, not *yet*. California.

It's nearly eleven. I stand in the cool rush of the refrigerator door, forgetting what I came for, and strain to hear. The train is passing, a bit late, over behind the campus. My windows are open, so the air conditioning is pouring out into the yard and fat bugs are smacking themselves against the screen, but this way I can hear everything clearly. The rattle as my neighbor hauls down the garage door, secures everything for the night. On the other side, another neighbor trundles a trash can out to the curb, then plods back. I am standing at the kitchen counter now. Behind me the refrigerator door is swinging shut, or close enough. I hear a car coming.

The same car.

I move to the living room, to the front door. I part the curtain. The car is coming closer, but even more slowly than before. Nearly stopping. It must be in first gear by now. There was always that slight rattle, just within the threshold of hearing, when you put it in first gear. Yes. And the slightly cockeyed headlights, yes, and the dent in the side. I can't clearly see the interior even under the streetlight but it looks like two people in the front.

Two people? Or just one?

And then it's on the other side of the neighbor's hedge, and gone, but I still can hear the engine, and I know that it's going to turn, and come back.

My hand is on the doorknob. The map is in my pocket. The night air is surprisingly cool. I flip on the porch light as I step out, and I stand illuminated in a cloud of tiny beating wings, waiting for them to come back, come back and see me standing here, waiting, waiting, oh my God how long I've been waiting, I want to walk out there and stand in front of the car and make it stop, really I do, but I can't, I can't move, I'm trapped here, trapped in this place, trapped in this time, don't drive past again, I'm here, I'm ready, I wasn't then but now I am, really I am, please, please stop. Present or past, alive or dead, what does it matter, what did it ever matter? Please. Stop.

Please.

CAITLÍN R. KIERNAN

Emptiness Spoke Eloquent

CAITLÍN R. KIERNAN WAS BORN NEAR DUBLIN, Ireland, but has lived most of her life in the southeastern United States. Trained as a vertebrate palaeotologist, she began writing fiction full time in 1992. Since then, her Gothic and Gothnoir short stories have appeared in numerous anthologies, including *The Sandman: Book of Dreams, Love in Vein II, Lethal Kisses, Darkside: Horror for the Next Millennium, Noirotica 2, Song of Cthulhu, The Crow: Shattered Lives and Broken Dreams, Brothers of the Night, Secret City: Strange Tales of London, Dark of the Night, White of the Moon, High Fantastic, Dark Terrors 2* and *3*, and *The Year's Best Fantasy and Horror Eleventh Annual Collection*. Her first novel, *Silk*, was published in 1998, and Meisha Merlin Press has recently released a limited-edition chapbook of her short fiction, *Candles for Elizabeth*. She is currently scripting *The Dreaming* and other projects for DC Comics' Vertigo line. She lives in a renovated overalls factory in Birmingham, Alabama.

"I started working on this piece in November 1993," reveals the author. "It was my third short story, and it would remain unfinished until May 1997. November 1993 also saw the release of Francis Ford Coppola's *Bram Stoker's Dracula* and, regardless of whether or not it was the most faithful screen adaptation of Stoker's novel, it certainly affected me more deeply than any other ever has. But it did leave me with a nagging question that I often have at the end of good films and books, especially good horror and dark fantasy: 'What happens next?'

"It isn't that Coppola didn't find a wonderful place to close the film, just that I couldn't possibly imagine the woman that Mina Harker had become returning to her previous life as a meek typist, going back to her middle-class existence as Jonathan Harker's wife. So I started asking myself questions, and 'Emptiness Spoke Eloquent' was the eventual outcome."

L UCY HAS BEEN AT the window again, sharp nails tap-tapping on the glass, scratching out there in the rain like an animal begging to be let in. Poor Lucy, alone in the storm. Mina reaches to ring for the nurse, stops halfway, forces herself to believe all she's hearing is the rasping limbs of the crape myrtle, whipped by the wind, winterbare twigs scritching like fingernails on the rainslick glass. Forcing her hand back down onto the warm blanket. And really, that simple action says so much, she knows. Retreat, pulling back from the cold risks; windows kept shut against night and chill and the thunder.

There was so much of windows.

On the colour television bolted high to the wall, tanks and soldiers in the Asian jungle and that bastard Nixon, soundless.

Electricwhite flash and almost at once, a thunderclap that rattles the sky, sends a shudder through the concrete and steel skeleton of the hospital and the windows and old Mina in her safe and warm blanket hidey-hole.

Old Mina.

She keeps her eyes open, avoiding sleep, and memories of other storms.

And Lucy at her window.

Again she considers the nurse, pale angel to bring pills to grant her black and nothing, dreamless space between hurtful wakings. Oh, if dear Dr Jack, with his pitiful morphine, his chloral and laudanums, could see the marvels that men have devised to unleash numbness, flat calm of mind and body and soul. And she *is* reaching then, for the call button and for Jonathan's hand, that he should call Seward, anything against the dreams and the scritching at the window.

This time she won't look, eyes safe on the evening news, and the buzzer makes no sound in her room. This time she will wait

for the soft and rubberquiet footsteps, the door to open and
Andrea or Neufield or whoever is on duty to bring oblivion in a
tiny paper cup.

But after a minute, minute and a half, and no response, Mina
turns her head, giving in by turtleslow degrees, and she watches
the rain streaking the dark glass, the restless shadows of the crape
myrtle.

June 1904

The survivors of the Company of Light stood in the rubble at the
base of the castle on the Arges and looked past iron and vines, at
the empty, soulless casements. It seemed very little changed,
framed now in the green froth of the Carpathian summer instead
of snow, ice, and bare grey stone.

The trip had been Jonathan's idea, had become an obsession,
despite her protests and Arthur's and in the end, seeing how much
the journey would cost her, even Van Helsing's. Jack Seward,
whose moods had grown increasingly black since their steamer had
docked in Varna, had refused to enter the castle grounds and stood
alone outside the gates. Mina held little Quincey's hand perhaps
too tightly and stared silently up at the moss-chewed battlements.

There was a storm building in the east, over the mountains.
Thunder rumbled like far-off cannon, and the warm air smelled of
rain and ozone and the heavy purplish blooms hanging from the
creepers. Mina closed her eyes and listened, tried to listen the way
she had that November day years before. Quincey squirmed,
restless six, by her side. The gurgle and splash of the swollen river,
rushing unseen below them, and the raucous calls of birds, birds
she didn't recognise. But nothing else.

And Van Helsing arguing with Jonathan.

". . . now, Jonathan, now you are satisfied?"

"Shut up. Just shut the bloody hell up."

What are you listening for, Mina?

Lord Godalming lit his pipe, some Turkish blend, exotic spice
and smoke, sulphur from his match. He broke into the argument,
something about the approaching storm, about turning back.

What do you expect you'll hear?

The thunder answered her, much closer this time, and a
sudden, cold gust blown before the storm.

He's not here, Mina. He's not here.

Off in the mountains, drifting down through passes and trees, a wild animal cried out, just once, in pain or fear or maybe anger. And Mina opened her eyes, blinked, waited for the cry to come again, but then the thunder cracked like green wood overhead and the first drops of rain, fat and cold, began to fall. The Professor took her arm, leading her away, mumbling Dutch under his breath, and they left Jonathan standing there, staring blankly up at the castle. Lord Godalming waited, helpless, at his side.

And in the falling rain, her tears lost themselves, and no one saw them.

November 1919

Fleeing garish victory, Mina had come back to Whitby hardly two weeks after the armistice. Weary homecomings for the living and maimed and flag-draped caskets. She'd left Quincey behind to settle up his father's affairs.

From the train, the lorry from the station, her bags carried off to a room she hadn't seen yet; she would not sleep at the Westenra house at the Crescent, although it was among the portion of the Godalming estate left to her after Arthur Holmwood's death. She took her tea in the inn's tiny dining room, sitting before the bay windows. From there she could see down the valley, past red roofs and whitewash to the harbour pilings and the sea. The water glittered, sullen under the low sky. She shivered and pulled her coat tighter, sipped at the Earl Gray and lemon in the cracked china, the cup glazed as dark as the brooding sky. And if she looked back the other way, towards East Cliff, she might glimpse the ruined abbey, the parish church, and the old graveyard.

Mina refilled her cup from the mismatched teapot on the table, stirred at the peat-coloured water, watching the bits of lemon pulp swirl in the little maelstrom.

She'd go to the graveyard later, maybe tomorrow.

And again the fact, the cold candour of her situation, washed over and through her; she had begun to feel like a lump of gravel polished smooth by a brook. That they were all dead now, and she'd not attended even a single funeral. Arthur first, almost four years back now, and then Jack Seward, lost at Suvla Bay. The news about Jonathan hadn't reached her until two days after the drunken cacophony of victory had erupted in Trafalgar Square and had finally seemed to engulf the whole of London. He'd died in some unnamed village along the Belgian border, a little east of Valenciennes, a senseless German ambush only hours before the cease-fire.

She laid her spoon aside, watched the spreading stain it made on her napkin. The sky was ugly, bruised.

A man named MacDonnell, a grey-bearded Scotsman, had come to her house, bearing Jonathan's personal things – his pipe, the brass-framed daguerreotype of her, an unfinished letter. The silver crucifix he'd worn like a scar the last twenty years. The man had tried to comfort her, offering half-heard reassurances that her husband had been as fine a corporal as any on the Front. She thought sometimes that she might have been more grateful to him for his trouble.

The unfinished letter carried with her from London, and she might look at it again later, though she knew it almost by heart now. Scribblings she could hardly recognise as his, mad and rambling words about something trailing his battalion through the fields and muddy trenches.

Mina sipped her tea, barely noticing that it had gone cold, and watched the clouds outside as they swept in from the sea and rushed across the rocky headland.

A soupy fog in the morning, misty ghosts of ships and men torn apart on the reef, and Mina Harker followed the curve of stairs up from the town, past the ruined Abbey, and into the old East Cliff churchyard. It seemed that even more of the tombstones had tumbled over, and she remembered the old sailors and fishermen and whalers that had come here before, Mr Swales and the others, and wondered if anyone ever came here now. She found a bench and sat, looking back down to where Whitby lay hidden from view. The yellow lantern eyes of the lighthouses winked in the distance, bookending the invisible town below.

She unfolded Jonathan's letter and the chilling breeze fingered the edges of the paper.

The foghorns sounded, throaty bellow, perplexed and lonesome.

Before leaving London, she'd taken all the papers, the typed pages and old notebooks, the impossible testament of the Company, from the wall safe where Jonathan had kept them. Now they were tucked carefully inside the brocade canvas satchel resting on the sandy cobbles at her feet.

". . . *and burn them, Mina, burn every trace of what we have seen,*" scrawled in that handwriting that was Jonathan's, and no one's she'd ever met.

And so she had sat at the hearth, these records in her lap, watching the flames, feeling the heat on her face. Had lifted a letter to Lucy from the stack, held the envelope a moment, teasing the fire as a child might tease a cat with table scraps.

"No," she whispered, closing her eyes against the hungry orange glow, putting the letter back with the rest. *All I have left, and I'm not that strong.*

Far out at sea, she thought she heard bells, and down near Tate Hill Pier, a dog barking. But the fog made a game of sound and she couldn't be sure she'd heard anything but the surf and her own breathing. Mina lifted the satchel and set it on the bench beside her.

Earlier that morning she'd stood before the looking glass in her room at the inn, staring into the soft eyes of a young woman, not someone who had seen almost forty-two years and the horrors of her twentieth. As she had so often done before her own mirrors, she'd looked for the age that should have begun to crease and ruin her face and found only the faintest crow's feet.

". . . *every trace, Mina, if we are ever to be truly free of this terrible damnation.*"

She opened the satchel and laid Jonathan's letter inside, pressed it between the pages of his old diary, then snapped the clasp shut again. *Now,* she thought, filled suddenly with the old anger, black and acid, *I might fling it into the sea, lose these memories here, where it started.*

Instead, she hugged the bag tightly to her and watched the lighthouses as the day began to burn the mist away.

Before dusk, the high clouds had stacked themselves out beyond Kettleness, filling the eastern sky with thunderheads, bruise-black underbelly already dumping sheets of rain on a foamwhite sea. Before midnight, the storm had reared above Whitby harbour and made landfall. In her narrow room above the kitchen, framed in wood and plaster and faded gingham wallpaper haunted by a hundred thousand boiled cabbages, Mina dreamed.

She was sitting at the small window, shutters thrown back, watching the storm walk the streets, feeling the icy salt spray and rain on her face. Jonathan's gold pocket watch lay open on the writing desk, ticking loud above the crash and boom outside. MacDonnell had not brought the watch back from Belgium, and she'd not asked him about it.

Quick and palsied fingers of lightning forked above the rooftops and washed the world in an instant of daylight.

On the bed behind her, Lucy said something about Churchill and the cold wind and laughed. Chandelier diamond tinkling and asylum snigger between velvet and gossamer and rust-scabbed iron bars.

And still laughing, "Bitch . . . apostate, Wilhelmina coward."

Mina looked down, watching the hands, hour, minute, second, racing themselves around the dial. The fob was twisted and crusted with something dark.

"Lucy, please . . ." and her voice came from very far away, and it sounded like a child asking to be allowed up past her bedtime.

Groan and bedspring creak, linen rustle and a sound wetter than the pounding rain. Lucy Westenra's footsteps moved across the bare floor, heels clocking, ticking off the shortening distance.

Mina looked back down, and Drawbridge Road was absurdly crowded with bleating sheep, soppy wool in the downpour, and the gangling shepherd, a scarecrow blown from the wheat fields west of Whitby. Twiggy fingers beneath his burlap sleeve, driving his flock towards the harbour.

Lucy was standing very close now. Stronger than the rain and the old cabbage stink, anger that smelled like blood and garlic and dust. Mina watched the sheep and the storm.

"Turn *around*, Mina. Turn around and look at me and tell me that you even loved Jonathan."

Turn around Mina and tell

"Please, Lucy, don't leave me here."

and tell me that you even loved

And the sheep were turning, short necks craning up and red little rat eyes and the scarecrow howled.

Lucy's hands were cool silk on Mina's fevered shoulders.

"Don't leave, not yet . . ."

And Lucy's fingers, hairless spider legs, had crawled around her cheeks, seized her jaw. Something brittle dry, crackling papery against her teeth, forced past her lips.

On the street, the sheep were coming apart in the storm, yellowed fleece and fat-marbled mutton; a river of crimson sluiced between paving stones. Grinning skulls and polished white ribs, scarecrow turning away, breaking up in the gale.

Lucy's fingers pushed the first clove over Mina's tongue, shoved another into her mouth.

And she felt the cold steel at her throat.

loved you, Mina, loved as much as the blood and the night and even as much as

Mina Harker woke up in the hollow space between lightning and thunderclap.

Until dawn, when the storm tapered to gentle drizzle and distant echoes, she sat alone on the edge of the bed, tasting bile and remembered garlic.

January 1922

Mina held the soup to the Professor's lips, chicken steam curling in the cold air. Abraham Van Helsing, eighty-seven and so much more dead than alive, tried to accept a little of the thin, piss-yellow broth; clumsy sip, and the soup spilled from his mouth, dribbled down his chin into his beard. Mina wiped his lips with the stained napkin lying across her lap.

He closed his grey-lashed eyes and she set the bowl aside. Outside, the snow was falling again, and the wind yowled wolf noises around the corners of his old house. She shivered, tried to listen instead to the warm crackle from the fireplace, the Professor's laboured breath. In a moment, he was coughing again, and she was helping him sit up, holding his snotgreen handkerchief.

"Tonight, Madam Mina, tonight . . ." and he smiled, wan smile, and his words collapsing into another fit, the wet consumptive rattle. When it passed, she eased him back into the pillows, noticed a little more blood on the ruined handkerchief.

Yes, she thought, *perhaps*. And once she would have tried to assure him that he would live to see spring and his damned tulips and another spring after that, but she only wiped the strands of feversweaty hair from his forehead, pulled the moth-gnawed quilt back around bony shoulders.

Because there was no one else and nothing to keep her in England, she'd made the crossing to Amsterdam the week before Christmas; Quincey had been taken away by the influenza epidemic after the war. Just Mina now, and this daft old bastard. Soon enough just her.

"Shall I read for a bit, Professor?" They were almost halfway through Mr Conrad's *The Arrow of Gold*. And she was reaching for the book on the nightstand, saw that she'd set the soup bowl on it, when his hand, dry and hot, closed softly around her wrist.

"Madam Mina," and already he was releasing her, his parchment touch withdrawn and something now in his eyes besides cataracts and the glassy fever flatness. His breath wheezed in, forced itself harshly out.

"I am *afraid*," barely a rasping whisper, slipped into and between the weave of the night.

"You should rest now, Professor," she said, wished against anything he might say.

"So much a fraud I was, Madam Mina."

did you ever even love

"It was *my* hand that sent her, by my *hand*."

"Please, Professor, let me call for a priest. I cannot . . ."

The glare that flashed behind his eyes, something wild and bitter, vicious humour, made her look away, scissored her fraying resolve.

"Ah," and "Yes," and something strangled then that might have been laughter, "So I confess my guilt, so I scrub the blood from my hands with that other blood?"

The wind banged and clattered at the shuttered windows, looking for a way inside. And for a helpless moment, empty space filled with mantle clock ticking and the wind and his ragged breathing, nothing.

Then, "Please, Madam Mina, I am thirsty."

She reached for the pitcher, the chipped drinking glass.

"Forgive me, sweet Mina . . ."

The glass was spotty and she wiped roughly at its rim with her blue skirt.

". . . had it been hers to choose . . ." and he coughed again, once, harsh and broken, and Mina wiped at the glass harder.

Abraham Van Helsing sighed gently and she was alone.

When she was done, she carefully returned the glass to the table with the crystal pitcher, the unfinished book, the cold soup. When she turned to the bed, Mina caught her reflection in the tall dressing mirror across the room; the woman staring back could easily have passed for a young thirty.

Only her eyes, hollow, bottomless things, betrayed her.

May 1930

As twilight faded from the narrow rue de l'Odéon, Mina Murray sipped her glass of chardonnay and roamed the busy shelves of Shakespeare and Company. The reading would begin soon, some passages from Colette's new novel. Her fingers absently traced the spines of the assembled works of Hemingway and Glenway Wescott and D.H. Lawrence, titles and authors gold or crimson or flat-black pressed into cloth. Someone she half-recognised from a café or party or some other reading passed close, whispered a greeting, and she smiled in response, went back to the books.

And then Mlle. Beach was asking everyone to find their seats, a few straight-backed chairs scattered among the shelves and bins. Mina found a place close to the door, watched as the others took their time, quietly talking among themselves, laughing at unheard jokes. Most of them she knew by sight, a few by name and casual conversation, one or two by reputation only. Messieurs Pound and Joyce, and Radclyffe Hall in her tailored English suit and sapphire cuff links. An unruly handful of minor Surrealists she recognised from the rue Jacob bistro where she often took her evening meals. And at first unnoticed, a tallish young woman, unaccompanied, choosing a chair off to one side.

Mina's hands trembled, and she spilled a few drops of the wine on her blouse.

The woman sat down, turning her back on Mina. Beneath the yellowish glow of the bookstore's lamps, her long hair blazed red-gold. The murmuring pack of Surrealists seated themselves in the crooked row directly in front of Mina and she looked away. Sudden sweat and her mouth dry, dull undercurrent of nausea, and she quickly, clumsily, set her wine glass on the floor.

And the name, held so long at bay, spoken in a voice she thought she'd forgotten.

Lucy.

Mina's heart, irrhythmic drum, raced inside her chest like a frightened child's.

Sylvia Beach was speaking again, gently hushing the murmuring crowd, introducing Colette. Measured applause as the writer stepped forward, something sarcastic mumbled by one of the Surrealists. Mina closed her eyes tightly, cold and breathing much too fast, sweatslick fingers gripping the edges of her chair.

Someone touched her arm and she jumped, almost cried out, gasped loud enough to draw attention.

"Mademoiselle Murray, êtes vous bien?"

She blinked, dazed, recognising the boy's unshaven face, one of the shop's clerks, unable to negotiate his name.

"Oui, je vais bien." And she tried to smile, blinking back sucking vertigo and dismay. "Merci . . . je regrette."

He nodded, doubtful, reluctantly returning to his windowsill behind her.

At the front of the gathering, Colette had begun to read, softly relinquishing her words. Mina glanced to where the red-haired woman had sat, expecting to find the chair empty or occupied by someone else entirely, whispering a faithless prayer that she'd merely hallucinated or suffered some trick of light and shadow.

The woman had turned slightly in her chair, so that Mina could see her profile, her full lips, familiar cheekbones.

The smallest sound, bated moan, from Mina's pale lips, and she saw herself rising, pushing past bodies and through the book-store's doors, fleeing headlong through the dark Paris streets to her tiny flat on Saint-Germain.

Instead, Mina Murray sat perfectly still, watching, in turn, the reader's restless lips and the delicate features of the nameless red-haired woman wearing Lucy Westenra's face.

After the reading, as the others milled and mingled, spinning respectful pretensions about *Sido* and Madame Collete in general, Mina inched towards the door. The crowd seemed to have doubled during the half-hour, and she squeezed, abruptly claustrophobic, between shoulders and cigarette smoke. But four or five of the rue Jacob Surrealists were planted solidly, typically confrontational, in the shop's doorway, muttering loudly among themselves, the novelist already forgotten in their own banter.

"Pardon," she said, speaking just loudly enough to be heard above their conversation, "puis-je . . ." Mina pointed past the men to the door.

The one closest, gaunt and unwashed, almost pale enough to pass for albino, turned towards her. Mina remembered his face, its crooked nose, had once seen him spit at a nun outside the Deux Magots. He gave no sign that he intended to let her pass, and she thought that even his eyes looked unclean. Carrion eyes.

"Mademoiselle Murray, please, one moment."

Mina matched the man's glare a second longer, and then, slowly, turned, recognising Adrienne Monnier; her own shop, the Maison des Amis des Livres, stood, dark-windowed tonight, across the street. It was generally acknowledged that Mlle. Monnier shared considerable responsibility for the success of Shakespeare and Company.

"I have here someone who would very much like to meet you," and the red-haired woman was standing at her side, sipping dark wine, faint smile and hazel-green eyes.

"This is Mademoiselle Carmicheal from New York. She says that she is a great admirer of your work, Mina. I was just telling her that you've recently placed another story with the *Little Review*."

"Anna Carmicheal," the woman added, eager and silken-voiced, offering Mina her hand. Detached, drifting, Mina watched herself accept it.

Anna Carmicheal, from New York. Not Lucy.

"Thank you," she said, her voice the same dead calm as the sea before a squall.

"Oh, Christ no, thank *you*, Miss Murray."

Not Lucy, not Lucy at all, and she noticed how much taller this woman was, her hands more slender, a small mole at the corner of her rouged lips.

Then Adrienne Monnier was gone, pulled back into the crowd by a fat woman in an ugly ostrich-plumed hat, leaving Mina alone with Anna Carmichael. Behind her, the divided Surrealists argued, threadbare quarrel and wearisome zeal.

"I've been reading you since 'The White Angel of Carfax', and last year, my God, last year I read 'Canto Babel' in

Harper's. In America, Miss Murray, they're saying that you're the new Poe, that you make Le Fanu and all those silly Victorians look . . ."

"Yes, well," she began, uncertain what she meant to say, only meaning to interrupt. The dizziness, sharpening unreality, was rushing back and Mina leaned against a shelf for support.

"Miss Murray?" And a move, then, as if to catch someone who had stumbled, long fingers alert. Anna Carmichael took a cautious step forward, closing space.

"Mina, please, just Mina."

"Are you . . ."

"Yes," but she was sweating again. "Forgive me, Anna. Just a little too much wine on an empty stomach."

"Then please, let me take you to dinner."

Lips pursed, Mina bit the tip of her tongue, hard enough to bring a salted hint of blood, and the world began to tilt back, the syrupy blackness at the edges of her vision withdrawing by degrees.

"Oh, no. I couldn't," she managed, "really, it's not . . ."

But the woman was taking her by the arm, crescent moon smile baring teeth like perfectly spaced pearls, every bit the forceful American. She thought of Quincey Morris and wondered if this woman had ever been to Texas.

"But I insist, Mina. It'll be an honour, and in return, well, I won't feel so guilty if I talk too much."

Together, arm in arm, they elbowed their way through the Surrealist blockade, the men choosing to ignore them. Except her gaunt albino, and Mina imagined something passing between him and Anna Carmichael, unspoken, or simply unspeakable.

"I hate those idiot bastards," Anna whispered as the door jangled shut behind them. She held Mina's hand tightly, squeezing warmth into her clammy palm, and surprising herself, Mina squeezed back.

Out on the gaslit rue de l'Odéon, a warm spring breeze was blowing, and the night air smelled like coming rain.

The meal had been good, though Mina had hardly tasted the little she'd eaten. Cold chicken and bread, salad with wild thyme and goat cheese, chewed and swallowed indifferently. And more than her share from a large carafe of some anonymous red Bordeaux. She'd listened to the woman who was not Lucy talk, endless talk of Anna Carmichael's copious ideas on the macabre and of Mina's writing.

"I actually went to the Carfax estate," she'd said, pausing as if she had expected some particular reaction, "just last summer. There's some restoration underway there now, you know."

"No," Mina answered, sipping her wine, picking apart a strip of white meat with her fork. "No, I wasn't aware of that."

Finally, the waitress had brought their bill and Anna had grudgingly allowed Mina to leave the tip. While they'd eaten, the shower had come and gone, leaving the night dank and chilly, unusually quiet. Their heels sounded like passing time on the wet cobblestones.

Anna Carmichael had a room in one of the less expensive Left Bank hotels, but they walked together back to Mina's flat.

When Mina woke, it was raining again, and for a few uncounted minutes she lay still, listening, smelling the sweat and incense, hint of rose and lilac in the sheets. Finally there was only a steady drip, falling perhaps from the leaky gutters of the old building, maybe from the eaves, striking the flagstones in the little garden. She could still smell Anna Carmichael on her skin. Mina closed her eyes and thought about going back to sleep, realised slowly that she was alone in the bed now.

The rain was over and the drip, minute and measured splash of water on water, clockwork cadence, wasn't coming from outside. She opened her eyes and rolled over, into the cold and hollow place made by Anna's absence. The lavatory light was burning; Mina blinked, called her name, called

Lucy

"Anna?"

drip and drip and drip and

"Anna?" and her throat tightened, whatever peace she'd awakened with leached away by fear and adrenaline. "Anna, are you all right?"

did you call for Lucy, at first, did I

drip and drip and

The floor was cold against her feet. Mina stepped past the chiffonier, bare wood becoming a time- and mildew- and foot-dulled mosaic of tile polygons. Some of the tiles were missing, leaving dirty, liver-coloured cavities in the design. The big tub, chipped enamel, alabaster and black iron showing beneath. Lion's feet claws, moulded rictus, grappling for some hold on the slick tiles.

Lucy Westenra lay, empty again, in the tub filled almost to overflowing. Each drop of water swelled like an abscess until its own weight tore it free of the brass faucet and it fell, losing itself in the crimson water. Her wrists hung limply over the sides, hands open; her head tilted back at a broken angle. And three cruel-bright smiles. All offered to Heaven or Mina.

The razor lay, wet and scarlet-glinting blade, on the floor where it had fallen from her hand. And, like the dripping water, Mina stood until the weight pulled her free and she fell.

October 1946

After the war and the ammonia antiseptic rooms where electrodes bridged the writhing space between her eyes with their deadening quick sizzle, after the long years that she was kept safe from herself and the suicidal world kept safe from her, Mina Murray came back to London.

A new city to embrace the mopwater grey Thames, changed utterly, scarred by the Luftwaffe's firestorms and aged by the twenty-four years of her absence. Three days walking the streets now, destruction like a maze for her to solve or discard in frustration, and at Aldermanbury she'd stood before the ruins of St. Mary's and imagined, wished, her hands around Van Helsing's neck. Brittle bones to break apart like charred timbers and shattered pews; *Is this it, you old bastard? Is this what we saved England for?*

And the question, recognising its own intrinsic senselessness, knowing that it did not even make sense, and certainly didn't matter, had hung nowhere, like the blown-out windows framing autumnblue sky, the hallways ending only in rubble. Or her reflection, the woman a year from seventy looking back from a pane that seemed to have somehow escaped destruction especially for the purpose, this moment; a year from seventy and she almost looked it.

*　　*　　*

The boy sitting on the wall watched the woman get out of the taxi, old woman in black stockings and a black dress with a high collar, eyes hidden behind dark spectacles. He absently released the small brown lizard he'd been tormenting and it skittered gratefully away into some crack or crevice in the tumbledown masonry. The boy thought the woman looked like a widow, but better to pretend she was a spy for the Jerrys on a clandestine rendezvous, secrets to be exchanged for better secrets, and she walked in short steps that seemed like maybe she was counting off the distance between them. In the coolbright morning her shoes clicked, coded signal click, Morse click, and he thought perhaps he should hide behind the crumbling wall but then she saw him, paused, and waved hestitantly as the taxi pulled away. Too late, so he waved back and she was just an old woman again.

"Hello," she said and fishing about then for something in her handbag, a cigarette out and when he asked, the widow gave him one also. Lit it for him with a silver lighter and turned to stare at the gutted ruins of Carfax, broken, precarious walls braced against inevitable collapse. Noisy larks and sparrows singing to themselves in the blasted trees, and further on, the duck pond glinted in the sun.

The woman leaned against the wall and sighed out smoke, tired dragonsigh, and "They didn't leave much, did they?" she asked him and "No, Ma'am," he said. "It was one of them doodlebugs last year that got it," and he rocketwhistled for her, descending octaves and a big rumbling boom stuck on the end. The woman nodded and crushed her cigarette out against a raw edge of mortar, ground it back and forth, black ash smear against oatmeal grey and the butt dropped at her feet.

"It's haunted, you know," the boy told her, "Mostly at night, though," and she smiled, nicotine teeth glimpsed past the lipstick bruise, nodded again, unexpected agreement. "Yes," she said, "Yes, I guess that it is, isn't it?"

Mina killed the boy well back from the road, the straight razor she'd bought in Cheapside slipped out of her purse while he was digging about for bits of shrapnel to show her, jagged souvenirs of a pleasant fall afternoon in Purfleet. One gloved hand over his mouth and the smallest muffled sound of surprise before she drew the blade quick across his throat and his life sprayed out dark and wet against the flagstones. The first since she'd been back in England and so she sat with him a while in the chilly shade of a tilted wall, his blood drying to a crust around her mouth. Once, she heard a dog barking excitedly off towards the wreck that had been Jack Seward's asylum such a long time ago. Adrenaline shiver, heart jump and she'd thought maybe someone was coming, that she'd been discovered. But no one had, and so she sat with the boy and wondered at the winding knot of emptiness still inside her, unchanged, unchangeable.

An hour later she'd left the boy beneath a scraggly hedgerow and went to wash her hands and face in the sparkling pool. If there were ghosts at Carfax, they kept their distance.

August 1955

The cramped and cluttered office on West Houston even hotter than usual, Venetian blinds drawn to keep the sun out and only the soft glow from Audry Cavanaugh's brass desk lamp, gentle incandescence through the green glass shade, but no matter to the sticky, resolute Manhattan summer. Sweltering anyway, and Mina had to piss again, bladderache and sweat and the stale, heavy smell of the expensive English cigarettes the psychoanalyst chain-smoked. The framed and faded photograph of Carl Jung dangled on its hook behind the desk, his grey and knowing eyes on her, wanting inside.

"You're looking well today, Wilhelmina," Dr Cavanaugh said, terse smile, and she lit another cigarette, great cloud exhaled into the torpid air of the office, settling about her head like a shroud. "Sleeping any better?"

"No," which was true, "not really." The nightmares and the traffic sounds all night outside her SoHo apartment, the restless voices from the street that she could never be sure weren't meant for her. And the heat, like a living thing to smother, to hold the world perpetually at the edge of conflagration.

"I'm very sorry," and Dr Cavanaugh was squinting at her through the gauze of smoke, stingy smile already traded for familiar concern. Audry Cavanaugh never seemed to sweat, always so cool in her mannish suits, her hair in its neat, tight bun.

"Did you speak with your friend in London? You said you would . . ." and maybe the psychoanalyst heard the strain in

Mina's voice because she sighed, loud, impatient sigh and tilted her head back, and "Yes," she said, "I've talked with Dr Beecher. Yesterday, actually."

Mina licked her lips, dry tongue across dry lips, parched skin of dead fruit, pause, and then Audry Cavanaugh said, "He was able to find a number of references to attacks on children by a 'bloofer lady,' some articles from late in September, 1897 in *The Westminster Gazette* and a few other papers. A couple of pieces on the wreck at Whitby, also.

"But, Mina, I never *said* I doubted you. You didn't have to prove anything."

"I *had* the clippings," Mina mumbled around her dry tongue, "I used to have *all* the clippings."

"I always believed you did."

More silence, then, street sounds ten stories down to fill the void and then Dr Cavanaugh putting on her reading glasses, opening her yellow stenographer's pad, pencil scritch across the paper to record the date. "Are they still about Lucy, or is it the asylum again?"

And a drop of sweat ran slow down Mina's rouged cheek, pooled at the corner of her mouth, abrupt tang of salt and cosmetics to tease her thirst; she looked away, at the dusty, worn rug under her shoes, at the barrister shelves stuffed with medical books and psychological journals. The framed diplomas and, almost whispering, she said, "I had a dream about the world."

"Yes?" and Audry Cavanaugh sounded a little eager, something new, perhaps, in old Mina Murray's tiresome parade of delusions. "What did you dream about the world, Wilhelmina?"

Another drop of sweat dissolving on the tip of Mina's tongue, musky, fleeting taste of herself fading too soon, and "I dreamed that the world was dead," she said. "That the world ended a long, long time ago. But it doesn't know it's dead, and all that's left of the world is the dream of a ghost."

For a few minutes neither of them said anything, just the sound of the psychoanalyst's pencil and then not even that, and Mina listened to the street, the cars and trucks, the city. The sun made blazing slashes through the metal blinds, and Audry Cavanaugh struck a match, lit another cigarette. The stink of sulfur made Mina's nose wrinkle.

"Do you think that's true, Mina?"

And Mina closed her eyes, wanting to be alone with the weary, constant rhythm of her heart, afterimages like burnscar slashes in the dark behind her vellum eyelids. Too tired for confession or memory today, too uncertain to commit her scattered thoughts to words; she drifted, no intrusion from patient Cavanaugh, and in a few minutes she was asleep.

April 1969

After she's swallowed the capsules and a mouthful of plastic-flavoured water from the blue pitcher on her night stand, after Brenda Neufield and her white shoes have left the hospital room, Mina sits up. Safety bar wrestled down and her legs swung slowly, painfully, over and off the edge of the bed. She watches her bare feet dangling above the linoleum floor, age spots and skin parchment stretched too tight over kite frame bones, yellowed toenails.

A week ago, after her heart attack and the ambulance from her shitty little apartment, the emergency room and the doctor smiled. "You're a pip, Miss Murray. I have sixty-year old patients who should look half so good."

She waits, counting the nurse's footsteps, twelve, thirteen, fourteen, at the desk by now and her magazines. And Mina sits, staring across the room, her back to the window, cowardice to pass for defiance.

If she had a razor, or a kitchen knife, or a few more of Neufield's tranquilizer pills.

If she had the courage.

Later, when the rain has stopped and the crape myrtle has settled down for the night, the nurse comes back and finds her dozing, still perched upright on the edge of her bed like some silly parakeet or geriatric gargoyle. She eases Mina back, dull click as the safety bar locks again, and the nurse mumbles something so low Mina can't make out the words. So she lies very still, instead, lies on starchstiff sheets and her pillowcase and listens to the drip and patter from the street outside, velvet sounds after the storm enough to smooth the edges off Manhattan for a few hours. The blanket tucked rough beneath her chin and taxi wheels on the street, honk of a car horn, a police siren blocks away. And footsteps on the sidewalk below her window, and the soft and unmistakable pad of wolf paws on asphalt.

"The blood-dimmed tide is loosed, and everywhere
The ceremony of innocence is drowned . . ."
            – W.B. Yeats, "The Second Coming"

MICHAEL
MARSHALL SMITH

Save As . . .

MICHAEL MARSHALL SMITH has had his short stories published in anthologies and magazines on both sides of the Atlantic, including several volumes of the *Darklands, Dark Voices, Dark Terrors, The Year's Best Fantasy and Horror* and *The Best New Horror* series, along with *Omni* and *Interzone*. He is a three-time winner of the British Fantasy Award for Best Short Story, and has been nominated three times for the World Fantasy Award.

His debut novel, *Only Forward*, won the August Derleth Fantasy Award in 1995. His second novel, *Spares*, has been optioned by Steven Spielberg's DreamWorks SKG and translated into fourteen languages. The Overlook Connection recently published the book in a Special Edition with an introduction by Neil Gaiman. His latest novel, *One of Us*, is being developed as a movie by Di Novi Pictures and Warner Bros.

The author is currently working on a number of screenwriting projects, several as a partner in Smith & Jones, a London-based genre production company, as well as his first collection of short fiction. He lives in North London with his wife Paula and two Burmilla cats.

"'Save As . . .' came into being from the collision of two thoughts," recalls Smith. "One concerned the way in which we're prepared to put our trust in computers, despite the fact that we struggle with their inadequacies every day; the second was that actually, when compared to fate, computers are relatively trust-worthy.

"In a perfect world we would be able to take some of the metaphors of computing and put them to use in our 'real' lives: this is not, however, anything like a perfect world . . ."

A s soon as I walked out of the hospital I knew what I was going to do. It was 1:00 a.m. by then, for what little difference that made. I was on hospital time, crash time, blood time: surprised by how late it was, as if I'd believed that what happened must have taken place in some small pocket of horror outside the real world, where the normal rules of progression and chronology don't apply. Of course it must have taken time, for the men and women in white coats to run the stretcher trolleys down the corridors, shouting for crash teams and saline; to cut through my wife's matted clothes and expose wet ruins where only an hour ago all had been smooth and dry; to gently move my son's head so that its position in relation to his body was the same as it had always been. All of this took time, as did the eventual slow looks up at me, the quiet shakes of the doctors' heads, the forms I had to sign and the words I had to listen to.

Then the walk from the emergency room to the outside world, my shoes tapping softly on the linoleum as I passed rows of people with bandaged fingers. That took the most time of all.

The air in the car park was cool and moist, freshened by the rain. I could smell the grass which grew in the darkness beyond the lamps' pools of yellow light, and hear in the distance the sound of wet tires on the freeway. Tires which, I hoped, would retain their grip, safely transport the cars' passengers to their homes. Tires which wouldn't fail under a sudden braking to avoid a car which had slewed into their path, hurtling the vehicles together.

I suddenly realised that I had no means of getting home. The remains of the Lexus were presumably lying by the side of the road where the accident had taken place, or had been carted off to a wrecker's yard. For a moment the problem took up the whole of my mind, unnaturally luminescent: and then I realised both that I could presumably call a cab from reception, and that I didn't really care.

Two orderlies walked across the far side of the lot, a faint laugh carrying to me. The smell of smoke in their wake reminded me I was a smoker, and I fumbled a cigarette from the packet in my jacket pocket. The carton was perfectly in shape, the cigarette unbent. One of the very few things Helena and I had ever argued about was my continued inability to resist toying with death in the form of tubes of rolled tobacco. Her arguments were never those of the zealot, just measured and reasonable. She loved me, and Jack loved me, and she didn't want the two of them to be left alone. The fact that the crash which had crushed her skull had left my cancer sticks entirely unmolested was a joke which she would have liked and laughed at hard.

For a moment I hesitated. I couldn't decide whether Helena's death meant I should smoke the cigarette or not.

Then I lit it and walked back to reception. If I was going to go through with it, I didn't have much time.

The cab dropped me at the corner of Montague and 31st. I overtipped the driver – who'd had to put up with a sudden crying jag which left me feeling cold and embarrassed – and watched the car swish away down the deserted street. The cross-roads was bleak and exposed; an empty used car lot and burnt-out gas station taking two corners, run-down buildings of untellable purpose squatting kitty corner on the others. It couldn't have been more different from the place where I'd originally gone to visit the Same Again Corporation, an altogether more gleaming street in the heart of the business district. I guessed space was cheaper out here, and maybe they needed a lot of it: though I couldn't really understand why. Data storage is pretty compact these days.

Whatever. The card I'd kept in my wallet was adamant that I should go to the address on Montague in case of emergency, and so I walked quickly down towards 1176. I saw from across the street that a light was on behind the frosted glass of the door, and picked up the pace with relief. It was open, just as the card said it would be.

As I crossed the street a man came out of Same Again's front door, holding a very wet towel. He twisted the towel round on itself, squeezing as much of the water out of it as he could. It joined the rain already on the sidewalk and disappeared.

When he saw where I was heading he suddenly looked up.

"Help you?" he asked, warily. I showed him the card. An unreadable expression crossed his face. "Go inside," he said. "Be right with you."

The reception area was small but smart. And very quiet. I waited at the desk for a few moments, while the man finished whatever the hell he was doing. Then I noticed a soft dripping sound. A patch of carpet near one of the walls was damp, and there was a similar spot on the ceiling.

I turned to find the man reaching out a hand to me.

"Sorry about that," he said, but didn't offer any more explanation. "Okay, can I have that card?"

He took it and went behind the desk, tapped my Customer Number into the terminal there.

"My name's . . ." I said, but he held up his hand.

"Don't tell me," he said quickly. "Not a thing. I assume something pretty major has happened." He looked at my face for a moment, and decided he didn't have to wait for an answer. "So it's very important that I know as little as possible. How many people have already been involved?"

"Involved?"

"Are aware of whatever event it is that has brought you here."

"I don't know." I didn't know who counted. The doctors and nurses, presumably, and the people who'd loaded up the ambulance. They'd seen the faces. Others knew something had happened, in that they'd driven past the mess on the Freeway, or walked past me as I stood in the parking lot of the hospital. But maybe they didn't count, because they had no knowledge of who had been involved in what. "Maybe ten, twelve?"

The man nodded briskly. "That's fine. Okay, I've processed the order. Go through that door and a technician will take you from there. May I just remind you of the terms of the contract you entered into with Same Again, most specifically that you are legally bound not to reveal to anyone either that you are a subscriber to our service or that you have made use of it on this or any other occasion?"

"Fine," I said. It was illegal. We both knew that, and I was the last person who wanted any trouble.

The door led me into a cavernous dark area, where a young woman in a green lab coat waited for me. Without looking directly at my face she indicated that I should follow her. At the end of the room was a chair, and I sat in it and waited quietly while she applied conductant gel to my temples and attached the wires.

When she was finished she asked if I was comfortable. I turned my head towards her, clamping my lips tightly together. My teeth were chattering inside my head, the muscles of my jaw and neck spasming. I could barely see her through a haze of grief I knew I could not bear. In the end I nodded.

She loaded up a hypo and injected something into the vein on the back of my hand. I started counting backwards from twenty but made it no further than nine.

I got home about four o'clock that afternoon. After I'd locked the Lexus I stood in the driveway for a moment, savouring a breeze which softened the heat like a ceiling fan in a noisy bar. The weather men kept saying summer was going to burst soon, but they were evidently as full of shit as their genus had always been. Chaos theory may have grooved a lot of people's lives but the guys who stood in front of maps for a living were obviously still at the stage of consulting entrails. It hadn't rained for weeks and didn't look like it was going to start any time soon – and that was good, because in the evening we had a bunch of friends coming round for a cook-out in the back yard.

I let myself into the house and went straight through into the kitchen. Helena was standing at the table, basting chicken legs, half an eye on an old Tom Hanks film playing on the set in the corner. I noticed with approval that it was an old print, one which hadn't been parallaxed.

"Good movie," I said.

"Would be," she replied. "If you could see what the hell was going on."

I'm against the "enhancing" of classics: Helena takes the opposite view, as is her wont. We'd had the discussion about a hundred times and as neither of us really cared, we only put ourselves through it for fun. I kissed her on the nose and dunked a stick of celery in the barbecue sauce.

"Dad!" yelped a voice, and I turned in time to catch Jack as he leapt up at me. He looked like he'd been dragged through a hedge sideways by someone who was an internationally-acknowledged expert in the art of interfacing humans and hedges to maximum untidying effect. I raised an eyebrow at Helena, who shrugged.

"How many pairs of hands do you see?" she asked.

I set Jack down, endured him boxing my kneecaps for a while, and then sent him upstairs for a bath – promising I'd come up and talk to him. I knew what he really wanted was to rehearse yet again the names of the kids who'd be coming tonight. He's a sociable kid, much more than I was at his age – but I think I was looking forward to the evening as much as him. The secret of good social events is to only invite the people you like having in your life, not the ones you merely tolerate. Tonight we had my boss – who was actually my best friend – and his wife; a couple of Helena's old girlfriends who were as good a time as anyone could handle; and another old colleague of mine over from England with his family.

I hung with Helena in the kitchen for a while, until she tired of me nibbling samples of everything she'd painstakingly arranged on serving plates. She was too tall to box my knee caps and so bit me on the neck instead, a bite which turned into a kiss and became in danger of throwing her cooking schedule out of whack. She shooed me out and I left her to it and went through into the study.

There were screeds of e-mail to be sent before I could consign the day to history and settle down into the evening and weekend, but most of it was already written and the rest didn't take long. As my software punted them out I rested my chin on my hands and gazed out onto the yard. A trestle table was already set up, stacks of paper plates at the ready. The old cable spool we used as a table when it was just family had been rolled over by the tree, and bottles of red wine were open and breathing in the air. Beer would be frosting in the fridge and the fixings for Becky and Janny's drink of choice – Mint Juleps, for chrisake – ready and waiting in the kitchen. I could hear Helena viciously chopping some errant vegetable in the kitchen, and Jack hollering in the bath upstairs.

For a moment I felt perfectly at peace. I was thirty- six, had a wife I'd die for and a happy, intelligent kid; a job I actually enjoyed and more money than we needed; and a house that looked and felt like an advert for The American Way. So what if it was smaltzy: it was what I wanted. After my twenties, a frenetic nightmare of bad relationships and shitty jobs – and my early thirties, when no-one around me seemed to be able to talk about anything other than houses, marriage or children – my life had finally found its mark. The good things were in place, but with enough perspective to let me exist in the outside world too.

I was a lucky guy, and not too stupid to realise it.

The machine told me it had accomplished its task, and that I had new mail. I scanned the sender addresses: one from my sister in Europe, and a spam about "Outstanding business opportunities ($$$$$$)!". I was mildly surprised to see that there was also one from my own e-mail address – entitled "Read This!" – but not very. As part of my constant battle to design a kill file which would weed out e-mail invitations to business opportunities of any kind – regardless of the number of suffixed dollar signs – I was often sending test messages to myself. Evidently the new version of the kill file wasn't cutting it. I could tool around with it a little more on Sunday afternoon, maybe aided by a glass of JD. Right now it hardly seemed important.

I told the computer to have a nap and went upstairs to confront the dripping chaos that our bathroom would be.

John and Julia arrived first, as usual: they were always invited on a "turn up when you feel like it" basis. Helena was only just out of the shower so Julia went up to chat with her; meanwhile John and I stood in the kitchen with bottles of beer and chewed a variety of rags, him nibbling on Helena's cooking, me trying to rearrange things so she wouldn't notice.

We moved out into the yard when Becky and Janny arrived, and I started the Weber up, supervising the coals with foremanship from Helena at the table. I'd strung a couple of extension speakers out the door from the stereo in the living room, and one of Helena's compilation minidiscs played quietly in the background: something old, something new, something funky and something blue. Jack sat neatly on a chair at the end of the trestle in his new pants and checked shirt, sipping at a diet coke and waiting for the real fun to begin. Becky chatted with him in the meantime, while Janny re-ran horror stories of her last relationship: she's working on being the Fran Liebowitz of her generation, and getting there real fast. When everyone around the table erupted as she got to the end of yet another example of why her ex-boyfriend had not been fit to walk the earth, Helena caught my eye, and smiled.

I knew what she meant. There but for the grace of God, she was thinking, could have gone you or I.

Being funny is cool; being happy is better. I left the coals to themselves for a bit, and went and stood behind Helena with my hand on her shoulder.

But then the doorbell went and she jumped up to let Howard and Carol in. Jack stood uncertainly, waiting for them to come through into the garden. Their two kids, whose names I could never remember, walked out behind them. There was a moment of quiet mutual appraisal, and then all three ran off towards the tree to play some game or other. They'd only ever met once before, on a trip we took to England, but obviously whatever they'd got up to then was still good for another day. As the evening began to darken, and the adults sat around the table and drank and ate, I could hear always in the background one of my favourite sounds of all, the sound of Jack laughing.

And smell Helena's barbecue sauce, wafting over from the grill; and feel Helena's leg, her thigh warm against my leg, her ankle hooked behind mine.

At ten I came out of the house, clutching more beers, and realised two things. The first was that I was kind of drunk. Negotiating the step down from the kitchen was a little more difficult than it should have been, and the raucous figures around the trestle table looked less than clear. I shook my head, trying to get it back together: I didn't want to appear inebriated in front of my son. Not that he was on hand to watch – the kids were still tirelessly cavorting off in the darkness of the far end of the yard.

The second thing I noticed was less tangible. Something to do with atmosphere. While I'd been in the kitchen, it had changed. People were still laughing, and laughing hard, but they'd moved round, were sitting in different positions at the table. I guess I'd been in the kitchen longer than I thought. Becky and Jan were huddled at one end of the table, and I perched myself on a chair nearby. But they were talking seriously about something, and didn't seem to want to involve me.

There was another burst of laughter from the other end, and I looked blearily towards it. There was something harsh in the sound. Helena and Carol were leaned in tight together, their faces red and shiny. Howard was chortling with John and Julia. It was good to see them getting on together, but I hadn't realised they were all so chummy. Howard had only been with the firm for a year before upping stakes and going with Carol back to her own country. John and I had been friends for twenty years. Still, I guess it showed the evening was going well.

Then I saw something I couldn't understand. Helena's hand, reaching out and taking a cigarette from the packet lying on the table. I frowned vaguely, knowing something wasn't right, but she stuck the cigarette in her mouth and lit it with her lighter.

Then I remembered that she'd started a few months before, finally dragged into my habit. I felt guilty, wishing I'd been able to stop before she started. Too late now, I suppose.

I reached for the bottle of beer I'd perched on the end of the table, and missed. Well, not quite missed: I made enough contact to knock it off the table. Janny rolled her eyes and started to lean down for it, but I beat her to it.

"It's okay, I'm not that drunk," I said, slightly stiffly. This wasn't true, of course, because it took me rather longer than it should to find the bottle. In the end I had to completely lean over and look for where it had gone. This gave me a view of all the legs under the table, which was kind of neat, and I remained like that for a moment. Lots of shins, all standing together.

Some more together than others, I realised. Helena's foot was resting against John's.

I straightened up abruptly, cracking my head on the end of the table. Conversation around the table stopped, and I found myself with seven pairs of eyes looking at me.

"Sorry," I said, and went back into the kitchen to get another beer.

A couple later, really pretty drunk by then. Didn't want to sit back down at the table, felt like walking around a bit. Besides, Janny and Becky were still in conference, Janny looking odd; Howard and Carol and Julia talking about something else. I didn't feel like butting in.

Headed off towards the tree, thinking I'd see what the kids were up to. Maybe they'd play with me for a while. Better make an effort to talk properly – didn't want Jack to see daddy zonked. Usually it's okay, as my voice stays pretty straight unless I'm

completely loaded, and as I couldn't score any coke that afternoon, that wasn't the case.

Coke? What the fuck was I talking about?

I ground to a halt then, suddenly confused. I didn't take coke,
never had. Well, once, a few years back: it had been fun, but not
worth the money – and an obvious slippery slope. Too easy to
take until it was all gone, and then just buy some more. Plus
Helena would have gone ballistic – she didn't even like me
smoking, for God's sake.

Then I remembered her taking a cigarette earlier, and felt cold.
She hadn't started smoking. That was nonsense.

So why did I think she had?

I started moving again, not because I felt I'd solved anything,
but because I heard a sound. It wasn't laughing. It was more like
quiet tears.

At the far end of the yard I found Jack's camp, a little clearing
which huddled up against the wisteria that clung to the fence. I
pushed through the bushes, swearing quietly.

Jack was sitting in the middle, tears rolling down his moon-like
face. His check shirt was covered in dirt, the leg of his pants torn.
Howard's kids were standing around him, giggling and pointing.
As I lumbered towards them the little girl hurled another clump of
earth at Jack. It struck him in the face, just above the eye.

For a moment I was totally unable to move, and then I lunged
forward and grabbed her arm.

"Piss off, you little bastards," I hissed, yanking them away
from my son. They stared up at me, faces full of some thought I
couldn't read. Then the little boy pulled his arm free, and his sister
did the same. They ran off laughing towards the house.

I turned again to Jack, who was staring at the fence.

"Come on, big guy," I said, bending down to take him in my
arms. "What was that all about?"

His face slowly turned to mine, and my heart sank at what was
always there to see. The slight glaze in the eyes, the slackness at
one corner of his mouth.

"Dada," he said. "They dirt me."

I fell down onto my knees beside him, wrapping my arms
around his thin shoulders. I held him tight, but as always sensed
his eyes looking over my shoulder, gazing off into the middle
distance at something no-one else could see.

Eventually I let go of him and rocked to my feet again, hand held down towards him. He took it and struggled to his feet. I led him out of the bushes and into the yard.

As we came close to the tree I saw Helena and John were approaching out the darkness. I sensed some kind of rearrangement taking place as they saw us, but couldn't work out what it might have been.

"Oh shit, what's happened now?" Helena said, reading Jack's state instantly and stepping towards us. John hung back, in the deep shadows.

I couldn't answer her. Partly just because I was drunk; I'd obviously over-compensated for my dealer's coke famine by drinking way more than usual. But mainly because there was something wrong with her face. Not her face, which was as beautiful as ever. Her lipstick. It was smudged all round her face.

"Christ you're useless," she snapped, and grabbed Jack's hand. I didn't watch as she hauled him back towards the house. Instead I stared into the darkness under the tree, where a faint glow showed John was lighting a cigarette.

"Having a good evening?" I asked.

"Oh yeah," he said, laughing quietly. "You guys always throw such great parties."

We walked back to the trestle table, neither of us saying anything.

I sat down next to the girls, glanced across at Becky. She looked a lot worse than the last time we'd seen her. The chemo obviously wasn't working.

"How are you feeling?" I asked.

She looked up at me, smiled tightly. "Fine, just fine," she said. She didn't want my sympathy, and never had since the afternoon I'd called round at her place, looking for some company.

Behind me I heard John getting up and going through into the kitchen. I'd never liked Julia, nor she me, and so it would be no comfort to look round and see her eyes following her husband into the house, where Helena would already have dispatched Jack up to bed with a slap on the behind, and would maybe be standing at the sink, washing something that didn't need washing.

Instead I watched Howard and Carol talking together. They at least looked happy.

*		*		*

I stood at the front door, as the last set of tail lights turned into the road and faded away. Helena stood behind me. When I turned to take her hand she smiled meaninglessly, her face hard and distant, and walked away. I lumbered into my study to turn the computer off.

Instead I found myself waking it from sleep, and clicked into my mail program. I read the letter from my sister, who seemed to be doing fine. She was redecorating her new house with her new boyfriend. I nodded to myself; it was good that things were finally going her way.

I turned at a sound behind me to find Helena standing there. She plonked a cup of coffee down on the desk beside me.

"There you go, Mister Man," she said, and I smiled up at her. I didn't need the coffee, because I hadn't drunk very much. Sitting close to Helena all evening was still all the intoxication I needed. But it would be nice anyway.

"Good evening?" she asked, running her fingers across the back of my neck.

"Good evening," I said, looping my arm around her waist.

"Well don't stay down here too long," she winked, "Because we could make it even better."

After she'd gone I applied myself to the screen, but before I could start writing a reply to my little sis I heard Helena's voice again. This time it was hard, and came as usual from outside the study.

"Put your fucking son to bed," she said. "I can't deal with him tonight."

I turned, but she was already gone. I sat with my head in my hands for a little while, then reached out for the coffee. It wasn't there.

Then something on the screen caught my eye. Something I'd dismissed earlier. "Read This!" it said.

As much to avoid going upstairs as anything, I double-clicked on the mail icon. A long text message burped up onto the screen, and I frowned. My kill file tests usually only ran a couple of lines. Blinking against the drunkenness slopping through my head I tried to focus on the first sentence.

I managed to read it, in the end. And then the next, and as I read all the way through I felt as if my chair was sinking, dropping lower and lower into the ground.

The message was from me, it was about Same Again, and finally I remembered.

Before I'd come home that afternoon, I'd driven over to their offices in the business district. It was the second time I'd been, the first when I signed up for the service and had a preliminary backup done a year before. When I'd got up that morning, awakened by Jack's cheerful chatter and feeling the warmth of Helena's buttocks against mine under the sheets, I'd suddenly realised that if there were any day on which to make a backup of my life, today was surely that day.

I'd sat in the chair and they'd done their thing, archiving the current state of affairs into a data file. A file which, as their blurb promised, I could access at any time life had gone wrong and I needed to return to the saved version.

I heard a noise out in the hallway, the sound of a small person bumping into a piece of furniture. Jack. In a minute I should go out and help him, put him to bed. Maybe read to him a little, see if I could get a few more words into his head. If not, just hold him a while, as he slipped off into a sleep furnished with a vagueness I could never understand.

All it takes is one little sequence of DNA out of place, one infinitesimal chemical reaction going wrong. That's all the difference there is between the child he was, and could have been. Becky would understand that. One of her cells had misbehaved too, like a 1 or 0 out of place in some computer program.

Wet towels. Heavy rain. A leaking ceiling.

Suddenly I remembered going to a dark office on Montague in the wet small hours of some future morning. The strange way the man with the towel had reacted when I said I needed to do a restore from a backup they held there. And I knew what had happened. There'd been an accident. Or there was going to be.

The same rain that would total the car which for the moment still sat out in the drive, was going to corrupt the data I'd spent so much money to save.

At the bottom of the mail message was a number. I called it. Same Again's twenty-four hour switchboard was unobtainable. I listened to a recorded voice for a while, and then replaced the handset.

Maybe they'd gone out of business. Backing up was, after all, illegal. Too easy for criminals to leap backwards before their mistakes, for politicians to run experiments. Wide scale, it would have caused chaos. So long as not many people knew, you could get away with it. The disturbance was undetectable.

But now I knew, and this disturbance was far too great.

I could feel, like a heavy weight, the aura of the woman lying in the bed above my head. Could predict the firmness with which her back would be turned towards me, the way John and I would dance around each other at work the next day, and the endless drudgery of the phone calls required to score enough coke to make it all go away for a while.

"Hi dad – you still up?"

Jack stood in the doorway. He'd taken three apples from the kitchen, and was attempting to juggle them. He couldn't quite do it yet, but I thought it wouldn't be too long now. Perhaps I would learn then, and we could do that stuff where you swap balls with one another. That might be kind of cool.

"Yep," I said, "But not for much longer. How about you go up, get your teeth brushed, and then I'll read you a story?"

But he'd corrupted again by then, and the apples fell one by one, to bruise on the hardwood floor. His eyes stared, slightly out of kilter, at my dusty bookcase, his fingers struggling at a button on his shirt. I reached forward and wiped away the thin dribble of saliva that ran from the bad corner of his mouth.

"Come on, little guy," I said, and hoisted him up.

As I carried him upstairs into the darkness, his head lolling against my shoulder, I wondered how much had changed, whether in nine months the crash would still come as we drove back from a happy evening in Gainesville.

And I wondered, if it did, whether I would do anything to avoid it.

Or if I would steer the car even harder this time.

KIM NEWMAN

Coppola's Dracula

KIM NEWMAN'S SHORT FICTION IS COLLECTED in *The Original Dr. Shade and Other Stories* and *Famous Monsters*, while his novels include *The Night Mayor, Bad Dreams, Jago, The Quorum, Back in the USSA* (with Eugene Byrne) and *Life's Lottery*. Also, under his "Jack Yeovil" pseudonym, there are a string of gaming novels: *Drachenfels, Demon Download, Krokodil Tears, Comeback Tour, Beasts in Velvet, Genevieve Undead* and *Route 666*, plus *Orgy of the Blood Parasites*.

His epic historical vampire novel, *Anno Dracula*, has won the Dracula Society's Children of the Night Award; The British Science Fiction Award; the Fiction Award of the Lord Ruthven Assembly, and the International Horror Critics Guild Award. He has followed it up with the sequels *The Bloody Red Baron*, which takes place during the First World War, and *Dracula Cha Cha Cha*, set in Rome in 1959. A fourth book in the sequence is planned, *Johnny Alucard*, which will use the following Bram Stoker Award-nominated novella as a starting point.

"It's pretty obvious that the premise of this story is what it would have been like if Francis Ford Coppola had made *Dracula* as one of his good films," explains the author. "Originally I was going to write it as a parodic skit consisting of the film itself, but it became more substantial as I thought of the process of the making of *Apocalypse Now*. Of course, I owe a debt to Eleanor Coppola's book *Notes* and George Hickenlooper's documentary *Hearts of Darkness: A Filmmaker's Apocalypse*.

"Having considered what Coppola might have made of *Dra-*

cula, I'm struck with the thought of the other film-makers who at various times promised but didn't deliver versions of the story – Orson Welles, Ingmar Bergman, Ken Russell – or by those who made *Dracula*s that don't quite fit their filmographies _ what if John Badham's *Dracula* had been the *Saturday Night Fever* follow-up, with John Travolta as a disco Dracula . . . ?"

A treeline at dusk. Tall, straight, Carpathian pines. The red of sunset bleeds into the dark of night. Great flapping sounds. Huge, dark shapes flit languidly between the trees, sinister, dangerous. A vast batwing brushes the treetops.

Jim Morrison's voice wails in despair. "People Are Strange".

Fire blossoms. Blue flame, pure as candle light. Black trees are consumed . . .

Fade to a face, hanging upside-down in the roiling fire.

Harker's Voice: *Wallachia . . . shit!*

Jonathan Harker, a solicitor's clerk, lies uneasy on his bed, upstairs in the inn at Bistritz, waiting. His eyes are empty.

With great effort, he gets up and goes to the full-length mirror. He avoids his own gaze and takes a swig from a squat bottle of plum brandy. He wears only long drawers. Bite-marks, almost healed, scab his shoulders. His arms and chest are sinewy, but his belly is white and soft. He staggers into a program of isometric exercises, vigorously Christian, ineptly executed.

Harker's Voice: *I could only think of the forests, the mountains . . . the inn was just a waiting room. Whenever I was in the forests, I could only think of home, of Exeter. Whenever I was home, I could only think of getting back to the mountains.*

The blind crucifix above the mirror, hung with cloves of garlic, looks down on Harker. He misses his footing and falls on the bed, then gets up, reaches, and takes down the garlic.

He bites into a clove as if it were an apple, and washes the pulp down with more brandy.

Harker's Voice: *All the time I stayed here in the inn, waiting for a commission, I was growing older, losing precious life. And all the time the Count sat on top of his mountain, leeching off the land, he grew younger, thirstier.*

Harker scoops a locket from a bedside table and opens it to look at a portrait of his wife, Mina. Without malice or curiosity, he dangles the cameo in a candle flame. The face browns, the silver setting blackens.

Harker's Voice: *I was waiting for the call from Seward. Eventually, it came.*

There is a knock on the door.

"It's all right for you, Katharine Reed," Francis whined as he picked over the unappetising craft services table. "You're dead, you don't have to eat this shit."

Kate showed teeth, hissing a little. She knew that despite her coke-bottle glasses and freckles, she could look unnervingly feral when she smiled. Francis didn't shrink: deep down, the director thought of her as a special effect, not a real vampire.

In the makeshift canteen, deep in the production bunker, the Americans wittered nostalgia about McDonald's. The Brits – the warm ones, anyway – rhapsodised about Pinewood breakfasts of kippers and fried bread. Romanian location catering was not what they were used to.

Francis finally found an apple less than half brown and took it away. His weight had dropped visibly since their first meeting, months ago in pre-production. Since he had come to Eastern Europe, the insurance doctor diagnosed him as suffering from malnutrition and put him on vitamin shots. *Dracula* was running true to form, sucking him dry.

A production this size was like a swarm of vampire bats – some large, many tiny – battening tenaciously onto the host, making insistent, never-ending demands. Kate had watched Francis – bespectacled, bearded and hyperactive – lose substance under the draining siege, as he made and justified decisions, yielded the visions to be translated to celluloid, rewrote the script to suit locations or new casting. How could one man throw out so many ideas, only a fraction of which would be acted on? In his position, Kate's mind would bleed empty in a week.

A big budget film shot in a backward country was an insane proposition, like taking a touring three-ring circus into a war zone. Who will survive, she thought, and what will be left of them?

The craft table for vampires was as poorly stocked as the one for the warm. Unhealthy rats in chickenwire cages. Kate watched one of the floor effects men, a new-born with a padded waistcoat and a toolbelt, select a writhing specimen and bite off its head. He spat it on the concrete floor, face stretched into a mask of disgust.

"Ringworm," he snarled. "The commie gits are trying to kill us off with diseased vermin."

"I could murder a bacon sarnie," the effects man's mate sighed.

"I could murder a Romanian caterer," said the new-born.

Kate decided to go thirsty. There were enough Yanks around to make coming by human blood in this traditionally superstitious backwater not a problem. Ninety years after Dracula spread vampirism to the Western world, America was still sparsely populated by the blood-drinking undead. For a lot of Americans, being bled by a genuine olde worlde creature of the night was something of a thrill.

That would wear off.

Outside the bunker, in a shrinking patch of natural sunlight between a stand of real pines and the skeletons of fake trees, Francis shouted at Harvey Keitel. The actor, cast as Jonathan Harker, was stoic, inexpressive, grumpy. He refused to be drawn into argument, invariably driving Francis to shrieking hysteria.

"I'm not Martin Fucking Scorsese, man," he screamed. "I'm not going to slather on some lousy voice-over to compensate for what you're not giving me. Without Harker, I don't have a picture."

Keitel made fists but his body language was casual. Francis had been riding his star hard all week. Scuttlebutt was that he had wanted Pacino or McQueen but neither wanted to spend three months behind the Iron Curtain.

Kate could understand that. This featureless WWII bunker, turned over to the production as a command centre, stood in ancient mountains, dwarfed by the tall trees. As an outpost of civilisation in a savage land, it was ugly and ineffective.

When approached to act as a technical advisor to Coppola's *Dracula*, she had thought it might be interesting to see where it all started: the Changes, the Terror, the Transformation. No one seriously believed vampirism began here, but it was where Dracula came from. This land had nurtured him through centuries

before he decided to spread his wings and extend his bloodline
around the world.

Three months had already been revised as six months. This
production didn't have a schedule, it had a sentence. A few were
already demanding parole.

Some vampires felt Transylvania should be the undead Israel, a
new state carved out of the much-redrawn map of Central
Europe, a geographical and political homeland. As soon as it
grew from an inkling to a notion, Nicolae Ceauşescu vigorously
vetoed the proposition. Holding up in one hand a silver-edged
sickle, an iron-headed hammer and a sharpened oak spar, the
Premier reminded the world that "in Romania, we know how to
treat leeches – a stake through the heart and off with their filthy
heads." But the Transylvania Movement – back to the forests,
back to the mountains – gathered momentum: some elders, after
ninety years of the chaos of the larger world, wished to withdraw
to their former legendary status. Many of Kate's generation,
turned in the 1880s, Victorians stranded in this mechanistic
century, were sympathetic.

"You're the Irish vampire lady," Harrison Ford, flown in for
two days to play Dr Seward as a favour, had said. "Where's your
castle?"

"I have a flat in Clerkenwell," she admitted. "Over an off-
license."

In the promised Transylvania, all elders would have castles,
fiefdoms, slaves, human cattle. Everyone would wear evening
dress. All vampires would have treasures of ancient gold, like
leprechauns. There would be a silk-lined coffin in every crypt, and
every night would be a full moon. Unlife eternal and luxury
without end, bottomless wells of blood and Paris label shrouds.

Kate thought the Movement lunatic. Never mind cooked
breakfasts and (the other crew complaint) proper toilet paper,
this was an intellectual desert, a country without conversation,
without (and she recognised the irony) life.

She understood Dracula had left Transylvania in the first place
not merely because he – the great dark sponge – had sucked it dry,
but because even he was bored with ruling over gypsies, wolves
and mountain streams. That did not prevent the elders of the
Transylvania Movement from claiming the Count as their inspiration and using his seal as their symbol. An Arthurian whisper

had it that once vampires returned to Transylvania, Dracula would rise again to assume his rightful throne as their ruler.

Dracula meant so much to so many. She wondered if there was anything left inside so many meanings, anything concrete and inarguable and true. Or was he now just a phantom, a slave to anyone who cared to invoke his name? So many causes and crusades and rebellions and atrocities. One man, one monster, could never have kept track of them all, could never have encompassed so much mutually exclusive argument.

There was the Dracula of the histories, the Dracula of Stoker's book, the Dracula of this film, the Dracula of the Transylvania Movement. Dracula, the vampire and the idea, was vast. But not so vast that he could cast his cloak of protection around all who claimed to be his followers. Out here in the mountains where the Count had passed centuries in petty predation, Kate understood that he must in himself have felt tiny, a lizard crawling down a rock.

Nature was overwhelming. At night, the stars were laser-points in the deep velvet black of the sky. She could hear, taste and smell a thousand flora and fauna. If ever there was a call of the wild, this forest exerted it. But there was nothing she considered intelligent life.

She tied tight under her chin the yellow scarf, shot through with golden traceries, she had bought at Biba in 1969. It was a flimsy, delicate thing, but to her it meant civilisation, a coloured moment of frivolity in a life too often preoccupied with monochrome momentousness.

Francis jumped up and down and threw script pages to the winds. His arms flapped like wings. Clouds of profanity enveloped the uncaring Keitel.

"Don't you realise I've put up my own fucking money for this fucking picture," he shouted, not just at Keitel but at the whole company. "I could lose my house, my vineyard, everything. I can't afford a fucking honourable failure. This has abso-god-damn-lutely got to outgross *Jaws* or I'm personally impaled up the ass with a sharpened telegraph pole."

Effects men sat slumped against the exterior wall of the bunker – there were few chairs on location – and watched their director rail at the heavens, demanding of God answers that were not forthcoming. Script pages swirled upwards in a spiral, spreading out in a cloud, whipping against the upper trunks of the trees, soaring out over the valley.

"He was worse on *Godfather*," one said.

Servants usher Harker into a well-appointed drawing room. A table is set with an informal feast of bread, cheese and meat. Dr Jack Seward, in a white coat with a stethoscope hung around his neck, warmly shakes Harker's hand and leads him to the table. Quincey P. Morris sits to one side, tossing and catching a spade-sized bowie knife.

Lord Godalming, well-dressed, napkin tucked into his starched collar, sits at the table, forking down a double helping of paprika chicken. Harker's eyes meet Godalming's, the nobleman looks away.

Seward: *Harker, help yourself to the fare, Jon. It's uncommonly decent for foreign muck.*

Harker: *Thank you, no. I took repast at the inn.*

Seward: *How is the inn? Natives bothering you? Superstitious babushkas, what?*

Harker: *I am well in myself.*

Seward: *Splendid . . . the vampire, Countess Marya Dolingen of Graz. In 1883, you cut off her head and drove a hawthorne stake through her heart, destroying her utterly.*

Harker: *I'm not disposed just now to discuss such affairs.*

Morris: *Come on, Jonny-Boy. You have a commendation from the church, a papal decoration. The frothing she-bitch is dead at last. Take the credit.*

Harker: *I have no direct knowledge of the individual you mention. And if I did, I reiterate that I would not be disposed to discuss such affairs.*

Seward and Morris exchange a look as Harker stands impassive. They know they have the right man. Godalming, obviously in command, nods.

Seward clears plates of cold meat from a strong-box that stands on the table. Godalming hands the doctor a key, with which he opens the box. He takes out a woodcut and hands it over to Harker.

The picture is of a knife-nosed mediaeval warrior prince.

Seward: *That's Vlad Tepes, called "the Impaler". A good Christian, defender of the faith. Killed a million Turks. Son of the Dragon, they called him. Dracula.*

Harker is impressed.

Morris: *Prince Vlad had Orthodox Church decorations out the ass. Coulda made Metropolitan. But he converted, went over to Rome, turned Candle.*

Harker: *Candle?*

Seward: *Roman Catholic.*

Harker looks again at the woodcut. In a certain light, it resembles the young Marlon Brando.

Seward walks to a side-table, where an antique dictaphone is set up. He fits a wax cylinder and adjusts the needle-horn.

Seward: *This is Dracula's voice. It's been authenticated.*

Seward cranks the dictaphone.

Dracula's Voice: *Cheeldren of the naight, leesten to them. What museek they maike!*

There is a strange distortion in the recording.

Harker: *What's that noise in the background?*

Seward: *Wolves, my boy. Dire wolves, to be precise.*

Dracula's Voice: *To die, to be reallllly dead, that must be . . . glorioussss!*

Morris: *Vlad's well beyond Rome now. He's up there, in his impenetrable castle, continuing the crusade on his own. He's got this army of Szekeley Gypsies, fanatically loyal fucks. They follow his orders, no matter how atrocious, no matter how appalling. You know the score, Jon. Dead babies, drained cattle, defenestrated peasants, impaled grandmothers. He's god-damned Un-Dead. A fuckin' monster, boy.*

Harker is shocked. He looks again at the woodcut.

Seward: *The firm would like you to proceed up into the mountains, beyond the Borgo Pass . . .*

Harker: *But that's Transylvania. We're not supposed to be in Transylvania.*

Godalming looks to the heavens, but continues eating.

Seward: *. . . beyond the Borgo Pass, to Castle Dracula. There, you are to ingratiate yourself by whatever means come to hand into Dracula's coterie. Then you are to disperse the Count's household.*

Harker: *Disperse?*

Godalming puts down his knife and fork.

Godalming: *Disperse with ultimate devotion.*

*　　*　　*

"What can I say, we made a mistake," Francis said, shrugging nervously, trying to seem confident. He had shaved off his beard, superstitiously hoping that would attract more attention than his announcement. "I think this is the courageous thing to do, shut down and recast, rather than continue with a frankly unsatisfactory situation."

Kate did not usually cover showbiz, but the specialist press – *Variety*, *Screen International*, *Positif* – were dumbstruck enough to convince her it was not standard procedure to fire one's leading man after two weeks' work, scrap the footage and get someone else. When Keitel was sent home, the whole carnival ground to a halt and everyone had to sit around while Francis flew back to the States to find a new star.

Someone asked how far over budget *Dracula* was, and Francis smiled and waffled about budgets being provisional.

"No one ever asked how much the Sistine Chapel cost," he said, waving a chubby hand. Kate would have bet that while Michelangelo was on his back with the brushes, Pope Julius II never stopped asking how much it cost and when would it be finished.

During the break in shooting, money was spiralling down a drain. Fred Roos, the co-producer, had explained to her just how expensive it was to keep a whole company standing by. It was almost more costly than having them work.

Next to Francis at the impromptu press conference in the Bucharest Town Hall was Martin Sheen, the new Jonathan Harker. In his mid-thirties, he looked much younger, like the lost boy he played in *Badlands*. The actor mumbled generously about the opportunity he was grateful for. Francis beamed like a shorn Santa Claus on a forced diet and opened a bottle of his own wine to toast his new star.

The man from *Variety* asked who would be playing Dracula, and Francis froze in mid-pour, sloshing red all over Sheen's wrist. Kate knew the title role – actually fairly small, thanks to Bram Stoker and screenwriter John Milius – was still on offer to various possibles – Klaus Kinski, Jack Nicholson, Christopher Lee.

"I can confirm Bobby Duvall will play Van Helsing," Francis said. "And we have Dennis Hopper as Renfield. He's the one who eats flies."

"But who is Dracula?"

Francis swallowed some wine, attempted a cherubic look, and wagged a finger.

"I think I'll let that be a surprise. Now, ladies and gentlemen, if you'll excuse me, I have motion picture history to make."

As Kate took her room-key from the desk, the night manager nagged her in Romanian. When she had first checked in, the door of her room fell off as she opened it. The hotel maintained she did not know her own vampire strength and should pay exorbitantly to have the door replaced. Apparently, the materials were available only at great cost and had to be shipped from Moldavia. She assumed it was a scam they worked on foreigners, especially vampires. The door was made of paper stretched over a straw frame, the hinges were cardboard fixed with drawing pins.

She was pretending not to understand any language in which they tried to ask her for money, but eventually they would hit on English and she'd have to make a scene. Francis, light-hearted as a child at the moment, thought it rather funny and had taken to teasing her about the damn door.

Not tired, but glad to be off the streets after nightfall, she climbed the winding stairs to her room, a cramped triangular space in the roof. Though she was barely an inch over five feet, she could only stand up straight in the dead centre of the room. A crucifix hung ostentatiously over the bed, a looking glass was propped up on the basin. She thought about taking them down but it was best to let insults pass. In many ways, she preferred the camp-site conditions in the mountains. She only needed to sleep every two weeks, and when she was out she was literally dead and didn't care about clean sheets.

They were all in Bucharest for the moment, as Francis supervised script-readings to ease Sheen into the Harker role. His fellow coach-passengers – Fredric Forrest (Westenra), Sam Bottoms (Murray) and Albert Hall (Swales) – had all been on the project for over a year, and had been through all this before in San Francisco as Francis developed John Milius's script through improvisation and happy accident. Kate didn't think she would have liked being a screenwriter. Nothing was ever finished.

She wondered who would end up playing Dracula. Since his marriage to Queen Victoria made him officially if embarrassingly a satellite of the British Royal Family, he had rarely been

represented in films. However, Lon Chaney had taken the role in
the silent *London After Midnight*, which dealt with the court
intrigues of the 1880s, and Anton Walbrook played Vlad opposite Anna Neagle in *Victoria the Great* in 1937. Kate, a lifelong
theatregoer who had never quite got used to the cinema, remembered Vincent Price opposite Helen Hayes in *Victoria Regina* in
the 1930s.

Aside from a couple of cheap British pictures which didn't
count, Bram Stoker's *Dracula* – the singular mix of documentation and wish-fulfilment that inspired a revolution by showing
how Dracula could have been defeated in the early days before his
rise to power – had never been made as a film. Orson Welles
produced it on radio in the 1930s and announced it as his first
picture, casting himself as Harker *and* the Count, using first-
person camera throughout. RKO thought it too expensive and
convinced him to make *Citizen Kane* instead. Nearly ten years
ago, Francis had lured John Milius into writing the first pass at
the script by telling him nobody, not even Orson Welles, had ever
been able to lick the book.

Francis was still writing and rewriting, stitching together scenes
from Milius's script with new stuff of his own and pages torn
straight from the book. Nobody had seen a complete script, and
Kate thought one didn't exist.

She wondered how many times Dracula had to die for her to be
rid of him. Her whole life had been a dance with Dracula, and he
haunted her still. When Francis killed the Count at the end of the
movie – if that was the ending he went with – maybe it would be
for the last time. You weren't truly dead until you'd died in a
motion picture. Or at the box office.

The latest word was that the role was on offer to Marlon
Brando. She couldn't see it: Stanley Kowalski and Vito Corleone
as Count Dracula. One of the best actors in the world, he'd been
one of the worst Napoleons in the movies. Historical characters
brought out the ham in him. He was terrible as Fletcher Christian
too.

Officially, Kate was still just a technical adviser – though she
had never actually met Dracula during his time in London, she
had lived through the period. She had known Stoker, Jonathan
Harker, Godalming and the rest. Once, as a warm girl, she had
been terrified by Van Helsing's rages. When Stoker wrote his

book and smuggled it out of prison, she had helped with its underground circulation, printing copies on the presses of the *Pall Mall Gazette* and ensuring its distribution despite all attempts at suppression. She wrote the introduction for the 1912 edition that was the first official publication.

Actually, she found herself impressed into a multitude of duties. Francis treated a $20,000,000 (and climbing) movie like a college play and expected everyone to pitch in, despite union rules designed to prevent the crew being treated as slave labour. She found the odd afternoon of sewing costumes or night of set-building welcome distraction.

At first, Francis asked her thousands of questions about points of detail; now he was shooting, he was too wrapped up in his own vision to take advice. If she didn't find something to do, she'd sit idle. As an employee of American Zoetrope, she couldn't even write articles about the shoot. For once, she was on the inside, knowing but not telling.

She had wanted to write about Romania for the *New Statesman*, but was under orders not to do anything that might jeopardise the co-operation the production needed from the Ceausescus. So far, she had avoided all the official receptions Nicolae and Elena hosted for the production. The Premier was known to an be extreme vampire-hater, especially since the stirrings of the Transylvania Movement, and occasionally ordered not-so-discreet purges of the undead.

Kate knew she, like the few other vampires with the *Dracula* crew, was subject to regular checks by the *Securitate*. Men in black leather coats loitered in the corner of her eye.

"For God's sake," Francis had told her, "don't *take* anybody local."

Like most Americans, he didn't understand. Though he could *see* she was a tiny woman with red hair and glasses, the mind of an aged aunt in the body of an awkward cousin, Francis could not rid himself of the impression that vampire women were ravening predators with unnatural powers of bewitchment, lusting after the pounding blood of any warm youth who happens along. She was sure he hung his door with garlic and wolfsbane, but half-hoped for a whispered solicitation.

After a few uncomfortable nights in Communist-approved beer-halls, she had learned to stay in her hotel room while in

Bucharest. People here had memories as long as her lifetime. They crossed themselves and muttered prayers as she walked by. Children threw stones.

She stood at her window and looked out at the square. A patch of devastation, where the ancient quarter of the capital had been, marked the site of the palace Ceausescu was building for himself. A three-storey poster of the Saviour of Romania stood amid the ruins. Dressed like an orthodox priest, he held up Dracula's severed head as if he had personally killed the Count.

Ceausescu harped at length about the dark, terrible days of the past when Dracula and his kind preyed on the warm of Romania to prevent his loyal subjects from considering the dark, terrible days of the present when he and his wife lorded over the country like especially corrupt Roman Emperors. Impersonating the supplicant baker in *The Godfather*, Francis had abased himself to the dictator to secure official co-operation.

She turned on the radio and heard tinny martial music. She turned it off, lay on the narrow, lumpy bed – as a joke, Fred Forrest and Francis had put a coffin in her room one night – and listened to the city at night. Like the forest, Bucharest was alive with noises, and smells.

It was ground under, but there was life here. Even in this grim city, someone was laughing, someone was in love. Somebody was allowed to be a happy fool.

She heard winds in telephone wires, bootsteps on cobbles, a drink being poured in another room, someone snoring, a violinist sawing scales. And someone outside her door. Someone who didn't breathe, who had no heartbeat, but whose clothes creaked as he moved, whose saliva rattled in his throat.

She sat up, confident she was elder enough to be silent, and looked at the door.

"Come in," she said, "it's not locked. But be careful. I can't afford more breakages."

His name was Ion Popescu and he looked about thirteen, with big, olive-shiny orphan eyes and thick, black, unruly hair. He wore an adult's clothes, much distressed and frayed, stained with long-dried blood and earth. His teeth were too large for his skull, his cheeks stretched tight over his jaws, drawing his whole face to the point of his tiny chin.

Once in her room, he crouched down in a corner, away from a window. He talked only in a whisper, in a mix of English and German she had to strain to follow. His mouth wouldn't open properly. He was alone in the city, without community. Now he was tired and wanted to leave his homeland. He begged her to hear him out and whispered his story.

He claimed to be fifty-two, turned in 1937. He didn't know, or didn't care to talk about, his father- or mother-in-darkness. There were blanks burned in his memory, whole years missing. She had come across that before. For most of his vampire life, he had lived underground, under the Nazis and then the Communists. He was the sole survivor of several resistance movements. His warm comrades had never really trusted him, but his capabilities were useful for a while.

She was reminded of her first days after turning. When she knew nothing, when her condition seemed a disease, a trap. That Ion could be a vampire for forty years and never pass beyond the new-born stage was incredible. She truly realised, at last, just how backward this country was.

"Then I hear of the American film, and of the sweet vampire lady who is with the company. Many times, I try to get near you, but you are watched. *Securitate.* You, I think, are my saviour, my true mother-in-the-dark."

Fifty-two, she reminded herself.

Ion was exhausted after days trying to get close to the hotel, to "the sweet vampire lady", and hadn't fed in weeks. His body was icy cold. Though she knew her own strength was low, she nipped her wrist and dribbled a little of her precious blood onto his white lips, enough to put a spark in his dull eyes.

There was a deep gash on his arm, which festered as it tried to heal. She bound it with her scarf, wrapping his thin limb tight.

He hugged her and slept like a baby. She arranged his hair away from his eyes and imagined his life. It was like the old days, when vampires were hunted down and destroyed by the few who believed. Before Dracula.

The Count had changed nothing for Ion Popescu.

Bistritz, a bustling township in the foothills of the Carpathian Alps. Harker, carrying a Gladstone Bag, weaves through crowds towards a waiting coach and six. Peasants try to sell him cruci-

fixes, garlic and other lucky charms. Women cross themselves and mutter prayers.

A wildly-gesticulating photographer tries to stop him slowing his pace to examine a complicated camera. An infernal burst of flash-powder spills purple smoke across the square. People choke on it.

Corpses hang from a four-man gibbet, dogs leaping up to chew on their naked feet. Children squabble over mismatched boots filched from the executed men. Harker looks up at the twisted, mouldy faces.

He reaches the coach and tosses his bag up. Swales, the coachman, secures it with the other luggage and growls at the late passenger. Harker pulls open the door and swings himself into the velvet-lined interior of the carriage.

There are two other passengers. Westenra, heavily moustached and cradling a basket of food. And Murray, a young man who smiles as he looks up from his Bible.

Harker exchanges curt nods of greeting as the coach lurches into motion.

Harker's Voice: *I quickly formed opinions of my travelling companions. Swales was at the reins. It was my commission but sure as shooting it was his coach. Westenra, the one they called "Cook", was from Whitby. He was ratcheted several notches too tight for Wallachia. Probably too tight for Whitby, come to that. Murray, the fresh-faced youth with the Good Book, was a rowing blue from Oxford. To look at him, you'd think the only use he'd have for a sharpened stake would be as a stump in a knock-up match.*

Later, after dark but under a full moon, Harker sits up top with Swales. A wind-up phonograph crackles out a tune through a sizable trumpet.

Mick Jagger sings 'Ta-Ra-Ra-BOOM-De-Ay'.

Westenra and Murray have jumped from the coach and ride the lead horses, whooping it up like a nursery Charge of the Light Brigade.

Harker, a few years past such antics, watches neutrally. Swales is indulgent of his passengers.

The mountain roads are narrow, precipitous. The lead horses, spurred by their riders, gallop faster. Harker looks down and sees a sheer drop of a thousand feet, and is more concerned by the foolhardiness of his companions.

Hooves strike the edge of the road, narrowly missing disaster.

Westenra and Murray chant along with the song, letting go of their mounts' manes and doing hand-gestures to the lyrics. Harker gasps but Swales chuckles. He has the reins and the world is safe.

Harker's Voice: *I think the dark and the pines of Romania spooked them badly, but they whistled merrily on into the night, infernal cake-walkers with Death as a dancing partner.*

In the rehearsal hall, usually a people's ceramics collective, she introduced Ion to Francis.

The vampire youth was sharper now. In a pair of her jeans – which fit him perfectly – and a *Godfather II* T-shirt, he looked less the waif, more like a survivor. Her Biba scarf, now his talisman, was tied around his neck.

"I said we could find work for him with the extras. The gypsies."

"I am no gypsy," Ion said, vehemently.

"He speaks English, Romanian, German, Magyar and Romany. He can co-ordinate all of them."

"He's a kid."

"He's older than you are."

Francis thought it over. She didn't mention Ion's problems with the authorities. Francis couldn't harbour an avowed dissident. The relationship between the production and the government was already strained. Francis thought – correctly – that he was being bled of funds by corrupt officials, but could afford to lodge no complaint. Without the Romanian army, he didn't have a cavalry, didn't have a horde. And without the location permits that still hadn't come through, he couldn't shoot the story beyond Borgo Pass.

"I can keep the rabble in line, maestro," Ion said, smiling.

Somehow, he had learned how to work his jaws and lips into a smile. With her blood in him, he had more control. She noticed him chameleoning a little. His smile, she thought, might be a little like hers.

Francis chuckled. He liked being called "maestro". Ion was good at getting on the right side of people. After all, he had certainly got on the right side of her.

"Okay, but keep out of the way if you see anyone in a suit."

Ion was effusively grateful. Again, he acted the age he looked, hugging Francis, then her, saluting like a toy soldier. Martin Sheen, noticing, raised an eyebrow.

Francis took Ion off to meet his own children – Roman, Gio and Sofia – and Sheen's sons Emilio and Charley. It had not sunk in that this wiry kid, obviously keen to learn baseball and chew gum, was in warm terms middle-aged.

Then again, Kate never knew whether to be twenty-five, the age at which she turned, or 116. And how was a 116-year-old supposed to behave anyway?

Since she had let him bleed her, she was having flashes of his past: scurrying through back-streets and sewers, like a rat; the stabbing pains of betrayal; eye-searing flashes of firelight; constant cold and red thirst and filth.

Ion had never had the time to grow up. Or even to be a proper child. He was a waif and a stray. She couldn't help but love him a little. She had chosen not to pass on the Dark Kiss, though she had once – during the Great War – come close and regretted it.

Her bloodline, she thought, was not good for a new-born. There was too much Dracula in it, maybe too much Kate Reed.

To Ion, she was a teacher not a mother. Before she insisted on becoming a journalist, her whole family seemed to feel she was predestined to be a governess. Now, at last, she thought she saw what they meant.

Ion was admiring six-year-old Sofia's dress, eyes bright with what Kate hoped was not hunger. The little girl laughed, plainly taken with her new friend. The boys, heads full of the vampires of the film, were less sure about him. He would have to earn their friendship.

Later, Kate would deal with Part Two of the Ion Popescu Problem. After the film was over, which would not be until the 1980s at the current rate of progress, he wanted to leave the country, hidden in among the rest of the production crew. He was tired of skulking and dodging the political police, and didn't think he could manage it much longer. In the West, he said, he would be free from persecution.

She knew he would be disappointed. The warm didn't really *like* vampires in London or Rome or Dublin any more than they did in Timisoara or Bucharest or Cluj. It was just more difficult legally to have them destroyed.

*   *   *

Back in the mountains, there was the usual chaos. A sudden thunderstorm, whipped up out of nowhere like a djinn, had torn up real and fake trees and scattered them throughout the valley, demolishing the gypsy encampment production designer Dean Tavoularis had been building. About half a million dollars' worth of set was irrevocably lost, and the bunker itself had been struck by lightning and split open like a pumpkin. The steady rain poured in and streamed out of the structure, washing away props, documents, equipment and costumes. Crews foraged in the valley for stuff that could be reclaimed and used.

Francis acted as if God were personally out to destroy him.

"Doesn't anybody else notice what a disaster this film is?" he shouted. "I haven't got a script, I haven't got an actor, I'm running out of money, I'm all out of time. This is the goddamned Unfinished Symphony, man."

Nobody wanted to talk to the director when he was in this mood. Francis squatted on the bare earth of the mountainside, surrounded by smashed balsawood pine-trees, hugging his knees. He wore a stetson hat, filched from Quincey Morris's wardrobe, and drizzle was running from its brim in a tiny stream. Eleanor, his wife, concentrated on keeping the children out of the way.

"This is the worst fucking film of my career. The worst I'll ever make. The *last* movie."

The first person to tell Francis to cheer up and that things weren't so bad would get fired and be sent home. At this point, crowded under a leaky lean-to with other surplus persons, Kate was tempted.

"I don't want to be Orson Welles," Francis shouted at the slate-grey skies, rain on his face, "I don't want to be David Lean. I just want to make an Irwin Allen movie, with violence, action, sex, destruction in every frame. This isn't Art, this is atrocity."

Just before the crew left Bucharest, as the storm was beginning, Marlon Brando had consented to be Dracula. Francis personally wired him a million-dollar down-payment against two weeks' work. Nobody dared remind Francis that if he wasn't ready to shoot Brando's scenes by the end of the year, he would lose the money and his star.

The six months was up, and barely a quarter of the film was in the can. The production schedule had been extended and re-worked so many times that all forecasts of the end of shooting were treated like forecasts of the end of the War. Everyone said it would be over by Christmas, but knew it would stretch until the last trump.

"I could just stop, you know," Francis said, deflated. "I could just shut it down and go back to San Francisco and a hot bath and decent pasta and forget everything. I can still get work shooting commercials, nudie movies, series TV. I could make little films, shot on video with a four-man crew, and show them to my friends. All this D.W. Griffith-David O. Selznick shit just isn't fucking necessary."

He stretched out his arms and water poured from his sleeves. Over a hundred people, huddled in various shelters or wrapped in orange plastic ponchos, looked at their lord and master and didn't know what to say or do.

"What does this cost, people? Does anybody know? Does anybody care? Is it worth all this? A movie? A painted ceiling? A symphony? Is anything worth all this shit?"

The rain stopped as if a tap were turned off. Sun shone through clouds. Kate screwed her eyes tight shut and fumbled under her poncho for the heavy sunglasses-clip she always carried. She might be the kind of vampire who could go about in all but the strongest sunlight, but her eyes could still be burned out by too much light.

She fixed clip-on shades to her glasses and blinked.

People emerged from their shelters, rainwater pouring from hats and ponchos.

"We can shoot around it," a co-associate assistant producer said.

Francis fired him on the spot.

Kate saw Ion creep out of the forests and straighten up. He had a wooden staff, newly-trimmed. He presented it to his maestro.

"To lean on," he said, demonstrating. Then, he fetched it up and held it like a weapon, showing a whittled point. "And to fight with."

Francis accepted the gift, made a few passes in the air, liking the feel of it in his hands. Then he leaned on the staff, easing his weight onto the strong wood.

"It's good," he said.

Ion grinned and saluted.

"All doubt is passing," Francis announced. "Money doesn't

matter, time doesn't matter, we don't matter. This film, this *Dracula*, that is what matters. It's taken the smallest of you," he laid his hand on Ion's curls, "to show me that. When we are gone, *Dracula* will remain."

Francis kissed the top of Ion's head.

"Now," he shouted, inspired, "to work, to work."

The coach trundles up the mountainside, winding between the tall trees. A blaze of blue light shoots up.

Westenra: *Treasure!*

Harker's Voice: *They said the blue flames marked the sites of long-lost troves of bandit silver and gold. They also said no good ever came of finding it.*

Westenra: *Coachman, stop! Treasure.*

Swales pulls up the reins, and the team halt. The clatter of hooves and reins dies. The night is quiet.

The blue flame still burns.

Westenra jumps out and runs to the edge of the forest, trying to see between the trees, to locate the source of the light.

Harker: *I'll go with him.*

Warily, Harker takes a rifle down from the coach, and breeches a bullet.

Westenra runs ahead into the forest, excited. Harker carefully follows up, placing each step carefully.

Westenra: *Treasure, man. Treasure.*

Harker hears a noise, and signals Westenra to hold back. Both men freeze and listen.

The blue light flickers on their faces and fades out. Westenra is disgusted and disappointed.

Something moves in the undergrowth. Red eyes glow.

A dire wolf leaps up at Westenra, claws brushing his face, enormously furred body heavy as a felled tree. Harker fires. A red flash briefly spotlights the beast's twisted snout.

The wolf's teeth clash, just missing Westenra's face. The huge animal, startled if not wounded, turns and disappears into the forest.

Westenra and Harker run away as fast as they can, vaulting over prominent tree-roots, bumping low branches.

Westenra: *Never get out of the coach . . . never get out of the coach.*

They get back to the road. Swales looks stern, not wanting to know about the trouble they're in.

Harker's Voice: *Words of wisdom. Never get out of the coach, never go into the woods . . . unless you're prepared to become the compleat animal, to stay forever in the forests. Like him, Dracula.*

At the party celebrating the 100th Day of Shooting, the crew brought in a coffin bearing a brass plate that read simply DRACULA. Its lid creaked open and a girl in a bikini leaped out, nestling in Francis's lap. She had plastic fangs, which she spit out to kiss him.

The crew cheered. Even Eleanor laughed.

The fangs wound up in the punch-bowl. Kate fished them out as she got drinks for Marty Sheen and Robert Duvall.

Duvall, lean and intense, asked her about Ireland. She admitted she hadn't been there in decades. Sheen, whom everyone thought was Irish, was Hispanic, born Ramon Estevez. He was drinking heavily and losing weight, travelling deep into his role. Having surrendered entirely to Francis's "vision", Sheen was talking with Harker's accent and developing the character's hollow-eyed look and panicky glance.

The real Jonathan, Kate remembered, was a decent but dull sort, perpetually 'umble around brighter people, deeply suburban. Mina, his fiancée and her friend, kept saying that at least he was real, a worker ant not a butterfly like Art or Lucy. A hundred years later, Kate could hardly remember Jonathan's face. From now on, she would always think of Sheen when anyone mentioned Jonathan Harker. The original was eclipsed.

Or erased. Bram Stoker had intended to write about Kate in his book, but left her out. Her few poor braveries during the Terror tended to be ascribed to Mina in most histories. That was probably a blessing.

"What it must have been like for Jonathan," Sheen said. "Not even knowing there were such things as vampires. Imagine, confronted with Dracula himself. His whole world was shredded, torn away. All he had was himself, and it wasn't enough."

"He had family, friends," Kate said.

Sheen's eyes glowed. "Not in Transylvania. *Nobody* has family and friends in Transylvania."

Kate shivered and looked around. Francis was showing off

martial arts moves with Ion's staff. Fred Forrest was rolling a cigar-sized joint. Vittorio Storaro, the cinematographer, doled out his special spaghetti, smuggled into the country inside film cans, to appreciative patrons. A Romanian official in an ill-fitting shiny suit, liaison with the state studios, staunchly resisted offers of drinks he either assumed were laced with LSD or didn't want other Romanians to see him sampling. She wondered which of the native hangers-on was the *Securitate* spy, and giggled at the thought that they all might be spies and still not know the others were watching them.

Punch, which she was sipping for politeness's sake, squirted out of her nose as she laughed. Duvall patted her back and she recovered. She was not used to social drinking.

Ion, in a baseball cap given him by one of Francis's kids, was joking with the girl in the bikini, a dancer who played one of the gypsies, his eyes reddening with thirst. Kate decided to leave them be. Ion would control himself with the crew. Besides, the girl might like a nip from the handsome lad.

With a handkerchief, she wiped her face. Her specs had gone crooked with her spluttering and she rearranged them.

"You're not what I expected of a vampire lady," Duvall said.

Kate slipped the plastic fangs into her mouth and snarled like a kitten.

Duvall and Sheen laughed.

For two weeks, Francis had been shooting the "Brides of Dracula" sequence. The mountainside was crowded as Oxford Street, extras borrowed from the Romanian army salted with English faces recruited from youth hostels and student exchanges. Storaro was up on a dinosaur-necked camera crane, swooping through the skies, getting shots of rapt faces.

The three girls, two warm and one real vampire, had only showed up tonight, guaranteeing genuine crowd excitement in long-shot or blurry background rather than the flatly faked enthusiasm radiated for their own close-ups.

Kate was supposed to be available for the Brides, but they didn't need advice. It struck her as absurd that she should be asked to tell the actresses how to be alluring. The vampire Marlene, cast as the blonde bride, had been an actress since the silent days and wandered about nearly naked, exposing herself to the winds. Her warm sisters needed to be swathed in furs between shots.

In a shack-like temporary dressing room, the brides were transformed. Bunty, a sensible Englishwoman, was in charge of their make-up. The living girls, twins from Malta who had appeared in a *Playboy* layout, submitted to all-over pancake that gave their flesh an unhealthy shimmer and opened their mouths like dental patients as fangs – a hundred times more expensive if hardly more convincing than the joke shop set Kate had kept after the party – were fitted.

Francis, with Ion in his wake carrying a script, dropped by to cast an eye over the brides. He asked Marlene to open her mouth and examined her dainty pointy teeth.

"We thought we'd leave them as they were," said Bunty.

Francis shook his head.

"They need to be bigger, more obvious."

Bunty took a set of dagger-like eye-teeth from her kit and approached Marlene, who waved them away.

"I'm sorry, dear," the make-up woman apologised.

Marlene laughed musically and hissed, making Francis jump. Her mouth opened wide like a cobra's, and her fangs extended a full two inches.

Francis grinned.

"Perfect."

The vampire lady took a little curtsey.

Kate mingled with the crew, keeping out of camera-shot. She was used to the tedious pace of film-making now. Everything took forever and there was rarely anything to see. Only Francis, almost thin now, was constantly on the move, popping up everywhere – with Ion, nick-named "Son of Dracula" by the crew, at his heels – to solve or be frustrated by any one of a thousand problems.

The stands erected for the extras, made by local labour in the months before shooting, kept collapsing. It seemed the construction people, whom she assumed also had the door contract at the Bucharest hotel, had substituted inferior wood, presumably pocketing the difference in leis, and the whole set was close to useless. Francis had taken to having his people work at night, after the Romanians contractually obliged to do the job had gone home, to shore up the shoddy work. It was, of course, ruinously expensive and amazingly inefficient.

The permits to film at Borgo Pass had still not come through. An associate producer was spending all her time at the Bucharest equivalent of the Circumlocution Office, trying to get the tri-lingual documentation out of the Ministry of Film. Francis would have to hire an entire local film crew and pay them to stand idle while his Hollywood people did the work. That was the expected harassment.

The official in the shiny suit, who had come to represent for everyone the forces hindering the production, stood on one side, eagerly watching the actresses. He didn't permit himself a smile.

Kate assumed the man dutifully hated the whole idea of *Dracula*. He certainly did all he could to get in the way. He could only speak English when the time came to announce a fresh snag, conveniently forgetting the language if he was standing on the spot where Francis wanted camera track laid and he was being told politely to get out of the way.

"Give me more teeth," Francis shouted through a bull-horn. The actresses responded.

"All of you," the director addressed the extras, "look horny as hell."

Ion repeated the instruction in three languages. In each one, the sentence expanded to a paragraph. Different segments of the crowd were enthused as each announcement clued them in.

Arcs, brighter and whiter than the sun, cast merciless, bleach-ing patches of light on the crowd, making faces look like skulls. Kate was blinking, her eyes watering. She took off and cleaned her glasses.

Like everybody, she could do with a shower and a rest. And, in her case, a decent feed.

Rumours were circulating of other reasons they were being kept away from Borgo Pass. The twins, flying in a few days ago, had brought along copies of the *Guardian* and *Time Magazine*. They were passed around the whole company, offering precious news from home. She was surprised how little seemed to have happened while she was out of touch.

However, there was a tiny story in the *Guardian* about the Transylvania Movement. Apparently, Baron Meinster, some obscure disciple of Dracula, was being sought by the Romanian authorities for terrorist outrages. The newspaper reported that he had picked up a band of vampire followers and was out in the forests somewhere, fighting bloody engagements with Ceausescu's men. The Baron favoured young get; he would find lost children, and turn them. The average age of his army was fourteen. Kate knew the type: red-eyed, lithe brats with sharp teeth and no compunctions about anything. Rumour had it that Meinster's Kids would descend on villages and murder entire populations, gorging themselves on blood, killing whole families, whole communities, down to the animals.

That explained the nervousness of some of the extras borrowed from the army. They expected to be sent into the woods to fight the devils. Few of them would come near Kate or any other vampire, so any gossip that filtered through was third-hand and had been translated into and out of several languages.

There were quite a few civilian observers around, keeping an eye on everything, waving incomprehensible but official documentation at anyone who queried their presence. Shiny Suit knew all about them and was their unofficial boss. Ion kept well away from them. She must ask the lad if he knew anything of Meinster. It was a wonder he had not become one of Meinster's Child Warriors. Maybe he had, and was trying to get away from that. Growing up.

The crowd rioted on cue but the camera-crane jammed, dumping the operator out of his perch. Francis yelled at the grips to protect the equipment, and Ion translated but not swiftly enough to get them into action.

The camera came loose and fell thirty feet, crunching onto rough stone, spilling film and fragments.

Francis looked at the mess, uncomprehending, a child so shocked by the breaking of a favourite toy that he can't even throw a fit. Then, red fury exploded.

Kate wouldn't want to be the one who told Francis that there might be fighting at Borgo Pass.

In the coach, late afternoon, Harker goes through the documents he has been given. He examines letters sealed with a red wax 'D', old scrolls gone to parchment, annotated maps, a writ of excommunication. There are pictures of Vlad, woodcuts of the Christian Prince in a forest of impaled infidels, portraits of a dead-looking old man with a white moustache, a blurry photograph of a murk-faced youth in an unsuitable straw hat.

Harker's Voice: *Vlad was one of the Chosen, favoured of God. But somewhere in those acres of slaughtered foemen, he found something that changed his mind, that changed his soul. He wrote letters to the Pope, recommending the rededication of the Vatican to the Devil. He had two cardinals, sent by Rome to reason with him, hot-collared – red-hot pokers slid through their back passages into their innards. He died, was buried, and came back . . .*

Harker looks out of the coach at the violent sunset. Rainbows dance around the tree-tops.

Westenra cringes but Murray is fascinated.

Murray: *It's beautiful, the light . . .*

Up ahead is a clearing. Coaches are gathered. A natural stone amphitheatre has been kitted out with limelights which fizz and flare.

Crowds of Englishmen take seats.

Harker is confused, but the others are excited.

Murray: *A musical evening. Here, so far from Piccadilly . . .*

The coach slows and stops. Westenra and Murray leap out to join the crowds.

Warily, Harker follows. He sits with Westenra and Murray. They pass a hip-flask between them.

Harker takes a cautious pull, stings his throat.

Into the amphitheatre trundles a magnificent carriage, pulled by a single, black stallion. The beast is twelve hands high. The carriage is black as the night, with an embossed gold and scarlet crest on the door. A red-eyed dragon entwines around a letter 'D'.

The driver is a tall man, draped entirely in black, only his red eyes showing.

There is mild applause.

The driver leaps down from his seat, crouches like a big cat and stands taller than ever. His cloak swells with the night breeze.

Loud music comes from a small orchestra.

"Take a Pair of Crimson Eyes", by Gilbert and Sullivan.

The driver opens the carriage door.

A slim white limb, clad only in a transparent veil, snakes around the door. Tiny bells tinkle on a delicate ankle. The toe-nails are scarlet and curl like claws.

The audience whoops appreciation. Murray burbles babyish delight. Harker is wary.

The foot touches the carpet of pine needles and a woman swings out of the carriage, shroud-like dress fluttering around her slender form. She has a cloud of black hair and eyes that glow like hot coals.

She hisses, tasting the night, exposing needle-sharp eye-teeth. Writhing, she presses her snake-supple body to the air, as if sucking in the essences of all the men present.

Murray: *The bloofer lady* . . .

The other carriage door is kicked open and the first woman's twin leaps out. She is less languid, more sinuous, more animal-like. She claws and rends the ground and climbs up the carriage wheel like a lizard, long red tongue darting. Her hair is wild, a tangle of twigs and leaves.

The audience, on their feet, applaud and whistle vigorously. Some of the men rip away their ties and burst their collar-studs, exposing their throats.

First Woman: *Kisses, sister, kisses for us all* . . .

The hood of the carriage opens, folding back like an oyster to disclose a third woman, as fair as they are dark, as voluptuous as they are slender. She is sprawled in abandon on a plush mountain of red cushions. She writhes, crawling through pillows, her scent stinging the nostrils of the rapt audience.

The driver stands to one side as the three women dance. Some of the men are shirtless now, clawing at their own necks until the blood trickles.

The women are contorted with expectant pleasure, licking their ruby lips, fangs already moist, shrouds in casual disarray, exposing lovely limbs, swan-white pale skin, velvet-sheathed muscle.

Men crawl at their feet, piling atop each other, reaching out just to touch the ankles of these women, these monstrous, desirable creatures.

Murray is out of his seat, hypnotised, pulled towards the vampires, eyes mad. Harker tries to hold him back, but is wrenched forward in his wake, dragged like an anchor.

Murray steps over his fallen fellows, but trips and goes down under them.

Harker scrambles to his feet and finds himself among the

women. Six hands entwine around his face. Lips brush his cheek, razor-edged teeth drawing scarlet lines on his face and neck.

He tries to resist but is bedazzled.

A million points of light shine in the women's eyes, on their teeth, on their earrings, necklaces, nose-stones, bracelets, veils, navel-jewels, lacquered nails. The lights close around Harker.

Teeth touch his throat.

A strong hand, sparsely bristled, reaches out and hauls one of the women away.

The driver steps in and tosses another vampire bodily into the carriage. She lands face-down and seems to be drowning in cushions, bare legs kicking.

Only the blonde remains, caressing Harker, eight inches of tongue scraping the underside of his chin. Fire burns in her eyes as the driver pulls her away.

Blonde Woman: *You never love, you have never loved* . . .

The driver slaps her, dislocating her face. She scrambles away from Harker, who lies sprawled on the ground.

The women are back in the carriage, which does a circuit of the amphitheatre and slips into the forests. There is a massed howl of frustration, and the audience falls upon each other.

Harker, slowly recovering, sits up. Swales is there. He hauls Harker out of the mêlée and back to the coach. Harker, unsteady, is pulled into the coach.

Westenra and Murray are dejected, gloomy. Harker is still groggy.

Harker's Voice: *A vampire's idea of a half-holiday is a third share in a juicy peasant baby. It has no other needs, no other desires, no other yearnings. It is mere appetite, unencumbered by morality, philosophy, religion, convention, emotion. There's a dangerous strength in that. A strength we can hardly hope to equal.*

Shooting in a studio should have given more control, but Francis was constantly frustrated by Romanians. The inn set, perhaps the simplest element of the film, was still not right, though the carpenters and dressers had had almost a year to get it together. First, they took an office at the studio and turned it into Harker's bedroom. It was too small to fit in a camera as well as an actor and the scenery. Then, they reconstructed the whole thing in the middle of a sound stage, but still bolted together the walls so they couldn't be moved. The only shot Storaro could take was from the ceiling looking down. Now the walls were fly-away enough to allow camera movement, but Francis wasn't happy with the set dressing.

Prominent over the bed, where Francis wanted a crucifix, was an idealised portrait of Ceausescu. Through Ion, Francis tried to explain to Shiny Suit, the studio manager, that his film took place before the President-for-Life came to power and that, therefore, it was highly unlikely that a picture of him would be decorating a wall anywhere.

Shiny Suit seemed unwilling to admit there had ever been a time when Ceausescu didn't rule the country. He kept looking around nervously, as if expecting to be caught in treason and hustled out to summary execution.

"Get me a crucifix," Francis yelled.

Kate sat meekly in a director's chair – a rare luxury – while the argument continued. Marty Sheen, in character as Harker, sat cross-legged on his bed, taking pulls at a hip-flask of potent brandy. She could smell the liquour across the studio. The actor's face was florid and his movements slow. He had been more and more Harker and less and less Marty the last few days, and Francis was driving him hard, directing with an emotional scalpel that peeled his star like an onion.

Francis told Ion to bring the offending item over so he could show Shiny Suit what was wrong. Grinning cheerfully, Ion squeezed past Marty and reached for the picture, dextrously dropping it onto a bed-post which shattered the glass and speared through the middle of the frame, punching a hole in the Premier's face.

Ion shrugged in fake apology.

Francis looked almost happy. Shiny Suit, stricken in the heart, scurried away in defeat, afraid that his part in the vandalism of the sacred image would be noticed.

A crucifix was found from stock and put up on the wall.

"Marty," Francis said, "open yourself up, show us your beating heart, then tear it from your chest, squeeze it in your fist and drop it on the floor."

Kate wondered if he meant it literally.

Marty Sheen tried to focus his eyes, and saluted in slow motion.
"Quiet on set, everybody," Francis shouted.

Kate was crying, silently, uncontrollably. Everyone on set, except Francis and perhaps Ion, was also in tears. She felt as if she was watching the torture of a political prisoner, and just wanted it to stop.

There was no script for this scene.

Francis was pushing Marty into a corner, breaking him down, trying to get to Jonathan Harker.

This would come at the beginning of the picture. The idea was to show the real Jonathan, to get the audience involved with him. Without this scene, the hero would seem just an observer, wandering between other people's set-pieces.

"You, Reed," Francis said, "you're a writer. Scribble me a voice-over. Internal monologue. Stream-of-consciousness. Give me the real Harker."

Through tear-blurred spectacles, she looked at the pad she was scrawling on. Her first attempt had been at the Jonathan she remembered, who would have been embarrassed to have been thought capable of stream-of-consciousness. Francis had torn that into confetti and poured it over Marty's head, making the actor cross his eyes and fall backwards, completely drunk, onto the bed.

Marty was hugging his pillow and bawling for Mina.

All for Hecuba, Kate thought. Mina wasn't even in this movie except as a locket. God knows what Mrs Harker would think when and if she saw *Dracula*.

Francis told the crew to ignore Marty's complaints. He was an actor, and just whining.

Ion translated.

She remembered what Francis had said after the storm, "What does this cost, people?" Was anything worth what this seemed to cost? "I don't just have to make *Dracula*," Francis had told an interviewer, "I have to *be* Dracula."

Kate tried to write the Harker that was emerging between Marty and Francis. She went into the worst places of her own past and realised they still burned in her memory like smouldering coals.

Her pad was spotted with red. There was blood in her tears. That didn't happen often.

The camera was close to Marty's face. Francis was intent, bent close over the bed, teeth bared, hands claws. Marty mumbled, trying to wave the lens away.

"Don't look at the camera, Jonathan," Francis said.

Marty buried his face in the bed and was sick, choking. Kate wanted to protest but couldn't bring herself to. She was worried Martin Sheen would never forgive her for interrupting his Academy Award scene. He was an actor. He'd go on to other roles, casting off poor Jon like an old coat.

He rolled off his vomit and looked up, where the ceiling should have been but wasn't.

The camera ran on. And on.

Marty lay still.

Finally, the camera operator reported "I think he's stopped breathing."

For an eternal second, Francis let the scene run.

In the end, rather than stop filming, the director elbowed the camera aside and threw himself on his star, putting an ear close to Marty's sunken bare chest.

Kate dropped her pad and rushed into the set. A wall swayed and fell with a crash.

"His heart's still beating," Francis said.

She could hear it, thumping irregularly.

Marty spluttered, fluid leaking from his mouth. His face was almost scarlet.

His heart slowed.

"I think he's having a heart attack," she said.

"He's only thirty-five," Francis said. "No, thirty-six. It's his birthday today."

A doctor was called for. Kate thumped Marty's chest, wishing she knew more first aid.

The camera rolled on, forgotten.

"If this gets out," Francis said, "I'm finished. The film is over."

Francis grabbed Marty's hand tight, and prayed.

"Don't die, man."

Martin Sheen's heart wasn't listening. The beat stopped. Seconds passed. Another beat. Nothing.

Ion was at Francis's side. His fang-teeth were fully extended and his eyes were red. It was the closeness of death, triggering his instincts.

Kate, hating herself, felt it too.

The blood of the dead was spoiled, undrinkable. But the blood of the dying was sweet, as if invested with the life that was being spilled.

She felt her own teeth sharp against her lower lip.

Drops of her blood fell from her eyes and mouth, spattering Marty's chin.

She pounded his chest again. Another beat. Nothing.

Ion crawled on the bed, reaching for Marty.

"I can make him live," he whispered, mouth agape, nearing a pulseless neck.

"My God," said Francis, madness in his eyes. "You can bring him back. Even if he dies, he can finish the picture."

"Yesssss," hissed the old child.

Marty's eyes sprang open. He was still conscious in his stalling body. There was a flood of fear and panic. Kate felt his death grasp her own heart.

Ion's teeth touched the actor's throat.

A cold clarity struck her. This undead youth of unknown bloodline must not pass on the Dark Kiss. He was not yet ready to be a father-in-darkness.

She took him by the scruff of his neck and tore him away. He fought her, but she was older, stronger.

With love, she punctured Marty's throat, feeling the death ecstasy convulse through her. She swooned as the blood, laced heavily with brandy, welled into her mouth, but fought to stay in control. The lizard part of her brain would have sucked him dry.

But Katharine Reed was not a monster.

She broke the contact, smearing blood across her chin and his chest hair. She ripped open her blouse, scattering tiny buttons, and sliced herself with a sharpening thumbnail, drawing an incision across her ribs.

She raised Marty's head and pressed his mouth to the wound.

As the dying man suckled, she looked through fogged glasses at Francis, at Ion, at the camera operator, at twenty studio staff. A doctor was arriving, too late.

She looked at the blank round eye of the camera.

"Turn that bloody thing off," she said.

*   *   *

The principles were assembled in an office at the studio. Kate, still drained, had to be there. Marty was in a clinic with a drip-feed, awaiting more transfusions. His entire bloodstream would have to be flushed out several times over. With luck, he wouldn't even turn. He would just have some of her life in him, some of her in him, forever. This had happened before and Kate wasn't exactly happy about it. But she had no other choice. Ion would have killed the actor and brought him back to life as a new-born vampire.

"There have been stories in the trades," Francis said, holding up a copy of *Daily Variety*. It was the only newspaper that regularly got through to the company. "About Marty. We have to sit tight on this, to keep a lid on panic. I can't afford even the rumour that we're in trouble. Don't you understand, we're in the twilight zone here. Anything approaching a shooting schedule or a budget was left behind a long time ago. We can film round Marty until he's ready to do close-ups. His brother is coming over from the States to double him from the back. We can weather this on the ground, but maybe not in the press. The vultures from the trades want us dead. Ever since *Finian's Rainbow*, they've hated me. I'm a smart kid and nobody likes smart kids. From now on, if anybody *dies* they aren't dead until I say so. Nobody is to tell anyone anything until it's gone through me. People, we're in trouble here and we may have to lie our way out of it. I know you think the Ceausescu regime is fascist but it's nothing compared to the Coppola regime. You don't know anything until I confirm it. You don't do anything until I say so. This is a war, people, and we're losing."

Marty's family was with him. His wife didn't quite know whether to be grateful to Kate or despise her.

He would live. Really live.

She was getting snatches of his past life, mostly from films he had been in. He would be having the same thing, coping with scrambled impressions of her. That must be a nightmare all of its own.

They let her into the room. It was sunny, filled with flowers.

The actor was sitting up, neatly groomed, eyes bright.

"Now I know," he told her. "Now I really know. I can use that in the part. Thank you."

"I'm sorry," she said, not knowing what for.

*   *   *

At a way-station, Swales is picking up fresh horses. The old ones, lathered with foamy sweat, are watered and rested.

Westenra barters with a peasant for a basket of apples. Murray smiles and looks up at the tops of the trees. The moon shines down on his face, making him look like a child.

Harker quietly smokes a pipe.

Harker's Voice: *This was where we were to join forces with Van Helsing. This stone-crazy double Dutchman had spent his whole life fighting evil.*

Van Helsing strides out of the mountain mists. He wears a scarlet army tunic and a curly-brimmed top hat, and carries a cavalry sabre. His face is covered with old scars. Crosses of all kinds are pinned to his clothes.

Harker's Voice: *Van Helsing put the fear of God into the Devil. And he terrified me.*

Van Helsing is accompanied by a band of rough-riders. Of all races and in wildly different uniforms, they are his personal army of the righteous. In addition to mounted troops, Van Helsing has command of a couple of man-lifting kites and a supply wagon.

Van Helsing: *You are Harker?*

Harker: *Dr Van Helsing of Amsterdam?*

Van Helsing: *The same. You wish to go to Borgo Pass, Young Jonathan?*

Harker: *That's the plan.*

Van Helsing: *Better you should wish to go to Hades itself, foolish Englishman.*

Van Helsing's Aide: *I say, Prof, did you know Murray was in Harker's crew. The stroke of '84.*

Van Helsing: *Hah! Beat Cambridge by three lengths. Masterful.*

Van Helsing's Aide: *They say the river's at its most level around Borgo Pass. You know these mountain streams, Prof. Tricky for the oarsman.*

Van Helsing: *Why didn't you say that before, damfool? Harker, we go at once, to take Borgo Pass. Such a stretch of river should be held for the Lord. The Un-Dead, they appreciate it not. Nosferatu don't scull.*

Van Helsing rallies his men into mounting up. Harker dashes back to the coach and climbs in. Westenra looks appalled as Van

Helsing waves his sabre, coming close to fetching off his own Aide's head.

Westenra: *That man's completely mad.*

Harker: *In Wallachia, that just makes him normal. To fight what we have to face, one has to be a little mad.*

Van Helsing's sabre shines with moonfire.

Van Helsing: *To Borgo Pass, my angels . . . charge!*

Van Helsing leads his troop at a fast gallop. The coach is swept along in the wake of the uphill cavalry advance. Man-lifting box-kites carry observers into the night air.

Wolves howl in the distance.

Between the kites is slung a phonograph horn.

Music pours forth. The overture to *Swan Lake*.

Van Helsing: *Music. Tchaikovsky. It upsets the devils. Stirs in them memories of things that they have lost. Makes them feel dead. Then we kill them good. Kill them forever.*

As he charges, Van Helsing waves his sword from side to side. Dark, low shapes dash out of the trees and slip among the horses' ankles. Van Helsing slashes downwards, decapitating a wolf. The head bounces against a tree, becoming that of a gypsy boy, and rolls down the mountainside.

Van Helsing's cavalry weave expertly through the pines. They carry flaming torches. The music soars. Fire and smoke whip between the trees.

In the coach, Westenra puts his fingers in his ears. Murray smiles as if on a pleasure ride across Brighton Beach. Harker sorts through crucifixes.

At Borgo Pass, a small gypsy encampment is quiet. Elders gather around the fire. A girl hears the Tchaikovsky whining among the winds and alerts the tribe.

The gypsies bustle. Some begin to transform into wolves.

The man-lifting kites hang against the moon, casting vast bat-shadows on the mountainside.

The pounding of hooves, amplified a thousandfold by the trees, thunders. The ground shakes. The forests tremble.

Van Helsing's cavalry explode out of the woods and fall upon the camp, riding around and through the place, knocking over wagons, dragging through fires. A dozen flaming torches are thrown. Shrieking werewolves, pelts aflame, leap up at the riders.

Silver swords flash, red with blood.

Van Helsing dismounts and strides through the carnage, making head shots with his pistol. Silver balls explode in wolf-skulls.

A young girl approaches Van Helsing's aide, smiling in welcome. She opens her mouth, hissing, and sinks fangs into the man's throat.

Three cavalrymen pull the girl off and stretch her out facedown on the ground, rending her bodice to bare her back. Van Helsing drives a five-foot lance through her ribs from behind, skewering her to the bloodied earth.

Van Helsing: *Vampire bitch!*

The cavalrymen congratulate each other and cringe as a barrel of gunpowder explodes nearby. Van Helsing does not flinch.

Harker's Voice: *Van Helsing was protected by God. Whatever he did, he would survive. He was blessed.*

Van Helsing kneels by his wounded Aide and pours holy water onto the man's ravaged neck. The wound hisses and steams, and the Aide shrieks.

Van Helsing: *Too late, we are too late. I'm sorry, my son.*

With a kukri knife, Van Helsing slices off his aide's head. Blood gushes over his trousers.

The overture concludes and the battle is over.

The gypsy encampment is a ruin. Fires still burn. Everyone is dead or dying, impaled or decapitated or silver-shot. Van Helsing distributes consecrated wafers, dropping crumbs on all the corpses, muttering prayers for saved souls.

Harker sits, exhausted, bloody earth on his boots.

Harker's Voice: *If this was how Van Helsing served God, I was beginning to wonder what the firm had against Dracula.*

The sun pinks the skies over the mountains. Pale light falls on the encampment.

Van Helsing stands tall in the early morning mists.

Several badly-wounded vampires begin to shrivel and scream as the sunlight burns them to man-shaped cinders.

Van Helsing: *I love that smell . . . spontaneous combustion at daybreak. It smells like . . . salvation.*

Like a small boy whose toys have been taken away, Francis stood on the rock, orange cagoul vivid against the mist-shrouded pines, and watched the cavalry ride away in the wrong direction. Gypsy extras, puzzled at this reversal, milled around their camp set.

Storaro found something technical to check and absorbed himself in lenses.

No one wanted to tell Francis what was going on.

They had spent two hours setting up the attack, laying camera track, planting charges, rigging decapitation effects, mixing kensington gore in plastic buckets. Van Helsing's troop of ferocious cavalry were uniformed and readied.

Then Shiny Suit whispered in the ear of the captain who was in command of the army-provided horsemen. The cavalry stopped being actors and became soldiers again, getting into formation and riding out.

Kate had never seen anything like it.

Ion nagged Shiny Suit for an explanation. Reluctantly, the official told the little vampire what was going on.

"There is fighting in the next valley," Ion said. "Baron Meinster has come out of the forests and taken a keep that stands over a strategic pass. Many are dead or dying. Ceausescu is laying siege to the Transylvanians."

"We have an agreement," Francis said, weakly. "These are my men."

"Only as long as they aren't needed for fighting, this man says," reported Ion, standing aside to let the director get a good look at the Romanian official. Shiny Suit almost smiled, a certain smug attitude suggesting that this would even the score for that dropped picture of the Premier.

"I'm trying to make a fucking movie here. If people don't keep their word, maybe they deserve to be overthrown."

The few bilingual Romanians in the crew cringed at such sacrilege. Kate could think of dozens of stronger reasons for pulling down the Ceausescu regime.

"There might be danger," Ion said. "If the fighting spreads."

"This Meinster, Ion. Can he get us the cavalry? Can we do a deal with him?"

"An arrogant elder, maestro. And doubtless preoccupied with his own projects."

"You're probably right, fuck it."

"We're losing the light," Storaro announced.

Shiny Suit smiled blithely and, through Ion, ventured that the battle should be over in two to three days. It was fortunate for him that Francis only had prop weapons within reach.

In the gypsy camp, one of the charges went off by itself. A pathetic phut sent out a choking cloud of violently green smoke. Trickles of flame ran across fresh-painted flats.

A grip threw a bucket of water, dousing the fire.

Robert Duvall and Martin Sheen, in costume and make-up, stood about uselessly. The entire camera crew, effects gang, support team were gathered, as if waiting for a cancelled train.

There was a long pause. The cavalry did not come riding triumphantly back, ready for the shot.

"Bastards," Francis shouted, angrily waving his staff like a spear.

The next day was no better. News filtered back that Meinster was thrown out of the keep and withdrawing into the forests, but that Ceausescu ordered his retreat be harried. The cavalry were not detailed to return to their film-making duties. Kate wondered how many of them were still alive. The retaking of the keep must have been a bloody, costly battle. A cavalry charge against a fortress position would be almost a suicide mission.

Disconsolately, Francis and Storaro sorted out some pick-up shots that could be managed.

A search was mounted for Shiny Suit, so that a definite time could be established for rescheduling of the attack scene. He had vanished into the mists, presumably to escape the American's wrath.

Kate huddled under a tree and tried to puzzle out a local newspaper. She was brushing up her Romanian, simultaneously coping with the euphemisms and lacunae of a non-free press. According to the paper, Meinster had been crushed weeks ago and was hiding in a ditch somewhere, certain to be beheaded within the hour.

She couldn't help feeling the real story was in the next valley. As a newspaperwoman, she should be there, not waiting around for this stalled juggernaut to get back on track. Meinster's Kids frightened and fascinated her. She should know about them, try to understand. But American Zoetrope had first call on her, and she didn't have the heart to be another defector.

Marty Sheen joined her.

He was mostly recovered and understood what she had done for him, though he was still exploring the implications of their blood link. Just now, he was more anxious about working with Brando – who was due in next week – than his health.

There was still no scripted ending.

The day that the cavalry – well, some of them – came back, faces drawn and downcast, uniforms muddied, eyes haunted, Shiny Suit was discovered with his neck broken, flopped half-in a stream. He must have fallen in the dark, tumbling down the precipitous mountainside.

His face and neck were ripped, torn by the sharp thorns of the mountain bushes. He had bled dry into the water, and his staring face was white.

"It is good that Georghiou is dead," Ion pronounced. "He upset the maestro."

Kate hadn't known the bureaucrat's name.

Francis was frustrated at this fresh delay, but graciously let the corpse be removed and the proper authorities be notified before proceeding with the shoot.

A police inspector was escorted around by Ion, poking at a few broken bushes and examining Georghiou's effects. Ion somehow persuaded the man to conclude the business speedily.

The boy was a miracle, everyone agreed.

"Miss Reed," Ion interrupted. She laid down her newspaper.

Dressed as an American boy, with his hair cut by the make-up department, a light-meter hung around his neck, Ion was un-recognisable as the bedraggled orphan who had come to her hotel room in Bucharest.

Kate laid aside her journal and pen.

"John Popp," Ion pronounced, tapping his chest. His J-sound was perfect. "John Popp, the American."

She thought about it.

Ion – no, John – had sloughed off his nationality and all national characteristics like a snake shedding a skin. New-born as an American, pink-skinned and glowing, he would never be challenged.

"Do you want to go to America?"

"Oh yes, Miss Reed. America is a young country, full of life. Fresh blood. There, one can be anything one chooses. It is the only country for a vampire."

Kate wasn't sure whether to feel sorry for the vampire youth or for the American continent. One of them was sure to be disappointed.

"John Popp," he repeated, pleased.

Was this how Dracula had been when he first thought of moving to Great Britain, then the liveliest country in the world just as America was now? The Count had practiced his English pronunciation in conversations with Jonathan, and memorised railway time-tables, relishing the exotic names of St Pancras, King's Cross and Euston. Had he rolled his anglicised name – Count DeVille – around his mouth, pleased with himself?

Of course, Dracula saw himself as a conqueror, the rightful ruler of all lands he rode over. Ion-John was more like the Irish and Italian emigrants who poured through Ellis Island at the beginning of the century, certain America was the land of opportunity and that each potato-picker or barber could become a self-made plutocrat.

Envious of his conviction, affection stabbing her heart, wishing she could protect him always, Kate kissed him. He struggled awkwardly, a child hugged by an embarassingly aged auntie.

Mists pool around Borgo Pass. Black crags project from the white sea.

The coach proceeds slowly. Everyone looks around, wary.

Murray: *Remember that last phial of laudanum . . . I just downed it.*

Westenra: *Good show, man.*

Murray: *It's like the Crystal Palace.*

Harker sits by Swales, looking up at the ancient castle that dominates the view. Broken battlements are jagged against the boiling sky.

Harker's Voice: *Castle Dracula. The trail snaked through the forest, leading me directly to him. The Count. The countryside was Dracula. He had become one with the mountains, the trees, the stinking earth.*

The coach halts. Murray pokes his head out of the window, and sighs in amazement.

Swales: *Borgo Pass, Harker. I'll go no further.*

Harker looks at Swales. There is no fear in the coachman's face, but his eyes are slitted.

A sliver of dark bursts like a torpedo from the sea of mist. A sharpened stake impales Swales, bloody point projecting a foot or more from his chest.

Swales sputters hatred and takes a grip on Harker, trying to hug him, to pull him onto the sharp point sticking out of his sternum.

Harker struggles in silence, setting the heel of his hand against Swales's head. He pushes and the dead man's grip relaxes. Swales tumbles from his seat and rolls off the precipice, falling silently into the mists.

Murray: *Good grief, man. That was extreme.*

Rising over Borgo Pass was Castle Dracula. Half mossy black stone, half fresh orange timber.

Kate was impressed.

Though the permits had still not come through, Francis had ordered the crew to erect and dress the castle set. This was a long way from Bucharest and without Georghiou, the hand of Ceausescu could not fall.

From some angles, the castle was an ancient fastness, a fit lair for the vampire King. But a few steps off the path and it was a shell, propped up by timbers. Painted board mingled with stone.

If Meinster's Kids were in the forests, they could look up at the mountain and take heart. This sham castle might be their rallying-point. She hummed "Paper Moon", imagining vampires summoned back to these mountains to a castle that was not a castle and a king who was just an actor in greasepaint.

A grip, silhouetted in the gateway, used a gun-like device to whisp thick cobweb on the portcullis. Cages of imported vermin were stacked up, ready to be unloosed. Stakes, rigged up with bicycle seats that would support the impaled extras, stood on the mountainside.

It was a magnificent fake.

Francis, leaning on his stake, stood and admired the edifice thrown up on his orders. Ion-John was at his side, a faithful Renfield for once.

"Orson Welles said it was the best train set a boy could have," Francis said. Ion probably didn't know who Welles was. "But it broke him in the end."

In her cardigan pocket, she found the joke shop fangs from the

100th Day of Shooting Party. Soon, there would be a 200th Day Party.

She snapped the teeth together like castanets, feeling almost giddy up here in the mists where the air was thin and the nights cold.

In her pleasant contralto, far more Irish-inflected than her speaking voice, she crooned "it's a Barnum and Bailey world, just as phoney as it can be, but it wouldn't be make-believe if you believed in me."

On foot, Harker arrives at the gates of the castle. Westenra and Murray hang back a little way.

A silent crowd of gypsies parts to let the Englishmen through. Harker notices human and wolf teeth strung in necklaces, red eyes and feral fangs, withered bat-membranes curtaining under arms, furry bare feet hooked into the rock. These are the Szekeley, the children of Dracula.

In the courtyard, an armadillo noses among freshly-severed human heads. Harker is smitten by the stench of decay but tries to hide his distaste. Murray and Westenra groan and complain. They both hold out large crucifixes.

A rat-like figure scuttles out of the crowds.

Renfield: *Are you English? I'm an Englishman. R.M. Renfield, at your service.*

He shakes Harker's hand, then hugs him. His eyes are jittery, mad.

Renfield: *The Master has been waiting for you. I'm a lunatic, you know. Zoophagous. I eat flies. Spiders. Birds, when I can get them. It's the blood. The blood is the life, as the book says. The Master understands. Dracula. He knows you're coming. He knows everything. He's a poet-warrior in the classical sense. He has the vision. You'll see, you'll learn. He's lived through the centuries. His wisdom is beyond ours, beyond anything we can imagine. How can I make you understand? He's promised me lives. Many lives. Some nights, he'll creep up on you, while you're shaving, and break your mirror. A foul bauble of man's vanity. The blood of Attila flows in his veins. He is the Master.*

Renfield plucks a crawling insect from Westenra's coat and gobbles it down.

Renfield: *I know what bothers you. The heads. The severed*

*heads. It's his way. It's the only language they understand. He
doesn't love these things, but he knows he must do them. He
knows the truth. Rats! He knows where the rats come from.
Sometimes, he'll say "they fought the dogs and killed the cats
and bit the babies in the cradles, and ate the cheeses out of the
vats and licked the soup from the cooks' own ladles".*

Harker ignores the prattle and walks across the courtyard.
Scraps of mist waft under his boots.

A huge figure fills a doorway. Moonlight shines on his great,
bald head. Heavy jowls glisten as a humourless smile discloses
yellow eye-teeth the size of thumbs.

Harker halts.

A bass voice rumbles.

Dracula: *I . . . am . . . Dracula.*

Francis had first envisioned Dracula as a stick-insect skeleton,
dried up, hollow-eyed, brittle. When Brando arrived on set,
weighing in at 250 pounds, he had to rethink the character as
a blood-bloated leech, full to bursting with stolen life, overflowing his coffin.

For two days, Francis had been trying to get a usable reading of
the line "I am Dracula". Kate, initially as thrilled as anyone else to
see Brando at work, was bored rigid by numberless mumbled
retakes.

The line was written in three-foot tall black letters on a large
piece of cardboard held up by two grips. The actor experimented
with emphases, accents, pronunciations from "Dorragulya" to
"Jacoolier". He read the line looking away from the camera and
peering straight at the lens. He tried it with false fangs inside his
mouth, sticking out of his mouth, shoved up his nostrils or
thrown away altogether.

Once he came out with a bat tattooed on his bald head in black
lipstick. After considering it for a while, Francis ordered the decal
wiped off. You couldn't say that the star wasn't bringing ideas to
the production.

For two hours now, Brando had been hanging upside-down in
the archway, secured by a team of very tired technicians at the end
of two guy-ropes. He thought it might be interesting if the Count
were discovered like a sleeping bat.

Literally, he read his line upside-down.

Marty Sheen, over whose shoulder the shot was taken, had fallen asleep.

"I am Dracula. I am Dracula. I am Dracula. I am Dracula."

"I am Dracula! I am Dracula?"

"Dracula am I. Am I Dracula? Dracula I am. I Dracula am. Am Dracula I?"

"I'm Dracula."

"The name's Dracula. Count Dracula.

"Hey, I'm Dracula.

"Me . . . Dracula. You . . . liquid lunch."

He read the line as Stanley Kowalski, as Don Corleone, as Charlie Chan, as Jerry Lewis, as Laurence Olivier, as Robert Newton.

Francis patiently shot take after take.

Dennis Hopper hung around, awed, smoking grass. All the actors wanted to watch.

Brando's face went scarlet. Upside-down, he had problems with the teeth. Relieved, the grips eased up on the ropes and the star dropped towards the earth. They slowed before his head cracked like an egg on the ground. Assistants helped him rearrange himself.

Francis thought about the scene.

"Marlon, it seems to me that we could do worse than go back to the book."

"The book?" Brando asked.

"Remember, when we first discussed the role. We talked about how Stoker describes the Count."

"I don't quite . . ."

"You told me you knew the book."

"I never read it."

"You said . . ."

"I lied."

Harker, in chains, is confined in a dungeon. Rats crawl around his feet. Water flows all around.

A shadow passes.

Harker looks up. A grey bat-face hovers above, nostrils elaborately frilled, enormous teeth locked. Dracula seems to fill the room, black cape stretched over his enormous belly and trunk-like limbs.

Dracula drops something into Harker's lap. It is Westenra's head, eyes white.

Harker screams.

Dracula is gone.

An insectile clacking emerged from the Script Crypt, the walled-off space on the set where Francis had hidden himself away with his typewriter.

Millions of dollars poured away daily as the director tried to come up with an ending. In drafts Kate had seen – only a fraction of the attempts Francis had made – Harker killed Dracula, Dracula killed Harker, Dracula and Harker became allies, Dracula and Harker were both killed by Van Helsing (unworkable, because Robert Duvall was making another film on another continent), lightning destroyed the whole castle.

It was generally agreed that Dracula should die.

The Count perished through decapitation, purifying fire, running water, a stake through the heart, a hawthorne bush, a giant crucifix, silver bullets, the hand of God, the claws of the Devil, armed insurrection, suicide, a swarm of infernal bats, bubonic plague, dismemberment by axe, permanent transformation into a dog.

Brando suggested that he play Dracula as a Green Suitcase.

Francis was on medication.

"Reed, what does he mean to you?"

She thought Francis meant Ion-John.

"He's just a kid, but he's getting older fast. There's something . . ."

"Not John. Dracula."

"Oh, him."

"Yes, him. Dracula. Count Dracula. King of the Vampires."

"I never acknowledged that title."

"In the 1880s, you were against him?"

"You could say that."

"But he gave you so much, eternal life?"

"He wasn't my father. Not directly."

"But he brought vampirism out of the darkness."

"He was a monster."

'Just a monster? In the end, just that?"

She thought hard.

"No, there was more. He was more. He was . . . he *is*, you know . . . big. Huge, enormous. Like the elephant described by blind men. He had many aspects. But all were monstrous. He didn't bring us out of the darkness. He was the darkness."

"John says he was a national hero."

"John wasn't born then. Or turned."

"Guide me, Reed."

"I can't write your ending for you."

At the worst possible time, the policeman was back. There were questions about Shiny Suit. Irregularities revealed by the autopsy.

For some reason, Kate was questioned.

Through an interpreter, the policemen kept asking her about the dead official, what had their dealings been, whether Georghiou's prejudice against her kind had affected her.

Then he asked her when she had last fed, and upon whom?

"That's private," she said.

She didn't want to admit that she had been snacking on rats for months. She had had no time to cultivate anyone warm. Her powers of fascination were thinning.

A scrap of cloth was produced and handed to her.

"Do you recognise this?" she was asked.

It was filthy, but she realised that she did.

"Why, it's my scarf. From Biba. I . . ."

It was snatched away from her. The policeman wrote down a note.

She tried to say something about Ion, but thought better of it. The translator told the policeman Kate had almost admitted to something.

She felt distinctly chilled.

She was asked to open her mouth, like a horse up for sale. The policeman peered at her sharp little teeth and tutted.

That was all for now.

"How are monsters made?"

Kate was weary of questions. Francis, Marty, the police. Always questions.

Still, she was on the payroll as an advisor.

"I've known too many monsters, Francis. Some were born,

some were made all at once, some were eroded, some shaped themselves, some twisted by history."

"What about Dracula?"

"He was the monster of monsters. All of the above."

Francis laughed.

"You're thinking of Brando."

"After your movie, so will everybody else."

He was pleased by the thought.

"I guess they will."

"You're bringing him back. Is that a good idea?"

"It's a bit late to raise that."

"Seriously, Francis. He'll never be gone, never be forgotten. But your Dracula will be powerful. In the next valley, people are fighting over the tatters of the old, faded Dracula. What will your Technicolor, 70mm, Dolby stereo Dracula *mean*?"

"Meanings are for the critics."

Two Szekeleys throw Harker into the great hall of the castle. He sprawls on the straw-covered flagstones, emaciated and wild-eyed, close to madness.

Dracula sits on a throne which stretches wooden wings out behind him. Renfield worships at his feet, tongue applied to the Count's black leather boot. Murray, a blissful smile on his face and scabs on his neck, stands to one side, with Dracula's three vampire brides.

Dracula: *I bid you welcome. Come safely, go freely and leave some of the happiness you bring.*

Harker looks up.

Harker: *You . . . were a Prince.*

Dracula: *I am a Prince still. Of Darkness.*

The brides titter and clap. A look from their Master silences them.

Dracula: *Harker, what do you think we are doing here, at the edge of Christendom? What dark mirror is held up to our unreflecting faces?*

By the throne is an occasional table piled high with books and periodicals. *Bradshaw's Guide to Railway Timetables in England, Scotland and Wales*, George and Weedon Grossmith's *Diary of a Nobody*, Sabine Baring-Gould's *The Book of Were-Wolves*, Oscar Wilde's *Salomé*.

Dracula picks up a volume of the poetry of Robert Browning.

Dracula: "*I must not omit to say that in Transylvania there's a tribe of alien people that ascribe the outlandish ways and dress on which their neighbours lay such stress, to their fathers and mothers having risen out of some subterraneous prison into which they were trepanned long time ago in a mighty band out of Hamelin town in Brunswick land, but how or why, they don't understand.*"

Renfield claps.

Renfield: *Rats, Master. Rats.*

Dracula reaches down with both hands and turns the madman's head right around. The brides fall upon the madman's twitching body, nipping at him greedily before he dies and the blood spoils.

Harker looks away.

At the airport, she was detained by officials. There was some question about her passport.

Francis was worried about the crates of exposed film. The negative was precious, volatile, irreplaceable. He personally, through John, argued with the customs people and handed over disproportionate bribes. He still carried his staff, which he used to point the way and rap punishment. He looked a bit like Friar Tuck.

The film, the raw material of *Dracula*, was to be treated as if it were valuable as gold and dangerous as plutonium. It was stowed on the aeroplane by soldiers.

A blank-faced woman sat across the desk from Kate.

The stirrings of panic ticked inside her. The scheduled time of departure neared.

The rest of the crew were lined up with their luggage, joking despite tiredness. After over a year, they were glad to be gone for good from this backward country. They talked about what they would do when they got home. Marty Sheen was looking healthier, years younger. Francis was bubbling again, excited to be on to the next stage.

Kate looked from the Romanian woman to the portraits of Nicolae and Elena on the wall behind her. All eyes were cold, hateful. The woman wore a discreet crucifix and a Party badge clipped to her uniform lapel.

A rope barrier was removed and the eager crowd of the *Dracula* company stormed towards the aeroplane, mounting the steps, squeezing into the cabin.

The flight was for London, then New York, then Los Angeles. Half a world away.

Kate wanted to stand up, to join the plane, to add her own jokes and fantasies to the rowdy chatter, to fly away from here. Her luggage, she realised, was in the hold.

A man in a black trenchcoat – *Securitate*? – and two uniformed policemen arrived and exchanged terse phrases with the woman.

Kate gathered they were talking about Shiny Suit. And her. They used old, cruel words: leech, *nosferatu*, parasite. The *Securitate* man looked at her passport.

"It is impossible that you be allowed to leave."

Across the tarmac, the last of the crew – Ion-John among them, baseball cap turned backwards, bulky kit-bag on his shoulder – disappeared into the sleek tube of the aeroplane. The door was pulled shut.

She was forgotten, left behind.

How long would it be before anyone noticed? With different sets of people debarking in three cities, probably forever. It was easy to miss one mousy advisor in the excitement, the anticipation, the triumph of going home with the movie shot. Months of post-production, dialogue looping, editing, rough cutting, previews, publicity and release lay ahead, with box office takings to be crowed over and prizes to be competed for in Cannes and on Oscar night.

Maybe when they came to put her credit on the film, someone would think to ask what had become of the funny little old girl with the thick glasses and the red hair.

"You are a sympathiser with the Transylvania Movement."

"Good God," she blurted, "why would anybody want to live here."

That did not go down well.

The engines were whining. The plane taxied towards the runway.

"This is an old country, Miss Katharine Reed," the *Securitate* man sneered. "We know the ways of your kind, and we understand how they should be dealt with."

All the eyes were pitiless.

*   *   *

The giant black horse is lead into the courtyard by the gypsies. Swords are drawn in salute to the animal. It whinnies slightly, coat glossy ebony, nostrils scarlet.

Inside the castle, Harker descends a circular stairway carefully, wiping aside cobwebs. He has a wooden stake in his hands.

The gypsies close on the horse.

Harker's Voice: *Even the castle wanted him dead, and that's what he served at the end. The ancient, blood-caked stones of his Transylvanian fastness.*

Harker stands over Dracula's coffin. The Count lies, bloated with blood, face puffy and violet.

Gypsy knives stroke the horse's flanks. Blood erupts from the coat.

Harker raises the stake with both hands over his head.

Dracula's eyes open, red marbles in his fat, flat face. Harker is given pause.

The horse neighs in sudden pain. Axes chop at its neck and legs. The mighty beast is felled.

Harker plunges the stake into the Count's vast chest.

The horse jerks spastically as the gypsies hack at it. Its hooves scrape painfully on the cobbles.

A gout of violently red blood gushes upwards, splashing directly into Harker's face, reddening him from head to waist. The flow continues, exploding everywhere, filling the coffin, the room, driving Harker back.

Dracula's great hands grip the sides of the coffin and he tries to sit. Around him is a cloud of blood droplets, hanging in the air like slo-mo fog.

The horse kicks its last, clearing a circle. The gypsies look with respect at the creature they have slain.

Harker takes a shovel and pounds at the stake, driving it deeper into Dracula's barrel chest, forcing him back into his filthy sarcophagus.

At last, the Count gives up. Whispered words escape from him with his last breath.

Dracula: *The horror . . . the horror . . .*

She supposed there were worse places than a Romanian jail. But not many.

They kept her isolated from the warm prisoners. Rapists and

murderers and dissidents were afraid of her. She found herself penned with uncommunicative Transylvanians, haughty elders reduced to grime and resentful new-borns.

She had seen a couple of Meinster's Kids, and their calm, purposeful, blank-eyed viciousness disturbed her. Their definition of enemy was terrifyingly broad, and they believed in killing. No negotiation, no surrender, no accommodation. Just death, on an industrial scale.

The bars were silver. She fed on insects and rats. She was weak. Every day, she was interrogated.

They were convinced she had murdered Georghiou. His throat had been gnawed and he was completely exsanguinated.

Why her? Why not some Transylvanian terrorist?

Because of the bloodied once-yellow scrap in his dead fist. A length of thin silk, which she had identified as her Biba scarf. The scarf she had thought of as civilisation. The bandage she had used to bind Ion's wound.

She said nothing about that.

Ion-John was on the other side of the world, making his way. She was left behind in his stead, an offering to placate those who would pursue him. She could not pretend even to herself that it was not deliberate. She understood all too well how he had survived so many years underground. He had learned the predator's trick: to be loved, but never to love. For that, she pitied him even as she could cheerfully have torn his head off.

There were ways out of jails. Even jails with silver bars and garlic hung from every window. The Romanian jailers prided themselves on knowing vampires, but they still treated her as if she were feeble-minded and fragile.

Her strength was sapping, and each night without proper feeding made her weaker.

Walls could be broken through. And there were passes out of the country. She would have to fall back on skills she had thought never to exercise again.

But she was a survivor of the night.

As, quietly, she planned her escape from the prison and from the country, she tried to imagine where the "Son of Dracula" was, to conceive of the life he was living in America, to count the used-up husks left in his wake. Was he still at his maestro's side, making himself useful? Or had he passed beyond that, found a new patron or become a maestro himself?

Eventually, he would build his castle in Beverly Hills and enslave a harem. What might he become: a studio head, a cocaine baron, a rock promoter, a media mogul, a *star*? Truly, Ion-John was what Francis had wanted of Brando, Dracula reborn. An old monster, remade for the new world and the next century, meaning all things, tainting everything he touched.

She would leave him be, this new monster of hers, this creature born of Hollywood fantasy and her own thoughtless charity. With Dracula gone or transformed, the world needed a fresh monster. And John Popp would do as well as anyone else. The world had made him and it could cope with him.

Kate extruded a fingernail into a hard, sharp spar, and scraped the wall. The stones were solid, but between them was old mortar, which crumbled easily.

Harker, face still red with Dracula's blood, is back in his room at the inn in Bistritz. He stands in front of the mirror.

Harker's Voice: *They were going to make me a saint for this, and I wasn't even in their fucking church any more.*

Harker looks deep into the mirror.

He has no reflection.

Harker's mouth forms the words, but the voice is Dracula's. *The horror . . . the horror . . .*

GWYNETH JONES

Grazing the Long Acre

GWYNETH JONES WRITES SCIENCE FICTION AND FANTASY for both adults and young people. She has also worked as a civil servant, freelance journalist and school dinner lady, among many other things.

She has been nominated for the Arthur C. Clarke four times, most recently for her 1994 novel *North Wind*, and acted as one of the judges for the award in 1996. The first novel in the same series, *White Queen*, was co-winner of the 1991 James Tiptree Award for science fiction exploring gender roles. Her teenage novel *The Fear Man* (written as "Ann Halam") won the Dracula Society's Children of the Night award in 1996. The same year, her fairy tale collection *Seven Tales and a Fable*, published by the Edgewood Press, won two World Fantasy Awards.

Recent publications include *Phoenix Café*, the third novel of the Aleutian trilogy, and *Crying in the Dark* (as "Ann Halam"). A collection of critical essays, *Deconstructing the Starships*, was published by the Liverpool University Press in 1998.

About "Grazing the Long Acre", she explains: "I wrote this story after I visited Poland, at Easter in 1997. The background details are all true. There is just such a stretch of the E75, next to the town where they keep the most sacred icon of the virgin, with just such a weird concentration of roadside girls.

"The Virgin Mary a suspected serial killer? Is nothing sacred?"

THE FIRST COUPLE OF girls I saw, I thought they were hitch-hikers. I'm not naïve, but that stretch of the E75, between Czestochowa and Piotrkow Tryb, must be the most lost, god-forsaken highway on earth. Talk about the middle of nowhere . . . It was so incongruous. You wondered how the hell *anyone* came to be there, least of all this plump unattractive young woman with thick thighs puce in the cold, in a crocheted mini-skirt and a strange little satin jacket, skipping about beside the traffic like a lonesome child; or this other girl, skinny as a rake, with her dishwater hair, black hot pants and pathetic thigh-high patent boots. After the third I got the idea. I sat up and watched, it was something to break the monotony. I couldn't work out why they were here in such numbers. I'd never seen whores plying beside a Polish freeway before. World War Two bomb craters, yes. Kids skateboarding on six-lane high speed curves abandoned half way through the building; potholes, crevasses; ambling horses and carts. But never anything like this line of shivering, primping ugly girls.

"How do they get here?"

My friend shrugged. "Their pimps drop them off, I suppose. It's none of my concern."

"But what makes this stretch so popular?"

"Habit. Police protection, how should I know? Word passes round."

He spoke excellent English, my friend. I went on staring, bemused, at the cabaret. The sex must be dirt cheap, but how could anyone get turned on in such a setting? I could tell that my friend thought my interest was in poor taste. He glanced at me, and settled his eyes back to the gliding, jolting grey road ahead with a frown.

"Something preys on them."

"What do you mean?"

"What I say. Something kills them. Sometimes they find a body, sometimes nothing but a heap of dirty clothing. Some devil . . . It's been going on for a while, maybe years. Many, maybe thirty, fifty girls have died. Or more. Of course the police do nothing."

"God, how awful."

"It's a pollution problem," he added. I was afraid for a moment that he was approving of the predator. But he was a decent enough guy, my friend. "There are monsters who feel they have a right to do away with women of this kind. They are a product of our crazy society, animals like that. A pollution, like the air and the water problems."

"But if they're getting killed, why do they keep on working here?"

"Why not? What else would they do?"

Sometimes you'd see an actual deal: a girl leaning into the open door of a halted car. Two of them getting down from the cab of a truck; the second slipped, scraped her bare buttocks on the crusted dirt of the bumper and recovered herself exclaiming, adjusting the grubby scarlet thong that divided her backside. "Grazing the long acre," I said.

"What's that?"

It was an expression my Irish grandmother had taught me. It's what peasants used to do in the old country, when they had a cow but no pasture. They'd send the kids out to lead her along the roadside and eat weeds. If you say someone's "grazing the long acre", it means something like making the best of a bad job, with a little cunning thrown in. I explained this to my friend. He liked "grazing the long acre". He said it sounded Polish. It made him laugh.

We drove on south to Czestochowa, where he had business. I went to see the famous icon of the Black Madonna, the most sacred object in Poland – which is saying something in this country full of sainted hallowed holy bones and swords and tombs. In the year 1430, some vandals tried to steal the picture. They couldn't shift it so they slashed her face instead. Apparently she started bleeding real blood, and that was the debut of her miraculous career. So the story goes, and there's still a mark on her cheek to prove it. I didn't see anything, actually. The place was far too crowded, thick with patriotic crocodiles of school-children and rattling with the brusque, hectoring voices of tour guides. But I bought a postcard.

Then we went on south to Kracow, where we stayed in a very nice hotel near the Slowacki Theatre. My friend left me alone for long stretches while he did whatever they do, these well-built Polish men in well-made suits, with their big-shouldered physical *presence* that you could cut with a knife. It was the beginning of April, very cold and still not really the tourist season, but I did a lot of sightseeing. One day I went to see what's left of the Jewish

Quarter: which is not much. I sat on a bench next to some dignified memorial or other, in a public garden by the Ariel cafe; which is fashionable with American tourists. I was brought up a Catholic as far as anything, but I'm Jewish enough in ethnic origin that I had a weird sense of belonging, sitting by that cold stone. I thought of the sixty thousand people who had been stripped out of these streets by the Nazis, and wondered how they'd feel about their errant child. Jewish Internationalism, that's me. I'm one place where the ancient, nation-stateless, assimilating spirit ended up . . . other than Auschwitz. I tried to visit the old Jewish cemetery, but it was all locked up. I walked along by the ballast of the railway line and picked up a blackened larch cone as a memento, which I keep still; I'm not sure why.

I don't think my friend liked the fact that I'd been to the ghetto. But we didn't quarrel. He was never nasty to me, never raised his voice. The day afterward we headed north again. I thought we were going back to Warsaw, but he didn't say. We went by the same route, on the good old E75. Most foreigners in Poland take the train or fly from one tourist destination to another, but my friend liked to drive. He didn't say so but I could tell. To have a big car, to travel big distances under his own power, was important to him; it was like the suits. As soon as we were in open country, clear of the commercial ring around Czestochowa, the whores in their tasteless little outfits were there again. But I was cool about it this time and pretended not to notice. About three in the afternoon, he pulled off into a bright, new service area. The middle of the afternoon is hungry-time in Poland, where many people haven't picked up the unhealthy twentieth century habit of dining in the evening; so I knew we were going to eat. He filled up with petrol, parked beside a black and chrome Cherokee jeep and guided me into the shiny "Modern Grill Bar"; sat me down and ordered me a pizza.

"Just stay there for a while," he said. "I have to talk to someone".

I had a funny feeling. The place was full. No one took any notice of me, but I was uneasy. Outside the big road went by, slicing through the flat, grey empty fields without a glance, on its way to somewhere real. I picked at my pizza, which was god-awful, and watched the family next to me tucking away sour soup, rice with dill and cream, slabs of fried fish, great heaps of meat and potatoes. Another decade of peasant meals without peasant labour, and the great-looking coltish blondes you see in Kracow and Warsaw will be vast as so many Mid-Westerners. The driver of the Cherokee jeep, a stylish dark-haired woman in a military-grey overcoat, was sitting a few tables away with a cup of coffee. I wondered how old she was. Probably younger than she looked to my foreigner's eyes, because she had the kind of face you meet more often in Europe than in America, beautiful but toughed-out, as if she'd been living hard and wasn't ashamed of it. I thought she looked Jewish, which even today is not the most popular ethnicity in this country. She saw me staring, and smiled a little. I glanced away.

At first I couldn't see where my friend had gone, then I spotted him at a table with two other men the same type as himself. This was normal. It would often happen in restaurants. He'd go off and talk to some buddies, and come back after a while. But I had that bad feeling. None of the men so much as glanced my way, and yet I was sure I was the subject of their conversation. And suddenly I knew what was happening. I went cold all over, because I am such a damned fool.

I was being passed on.

I stood up, casually as I could make it, thinking in my mind so my gestures would match *I am just taking a trip to the john, to powder my nose*. The woman in the grey overcoat had paid for her swift coffee and was leaving. I followed her out, and instead of going to the toilets I put my hand on her arm. I said, in my best Polish, "Can you give me a lift?"

She'd seen me come in with a middle-aged local guy. As soon as she heard me speak she knew I was a foreigner. She could probably work out the rest. She didn't hesitate.

"Sure, come along."

I guessed she might not have been so willing to help if she had known what a clown I was, and how richly I deserved the situation I was in. Luckily she didn't ask for my life story. We went out and climbed into the huge jeep, and drove away. If she'd asked me where I was heading I'd have had no answer. I couldn't speak more than ten words of Polish anyway. But she didn't ask. She didn't say a word until we'd been driving for about ten kilometres. "Would you mind," she said in English then, slowing down. "I have some business."

At this point the forest, which is always there on the edge of the cold flat fields, had closed right in on either side of the road. In Poland, you never lose the sense that this country really belongs to the trees. Sometimes they look pretty sick, but they never give up. There were trees in a thick crowd around the long wooden shack and its churned up parking lot. They made the place look kind of sinister, but appealing.

Inside, the shack was a fancy version of the old-fashioned Polish roadside diner: no plastic, everything wood; mud-coffee and a handwritten menu. For the coffee they don't use a pot or a filter or anything, they just dump boiling water on a heap of grounds and the rest is up to you. Getting anything other than a mouthful of grit is quite an art. She ordered for both of us without asking what I wanted (I was used to that) and we took our glasses of mud to a table. She offered me a cigarette and lit one herself. Close up she was both more good looking and more ravaged than she'd seemed back in the Modern Grill. There were crinkly smoker's creases around her big dark eyes, and a faded scar on her cheek that was only partly concealed by make-up. From the few words she'd spoken I could tell her English was good. I wanted to break the ice, and head off some of the questions she was bound to ask: but then I looked around and I got distracted.

Our diner was the whores' restroom. Here they all were, off duty, their peepshow nakedness looking less ridiculous: as if we, fully dressed, were the ones who had stumbled into a chorus-girls' dressing room. There were a few men, too, eating their meals and joking with the girls in a comradely way, as if this scene was perfectly normal. I couldn't stop staring. I am *not* naïve, but it was so interesting. There was a constant coming and going. A girl would rush in, pulling a bundle of notes out of her bra. She'd go up to the counter and have an intense discussion with the woman behind it; a narrow-eyed, respectable-looking dame in a rusty brown overall. Some notes would change hands. Sometimes the girl would enlist a friend to help resolve the transaction, and there'd be some sharp exchanges. Or two of them would dive into one of the toilet cubicles at the back of the room, and there'd be much laughter and banging before they emerged, eyes bright and make-up slipping. They came in from the road looking exhausted: they left again refreshed, tugging at their underwear; rearranging nearly naked tits in rats' nests of dirty polyester lace.

It jolted me a little when I realised that my new friend was equally fascinated. She smoked one cigarette and lit another, in silence: absorbed.

"Excuse me," she said at last. "I have to talk to someone."

Off she went, taking her coffee, to chat with a little blonde in a crumpled black vest dress, who'd just walked in.

Well, here I am again, I thought.

The great thing about these old East Bloc countries with the two-tier economies, is that when you find yourself on the street again, suddenly your last scraps of spare change turn into a month's wages. I looked in my purse. I could eat, I could buy a night's lodging if it came to that; wash my smalls out in the basin. I had my toothbrush and my lipstick, what more does a girl need? I went up to the counter and ordered a plate of *bigos*, the universal meat and sauerkraut stew. It came with fresh rye bread. The stew was very good. I wolfed it down and lit another cigarette. I felt like Lauren Bacall in *To Have and Have Not*, the ideal of all teenage runaways. I wished the diner was a hotel so I could stay, and become part of the louche scene. I wished it was Martinique out there instead of a slab of dour *Polsku* highway, but you can't have everything. Romance moves on, it changes locale with the changing times.

There was a flurry going on among the girls, around the blonde: who was slumped with her head on her folded arms, looking in sore need of a pep-up trip to the john. My friend was in the midst of it. I watched without seeming to care, I didn't want to be pushy. I wondered what I'd say when she asked me how did I get into this scrape?

I was at school in Paris. I wasn't failing, I had friends, I wasn't taking drugs. There are smart and pretty bourgeoise Paris school-girls who sell ass around the *Marechales* – that's a ring of Paris road junctions, all called after old generals – for jetset pocket money: I wasn't there. Maybe I just wanted my parents to take notice. Maybe I resented the way they'd brought me up inter-national, following Daddy's job over the world, when I'd have preferred to stay home with my grandmother. In short there was no big reason, no excuse. I wanted to be in a Howard Hawks movie. So I took a flight to Budapest, to see what I could see. I lost my credit cards to a mugger. When my cash had run out and I was thinking about phoning home, I met a guy, another American, in a picture gallery. I told him my troubles, he paid the rent I owed at my pension. He took me out to dinner, we went back to his hotel room. It was no different from having an older boyfriend, a grown-up who would naturally pay for everything: until one morning a couple of weeks later I woke up, my friend had checked out and there was money on the table. Then I understood, but it didn't matter. He was gone and I didn't have to face him.

Since then I'd been living on my wits. I could have stopped the adventure any time. I didn't want to. It had been fun riding up and down that big road with my Polish friend. It makes you feel part of something exciting, to be cruising with some guy whose mysterious business is like an intriguing foreign film without subtitles. It makes you feel different. I'd been scared by what had happened, or nearly happened, in the Modern Grill Bar. That had given me a shudder, like the time in Kracow's Jewish quarter when I'd suddenly realised I was easily Jewish enough to have been shipped out with the others, down the railway line to the death camp. I like to choose my friends. But it was okay, I'd escaped. Now here I was with this beautiful Jewish-looking woman, who had a thing for hanging out with whores. Another strange encounter, another adventure.

I recalled the story of the predator. Was that true, or something my ex-friend had said to scare me? On the wall behind the counter – where a small TV stood, playing a quiz show with the sound turned down – I saw some Wanted Posters – the kind of thing you get in big train stations: a poorly copied black and white photo of some girl or boy, missing or dead. Have You Seen Her? Do You Know Anything . . . ? I didn't have to know Polish or get close to get the message. There seemed to be a lot of them, scattered among the National Soccer Team pics and the gaudy advertising: graded in age from grey and battered to brand new. I fantasised that the Jewish woman and I would investigate. She'd be cynical and wary of getting involved, but my belief in her would swing it: we would be a team. Would she accept that role, playing reluctant good guy to my blunt tomboy, Humphrey Bogart to my Bacall? I wished I could make it happen. Trouble is, you can give yourself the illusion of choice but you can't really choose a new protector. They have to choose you.

I was just beginning to get melancholy when she came back to me. "I'm sorry about that," she said, with a smile that left her eyes pensive. "We can go now."

"What was going on?"

"Oh, another girl has disappeared, Malga's friend. The police think she's dead."

"Oh wow, I heard about that shit, the killer. They didn't find a body?"

She shook her head. Her frown said she didn't want to dwell on the subject, so I laid off.

This time she asked me where I was heading. I said Warsaw for the sake of argument. Her English was very good. We talked, neutral stuff about how I liked Poland and what other countries I'd visited. She knew damn well I wasn't a tourist, but she'd obviously decided to ask no awkward questions and I was too proud to throw myself on her mercy. A song I liked came on the radio. I asked her what the words meant and she translated the catch for me –

"If I could spend some time alone with you
In some place that's hard to find, but easy to remember . . ."

I started to sing along, chopping up the English to make it fit the tune. She laughed, but she didn't seem to take the hint. We got as far as the next roadside restaurant. When she pulled up again, I was puzzled. But somehow I knew she wasn't planning to dump me. It was business again, this *business* they always have, the people you meet when you've fallen or jumped out of the regular, law-abiding world.

"You did well to eat at the other place," she said. "The food here is terrible."

It was the same scene as before, except that the clientele was more mixed and the girls were more discreet. They wore coats. The same as before, she bought two coffees (granules from a Nescafe sachet, tasting of grease) and left me on my own. I watched her with the girls. You could see that the news about "Malga's friend" had hit this place too. They were like little birds, huddling together in an invisible storm. And my friend was in the middle of it again. But this time I saw the deal. I saw some kind of pills in a clear plastic envelope, slipped from the pocket of the military-grey coat into a hungry teenage hand. You wish there'd be a little more variety, but it's always either drugs or sex. Always.

"What was that?" I said, when she came back. I didn't want her to think I was naïve. "What kind of shit are you selling? Maybe I want some."

She shook her head. "I hope not."

"C'mon. What was it?"

"AZT."

"Oh," I said. "Oh . . ." I felt gauche and confused. "Is . . . is that what you do? You ride up and down here selling medical stuff? A kind of whores' paramedic?"

"Not exactly." She sat down, hands deep in the pocket of that excellent coat, gazed into space for a moment, then gave a nod towards the girl – who was leaving, getting back on the job. "How old, do you think?"

"Um . . . sixteen?" I hazarded. Making her two years younger than me, and dying. So it goes.

"Perhaps, barely. Once upon a time, I was a teenage Jewish girl, engaged to an older man. I had no choice about the marriage. I mean, in my heart I had no choice. Our community, my community was important to me." I nodded. I imagined how she might have felt, growing up Jewish in Communist Poland. "I got pregnant. He knew the baby wasn't his. He also knew that the other guy, the baby's father, was still in my life and always would be. He married me anyway, and brought up my kid as his own. But then he died."

"What about the other guy, the baby's father?"

"Oh, he was still around. Always will be. I'm part of his operation. I have no choice about that, either. You could say that is my big problem." She smiled at me. "So you see, I have a fellow-feeling for these girls. The drugs are only to gain their confidence. What I'm trying to do is to get them out of this life. Completely. But it's not easy to change even one girl's mind. Being a whore is like an addiction. Everything contributes: friends, circumstances, the idleness; a certain fascination."

I felt uncomfortable. "If you want to save the girls, why don't you go after the guys?"

"Ah!" She laughed, offered me a cigarette and lit one for herself. Her long fingers were stained with nicotine, and nervously beautiful. "And do what? Shoot them in the head? A person has to know he is sick, before he can be made well. It is hard for me to reach 'the guys', as long as they feel no pain. They have no sense of wrongdoing when they buy sex. The girls are suffering, and that opens the heart." She laughed. "My dear, I wish it were otherwise, but in this time and in this place *suffering* is definitely me."

I didn't say anything. I didn't really care what she was up to, though I guessed I wasn't getting the full picture. The fact that she was talking to me, intimately, was enough. I just loved the sound of her voice, the darkness in the depths of her smile: the sad and mocking laughter in her black eyes. I wanted nothing better than to stay quiet and listen while she gave me glimpses of her complex and mysterious life.

"In the heart of me," she said softly, "there is something that knows nothing of 'right' or 'wrong'. I have been many people, I have had many names. The forms, you know, are nothing. Inside, deep inside, I am still what I always was. I remember that I was born unstained, completely free. But since the great divide had to come into my world, I have to admit, *there is no contest* I must accept the work that has been given to me. As difficult and long as it may be, we must make things turn out for the best. Do you see what I mean? And the only way it can be done is one piece at a time."

She sipped her cold coffee for a while, preoccupied.

"Would you mind coming back with me to Pod Las now?"

"Huh?"

"The first place we stopped. It means, 'Under the Forest'."

So we went back. It was dusk, and getting very cold. We'd hit a slack moment, the room was nearly empty. Yellowish electric light glistened on the wooden walls. The raggedy blonde she'd talked with earlier was almost the only girl in the place. My friend said, "Wait here."

I got myself some tea, cheaper than coffee; and sat down. I wanted to be her sidekick, the fresh page for her experience to write upon. I wondered if she carried a gun, and how much should I believe the Scarlet Pimpernel story about saving fallen women; and was I going to meet this monster, the Mr Big from whom she couldn't escape, my dark lady with the chequered past. The blonde girl called Malga stood up. Her face was drawn and grey, her eyes blank. She headed for the door, my dark lady following.

My friend said quietly as she passed, "Stay here. Don't follow us!"

She went out. I sat for a few minutes. Then I started thinking, about the girl who had just walked by me with the mark of death on her face; about the scene I'd witnessed here earlier; about my friend who liked to hang out with whores, but told me that her mission was to rid the world of girls who sell sex for a living. Soon I had myself completely terrified. I decided that I'd been riding around with a psychopath. My dark lady was the predator! It had to be. Now I understood why she'd asked me no questions. She already knew everything she needed to know. I was alone, I was vulnerable, and the way she'd met me had left her in no doubt that I was her legitimate prey.

The sinister little diner was suddenly drained of romance. Everything changed shape and colour. My American, the one in Budapest, had two little daughters. He didn't tell me that, I looked in his wallet once while he was sleeping and found their pictures. I suppose when they grew up he wanted them to be dentists, or something. But when he met me, he thought it was perfectly okay that I should pay with sex for food and shelter. Was he right? I don't know. He didn't *force* me. But he didn't march me to a telephone and stand over me while I called my terrified parents. He didn't do anything to haul me back from the brink of the slippery slope. What went through his head? Am I an adult? Am I my brother's keeper? I was going hot and cold by turns. The parched and withered faces of the murdered girls were staring at me from the wall. I was so frightened that I couldn't see any way to resist. She would come back from whatever she did to Malga. She would lead me into her darkness . . .

The woman behind the counter was giving me strange looks. Finally she came over with a short man in a pork pie hat, one of her more prosperous customers. "Are you wanting a lift?" she asked. "This gentleman can help you."

"No thank you."

"You should take the lift," said the proprietress of the Pod Las. I couldn't ask about the Jewish-looking woman, because I couldn't speak Polish. But from the way she spoke and the look in her eye I knew that she was warning me to get away from here. She was right. The guy looked okay. I would do him and get him to drop me in a town, somewhere away from this damned road, where I would call my parents. Tomorrow or the next day I would call them, I would call them real soon. As soon I had a story worked out.

We went out into the night. He slipped his arm around my waist. I was looking up and down for the raggedy blonde. I saw something big parked a few hundred metres along the road, no lights. I thought it was the jeep. I could see what looked like a struggle going on. I shouted "Stop that!" and threw off the man's arm. He yelled after me, something like *it's not our concern!* I kept running, beside the stream of traffic, screaming *"Leave her alone!"* I reached the spot in time to see . . . Three men's pale faces, flashing angry guilty glances over their shoulders, as they stooped over what seemed like a bundle of dirty clothes. They dumped their burden, leapt into their big car, slammed the doors; and it roared away.

I don't know if they had meant to kill her. Probably not. The angel of death that stalks girls like my raggedy blonde has not one face but many: disease, neglect, accident, overdose. It's only sometimes murder; and bodies can vanish without much mystery, when no one cares. I was going to go to her, but someone else was there.

It was my dark lady, the figure of all my hopes and fears. The dead girl's body seemed to be lying in her arms, in the gesture of the *pieta*. And then, where she had been, there seemed to be a human shape cut out of clear darkness, cut into the uttermost abyss . . . What did I see? I tremble still at the memory, though I know even this belongs to me: to my sex, my culture, my situation. It is not She. For an instant I believe I saw unveiled – sexless, impersonal, absolute – what lies within and beyond all images of that lady. I saw the gateway between creation and the uncreated: the innocent, the immaculate void of all our desire, opening and flowering in that cold April night . . . with the traffic roaring by, exhaust fumes in the air, headlights splashing like shoreline waves on the forest eaves.

The man from the Pod Las came running up. He exclaimed and cried (I think) What a terrible thing! and that I mustn't look! He led me back to the diner and the proprietress called the police. There were sirens and lights and they took the girl's body away. I soon discovered that no one else had seen a Jewish-looking woman with a scarred cheek. I'd come into the Pod Las alone, once in the afternoon and then again in the evening. I didn't insist. They'd have thought I was crazy. When the police had found me a hotel for the night, I looked in my purse to see how much money I had left and discovered a wad of notes tucked into the back pocket, with a scrap of paper on which someone had written, in looping old-fashioned European handwriting: *go home*. It was enough for my air fare. I suppose my Polish friend must have tucked the money in there, when he decided to dump me at the Modern Bar Grill. I told you he was a decent enough kind of guy. The rest, the whole dark lady encounter, was my vivid imagination.

And that was the end of my adventure. There were no dreadful consequences, much as I deserved them. It was just a wild adolescent spree. But I kept the paper with the message I like to think she sent me (directly or indirectly); and I keep the picture of her I bought up on my wall. I think of her often, my impossible She. I wonder is she still driving up and down, between Czestochowa and Piotrkow Tryb, saving souls? And I think about going home.

DOUGLAS E. WINTER

The Zombies
of Madison County

DOUGLAS E. WINTER IS A WINNER OF the World Fantasy Award, and a multiple nominee for that award as well as the Hugo Award and the Bram Stoker Award.

A partner in the internationally based law firm of Bryan Cave LLP and a member of the National Book Critics Circle, he is the author or editor of eleven books (including *Stephen King: The Art of Darkness*, *Faces of Fear*, *Prime Evil*, and the epic anthology of apocalyptic fiction, *Revelations* [aka *Millennium*]). Winter has published more than 200 articles and short stories, appearing in such major metropolitan newspapers as the *Washington Post*, *Washington Times*, *Philadelphia Inquirer*, *Atlanta Journal-Constitution* and *Cleveland Plain Dealer*, and in magazines as diverse as *Harper's Bazaar*, *Saturday Review*, *Gallery* and *The Twilight Zone*. His short fiction has been selected seven times for inclusion in "Year's Best" anthologies, and he is also a book columnist for *The Magazine of Fantasy & Science Fiction* and the music columnist for *Video Watchdog*.

His forthcoming books include a critical biography of Clive Barker and *American Zombie*, a trilogy of literary pastiches illustrated by J.K. Potter, which will include "Less Than Zombie", "Bright Lights, Big Zombie" (reprinted in *Best New Horror 4*), and the following, Bram Stoker Award-nominated novella . . .

> *Jesus*
> *raised the dead*
> *but who*
> *will raise the living?*

– Pearls Before Swine

The End

THERE ARE SONGS THAT COME WEIGHTED with debt from the stormclouds of a hundred smokestacks, from the grey ashes of a thousand lives, a million deaths. This is the last of them. On another long morning after the dead began to walk, I'm at my desk, staring into the wide blank screen of my computer, waiting for the words that never come, the telephone that never rings.

Nothing but the manuscript is left. The world outside is gone, at least the world as I knew it, and in its place the New Age. Inside there is nothing more to say. Only the manuscript remains, a shuffled stack of pages, for the most part typed, but by its midpoint nicked and scratched with ink and at last given over entirely to handwriting. A story; perhaps a fable. Whether a book of lies, or of revelations, it is the final missive from Madison County.

Its writer has extracted a solemn promise: If I decide not to publish his manuscript, I must agree to tell in my own words what happened in Madison County, Illinois, in the late summer of this year – what, for all I know, is happening there still. As usual, his ambition and conceit are intense, his compulsion to tell a story so demanding as to try to make that story mine.

Still, with the manuscript complete, the puzzle parts in place, I read his story through to the end. At times I stop, put the pages aside and wish them away. But I cannot help myself; I read, and read again. As I read, I begin to see the images, black type on white paper blurring, finally swallowed up in a wash of grey. To see the images is to know the truth of words. And I begin to hear those words, rising like smoke off these brittle pages. The story whispers to me. At times it shouts; at other times it cries. Sometime just after midnight, I know that there is no alternative but to try to publish the story – if anyone is left alive, or cares, to read it –

though its telling may seal my fate as surely as it sealed that of Douglas Winter.

In a world where death is life, and life, in all its forms, seems nothing more than a rehearsal for death, I could feel the hunger created by this story, the need to know its truth or deception. I believed then that, in a world where movies have become reality, where the dead walk and eat the living, there was still a place for fiction. I believe even more strongly now that I was wrong. But I had read his story, and I needed to know if it was truly a story, or something more. And the knowing could bring me to one place, and one place only.

Journeying to Madison County through these pages – and now, as I must, by wing or wheel or foot – I felt that, in many ways, I had become Douglas Winter. Finding the way into his essence is something of a challenge. His story provides few certainties, and a handful of vague clues from which only the most cautious of deductions may follow. He is an enigmatic person. At times he seems mysterious yet mundane, for in the days before the dead, he was one of those Washington lawyers, walking and talking through corridors and courthouses, aloof in Armani suits, fast cars, fast tracks. At other times he seems ethereal, perhaps even imaginary. He was not simply a lawyer but a writer, lost so deeply in himself that he would fall into the well of the subconscious and emerge with a story, a book – not about the law, but about horror. In his legal work he sought, no doubt, to be a consummate professional; probably he worked too hard at it, worsening his own wounds in seeking cures for others. Since he saw the world through different eyes, in time he inevitably would count himself one of the hunted, not the hunters. Given the law's implacable need for order, consider the agony of his vision, which saw that very likely there was none. Consider his plight, in the darkest hours of the night, awake, watching, waiting, for the answer to come.

Too many questions remain without answer, and they, too, draw me onward, a wary moth to the flame of Madison County. I have been unable to determine what became of anything else Winter wrote there, which, as his story suggests, may have included other stories, perhaps in the hundreds of pages. The best guess – and this would be consistent with what I know of him – is that he destroyed it all before vanishing into the midnight existence that tells us nothing and everything. For, having reached this story's end, I know nothing more of Douglas Winter than is written here, nothing at all about his life, if indeed there is one, after the zombies of Madison County.

His story has revised the very way that I read, I write, I think – and, most of all, reminded me of how we lived for so very long in a fragile kind of light, that light known as faith. For some people, there was faith in God or some other spiritual source of goodness, but for most of us, there was simple faith in a neighbor, a friend, a lover, a parent, the proverbial fellow man. We slept our peaceful nights in a darkness that was incomplete, pierced and illuminated by the shining stars of our faith: holes in the floor of Heaven. Coming to know Stacie Allen and Douglas Winter as I have in reading, and now writing, this story, I think that we were lucky, far more lucky than we knew. When the dead finally rose to teach us, it was too late for us to learn.

A story is always something more than its writer; it is also its reader. If you approach what follows, as I did, with the willingness to believe, you may find yourself on a journey that leads inexorably to his unspoken words: The End. You may wonder if you were meant to be entertained. In the increasingly indifferent furnace of your heart, you may even find, as Stacie Allen did, room to die again.

Douglas E. Winter

At dawn in late August, in the year of the dead, Douglas E. Winter locked the door of his suburban split-level house in Alexandria, Virginia. He carried a black leather dufflebag filled with handguns and ammunition and pharmaceuticals, the currency of the day, down a short curve of cement steps to the driveway. There, his 1971 Ford Mustang, taken from a used car dealer for a song and six clips of Black Talons, was waiting to take him home. The Mustang's once-bright racing blue was tainted red with rust, but its tires were new, and he would ask it only to make one last ride. A knapsack containing notebooks, pens and a laptop computer snuggled in the tiny back seat among canned goods and bottled water, the box of novels, the sleeping bag, the Coleman lantern, the Mossberg .410 pump shotgun.

He sat in behind the wheel, fed an old Beatles cassette to the tape deck, and began the long and winding road that would lead, in two or three days, to the heart of the Midwest. Driving through the tranquil streets of Alexandria, he took in the familiar landscape for the final time before heading north on the Shirley Highway and then cutting onto the George Washington Parkway, which snaked west to the Beltway. Across the Potomac, invulnerable Washington, its ghettoes burned and streets patrolled by Marines, shone back its white wisdom: Order has been restored.

Above Langley, the Cabin John Bridge still stood, and took him through an armed checkpoint and out of Virginia. There was no looking back, not now, not after the knowledge, that thief in the night, had come to him and whispered its summons. Something was calling him, some uncomfortable urge that grew with each sleepless night; something he knew, in that place kept for secret knowledge, and that now needed to be confirmed. He had grown tired of the movie, the endless replay of images from horror films that flooded the television screen, which with each passing day became more unreal, more fictional than the words he would type onto the page. He realized then that he was expendable, that in a world made up of horror, there might be nothing left to tell, no one left who wished to read his words.

He had written books, he had written articles, he had written stories; for nearly twenty years he had scrawled his message on the wall. Often he had written about the human need for horror, the passion with which the films, the fiction, had been embraced as his nation slouched toward the Millennium. By then he had quit the law and begun to argue his case alone, facing a computer screen instead of short-tempered judges, recalcitrant witnesses, blankfaced jurors. It was a good life, one in which his pain could be managed, in which he could retreat to the interior world, where everything mattered, and be done with the outside, the surface that the years had lacquered with layer after layer of lies to keep him safe. But then, when the dead rose, nothing could keep him safe. The law had also quit him, its façade of lofty ideals fallen into grim rituals of revenge, at first overseen by lynchmobs and shooting parties, but in time made formal by military tribunals, death squads, detention camps.

The highways were restricted but clear, said the talking heads on the nightly news, for Interstate 70 was the throat for the food and fuel supplies that kept the Northeast, what was left of it, alive. The convoy was formed near Frederick, Maryland, where he pressed the eject on his tapedeck and inserted the soundtrack to *Dawn of the Dead*. A bored M.P. glanced at his papers and waved him into line. The Mustang clung close to the heels of a pack of vans and eighteen-wheelers. In his rearview he watched an ever-lengthening tail of land rovers and tractor trailers, ridden herd by full-throttled Humvees as helicopter gunships fluttered overhead. There were detours, delays, diversions, wide and weary loops around the free-fire zone south of Pittsburgh, the ravaged remains of Columbus, but as evening brought down its veil, he made his bed within the gates of Fort Benjamin Harrison, and slept there encircled by the victorious army of the righteous, the living.

He had secured the rarest of commodities, a travel pass, which, like everyone and everything, had its price. But money, lies and favors, the fair trade of the nation's capital, meant nothing to him now; their spending loosed him of what had become shackles, imprisoning him first in the law, and then at his writer's desk. Now he had the freedom to know. By midmorning of the second day, the convoy split at Indianapolis, and he was caught up in a new column that followed the great scythe of I-70 southwest toward St Louis, the Gateway to the West and now a mighty fortress for the cause of humanity, spared from the curse of the living dead by a trick of geography and a quick-tempered general who had seized power and levelled, in rapid order, its cemeteries, bridges and crowded ghettoes.

His destination was there, just a few miles east of St Louis, on the near shore of the Mississippi. Interstate 70 wove through the last of the Illinois countryside, through Vandalia and Highland, until reaching, just before Edwardsville, a cusp of low hills whose green had faded, the outpost of urban decay, erratic corridors of condominiums and convenience stores, acres of earth torn open, laid bare, mere symptoms of the suffering that lay beyond: the inner-city despair of East St Louis, the blue-collar barrios of Madison and Venice, and at their crest, his hometown, the great grey ghost of Granite City.

But first he sought the strength that only could be found in pain: the pain of remembering. It brought him from the protection of the armored escort to the two-lane twist of blacktop that carried up into the hills and to the marker, the place of departure and forgetting, the place where he had stopped nearly twenty years before, on the day he left Madison County. His mother was buried there, on a sleepy knoll named Sunset Hills; she had lived long enough to see him as a lawyer, but not to see him happy. When God in His cruelty took her, he had started to write again.

The cemetery, once secluded, as peaceful and precious as an autumn sunset, was blanketed in black, its innocent fields now cratered char where even the earth was dead, sacrificed on the altar of fuel-air explosives or napalm. He closed his eyes and saw the silver-winged fighter-bombers of Scott Air Force Base, their howling dive and breath of flame, and he prayed that she was there when the airplanes struck, that she suffered only one death – for that, indeed, was enough. He vowed not to think about it again, and then faltered, sitting in the ashes as he began to cry.

He wished for the thousandth time in his life that he had married, and unmade the wish, as he often did, with the thought that it would have meant another betrayal, another loss. Then he asked his mother for forgiveness, and asked his God, what was left of Him, for the mercy He had not shown to her.

As he returned to the Mustang, he looked to the west, where the sun retreated through a sky he had never forgotten, the sky that shadowed his dreams, his nightmares, his stories: the sky of burnt steel, smokestack lightning, roiling above the mighty forge of Granite City, whose mills, long dead, were alive like the zombies, burning again, burning brightly, churning thunder-clouds that never rained. A grey hope once, in the Forties, Fifties and Sixties; a grey hope that, like so many American dreams, had turned to dust and despair instead. Foreign imports, labor unions, environmentalists, Arabs and Israelis, Democrats and Republicans, the energy crisis, the recession – he had heard all the stories and in the end believed none of them. For growing up in this burning world, he had seen neither hope nor despair, only grey.

That the shadow lingered still, snuffed out the sun, was no surprise. This place was waiting for him, waiting for his return. If asked, he could not have told anyone why. There was only the knowledge that had come to him that long and lonely night the week before, as he watched the government's video footage from St Louis, the city of the miracle, the city that had escaped the dead, the city that stood at the banks of a mighty river, the promise of the New America. It was then that he saw this sky, the clouds that were not clouds but the dark breath of smokestacks, lingering in the distance. Just as he saw them now, saw them and felt their call.

At the First Baptist Church of Granite City, a little boy named Doug Winter had stood every Sunday morning, every Sunday night, as the evangelist closed each service with an invitation, arms upraised as if to embrace some invisible giant, *Just as I am, without one plea*, summoning those in the congregation who had heard the call of blessed Jesus, who had been touched by the hand of God, *But that thy blood was shed for me*, to join him before the altar, to join him in salvation, and when that little boy, seven or eight years old, had stumbled forward, down the long and lonely aisle and into that empty embrace, *And that thou bids't me come to thee*, he did not know why, he did not know what he heard, what had called him, just as he did not know now, or care to know, save that for once he had heeded the call: *O Lamb of God, I come . . . I come.*

Stacie

Darkness measured time for Stacie Allen, and darkness settled swiftly in this world of shadows. She watched the darkness, looked through it to the tall hurricane fence and its weave of barbed wire, thinking, if indeed there were thoughts, of the man who stood at the other side. Soon he would gesture to her, approach the wire, and soon she would stagger toward him from the crowded interior of the holding pen.

Sometimes it was hard for her to walk, and impossible for her to talk; the words she tried to speak coughed from her lips in immutable moans, and however she sought to form them, they meant only hunger. It was hard to remember her name, how she looked, hard to remember the man who waited on the outside, harder still to remember how she had looked to him then, twenty years before. A girl in a red turtleneck sweater, plaid skirt, red tights, black patent leather shoes, her hair long and dark and alive with the wind as she turned away, eyes wet – with tears or rain, he never knew. She kissed him goodbye, ran to the waiting car and ducked down out of the sudden spring shower, out of his life. Douglas Winter did not know then that she was pregnant with the child of another man, or that two months later she would be married and a housewife in a farm town somewhere in central Illinois. Certainly he did not know that some twenty years after that, he would be facing her again, their eyes still locked in that stare: his eyes filled with hope, hers blank and dead.

That he should find her here, at this time, this place, was the stuff of fiction. It was something that did not happen save in stories, including one that he had written. But it happened in movies, too, and the world, for all its dreaming, had at last become a motion picture.

If she could still read, she would know that she was fiction. His words had found her, or what remained of her, in sullen moments of introspection that he called stories. In their pages, her hair was black, her body lithe, her legs taut and athletic, curving into what her mother had called racehorse ankles; but her face was missing, without description, always in shadow, unseen, unknown – the cipher with raven hair. With three words, she had left him; with thousands upon thousands of words, he had brought her back.

It did not take long to find her. When he left his mother's grave, he followed the state highway down from the low hills and through the decades, past the ghost of the Bel Air Drive-In, whose screen still shone somewhere inside his head, past Pontoon Beach and its polluted pools and streams, past Tri-City Speedway and Bowland and the first of the housing projects, and then stopped at the railroad tracks, where he waited, counting the endless train of passing freight cars until, near one hundred, he noticed their cargo. Soon he crossed the web of tracks and was there, on Nameoki Road, driving into his hometown.

Thomas Wolfe was right: You can't go home again. The reason is that you have never left. Douglas Winter may have lived his adult life in places far from Granite City, but Granite City lived on in him. When he saw St Elizabeth's Church, made the left turn onto Johnson Road, he was not only driving the Mustang, but its immaculate twin, and then a 1968 Ford Galaxie 500, riding in the back of a 1956 Ford Woodie, the front of a Volkswagen Beetle, pedaling a bicycle, running, walking, carried along in his father's arms; it was a journey he had probably taken more often in dreams than in life. Twice he met police cars, first at the sharp turn of Johnson, where he offered his ID, and then at Fehling Road, where he had to offer a fifth of whiskey as well. In the few minutes it took to circle the east of town, going as far as Bellemore Village, he felt the old pains, the ones that cut through him as certain as his mother's cancer: the Ben Franklin five-and-dime where he had bought his first toys, the pharmacy where he had bought his comic books and paperbacks, the confectionery that had become a funeral home, all of them gone, replaced by mocking strip malls and merchandise marts whose windows were smashed, their goods as stolen as his youth.

He drove past Frohardt School, where his mother had taught and he had written his first stories, past all the houses where he had lived, down Lindell Boulevard, over to Franklin Avenue and then the short distance back to Riviera Drive and Miami Court, the town's middleclass neighborhood, home to the Catholic merchants, the Jewish dentists and doctors, and the few others, his father among them, who had stepped from the shadow of the steel mills into a life outside. Douglas Winter drove through that shadow, knowing, not knowing, simply trusting in that instinct that had called him home as inevitably as a sparrow in late autumn.

The town had closed in on itself, the homes and shops abandoned, what was left of life waiting in the armed camp that surrounded the smokestacks of Granite City Steel. He found Nameoki Road again, took it south past the high school, where troops in the hundreds were now billeted, then farther along to the sullen projects of Kirkpatrick Homes, where plainfaced men and women in workclothes stared past him with tired and uncaring eyes. And at last he reached the unholy hive in which they labored: the mills, the chemical plants, the furnaces, the pipelines, insectile monstrosities of metal and flame that stalked Route 203 like some vast alien war machines from the science fiction films of his childhood.

He parked the car at the Nash Street entrance of Granite City Steel and sat on the hood, waiting for something to come to him – inspiration, antagonism, admonition – through the smoke and fog of his youth. He bought off the civilian security guards and watched the trains pull through like clockwork. The night brought nothing, so he drank his way into the next day, sleeping when he could, curled in the tiny back seat of the Mustang, the laptop computer hugged to his chest like a firstborn child. When he woke, the faded, dying searchlight of the sun was almost gone. Darkness prowled down, but a brighter light, borne of the blast furnaces, kept his vigil. He could feel its warmth, breathe its fumes, a pungence that burned his lungs more than his brief foray with cigarettes, the smoke that cancelled vision, silenced life, and it moved him as it never had before. Home was a city dressed in grey, forever shrouded, eternally in mourning. A place where even the dead came to die.

In the distance he heard the shuffle of another train, the latest in the ceaseless caravan that hauled restless cargo into the mills. Its whistle mourned a new night of grief, a cry that had echoed down the miles of rail from decimated Minneapolis and St Paul, Milwaukee and Chicago and all points south, where parentless children, sundered spouses, the childless, the friendless, wept over a world gone so wrong that nothing could put it right but order. If only he had known – known and not seen what waited for him in Madison County – then perhaps he could have lived still in Virginia, watched his television with a bottle in hand like so many others, rested in the embrace of that greater sorrow. But the roaring furnaces burned through him now, heat melting the weariness of years spent in hiding; and he had touched the smoke, which gave back nothing to the world but a stain, a taint, that would never be washed away.

In the shriek of braking metal, the night's wailing engine found its resting place beneath the great burrow of corrugated steel that enclosed the railhead. He wiped the sleep and ash from his face as, in the deepening gloom, soldiers dropped from the cars, exchanged salutes and salutations with their kin at the yard, and then formed up into lazy ranks. The scene had been replayed with minor variations throughout this day, and the day before: the troops dispersing, reforming with weapons ready at the first of the boxcars as the process of unloading began. A huddle of zombies would be herded out of the car and into a jagged run of wooden chutes and fences that funnelled and divided them like cattle until, one by one, they emerged into a final chute. There, soldiers with air hammers would hobble them at ankle or knee before letting them stagger into the wide fields of slag that bordered the mills, a makeshift prison secured with wire and cinderblock and steel.

He was too tired to count the zombies, or to count the mass of undead bodies that already crowded each wide rectangle of fencework with emigrants from the grave. But he remembered each one of them, fascinated by the faces of the American dead; for here, at last, was a democracy where all men were created equal, mindless husks of grey with little to distinguish them but hair, clothing, shoes – and hunger. The tired, the poor, the huddled masses, yearning, yearning . . . to feed.

In time he watched the last of the passengers, what once had been a woman, stumble down the plank of the boxcar. Stop. Head lolling off to the side as if she were sleepwalking. Turn. Eyes raising to him. As if he had been waiting there for her.

And, of course, he was waiting. For her.

It was Stacie Allen.

The Book of Saturday

She could see him, vaguely, in the everslowing trickle of memory. Each moment she saw him, saw through him, a patchwork quilt, pieces of time sewn into what once was. He was tall, over six feet, weighted with the beginnings of middle age, and he moved like the smoke itself, tentative, ominous, hovering over her. His eyes were ice blue, now faded to grey, halfmoons of weariness etched beneath them, and there was only the trace of a smile, a mask to tame the world outside.

He was tired, that would have been the word she had tried to form while watching him. Tired for lack of sleep, and for lack of something else. He told her he had been a lawyer, though she knew that, and that his work had been long and hard, trials in distant places, trials about the dead and dying – dreadful accidents, air disasters – but Stacie could no longer imagine what this meant, could only see men in staid suits huddled among the victimized, the guilty, in courtrooms of winedark wood, shifting paper that meant money or life and sometimes both.

Douglas Winter was not meant to be a lawyer; he was a dreamer of sorts, who lived within himself in strange, almost threatening ways. Stacie had sensed as much on that distant Monday, the first day of school in that long-lost enigma of the

1960s, after a president had died but before his brother was killed, when Douglas Winter stopped by her desk in the Ninth Grade English class at Granite City Junior High School and asked if she were Clark Allen's sister.

She had been waiting for him, waiting for this question, for if it went unasked, she would have come to him and told him. She knew that from the moment she saw him. But she would wait, and wish, and across the room at the ringing of the bell he came, looking like a lost boy stepping painfully into that actor called a man.

He smiled, pushed at his glasses. "Are you Stacie?" A fat stack of books nearly wormed out from his hands. He set them carefully on her desk, and atop the shopping-bag-covered textbooks she could see a paperback novel: *The Puppet Masters* by Robert Heinlein. When her eyes returned to his, she felt something shift inside. The eyes, the voice, the face, the stance, the silence, an uncomfortable moment as something new, something disturbing, touches and then breaches the abyss that separates two hearts, makes them beat as one. Stacie knew this moment, though she had never known it before, might never know it again. And there began the thing that would change them both forever.

They spoke about that moment only once, late at night in a house emptied of her roommates, the beginning of a long holiday weekend together at the farthest point she had traveled from home: one hundred miles to college in Charleston, Illinois. She curled against him, naked yet chaste, and asked him if even then he knew that it would come, six years later, to this place where children no longer played at love but began to make love.

He leaned back into the pillow and looked at the poster scotchtaped above her bed, a sunny seascape whose caption told them VIRGINIA IS FOR LOVERS. "I don't know if I want to go back." That he was looking at the poster confused her, but only for a moment. "Back home. To Granite City . . . to Madison County."

"Yes." Stacie pulled in closer to him, placed her head upon his chest "I know what you mean." But even then she didn't know. His knapsack, a tattered mangle of surplus-store canvas and rope, huddled on the floor beside the bed. The flap was folded back to expose the sheaf of papers, unkempt manila envelopes and file folders from which typescript pages fanned out. The nearest of the envelopes, thick to overflowing, contained a novel, she knew – a novel that would never end, he said. Even though it was fiction, the novel was called *Autobiography*, and it was about violence and Vietnam, madness and the Mississippi; most of all, it was about Madison County.

This package of paper that wanted one day to become a book was good. At least the parts she understood. He had read it to her, parts of it, and it had given her an excuse to glance inside him, to those places he had not opened, even to her.

He was going places, she knew that. Law school, lawyer. And what then? Washington, he sometimes told her, and that was near Virginia, the place for lovers. People. Power. Wealth. Those words didn't seem to apply to him. He was still lost, and there was little she could do about it except hold him in the night and wait and wait until the day came, and in time it would, when another man would cross another room to ask if she were Stacie Allen.

"Write another poem for me." Douglas Winter had smiled then. "A poem about Virginia."

He had written through the night, sitting on a broken angle of sidewalk, balancing the computer between his knees as his fingers tap-tapped at its keyboard, the arcane code of the storyteller.

He wrote, saved files, wrote again, shifted his body, and talked quietly to her as he worked, forever telling her about her beauty and how much he loved her. "Stacie, I . . ." Admissions of love. Sometimes he stopped and simply stared at her, a moment of inexpressible rapture.

Her throat was torn open from just beneath the left jawline, a gash that widened as it zigzagged down to a gaping hollow where flesh and marrow had been scooped from above her breasts. Most of her left arm had been chewed away, the forearm dangling on threads of muscle. She was not concerned about the wounds, or the blood that had dried into mudbrown patterns on her ashen skin and foul, torn J.C. Penney clothes.

Douglas Winter asked questions of her, and the words upset her, confused her, until he had whispered, "No, no, please, stay there." Then he held his silence, but after a time he could not help himself. There was so much to say, so little time left in which to say it. He would start to tell her something, then stop and type instead. Sometimes he slipped into moments of self-conversation. But then he would look at her, and his face would fall from its anguish into a kind of peace.

Near dawn, his confused emotions and the battery of his laptop computer were drained. On the spiral of his homecoming tour, he had taken the time to hide his backup battery, along with most of his belongings, in a closet of the house on Lindell Boulevard, sold by his parents late in the Fifties, now abandoned, its roof partially collapsed – beneath the weight of time or explosives, it did not matter. He had taken back the house, the neighborhood, and it was home again.

He stood, shaking the aches from his back and hands, and stepped up to the fence, its heavy links, steel posts and coiled parapet of barbed wire no barrier to what he first said to her. Then, remembering perhaps, or drawn only by the sound of his footsteps, the smell of his flesh, she came toward him as far as the barrier would allow. Reaching carefully through the small hole that he had cut in the fence, he could almost touch her wounded face. But it was time to leave.

Just short of his car, Douglas Winter stopped, looking back at her as another train sighed out its blast of steam, its aching weight finding rest in the Nash Street terminal. Through the jigsaw puzzle of chain he could see the mountains of slag that still marked the city's southern boundary, the coke plant and its blast furnaces belching their dirty mist into the dead sky beyond. Stacie was framed in a perfect circle of light, the raging furnaces brighter than the rising sun.

She was about five feet four, and from what he could tell her face had not seemed to age, though her body, like his, had thickened. Two children could do that to a woman. Her physical attraction had been immense, at first, to his teenaged rage of hormones and happiness. But there was something in Stacie Allen that interested him still. There was no intelligence, he could see that. And there was no passion, though he never quite knew if there had been passion there for something other than stability, for a house and two cars and two children and a cat or a dog, in a town like Granite City, in a place like Madison County.

Later, he would tell her that in ways undefinable, finding her at the railyard that day was the most important moment of his life.

Why was not spoken. That was the way he approached his life. He would write, not speak, about what was important, and even then, what he wrote was veiled, hidden, encoded, protected.

"Why is it that you write, exactly – I mean, this stuff?"

He looked across another barrier, one no less daunting, to her. She stirred at her Coca-Cola with a straw, wrinkled her nose at the pile of pages on the dining room table between them. In the kitchen, only paces away, her mother made quiet noises, shuffling plates, rinsing silverware, letting them know she was still there.

"If I knew, do you think I would be writing it?" His smile went unreturned. "Sometimes I look down into my typewriter and there's this space there, white space, just emptiness. And it has to be filled. Like it's my job, that if these words don't get written down then they will never matter. I will never matter. And sometimes, when somebody, usually you, or my mother, sometimes a teacher, reads them and then looks at me a certain way, sometimes I think I've managed to matter. The rest of the time I'm just having fun. Trying to have fun. So why is it that you read what I give you?"

Stacie hadn't expected him to ask that question. He wondered if she thought before she spoke. She did stir again at her Coke; soon, he thought, the straw might become a cigarette.

"Well, because you gave it to me. So I thought that meant you wanted me to read it. That I was supposed to read it. Or that maybe you had written it for me." Her face brightened, a smile that held, waiting for him to respond.

"What if I didn't care?"

There was truth in there, somewhere. She knew it, and knew, for the first time, that she had looked into the soul of Douglas Winter.

"I'm supposed to say, 'Then I don't care, either.' Which is true, mostly. But I think you care. I think that you think you love me. And that you want me to love you. But you don't want me to love you, not really. You want me to love your poems, your stories. And" – she hesitated, glancing back over her shoulder toward the kitchen and the ghost of her mother – "it's not what I dreamed about as a girl."

Back in the house on Lindell he found the shower still working, though its water was cold and colored with corrosion. He could not remember ever bathing inside these walls. Perhaps the later dwellers had repainted, remodeled, rearranged the rooms. The tile was recent, only a decade or so old. The mirror above the sink was cracked, a jag of lightning that cut his face into a kind of Jekyll and Hyde. Like most people thought of him: Lawyer and writer and never the twain to meet.

During the last good days, before the dead returned, he had thought, more and more often, of giving into despair, of writing the John Grisham novel that everyone seemed to expect or demand of him. He had neglected this kind of thinking since the last months of their first love affair, in the Spring of 1971, when he had talked of a novel about the law, about the chaos they witnessed around them, the war in the streets, the war in the jungle. She watched in wonder as he slipped a joint from his pocket, raised it then in half-salute: "To steel mills and coke plants, Dow Chemical and napalm. Or better yet, to cold, coughed-up mornings in good old Granite City, Illinois."

Stacie said nothing, but looked off to the side of him and hugged herself against something, a chill in bright April, the University of Illinois campus alive with parties and protest. There were four dead in Ohio, and many, many more in Vietnam, and in another month or so he would be receiving his draft notice. He was the love of her past six years and yet a stranger, talking now about peace and justice and freedom, but writing through the night as if alive on the chaos spinning around him, watching the endless stream of helicopters and bodybags on TV, watching flags burn, stomach burning with an ulcer, living hard, drinking harder, now slipsliding to dope. It was the child finally grown, punching his way into manhood, and it was more than she could deal with. She had an answer, but as usual, he was not listening, and gave her his own instead.

"Jesus raised the dead," he told her, summoning up one of the strange songs that sobbed from his stereo. "But who will raise the living?"

He passed the joint over to her; she pushed his hand away. And at last she said it: "I've got something to tell you." Words that he could have written, should have written, then. He wished that he could find them now, always thought that he would remember – that, for as long as he lived, he would never forget them.

Words that slipped from her like a confession. "*I don't think* . . ." Words that seemed rehearsed. ". . . *that I should* . . ." And they were rehearsed, of course they were rehearsed. ". . . *see you* . . ." Words that gave way to tears, expected tears, scripted tears, soap opera tears. ". . . *anymore.*"

New Mornings, Distant Music

When, in the hour after dawn, he had returned to the house on Lindell Boulevard, its yard of dead grass was blackened with the curious wash of fading night and oncoming shade. He moved through the uncertainty of that evolving darkness, beer in one hand, pistol in the other, listening for its sound. Nothing spoke to him, not even bird or insect. He could hear only the distant drumming of the morning trains, arriving from the east with the sun.

Once inside the house, he checked the doors and boarded windows, then took his shower. He replaced the computer battery, printed out what he had written, and placed the pages inside his knapsack, loose and unsettled as ever. Everything obviously had its place, but in a pattern known only to him. He finished the beer and took another with him as he curled on the floor, his knapsack a pillow, and tried for a time to sleep. The sounds of the trains, implacable, mechanical, forever forceful, turning their great wheels around and around and around, lured him toward a calm, a peace, he had not felt in years. In a place where he had not slept for almost four decades, he tried but still could not feel safe.

"You're afraid," Stacie had told him. "You write because you're afraid. Not of the monsters, not of the dark, not of any of this stuff you make up . . . That isn't real to you, is it? You try to make it real to other people because it gets in their way. So they can't know you. Because that's what you're afraid of. Other people."

It was Christmas. Their last Christmas together. He had given her a sweater, perfume, a poem. She had given him a framed picture of her. It did not do her justice; the angle invoked her brother's face, and her smile was fixed and false. Later he wondered if even then she knew, even then the clock of their love was winding down.

"That's not fear," he said at last "That's living. I write because each day is like the twist of the handle on a jack-in-the-box. But they tell you that that's God in the box. You turn the handle, slowly, swiftly, however you live, but you know – or you think you know – that God is somewhere inside, and that sooner or later He's going to pop out and take you. Or maybe you don't believe in Him, so you keep winding and winding that crank. Maybe the box never opens. Maybe the crank breaks off, or you get tired of turning it. Maybe it just winds on forever."

She pulled the soft wool of her new sweater between her fingers and felt her brow wrinkle, felt a kind of desperate headache push its way up from somewhere deep inside, a guilty place where the hands and lips and cock of a phantom had touched her. Stacie supposed that, for Douglas Winter, this was everyday talk. For her, it was the stuff of danger, darkness, plague years. People in Madison County didn't talk this way, about these things. The talk was about weather and the steel mills and the labor problems, the high school wrestling team and the new environmental regulations and the dangerous Negro boys from East St Louis. Not about art or nightmares. Not about Gods who might or might not exist.

He put the framed photo aside, reached for her and brought her into his arms. She started to cry, for reasons he did not then know, and told him how much she loved him, wanted him, wanted to be with him.

As they kissed, slowly slipping to the floor, to lay entwined as the evening fell into night, he thought about what life would be like in twenty years. About the place on her poster, Virginia, with its sunny seascape, a beach on which a mother, unchanged by time, walked with a leopard's grace, her mane of black hair tied up in a knot, two children scurrying after her, dancing in the wash of salt water and sand, as her husband, their father, a happy man with a law degree and a fistful of novels, stood off-camera, watching.

He kissed her and told her something, something he had never said before. Outside the snow cut through the cloud cover and brought a blanket of white over the grey streets of Granite City. The lights of the Christmas tree twinkled like fallen stars. An angel watched over them. Stacie Allen was nineteen years old, and the Moody Blues sang of nights in white satin. Never reaching an end.

The Use of Ashes

Now what? thought Stacie Allen. But there could be only one thought: Food, always food.

He sat on the same bent angle of sidewalk he had used before and watched her and the city become one. The old ways, the old times, coming back to him again. He wondered at how much had returned; how far he had traveled, only to find himself back here. He wondered how her hair would feel to his touch, how the curve of her back would meet his hand, how she would fit beside him.

The old ways came to him so easily, despite all that was learned, dispensing so quickly with the lessons of the years, the hard rules of growing up and old. He tried to think of something else, writing or even the law. Anything but how she looked, now and then. But he failed and wondered again how it would feel to touch her, to put his face and hands and heart against hers.

He could feel her eyes on him constantly, hear her ceaseless back and forth, here and there, on her side of the barrier made of steel and time. He wanted to know, just as he wanted her to know, how much he cared.

Like the best of lovers, he fulfilled her desires. A newspaper, print blurred with greasy stains, brought from the folds of his knapsack and passed through the ragged portal in the wire. There he unfolded the paper for her and let the contents loose. They fell in a scramble at her feet. The air seemed wet, awash with seared metal. Her nostrils flared, head suddenly erect, like a dog capturing a scent.

She knelt, penitent, hands digging into the offering, not so much clutching at the wet meat than fondling it, the slick fat and strips of skin and sinew wound in her fingers as she brought it to her lips. He fell against the fence, the barbed wire cutting into one hand, the other seeking anxious purchase, a steady place, as he watched her eagerly press the meat to her mouth. Strings of fat leaked from her teeth and along her chin like ragged vomit; the sound of her chewing pained his own stomach. At last he turned away, unable to watch the guileless greed of her swallowing.

His uncertain steps trailed after the false beacon of the moon, cloaked in a sky of smoke whose lower reaches shined with the bloom of blast furnaces, replaying the nights of his childhood, when the mills, ferociously alight, marked the boundaries of his world. He stumbled on, deepbreathing the stench, the flurry of ashes, oblivious to the great grey hills that rose all around him. He had seen it all before: the heaps of coal and limestone, rusted metal and slag, all of it fodder or waste, and that the mounds had multiplied, grown taller with the years, meant nothing to him – nothing but the inevitable.

It had been too long since he had taken this kind of a walk, and soon he was short of breath, and his thigh ached, a quiet but lingering lament. He dryswallowed a Percoset and kept on going. In the distance the civilian guards and soldiers lit cigarettes and spoke of something, nothing. He had taken care of them and their clones on each shift: cigarettes, ration slips, dollars, drugs – every one of them had their price, and it was cheap. Enough to buy him the time he needed, though now it was almost gone, as shift replaced shift and day followed night, and soon there would be nothing left for him to trade. They would need her for their labors, and with the sound of a morning whistle, an angry foreman or NCO, the scuffle of the swing shift, a rattle of M-16s, he would awaken from this dream. Now that he had found her, she would be lost again.

Awakening always generated a summons. So did the zombies when they first appeared on the CBS News Bulletin. He had looked with surprise at the television screen, searching through the channels but finding only the same story, the old story, watching these shambling undead creatures rise from the grave as he had so many times before in horror movies – walking out of fields, forests, ruined cities, walking out of film after film and into reality.

For a short time, that first night, he wondered how many people knew that there was a difference, how many had died while watching their television sets, never thinking to look outside. But he lived in the sanctified shadow of the nation's capital: the body counts were for the most part distant, and as the days turned into weeks, and the weeks into months, the dead were simply statistics that tickertaped like stock market quotations beneath CNN broadcasts. He didn't need to be told to stay inside at night, to clean and load his shotgun, to walk calmly into the Drug Emporium and trade a fistful of Krugerrands for a shopping list of prescription drugs – painkillers, antibiotics, antidepressants. By then elements of the Rapid Deployment Force had moved into position, and soon the fifty-mile perimeter was drawn around the capital, while Marine Force Recon units prowled the streets within, shooting first, not even asking later.

Then came the night when the sky over the District of Columbia was lit, a patriotic celebration of superior firepower, a cleansing flame whipped by the wind of hovering helicopters. Just north of the Pentagon, a ruby rain showered down, the first of the gunship assaults on Arlington National Cemetery, where an army of the dead made their encampment. Later there would be airstrikes, napalm; and later, silence. More ashes.

After she walked out of his life, and the Army took him into its embrace, his father bought a car for him, a 1971 Mustang Mach 1 in racing blue, the sleek stuff of Team McLaren. He liked to drive the Mustang at night, to push the pedal down and down until he hit 100 miles per hour, letting the Interstate lead him into the dark, uncharted territory beyond Madison County. There he would find a dirt road, park on some quiet corner of farmland and wander into the embrace of fields of tall corn, convincing himself that he was lost, that if he went far enough, he could never be found; that no one could ever touch him again. In a year he was driving the car across the country to law school, and within three years more, to Washington, D.C.

Without any conscious plan, he reached the end of 21st Street, and looked west down a range of wall and wire as far as he cared to see. Inside were zombies by the thousands, tens of thousands, an inhuman ocean of grey whose restless tide washed up on shores of waste. Past them, across Route 203, the sickly cumulus brewed out from a hundred smokestacks. There, he knew, on the far side of the coke plant, lurked more avenues of rail, routes spiderwebbing north from Arkansas and Tennessee, Louisana, perhaps even Texas. He looked up at the long stretch of fencing, the angry furnaces, the eternal ghost dance of fire and smoke, and shook his head at the industry of men. And then he looked back, just before his view would be lost to plateaus and peaks of slag, and he saw her sitting crosslegged in the dust, her head in her hands.

By the time he returned to the cut in the wire, his leg taut and forcing him to limp, another dawn wept over them, the sun pulling itself reluctantly into the sky. Stacie said nothing, her eyes simply following a man to whom the idea of darkness seemed important. Empty eyes; accusing eyes. The question, unasked, unanswered, consumed him. The wire that separated her from him was nothing; it was the darkness, most of all, that kept them apart. The darkness defied him; and yet it defined him, made him into someone – someone who played at being a lawyer, who couldn't earn his living with words, so sold his soul to write them. Who once was lost. And who now, in the shadow of the smoke-stacks, had been found.

Soon she was only inches away. The wire blurred, almost disappeared from sight. Her face was slack, almost saddened; the meal seemed to calm her. Perhaps she was remembering. The image of glowing candles, the mills alight in stormclouds of smoke, had stalked her childhood, too, and now that darkness was returning again. There were so many memories: frail, un-certain flowers of flesh and blood that might blossom in the desert of her consciousness.

He embraced the darkness, wishing that it were her. "A grey hope," he told her, calmly reciting the words, another song out of another time. And slowly he raised his hand, brought it to the gap in the fence.

She looked up at him, past him. Her face, what was left of it, was without passion, without memory, eyes locked in a television game-show stare: all-seeing, never knowing. She remembered nothing, no one, then moonlight, a window, a flight of birds, the cry of a child, the pain of birthing, a grey hope . . . and then she remembered no more.

"Hope," he said again. Whether this night, alight with its furnaces, or another, it did not matter. There were few words left that mattered, and in the darkness there was only one:

"Love."

As if conjured by this word, the halo of a furnace flared over them, loosed by the opening of a distant gate. A team of workers, orange and yellow helmets, plaid flannel shirts, blue jeans and boots, faces and hands dark with grime and nightmare, emerged from the backdrop of flame, then melted into their counterparts, arriving for the morning shift.

"Love," he told her again, and his fingers touched her, softly, gently, on the curve of her wet cheek. From somewhere over an unseen rainbow rose the sigh of another train, bringing the zombies home.

The Wafer and the Wine

On that evening of another unnamed, unnumbered day after the Second Coming, Douglas Winter looked steadily at Stacie Allen. She looked back in kind. From ten feet apart, through a webwork of rusted metal, they were locked in to one another, solidly, intimately and eternally.

A train whistle blew. Still looking at him, she did not move on the first whistle, or the second. In the long silence after the second whistle, and before the third, he took a deep breath and looked down at his pants, the left leg streaked and shiny with new blood. In that instant of inattention, she urged herself forward, fingers twining in the chain links, face pressed against the barbed wire so tightly that her brow was etched and split.

He came closer, hesitated, and then moved closer still. She reached out with her hand, beckoning, bidding him to her. The fingers opened, clawed, pulled into a fist, then opened again. In only forty-eight hours she had come to remember Douglas Winter, to want him again, need him again. To love him again.

Her hand waved inches in front of him. The tear at his thigh was nothing, a tender scratch of the knife, the first of the wounds made flesh. He could feel the second cut, the awkward slice he had made from his neck along his shoulder, which took a layer of muscle from just back of the collarbone. Its urgent pain overwhelmed the latest, more cautious carving at his waist, where he had begun to run to fat. She was looking down at this wound, the freshest, where blood clotted in a wet stew against his shirt.

He was conscious of the warmth, the smell of his blood. The warmth came into her hand, moved up her arm, and from there spread to her mouth, her stomach, wherever it wanted to go, with no effort on his part. He kept his silence, watching this quiet power, this queer control.

Her hand spread like a talon, reaching, reaching, and when daunted, snaked back through the wire, fingers thrust into her mouth as if the taste of the air, warm with his blood, were enough.

He noticed all of this, just as he noticed all of her. He could have walked out on this earlier, could still walk. Rationality shrieked at him, but rationality had died long ago. In its place, the old slow song had begun. Somewhere it played, he could hear it, a 45 rpm single spinning inside a plastic-cased GE stereo, voices calling down an empty corridor that he had walked and walked until there was nowhere left to go, except toward Stacie Allen.

"We knew something once," he told her. Hands fumbling with the buttons of his shirt. Another sound in the distance, a voice calling, the bark of a guard dog; then the rattle of chain, the shuffle of restless feet, marching, marching.

By then he had reached out, placed his hand against the fence, felt her hand come up, slowly, slowly, to grasp it. Her head followed, the long flow of raven hair, now a crop, half curls, half shorn, slivered with the grey of age, the brown of dried blood. Then her lips, peeling back to offer a row of stained and broken teeth and a tongue that darted forward to kiss his hand.

"No." His hand pulled away. "No." Left her hand as she bit at air, chewed at nothing, turning to face him with a hiss of sour spittle. "No." That softened to a purr as she saw him ease open the left side of his shirt, his shoulder and chest bared to her, a swamp of cotton and tape and blood. As he peeled the pressure dressing back, slipped the knife from his belt, cut at the strands of tape.

Three shots came in rapid fire from the distance behind him, whether warnings or kills he did not know, or care to know. Here, on this small island in a sea of grey, the music had started again. A needle scratched at vinyl skin, and the music, spun from its black circle, played. And played. Strange how these songs aged, lost meaning, became the background noise of elevators and doctors' offices, then somehow, in the night, returned.

She felt cold. So did he. But he took her right hand, brought it through the opening in the wire, her fingers moving into the wound at his side, and the pain vanished. Somehow it vanished as her nails clawed at the puddle of blood and muscle. He moved her hand in tighter.

She could smell him, his breath on her face, his meat on her busy fingers. The inescapable smell of a man from whom the veneer of civilization had been stripped forever and who seemed, in every eager part of himself, ready to acknowledge his kinship with the animal.

They danced, slowly, each on their side of the fence. He could feel her hand digging relentlessly into his side, coming away with a piece of him, and then returning, now squirming into his pectoral muscle, somehow searching for his heart, their bodies touching again and again through the wire.

The song ended, but he held on to her, humming that distant melody into her unhearing ear, and they stayed as they were until at last she tore the strand of muscle from his chest. He stifled a cry, of pain, of loss, and leaned into her, face pushed against the wire, his flesh to her lips, and the dance went on and on.

Her hand found his shoulder next, tore at the thin shirt and then tore at him. She was real, this was real, more real than anything he'd ever known. He bent slightly as the nails of her hand tightened, tore, then brought his bounty to her lips.

During the last night they had spent together, in his half-sleep, he thought she had slipped the covers from his chest and kissed at him, gently, tenderly, lips moving over his abdomen and down between his legs. He never knew if it was a dream, or real. Now as he watched her tasting him, he knew that it was a dream. That only this could be real.

There was no denying the feeling. She felt so good to him, her breasts and stomach and legs rubbing against him. He wanted this to run forever. More old songs, more of his body taken into hers. She had become a woman again, his woman. In a slow, unremitting way, she was turning for home, toward a place they had been and now might never leave.

He was falling into her now. And she into him. The barrier between them was giving way, the wire parting as her hand thrust at him and he pressed back against her. She bit at him, teeth grazing his throat, tongue licking at the vein beneath the skin. She looked up at him with dark, uncaring eyes, and he kissed her, kissed her grey and riven and moldering and pustulent cheek, and she snapped back, biting, biting, razor cuts at his face and at last blood, a silent stream of it that she licked and lapped and drank in thirsty mouthfuls.

The images of their long night together were blurred, obscured by passion and pain. He remembered the vague storm of sleep, her body curled against the fence, against him, her face placid, her appetite at last fulfilled, and then her smile, eyes opening slowly to look into him, to drink up this picture, one memory that would last for her brief eternity. When she kissed at him again, he was helpless, could only fall back into the wire as her lips worked on him. And in the midst of it, this fatal act of love, she had whispered the totality of her knowledge to him, spoken that single sentence: "I love you."

With her face buried in his neck, his torn skin open to her, he could smell the old smells, the smells of smoke, could hear steaming trains in that grey gulley, could see soldiers in autumnal camouflage moving steadily along the railhead, the sounds of the night unloading, unloading, urging the sleepwalkers onward, ever onward. Granite City swept over him, again and again and yet again, like a dirty rain that would never end. As he bled into her mouth, he murmured into her unhearing ears, "Oh, Stacie, Stacie . . . You love me."

She who had ceased consciousness days before paused at the sound of his voice, swallowing. "That was what you told me, wasn't it?" Teeth chewing at air. "Wasn't it?" Then he heard the words she had once whispered to him, now spoken in a voice other than her own. "I love you," he said, to her, for her.

And in that moment, he knew, after so many years, the meaning of love.

That was when he began to write this story.

Room to Die Again

Douglas Winter wrote without stopping for the next several days. He spent most of his time with her, letting the old wounds, and the new ones, heal. Alcohol helped, poured onto his torn skin and then down his throat. Antibiotics and painkillers were his only other sustenance. Nothing but his story really mattered. The battery of the laptop computer soon expired, then its replacement, and he turned to paper instead, writing with an old pen whose bent nib seemed to weep with words.

Sometimes, when the need struck him, he would take the car on a long drive, finding this place or that, excavating memories, restoring the town to the museum of his mind. He pressed hard on the accelerator, trying to remember and trying to forget, weaving through silent streets on which ash danced like fallen snow, past the abandoned City Hall, the firegutted Public Library, the First Baptist Church and its blood-drenched sanctuary, where he had once walked a long and lonely aisle; where, he often thought, he had first found fear.

She rode with him, side-by-side, restored, like the town, to her youth. She was not a ghost, though only he could see this part of her. He kept wiping at his eyes, the sunlight and the smoke blurred into tears. If the songs could return, why not Granite City, and with it, Stacie Allen? All it took was love.

On the night that he finished writing, they made their new love again, touching at the fence until it was nearly sunrise, her fingers working endlessly at his flesh, her mouth tearing at the gift of his body and blood. Hers was a hunger that would not end. Soon, he knew, there would be nothing left to give.

When this sorrow, this pain that transcended any other pain, swept past the Percoset, past the fever, and into that place of secrets that was his heart, he cried out against the darkness. She did not move, just buried her face in the wire, teeth snapping at the remaining shreds of metal that kept them apart; he stumbled backward, fell prostrate into the dust, spent. Searching for the solace of sleep.

On that other endless night, after she told him that it was over, he wondered how she could sleep, and whether he would ever sleep again. She lay in his bed, wrapped in the covers of some hidden knowledge, while he lay awake, part of him forever torn away. In time he would sleep; in time, he knew, anyone would sleep. But time would heal no wounds. Time would only pass, and the wounds, once and forever open, would remain for her to touch and savor again.

"Tell them I love you," he had said the following morning, his last, helpless words as she pulled from a long and, until then, silent embrace and ran to the waiting car. He had no idea what those words meant: resignation, protestation, a dismal plea. Or to whom they should be spoken, save perhaps himself; that, whoever she was meant to speak them to, they were probably dead by now.

He imagined that he slept, and that as he slept, his fevered dreams gathered a circle of uniforms around him, dour and dreary faces peering out from beneath their helmets and gasmasks with expectancy. He wanted to tell these men and women something, but the words could not be spoken; he had to write them down. When he tried to take the pen from his pocket, he felt what must have been a kick, a combat boot that caught his elbow, then his stomach; but there was no pain. He knew pain, and this was nothing like it. "It's over." Were those his words? His tongue tasted dirt and rock, and he spat out the chalky grit, saw the blood that sprayed from his lips instead. He wanted to waken, at least to roll over and let his body lay more comfortably in the concrete and ash on which he made his bed. More movement; another kick, and he opened his eyes again, watched a rifle butt slam down twice into the plastic case of the computer, watched shattered pieces spin away in all directions. He joined in the laughter; at least this time he could hear his voice. Then something hit his head, and the dream faded, far and away, and he found his black sleep.

Toward morning, he raised himself from the sidewalk, saw with muddled vision the stains where his blood had leaked into the earth. He turned anxiously to the holding pen, but she stood there, watching, waiting. He tried to meet her unseeing eyes, asked himself if she indeed could hear his words, understand them as something more than the grunt of an animal. He knew what had to happen, but he had been delaying the moment, wishing it away. The voice that echoed his knowledge was his own. "It's over." The great yards to the left and right were vacant, emptied; even the ranks of her holding pen had thinned. But she was still there, watching, waiting, watching, waiting.

Standing by the picture window on her twentieth birthday, sipping but not tasting a Diet Rite Cola, feeling the weight of the child growing inside her, Stacie Allen watched the bright August sunlight and decided that she would no longer imagine. She had looked into the sudden cloud that swelled high above the birch tree, and found a place where the two of them would stand, divided by a barrier more profound than that of marriage or years. The feelings inside her would change, of that she was sure. Sure enough that she would return to that place only once or so a year, and perhaps, if she were lucky, never again.

Her abstinence from imagining had been the first of the concessions. In the early years of her marriage, there had been many more: the new house, the children, the bills, the lack of money, the constant call of the real. She had needed nothing to stop him from coming into her. Until the night, one Halloween, that she saw the movie. The images were warped, fractured, as if seen from a distance through a veil of smoke, a maze of wire and steel. Twenty years forward, and quickly, so very quickly, twenty years back. With a flick of the dial, these frightening dreams, these fantasies, were banished, and she gave herself over to the here and now, marriage and motherhood, Taco Bell and TV, the only reality in which she cared to live.

She knew she was twenty and accepted it, but she could not imagine Douglas Winter being forty. Could not think of it, would not think of it. He was here with her, somewhere inside of her, as palpable as her unborn child. He was here with his long hair and wire-rimmed glasses and wrinkled fatigue jacket and that knapsack with its frantic sheaf of papers. No other version of him could exist, would exist; certainly not one older or wiser. Or that could be desired.

He hobbled across the uncertain path from the broken concrete to the fence, each few steps bringing the drillbit of pain to play at his chest, his shoulder, his leg, his side. But he wandered through the pain, jazzed by his morning cocktail of pharmaceuticals and the vision of her. There was little he could say, but it took some time for him to try to find the words.

"What are we going to do?" he said.

She was silent, walking-dead silent. Then: "I don't know," he answered, softly, for her. But he knew, in that part of him that believed she was inside of him, that knew he was inside of her, that wanted so desperately to believe in another being the two of them had created called "us." They had lost themselves and tried to create something else, something that existed only as an intermingling of the two of them. They were in love.

He pulled the pages of his manuscript from his back pocket, opened them and brought them to her, a final offering, a piece of him more intimate than flesh or blood.

"You can't come with me, Stacie. To that place, faraway, to that beach, the one in the poster. Virginia. Or anywhere."

Something brought her closer. He willed himself to believe it was the pages, everything that he had written; not the blood, not the sick smell of his life.

"But I can go with you."

He folded the pages into a tight square and slipped them through the break in the wire and into the pocket of her blouse.

There was only one thing left to do. He turned, wincing with the shift of his weight, and made his way back to the car. He opened the door, reached down into his knapsack, pulled free the pistol that had called to him with each new dawn. Knowledge in his eyes. Tears stealing down his cheeks. Gauze webbed around his breast, his side, his left arm; the wrappings of her love.

His hands trembled as he limped toward her, stopped ten feet short of the fence. Finally he flicked the slide of the Glock 17, chambering the first round. Just keep firing until it's empty, his friend Michael had told him once, on a day of blue skies and sunshine that must have been a dream. Until it's empty.

Only this was real: a man, a woman, and the grey hope that clouded over them. But when he readied himself, raising the pistol to stare over its unblinking eye into the face of Stacie Allen, he found that there was one more thing he wanted to do: He wanted to pray. Trying to find the old words, the words that had brought him down the aisle of the Interstate, to the altar of this city, to the faith that at last was his only faith: the faith in the artist, the writer, to tell the truth. And thus to know the truth before it is finally told. He had no faith in those distant, ever-dwindling stars above – the light, they had told him, that flickered through holes in the floor of Heaven.

He knew that he could not pray to that God above, but only to this idiot Goddess who reigned eternal in the shadows of the mills, the shadows of his heart. Her love would live forever; but his love? His love had to die.

He looked down the barrel, his unsteady hands lining the sight between the empty eyes that stared back at him, and he swallowed a long breath. His finger closed down on the trigger. And in that moment, he saw the same eyes, staring back at him across the gulf of years as he stood beside her desk and asked her name.

"Are you Stacie?" he had said then; and now, again, aloud: "Are you Stacie?"

And at last, swathed in the smoke of this burning world, he found the answer to his riddle, the conclusion of his story. He tossed the pistol aside.

He could not kill that which was already dead.

Postscript: The Furnace of the Heart

As I read the story of Douglas Winter and Stacie Allen, I understood how little any of us knew, or cared to know, about the zombies of Madison County. When I found its final words, there was little choice: I needed to know the truth – or the lie. I talked my way aboard one of the newly resumed commercial flights to St Louis, and paid whatever it took for an enterprising cabbie to cross one of the precarious bridges laid by the Corps of Engineers to span the wide and swollen Mississippi.

On the Illinois side, a potholed four-lane road veered away from the flatland of crushed concrete and glass that once had been East St Louis and north into ghostly villages named Venice and Madison. There the smoke descended, and with each minute dimmed the red brick houses, the pillaged storefronts, into a long forgotten past. It was like driving into a black-and-white photograph from the 1950s, worn and faded, a mist-shrouded landscape watched over by an anemic sun.

After the gypsy taxi made a confusing series of turns, and then found the wide lanes of Madison Avenue, we faced a phalanx of tanks and armored personnel carriers: the end of my ride, and the beginning of the long walk into Hell. That the soldiers let me pass was no surprise; their weapons were pointed away, in the other direction, guarding the world from whatever waited inside.

I needed no guide but the smoke and the flame. I walked in a snow of grey ash, following the curve of Madison Avenue until the great demon of Granite City Steel roared into view. The heat pulsed over me in waves, bringing sweat in December and, in time, tears. In row after row the smokestacks cut into the sky, venting the angry furnaces where once iron and carbon had melted, mated, formed the backbone of a nation, where once the locomotives had hauled in coal, hauled out shining steel. Now no kind word could describe this place; it was no city, no town, but an inferno whose fires had raged throughout eternity. It was where the dream that was America had come to die.

When I reached Nash Street and, at its midpoint, the entrance to the terminal where he had waited with sanguine expectancy, there were no longer civilian guards: I was questioned at length, turned away by a squad of black-bereted Army Rangers. Something was happening; I heard talk of shutting down, a laugh, and then stony silence. The railhead inside was barely visible, a rusted locomotive fallen from the nearest siding like an ancient, toppled monument. There was nothing else to be seen, they told me. Hands gripped at gunbelts; eyes offered a mortal desire. So I turned away, taking the same path he had taken, across 14th Street, following the high fences that stretched down and along Route 203, finally confronting the raging furnaces, the mountains of slag.

At first I believed them: nothing could be seen, nothing but grey. Yet I walked his path, and the smoke walked with me. I searched the miles of wire strung along steel girders that had been driven into the ground at fifty-meter intervals. In time I found the car, the rusted memory of a Ford Mustang, its tires stolen, interior picked over by scavengers. I found a broken angle of sidewalk and scattered pieces of a laptop computer. I even found a pen. And as I approached the fence nearby, I found something else: something that was nothing, a space torn in the wire and painted with dried blood, the space where, for a time, a kind of love had been made. On the other side of the fence, in what he had called a holding pen, there was only dust, slag in endless heaps and mounds, the waste dumped from the furnaces, the grey that had risen from the smokestacks to bleach every inch of the earth with its sadness.

It was the absence, I realized then, that was the presence of Madison County. The absence of life, and the presence, all around me, of every element of death. And at last I saw, I truly saw, where I stood, not just at this place, this moment in time, but in all places, at all times, lost in this burning world.

Standing there before me, he had seen Stacie Allen, or what he thought or wished or dreamed was Stacie Allen; but what he had written there made me see something else: the terrible something that is nothing. The hills, the mounds – there were so many grey rises that to the eye they seemed like so much litter, the refuse of the mills, and though of course they were, the act of seeing was one that for some time defied belief. But the smell could not be ignored. The smell is what made me believe.

The hills nearest to me were made up of shoes, piles and piles of shoes – leather and rubber and Corfam, women's pumps, children's Keds and Nikes, sandals, work boots, high heels and low, all shapes and all sizes, all kinds and all colors, and all of them empty. Whether it was the smell of them or the sight inside, that first instant of understanding, that bent me, I do not know. I simply wanted, so very desperately, to be sick, to vomit out their teaching.

But still I walked on, forced entry through that breach in the wire and into those forlorn hills, where clothing was heaped to the height of houses, sweaters mingled with suits, pyjamas with parkas, anything with everything: dirty, clean, wet, dry, bloody, white, synthetic, woolen. At uneven intervals I found troves of cheap jewelry, watches, eyeglasses, belts that curled like sleeping snakes; I stumbled over a prosthetic arm, pink with the tint of blood, and found a torn and empty baby blanket. Still I walked on and on, until I was to the farthest reaches of this place, and of my comprehension: to the dark, unsettled hills that dared me to approach, to know them, to caution me never to forget them. I could not deny their mystery, their gentle weave of brown and black, laced with auburn and gold, grey and white; and when I touched them, felt their silky yet brittle threads – felt my fingers flecked with hair – I did not need to look back to the smokestacks, the furnaces, the ovens, to know what burned inside.

First it was the dead, the things we called zombies, who had passed out of what we knew as life and into an existence of their own. But the fires are eager, they are hungry, they burn and they burn and, while we still live to stoke them, they will never stop. It was not long until the living dead would have given way to the legally dead – the prisoners, from the penitentiaries at Marion and Springfield, Leavenworth and Little Rock – and in time to the mental patients from Columbia and Alton, and then the near-dead, the dying, the defective, the disabled, and sooner or later the dissidents, the white-hot ovens forging a new world for a new age of harmony and love. For it was love that brought the zombies, like it brought Douglas Winter, to Madison County – a love made of fragile lies, the love of storybooks and sociopaths who believe in such conceits as love at first sight, a love that lasts forever, a love without consequences; a love without the effort that itself is love. A love that makes for bestsellers and bad movies. A love that denies the certain truth: that love, like any miracle, does not happen; it must be made.

I know these things, of course, because I know that I invented Douglas Winter, that he is just a character in what is, after all, just a story. I created him and the ground on which he walked. It did not take seven days. But now, having found my way to this place that he once called home, this trap of smoke and steel, I wonder how much I understand. The dead and the living, the living and the dead . . . what difference does it make? In the end they are the same; they are us. Now that I have seen his world, seen through the veil of grey that most of us mistake for clouds or mist or fog, I wonder if perhaps he created me, crafted me from the clay of this place of shadow and sorrow, in order to bring you here with me.

There is no end to his story, only the end of mine. In my dreams I want to believe that he somehow made his way to a world where words may still be spoken freely, if such a place exists – to Toronto or Quebec or some other unlikely Valhalla where he would find an audience that could still know horror, understand its meaning, its lessons. Who would read and perhaps be moved, swayed, cajoled into caring. Into waking, and living.

In my dreams he has found the right weapons. For it is possible that mere words are no longer enough; their powder, wet with so much blood, so many tears, may never again ignite the imagination. It is the time of the gun; perhaps it always has been, and those of us who thought otherwise were indeed poets, dreamers, fools.

In my dreams he lives, and he has finally found the nerve to fire back. But in my nightmares I know better; I know that he walked with her, hand in hand, into the steaming shadow of the mills, shorn of shoes and clothes and at last of his hair, and then cast, like Daniel, into the flames.

Yet my dreams and my nightmares, like my story, have come to an end, because I know one other thing: I have the courage that Douglas Winter lacked.

I grip the slide of the pistol and chamber the only round I need. The barrel is black and tastes of blood and magazine oil as I press it into my mouth. My hand is steady; my will, not his, be done.

I stand in the smoke of his childhood and I watch the signal fires, a burning world whose only gift is grey. In the ever-darkening sky above, nothing shines down. The stars have gone out; the holes in the floor of Heaven are sealed.

The only light now is the light of man, burning brightly in the furnace of the heart.

for Lynne
without whom

STEPHEN JONES &
KIM NEWMAN

Necrology: 1997

A S WE NEAR THE END OF THE DECADE, we remember the following writers, artists, performers and technicians who made significant contributions to the horror, science fiction and fantasy genres during their lifetimes, and who died in 1997 . . .

AUTHORS/ARTISTS

Screenwriter **William Lancaster**, the son of actor Burt, died from a heart attack on 4 January, aged 49. His credits include John Carpenter's 1982 version of *The Thing*.

The same day, writer and editor **Mike Baker** died of pneumonia in Las Vegas, aged 31. He was the assistant editor of *New Blood* magazine and edited and published thirty-three issues of the horror news magazine *Afraid* and two issues of the short-lived fiction title *Skull*. His short stories appeared in a number of anthologies and magazines and he edited the anthology *Young Blood*. At the time of his death, he left behind the completed manuscripts for another anthology, *The Ultimate Horror*, and a novel entitled *Vampires*.

Songwriter **Burton Lane**, whose credits include the stage and screen versions of *Finian's Rainbow* and *On a Clear Day You Can See Forever*, died on 5 January, aged 84. "Ol' Devil Moon" and "How Are Things in Glocca Morra?" are among the many hit songs he composed.

SF writer **Charles V. De Vet** also died the same day, aged 85. He sold his first story to *Amazing* in 1950 and over the next fifteen years published around fifty more. He collaborated with Katherine MacLean on the novel *Cosmic Checkmate* and produced just one book on his own, *Special Feature*.

Belgian comic strip cartoonist **André Franquin** died on 5 January, aged 73. During a fifty year career he created the characters Marsupilami (half-chimp, half-leopard) and Gaston Lagaffe, while his *Idées Noires* presented a pessimistic view of a world dominated by pollution, genocide and despair.

Hollywood scriptwriter **Harry Essex**, best remembered for such films as *Man-Made Monster* (original story), *Creature From the Black Lagoon*, *It Came from Outer Space*, *He Walked by Night*, and for writing/directing *I the Jury*, *Octaman* and *The Cremators*, died of heart failure on 6 January, aged 86.

Penelope Wallace, the daughter of Edgar Wallace and a former chairman of the Crime Writers' Association (1980-81), died on 13 January, aged 73. She founded the Edgar Wallace Society in the 1970s and her story "Tell David . . ." was made into an episode of TV's *Night Gallery* starring Sandra Dee.

Songwriter **Richard Berry**, whose hits included "Louie, Louie'", died on 23 January at the age of 61.

Comics artist **Dan Barry**, who illustrated the daily and Sunday *Flash Gordon* newspaper strip from 1951 until the early 1990s, died on 25 January, aged 73. More recently, he also worked on the *Indiana Jones* comics.

Gerald Marks, who wrote the song "All of Me", died from natural causes on 27 January, aged 96.

Author **Daniel P.** (Pratt) **Mannix**, who wrote the book *The Fox and the Hound* (the basis of the 1981 Disney cartoon), died after a lengthy illness on 29 January. He was 85.

Publisher **Arthur Ceppos**, whose Heritage House first published *Dianetics* by L. Ron Hubbard, died in early February, aged 87.

Veteran comedy screenwriter **Frank Launder**, best known for his long association with Sidney Gilliat and for such movies as *Oh Mr. Porter*, *The Lady Vanishes* and *They Came by Night*, and director of *The Blue Lagoon* and some of the *St. Trinians* films, died in Monaco on 23 February, aged 91.

Pulp writer **Floyd Clifford Gold**, the younger brother of *Galaxy* editor H.L. Gold, died of a stroke the same day, aged 78. He wrote book reviews for that magazine for eight years under the pen-name "Floyd C. Gale".

James Dickey, who scripted his novel *Deliverance* in 1972, died in February, aged 73.

Maurice Goldsmith, one of the founding fathers and administrator of the judging panel for the Arthur C. Clarke Awards, died on 1 March after a long illness.

William S. Roberts, who scripted *The Wonderful World of the Brothers Grimm* for George Pal, died of respiratory failure on 5 March, aged 83.

The Welsh-born creator of The Daleks, **Terry Nation**, died in Los Angeles of a respiratory illness on 9 March at the age of 66. His numerous TV credits include episodes of *Doctor Who*, *Survivors*, *Blake's 7*, *The Avengers*, *Out of This World*, *The Champions*, an adaptation of Asimov's *The Caves of Steel* and *The Incredible Robert Baldick*. He also co-scripted and produced the 1973 comedy movie *The House in Nightmare Park* (aka *Night of the Laughing Dead*).

British novelist **Ursula Torday** died on 16 March, aged 85. She wrote under her own name as well as a number of pseudonyms, including "Charity Blackstock", "Charlotte Keppel" and "Paula Allardyce", and her books included *The Exorcism* (aka *A House Possessed*), *Sabbath*, *The Ghost of Archie Gilroy*, *Ghost Town*, *Haunting Me* and *The Ghosts of Fontenoy*.

Composer **Fritz Zpielman**, whose Broadway show *The Stingiest Man in Town* was a musical version of Dickens' *A Christmas Carol*, died of natural causes on 21 March, aged 90.

The same day saw the death of **V.S. Pritchett** (Sir Victor Sawdon Pritchett), aged 96. His non-fiction books include acclaimed biographies of Balzac and Chekhov and a collection of essays on E.F. Benson and other writers, while his story "A Tale of Don Juan" first appeared in Cynthia Asquith's *The Second Ghost Book*.

Author and aviation expert **Martin** (Strasser) **Caidin** died of thyroid cancer on 24 March, aged 69. The author of more than 200 books, his novel *Marooned* was filmed in 1969, while his 1972 novel *Cyborg* became the basis of the popular TV series *The Six Million Dollar Man*. More recently he wrote a series of thrillers and such novelizations as *Indiana Jones and the Sky Pirates* and *Indiana Jones and the White Witch*.

Influential '60s beat poet **Allen Ginsberg** died of liver cancer on 5 April, aged 70. He once tried to exorcise the Pentagon, and appears as a character in William Burroughs' *The Naked Lunch*.

Singer-songwriter **Laura Nyro** (Laura Nigro), whose hit albums include *Stoned Soul Picnic* and *New York Tendaberry*, died from ovarian cancer on 8 April, aged 49. F. Paul Wilson wrote about her in the anthology *In Dreams*.

Editor, critic and genre expert **Sam** (Samuel) **Moskowitz** died on 15 April from complications following a massive heart attack he suffered on 8 April. He was aged 76. His non-fiction books about the SF field include *The Immortal Storm: A History of Science Fiction Fandom*, *Explorers of the Infinite: Shapers of Science Fiction* and *Seekers of Tomorrow: Masters of Modern Science Fiction*, while he edited numerous anthologies including *The Man Who Collected Poe*, *Great Untold Stories of Fantasy and Horror*, *Ghostly by Gaslight*, *Horrors in Hiding*, *Horrors Unknown* and *Horrors Unseen*. In 1973-74 he also edited a brief four-issue revival of *Weird Tales* magazine.

Mexican screenwriter/director **Carlos Enrique Taboada** died the same day from a heart attack, he was 67. His writing credits include the four-film *Nostradamus* vampire series, *The Witch's Mirror* and *Orlak, The Hell of Frankenstein*.

French author/artist **Roland Topor**, best known for his novel *The Tenant* (filmed by Roman Polanski in 1976) died of a cerebral haemorrhage or aneurysm in Paris on 16 April, aged 59. His work encompassed film, TV, theatre, sculpture and painting – he designed the animated movie *Fantastic Planet*, illustrated the poster for *The Tin Drum*, created the TV puppet series *Telechat* and portrayed Renfield in Werner Herzog's 1979 version of *Nosferatu the Vampyre*.

Australian film composer **Brian May** died of a heart attack on 24 April, aged 63. His credits include *Mad Max*, *Mad Max 2* (aka *Road Warrior*), *Gallipoli*, *The Survivor*, *Steel Dawn*, *Patrick*, *Thirst*, *Harlequin*, *The Day After Halloween*, *Bloodmoon*, *Dead Sleep*, *Deadline*, *Stage Fright*, *Dr. Giggles* and *Freddy's Dead The Final Nightmare*,

Lou Stathis, the editor of DC Comics' upmarket Vertigo line, died on 4 May following chemotherapy and surgery for brain cancer, aged 44. He also worked as an assistant editor for Dell and such magazines as *Amazing* and *Fantastic*, and was associate editor of *Heavy Metal*.

Irish author **Mervyn Wall**, whose fantastic novels include *The Unfortunate Fursey* and *The Return of Fursey* (both collected in *The Complete Fursey*), died in Dublin on 18 May, aged 88.

William Derry Eastlake, whose fantasy war novel *Castle Keep* was filmed in 1969 starring Burt Lancaster, died on 1 June, aged 79.

Australian author and critic **George** (Reginald) **Turner**, aged 80, suffered a stroke on 5 June and died three days later without regaining consciousness. His novels include *Beloved Son*, *Yesterday's Men*, *The Destiny Makers* and the Arthur C. Clarke Award-winning *The Sea and Summer* (aka *Drowning Towers*). He was to be a guest of honour at Aussiecon 3, the 1999 World Science Fiction Convention. Transworld Australia announced plans for the George Turner Prize for unpublished science fiction or fantasy novels.

Screenwriter **Mark Patrick Carducci** shot himself to death in Los Angeles on 18 June, aged 42. In a suicide note he apparently blamed his dysfunctional childhood. His many credits include *Neon Maniacs*, *Pumpkinhead*, *Flying Saucers Over Hollywood: The Plan Nine Companion* (which he also directed), the *Josh Kirby . . . Time Warrior* series, the TV movie *Buried Alive* and the *Tales from the Darkside* episode "The Spirited Photographer". He also executive produced *Vampirella*.

The same day, Mexican screenwriter **José Maria Fernandez Unsaun** died of peritonitis, aged 77. His more than two hundred film credits include *The Ship of Monsters*, *Museum of Horror*, *Adventure at the Center of the Earth*, *Dr. Satan*, *Dr. Satan and Black Magic* and *Conquest of the Moon*.

New Zealand-born author **Caroline Macdonald** died after a long battle with cancer in Australia on 24 July, aged 48. Her young adult science fiction novels won numerous awards, while more recent work such as the novel *Secret Lives* and the collection *Hostilities* were oriented toward dark fantasy and horror.

William S. (Seward) **Burroughs**, iconoclastic author of such novels as *The Naked Lunch* (filmed by David Cronenberg), *Nova Express*, *The Place of Dead Roads* and *Towers Open Fire*, died on 2 August, aged 83, twenty-four hours after suffering a heart attack. He was the grandson of the inventor of the adding machine, a heroin junkie and one of the most original voices in post-war American literature. In 1940s Manhattan he was mentor to Jack Kerouac and Allen Ginsberg. His film appearances include *Chappaqua*, *Bloodhounds of Broadway* and *Even Cowgirls Get the Blues*, and he narrated the 1960s reissue of Benjamin Christensen's *Witchcraft Through the Ages* (1918/21).

Photo-journalist **Horace Bristol**, whose pictures of migrant families helped inspire John Steinbeck's Pulitzer Prize-winning novel, *The Grapes of Wrath*, died on 4 August, aged 88.

Screenwriter **Orville H. Hampton** died on 8 August, aged 80. His films include *The Four Skulls of Jonathan Drake*, *The Alligator People*, *The Snake Woman*, *Jack the Giant Killer* and the 1963 *Beauty and the Beast*.

TV producer **John Elliott**, who co-scripted the early 1960s BBC series *A for Andromeda* and *The Andromeda Breakthrough* with astronomer Fred Hoyle, died on 14 August, aged 78.

Publisher **Donald I. Fine**, founder of Arbor House and Donald I. Fine books, died of cancer the same day, aged 75.

British showbiz gossip columnist, author and bit-part actor **Peter Noble** died on 16 August, aged 80. Best known for his long association with the Light Programme's *Movie-Go-Round*, from 1945 until the 1990s' he edited the *British Film Yearbook* he became the editor of *Screen International* in 1975 and continued to write for the magazine until 1992, and he was a radio and TV "personality" through such game shows as *Find the Link* and *Looks Familiar*.

Canadian-born publisher **Alfred Saunders**, whose Newcastle Publishing Company was responsible for five issues of *Forgotten Fantasy: Classics of Science Fiction and Fantasy* and twenty-four volumes of The Newcastle Forgotten Fantasy Library in the 1970s, died of prostate cancer in Los Angeles on 23 August, aged 68.

Veteran short story writer and journalist **Carl** (Richmond) **Jacobi** died at a nursing home in Minneapolis on 25 August, aged 89. Starting out as a reporter, he sold his first story in 1928 and soon became a regular contributor to *Weird Tales* and other pulp magazines such as *Ghost Stories*, *Strange Stories* and *Thrilling Mystery*. His fiction was collected by Arkham House in *Revelations in Black*, *Portraits in Moonlight* and

Disclosures in Scarlet and by Fedogan & Bremer in *Smoke of the Snake*. A fifth collection of adventure tales, *East of Samarinda*, was his only fiction outside the horror genre, and he compiled a high school text book in the 1930s entitled *Paths to the Far East*. His story "The Satanic Piano" was adapted for TV's *Tales from the Darkside*, and R. Dickson Smith's biography of the author, *Lost in the Rentharpian Hills*, was published in 1985.

Hollywood writer/producer **Samuel A. Peeples** died the same day from the effects of cancer, aged 79. He helped Gene Roddenberry develop *Star Trek* and wrote the second pilot episode "Where No Man Has Gone Before". He also wrote the pilot for the animated *Star Trek* series, contributed to the screenplay of the movie *The Wrath of Khan*, and scripted the cartoon TV movie *Flash Gordon The Greatest Adventure*.

Pioneering SF fan **Conrad H. Ruppert** died in hospital from heart and lung failure on 28 August, aged 84. During the 1930s he was involved in the typesetting and printing of such early fanzines as *The Time Traveller*, *Science Fiction Digest/Fantasy Magazine*, *The Fantasy Fan* and the Stanley G. Weinbaum memorial volume *Dawn of Flame and Other Stories*. He also printed the souvenir book for the First World Science Fiction Convention in New York in 1939.

Professor **Leon Endel**, the foremost Henry James scholar of the past fifty years, died in Honolulu on 6 September, aged 89. His five-volume biography of the author (1953-72) was revised into a single book in 1987, and he also compiled *The Ghostly Stories of Henry James*.

American-born author, editor and reviewer **Judith Merril** (Josephine Juliet Grossman), one of the first women to gain recognition in science fiction, died of congestive heart failure in Toronto on 12 September, aged 74. She became associated with the Futurians in the 1940s and her first short story appeared in *Astounding* in 1948. As an anthologist and champion of feminism, she regularly included new writers in her twelve "year's best" *SF* anthologies, starting in 1956. Her other books include the anthologies *Galaxy of Ghouls* and *England Swings SF* (aka *The Space-Time Journal*), the collections *Out of Bounds: Seven Stories*, *Daughters of Earth* and *Survival Ship and Other Stories*, and she created the *Tesseracts* anthology series in Canada. Her

1950 novel *Shadow on the Hearth* was later adapted for TV as *Atomic Attack*. The Merril Collection, based on her donation in 1970 to the Toronto Public Library, is one of the major SF research libraries in the world, containing more than 35,000 books and 18,000 periodicals.

South African-born **Kathy Keeton**, the wife of Bob Guccione and founder of *Omni* magazine in 1979 and *Longevity* in 1989, died on 19 September after undergoing surgery for cancer. She was 58.

Children's author **Merian Lovelace Kirchner**, who created the popular Betsy-Tracy series of books from 1940-55, died from emphysema on 25 September, aged 66. She was the daughter of journalist Delos W. Lovelace, who wrote the novelization of *King Kong*, and was named after the movie's director, Merian C. Cooper.

Screenwriter **Dorothy Kingsley**, whose credits include *Kiss Me Kate*, *Angels in the Outfield* and *Angels*, died of heart failure on 26 September, aged 87.

British author, editor and tireless promoter of science fiction **George Hay** (Oswyn Robert Tregonwell Hay) died on 3 October following an operation, aged 75. The co-founder in 1971 of the Science Fiction Foundation and its magazine *Foundation*, he spent his life promoting the idea of SF as a teaching tool, and his many books include four 1950s SF novels, the anthology *Hell Hath Fury*, and the 1978 spoof *The Necronomicon*. He also contributed stories to *Ghosts & Scholars*, *More Ghosts & Scholars* and *The Year's Best Horror Stories: Series VIII*.

The same day saw the death of historian **A.** (Alfred) **L.** (Leslie) **Rowse**, aged 93. Five stories from his collection *West Country Stories* were reprinted by Denys Val Baker, who also commissioned two more for his Kimber anthologies.

Doctor Who scriptwriter **Ian Stuart Black** died on 13 October, aged 82. He created the TV show *Danger Man* (US: *Secret Agent*) for Patrick McGoohan, and also worked on such series as *Adam Adamant Lives!* and *The Invisible Man*. The author of nine novels, including the ghost story *Creatures in a Dream*, his actress daughter Isobel appeared in Hammer's *Kiss of the Vampire*.

Bestselling author **Harold Robbins** (Francis Kane) died on 14

October, aged 81. His steamy novels include *Never Love a Stranger*, *The Carpetbaggers* and *The Betsy* and, despite a stroke in 1982 that left him with a slight case of aphasia, he continued to write.

Another bestseller, **James A. Michener**, whose books include the Pulitzer Prize-winning novel *Tales of the South Pacific* (the basis for the stage and screen musical *South Pacific*), *Hawaii* and *Space* (made into an all-star TV mini-series in 1985) died of complications following renal failure on 16 October, after discontinuing kidney dialysis earlier in the month. He was 90, and donated millions of dollars to educational institutions, and was considered one of America's leading philanthropists.

Fantasy author **Paul Edwin Zimmer**, the brother of Marion Zimmer Bradley, died of a heart attack while attending a convention on 17 October, aged 54. His books include *The Survivors* (with his sister), *The Lost Prince*, *King Chondo's Ride*, *A Gathering of Heroes* and *Ingulf the Mad*.

SF novelist, photographer, sculptor and fan cartoonist **William Rotsler** died in his sleep on 19 October after a long battle with throat cancer, a heart attack and bypass surgery. He was 71, and his books include *Contemporary Erotic Cinema*, *Patron of the Arts*, *To the Land of the Electric Angels* and, in collaboration with Gregory Benford, *Shiva Descending*. He knew Marilyn Monroe, discovered Kitten Natividad, and was involved in such softcore movies as *Notorious Daughter of Fanny Hill* (1966), *Mantis in Lace* (1968) and *The Secret Sex Life of Romeo and Juliet* (1970). He won his fifth Best Fan Artist Hugo in 1997.

Former agent, author and SF editor at Pyramid, Berkley, Dell/ Dial Press and Ballantine, **Donald R.** (Roynold) **Bensen**, died on 19 October from an apparent stroke, aged 70. He wrote westerns, one humorous SF novel, and edited the early 1960s anthologies *The Unknown* and *The Unknown Five*.

Self-confessed Satanist **Anton Szandor LeVey** (Anthony Levy), aged 67, died on 29 October from pulmonary edema. The founder of the Church of Satan in 1966, and the author of *The Satanic Bible* and *The Secret Life of a Satanist*, he appeared in *Witchcraft '70*, *Satanis The Devil's Mass* and had a small role in *Rosemary's Baby* (as the Devil). He also claimed to have been an uncredited consultant on the two *Dr. Phibes* films.

Margaret Adiss died from pancreatic cancer in early November, aged 64. She had been married to author Brian Aldiss since 1965 and was the author of three bibliographic works about her husband.

G. (George) **Harry Stine** died from an apparent stroke while writing in his Arizona home on 2 November, aged 69. He was the author of many non-fiction books about science and rocketry and wrote juvenile science fiction novels under his own name and as "Lee Correy". These include *Starship Through Space, Star Trek: The Abode of Life*, and *A Matter of Metalaw*. The twelve-book *Warbots* series (1988-92) was published under his own byline.

Richard Hornberger (aka Richard Hooker) author of the bestselling semi-autobiographical novel *M*A*S*H* and its lesser-known sequel *M*A*S*H Goes to Maine*, died of leukaemia on 4 November, aged 73.

Musical director/composer **Saul Chaplin** died on 15 November from injuries sustained in a fall. He was 85, and his many credits include *An American in Paris, Crazy House, Kiss Me Kate, On the Town*, and *The Sound of Music*.

Pulp writer **H.** (Horace) **B.** (Bowne) **Fyfe**, who contributed a number of stories to *Astounding* during the 1940s and '50s, died on 17 November after a long illness. He was 79.

Early TV presenter/author/photographer **Daniel** (Negley) **Farson**, aged 70, died of cancer of the pancreas on 27 November, during the centenary year of his great-uncle Bram Stoker's novel, *Dracula*. He became a full-time writer in 1964 and his books include the non-fiction studies *Jack the Ripper* and *The Man Who Wrote Dracula, The Beaver Book of Horror, Ghosts* and *Monsters* for Hamlyn Books, and the horror novels *Curse* and *Transplant*. A few months before his death he contributed the foreword to *The Mammoth Book of Dracula*.

Author and journalist **Kathy Acker** died of cancer in Mexico on 29 November, aged 49.

Composer **Wilfrid Josephs** also died in November. Born in 1927, his credits include such films as *The Deadly Bees, The Uncanny* and an unused score for *Cry of the Banshee*.

Science writer **Kenneth Gatland**, who was the technical advisor on the 1953 BBC-TV serial *Journey Into Space*, died on 11 December, aged 74.

Writer and philosopher (Arthur) **Owen Barfield**, the last surviving member of C.S. Lewis' group of Oxford intellectuals, the Inklings, died at his home in East Sussex on 14 December. He was 99. His books include the 1925 children's fantasy *The Silver Trumpet* and *Poetic Diction: A Study in Meaning* (1928), which had a great influence on fellow Inkling J.R.R. Tolkien. Lewis' classic *The Lion, the Witch and the Wardrobe* is dedicated to Barfield's daughter, Lucy.

TV writer/producer **Charles D. Webster**, whose credits include *Fantasy Island*, *Wonder Woman* and *Knight Rider*, died after a prolonged illness the same day. He was 73.

British Film composer **Buxton Orr**, whose credits include '50s and '60s cult favourites *Grip of the Strangler* (aka *The Haunted Strangler*), *Fiend Without a Face*, *Corridors of Blood*, *First Man Into Space*, *Snake Woman* and *Doctor Blood's Coffin*, died on 27 December.

Historian, conservationist and executive of the National Trust's Country Houses scheme since it began in 1936, **James Lees-Milne** died on 28 December, aged 89. Apart from his many non-fiction works, he also wrote three Gothic romances and Robinson published his short novel, *Ruthenshaw – A Ghost Story*, in 1994.

Japanese SF pioneer **Shin'ichi Hoshi** died on 30 December, aged 71. He had been in hospital since April in a coma following pneumonia. He wrote more than a thousand fantasy and science fiction stories plus two novels.

ACTORS/ACTRESSES

Veteran cigar-chewing character actor **Jesse White** (Jesse Marc Wiedenfeld), who appeared in more than sixty movies, including *Harvey* (both 1950 and 1972 versions), *Frances Goes to the Races*, *The Bad Seed*, *Pajama Party*, *The Ghost in the Invisible Bikini*, *The Spirit is Willing*, *The Reluctant Astronaut*, *The Cat from Outer Space*, *Monster in the Closet* and *Matinee*, died on 8 January from a heart attack following surgery for colon cancer. He was 79, and although he made numerous guest appearances on TV, he is best remembered as the lonesome Maytag repairman in a long-running series of American commercials (1967-89).

Tough-guy actor-turned-producer **Sheldon Leonard** (Sheldon Bershad) died on 11 January from natural causes. He was 89, and his movie credits include the 1935 *Love Wanga*, *It's a Wonderful Life* (as the bartender who throws out James Stewart), *Drums of the Jungle*, *To Have and Have Not*, *Zombies on Broadway* (with Bela Lugosi), *The Fabulous Joe*, *Sinbad the Sailor* and *Abbott and Costello Meet the Invisible Man*. As a producer he was responsible for such TV series as *The Dick Van Dyke Show*, *I Spy*, *The Andy Griffith Show* and the Emmy Award-winning *My World and Welcome to It*.

Adriana Caselotti, who was paid just $20.00 a day to supply the voice of Walt Disney's Snow White when she was eighteen years old and had a very small part in *The Wizard of Oz*, died of cancer on 19 January, aged 80.

American character actor **Guy Raymond**, who appeared in the classic *Star Trek* episode "The Trouble With Tribbles", died on 26 January, aged 85. He also appeared in such films as *The 4-D Man* and *The Reluctant Astronaut*.

Actor **Richard X. Slattery** died from a stroke on 27 January, aged 72. Best known for his TV work, he also appeared in *Herbie Rides Again* and the mini-series *Space*.

A former child actress in silent films, **Marjorie Reynolds** (Marjorie Goodspeed) died of congestive heart failure on 1 February, aged 79. Her many adult credits include *Sky Pirates*, *The Time of Their Lives*, *Heaven Only Knows*, *No Holds Barred*, *Holiday Inn*, *Ministry of Fear* and, with Boris Karloff, *Mr. Wong in Chinatown*, *The Fatal Hour* and *Doomed to Die*.

Cleveland-area TV horror host **Ernie Anderson**, better known as "Ghoulardi", died from cancer on 6 February, aged 73. He appeared in such films as *Tunnelvision* and *Hard Eight*, and later did voice-overs for such shows as *The Love Boat*.

Actor **Robert Ridgeley**, who portrayed Dracula in the 1968 *Get Smart* episode "The Wax Man", died from cancer the same day, aged 65. His movie credits include *Blazing Saddles*, *Multiplicity* and *Boogie Nights* (directed by Ernie Anderson's son, Paul Thomas Anderson).

British actor **Barry Evans**, who had been working as a taxi driver, was found murdered on 10 February, aged 52. Two men were subsequently held by police. He starred in *Here We Go*

Round the Mulberry Bush, *Die Screaming Marianne*, the 1993 *Mystery of Edwin Drood*, and in the TV series *Doctor in the House* (1970-72).

Actor **Don Porter**, whose credits include *Night Monster* (with Lugosi), *She-Wolf of London*, *Who Done It?*, *The Norliss Tapes*, *Legend of Lizzie Borden* and numerous TV shows, died on 11 February, aged 84, from natural causes.

British character actor **James Cossins** died after a long illness on 12 February, aged 63. Best remembered as the first victim of the Underground cannibal in *Deathline* (US: *Raw Meat*), he also appeared in Hammer's *The Anniversary*, *The Lost Continent* and *Blood from the Mummy's Tomb*.

David Doyle, best known for his recurring role as Bosley on TV's *Charlie's Angels*, died from a heart attack on 27 February, aged 67. His other credits include *No Way to Treat a Lady*, the 1973 *Miracle on 34th Street*, *The Stranger Within*, *Capricorn One*, *The Comeback*, *Ghost Writer* and *The Invisible Woman* (1983).

Mexican actor/director **Raoul da Anda**, "El Charro Negro", died in February. He had more than 250 films to his credit.

Veteran Hollywood stuntman **Carey Loftin**, who portrayed the mysterious truck driver in Steven Spielberg's *Duel*, died on 4 March, aged 83. He began his career doing stunts in such serials as *Spy Smasher*, *Haunted Harbour*, *The Purple Monster Strikes*, *The Crimson Ghost*, *King of the Rocket Men* and *Canadian Mounties vs. Atomic Invaders*.

After a fall at home, British comedy actor **Ronald Fraser** died from an unexpected internal haemorrhage on 13 March, aged 66. His film credits include *Bobbikins*, *The Bed-Sitting Room* and *The Mystery of Edwin Drood* (1993) along with guest spots on numerous TV shows, including *The Avengers*, *Doctor Who*, *Star Maidens* and *The Young Indiana Jones Chronicles*.

British leading man-turned-producer/director **Anthony Bushell** died on 2 April, aged 92. He appeared alongside Karloff in *The Ghoul* (1933), co-produced Olivier's *Hamlet* (1948), was featured in the 1950s BBC production of *Quatermass and the Pit* and directed Hammer's *Terror of the Tongs* starring Christopher Lee.

American TV actor **Michael Stroka** died from cancer on 14 April, aged 58. He appeared as Bruno on *Dark Shadows* (1966-

71) and the spin-off movie *House of Dark Shadows*, plus episodes of *Psi Factor*, *Whodunit*, *The Next Step Beyond*, *The New Adventures of Wonder Woman*, *Buck Rogers in the 25th Century* and *The Twilight Zone*.

BBC Radio 1 disc jockey **Mike Raven** (Austin Fairman) died in April, aged 72. Looking like a cross between Christopher Lee and Vincent Price, he made an unsuccessful attempt to turn himself into a horror star in the early 1970s with such films as *Lust for a Vampire*, *I Monster*, *Crucible of Terror* and *Disciple of Death*. However, his career fizzled when it became obvious that he couldn't act and he retired to Cornwall to run a farm, and later worked as a wood carver until his death.

American comedian **Pat Paulsen** died from cancer on 24 April following surgery. He was 69 and his film credits include *Auntie Lee's Meat Pies* and *Bloodsuckers from Outer Space* (in which he plays the President, after a number of joke campaigns to run for the office).

Actor **Paul Lambert**, who made his screen debut in *Spartacus* (1960), died from cancer on 27 April, aged 74. He also appeared in *Planet of the Apes*, *Wrong is Right*, *Blue Thunder* and numerous TV shows, including the classic "Masquerade" episode of *Thriller*.

Canadian-born child star turned British TV quiz show host **Hughie Green** died in May. Born in 1920, it was belatedly revealed that he was the father of Paula Yates.

Character actor **Alvy Moore**, who played Hank Kimball on TV's *Green Acres* (1965-71), died on 4 May from heart failure, aged 75. His films include *A Boy and His Dog*, *The Witchmaker*, *War of the Worlds*, *Everything's Ducky*, *The Gnome Mobile*, *The Brotherhood of Satan*, *The Horror Show*, *Intruder*, *The Outing*, *Mortuary* and *They're Playing With Fire*, along with many other TV appearances.

Walter Gotell, who played the recurring role of General Gogol in such James Bond films as *From Russia With Love*, *The Spy Who Loved Me*, *Moonraker*, *For Your Eyes Only*, *Octopussy*, *A View To a Kill* and *The Living Daylights*, died in May. Born in 1924, his other movie credits include *Circus of Horrors*, Hammer's *The Damned*, *The Devil's Daffodil*, *Road to Hong Kong*, *Sleepaway Camp 2* and *Puppet Master III*.

TV actor **Howard Morton**, who played the vampiric Grandpa

in *The Munsters Today* (1988-91), died on 11 May from complications following a stroke. He was 71, and also appeared in the movie *Rhinoceros* and many other TV shows.

Stage magician **Harry Blackstone, Jr.**, who appeared in the 1979 TV movie *Mandrake*, died on 14 May from complications from pancreatic cancer. He was 62.

Singer-actress **Thelma Carpenter**, whose credits include *The Wiz*, died from a massive heart attack in May.

American actor **Donald Curtis** died around 22 May, aged 82. He appeared in the 1940 serial *Flash Gordon Conquers the Universe*, *Invisible Agent* and *The Spiritualist* (aka *The Amazing Mr. X*), and starred in *It Came from Beneath the Sea* and *Earth vs. the Flying Saucers*.

Irish-born TV actor **Edward Mulhare**, best remembered for his roles as the ghost of Captain Daniel Gregg in *The Ghost and Mrs. Muir* (1968-70) and Devon Miles in *Knight Rider* (1982-85) died of lung cancer on 24 May, aged 74. His film credits include *Our Man Flint*, *Eye of the Devil* (aka *13*) and *Megaforce*, and he starred as Henry Higgins in several stage versions of *My Fair Lady*, playing the part on Broadway in more than 1,000 performances.

Hollywood leading man **John Beal** (James Alexander Bliedung) died on 26 May of complications from a stroke, aged 87. His many films include *The Cat and the Canary* (1939), *The Vampire* (1957), *The Funhouse*, *Here Comes the Bride*, *Amityville 3-D* and *The Legend of Lizzie Borden*.

Italian actor/producer **Walter Brandi** died in May. His films include *Playgirls and the Vampire*, *Vampire and the Ballerina*, *Slaughter of the Vampires*, *Bloody Pit of Horror* and *Terror Creatures from Beyond the Grave* (with Barbara Steele).

George Fenneman, who appeared in the original version of *The Thing*, died on 29 May, aged 77. On radio and TV he was Groucho Marx's sidekick and straight man on *You Bet Your Life* and was one of the opening narrators of *Dragnet*.

Dependable character actor and former Twentieth Century Fox mail boy **Richard Jaeckel** died on 14 June from cancer, aged 70. Among his many films are *The Green Slime*, *Latitude Zero*, *Chosen Survivors*, *Grizzly*, *Mako Jaws of Death*, *Day of the Animals*, *Twilight's Last Gleaming*, *The Dark*, *Blood Song*,

Airplane II the Sequel, Starman and *Black Moon Rising*. He was nominated for a Best Supporting Oscar in 1971.

Born in 1944, actress **Olga Georges-Picot** who appeared in *The Man Who Haunted Himself* and *Persecution* (aka *The Terror of Sheba*), died in June.

British character actor **Don Henderson,** who made his debut as the eponymous character in *The Ghoul* (1975), died in June. His other credits include *Star Wars* (as General Taggi), *The Island, Brazil, The Adventures of Baron Munchausen* and TV's *Bulman.*

American leading man **Brian Keith** (Robert Brian Keith, Jr.) shot himself to death on 24 June, aged 75. Suffering from cancer, he was also apparently depressed about the death of his daughter, Daisy, who had died of a self-inflicted gunshot wound to the head on 17 April. Most of Hollywood stayed away from the funeral of the actor who appeared in *Moon Pilot, Way . . . Way Out, Moonraker, Meteor, Charlie Chan and the Curse of the Dragon Queen, World War III, Cry for the Strangers* and TV's *Hardcastle & McCormick* and *Family Affair.*

Creepy-looking character actor **William Hickey** died in New York City on 29 June of complications from emphysema and bronchitis. He was aged 69, and his film credits include *Prizzi's Honor, Tales from the Darkside The Movie, The Runestone, Puppet Master* and *Mouse Hunt.*

Tough-guy Hollywood star **Robert Mitchum** died on 1 July from emphysema and lung cancer, aged 79. He starred in more than 120 movies, including the classic *Night of the Hunter* (1955), *Cape Fear* (both versions), *Agency, Scrooged* and *Dead Man.* He was arrested for possessing marijuana in 1948.

Another Hollywood giant, 89-year-old **James Stewart** (*It's a Wonderful Life, Harvey* [1950 and 1972], *Bell Book and Candle, Vertigo, Mr. Krueger's Christmas, An American Tail 2: Fieval Goes West* etc), died from cardiac arrest on 2 July as a result of a blood clot in the leg. Gloria, his wife of forty-four years, had died in February 1994 and he had been depressed since. He won a Best Actor Academy Award for *The Philadelphia Story.*

American actress **Carol Forman,** who portrayed Sombra in the 1947 serial *The Black Widow* and the Spider Lady in the 1948 serial *Superman,* died on 9 July, aged 78. She also appeared in the 1952 serial *Blackhawk.*

Stage actor **Alan Mixon**, who made his first New York appearance in 1957 in the off-Broadway premiere of Tennessee Williams' *Suddenly Last Summer*, died on 19 July, aged 64.

1940s and '50s serial queen **Linda Stirling**, who starred in *Tiger Woman*, *Zorro's Black Whip*, *Manhunt on Mystery Island*, *The Purple Monster Strikes* and *The Crimson Ghost*, died of cancer on 20 July, aged 75. A former model, she was signed by Republic Pictures in 1944 to make a string of adventure film serials and westerns.

New Zealand-born British actor **David Warbeck** (David Mitchell), who became a likable leading man in such British and Italian horror films as *Trog*, *Tam Lin*, *Craze*, Hammer's *Twins of Evil*, *The Black Cat* (1980), *The Beyond*, *Miami Golem*, *Ratman*, *Breakfast With Dracula*, *Razor Blade Smile* and many others, died after a long battle with cancer, on 23 July, aged 55.

British character actor **Brian Glover**, who appeared in *An American Werewolf in London*, *Jabberwocky*, *Britannia Hospital*, *The Company of Wolves*, *Alien^3*, *Kafka*, *Snow White: A Tale of Terror* and other films, died from a brain tumour, in his sleep on 25 July, aged 63.

Thin-faced British stage actress **Rosalie Crutchley** died on 28 July, aged 77. Her occasional film appearances include *The Gamma People*, *The Haunting*, *Wuthering Heights* (1970), *Whoever Slew Auntie Roo?*, Hammer's *Creatures the World Forgot* and *Blood from the Mummy's Tomb*, *The House in Nightmare Park*, – *And Now the Screaming Starts!*, *The Hunchback of Notre Dame* (1982) and *The Keep*.

Pioneering American disc jockey/actor 'The Real' Don Steele died on 5 August from lung cancer, aged 61. Famous for the way he announced the records he played, his occasional film and TV appearances include *Death Race 2000* (as Junior Bruce), *Kiss Meets the Phantom of the Park*, *Gremlins*, *Eating Raoul*, *Bordello of Blood* and *Bewitched*. He was honoured with a star on the Hollywood Walk of Fame in 1995.

Pakistan's most popular singer, **Nusrat Fateh Ali Khan**, died in London on 16 August, aged 48. His songs were used in such films as *Dead Man Walking* and *Natural Born Killers*.

American character actress **Cathleen Cordell**, who trained at England's Royal Academy of Dramatic Art, died on 19 August, aged 81. She spent most of the Second World War in Britain, where she appeared in radio dramas and in the original version of *Gaslight*. Her subsequent credits include such movies as *M*A*S*H* and *Airport* and the TV series *I Dream of Jeannie*.

Sally Blane (Elizabeth Jane Young), the actress-sister of Loretta Young, died on 27 August, aged 87. She appeared in more than 100 films, including *Night of Terror* (with Lugosi) and *Charlie Chan at Treasure Island* (directed by her husband, Norman Foster). Her last film was *A Bullet for Joey* in 1954.

Sultry-looking American actress **Elisabeth Brooks** died on 7 September from cancer, aged 46. She appeared in *The Howling* (as Marsha the werewolf witch), Hitchcock's *Family Plot*, *Deep Space*, *The Forgotten One* and TV's *Kolchak: The Night Stalker*.

Ubiquitous character actor **Burgess Meredith** (George Burgess) died on 9 September from skin cancer, internal bleeding and Alzheimer's disease at his Malibu home. He was 89, and best known for his role as The Penguin in the *Batman* TV series (1966-68) and the 1966 feature version, as well as the classic "Time Enough at Last" episode of *The Twilight Zone*, and the *Rocky* films. His numerous credits also include *Of Mice and Men* (1939, with Lon Chaney, Jr.), *Torture Garden*, *Beware! the Blob* (aka *Son of Blob*), *Burnt Offerings*, *The Sentinel*, *The Manitou*, *Magic*, *The Last Chase*, *Clash of the Titans*, *Twilight Zone The Movie* (as narrator), *Santa Claus*, *Night of the Hunter* (1991) and the mini-series *The Return of Captain Nemo*.

Radio, film and TV comedy actor **Red Skelton** (Richard Bernard Skelton) died on 17 September after a long illness. He was 84, and his many credits include *Whistling in the Dark* ("Ah-woo, it's the Fox!"), *Whistling in Dixie*, *Whistling in Brooklyn*, *I Dood It*, *Merton of the Movies* and *Around the World in Eighty Days*. On TV he was the comedian whose ad-libs threw off Bela Lugosi, as recreated in Tim Burton's *Ed Wood*. Milton Berle gave the eulogy at the Forest Lawn services.

British character actor **Jack May** died in September. His films include *Cat Girl*, *Trog*, *The Man Who Would Be King* and *Night After Night After Night* (as a murderous transvestite judge). However, he was best known for forty-five years as Nelson Gabriel on the radio drama *The Archers*.

Teen actor-turned-producer **John Ashley** died in New York City from a heart attack on the set of his latest film, *Scarred City*, on 4 October. Aged 62, his film credits include *Frankenstein's Daughter*, *How to Make a Monster*, *Bikini Beach*, *The Eye Creatures*, *Sergeant Deadhead*, *Brides of Blood*, *The Mad Doctor of Blood Island*, *Beast of Blood*, *Beast of the Yellow Night*, *The Twilight People*, *Womanhunt*, *Beyond Atlantis* and a walk-on in *2001: A Space Odyssey*. On TV he co-produced such series as *The Quest*, *The A-Team*, *Werewolf*, *Something is Out There* and *Dark Avenger*.

Dependable Scottish character actor **Andrew Keir** died on 5 October, aged 71. He made his screen debut in an early Hammer thriller, *The Lady Craved Excitement* (1950), returning in substantial roles like the vampire-hunting Father Sandor in *Dracula Prince of Darkness*, the titular scientist of *Quatermass and the Pit* (a role he recreated in 1996 for BBC Radio 3's *The Quatermass Memoirs*) and an obsessed Egyptologist in *Blood from the Mummy's Tomb*. His other credits include *The Pirates of Blood River*, *Daleks' Invasion Earth 2150 A.D.*, *The Night Visitor*, *Absolution*, *Haunters of the Deep*, *Dragonworld* and *Dragonworld The Legend Continues*.

Country singer/songwriter **John Denver** (Henry John Deutschendorf), aged 54, was killed when his experimental one-seat plane crashed off the coast of Monterey Bay on 12 October. A well-known environmentalist, his many hit songs include "Leaving on a Jet Plane", "Rocky Mountain High" and "Take Me Home, Country Roads", while in 1977 he starred in *Oh, God!* opposite George Burns as the eponymous deity.

American supporting actress **Joyce Compton** (Eleanor Hunt) died on 13 October, aged 90. She made her movie début in 1920 and appeared with Bela Lugosi in *Scared to Death* (1946), while her other credits include *Trapped by Television*, *Mighty Joe Young*, *Turnabout* and *Sorry, Wrong Number* (1948).

American TV actress **Audra Lindley**, best known for her role as Helen Roper in the series *Three's Company* (1977-79) and *The Ropers* (1979-80), and her recurring roles in *Cybill* and *Friends*, died on 16 October of complications from leukemia, aged 79. Divorced from actor James Whitmore, her film credits include the 1975 *Canterville Ghost*, *Revenge of the Stepford Wives*, *Spellbinder* and *The Relic*.

British-based American character actor **Michael Balfour** died on 19 October, aged 79. He appeared in *The Diamond Wizard*, Hammer's *Quatermass 2* (aka *Enemy from Space*), *Fiend Without a Face*, *The Flesh and the Fiends*, *The Hellfire Club*, *The Monster of Highgate Ponds*, *Fahrenheit 451*, *The Oblong Box* (with Vincent Price and Christopher Lee), *The Private Life of Sherlock Holmes*, *Batman* (1989) and *The Revenge of Billy the Kid*.

Don Messick, the voice of cartoon character ScoobyDoo for thirty years, died on 25 October. Born in 1927, he also created the voices for ScrappyDoo, Astro Jetson, Dr. Benton Quest, Bamm Bamm, Ranger Smith, Atom Ant, Muttley, Papa Smurf and numerous other animated characters.

Hong Kong Chinese actor and martial arts expert **Lam Ching-Ying** (Lin Zhengying) died on 8 or 9 November from liver cancer, aged 56. After stuntwork with Bruce Lee, Lam became a star as a Taoist vampire hunter in the popular *Mr. Vampire* (*Jianghsi Xiansheng*) series. His many other films include *Encounters of the Spooky Kind* and *Encounters of the Spooky Kind II*, *The Dead and the Deadly*, *Crazy Safari*, *Vampire vs. Vampire* (which he also directed), *Magic Cop*, *Gambling Ghost*, *Skin-Stripper* and *Exorcist Master*.

American character actor **George O. Petrie** died on 16 November of lymphoma, aged 85. His credits include *What's So Bad About Feeling Good*, *A Fire in the Sky*, *The Day After* and *Wavelength*.

The lead singer with Australian band INXS and husband of Paula Yates, **Michael Hutchence** hanged himself in a Sydney hotel room on 21 November. He was 37, and appeared as a foppish Lord Byron in Roger Corman's *Frankenstein Unbound*.

American actor **Charles Hallahan**, aged 54, died on 25 November from an apparent heart attack – just like his character's death in John Carpenter's *The Thing*! His other films include *Pale Rider*, *Space Jam* and *Dante's Peak*.

British character actor **Richard Vernon** died on 4 December, aged 72. His numerous film credits include *Village of the Damned* (1960), *Goldfinger*, *The Tomb of Ligeia*, Hammer's *The Satanic Rites of Dracula*, *Loch Ness*, *The Pink Panther Strikes Again* and *A Hard Day's Night*. He played Slartibartfast in both the radio and TV versions of *The Hitchhiker's Guide to the Galaxy*.

300-pound Canadian comedy actor **Chris Farley** died in December from a drugs overdose. A regular on TV's *Saturday Night Live* (1990-95), he appeared in such movies as *Wayne's World* and *Wayne's World 2*, *Coneheads* and *Beverly Hills Ninja*. At the time of his death he was 33, the same age at which his idol, John Belushi, died.

American comedy actor **Stubby Kaye** died from lung cancer on 14 December, aged 79. His films include *Guys and Dolls*, *Li'l Abner*, *The Monitors*, *Cat Ballou* and *Who Framed Roger Rabbit?*

Character actor **Edward Walsh**, who appeared as the vampire's hunchbacked henchman in *Count Yorga, Vampire*, died in Texas on 15 December, aged 62. He also appeared in the sequel, *The Return of Count Yorga*.

Veteran character actor **Denver Pyle** died on 23 December from lung cancer, aged 77. Best known for his westerns, he also appeared in *The Flying Saucer*, *Terrified*, *The Legend of Hillbilly John*, *Escape to Witch Mountain* and *Return from Witch Mountain*, and was a regular on such TV series as *Gunsmoke* (as Caleb) and *The Dukes of Hazard* (as Uncle Jesse).

Japanese star **Toshiro Mifune** died from organ failure on Christmas Eve, aged 77. A favourite of director Akira Kurosawa, his films include *Rashomon*, *Seven Samurai*, *Throne of Blood*, *Yojimbo*, *The Lost World of Sinbad* and Steven Spielberg's *1941*.

Billed as "The American Beauty", **Billie Dove** (Lillian Bohny), a leading lady of the silents who could not adapt to sound, died from pneumonia on 31 December, aged 96. A former Ziegfeld Follies dancer, she appeared in more than thirty films, including *The Black Pirate* (1926) opposite Douglas Fairbanks, and she emerged from retirement in 1962 to appear in *Diamond Head*, starring Charlton Heston.

FILM/TV TECHNICIANS

Chinese director **King Hu** (Hu Jinquan), whose films include *A Touch of Zen*, died from a stroke on 14 January, aged 65.

Mexican director **Gilberto Martinez Solares** died from a heart attack on 18 January, aged 90. His many films include *La Casa del Terror/Face of the Screaming Werewolf* (with Lon Chaney, Jr), *Santo and Blue Demon vs. the Monsters*, *World of the Dead*, *Blue Demon and the Seductresses*, *Chanoc vs. the Tiger and the*

Vampire and *Satanico Pandemonium*. He also scripted *Attack of the Mayan Mummy* and *Phantom of the Operetta*.

Bud Abbott, Jr., a partner in Abbot & Costello Enterprises, died from a heart attack on 19 January, aged 57.

American writer/director **Robert Clouse** died from kidney failure on 4 February, aged 68. His films include *The Pack, Golden Needles, Enter the Dragon, The Rats* (based on the novel by James Herbert), *Darker Than Amber* and *The Ultimate Warrior*. He also scripted the Spielberg TV movie *Something Evil* and *Happy Mother's Day Love George*.

Cinematographer **Enzo Martinelli** died on 5 February from natural causes, aged 89. He worked as an apprentice to his uncle, Arthur Martinelli, on the 1932 Bela Lugosi movie *White Zombie*, and his TV credits include *The Munsters, The Six Million Dollar Man, The Bionic Woman* and the pilot for the 1970s *Invisible Man*.

Costume designer **Mary Lillian Wills**, who won an Academy Award for her work of *The Wonderful World of the Brothers Grimm*, died on 7 February, aged 82. Her other films include *Hans Christian Andersen, Carousel, Camelot, Cape Fear* (1962) and *Song of the South*.

Former child actor (*Captain Video and His Video Rangers, Blackhawk* etc) turned TV director **Larry Stewart** died from a bacterial infection/heart failure on 26 February, aged 67. His credits include episodes of *Perry Mason, The Bionic Woman, The Incredible Hulk, Spider-Man, Fantasy Island* and *Buck Rogers in the 25th Century*.

Animator **Harry Love**, a long-time colleague of Friz Freleng, died in February.

Polish-born producer **Alexander Salkind** died in a Paris hospital from leukaemia on 8 March, aged 76. With his son Ilya, he co-produced the first three *Superman* movies starring Christopher Reeve, plus *Supergirl, Santa Claus*, Orson Welles' *The Trial, The Light at the Edge of the World, Bluebeard* with Richard Burton, *The Three Musketeers* (1974) and its sequels, and the *Superboy* TV series.

Austrian-born director **Fred Zinnemann** died on 14 March, aged 89. After beginning his career as an extra in such films as *All Quiet on the Western Front*, he became a director, winning Academy Awards for *From Here to Eternity* and *A Man for*

All Seasons. His other credits include *High Noon* (with Chaney, Jr.), *Oklahoma!*, *Kid Glove Killer*, *Eyes in the Night* and the original *Day of the Jackal*.

Tomoyuka Tanaka, a former chairman of Japan's Toho Studios, died from a cerebral infarction on 2 April, aged 86. In the mid-1950s he had the idea for Gojira/Godzilla, and produced twenty-two films in the series (seen by an estimated 85 million Japanese), plus many other Toho movies, including six films with Akira Kurosawa.

Argentine-born Spanish director **León Klimovsky** died on 8 April, aged 89. He guided Paul Naschy through his medallion-man werewolf movies *Shadow of the Werewolf* and *Dr. Jekyll and the Werewolf*, plus *Vengeance of the Zombies*. His other films include *The Dracula Saga*, *The Vampires' Night Orgy*, *La Noche de Walpurgis*, *Planeta Ciego* and *The People Who Own the Dark*.

Costume designer **Jean Louis** died from natural causes on 20 April, aged 89. His films include *Bell, Book and Candle*, *From Here to Eternity*, *A Star is Born*, *Thoroughly Modern Millie*, *1001 Nights*, *Gilda*, *Down to Earth*, *Lady from Shanghai*, *Suddenly Last Summer* and the 1973 version of *Lost Horizon*.

Thomas Carr, who directed the 1948 serial *Superman* and numerous episodes of the 1950s TV series, died on 23 April, aged 89.

Mexican cinematographer **Gabriel Figueroa**, aged 90, died on 27 April from a stroke following heart surgery. His films include *The Exterminating Angel* and *Simon of the Desert*.

Swedish director **Bo Widerberg**, whose credits include *Elvira Madigan*, died on 1 May, aged 66.

Italian director **Marco Ferreri**, once described by the *Sunday Times* as "The master of bad taste", died from a heart attack on 9 May, aged 68. His films include *La Grande Bouffe*, *La Carne* and *Bye Bye Monkey* (with a cameo by a dead King Kong).

American director/editor **John Rawlins** died on 20 May from pneumonia, aged 94. His many films and serials include *The Green Hornet Strikes Again*, *Arabian Nights*, *Sherlock Holmes and the Voice of Terror*, *Dick Tracy's Dilemma*, *Dick Tracy Meets Gruesome* (with Karloff), *The Missing Guest*, *Junior G-Men* and *The Great Impersonation*.

Sydney Guilaroff, who was the chief hairdresser at Metro-

Goldwyn-Mayer for many years, died on 28 May following a lengthy illness, aged 89. He created Judy Garland's braids for *The Wizard of Oz*, turned Lucille Ball into a redhead, and worked on *Dr. Jekyll and Mr. Hyde* (1931) and numerous others movies.

Animator **Stan Green**, whose credits include Disney's *The Rescuers* and *Who Framed Roger Rabbit?* died in May.

Actor-turned-special effects supervisor **George E. Mather** died from an apparent heart attack on 4 June, aged 77. He appeared in *Man of a Thousand Faces* and worked on the effects for *Star Wars, Ghostbusters, Fright Night, Poltergeist II The Other Side* and many other films.

BBC director/producer **Julia Smith**, the co-creator of *EastEnders* whose credits also include *Doctor Who*, died on 19 June, aged around 70.

French oceanographer **Jacques-Yves Cousteau** died on 25 June, aged 87. His exploits were chronicled in *The Silent World, World Without Sun* and other films.

British nudie photographer/producer/director/star **George Harrison-Marks**, described by *Sight and Sound* magazine as "the semi-acceptable face of smut in Britain thirty or forty years ago", died from sclerosis of the liver while battling cancer on 27 June, aged 71. His exploitation films include *The Naked World of Harrison Marks* and *Nine Ages of Nakedness*.

Academy Award-winning costume designer **Marjorie Best** (*The Adventures of Don Juan, Giant* etc) died in June.

Max E. Youngstein, the last survivor of five partners who in the 1950s were promised fifty per cent of United Artists if they could return the studio to profitability within three years, died on 8 July, aged 84. As head of production and marketing he green-lighted such films as *Marty* and *Around the World in Eighty Days*. With his associates he succeeded in saving the company, and they subsequently bought the remaining shares.

Prolific film editor **William H. Reynolds**, whose credits include *The Day the Earth Stood Still* and who won Academy Awards for *The Sound of Music* and *The Sting*, died on 16 July of cancer, aged 87.

Academy Award-winning special effects supervisor **Gene** (Francis) **Warren Sr.** died from cancer on 17 July, aged 80. He started his career as an animator with George Pal's Puppetoons in the 1940s and moved on to such films as *Monster from Green Hell*, *Tom Thumb*, *The Time Machine*, *Dinosaurus!*, *Atlantis the Lost Continent*, *Master of the World*, *The Wonderful World of the Brothers Grimm*, *Jack the Giant Killer*, *7 Faces of Dr. Lao*, *Around the World Under the Sea*, *The Power*, *The Andromeda Strain*, *The Legend of Hillbilly John*, and such classic TV shows as the original *Outer Limits*, *The Twilight Zone* and *Star Trek*.

The founder of Cobb Theaters, **Rowland Chappel Cobb**, who pioneered the multiplex theatre in 1971 by putting four screens into a single building, died on 1 August, aged 76.

British director of photography **Dick Bush** died suddenly on 4 August. Born in 1931, he photographed Jonathan Miller's TV version of *Alice in Wonderland* and such movies as *Mahler*, *Savage Messiah*, *Tommy*, *Lair of the White Worm* and *Crimes of Passion*, all for director Ken Russell.

Former Hollywood executive **Leo Jaffe**, who for eight years steered Columbia Pictures from near-bankruptcy in 1973, through an embezzlement scandal to box office success with such pictures as *Taxi Driver*, *Midnight Express* and *Close Encounters of the Third Kind*, died on 20 August, aged 88.

Brandon Tartikoff, former president of NBC-TV and chairman of Paramount (1991-92) died of Hodgkin's disease on 27 August, aged 48. As the youngest entertainment president in network history, taking over NBC programming in 1980 at the age of thirty, he is credited with transforming prime-time TV with such shows as *Hill Street Blues*, *L.A. Law* and *The Cosby Show*.

Executive producer/financier **Dodi Fayed** was killed with his girlfriend in a car crash in Paris on 31 August, aged 42. His film credits include *Hook*, *FX Murder by Illusion* and *FX2*.

Award-winning television, theatre and film producer/director **George Schaefer** died in September, aged 76. In a career spanning sixty years, he directed nearly one hundred TV productions, including the first live broadcasts of *Hamlet* and *Macbeth* in the 1950s. His autobiography is titled *From Live to Tape to Film*.

Television producer/director **Paul Bernard** died on 25 September, aged 68. After working as a designer in the 1950s, he went on to direct the episodes "Day of the Daleks", "The Time Monster" and "Frontier in Space" for the Jon Pertwee *Doctor Who* in the

1970s. He also directed the first three episodes of *The Tomorrow People* in 1973.

New Guinea-born TV producer/director and film historian **David Gill**, who collaborated with Kevin Brownlow on such series as *Hollywood The Pioneer Years* and *The Other Hollywood*, died from a heart attack on 28 September, aged 69. Together they formed Photoplay Productions in 1990 and worked on the restoration and presentation of such silent classics as *Napoléon*, *Ben Hur*, *Intolerance*, *The Four Horsemen of the Apocalypse*, *The Thief of Bagdad* and *The Phantom of the Opera*.

Michael L. Bender, who produced *Beetle Juice*, died on 3 October of complications from HIV. He was 51, and began his career as an entertainment lawyer for Warner Bros. and Avco-Embassy.

British cinematographer **Arthur Ibbetson** died in October. Born in 1922, his credits include *Willy Wonka and the Chocolate Factory*, *The Medusa Touch*, *Santa Claus*, *11 Harrowhouse* and TV's *Frankenstein: The True Story*.

British TV producer **Sydney Newman**, who was involved in the creation of both *Doctor Who* and *The Avengers*, died on 30 October, aged 80.

American director/producer/writer **Samuel** (Michael) **Fuller** died on Halloween, aged 86. His films include *The Baron of Arizona*, *Hell and High Water*, *Shock Corridor*, *White Dog*, *Run of the Arrow* and *The Naked Kiss* (1966). In later years he appeared in a number of cameo roles, including *Slapstick of Another Kind*, *Hammett* and as a testy Nazi hunter confronting vampires in Larry Cohen's *A Return to Salem's Lot*.

Actor-turned-comedy director **Hy Averback** died in October, aged 76. His films include the 1966 *Chamber of Horrors*.

Cinematographer **Robert Caramico**, whose credits include *Spawn of the Slithis* and *The Happy Hooker Goes to Washington* also died in October.

Special effects photographer **David Stewart** died in October. His credits include *Blade Runner*.

William Alland, a former actor with Orson Welles' Mercury Theatre (he played the enquiring reporter in *Citizen Kane*) and later a producer at Universal-International, died on 10 November of complications from heart disease. He was 81, and his films include *Creature from the Black Lagoon*, *The Black Castle*, *It Came from Outer Space*, *The Mole People*, *Revenge of the Creature*, *Tarantula*, *The Land Unknown*, *The Creature Walks Among Us*, *The Deadly Mantis*, *The Colossus of New York* and *The Space Children*. In later years he manufactured sailboats.

Special effects supervisor **Tom Cranham** died of cancer on 19 November, aged 63. He worked with Irwin Allen on the TV series *Time Tunnel*, *Lost in Space* and *Land of the Giants* and such movies as *The Poseidon Adventure*, *The Towering Inferno* and *The Swarm*. His other credits include *Honey I Shrunk the Kids*, *Blade Runner*, *Ghost*, *Jumanji*, *Jurassic Park* and TV's *Buck Rogers in the 25th Century*.

Choreographer **David Toguri**, whose credits include *The Rocky Horror Picture Show* and *Absolute Beginners*, died in November.

Child actor-turned-BBC radio producer **Glyn Dearman** died after a fall in his London home on 30 November. He was 57, and he appeared in the 1951 version of *Scrooge* and Hammer's *Four-Sided Triangle*.

Walt's widow **Lillian Disney** died in December. She was credited with naming Mickey Mouse.

American director and *Famous Monsters* contributor **David Bradley**, who made amateur versions of *Julius Caesar* and *Peer Gynt* with Charlton Heston, died on 21 December, aged 78. His other films include *Dragstrip Riot*, *12 to the Moon* and *They Saved Hitler's Brain*. He owned one of the largest private film collections in the world.

Studio executive **Dawn Steel** died of a brain tumour on the same day, aged 51. She handled the merchandising on *Star Trek, the Motion Picture*, was the studio head for *Fatal Attraction* and *Ghostbusters*, and produced *Twelve Monkeys*.

Superlative American cinematographer and the brother of actor Ricardo, **Stanley Cortez** (Stanislaus Kranz) died of a heart attack on 23 December, aged 92. His many credits include *The Black Cat* (1940), *The Magnificent Ambersons*, *Flesh and Fantasy*, *Secret Beyond the Door*, *Riders to the Stars*, *The Neanderthal Man*, *The Night of the Hunter* (1955), *The Angry Red Planet*, *Dinosaurus!*, *They Saved Hitler's Brain*, *Shock Corridor*, *The Navy vs. the Night Monsters* and *The Ghost in the Invisible Bikini*.

Actor-turned-TV writer/producer **James Komack** died of heart failure on Christmas Eve, aged 67. He appeared in *Damn Yankees* and his TV credits include *Get Smart* and *My Favorite Martian*.

Walt Disney producer **Bill Anderson**, who produced the TV series *Zorro*, died on 28 December, aged 86. He had been with the studio for forty-four years.

American physical special effects pioneer **Joe Lombardi** died from bronchial pneumonia while on location in London on 28 December, aged 74. The founder of Special Effects Unlimited Inc. in Hollywood in 1962, his more than sixty movies include *Apocalypse Now*, *The Godfather* and *Con Air*.

American director **Bernard Girard**, whose credits include *The Mad Room*, *A Name of Evil*, *The Mind Snatchers* and episodes of TV's *Alfred Hitchcock Presents*, *Twilight Zone* and *The Sixth Sense*, died on 30 December, aged 79.

USEFUL ADDRESSES

T HE FOLLOWING LISTING OF ORGANIZATIONS, publications, dealers and individuals is designed to present readers with further avenues to explore. Although I can personally recommend all those listed on the following pages, neither myself nor the publisher can take any responsibility for the services they offer. Please also note that all the information below is subject to change without notice.

ORGANIZATIONS

The British Fantasy Society (http://www.geocities.com/SoHo/6859/) began in 1971 and publishes the bi-monthly *British Fantasy Newsletter*, other periodicals including *Dark Horizons*, and organizes the annual British FantasyCon and semi-regular meetings in London. Yearly membership is £20.00 (UK), £25.00 (Europe) and £40.00 (America and the rest of the world) made payable in sterling to "The British Fantasy Society" and sent to The BFS Secretary, c/o 2 Harwood Street, Stockport, SK4 1JJ, UK. E-mail: syrinx.2112@btinternet.com

The Ghost Story Society (http://www.ash-tree.bc.ca/gss.html) publishes *All Hallows* magazine three times a year. The annual subscription is $23.00 (USA), Cdn$34.00 (Canada) or £14.50/$25.00 (rest of the world). Write to joint organizers Barbara and Christopher Roden at "The Ghost Story Society", PO Box 1360, Ashcroft, British Columbia, Canada V0K 1A0. E-mail: ashtree@ash-tree.bc.ca

Horror Writers Association (http://www.horror.org/) was formed in the 1980s and is open to anyone seeking Active, Affiliate or Associate membership. The HWA publishes a regular

Newsletter and organizes the annual Bram Stoker Awards ceremony. Standard membership is $55.00 (USA), £38.00/$65.00 (overseas); Corporate membership is $100.00 (USA), £74.00/$120.00 (overseas), and Family Membership is $75.00 (USA), £52.00/$85.00 (overseas). Send to "HWA", 8490 Zephyr Street, Arvada, CO 80005, USA.

World Fantasy Convention (http://www.farrsite.com/wfc/) is an annual convention held in a different (usually American) city each year.

MAGAZINES

Cinefantastique is a monthly SF/fantasy/horror movie magazine with a "Sense of Wonder". Cover price is $5.99/£4.20 and a twelve-issue subscription is $48.00 (USA) or $55.00 (Canada and overseas) to PO Box 270, Oak Park, IL 60303, USA.

Interzone is Britain's leading magazine of science fiction and fantasy. Single copies are available for £3.00 (UK) or £3.50/$6.00 (overseas) or a twelve-issue subscription is £32.00 (UK), £38.00/$60.00 (USA) or £38.00 (overseas) to "Interzone", 217 Preston Drove, Brighton, BN1 6FL, UK.

Locus (http://www.Locusmag.com) is the monthly newspaper of the SF/fantasy/horror field. $4.95 a copy, a twelve-issue subscription is $43.00 (USA), $48.00 (Canada), $70.00 (Europe), $80.00 (Australia, Asia and Africa) to "Locus Publications", PO Box 13305, Oakland, CA 94661, USA.

Necrofile (http://www.necropress.com) is a quarterly review of horror fiction. $3.00 a copy, a four-issue subscription is $12.00 (USA), $15.00 (Canada) or $17.00 (overseas) in US funds only to "Necronomicon Press", P.O. Box 1304, West Warwick, RI 02893, USA.

Science Fiction Chronicle is a monthly news and reviews magazine that covers the SF/fantasy/horror field. $3.50 a copy, a twelve-issue subscription is $35.00 (bulk USA), $42.00 (1st class USA and + GST in Canada), £29.00 (UK) and $A59.00 (Australia). Make cheques payable to "Science Fiction Chronicle" and send to Science Fiction Chronicle, PO Box 022730, Brooklyn, NY 11202-0056, USA or payable to "Algol Press" and send to Rob Hansen, 144 Plashet Grove, East Ham, London E6 1AB, UK.

SFX (http://www.sfnet.co.uk) is a monthly multi-media magazine of science fiction, fantasy and horror. Single copies are £3.25 or a twelve-issue subscription is £24.00 (UK), £42.00 (Europe), £60.00 (USA) or £62.00 (rest of the world) to "Future Publishing", SFX Subscriptions, FREEPOST (BS900), Somerton, Somerset TA11 6BR, UK, or overseas subscribers to "Future Publishing", SFX Subscriptions, Somerton, Somerset TA11 6TB, UK.

Shivers is the monthly magazine of horror entertainment. Single copies are £2.99 (UK) or $5.99 (USA), and a yearly subscription is £33.00 (UK), $66.00 (USA), £43.00 (Europe airmail and rest of the world surface) or £47.00 (rest of the world airmail) to "Visual Imagination Limited", Shivers Mail Order, PO Box 371, London SW14 8JL, UK, or PO Box 156, Manorville, NY 11949, USA. Please mark your envelope clearly as "Subscription".

Starburst is a monthly magazine of sci-fi entertainment. Cover price is £2.99 (UK) or $4.99 (USA). Yearly subscriptions comprise twelve regular issues ('budget') or twelve regular issues and four quarterly Specials ('full') at £46.00 full/£32.00 budget (UK), $82.00 full/$53.00 budget (USA), £56.00 full/£39.00 budget (Europe airmail and rest of the world surface) or £71.00 full/ £49.00 budget (rest of the world airmail) to "Visual Imagination Limited", Starburst Mail Order, PO Box 371, London SW14 8JL, UK, or PO Box 156, Manorville, NY 11949, USA. Please mark your envelope clearly as "Subscription".

Video Watchdog (http://www.cinemaweb.com/videowd) is a bi-monthly magazine described as "the Perfectionist's Guide to Fantastic Video". $6.50 a copy, an annual six-issue subscription is $24.00 bulk/$35.00 first class (USA), $33.00 surface/$45.00 airmail (overseas). US funds only to PO Box 5283, Cincinnati, OH 45205-0283, USA.

BOOK DEALERS

Cold Tonnage Books offers excellent mail order new and used SF/ fantasy/horror, art, reference, limited editions etc, with regular catalogues. Write to Andy Richards, 22 Kings Lane, Windlesham, Surrey GU20 6JQ, UK. Tel: +44 (0)1276-475388. Credit cards accepted.

Ken Cowley offers mostly used SF/fantasy/horror/crime/supernatural, collectibles, pulps etc. by mail order with occasional catalogues. Write to Trinity Cottage, 153 Old Church Road, Clevedon, North Somerset, BS21 7TU, UK. Tel: +44 (0)1275-872247.

Dark Delicacies is a friendly store specialising in horror books, vampire merchandise and signings. They also publish a regular newsletter. Contact them at 3725 West Magnolia Blvd, Burbank, CA 91505, USA. Tel: (818) 556-6660. Credit cards accepted.

Fantastic Literature (http://www.netcomuk.co.uk/~sgosden) mail order offers new and used SF/fantasy/horror etc, with regular catalogues. Write to Simon G. Gosden, 35 The Ramparts, Rayleigh, Essex SS6 8PY, UK. Tel: +44 (0)1268-747564. Credit cards accepted.

Fantasy Centre shop and mail order has mostly used SF/fantasy/horror, art, reference, pulps etc. at reasonable prices with regular catalogues. Write to 157 Holloway Road, London N7 8LX, UK. Tel: +44 (0)171-607 9433. Credit cards accepted.

Mythos Books mail order presents books and curiosities for the Lovecraftian scholar, and collectors of horror, weird and supernatural fiction, with regular catalogues and e-mail updates. Write to 218 Hickory Meadow Lane, Poplar Bluff, MO 63901-2160, USA. Tel: (573) 785-7710. Credit cards accepted.

PDW Books mail order offers many speciality press items plus new and used SF/fantasy/horror etc, with regular catalogues. Write to 3721 Minnehaha Avenue South, Minneapolis, MN 55406, USA. Tel: (612) 721-5996.

Richard Dalby issues semi-regular mail order lists of used ghost and supernatural volumes at very reasonable prices. Write to 4 Westbourne Park, Scarborough, North Yorkshire YO12 4AT, UK. Tel: +44 (0)1723 377049.

Weinberg Books at The Stars Our Destination is a mail order list of mostly new horror/fantasy/SF/media and gaming tie-ins/mystery and suspense etc, with regular catalogues. Write to the store at 1021 West Belmont, Chicago, IL 60657-3302, USA. Tel: (773) 871-6381. Credit cards accepted.

Zardoz Books are mail order dealers in used vintage and collectable paperbacks, especially movie tie-ins, with regular catalogues. Write to 20 Whitecroft, Dilton Marsh, Westbury, Wilts BA13 4DJ, UK. Tel: +44 (0)1373 865371.

MARKET INFORMATION AND NEWS

DarkEcho is an excellent service offering news, views and information of the horror field every week through e-mail. To subscribe, e-mail editor Paula Guran at darkecho@aol.com with "Subscribe" as your subject.

The Gila Queen's Guide to Markets (http://www.geocities.-com/Athens/Aegean/7844/gila/index.html) is a regular publication detailing news of new markets for SF/fantasy/horror plus other genres. A sample copy is $6.00 and subscriptions are $34.00 (USA), $38.00 (Canada) and $50.00 (overseas). Back issues are also available. Cheques or money orders should be in US dollars and sent to "The Gila Queen's Guide to Markets", PO Box 97, Newton, NJ 07860-0097, USA. E-mail: GilaQueen@aol.com or GilaQueen@worldnet.att.net

Hellnotes (http://www.hellnotes.com) is described as "Your Insider's Guide to the Horror Field". The weekly newsletter is available on e-mail for $10.00 per year to mailto:dbsilva@ hellnotes.com and the Hellnotes Bookstore can be found at http://www.hellnotes.com/book-store

Scavenger's Newsletter (http://www.cza.com/scav/index.html) is a monthly newsletter for SF/fantasy/horror writers with an interest in the small press. News of markets, along with articles, letters and reviews. A sample copy is $2.50 (USA/Canada) and £2.40/$3.00 (overseas). An annual subscription is $17.00 (USA), $20.00 (Canada) and £18.00/$26.00 (overseas). *Scavenger's Scrapbook* is a twice yearly round-up, available for $4.00 (USA/Canada) and $5.00 (overseas). A year's subscription to the *Scrapbook* is $7.00 (USA/Canada) and $8.00 (overseas). Make cheques or money orders in US funds payable to "Janet Fox" and send to 519 Ellenwood, Osage City, KS 66523-1329, USA. E-mail: foxscav1@jc.net. In the UK, contact Chris Reed, BBR Distribution, PO Box 625, Sheffield S1 3GY, UK. (http://www.bbr-online.com). E-mail: c.s.reed@bbr-online.com